WHAT I CALL LIFE

JILL WOLFSON

SQUARE FISH

HENRY HOLT AND COMPANY

SQUARE
FISH
An Imprint of Macmillan

Square Fish and the Square Fish logo are trademarks of Macmillan and are used by Henry Holt and Company under license from Macmillan.

Library of Congress Cataloging-in-Publication Data
Wolfson, Jill.
What I call life / Jill Wolfson.—1st ed.
p. cm.
Summary: Placed in a group foster home, eleven-year-old Cal Lavender learns how to cope with life from the four other girls who live there and from their storytelling guardian, the Knitting Lady.
ISBN-13: 978-0-312-37752-6
ISBN-10: 0-312-37752-5
[1. Foster home care—Fiction.   2. Self-perception—Fiction.   3. Storytelling—Fiction.   4. Conduct of life—Fiction.   5. Knitting—Fiction.]   I. Title.
PZ7.W8332Wh 2005   [Fic]—dc22   2004060742

Originally published in the United States by Henry Holt and Company
Square Fish logo designed by Filomena Tuosto
First Square Fish Edition: April 2008
10 9 8 7 6 5 4 3 2 1
www.squarefishbooks.com

To Alex and Gwen—
my inspiration for everything,
even sunflower seeds

CHAPTER 1

Everyone is always living her story.

When I first heard this, I thought: *What kind of nutty philosophy is that? Who would buy it? Everyone? Always?*

All I had to do was look at my own personal situation to see how wrongheaded this kind of thinking happened to be. I looked around at where I was living at the time and with whom I was living and shook my head. *No, sir. This isn't MY story. This is nothing like MY life.*

My life—what I call life—had been running its usual course up until recently. Until everything came to a complete and total halt. That was the day my mother happened to have one of her episodes in full public view at the library (more on that later). I, for a fact, knew that things weren't as bad as they might look. Anyone who knew my mother knew that she'd snap out of it eventually. She always did.

But certain people in the library didn't look too kindly on some of the things she was doing during her episode. So these certain people called the police, and, while one of the officers whisked my mother one way, another whisked me outside and loaded me into the back seat of his patrol car.

That had been my first time ever in a police car, and, while I suppose that most eleven-year-old girls would have thrown a full-blown emotional conniption, I didn't put up a fuss, no fuss at all.

Which brings me back to the subject of life stories. If I was going to tell mine, that's one of the first things I would put in about myself: *Cal Lavender is known far and wide for never fussing.*

No crying. No whining. No complaining. No fuss. Not even when she has to sit in a police car, breathing in the smell of sweat, stale cigarettes, and worn, cracked leather. Whew! I'll tell you one thing. If that vehicle is any indication of what the rest of the police cars in our city are like, they could definitely use a good airing out. But even though I have the ability to clean up far worse messes, I wasn't about to volunteer to do it. Let that officer and his criminal riders clean out their own car.

There was a sharp crackle of static from the police radio, and that's when I decided that I would fold up and die right then and there if the policeman put on the siren. I cringed at the thought of being paraded through downtown in such an embarrassing manner, especially so soon after the previous embarrassing situation at the library. (Like I already said, more on that later.)

That's another thing you could put in any story about my life: *Cal Lavender hates it when nosy strangers think it is perfectly okay to stare at people in situations that they know nothing about.*

But thank goodness the siren didn't happen. There were only the usual traffic noises. I was perfectly anonymous, just the way I like to be. I pressed my nose against the window. I looked out at the streaks of stores and buses and people rushing by, but nobody could see in. For all anyone knew, the car contained a cold-blooded killer/arsonist/drug dealer on her way to the electric chair, instead of an eleven-year-old girl with a mother who unfortunately happens to have episodes every once in a while. Which, to my way of thinking, does not come anywhere near qualifying as a criminal offense.

Every so often, I caught the policeman sneaking peeks at me through the rearview mirror. When he saw me looking back, he snapped his eyes away. But then he would look again when he thought I wasn't looking. Then I would snap *my* eyes away. We went back and forth like that for a while, until we stopped at a red light. This time, he didn't drop his eyes. "No problems back there—right, young lady?"

His eyes held on to mine, which made me feel kind of funny in the stomach, even though I'm sure I didn't show it. I have spent many hours in front of a mirror, imagining embarrassing situations even worse than this one and making sure that, whatever jumpy feeling was going on inside of me, I, Cal Lavender, would have the same fixed expression on my face. I call it My Face for Unbearably Unpleasant and Embarrassing Situations. It looks like this: Eyes like two black checkers. Mouth, a thin line with only the slightest curve at the corners. I'm naturally olive-skinned and thin, with one long eyebrow instead of the two short ones that ordinary people have. This gives me the ability to scowl without even trying. My mother, who has the same line across her forehead, says it's an awning over our eyes, protection against whatever life throws at us.

That's the face I showed the policeman, which made him cough nervously and then say, "Hey, would you like one of these breath-mint things? Sure, all kids like breath mints." A tin of Altoids landed next to me. I didn't touch it. "Not *all* kids think that their breath needs help," I said.

"No offense intended," he said back.

I forgave him. I had seen the name on his tag—Officer Quiggly—and immediately renamed him in my mind. Officer Quiggly Wiggly. That's another thing I inherited from my mother. She has a way of finding the perfect name for everyone, me included. (More on that later, too.)

Then there was more crackling from the radio. "Yeah, that's where we're headed," Quiggly Wiggly said into the receiver. The light changed to green, and the car moved forward.

Now, your average eleven-year-old would probably have been scared out of her wits, not knowing where she was headed, where the ride was taking her, not knowing what waited ahead.

But not me. Not Cal Lavender. I wasn't scared at all. My knees were aligned, my thighs pressing together and perfectly matched. My hands were folded on my lap.

Why should I have been scared? After all, this wasn't my story. This was just a short, temporary detour from what I call life.

CHAPTER 2

When I first made the acquaintance of the Knitting Lady, the first thing she said to me was not *Everyone is always living her story.* That came later when she was telling us a fascinating tale that took us from coast to coast and covered about one hundred years of human history.

I have to say she turned out to be an excellent story-teller, even though I had my doubts when I first met her. There was the fact that she stuttered, not all the time, but enough that— Now there I go, jumping ten steps ahead.

I haven't even explained yet about the Knitting Lady. Who is she? How did I wind up on her doorstep? How did I meet the other girls who became my friends—no, they became more than friends—despite the fact that they drove me absolutely crazy?

I need to take a giant step back, return myself to the police car, and explain how I, Cal Lavender, came to be living a life that wasn't my own.

So.

I was in the police car, and we traveled on the freeway for a while. So far, I was doing fine with all this. To my way of thinking, travel can be very educational. Officer Quiggly Wiggly took an exit, then went a few more blocks before turning onto a narrow street with a one-way arrow. "Hang in there, young lady," he said. "We're just about home."

Home? Whose home? Not my home. I looked out the window and asked myself: *If this is home, where are all the rooming houses? Where's the bus station? Where's the Sacred Heart Community Center, where an eleven-year-old girl and her mother can walk in and pick out any kind of outfit she wants and it doesn't cost them one red cent?*

No, this definitely wasn't home. Here, all the houses were exactly alike and painted the exact same shade of not-exactly-white. The flowers on the lawns were perky and perfectly spaced, like they were doing a line dance. When the policeman clicked off the motor, everything came to a stop that felt strange and permanent, like nothing would ever move again.

I would say that this feeling was caused by a case of the nerves—if Cal Lavender was the type of person to have a case of the nerves, which she definitely is not.

I must have opened the car door. I must have walked, because the next thing I knew, Officer Quiggly Wiggly and I were standing on the front step of the only house that was orange instead of not-exactly-white. And I do mean orange. What had the painter been thinking? Officer

Quiggly Wiggly knocked on the door, and from the other side I heard footfalls and the shouting, laughing voices of what sounded to be about a million girls.

Then the door opened and I was standing forehead to forehead, eye to eye, with a woman. Even though I'm eleven and she looked to be about 111, we were the same height. Her cheekbones sat high on her face in two peaks. Her nose came to a point. That was my first impression of the Knitting Lady, sort of a Munchkin with white-gray hair pulled back into a neat, tight bun.

Behind her, the million girls were jostling one another to get a better opportunity to stare and point at me. "Officer," the woman said.

"Yes, ma'am. I'm assuming you got the call about this one."

"We're all r-ready for her."

"She's a nice, quiet one. Didn't give me a moment's trouble."

I made sure that My Face for Unbearably Unpleasant and Embarrassing Situations was perfect. I spoke clearly and slowly like a microphone was being held in front of my face. If I do say so myself, Cal Lavender is known for having a mature manner of speaking. "I assure you that I am never any trouble to anyone."

"Of course, you're no trouble, d-dear." Then she squinted at the policeman's badge. "Thank you, Officer Wiggly."

"Quiggly," he corrected.

"Quiggly?" she asked.

"Yes. It's Officer Quiggly, ma'am. You said 'Officer Wiggly.'"

"Oh, did I? Well, aren't I the silly one? Thanks again, Officer Wiggly. No! Officer Quiggly, not Wiggly. I'm sure she will fit in just w-wonderfully."

By this point, all the million girls were busting a gut from the Quiggly-Wiggly confusion. The Knitting Lady didn't smile though. But there was something behind her eyes—the look of club soda that had been shaken hard—that told me she knew exactly what she was doing. That was very interesting to me because I had never met any grown ups—except my mother, of course—who didn't mind acting not too bright every once in a while.

Poor Officer Quiggly Wiggly. His mustache trembled a little in confusion as he tried to figure out whether or not she was making fun of him. Then he patted me on the shoulder. I gave him a polite, no-fuss-from-me smile and watched him walk away. "Okay, young lady," he yelled from the police car. "You're in good hands now."

Behind me, the woman laughed. She had a high, tinkling laugh, like it was bouncing off broken glass. "Hmmmm, good hands?" she asked. "Do these look like good hands to you?"

When I turned, she held her gnarled hands up to my face, all the fingers stretched out like she was teaching the number ten to a little kid. "I'd say these look more like old m-man hands, wouldn't you? I've seen people drop spare change into hands that look like these. But believe you me, they can still work the knitting needles."

"Knitting?" I asked.

"Knitting," she repeated. "Everyone here calls me the Knitting Lady. M-maybe I can teach you sometime. Think you might like to knit?"

"Perhaps that would be something I would enjoy," I said, but only to be polite.

"I knew it. I took one l-look at those nervous hands of yours and knew they were itching to try something new."

I had not even realized that my right hand was winding a strand of my hair around and around. Immediately, I dropped it, held both arms tight to my sides as though they were stitched there.

"Oh, don't be insulted," she said. "We all have our nervous habits. You should h-hear me stutter when my system gets overloaded. Besides, nervous hands are the best hands for knitting."

"My hands," I insisted, "are *not* nervous!" I closed my eyes to think better, and when I opened them again, I was ready to show that Cal Lavender was *never* nervous. "It's very kind of you to offer knitting instructions. But my mother will be coming for me soon. She doesn't do very well without me for long."

I couldn't help but notice how the Knitting Lady's forehead wrinkled with soft creases. Her mouth opened, then shut. Whatever it was that came to her mind, she forced it back in favor of just saying, "Ahhhh," accompanied by a dozen quick, light little pats on my shoulder.

I wondered, *What does "Ahhhh" mean?*

CHAPTER 3

"Girls," the Knitting Lady said, "the newest m-member of the household—Carolina Agnes London Indiana Florence Ohio Renee Naomi Ida Alabama Lavender."

I wanted to die. They didn't even try to do the polite thing and fight back the giggles.

We were in a large, sparsely furnished room that everyone referred to as Talk Central. It was the largest room in the house, probably some regular family's den before it got taken over by a bunch of girls with knitting needles in their hands and balls of yarn on their laps.

I was wrong about there being a million of them. It was more like four.

From what the Knitting Lady had explained so far, I had wound up in something called a group home. Which, from what I gathered, was a place that looked like a regular home from the outside, even if it was pumpkin-colored. But instead of one family living inside, this was where they put girls when their mothers had problems—like throwing an episode in a public place—and couldn't take care of them for the time being.

"That name's too long," one girl moaned. She was holding a pillow to her stomach. "I can't remember all that. I *caaaan't*."

The girl sitting next to her started giggling and looking around the room with a spaced-out smile.

Another girl, this one so pale it looked like she had been through the wash too many times, bounded into the room like she owned it. Then she plopped on the floor and stared and stared like she also owned me.

This was my introduction to Whitney, one of my roommates-to-be. Didn't that girl ever comb her hair? She looked like she had a special brush just for *unbrushing* it. Plus, she had two silver front teeth instead of pearly white ones like the rest of us had. Her head was also way too big for her body.

That's when I noticed that Whitney wasn't the only one who looked like something had backed up and dinged her. The girl with the pillow was wearing a bright pink cast on her arm. And I don't know what the girl with the dopey smile had to smile about, since she had a right eye that was purple and swollen shut.

But strangest of all was the girl who had not yet said a word. Her problem was her hair. There's no way to put this politely. She had no hair. Well, it wasn't exactly *no* hair—she had something on her head, but it looked like a lawn mower had run wild on it. Her eyelashes and eyebrows were especially creepy. There *were* no eyelashes or eye-brows!

If I do say so myself, I'm very good at remembering names. Whitney was the one who never sat still. Monica was the big, doughy girl with the cast. Fern, thin with a face full of freckles, had the black eye. Amber was the one without hair, which made her face look like a lightbulb.

"Well, what's the story?" Whitney demanded.

The Knitting Lady clapped for silence. "Don't mind Whitney. She's a little, w-well, overly enthusiastic some-times. We'd all like to know the story of your name."

As I previously mentioned, I don't get nervous. I wasn't nervous then, definitely not. So probably I was hav-ing some kind of dust attack, because my voice came out in a squeak. "My mother . . . her name is Betty. I call her Betty." I hesitated. Just saying Betty's name out loud made me feel something like insects jumping around in my stomach. But for some reason, I wanted to keep saying her name as much as I could. So I did.

"Betty, you see, Betty named me for all the people she liked and all the places she passed through where good things happened to her. These are only a few of the places Betty has traveled. Betty is very well traveled. Betty says that traveling is very educational."

The whole time I was talking—which felt like about six hours—Fern kept giggling and the girl with no hair,

Amber, stared like she was storing up everything I was saying for an important test. On the other hand, Whitney was obviously the type who said every interesting and uninteresting thing that went through her mind. "That's a good one, all right. I like that story plenty. So what do we call you? You're gonna be my roommate, but I ain't gonna call you Alabama Alaska Ohio, or whatever you said."

The Knitting Lady had been quiet this whole time, looking very thoughtful, and then she said, "Oh!" Then "Oh!" again. "If you take the first letter from each name and state and line them up, it spells out *California*."

Most people I have run into in my life are nowhere near that smart. I was impressed that she figured it out on her own. "Yes, California is where I was born. Betty says her luck had been running pretty good in California."

The Knitting Lady put down her needles. "So, you like it when people call you . . ."

"Cal," I said. "Everyone here can call me Cal."

CHAPTER 4

I was assigned to the largest bedroom on the second floor of the house. The walls were covered in pink paper with little embossed flowers. It was kind of pretty, except for the section where Whitney had scrawled her name—WHITNEY—all over it in printing that looked like it was done by a first grader. Three beds were lined up on one side. Mine was the middle one. It sat under a window that looked out onto a patio that had some dried-out crabgrass and a few spindly rosebushes.

Whitney threw herself on the bed to my right. Fern and Monica, who shared a room down the hall, stood between us. They were so close together, they could have been Siamese twins, except one was dark and little and the other was about twice her size.

"So Cal gal—" Whitney began.

"Cowgirl?" Fern interrupted. "Is she really a cowgirl?"

"Don't mind her," Whitney said to me. Then to Fern, "Fern, beat it, okay?"

I was shocked by such impoliteness, but Fern didn't seem to mind at all. She just shrugged, giggled, and headed out of the room. Monica followed close behind, complaining about being hungry.

"Are they always like that?" I wondered aloud.

"Like what?" Whitney asked.

"Like—" But that's all I got out because Whitney, who obviously lived to interrupt, interrupted me: "Forget about them. Who you really want to know about is me. I'm the girl who kicked heart disease's butt."

Then she reached for the edges of her shirt, and, just like that, pulled it up to her chin. A scar ran down from the hollow of her skinny neck and kept going until it disappeared over the edge of her belly button. Whitney noticed when I cringed, which seemed to please her no end. "Yop," she said. "Everyone gets grossed out."

After the unveiling of her scar, Whitney made a big production about showing me my dresser, which is where I was supposed to store all my personal belongings.

Now here's another thing that would go in any life story about me: *What Cal Lavender's brain is thinking often doesn't match what her mouth is saying.* For example, when Whitney pulled out the empty top drawer of the dresser, I was thinking: *Why are you showing this to me since anyone with any eyes can see that I don't have any personal belongings to store and Betty is coming for me anyway?*

What I said was "Hmmm. Empty."

Then Whitney took me by the hand and conducted a very detailed, guided tour of her own dresser, which had six overstuffed drawers with all sorts of shirts and underwear hanging out. Plus there was a whole collection of fossilized Bazooka stuck to the side. Very tasty. She held up a smelly old cloth dog with a chewed-up tail. "See this?" she said. "Stole it from my second fosters. Served them right."

I noticed her looking hard at me, probably waiting for me to ask naively, *Fosters? Do you mean The Fosters Freeze downtown?* But Cal Lavender has certainly been around enough to know that she meant a foster home, and I don't like people thinking I haven't been around, so I pointed to the cracked flowerpot on her dresser. "Stolen from a *foster home,* too?" I asked.

"You bet," she said. "Fourth fosters. I call them my souvenirs. Get it? Souvenirs?"

I picked up an old mayonnaise jar filled with leaves. "What's this?"

"Give that back!" She grabbed it out of my hands.

"Sorry," I said, annoyed. "What is it anyway?"

"That's the home of Ike Eisenhower the Fifth."

I knew my history. "Eisenhower? The former president of the United States?"

"What are you talking about?" Whitney was tapping on the glass with her fingernail, which definitely needed cutting. "Ike Eisenhower the Fifth's my pet pill bug. He's named after my favorite candy, Mike and Ike. I made up the last name. Came to me like that." She snapped her fingers.

"Like that?" I asked suspiciously. "Tell me that you never heard of Ike Eisenhower."

"Nope," she stated flatly, then she said, "Mike the Fifth died."

"Mike?"

"Ike's brother. Now it's just Ike the Fifth and me, together since I came to this fosters. How many fosters for you? Does your mother have funny eyebrows, too? I'm ten, but I look eight, which is a good thing 'cause when people are looking for kids to adopt, the younger the better, and I'm plenty young-looking, so I still have a chance. What do you think about spaghetti? I hate spaghetti."

"I'm eleven," I said proudly. "Actually, eleven and one month. But I'm very mature for my age."

She studied me. "Yeah, I figured. Are you at that hormonal age yet?"

I was not about to discuss my personal hormonal situation with a perfect stranger, so I changed the subject. "Is this room always a mess like this?"

She scanned my face like I was talking a foreign language. "We just cleaned yesterday."

She had to be kidding, or blind. When Whitney's life story is written, it will definitely say: *When it comes to slobs, Whitney takes the cake! And her bed is full of it!* Crumbs and gum wrappers and dirty socks. She didn't even seem to notice. How could someone not notice sunflower-seed shells on her pillow?

And I have to say that my other roommate, Amber, was not much better in the cleanliness department. I haven't mentioned that Amber was in the room this whole time, but I guess it's an easy thing to overlook. Amber was by far the quietest person I had ever met in my life, except maybe for Betty when she slid into one of her ultraquiet moods. Amber wasn't politely quiet. She was creepy quiet. The whole time, she sat on her bed looking that *I can see inside of you* look at me, while Whitney did enough talking for both of them.

Within a half hour of being her official temporary roommate, I heard the full and complete list of all the awful, no good, rotten, miserable things that had ever happened to Whitney.

1. Born with a hole in her heart.
2. Fought off death during the surgery to repair the above-mentioned hole. "Yep," she told me, "I heard the doctor say in a real sad voice, 'Too bad. She's dead.' But then I decided, *That's a lie. Whitney, you're not the type to die.*"
3. Kicked out of first fosters. Doesn't know why.

4. Recurring nosebleeds.
5. Almost adopted except lady and man decided they wanted a boy.
6. Head lice and chicken pox at the same time.
7. Kicked out of second fosters 'cause family moved to Alaska.
8. Stuffed into a clothes dryer by other kids at third fosters.
9. Bitten by parrot at this same fosters.
10. Food poisoning on her eighth birthday.
11. Front teeth knocked out in a bike accident and hasn't gotten real fake ones yet.
12. Almost adopted again but lady got cancer and died.
13. Doesn't like to talk about what happened at fourth fosters.
14. Dropped on head by Santa at a group-home Christmas party.

I made a mental note—*Ask Whitney how she got into foster homes in the first place*—but it had to remain a mental note. She didn't stop talking long enough and everything she said came out in one uninterruptible exhale—

"Poisoneddroppedsplitinhalfandmadewholeagain! I have one word to say about that fourth fosters. Messed up, awful, polluted, hellhole, sicko!"

"Whitney, that's six words," I managed to point out.

"Well, la-de-dah. Who cares about numbers? If they ever try to put you in that fosters, you should run away. Remember that!"

"How many fosters have you *been* in, Whitney?" I asked.

"Nine? Ten? I don't know. I lost count."

I know that some people might find it hard to believe that anyone wouldn't know exactly how many different houses they've lived in. But this was something that I could definitely relate to because of all the times that Betty and I just picked up in the middle of the day or night and decided to change addresses. So if anyone had asked me how many places I had lived, how many different schools I had gone to since kindergarten, I would have given the same answer as Whitney: "I lost count."

All the time we were talking—or all the time that Whitney was talking—Amber still had not yet said a word, which, as I said before, was giving me the creeps. One of the things that I've learned by changing schools a million times is how to work my way into a new group of kids. Teachers have always written on my report cards: *Cal Lavender knows how to make herself feel right at home and can make others feel welcome, too.* So even though I was the new kid, I felt responsible for getting Amber involved in the conversation. I tried my best. "What about you, Amber?"

Silence.

"Um, have you been in a lot of um, er, fosters?"

Whitney answered for her. "Yeah, she's been in tons. Even more than me."

I wondered if maybe Amber didn't speak because she *couldn't* speak. Which—because of the logical way that my mind works—reminded me of my mother's friend Harry who had a hole the size of a quarter cut right into his throat. He didn't speak much either. Just the thought of him made me shudder. And since Whitney had been born with an extra hole in one of *her* essential organs, I thought this would be an interesting item of conversation for all of us. I said, "This man I know has a hole in his throat."

"So?" Whitney said sharply.

"He can light up a cigarette and smoke it, not through his mouth like an ordinary person, but through the hole." I held two fingers together, then pressed them to my throat. I made a drawing-in sound that made the inside of my cheeks vibrate.

"Puff, puff," I said. "I swear, you can see smoke and everything."

To me, this was about as fascinating as a conversation could get. So it startled me when Whitney snapped, "Who cares? Anybody can have a hole in their throat."

Any other eleven-year-old girl would have gotten snappy right back. But I tactfully changed the topic. "So Whitney, when are you going back to your real home?"

A look like she had been slapped passed across her

face. She ignored my question and continued in an extremely bratty way, "I bet you think you're going home tomorrow."

"Of course I'm not going home tomorrow," I said. "I'm going home tonight."

What I was thinking was: *I need to go home because if I'm not there, things will "go to hell in a handbasket," as Betty always says. The medicine! Who will make Betty take her medicine? And what will she eat? And who will make sure she gets to the Laundromat? Walking around in dirty underwear is no way for a person to walk around!*

That's what I was thinking, but I said, "Betty's coming for me any time now."

Whitney snorted. "Fat chance. You may talk in perfect complete sentences, but you don't know squat. You're going to be here for a long time."

"No, I'm not," I said.

"A long, *long* time!"

"No!"

"A long, long, *long* time."

By this point, we were glaring at each other, arms crossed against our chests as though we were tied up in knots. There was no reason to believe someone as stupid and rude and messy as Whitney. Why would I believe someone like that? I turned to Amber, hoping that she would shake her head or give some sign that I was right. But without eyebrows to go up and down, her face remained expressionless. It was impossible to know what she was thinking. *If* she was thinking. I guess eyebrows are like street signs. You never know how important they are until they're missing.

But who cared about what Amber was thinking? I didn't need Amber. Or Whitney. I was going home any minute now.

CHAPTER 5

Cal Lavender looks truth square in the eye. I'd be the first to admit that Betty wasn't always the most reliable person in the world. There was the time she went to get popcorn in the movies and decided that she just wasn't in the mood to sit still and didn't remember to come back until I had seen the same picture three times straight through. But forget about me all night? Leave me stranded in an orange-colored house with strangers? Never!

At 8:30, I joined the lineup of girls outside the bathroom, getting ready for bed. While we waited for Amber to finish up inside, Monica tossed a pencil down the hallway. Whitney got down on her hands and knees, crawled after it, and brought it back in her mouth for Monica to throw again. Fern thought this childish doggie behavior was the funniest thing ever. I ignored them. I most especially ignored Whitney.

At 8:35, I brushed my teeth and washed my face.

At 8:50, I put on the nightgown the Knitting Lady handed me. It was a nice soft cotton with kittens on it that I might have liked under different circumstances.

At 8:53, I pulled back the sheets and blanket and got into bed. Whitney kept making *la-de-dah* faces at me, but I'm good at ignoring annoying people.

At 8:55, I got out of bed and changed back into my clothes. I folded the blanket and then the nightgown into two tidy packages. I sat on the edge of the cot, my hands folded on my lap.

When the Knitting Lady sat next to me on the bed, I glanced out of the corner of my eye and could see that she looked worried. I thought, *You don't have to worry about Cal Lavender. I can take care of myself, thank you very much.*

I said nothing. I stared past her and put all my focus on the flowered wallpaper.

"H-hey," she said. "Having trouble settling in?"

I gave my chin a stiff shake. "Betty is coming any minute. It's pointless for me to get into bed."

The Knitting Lady started to say something, but Whitney the Interrupter interrupted. "You're the pointless one. You don't get the point! This is a group home. Parents never, ever come at night to pick up their kid."

That was it! I whirled around to face her. "You don't know what Betty will do!"

"They won't let her come! That's the law!"

"Who's *they?* What law? You don't know what's going to happen!"

The Knitting Lady's voice was soft and firm at the same time: "Whitney, Cal's right. We never know from one minute to the next what will happen. Do we, Cal?"

"That's right," I said. "She doesn't know anything."

"N-none of us know. Anything can happen. What about a compromise? You go to sleep. And if your mother comes tonight—"

"*When* my mother comes," I said.

"I'll wake you. P-promise."

"No," I said. "I'll wait up."

"Let her learn the hard way," Whitney said.

The Knitting Lady shot her a look, which I was glad to see. "That's enough now, Whitney. You more than anyone know how hard the first night is." And then she turned back to me, and I guess she was having one of her system overloads because she really started stumbling over her words: "T-take your time. Sit up awhile. If you n-need anything, I'm-m—"

"I'm just fine!" I blurted out. Her stuttering was making me even more impatient. I know it was impolite, but I couldn't sit there waiting for her to say what she was trying to say. I didn't need anything from her. I just wanted to get out of this place.

When the Knitting Lady stood, I felt the bed tip slightly. I heard the click of the overhead light. Thank goodness she was gone. Darkness fell around me. There was the sound of slow, steady footsteps as the Knitting Lady walked down the stairs. I listened to Fern's giggling coming through the wall. Monica was whining about something. A toilet flushed. I could hear Whitney chewing gum in bed and the crinkle-crinkle noises of Amber's sheets as she tossed around.

And I waited. I waited for Betty to charge in Betty-style and rescue me. As I waited, I tried to draw calmness from all the sounds—the chewing, the tossing, the flushing—but all I could think was *Now!*

Now! Now! Now! Now! Now! Now! Now! Now! Now! Now! Now! Now! Now! Now! Now! Now! Now! Now! Now! Now! Now! Now! Now! Now! Now! Now! Now!

Betty is coming for me NOW! She is!

And then two more ice ages passed, and a whole flood of thoughts came at me: *Betty is lost. Of course, she's lost! Betty can't do anything without me. She's wandering the streets, not knowing what bus to take, whether to go left or right, north or south. Or maybe she's hurt. That's it! Horrible things happen all the time to people, and Betty is never, ever careful enough. A car ran a red light and hit her. She was bitten by a rat, fell down a long flight of steps, was run over by a garbage truck. Maybe Betty is dead.*

I pictured her in a coffin, her hands resting lightly on her chest. There would be makeup on her face because that's what they do with dead people. They put makeup all over them so that they don't look so dead. I saw that in a movie once. Betty would hate that. She hates makeup when she's living, and she'd really hate it when she's dead. She'd never stand for it. Never!

So maybe she isn't dead. Maybe . . . maybe . . . maybe it's something worse.

A dread, something even more horrible than the thought of Betty in a coffin, started at the base of my spine and slithered its way to the top of my head. I couldn't let myself think what I was starting to think. I couldn't think it. I couldn't!

Then I thought it: *Betty isn't dead. Betty isn't lost. Betty isn't here because she doesn't want to be here.*

It felt like someone stuck a vacuum cleaner hose down my throat and sucked my heart right up out of me.

I suddenly felt more tired than I had ever been in my entire life. Every muscle gave up at once. My stomach hurt something awful. It took every bit of energy I had left to crawl beneath the blanket. I turned my face into the pillow and held it there. There was a smell I didn't recognize. It wasn't my smell. It wasn't Betty's smell. I guess it was the smell of every kid who had ever wound up in this bed.

I guess maybe I started to cry.

"Cal, are you crying?" It was Whitney's voice.

"No," I said. My jaw was quivering from the strain of holding it in. "I never cry."

"Good. Because I can't invite a crybaby for a sleep-over. My bed would get wet."

I lifted my face from the pillow and looked across the narrow gulf that separated our beds. When I saw Whitney reach across to touch my mattress, I let my right hand drop over the side. She fumbled and took it in hers. Whitney's hand was soft and as light as a piece of paper. And she was grinning, her two big glinting silver front teeth catching the sliver of streetlight that was peeking in through the blinds. That did something to me. It made me feel better somehow, like there were two glowing lights so that I wouldn't have to be all alone in the dark.

"But Betty doesn't let me have sleepovers," I whispered.

"Come on! Don't be so goody-goody. Betty's not here now!" She held open her blanket. Why not? After a slight hesitation, I scooted into the tent of it. I was surrounded by the smell of sunflower seeds and dirty socks and, beneath it, what I would come to recognize as a distinctive Whitney smell. I whispered, "Whitney, is your mom coming for you, too?"

"Nah," she said. "Don't have one."

"No mom?"

There was a long silence. Then, "I got a different kind of mom. A dead one."

I felt another shiver go through me, and I didn't have a clue of what to say to that. "I'm sorry" didn't feel right, and asking questions didn't feel right either. Luckily, I didn't have to say anything because Whitney bolted upright. "Hey, Knitting Lady. Don't worry. She didn't take off. She's in here with me."

I peeked out of the blanket and saw the short silhouette framed in the doorway.

"No one's sleepy in here yet," Whitney went on. "Right, Cal?" Then she knocked on the wall—three short, quick knocks; a pause, then two more.

It must have been their secret code because Monica and Fern came rushing in and threw themselves on my now-empty bed. Monica immediately started whining, "Stop it, Fern. Your feet are in my face. It's not fair."

"Whose bed is this?" Fern asked.

"The new girl."

"The new girl? There's a new girl? Oh, I forgot! The new girl."

I waited for the Knitting Lady to order us all back into our own beds. But instead, she asked, "Well girls, if you're not sleepy, what do you have in mind?"

Whitney started butt-bumping the mattress. "You know!"

"I d-do? Cal, do you have a clue as to what she's talking about?"

"Me? How would I know?"

Monica switched on a small lamp. The room glowed with warm light. She said to the Knitting Lady, "Why do you always do that? Pretend you don't know what we want?"

And then Whitney said to me, "She tells the world's best stories. But she makes us beg first."

The Knitting Lady laughed. "You girls have really got my number! Is there any particular story you want to hear?"

There was some movement behind me, which made me jump. Once again, I had forgotten all about Amber being in the room. Her bed squeaked when she got out and walked to her dresser. She reached into the top drawer and pulled out something that was dangling from a long chain.

"Oh, *that* story," the Knitting Lady said, sounding surprised but somehow not surprised at all. "Aren't you tired of that story yet? N-no, of course you're not tired of it. Truth is, I never get tired of telling it."

So Amber got back into bed. Monica and Fern curled up against each other, hooked together like snails.

"The s-story of Amber," the Knitting Lady began. "A valuable jewel that was born out of destruction.

CHAPTER 6

"Picture a long time ago," the Knitting Lady continued. "There was a storm. Amber was born from this—low-pressure zones that had built up over time and space."

"I have a question already," I said.

"G-go ahead, Cal."

"I don't understand."

"What part?"

"This story. Is this about Amber—her?" I pointed to the girl.

Whitney snorted. "Man-oh-man, that's like a dumb question Fern would ask. It's about a rock. A rock! Amber, show her."

Amber held up the necklace that she had taken from her dresser. Dangling from the chain was a polished orange-yellow nugget cradled in a cobweb of silver.

The Knitting Lady nodded in agreement and said, "That's amber. But Cal's question is actually quite a good one. Hold on to that question as I tell the story. So, where was I? The storm. It was a humdinger. Picture a tree in the midst of it. This wasn't a very big tree. In fact, it was little more than a sapling."

"Oh, the poor tree," Monica said. "I'm glad I'm not the tree. I'd be *soooo* scared."

Whitney nudged me and rolled her eyes. "She says that every time. She's scared of everything!"

"Well, I *would* be scared," Monica insisted.

"B-being scared is nothing to be ashamed of. Everyone gets scared in scary situations. We each learn to handle frightening things in our own way. This tree had been through so many storms, it had learned to be very flexible, to bend and sway in order to survive. But not—"

"Not in this storm," Whitney interrupted.

"T-true. This storm proved too much for it. Its bark was no more protection than lace. Leaves blew to kingdom come. Can you hear the branches of this young tree snap with a sickening crack?" The Knitting Lady gave her hands one loud clap.

Fern started giggling. "Why are you laughing?" I asked.

"Don't ask. Fern's always laughing, except when she's crying," Whitney said.

Monica took a sharp inhale of breath. "This next part is so scary. I don't like this part."

"Man-oh-man, Monica, you are such a wimp," Whitney said. "You always—"

"Wh-Whitney, you know how this story goes. What happens next?"

"And then, the plunderers and marauders came forth!" she recited.

"Exactly! W-when the bark broke, it was like skin splitting. Everything underneath—the bones of the tree, its fragile inside, its delicate heart—became vulnerable. Then an army of insects, parasites, and diseases marched forth with their pinching jaws and big appetites. They seemed unstoppable. What could the tree do?"

"I'd run," Monica said. "I'd get out of there so fast!"

Whitney said sarcastically, "Man-oh-man, Monica, you can't even walk a half a block without dying of heat frustration."

"Heat prostration," I corrected.

"Heat *is* frustrating," Monica moaned. "I die from the heat."

"Where's Monica walking?" Fern asked.

"Jeez-Louise, not Monica," Whitney said.

I wanted them all to be quiet so that I could hear the rest of the story, so I took it upon myself to sort things out for them. I said to Fern, "To begin with, Monica's not going anywhere." Then I pointed out to Monica, "And secondly, a tree is rooted to the ground. It can't just pick itself up and run."

Whitney said, "Hey, I never asked this before. Did the

tree try yelling for help? If it was me, I'd be screaming my head off."

"Trees can't yell," I said. "That's just not logical."

"It doesn't have to be logical! It's a story. Animals can talk. Trees can yell. So did it? Yell, I mean."

"P-perhaps it did try. Y-yes, I know it did. But unfortunately, it spoke a special tree language that no one understood. Or maybe no one believed. Not many people pay much attention to the complaints of young trees. So next— That's right, Whitney. You know."

"It found a way to protect itself!" she said.

"What a clever w-weapon it found. That young hurting tree went deep within itself and discovered a steady flowing fountain of resin."

"Resin. That's the same as pancake syrup," Whitney tried to inform me, but I informed her, "I know what resin is. But how can that be a weapon?"

"G-good question, Cal. This resin had a sharp, pungent smell. Big globs oozed out of the tree's wounds. Those plunderers and marauders didn't know what hit them! Some hightailed it away as fast as possible. The slower villains thought, *My-oh-my, what is that mouthwatering smell?* But their first taste was their last because they found themselves trapped in a flypaper of syrup."

Fern waved her hand in the air. "Another question!"

"Y-yes, Fern?"

"Are we?"

"Are we what?"

"Having pancakes for breakfast tomorrow morning?"

"Ignore her," Whitney said. "Get to the next part—the part where the sap hardened!"

"R-right! The resin hardened, trapping all the villains and sealing the wound of the tree. Over time, the sap continued to harden. The shell grew thicker and more impenetrable. That's amber. Nothing can get in and nothing can get out."

"The end," Whitney announced.

"So when did all this happen?" Fern asked.

Monica rubbed her eyes and yawned. "Fern, you've heard this story a million times. It happened about a million years ago."

Whitney spoke directly to me: "See? I told you she tells a good story. Her stuttering doesn't wreck it at all."

My eyes darted to the Knitting Lady and back. "Whitney, that's incredibly rude."

"But it's true. If something's true, it can't be rude, right? And *she* doesn't mind." She addressed the Knitting Lady. "You don't mind, right?"

The Knitting Lady didn't answer, but you could see that it didn't bother her a bit. "A-Amber, what do you see when you hold up your necklace? That's right. Tilt it so that the light is to your advantage. What do you see inside?"

I twisted around. I was very interested in hearing her

answer, but even more I wanted to hear her voice. Maybe it would be squeaky. Maybe she would have some kind of accent. I waited. But Amber remained silent and held the necklace out in my direction.

"Me?" I asked, and she nodded.

"Go on," Whitney urged.

I walked to her bed, and, when I took the jewel, Amber watched me carefully, as though I might never give it back. I held it to the light. "Something in there looks like a bug!"

"It *is* a bug!" said the Knitting Lady.

"I hate bugs!" Monica said.

"You like Ike, right? So, don't be a baby," Whitney said. "It can't hurt you."

"That's r-right. It's probably a termite that was stopped cold in the act of destroying the tree. There are also things in there too small to see, like bacteria. So much dangerous debris of the past, but all trapped safely inside. None of those old hurts are a problem anymore."

↩

That night, I was allowed to sleep in Whitney's bed. Fern and Monica took over mine. "A real sleepover," the Knitting Lady said. "One night only."

A minute after the lights went out, Whitney's body jolted and went still. I never thought anyone could fall asleep as fast as that. It was like she had been unplugged.

Her breathing lengthened. It turned so quiet that it worried me. I kept putting my ear to her back to make sure her breath was still there.

Pretty soon, Fern was snoring slightly. Monica mumbled a few words. She was already dreaming. But I still wasn't anywhere near ready to sleep.

I wondered what Betty was doing. She can't fall asleep unless I talk her to sleep.

I wondered: *Why is Monica so scared of everything? Why does Fern laugh at everything?*

What did the Knitting Lady mean: We each handle scary things in our own way?

Was I supposed to make my own breakfast?

What did Whitney's scar feel like? Was it rough and even, like a zipper to her heart?

What if I *never* fell asleep?

I wondered: *What was the Knitting Lady's story really about?*

And still, I was awake. I thought of the other things that might have been trapped inside of amber. Seeds and feathers and molecules of air from another era. It wasn't until I started thinking about what melted amber would look like, imagining it turning to liquid gold, that I started drifting off. I hopped on a million-year-old bubble of air and the next thing I knew, it was morning.

CHAPTER 7

Sunlight was pouring in on me. I couldn't tell where I was, what day, what planet I had landed on. I felt like I weighed nothing in all that light. Out of habit, I reached over, patted the space next to me, felt nothing. No Betty!

A voice said: "Man-oh-man, what is that mouthwatering smell?"

What? Plunderers and marauders! Termites trapped in amber! Was I dreaming?

I bolted upright. I was in a bed. A girl—I remembered now, *that* girl, Whitney—was sitting in the middle of the room, tearing through a pile of clothes. Without glancing at me, she said, "Cal, breakfast! Smells like pancakes and resin," then pulled off her pajama top—that scar again!—and put on a wrinkled shirt.

She asked, "Wanna play cards later?"

My brain felt fuzzy, which most definitely is not the usual state of my brain. "Cards?"

"You know." She made a motion like she was dealing. "Wanna play?"

"Sure," I said. "Why not?"

"Good. Because when I'm done with you, your life won't be worth a penny."

◌◌

I, Cal Lavender, was definitely not myself. A fuzz brain, crying and whiny the night before. Definitely not me. But after I brushed my teeth, checked the mirror, and adjusted My Face for Unbearably Unpleasant and Embarrassing Situations, I felt more myself. Or at least as close to myself as an eleven-year-old can be when she is being forced to live not her real life.

So.

On the first morning of not really living my story, Fern and Amber had pancake-making duty. Now, I know how to make pancakes. You can count on any pancakes made by Cal Lavender to be light and fluffy the way Betty and I like them. But the way the others attacked the tall stack made by Fern and Amber, you'd think they actually liked their pancakes to have the taste and texture of a sponge. Well, there's no accounting for taste, as Betty always says.

After eating, we were all supposed to pitch in and clean up. That seemed fair enough to me, but everyone else complained their heads off, especially Monica. Because of the cast on her arm, she got to do just about nothing, but still she whined.

"I *caaaan't* wipe down the table."

44

And, "My arm itches *soooo* much."

And, "I'm tired. Fern snored all night."

And, "Whitney is being mean to me. She called me a big baby."

At first, I got drying duty and Whitney got to wash. As you can imagine, she did not do an acceptable job. I had to keep handing back the dishes because she never got off all the suds.

After her fifteenth unacceptable dish, she snapped at me, "Okay, then. You wash! I'll dry!" But then she also got snippy because each time I handed her a knife to dry, I yelled "Sharp!" which to my way of thinking is a very safety-conscious thing to do.

When the kitchen was finally clean, all of us—minus the Knitting Lady—went into Talk Central and started watching a monster movie on TV. Every time the vampire came on screen and bared his blood-dripping fangs, Whitney yelled "Sharp!" Fern thought that that was hysterical, and pretty soon she and Monica were also yelling "Sharp!" Maybe it was a little funny the first time, but by the hundredth time, there was no humor left at all.

So immature!

At the first commercial, Monica made us change the channel because the movie was getting too scary for her. Nothing else remotely interesting was on. Then we helped the Knitting Lady with the laundry, only I didn't have any laundry. Still, I was the only one who didn't act as though helping was the end of the world.

After laundry, I played blackjack with Whitney. She wasn't as good as she had bragged about. As I suspected, I was a much better counter. I usually get straight A's in math, even when Betty moves me to a new school in the middle of the term. Right in the middle of the game, right when I was about to wipe her out of cards, Whitney made a big announcement: "It's time to educate Cal."

I couldn't imagine what *she* had to teach *me,* since I was winning just about every hand. Still, I followed her upstairs to the bedroom. It was just the two of us. She got all mysterious, locked the door, and told me to listen very, very carefully.

Let it be known: Cal Lavender is a very, very good listener.

According to Whitney, this was not just an ordinary house I had landed in; it was a whole world that was nothing like my old world.

"Orange is just the tick of the iceberg," she said.

"Tip," I corrected.

"Tick," she insisted. "If you don't understand what's going on, man-oh-man, you're going to be ticked-off 24/7."

My new world, she explained, has its own language, secret codes, and horror stories. She said, "You need to know who's who and what's what, or it's— What's it for you?" She made a slicing motion across her neck.

"Curtains?" I said.

"Yeah, curtains for you."

I said, "You make it sound like I'm in one of those lost civilizations on the Discovery Channel. Why do I have to know anything? I'm only here by mistake."

She was eating sunflower seeds at the time and making a pile of the shells on her bed. "That's what"—*crack, crack*—"every new kid thinks at first." *Crack, crack.*

"What does everyone think?"

"That they're here by mistake." *Crack-crack.* "The crybabies are the ones who drive me crazy. Don't even"—*crack*—"get me started on the crybabies."

"You mean like Monica?" I asked.

"Not Monica! Monica's a whiner. The crybabies are new kids who"—*crack*—"say they don't"—*crack*—"care where they live, but they sweat a lot, which is"—*crack, crack*—"how you can tell they're"—*crack*—"scared to death." *Crack!*

"Could you *please* stop that?" I put my hands over my ears.

"The sunflower seeds?"

"Yes! No! Yes, the seeds! Not just the seeds. Stop acting like I'm everyone else. Like I'm going to be here forever."

"Well, maybe not forever." *Crack.* "But you're going to be here longer than you"—*crack*—"think. Everyone is. So you might as well know what's what. To start with"—*crack*—"you should know that you're a Code 300 kid."

"What's that?"

"It means you're not a Code 600 kid."

"That's great, Whitney. Very helpful."

She missed the sarcasm. "Thanks. I mean to be help-ful. And you should know about the social worker. It's a good news/bad news situation. Which first?"

"Good."

"The good thing is that everyone here has the same social worker, so I can tell you everything you need to know and save you from learning the hard way. The bad news is that when you see her, you're going to ask your-self: *Man-oh-man, is that animal, vegetable, or mineral?* You *do* know what a social worker is, right? If you don't, it's nothing to burn in shame about."

Did she think I was an idiot? "Of course, I know. I already have a social worker. I mean, Betty does. That's who gives us our food stamps and—"

"Not *that* kind! A special *kid* social worker just for you. Her name is Mrs. S-something-long-in-the-middle-that-no-one-can-pronounce-with-*ski*-at-the-end, so everyone just calls her Mrs. S. There's something you got to know about her."

"What?" I asked. Only I guess I had the wrong tone of voice because Whitney snapped, "Don't get la-de-dah again! This is important information. It isn't for babies. Are you listening?"

I blinked once.

"Well, are you?"

"Yes!"

"Good. Because this is reality TV, starring guess who."

"Who?"

"You!" she said in exasperation. "Now, about Mrs. S. The big thing is to always be super-polite. Don't get pissed off and spit in her eye because Mrs. S. has the power to get you in and out of certain foster homes. Take it from me personally, it doesn't pay to spit in her eye." Whitney took measure of me. "You won't have any trouble with sucking up. You have the la-de-dah act down pat. Now, quiz time. You have a choice between being on the bad side of Mrs. S. or diving into a pit of hot lava. Which do you choose?"

"Mrs. S."

"No! No! No! What do you choose?"

"Hot lava?" I answered hesitantly.

"Right. I could tell that you were smart! Now you're learning!"

That was just the start of my first educational session. That day in the Pumpkin House, I also learned the following:

1. The social worker—the dreaded Mrs. S.—would help decide when and whether I could go back home with Betty again.

2. Whitney and Amber had their parental ties severed, which sounded to me like something out of a horror movie, with a parent sliced away and rolling down a flight of stairs like a decapitated head. But Whitney explained that it's the opposite of a horror show. It means that they can both be adopted as soon as the perfect new parents are found for them.

3. Flush the downstairs toilet after every pee or it over-flows.

4. Code 300 kids are the ones who had something wrong done to them (or have a mother who has episodes). Code 600 kids are the cold-blooded killer/arsonist/drug-dealer types who are locked up in kid jail.

5. Fern didn't have her parental ties severed, which means that she gets to go home and live with her mother sometimes. She loves going home. Only something bad always happens and she has to come back into foster care.

6. Ditto with Monica.

7. Amber doesn't have cancer, which is what I first thought. It turns out that she has this nervous prob-lem and, when her nerves kick up, she actually pulls out her hair. "*Ouch* is right," Whitney said. "She doesn't do it on purpose or anything. It's all in her head. And her noggin. Her brain, too."

8. The Knitting Lady won't let me call Betty no matter how much I beg. So don't beg.

"I know this isn't the easiest stuff to have dumped on you all at once," Whitney said. "I bet you want to run off somewhere and puke."

"I'm fine," I said quickly. "So out of all that, what's the *most* important thing to know?"

She thought for a moment. "You know the expression 'God helps those who . . . who . . .' Who does God help?"

I nodded eagerly. "Who help themselves!" I was very good at helping myself.

"Yeah, that's what I mean. Only, don't count on that to work around here. Everything gets decided behind your back, and there's not much you can do about it."

CHAPTER 8

Later that first day, the Knitting Lady told us to get ready for a short road trip. "We have things to do!"

Transportation was an old-model van with all sorts of dents and bruises. Since the paint was peeled off and faded, there was no way to tell the original color. Maybe it was once orange like the house. Only now it was somewhere between puke green and dog-poop brown. But as long as it didn't have a siren and something embarrassing written along the side like "Pathetic Group-Home Girls," dog poop–puke brown-green was okay with me. Cal Lavender is no snob when it comes to minivans. I'm more of a public-transportation type of individual.

Since I was the new girl, I got to sit up front, which made Monica start whining. "I get carsick in the back. I *do*! Don't blame me if I puke. It feels like a million degrees in here."

I rolled down the window. Then it felt like a million degrees minus one. But I didn't care. I was getting out. That's another way that Betty and I are exactly alike. Don't fence us in! I felt like one of those dogs you see in the back of pickup trucks, her head tilted up, her mouth open and trying to swallow as much fresh air as she can.

The Knitting Lady looked pretty funny in the driver's seat. She was one of those gray-haired ladies that you see driving down the road, her head barely clearing the steering wheel. From the back, I bet it looked like the van was driving itself. Her feet didn't even reach the pedals, so everything she needed was right there on the dash. That was very interesting to me, since I had never seen anything like that before. She pushed a button, pulled a lever, and we were off.

"There! Look there!" Unfortunately, Whitney was sitting directly behind me, cracking sunflower seeds, yelling in my ear, and kicking me in the bottom through the seat. "Mountain Mike's Pizza. Nobody here likes pepperoni. Do you?"

When I didn't respond immediately, she kicked harder. "Pepperoni? Do you?" And when we drove by a rec center, she jabbed me in the shoulder. "That's where the pool is. Did I tell you about the pool yet? It's gotta be the best pool ever. Man-oh-man, you have to take a test before they let you in the deep part, so now I'm taking swim lessons. I didn't want to take swim lessons, not because I'm scared or anything and— Look! That's Horace Mann Middle School. Memorize that! *Horace. Mann. Middle. School.* We all walk together."

She reached over and tapped the Knitting Lady's

shoulder—"She's in sixth, right?"—then tapped me—
"You didn't flunk or anything, right?"—then poked
Monica—"She'll walk with us, right? And eat lunch with
us, right? Everything together, right?"

I did not say anything, but I was thinking: *Wrong!
This is July, and there is no way that I will still be living
not-my-real-life when school starts. No way.*

Besides, if I did have to go to a school, it would certainly not be *that* one. As we drove by, I saw that Horace
Mann was mostly a cluster of portables surrounding the
main building, which to me looked like a very bad school.
Perhaps the worst school that ever existed. I thought: *Not
that it matters because I won't go there. And even if I did
have to go there—which definitely is not going to happen—
maybe I would walk with them sometimes, but there is no
way that I would do everything with them. I would have
to make it very clear very quickly that Cal Lavender is
never joined at the hip with anyone. I am an extremely
independent type of person.*

Whitney kicked again: "Everything together? Right?"

෴

Whitney had told me so many things that day, I could not
believe that she had forgotten one of the most important.
I would have to get examined by the nurse from the
Department of Children's Services. No kid ever got out of

it. That was our first stop of the day. Everyone else got to stay in the waiting room, playing with little-kid toys and eating junk from the vending machine, while I followed Nurse Francine. That's what her name tag said. *Nurse Francine.* She led me into an examination room and asked, "So?"

I said, "I'm not the type to get sick. Put that down on my chart."

Nurse Francine bent her head and took my blood pressure. I had never met anyone who talked only in questions. First, she shoved a tongue depressor far down my throat, and, while I was gagging, she asked, "Make you gag?" She pulled out my eyelids by the eyelashes and shined a light onto the inner linings. Then came other questions, strange, embarrassing ones that she asked in a flat, bored voice. "Do you currently have diarrhea? Do you have itching in your vaginal area? Do you ever wet the bed? Do you ever hear voices?"

"No!" I said, outraged. "No diarrhea. No itching. No wetting. No voices."

Then she picked up a clipboard and began turning pages. Her hands were a whirl. "How are you feeling in general?"

That was the first question she asked that I actually had to stop and think about. I was feeling . . . ? How? There must have been ten thousand words for what I was feeling. Words for missing Betty. Words for wondering when I could go home. Is that what she wanted?

I suddenly suspected that without a doubt this must be a trick question. If I answered wrong, a trapdoor was going to spring open beneath my feet—whoosh!—and suck me away someplace where Betty would never find me.

I, Cal Lavender, who never, ever felt nervous, measured every word. "I feel . . . I feel . . ." I looked at my feet. "I feel full of feelings."

Nurse Francine's face dropped and she lowered her eyes, like she was the one who was embarrassed instead of me. "Hmmmm. Is that so?" She marked something on her clipboard. Was it a black mark? Something that was going to get me in trouble? But when I strained to see it, she flipped my chart closed.

꩜

After that, we got back into the van and then stopped at the drugstore to pick up some head lice–treatment shampoo because Nurse Francine said that I had nits, which I certainly did not. And if I did, it must have come from sharing a room with someone who keeps a bug as a pet.

After that, we went grocery shopping, and the Knitting Lady said that, because I was the new girl, I could pick three things that I especially liked or wanted to try.

Whitney kept chanting, "Pop-Tarts, Pop-Tarts, Pop-Tarts." Fern said that maybe she *does* like pepperoni, but she forgets. Maybe it's sausage she doesn't like. Or anchovies. Monica said that she's definitely highly allergic to pepperoni and sausage and anchovies and begged me— "Please, please, please!"—to get plain pizza because that was one of only three things that she could eat without getting a stomachache. The other two things were pancakes and frozen chicken sticks, but only the supermarket generic brand.

I ignored them. Unlike most eleven-year-old girls, I believe in eating nutritionally. Betty is fond of saying, *Your body is your temple,* so I set a good example for the others by filling our cart with lettuce, tomatoes, cucumbers, avocados, mustard, mayonnaise, and tortillas in order to make Cal Lavender's Infinitely Superior Lettuce, Tomato, Cucumber, Avocado, Mustard, and Mayonnaise Tortilla Roll-Ups.

"Very creative," the Knitting Lady said. She clearly approved of my nutritional standards because even though Whitney kept calling avocados "slimy, green fat balls" and Monica was whining, "That's seven things, not three," the Knitting Lady didn't make me put anything back.

∽

So that was that—the condensed version of the first day of living not really my life. I also came to some specific conclusions about the other girls in the house. That's something else to note in my life story: Cal Lavender can tell everything there is to know about a person within fifteen minutes of meeting them. So without a doubt, I knew that these girls were strange. By this, I mean strange in their own unique way, which is the definition of being truly strange. I've seen plenty of kids who put on a big act of being strange—like dressing gothic or doing something purple with their hair—but then they're all strange in the same way, which makes them not strange at all.

But the girls in the Pumpkin House didn't fall into any of the usual groups. They weren't jocks or math nerds or school-play kids. For example, I can say without a doubt that I have never come across a group for hair-plucking girls.

Later that evening, when the Knitting Lady and I were alone in the kitchen, I brought up this observation. She more or less agreed with my conclusion. She said, "We have our own groups. For example, there are the girls who refuse to think or feel anything bad about their parents, no matter how much their parents disappoint and hurt them."

"How do they do that?" I asked.

"It's quite a trick, all right. Some of these girls get so

silly that there's no space for anything serious. You'd think they didn't have brain or a care in the world. They laugh at anything. Sometimes, they can't stop laughing."

"Fern?" I asked, and the Knitting Lady said, "That's for you to decide. And then, we have girls who can't stand change. They're t-terrified of it. Sound like anyone you know? And I can't forget the runners. They blow out of every foster home, even the good ones."

"Why do they do that?"

"It's c-complicated. Maybe someday you can help me figure that out."

"I'd be very glad to help. I'm good at figuring things out. What about Whitney's group?"

"Some children have been in foster care so long, they know more about the way things work than any social worker. Whitney's something of a genius in that respect, isn't she? Then there are the failure-to-thrive children—"

"Failure to drive?" I asked.

"Thrive," she corrected. "Some girls have such difficult lives that they somehow will themselves to stop growing. Stop *thriving*."

"I don't like the sound of that," I said.

"It's no p-picnic. But you're not that type."

"I'm not any type at all. I don't fit in a group because I don't belong here," I pointed out.

"Ahhhh," the Knitting Lady said. "That's another type."

"What do you mean 'ahhhh'? You say 'ahhhh' a lot."

"I'll tell you a story about it sometime. But the bottom line is that whatever you're thinking, whatever you might be afraid of, whatever you're proud of, you, Cal Lavender, are far from being alone."

CHAPTER 9

The second day of *not really my life* was the hottest day in the history of the universe. We were all in Talk Central, all moping around except Whitney. While we moped, she danced, skipped, and swirled, the same bouncing rubber band–ball girl no matter what the weather. She insisted that we play AA, her all-time favorite game. *AA* happens to stand for "Alcoholics Anonymous," which is a club that grown-ups go to in order to help them stop drinking. I could tell that Monica and Fern already knew about AA the way some kids know about PTA meetings. They didn't come out and say so, but I concluded that their parents stopped going to meetings, which was part of the reason why they now had to live in a group home.

Whitney was tapping her right foot, waiting for us to give her our full attention. "My name is Whitney P.," she said. "This is my first time here."

Of course, it wasn't her first time. It was just part of the game to say so. I caught on quickly and said, "Hi, Whitney!" when everyone else did. I think we were supposed to have tons of warm enthusiasm, only our "Hi,

Whitney" came out limp because of the heat that I already mentioned.

Whitney gave us a disappointed and annoyed look, but continued anyway. "I am"—*dramatic pause*—"an alcoholic." She pressed her hands to her heart. "It all started way back when I was born with a big old hole in my heart. *Not* in my throat, which is something any old Harry in the street can have and is nothing to brag about. And if that's not enough, well, man-oh-man, there were plenty other things that ran wild in my life. To begin with . . ."

Whitney then provided us with her usual rundown of the awful, no good, rotten, miserable things that have happened to her and then threw in some other juicy tidbits, which were more or less a pack of lies. I have to admit that Whitney was a pretty entertaining reforming alcoholic. When she got to the end and was crying fake tears, she reminded us that we were all supposed to start saying peppy AA things like "Thanks for sharing, Whitney!"

However, as I mentioned before, no one was in the mood for peppy. Fern didn't even have the energy to giggle. Monica sunk further into the couch and whined, "Be quiet, Whitney. I have a headache. You're talking too much. You always talk too much."

"Me? Talk too much?" Whitney looked genuinely surprised, then she lashed out. "You snore."

"I don't!" Monica protested. "I just breathe heavy. It's my allergies."

"Nope. You snore." As soon as Whitney started making piggy sounds, that did it. The lid of Pandora's box lifted, which is something that I learned about during Betty's Greek-mythology, library phase. What this means in regular English is that it was as if dozens of mean spirits came screaming out. As the only sensible, polite person in the room, I was the only one who didn't unleash something mean about someone else.

"You smell like armpits."

"Your teeth have green fuzz."

"Stop laughing at everything."

"You stop laughing at me!"

"You'll never be adopted!"

"No, you'll never be adopted!"

"I don't want to be adopted!"

Of course, Amber didn't say anything either. At this point, I had given up any hope of ever hearing her voice. But I could tell the whole scene was making her nervous because she started plucking at the few eyebrow hairs that were still left on her face.

It wasn't shaping up to be a very good day.

The Knitting Lady came into the room then, took a seat next to Amber, and gently sandwiched the girl's hands between her own. The Knitting Lady herself wasn't holding up too well with the weather either. She had cracked lips and instead of looking 111, she looked 112. Even though she was sweating, her lips and teeth started chattering like they belonged to a little kid who had been in the water too long. She was definitely having a bad speaking day.

"S-stop it! S-stop it, already. All this b-bickering and squabbling! If everyone stops c-complaining for ten seconds, I'll tell a story."

Story. That was the magic word.

"A true story!" Whitney demanded.

"All my stories are t-true. They're all about your ancestors."

Whitney took a sharp inhale and then released it through her nose. "I don't have ancestors. That's why I'm here."

"Now, Whitney, why do you think that? You have h-hundreds of ancestors. You all do. I've told you about some of them. Do you know who I mean?"

Monica shrugged.

"H-how about you, Fern?"

"Huh?" she said.

I said, "I don't belong here, so I can't be expected to know."

The Knitting Lady looked disappointed, as if we had let her down in a small but very important way. "S-Superman, for instance. His p-parents couldn't raise him, so some kind earthlings took him in. And what about the story I told you the other day? He's one of your ancestors, too, each and every one of you."

"What story?" Fern asked.

"Basket Boy!" Whitney exclaimed.

"The one adopted by the fairy?" Fern asked.

"Pharaoh," the Knitting Lady corrected.

Whitney was nodding her big head so fast, she looked like a bobble-head doll in the back window of a car. "I knew Basket Boy was my kind of kid! When his mother stuck him in those river reeds, did he scream his head off? No! Did he get all mealymouthed and wimpy around the guy who adopted him? No! Not even when he found out that his new father was king of half the world and everything."

"Th-that's the story I mean! That boy who was put into a basket by his mother went on to greatness. He did amazing things to help his people."

By Basket Boy, I figured that she meant Moses. Betty was a great reader, and as I mentioned before, we spent a lot of time in the public library, studying whatever caught her attention. The Bible happened to be one of Betty's favorites, so I knew all about Moses and how he never lived with his real mother again.

I pointed that out. Then I pointed out that my mother was coming for me any time now. "Therefore," I concluded, "Basket Boy can't be my ancestor, too."

"Are you calling the Knitting Lady a liar?" Whitney challenged.

"No, but—"

"The Knitting Lady makes things up, but she doesn't lie," Monica insisted.

"No, but—"

"Who's a liar?" Fern asked. "Basket Boy?"

I stayed firm. "Nobody's a liar. But the fact is, I'm not going to be adopted. I have a mother."

The Knitting Lady patted Whitney on the shoulder to calm her down, but she talked to me. "I didn't say that you'll never see your m-mother again. Some of our ancestors get adopted, some don't. You still share a common history."

"History?" I asked.

"It means that you have similar experiences. You have some of the same heroes. You know the same stories. You're members of the same tribe."

Whitney looked lost. So did the others. But for me, a thought took shape, and I guess the Knitting Lady caught me thinking it. "Cal, do you see what I'm getting at?"

"Well, if Basket Boy—I mean, Moses—is Whitney's ancestor and he's Monica's ancestor and he's Amber's and Fern's, that means . . ."

The Knitting Lady was nodding her head in encouragement. "Go ahead, Cal. Work through the logic."

"It means that Whitney, Monica, Fern, and Amber are all related. And me, too, only of course, I'm not."

"Like cousins?" Whitney asked. "We're all cousins?" Then she pointed to Fern and said, "I'm not related to *her.*"

"You wish," Monica said back.

"When you wish upon a star . . . ," Fern started singing.

"See!" Whitney said. "See what I mean?"

The Knitting Lady scratched her head. "What I see is that I'm failing to make my point here. You're all resisting the connection. Why am I not g-getting through?"

Nobody had the answer for her, of course. I wanted to understand. I really did. But I couldn't believe that I was related to them. Any of them. Betty was my family.

Whitney didn't buy it either. "Jeez-Louise, just tell the story."

At that, the Knitting Lady froze. Her teeth were giving her bottom lip a good hard chew, so you could tell she was getting ready to say something important. If it had been me, I would have given Whitney a much-needed lecture about rudeness. But instead, the Knitting Lady's features softened. "You're right. It's best to just tell the story."

"A new one," Whitney demanded. "Something we haven't heard before."

"There is one sp-special story. But I don't think you're ready for it."

"Man-oh-man, that's what you always say about this story! We're ready for it!"

"It's c-complicated with lots of ancestors to keep track of."

Monica made a moaning sound. "I don't think I can follow it. I'm not good at complicated things."

"Me neither," Fern said. "But I'll try. I'll help you, Monica."

"If she tells it, you can't start laughing at everything," Whitney ordered.

Fern crossed her heart.

Meanwhile, the Knitting Lady's eyes were narrowing like two hands trying to hold on to something. I knew how *that* was—wanting to do something and not knowing if it's the right thing to do.

"Is it about a girl or a boy?" I asked.

The eyes let go. "Okay, you get your story. Take from it what you will."

"How does it start?" I asked.

The Knitting Lady closed her eyes and tilted her head up to the ceiling, like the story was written on the inside of her lids. All the tension around her face was gone. And when she opened her mouth, her voice was smooth and easy, no stutter at all, like she was singing us a song that began "The story of a girl who began to remember.

CHAPTER 10

"This is the story of a girl who began to remember. You don't need to hop on a magic carpet like in many stories you hear. The real distance is time."

"So this *is* a fairy tale!" Whitney said.

"No," Monica said. "It didn't start 'Once upon a time,' so it's true."

"True or not true, you have to start by imagining an old-fashioned, countrified past. There were acres of soil, rich and black enough to make you shiver. There were plum trees, an orchardful that had to be picked in late summer or else the fruit fell and rotted on the ground. What a stink! One by one, the plums were handpicked and then set out to bake in the sun. At first, it looked like chickens had laid little purple eggs in long, neat rows. But after a while, the fruit shriveled and turned into prunes."

"Ewww! I hate prunes," Monica said. "It means you're constipated, and I hate being constipated."

Whitney waved her off. "Forget about prunes! Go on with the story."

"The opening scene takes place in a building, a long,

no-nonsense rectangle, three floors high with more windows than you can count. Anyone could see that this was a building not to be questioned. It was painted such a gleaming white, it looked like it could deflect anything, even the impurities of the world."

Fern was all dreamy-eyed. "It sounds like a castle. I love a story with a castle."

"But a true story can't have a castle in it," Whitney complained.

"As a matter of fact," I said, "real castles exist, not only those in fairy tales."

The Knitting Lady continued. "All I'll say right now is that it looked like a castle. Every time people saw it nestled against the parched brown foothills, it startled them. The citizens of the nearby town said it looked like a great, white throne set against a carpet of wheat. They wanted to imagine that it was filled with princesses, poor but noble, being groomed to take their rightful place in the world. But for the people living inside, there was nothing romantic about the place."

"What was it?" I asked.

"There are so many names, and they all mean the same thing. An asylum, an institution, a mission, the Society, the Orphanage. It was a group home."

"Like this one?" Whitney asked.

"Much, much larger. There were a hundred girls at any

one time. And things were more permanent back in those days. It wasn't like today when you go in and out of various foster homes, or back and forth between your own family and group homes. Once a girl came in, she usually stayed."

Monica asked the question I was going to ask: "Did it have a name?" And the Knitting Lady answered: "The full and complete name was the Home for Orphaned and Indigent Children. The girls living there called it the Home. Many of them even came to think of it as home, even though most people in the world—if you could ask them— would say that a real home doesn't have a capital *H* and *the* in front of it. And now for the main character."

"A she!" Fern said, then turned to Whitney to brag. "See, I told you I could pay attention."

"The m-main character. Yes, a girl. The girl who began to remember. Like anyone who begins to remember, she first has things to forget. She was young when this story starts—about seven—and many things for the young are like a half-forgotten dream."

"She needs to have a name," Whitney insisted. "And don't just say *the girl*. You've pulled that one too much!"

"I agree. I call her Brenda. If you look up that name in a baby book, it means 'Little Raven.' Can you picture her? Her hair was raven black, so dark it had purple streaks. And shiny! A beautiful child. Her mother wasn't beautiful. She was glamorous, but only her hands—"

Fern interrupted. "Brenda's hands?"

"No, her mother's hands. They were something to behold, as wide as they were long and knotted with muscle."

Fern was still confused. "Knotted Hands is . . . ?"

Monica answered, "Brenda," but Whitney said, "No! The other one!"

The Knitted Lady made two fists and tapped one on top of the other. "Ahhh, I can see that I'm making this story way too confusing too soon. Let's go back to where Brenda's story begins. She's seven years old and she remembers arms lifting her from a bed and putting her into a car. She remembers a long drive in the middle of the night. She falls in and out of consciousness to the drone of the motor and the rhythm of voices from the front seat of the car. Her mother—"

"The glamorous one," I reminded everyone.

"Yes, that's her. Her mother muttered, 'Save me from one more town that ends in *ville.*'"

"In *ville,*" Fern mimicked, and started to laugh, but Whitney told her to zip it. "Go on," she urged the Knitting Lady.

"The man behind the wheel, who had a head of thick chestnut-colored hair, lit a cigarette, then blew smoke out the window. There were other memories attached to this particular day. Brenda's first sight of the Home off in the distance. The sound of her mother's voice, both wary and too enthusiastic: 'Look how white the building is. I'll say that for it. At least we know it's clean.' The man's wordless grunt. The long drive into the hills.

"When the car finally stopped, the man lifted Brenda, still dazed with sleepiness, out of the back seat. Her nose pressed against his jacket, the scent of tobacco mixing with the thick perfume of flowering plum trees in the morning air. An unfamiliar voice pulled Brenda out of her sleepy haze. A short, plain-faced woman, hands in the pockets of her apron, was looking at her and said, 'She does walk, doesn't she? We don't have no amenities here for a lame girl.'

"And then, her mother's voice again, 'She walks.'

"Without warning, Brenda's feet hit the ground, and she felt the man's hand in the small of her back, pushing her forward. 'Show the lady,' he ordered. 'Walk.'

"Brenda made a few hesitant marching steps, looking at her mother for approval. In return, Brenda got a weak smile. *This is not right,* she thought, and felt an uncomfortable twinge running through her, like when you drink something too cold and it goes right to your forehead. She looked around in a panic. There were girls everywhere, dozens of girls, some still in diapers, some already looking like adults, all dressed alike in white blouses and gray jumpers. Girls leaned on brooms, girls propped themselves on rakes, staring at her.

"Then Brenda's mother was down on one knee in front of her daughter. 'My darling girl, maybe a farm life will do you some good.' And then the man with the handsome head of hair took Brenda's mother by the arm, urging her back to her feet.

"'One minute,' she said to him, then turned back to Brenda. 'To remember me by.' She pressed something into Brenda's hand."

"What was it?" Monica asked.

"An unusual and very fancy pair of eyeglasses with a French name. Lorgnette. These glasses didn't hook around your ears, but had a gold handle to hold them up by. They were all the rage of glamorous ladies."

"What did Brenda say back?" I asked.

"Nothing. All she could do was watch her mother walk away."

"It was a big mistake," I said. "Her mother will come back."

"What m-makes you think that?"

"Because she will! It was a big mistake."

"N-no, Cal, it wasn't fair. But it wasn't a mistake."

"And then?" Whitney asked.

"And then— Girls, I'm sorry to say, we need to stop here."

"No! Don't stop!" Whitney begged.

"That's it?" Fern asked. "The end of the story? Did I miss something?"

"Come on," Monica whined. "I won't be able to sleep tonight. I'll be up *all* night worrying."

"Me too," Whitney said. "I have a thousand questions!"

Still, the Knitting Lady couldn't be persuaded to continue. It was my first sign of just how stubborn she could be. She pushed herself to standing. "Brenda's story has w-way too many twists and turns for one sitting. But don't worry. We'll get to them all. Brenda isn't going anywhere for a long time."

Fern's arm shot up. She waved it around. "One question. Please, just one? Please, it's important." The Knitting Lady held up one finger, and we all waited to see which of the thousand questions would be answered.

"So my question is," Fern said, "are we having prunes for dinner or not?"

CHAPTER 11

Later that afternoon, we all went to a park. It was only a few blocks away, but by the time we got there, we were dragging from the heat. The Knitting Lady had a conversation with a Parks and Rec type of person who turned on the sprinklers and let us run through them. Monica and Fern held hands and squealed, glowing like this was the best day of their lives. Amber looked happy, too. It was the first time I had actually seen her smile. She had the straightest whitest teeth. Whitney, soaking wet, took a flying leap and flung herself belly first on a swing.

After running through the sprinkler, I shook myself off like a dog and found a tree to sit under. Whitney motioned for me to join her on the swings, but I waved her off. That's another way I'm like Betty. I can stand being around people only for so long without needing to get off by myself. How else can a person think?

And I had things to think about, such as those fancy French glasses that had been placed in Brenda's hands. The look of them. The feel of them. Brenda's situation was certainly bad, but at least she had her mother's fancy glasses. What did I have of Betty's? Nothing! Not even a piece of hair, not a scarf with her smell, not a scrap of paper with her tight handwriting that always reminded me of barbed wire. This thought turned around and around in my head until I realized with a sick feeling that I had no proof that my mother was my mother, that she ever even existed.

I shivered, and it had nothing to do with being wet.

Stop! Stop! Stop! I, Cal Lavender, refused to give in to thoughts like that. I would just have to keep myself busy until Betty came for me. Put *that* in the story of my real life: *Cal Lavender knows the secret of avoiding certain thoughts. She keeps busy.*

By the time we got back to the Pumpkin House, I had the perfect "keeping busy" project in mind. My temporary roommates definitely needed some serious help in the room-cleaning-and-organization department. Most typical, average eleven-year-old girls would rather clip their toenails with a chain saw than clean their rooms, but organization is something that I really excel at. It was practically a requirement for living with Betty. If I didn't have an orderly system for just about everything, meals would never be made, my homework would wind up in the trash, we would have to wear dirty underwear, and, as I mentioned before, that's no way to walk around. To my way of thinking, organization is a beautiful and necessary thing.

That's exactly what I said to Whitney and Amber. I stood in the middle of the messy bedroom and said, "Organization is a beautiful and necessary thing. What on earth is *this* doing here?"

Whitney was on her bed reading a comic book. "What's *what* doing *where*?"

I held up a toothbrush. "This." Then I hooked my finger into the back of one of her shoes and let it dangle. "This doing in here."

"That's where I keep it," she said.

"Why?"

"Because then I know exactly where my toothbrush is."

I thought: *This is going to be a long road. It will take me several days to just make a dent in this mess, but I'm not going to be here that long. Still, I'll do what I can. This will be my legacy to them. Years from now, Whitney and Amber will recall fondly: Remember that girl who was here for only a day or two? That Cal Lavender really taught us a thing or two about the beauty of organization.*

"I'm going to clean," I said. "Yes, that's what I'm going to do." I began my attack by giving the toothbrush a proper home in the bathroom down the hall. Then I picked up the pile of Whitney's clothes that were all over the floor like roadkill. I folded each piece and you couldn't find better folding in the finest department stores.

But where was I supposed to put all the perfectly

folded laundry? Whitney's drawers were already overflowing. And what should I do with her shoes? The closet, I guess. I opened the door. They joined about a million other things stuffed in there. From the floor, I started picking up candy wrappers, gum wrappers, toothpicks, and about two dozen cellophane sleeves, the kind that keeps string cheese in fresh and sanitary individual portions. I moved Ike Eisenhower the Fifth from the messy dresser top to a messy desktop. Then I picked up what I thought were pieces of broken greenish plastic, but they turned out to be old, moldy, unsanitary pieces of string cheese.

By this point, I was hoping that my temporary roommates would catch some of my cleaning fever and join in enthusiastically. I sighed. I gave a bigger sigh. I sighed again. I know they heard me, but they went deaf all of a sudden. Amber sat watching me like I was a stage show, *The Sound of Scrubbing.* It was creepy. But to my mind, being creepy is absolutely no excuse for being a slob.

I asked, "Can she talk?"

Whitney looked up. "Huh?"

"Can Amber talk?"

"Can a . . . can a *what* poop in the woods?"

"A bear," I answered.

"Yeah, a bear can poop in the woods, and Amber can talk. Can't you, Amber?"

Amber nodded, which was infuriating because, if she

could talk, that was the time to do it. Whitney kept eating her sunflower seeds—*crack, crack*—which covered the carpet, like she expected April showers to come in and turn them into May flowers.

I said, "Whitney, are you afraid of getting lost in here?"

She looked up from the comic book. "Huh?"

I paused for effect. "Like Hansel and Gretel? Are you leaving a trail of seeds so that you can find your way back to your bed?"

Whitney started humming "Whistle While You Work." When she got to the chorus, she stopped and said, "My fifth foster mother was like you. A real cleaning nut. Once a week, she made us do 'Cleaning Madness.' It took hours and wrecked a perfectly good Saturday afternoon. My job was to rake the wall-to-wall carpet. Man-oh-man, all the nap had to go in the same direction."

Personally, I did not see what was so outrageous about that. I bet it looked a whole lot nicer than wall-to-wall shells. "Well, no offense, but anyone would be a cleaning nut compared to you. Face it, Whitney. You're organizationally challenged!" I turned to Amber and said, "You, too."

Whitney laughed like *How amusing,* crossed her legs, and pretended to be smoking a cigarette in a glamorous way. "You may clean the toilet next."

"Well, it *does* need it," I said.

"Go wild," she said.

Some people would have stopped cleaning on the spot and let Whitney and Amber roll around in their own mess. But when Cal Lavender gets mad, she gets cleaning. Come to think of it, when I get sad, I also clean. I really throw myself into it until I get lost in all the moving and dusting and organizing and scrubbing. It's my way of forgetting about everything else.

I ricocheted around the room, squirting Endust and wiping down every surface. Door frames, door handles, table legs, baseboards. I must have taken an inch layer of dust off the windowsill alone. An *inch*! I wiped the outside of Ike Eisenhower the Fifth's home. I emptied the overflowing trashcan. I was about to tackle the black hole of a closet when Whitney called me back from the Land of Spic-and-Span by saying, "Whatever you do, don't look in there."

"In where?" I asked. "The closet?"

"No, there." She pointed across the room at her dresser.

"I'm not anywhere near your dresser."

"Good. Whatever you do, don't look in there. Especially the bottom drawer."

I tried to ignore her, but it was no use. Most people are like that, right? You tell them not to think about pink elephants, and all they can do then is think about pink elephants. "Why shouldn't I look in there?" I took two steps closer.

Whitney glanced around the room suspiciously like she was certain that foreign agents, the CIA, the county school board, and the anchorman on the nightly news were all eavesdropping. "It's the PICTURE," she said. That's the way she said it, like the word *picture* was in capital letters or in special print.

"What picture?"

"Amber has seen the PICTURE. Right, Amber?"

Amber nodded.

Whitney's hand went to her mouth. *Crack-crack.* Her eyes narrowed into slits. *Crack-crack.* "You wanna see it?"

"Sure," I said.

"Say *really, really.*"

"Really, really."

"Okay then." She hopped out of bed, opened the drawer, dug to the very bottom, and handed something flat to me. "Don't bend it!" she ordered.

It was a photograph of a little girl and was already bent, crumpled too, like she had pulled it in and out of the drawer three times a day for the past five years. The girl in the picture was about three. Her back was to the camera, but she was peeking over her shoulder so that you could see part of her face. She also happened to be buck naked in that cute, Jell-O–bottom, three-year-old way.

I looked up for an explanation. Whitney was beaming. "That's her."

"Her?"

"Tell her, Amber. That's my sister. Right, Amber?"

The Amber nod again.

I looked closer at the photo. "I thought you said you don't have any family."

"I *said* I don't have any parents. I have a sister. She got adopted because she didn't have a hole in her heart. Now she's looking for me. Tell her, Amber."

Amber's eyes went wide, and for a moment, I actually thought she was going to speak. But even if she had wanted to, there was no breaking in on Whitney, who was really on a roll: "Amber had a dream about her. A dream! That's a sign, all right. She's the older sister, two years older. But she needs me. I have to go to her."

I asked, "Where does she live?"

Again that Whitney look of disgust that told me I did not know much about anything worth knowing. "How would I know where she lives? When someone gets adopted, they don't tell you anything about where they went. Sometimes, the new parents even change the kid's name just because they feel like it."

"So how are you going to track her down?"

Whitney waved the picture like she was drying it. "I'll recognize her, of course."

"By that?" I asked in disbelief. "It's all out of focus. Besides, she won't look like this anymore."

"Look here!" Whitney was stabbing the end of her fingernail at the photo.

I looked over her shoulder. "What am I supposed to be looking at?"

"The birthmark! My sister has a little veiny thing, a bump, right on her left butt cheek. It's shaped like a heart."

I was looking hard. I was really trying to see something, but there was nothing to see. I pressed my tongue against my front teeth and ran Whitney's plan—if you could call it a plan—through my mind: *Let me see if I have this right. The last time Whitney saw her sister, the girl was running around in diapers, only without the diaper. She doesn't know her sister's name. She doesn't know where she lives. The only thing she has to go on is an old photo and a birthmark that hardly exists. Wrong, wrong, wrong.*

There was something definitely not normal about Whitney's logic. I said in a very polite way, "Excuse me, Whitney, but are you intending to walk up to every twelve-year-old girl in the world and ask to see her bottom?"

Whitney: *Crack-crack.*

I continued politely and logically. "Frankly, your plan has problems."

Whitney: Louder, faster *crack-crack-crack*. She stopped cracking. "It does not."

"I have to be honest," I said. "It's totally illogical. Frankly, it's a touch not normal. Truthfully, it's insane."

Whitney ripped the picture away from my eyes. "Well, you should know plenty about insane."

I asked cautiously, "What do you mean by that?"

"I snuck a peek at your social-worker file and your mother is plenty insane. She insaned all over the library!"

I said nothing.

"Crazy," she said. "C-R-A-Z-I-E."

Whitney's words were making me feel like I had just fallen off a jungle gym and landed so hard on my back that all my breathing caught high in my chest. What did Whitney know about Betty? What did she know about anything?

She turned to Amber. "Betty's in the funny farm. What do people *do* in the funny farm anyway? They must plant seeds and water the clowns that grow. Get it? The *funny* farm."

Whitney kept saying "funny farm, funny farm," and I had my hands clamped over my ears, ordering myself to ignore her. I called on my special power, not a superpower or anything like that, but a strength that I taught myself to conjure up whenever I need it. *You will not cry. You will not cry!!*

I WILL NOT CRY! And when I was absolutely, one hundred percent sure that I wouldn't, I looked Whitney right in the face and said, "At least I have a mother."

That stopped her. That shut her up! She winced like someone getting a scraped knee cleaned with alcohol. Then her eyes began widening, wider and wider like she was trying to inhale me through them. She reached out and pressed her hand over my mouth like a gas mask. I slapped it away. She started to say, "Library," so I yelled, "Mother!"

Through the walls, I could hear Monica and Fern yelling, "Fight! Fight!" I turned to Amber—"What are you looking at?"—and took giant steps out of the room.

On my way down the stairs, I vowed: *Nobody will ever know what happened in the library!*

CHAPTER 12

Here's what happened in the library:

From what I can tell, average grown-ups have trained themselves not to think about all the stupid, scary, and hurtful things in the world. If they thought too much about them, they couldn't get out of bed in the morning. And if they couldn't get out of bed in the morning, who would take care of the cooking, cleaning, teaching, shopping, taxpaying, and all that other adult business? Who would drive the buses?

But anyone who knows Betty knows that she is not an average grown-up. She's more like a kid. Things get to her. Usually I could sense when trouble was starting to build up inside. She'd sleep too much, then stop sleeping altogether. She'd talk and talk, but then suddenly I wouldn't be able to get a word out of her. Mostly though, it showed in her eyes, the way they'd be burning way too bright, like supernovas, two distant unreachable stars that are ready to explode.

That day at the library, I must have fallen asleep. Because the next thing I remember was seeing volume F of the *World Book Encyclopedia* flying through the air. Then, *The Complete Guide to Learning and Loving Ballet* hit the floor across the room. All over the reading room, heads lifted from their necks and swiveled in our direction like they were controlled by machinery. Betty threw more books, and arms went up in defense.

I remember an alarm ringing. Shouts. Screams. People running. Elbows pushing this way and that. I remember ordering myself, *Do something! Do something!*

And then all went silent for a second as Betty sat back down at our table and plopped forward at the waist. Her arms were spread, and her face lay flat against the table. She looked like a puppet whose strings had been cut. I heard someone say, "Don't put the child at risk."

The child. That was me. I wanted to say: *I'm not at risk. Just leave us alone. Let me take care of things. I always know what to do.* But I didn't say anything.

Why didn't I say anything? In the Knitting Lady's story, Brenda didn't say anything either. Why?

And then another voice in the library said, "I'm going to try to get closer. She's calm now."

But I knew better. They should have asked me. I knew that Betty was only on hold. Her eyes opened—*thwock!*—like parachutes. A wail went up and then her wails filled the room, like she was drawing sadness from every sad story in every sad book in the library.

Why didn't I notice her eyes earlier? Why didn't I see the signs? If I had only looked closer. If only I hadn't fallen asleep.

So that's what happened in the library. But nobody in the Pumpkin House will ever know. They would never understand. Nothing like that ever happened to them. Ever!

CHAPTER 13

"I am *not* staying in that bedroom."

I found the Knitting Lady alone in Talk Central. Her hands were a whirl of yarn and needles. "What's wrong with the b-bedroom? You have the nicest room, in my opinion. But don't tell Fern and Monica I said that."

"It's not the bedroom. Something's wrong with Whitney. Amber, too. I'm sure you've noticed." I tapped my index finger to my temple and made little cuckoo circles. "The polite term for them is head cases."

"P-polite? I'd hate to hear the— Dang!" She held up the long rectangle she was knitting. There was a puzzled look on her face.

"Did you mess up?" I asked.

She shushed me. "Give me a sec." She began counting the number of loops on her needle. "One, two . . ." At seventy-one, she said "Dang!" again. "I knew it. I dropped a stitch somewhere. Help me find it."

I knew zilch about knitting, but finding things was my specialty. Betty was always losing something, and it was always up to me to find it. But where should I look? When you drop a stitch, how far can it go? Does it bounce or roll? I don't like admitting that I don't know something, so I started checking in the most logical place, under the couch.

Above me, I heard the Knitting Lady laugh. "It doesn't take off *that* far."

She held up her knitting to study it. I looked closely at the shades of purple, but I didn't see anything that looked like a dropped stitch. Not that I knew what a dropped stitch looked like, but I expected to see something cracked or hanging off at least.

"Nothing," I said.

"I don't see it either. But I know it's h-here somewhere."

"How do you know you dropped it if you don't see it?"

"I've been at this long enough to feel it in my bones. My rhythm felt off. So I counted, and sure enough one is missing."

"Can you fix it?"

"S-sure. Everything can be fixed. I go backward and find the source of the mistake."

She slipped the needle out of her work and started unraveling. My stomach winced as I watched all those nice, even rows disappearing. That's another thing you can say about me: *Cal Lavender is a stomach person, the way some people are headache people or ache-in-the-back people.* The stomach is where I feel things first.

I asked, "How long did it take you to knit all that?"

"This? A couple of hours. This y-yarn isn't the easiest to work with. And the needles are small. It's a new pattern for me, and a hard one at that. But the hardest ones are the most rewarding when you finally get it right."

She handed me the balls of yarn and showed me how to wind the unraveled strands onto their matching color.

"Doesn't this make you frustrated?" I asked.

"Of c-course. I'm like everyone else. I like things to run nice and smooth. When I first started knitting, I was younger than you and used to get furious when I had to rip out my work. Furious! But mistakes are inevitable. Especially when you're working with something new, before you get in sync with it."

"What if you ignored the mistake? Does one . . . what did you call it?"

"A dr-dropped stitch."

"One of those doesn't sound like the end of the world. You have so many others. What does one matter?"

"B-believe you me, you're not the first to come up with that bright idea. It seems logical enough, and I have personally tried ignoring my mistakes, only to find myself in a real knitting pickle later on. One little mistake influences every stitch that comes after it. Trust me, in the long run it's best to go back and clear it up. There's no way around it."

I repeated after her, "Clear it up?"

"Start fresh," she said. "Sometimes you just get off on the wrong f-foot. You're a smart girl. You see what I'm getting at."

I didn't. Not until just that moment anyway. Then I recognized the tone that grown-ups get when they're trying to slip in some advice or a really big life lesson. As I rewound the conversation in my head, all the telltale words were there.

Ignoring mistakes. Going back to the beginning. Getting in sync. Starting fresh.

"Are you talking about knitting? Or something else?"

She didn't miss a beat. "What else do you have in mind? What else do you think I might be talking about?"

But before I had a chance to answer, she shouted, "Got it!"

"Got what?"

"The dropped stitch. See, it wasn't very far back. Now it's no problem at all to correct. I join it to the others. Then I can move forward again."

I knew what she was trying to say. It was one of those life lessons, all right. Whitney and Amber and I had gotten off on the wrong foot, and I should go back and correct my mistake so that I don't find myself in a pickle down the line.

"I know what you're saying, but I still want to change my room," I insisted.

"Ahhhh," she said. "If you're going to bitch, then you might as well stitch."

It was funny hearing something like that coming out of her mouth. *Stitch* and *bitch.* That sounded more like something Betty would come up with, which made me wonder what my mother would think of the Knitting Lady and vice versa. They definitely weren't anything like each other. They were more like exact opposites. Betty was . . . well, Betty. And the Knitting Lady had a way of being calm that made you think that everything is running smoothly, that there really aren't any problems in the world, at least no problems that can't somehow be fixed.

But still, they would hit it off. I just knew they would. Betty would tell the Knitting Lady her stories. The Knitting Lady wouldn't rub her temples as if it gave her a headache just to be around Betty. They would like each other. They would.

"Your turn," the Knitting Lady said, and handed me a pair of knitting needles. They were different than hers. These were as long and thick as drumsticks. "Ready for a good old-fashioned stitch-and-bitch?"

CHAPTER 14

Knitting lesson number one: A dropped stitch is only the beginning of all the possible mistakes a person can make. You can add a stitch. You can twist a stitch. You can purl when you are supposed to knit and knit when you are supposed to purl. A purl, by the way, is a backward knit stitch, which is sometimes exactly what you want. But when you don't do it on purpose, a purl is an ugly screwup that sticks out like a pimple on your nose.

The Knitting Lady began by teaching me the basic knit stitch, which was easy enough, especially when she put the rhyme to it. She said, "In through the front door / run around the back / peek through the window / off jumps Jack."

Translation: You stick the needle into the first loop, wrap the yarn around it, then pull it through, up and off the top.

Normally I'm not the braggy type, but I was a total and complete natural at knitting. I'm sure the Knitting Lady had never seen anyone take to it like I did. I made one stitch, then another. Pretty soon, my hands were flying and I found myself at the end of the row. Then with just about no help at all, I flipped the needles around and started back down the other side.

Only, by the time I got to the seventh row, things were not going quite so smoothly. I couldn't get in the front door. In frustration, I jammed a needle through the loop. There, that worked. Only the loop looked all mangled. Plus it had a death grip around both needles.

I was deep in a knitting pickle.

"Got a problem with Jack?" the Knitting Lady asked. She took my knitting and examined it. "Ahhhh, the tight-stitch type."

"What's that mean?" I asked.

"Everyone has a t-tendency. I could tell from the minute I looked at you. I said to myself, *Cal Lavender is the tight-stitch type.* I'm a stitch reader."

"Like a palm reader?"

"Sort of. Only I don't care so much about the future. The present is much more interesting, and that's what your stitches reveal. They tell me all about who you are right n-now, at this very moment."

She picked up a tangle of yarn and needles that were bunched up on the floor by her feet. What a mess! It was the wildest looking thing, oranges and purples with a whole lot of loose ends snaking out. Somebody had no taste in colors at all!

"Take this, for instance. A loose-stitch type. Definitely,"

she said. "I look at this, and I see someone whose personality is all loosey-goosey, the opposite of yours."

It didn't take a genius to know who did it. "Whitney," I said. "It's an obvious mess. It is so . . ."

"*So* Whitney, isn't it? Who else would put these wacky colors together? It's so much fun, it makes me laugh."

Personally, I didn't see what kind of fun she saw in it. It made me laugh—*Ha!*—but not in the nice way the Knitting Lady meant. "Tight definitely has it over being loosey-goosey," I decided. "A million to one."

"One's not better than the other. They can both be strengths. But they can both also be w-weaknesses. Whitney's knitting has trouble holding together. But it's so full of surprises. Sort of like Whitney."

"What does Monica's knitting reveal?"

"W-what do you think?"

"My guess is that she won't even try. She would say that she can't do it, that she doesn't know how, even before she tried."

"I-I'm working on her!" the Knitting Lady said cheerfully.

"And Fern? Hmmm. I bet she starts something and can't remember where she put it and then starts something else new. Am I right?"

The Knitting Lady nodded with encouragement. "Hey, you have the stitch-reading power in you, too."

I held up my knitting. "So what does mine say?"

She put her hand to her temple and did a corny swirling motion like she was going into a trance. "I see precision, a love of order. I see a girl who likes to do things perfectly and often succeeds at it."

Definitely right! "So what's the weakness?"

She patted my knitting like it was her favorite pet, then handed it back. "You tell me. You're the one w-working with it."

It *was* precise. It *was* perfect. It was really something! Except . . . "I guess if I don't loosen up a little, I'll be stuck in the same place forever. How do I loosen up?"

She pulled the needle off the tight stitches. I thought I heard them sigh in relief. "You loosen up your knitting by loosening up yourself. You feel the looseness starting here." She tapped the crown of my head. "Let the looseness travel down through your neck into your hands and out your fingers. Think loose. No! Don't *think* loose. *Be* loose."

I unraveled. "Loose," I said aloud. Then in my head: *Loose, loose.*

I was back to the beginning. This time I was sure I would get it right. I will be loose. I WILL be loose. I WILL BE LOOSE! Only by the time I got to row five, the stitches were strangling the needle again. I didn't even get as far as the last time. How did this happen? Why couldn't I do it right? When the Knitting Lady examined my work, all I wanted to do was apologize.

"For what?" she asked. "For not immediately getting it right? For not being p-perfect? You'll get it. It takes time. Let me ask you an important question: What's the first thing you need when you start a piece of knitting?"

What kind of riddle was this? I tried, "Needles?"

She shook her head no. "Try again."

"Yarn?"

"Nope. Whitney, you want to tell her?"

I had been so engrossed in staying *loose, loose* that I didn't notice Whitney standing at the door. I looked up, then quickly away.

"Uh? Tell her what?" she asked.

"What is the f-first thing you need when you start knitting?"

Whitney answered quickly: "Peace of mind."

CHAPTER 15

Whitney plopped on a chair. She gave me a *glad to see you, glad to see your face* look, which took me by surprise. She didn't look mad or embarrassed or like her stomach hurt, any of the things that a logical person feels right after she's made a brand-new enemy for life. I put on My Face for Unbearably Unpleasant and Embarrassing Situations to show her that I would never fall for phony friendliness. But that was a waste of time, since she didn't even notice. She was too busy bobbing up and down in front of the Knitting Lady, blurting things out. "Come on, come on! It's time. We've waited. Can we? Can you? Come on! Pleeeeease. You promised. Where were we?"

I don't know how the Knitting Lady had the slightest clue what Whitney was talking about, but she answered, "Brenda."

"Get on with it," Whitney ordered.

"Okay. But first, g-gather everyone together."

ᔓ

"Do you r-remember where I stopped? Brenda has arrived at the Home. More than anything, she wanted her life to remain the way it had always been. Now, some people might have trouble understanding that. They would have looked at Brenda's life and thought that it was no life at all for a child. Her mother had dragged Brenda from one town to another and had never given her a permanent home. Many people would have been shocked by the number of boyfriends who had passed through her mother's life. *Shocked!* But Brenda didn't remember any of that. A child remembers what she needs to. This was what Brenda called life, and now she felt everything familiar slipping away.

"Her mother got into the car and said something to the man next to her. He started the engine. The car turned around and headed down the long driveway. The whole time Brenda just stood there gazing out into the distance and waiting for the car to make a U-turn and fly back, tires squealing. But when the car disappeared into a tiny dot on the horizon—*Oh!*—she was outraged. Anger rose from her pores like a gas. A voice screamed. A hand hurled those fancy French glasses to the ground. Brenda barely recognized the voice and the hand. They were hers, of course, but she was too furious to stop herself."

"I like Brenda," Whitney said. "She didn't just stand there and take it."

"Go on," Monica encouraged. "What happened next?"

"I s-suppose I could do that. I could move on from there and tell the story in a nice straightforward, logical manner. But that won't do. It would make it seem like Brenda was just the beginning and the end of her own separate line. What nonsense! So let's leave Brenda now."

"No!" Whitney shouted.

"D-don't worry. Her story isn't going anywhere. There are too many connections. Everything that happened in the past leads to it; the future backs right up to it. We have to go back to the story of Brenda's mother. Let's call her Lillian."

"She's the glamorous one, right?" Fern asked.

"Exactly! G-good for you for remembering. Now, all of you, close your eyes and go back even further in time. There was no TV yet. People had to leave their homes to get entertainment. Now picture a butcher shop on the main street of a small town. In the window, there is a thick cardboard placard."

J. S. BERRY'S DRAMA-VARIETY THEATER,
the Grand Inaugural of the Summer Season.

FEATURING **ARCHEY HUGHES**, *an Old-Timey Singer.*
TOMMY GRANGER—*Bringing a Lifelike Imitation of a Jockey after a Ride.*
SWAIN'S BIRDS—*a Bevy of Feathered Thespians.*

I started laughing. I couldn't help it. Whitney was doubled over. Amber had a small grin, which was a major show of emotion for her. Monica was cracking up. Fern was really out of control—Ha! Ha! Ha! Ha! Ha! Ha! Ha! Ha! Ha! Even when the rest of us stopped laughing, she was still going Ha! Ha! Ha! Ha! Ha! Ha!—until she finally caught her breath and asked the Knitting Lady, "So *what* are we laughing at again?"

"V-vaudeville! You girls have to understand that there were posters like that all across the country, in every small town. That's what entertainment was in those days. Nothing today—not even a circus—comes close to the amazing events you could see for only twenty-five cents! On this same bill there was also *Lovely Lillian with Her Delightfully Dexterous Digits!!!!!!!!!!* Ten exclamation points after her title! One for each digit! She must have been something!"

"Digits?" Whitney asked

"Fingers," I explained. "Or toes."

Monica was shaking her head. "What kind of entertainment is digits?"

"We'll g-get to that. But first, we need to go back even further to before Lillian became the *Lovely Lillian*. Her story opens when she was a young girl in New York City. This was a long time ago, around the turn of the previous century. Back then, it was always hard times, never a break. A lot of people couldn't even manage to squeak by. Groups of kids ran wild all day and all night. Lillian lived in a small, noisy apartment with her mother and—"

"No father?" Monica asked.

"No father. Lillian's father left before she was born. It had always been just her and her mother. On a shelf in their tiny apartment sat a pair of fancy spectacles. They were gold—real gold—thin and light as wire."

"The . . . the . . . you know . . . the whatchamacallits!" Fern called out.

I translated for everyone in a very proper French accent, "The word is *lorgnette*."

"Exactly. K-keep in mind that Lillian and her mother were so poor that they owned nothing that didn't serve some practical use. Except for the lorgnette. These stood in such sharp contrast to their pitiful surroundings that Lillian couldn't keep her eyes off them.

"Lillian's mother was very young and different from a lot of the other adults in this run-down neighborhood. For one thing, she knew how to read and write. And what a lovely voice came out of her mother's mouth. That was their bread and butter. Each morning, Lillian and her mother trudged off to the docks. All day, they stood singing and begging for coins."

"Lillian had a lovely voice, too?" I asked.

"To put it bluntly, n-no. The poor child could not carry a tune, couldn't dance either. When it came to performing, truthfully, our Lillian was pathetic."

"How embarrassing!" Monica said. "I would die of embarrassment."

"B-but not Lillian. She was quite an individual. Most children normally shy away from what they can't do well. But a complete and total lack of talent didn't stop Lillian. Not for a minute! She was a plain little thing, but she already knew that she liked being looked at. Really liked it! On the street corners, she caterwauled and stomped and stumbled over her own feet. She was unstoppable."

"Like this?" Whitney stood and shuffled her feet.

Fern jumped up, too, and moved so fast that her feet slipped out in front of her and she fell to the floor, laughing of course.

"That's exactly the style. Whitney, Fern, you both definitely have some Lillian in you! Even though Lillian was wearing rags, she presented herself to the world as if she were dressed in silk and crinolines. Then one day, everything changed."

"Oh, no!" Monica said.

"Oh, no, what?" Fern asked. "What?"

The Knitting Lady paused. She put down her yarn and needles and looked at us in a serious way. I felt that she was most especially looking at me. "It can happen that way, can't it? One day, things are one way. And the next day, the life you are living, what you call life, changes forever."

CHAPTER 16

"Not forever!" I insisted.

"In this case, yes, forever." The Knitting Lady shook her head. "It's sad. Very, very sad."

Monica took a pillow from the couch and hugged it to her middle. "This is going to be scary. I'm going to have nightmares about this. I know I will."

"Sad?" Fern asked. She scanned faces frantically. "What did I miss? Who's sad? Who's having nightmares?"

Something hard and heavy dropped to the pit of my stomach. *Someone died. The last thing I want to hear is a story where someone dies because dead, dead, dead, that's all I'll think about. Betty and a coffin and that pie-crust makeup. Dead is dead is dead. Forever.*

Monica said what I was thinking, "I hope no one died. I hate a story where somebody dies."

"Not me," Whitney said. "It hardly counts as a story unless someone dies. Especially a mysterious, gruesome death. I saw a dead body once. It had maggots and everything coming out of its eyes."

Monica blanched. "Stop it. You never saw a dead person. You're saying that to scare me. Don't do that!"

Whitney crossed her heart. "Hope to die, it's the truth. Get it? Hope to *die*." Then, she addressed the Knitting Lady, "Did someone die or not?"

"Unfortunately, y-yes. There was a death. It was Lillian's mother. I think you all suspected that. I'm sorry, but that's what happened. One day she was singing and the next day she got a cough and the day after that, the cough got worse. Pneumonia."

"I had pneumonia once, in my sixth foster home," Whitney said. "But I didn't die. At least then, I didn't die. There was the other time when—"

I interrupted, "There's a time for silence, Whitney, and this is it." I pressed the Knitting Lady. "Go on."

"For L-Lillian, there were so many memories attached to this tragedy. For instance, her mother's casket and how it sat on top of a large tank of ice in their apartment."

"Gross!" Monica blurted out.

"That's h-how they did things in those days. Everyone in the apartment building came to pay their respects. Neighbors filtered in and out. The religious ones crossed themselves. Nobody knew the dead woman well, and, if the truth be told, none of them cared much for what little they knew. She had always seemed to be putting on airs, the way she carried herself in a straight-backed way like she was better than her surroundings. Still, a great many neighbors cried when they looked at the young mother on a block of ice."

"Did Lillian look at her mother?" I asked.

Monica covered her face: "No, I wouldn't look. Never, ever!"

"Wh-what do you think, Cal? Can you put yourself in Lillian's shoes?"

"I think she wanted to look," I began. "But then again, she wouldn't want to. Like when you know there's a really scary part in a movie and you try to keep your eyes open, but at the last second, you put your hands over them."

"It was a l-lot like that. Lillian would approach, then at the last second scurry off to a closet or dive under a table, her heart pounding. Then for hours, she sat on the floor in a corner of the room, knees drawn to her chest, silent. For probably the first time in her life, the girl wanted no attention at all. Still, neighbors kept urging her to say a final farewell to her mother. A woman with big teeth came right up to Lillian's eyes. 'Come on and be a big girl,' she insisted. 'Pay your respects. Say something.'

"But Lillian put on a face she invented herself, a hard, scowling face that drove the woman away. It wasn't that Lillian wasn't thinking about her mother. Of course, she was thinking about her. For days, she had been thinking of nothing else. But after a while, Lillian just didn't know what to think anymore. She had run out of thoughts, the way you can run out of tears. Everything was numb. So what could she say? What does a girl say when her mother has died? What words are there?"

Fern gave a nervous laugh.

"None," Monica said. "There are no words."

"So in her h-head, where no one could hear, Lillian conducted her own farewell ritual. She sang a song her mother was always singing. Then she sang another. We all have our own way of mourning and of saying good-bye to the people we love. This was Lillian's homage.

"At some point, without even realizing it herself, she began to sing her mother's favorite tunes aloud. She sang 'Take Me Out to the Ball Game.' And she sang 'In the Good Old Summertime.' How does that song go again? It was so popular way back when. *You hold her hand, and she holds yours, / and that's a very good sign. / That she's your tootsy-wootsy, / in the good old summertime.* Lillian got so caught up in her singing—her loud, off-key singing that she didn't notice when two strangers, a woman and a man, walked into the apartment."

"Uh-oh," Whitney said. "Here comes trouble."

"How do you know that?" I asked.

"It's obvious. In stories, strangers are trouble." Whitney turned to the Knitting Lady. "Trouble, right? So they walked in and—"

"*Walked* is the wrong w-word for the way these two entered. They made an entrance. They floated. They seemed to take up all the space and air in the room even though there were only two of them. Once or twice, Lillian and her mother had ventured out of their neighborhood to gaze at the clothing in the windows of fancy shops on fancy streets. Fancy was how the woman dressed, all lace and silk and satin that made a swishing noise when she turned. The man wore a thick black cloak made of the finest wool and carried a broad-brimmed hat.

"As the man looked around the apartment, his eyebrows shot up in a judgmental arch. The woman's nose crinkled and twitched as though it was the first time in her life that she had ever smelled anything that wasn't fresh from the laundry. She cleared her throat: 'We hear there is a child. Is that the child over there?'"

Fern started singing: "'She's your wootsy-tootsy. In the one, two, three strikes you're out time.'"

"Exactly!" the Knitting Lady said. "Lillian was still singing her heart out. The man in the black cloak got a distasteful expression on his face.

"'Tsk, tsk,' he said. 'Singing at a tragic time like this!' And the woman in satin and lace responded, 'What do you expect? Look at how she was raised.' Then she pointed at one of the neighbors, a man from down the hall who had arms the size of hams. 'You! Yes, you. Bring the child here!' Before Lillian realized what was happening, a pair of thick, hairy arms lifted her and carried her across the room. Then she felt her feet hit the ground, her ankles buckling slightly.

"The rich woman studied her. 'Not at all delicate and

fair like Cousin. Must take after the father.' She made that last word—*father*—sound slick and oily. 'Still, she appears strong.'

"Then the strangers formed a tight twosome, their heads bowed, their shoulders touching. There was a lot of whispering, and Lillian heard many hard, hissing *S*s. 'Yes, yes, Reverend, I simply agree. She must say good-bye. After all, Cousin was her mother.'

"At that, the man, this well-dressed reverend, approached Lillian. His lower lip was pressed forward. He lifted her up and when she looked down, she saw her mother who wasn't her mother.

"'Say good-bye, child,' the Reverend coaxed. 'She's at peace now.'

"'Peace?' the rich woman said with scorn. 'After the pain she caused to her family? After she threw away everything for . . . this?'

"The woman's arm made a sweeping motion around the room, and then her face widened with surprise. She walked to the shelf and picked up the only thing of luxury and refined taste in the room."

"The lorgnette," I said.

"S-she ran her fingers over the engraving and held it up to her face. Lillian, still suspended in the air, nothing solid under her feet, was struck for the first time in her life by a great desire to escape."

III

CHAPTER 17

"So," Fern said. "I guess the mother died, huh?"

Whitney threw up her hands: "Is the pope . . . Is the pope . . . Is the pope what, Cal?"

"Catholic," I answered.

"Yeah, the pope is Catholic and the mother died!" Whitney snapped. Then she went on with a million questions: "Who are the rich people? What did Lillian's mother do wrong? Why is the pope Catholic? Can you sing the funny song again?"

The Knitting Lady pushed down the air with her palms. "Slow down, Whitney. Anyone want to take a stab at the first question? Who are the rich people?"

I was about to answer, "Lillian's relatives," when the Knitting Lady said, "That's right, Amber. You know."

My head snapped around. This was not a yes-or-no question that Amber could answer with a nod. She couldn't get away with that! Finally, the moment I had been waiting for. Would she or wouldn't she? Could she or couldn't she? Amber's lips began moving and something was coming out. Words. They were so soft that I had to strain to hear them. "The rich people are . . ."

The Knitting Lady encouraged her. "Go on, Amber. You've got it."

A little louder now, more secure. "They're Lillian's mother's la-de-dah relatives."

"La-de-dah?" Monica asked.

"She used to be rich, too."

Fern still didn't get it. "Who used to be rich?"

Whitney nudged me. "I don't get it either."

But I understood. I got it! And Amber understood. I exchanged a knowing look with her and she gave me a smile—more of a half smirk really—that confirmed what I was thinking. *At least someone else in this room is mature enough to follow such a complicated story.* That's when I also noticed something in Amber's face that I had not noticed before. I mean, when someone has just about no hair, it's hard to get past that person's no-hairness. At first, that's all you see. But now I noticed how much Amber reminded me of a flower, her mouth with its curly upper lip, her features bunched together in the center of her face.

"It's all very logical," I explained. "Point number one: Lillian's mother had been born very rich."

"Like with a fork in her mouth?" Whitney asked.

"A spoon," Amber corrected.

"Yes, a silver spoon," I went on. "Until—point number two—she had a baby—by a guy who wasn't la-de-dah like her family. Point number three: Lillian is the baby.

And finally point number four: Her rich family threw Lillian's mom out."

"Oh!" Whitney said. "Suck a duck! Suck a big, quacking duck! That makes me sore. That rich family can just kiss my skinny butt. If you say that Lillian went to live with them, man-oh-man, I won't believe it! I wouldn't let myself get adopted by people like that!"

"What about her desire?" Fern asked. "What about that?"

"Desire? Really, Fern, what are you talking about?" I said.

"Ahhhh," said the Knitting Lady. "But she did have a desire."

"To escape!" Fern said with pride. "I remembered! I'm the only one who did! So did she?"

"Y-yes, she did. But not right away. Before that . . ."

"Before that?" Monica encouraged.

"Before that, I have to s-say, must wait for another day."

❧

I quickly discovered that one of the most unpleasant and unbearable things about living in a group home is that someone is always around, breathing the same air as you. You go into the kitchen and someone is sneaking a snack. You go to the bathroom, someone is banging on the door to get in. So while everyone else rushed outside to take a walk, I escaped to my room. It really wasn't *my* room because this wasn't my life, but it would have to do right then.

I needed to think. The Knitting Lady's story had given me so many things to think about.

For instance, Lillian had her mother. They did everything together. But did she ever wonder about her father? Did she think that someday, somewhere, a door would swing open and a man would come in and she would recognize him immediately even though they'd never met, and they wouldn't even have to be introduced because he would recognize her, too? They would just recognize each other, and he would say, *Gee, you remind me so much of me.* And she would say, *Likewise!* Did Lillian ever wonder about her father like that?

I was on my bed with a pillow propped under my head so that I could look out the window. There were some robins out there. And a tree. That's when I decided that, as long as I had to stay here, the world outside the window would belong to me. No one else had a window. Why shouldn't the outside—all of it—belong to me?

I picked up my knitting and knit a row. I knit another row. *My* tree was swaying in a light breeze. *My* cloud floated by. I knit four more rows. My stitches were definitely getting looser.

That night before I went to bed, I wrote on a piece of paper: If I were writing the story of my life, how would I begin?

I wrote: I'm in the wrong story.

When I woke the next morning, the paper was still on the floor next to my bed where I had left it. Only now, one side was covered with the prettiest handwriting I had ever seen. I never knew handwriting could be music.

Sometimes, fears come at me like genies released from a bottle.

Sometimes, I feel like everyone else has an important phone number—like God's phone number—except me.

Amber is the story of a girl who is also trying to remember.

CHAPTER 18

The next morning, I had two major accomplishments. When Whitney started talking again about her brilliant plan to look for her sister, I did *not* remind her that it was the most lame plan in the history of all lame plans ever planned. My other accomplishment was not getting on the bad side of Mrs. S., the social worker. No thanks to Whitney. Thanks to her, it was almost another story.

Our meeting started off just fine, everything under control. We were in the upstairs bedroom for "a little private tête-à-tête," as Mrs. S. called it. "I want you to feel perfectly relaxed around me," she said.

I thought: *Hot lava.*

"I want you to tell me everything's that going on around here." She was smiling so hard her gums showed.

I recited to myself: *Hot lava. Hot lava. Hot lava.*

I said nothing. I had created a new face just for the occasion. I called it My Face for Sucking Up to Social Workers, and it was almost like My Face for Unbearably Unpleasant and Embarrassing Situations, only with wider eyes. It seemed to be working. I could tell that Mrs. S. completely understood that Cal Lavender was not the type of person to spit in anyone's eye. She said, "I can tell we are going to get along just fine."

She continued the way Whitney said she would, by asking questions and more questions. *Being treated well? Getting plenty to eat?* Which I answered in complete sentences in a very mature manner. So far, so good. She nodded, wrote, and then she broke the news: I would not be going home anytime in the immediate future.

It took a lot of willpower to keep the panic from showing on My Face for Sucking Up to Social Workers. "What does the immediate future mean?" I asked. "A few more days? A week?"

Mrs. S. said that she could not give me an answer because it wasn't up to her. It was up to Betty. The social worker really emphasized that. "If Betty follows all the rules, if Betty does what she's told, if Betty makes commitments and follows through, if Betty does this and that, then—and only then—will you be released to her."

I thought, *What kind of commitments? What kind of this and that? How can* anything *be up to Betty? How can Betty follow rules when anyone who knows Betty knows that she can never, ever follow rules? In the life story of Betty, the first sentence would be: Betty Lavender lives to* break *rules. I'm the only one in the history of the universe who can get Betty to follow rules, so how will she follow them if I'm stuck here and she's stuck somewhere else?*

But I certainly didn't say any of this. My personal thoughts were none of the social worker's business. I said, "Betty will certainly follow the rules." Then I asked, "Where is she?"

Big mistake.

"You can't ask me that. A rule is a rule is a rule. And if you are even thinking about it, don't!"

"Don't what?"

"Blow this placement. Don't *think* about running away to find your mother. This is a good placement. You're lucky to have a placement this good."

I nodded with my most polite and sincere head nod. "I have a request. Whatever you do, don't put me in Whitney's fourth foster home."

Her eyes blinked twice, then widened. "Whitney!" she exclaimed. "That girl! She's a Code 600 waiting to happen."

Code 600, I reminded myself, *cold-blooded killer/ arsonist/drug-dealer types who are locked up in kid jail.*

"So," Mrs. S. probed, "what kind of malarkey has Whitney been feeding you?"

"No malarkey," I said, probably too quickly.

Her voice turned all syrupy. "Hmmm. About Whitney. Does she have any particular schemes cooking right now? Something that you are going to stay away from if you know what's good for you? So does she?"

Truthfully, I had no reason to protect Whitney. A part

of me was even thinking that I would be doing her a favor. Someone with some authority should know about her "c-r-a-z-i-e" scheme to find her sister. But the way the social worker's eyes kept scanning my face, trying to get behind my eyes and into my thoughts . . . well, it did something to me. Even though Cal Lavender is a firm believer in following the rules and even though Whitney's scheme was likely to turn into a big mess, I wasn't going to tell Mrs. S. anything. Nothing!

"No," I said. "Nothing's cooking."

The social worker hunched over some papers and started writing. I looked up. Behind Mrs. S., peeking out of the closet—guess who. Whitney, of course. How did she manage to stuff herself in there with all the clutter? She was signaling to me with hand motions like she was on a ship lost at sea. What did she want? She was making stabbing motions with her index finger.

Was she pointing at the table? Her head shook. No, not that. I pointed at the stack of files on the social worker's left.

Bingo! Okay, the files. But what did she want me to do with them?

"Don't move!" the social worker said suddenly.

I didn't. Believe me, I didn't.

Mrs. S. slowly lifted her bulk from the chair and wiggled her panty hose straight. "I need to talk to her," she said. "See if she has any questions or complaints."

I assumed she meant the Knitting Lady. "Should I come, too?" I asked.

"Wait here," she ordered, then went out the bedroom door.

Whitney charged out of the closet and began rummaging through the files that the social worker had left behind.

"What are you looking for?" I asked.

She answered, "I'm not sure." Then, "Here it is." Then, "Go stand guard."

"No," I said.

"Yes! If she catches me, you're in for it, too."

I dashed to the door and stuck my head out, looked up and down the hallway. I gave her a thumbs-up. Whitney opened a file, took out all the papers except the top few and replaced them with a stack of blank white paper.

"You can't do that!" I said. "That's got to be against the rules."

"It's my file," she hissed back. "It's got my name on it. It's all about me. Why can't I have it?" And with that, she and the papers were out the door.

I went back to the table and drummed my fingers on the top. I waited. I waited some more. I took a slow, rambling walk to the door and looked out. No one. I stood at the top of the stairs and could hear the social worker going on and on. Her voice really carried.

I charged back to the room and found the file I was

looking for. It was the fattest one there, even fatter than Whitney's. I grabbed a few papers, some from the front, the rest from the middle and back. That file, the one with Amber's name on it in block letters, was at least three inches thick.

ભ

The typical average American kid has a scrapbook that her parents start putting together even before she's born. There are photographs of her mother's big belly and all the "Welcome to the World" cards from the wildly happy relatives. Over the years, the book keeps filling up—with pictures of the first birthday party, pictures of the kid when she catches her first fish and when she wore the funny Halloween costumes, and the report card with all A's and B's is there, too. The book becomes so thick that it practically splits the binding. At family parties, the book comes out and everyone sits around making comments and cracking jokes about all the honors and wonderful events that have happened in their child's life.

Amber's social-work file—the papers that I *borrowed*—was like that, only in the opposite way. It started out bad and kept getting worse. I didn't think that any life could get worse after being born in a public restroom and left to scream your head off. But Amber's life did. It started with her mother giving birth to her on the cold linoleum floor, and from there her life just seemed to get worse.

There were not a lot of details. Just a couple of lines for each time she changed foster homes and a few more lines for each time she wound up in the hospital, a part of a page for each person who hurt her and another sentence for each promise to her that was broken.

In a way, the lack of details made it even worse. It was like reading an outline for the saddest story anyone would ever write about any kid. I know I didn't see half of it. But I didn't need to. What was left out, my imagination had no trouble filling in.

I had wanted to know more about Amber. Why was she so quiet? What made her pull out her hair? What made her the way she is? Now I knew.

CHAPTER 19

I stuffed Amber's papers back under my mattress just in time. Whitney burst into the room, waving her stolen goods over her head. "Interesting! Very interesting!" she was saying. "Man-oh-man, if I didn't know this was me, I would read this stuff and think: *Now this is a* very *interesting person.* Everyone come in. You gotta hear this, too."

I couldn't look directly at Amber as she entered the room. I felt like I had just broken into her past and tiptoed around like a trespasser. She entered as quietly as someone afraid of even disturbing the dust.

Monica was next, rubbing her hands together and fretting. "I can't believe you stole those. We are going to get in so much trouble. *So* much! She's gonna find out and kill all of us."

Whitney shook an old, yellowed piece of newspaper in my face. I pushed it aside. "What's that?"

"I was"—dramatic pause—"the Child Who Waits."

What was she talking about? "The child who . . . ?"

"Who waits!" she said. "Once a month, in every newspaper in the entire county, out of all the foster kids in the entire county, they pick one kid to put in the newspaper and talk about. And in"—she stopped, ran her finger along the paper—"in May a couple years ago, I was her. I was the Child Who Waits."

I still didn't understand, so I took the paper from her and read aloud:

"'The County Department of Children's Services is looking for an adoptive family for Whitney S., a high-spirited girl of seven, small for her age because of a congenital heart problem that has been surgically corrected. Whitney is a real leader among her peers.'"

"That's right!" she said. "A real leader."

"'She has a very well-developed imagination.'"

"Told you that's me!"

I continued, "'After experiencing severe abuse by her parents, she has lived in several foster homes and has had to deal with feelings of abandonment and a lack of a stable family environment.'"

"Well, that's not entirely wrong. Go on," she said.

"'Because of her difficult childhood, Whitney can tend to live in a fantasy world. She would best be served by a patient, well-grounded family with other children to help—'"

"What do they mean? Living in a fantasy world? I don't—"

"'—with other children to help satisfy her immense longing for siblings.'"

"And what the heck is a sibling?" she asked.

"A sister. Or a brother," I answered.

Whitney grabbed the paper and sneered at it. "What do they know? I don't need somebody else's sibling. I already have one of my own. I just have to find her." Whitney whirled to face me. "And now I have all the clues I need." She patted the pile of social-work papers. "Everything I need."

"Let me see!" Monica demanded.

Whitney's voice lowered. "Not yet, but soon. And it all depends."

"On what?" I asked.

"If all of you are going to help me find her."

Amber was nodding rapidly. Yes, of course she would help. Even timid, tired-all-the-time, scaredy-cat Monica with a broken arm was saying yes. And if *she* said yes, I knew that Fern, her personal shadow, would also go along with it.

As a group, they turned and looked at me.

Luckily, I didn't have to answer yes or no because the door flung open and Fern was standing there waving her needles. "She said to bring your knitting and come down. She's ready to tell the next part of the story."

Like I said, I didn't say anything, but I could tell from the satisfied look that Whitney gave me that I might as well have said, *Yes! Cal Lavender will help you with your nutty plan!*

"Do you like the story so far?" the Knitting Lady asked.

The answer seemed important to her. "A lot," Fern said.

"I'm s-so glad because I always worry that, with my stutter, I never do the stories justice. When I was your age, I hated that I stuttered. I hated that I hated that I stuttered. Then I hated that I hated that I hated that I stuttered. Which just seemed to make me stutter even more. Even now, at my age, after a lifetime of stuttering, I can't stop looking at my listeners and asking myself: *Do I look stupid when I talk? Are they bored? Am I taking too long to tell it?*"

"But you hardly stutter at all when you're telling a story," I said.

"Especially this story," Whitney added.

"I th-think I also noticed that. It's like something outside of myself comes along and unloosens the knot from my tongue. This must be a pretty important story for something like that to happen. Still, I worry that . . ."

"Don't worry so much," Whitney said. "Just tell the story."

The Knitting Lady gave a little snort of amusement. "So I will. Do you remember where we left off?"

"The dead mother." Monica shivered at the memory. "How could I forget?"

"Escape, something about escape," Fern added.

Amber was very precise: "Suspended in the air, nothing solid under her feet."

"Y-yes. After that day, after her mother was buried, Lillian was passed around from one rich cousin to another like a puppy no one wanted. Then one day, the Reverend sat before Lillian, took her by the hand.

"'So, young lady,' he said, 'have you ever traveled before?'

"And Lillian said, 'Damn straight, I've been all over the Lower East Side of New York.'"

At that, we all cracked up because the Knitting Lady was a good mimic, and it sounded exactly like something Whitney would say.

"You laugh, but I can t-tell you that the Reverend did not see the humor one little bit. He looked like he was choking on a chicken bone. The Reverend was of the belief that children are innocent jewels, and it shook him to his very core to hear a little girl swearing like a sailor. You girls and I know that cussing never killed anyone, but that's not the way this man thought. His whole purpose in life was to rescue poor, cussing, orphaned waifs like Lillian.

"'Well, young lady,' he continued, 'now you are *really* going to do some traveling—far from New York City. Most people just dream of heading west. But you are going to join with other lucky boys and girls just like yourself, to be part of the biggest migration of children that the world has ever known.'

"The Reverend was a man of the church, but he spoke like a salesman. Escape! Adventure! He told Lillian that she would have the opportunity to ride ponies, which for a city girl was like promising a rocket trip to Mars. She would be whisked away on a train to a place where the air was so clean, she could run for miles without coughing. And there would be so much food—not just cabbage and more cabbage like she was used to, but fresh milk and cakes that dripped with honey and chocolate.

"He said to her, 'Don't you want to learn how to milk a cow? Don't you want to get a good upbringing and learn to speak a refined English? Out west, you will learn to churn butter and stitch quilts.'

"About churning and quilting, Lillian knew nothing. But when the Reverend started speaking of dresses— pretty, fancy, new dresses, not rags like she was used to wearing—he tapped into her deepest fantasy. Her eyes began rolling to the top of her head like Dorothy in the field of poppies. She practically swooned as he spoke of calico prints, gingham, and satin sashes.

"It was all so much like a fairy tale coming true that Lillian did not think to ask certain questions. Like, What did the Reverend mean by *boys and girls like her*? Or,

Why would people Lillian had never met want to drape her in gingham dresses?

"So when the Reverend asked, 'So, you lucky little girl, what do you say to this blessed opportunity?' what could Lillian say? She had never been so intoxicated! Suddenly her mother's death was the furthest thing from her mind.

"No! That's not quite true. Nobody's mother's death is ever the furthest thing from her mind. But Lillian did not really, truly understand that dead means you are never, ever going to see the dead person again. 'Heck yes!' she said. 'I want to go.'

"After that, so much happened so fast. Strangers scrubbed Lillian until her skin felt raw. They probed her ears and dug around in her nose. As the Reverend had said, a lot of boys and girls had been rounded up for this great trip west. Like Lillian, each one assumed they had been especially selected, but it was just a matter of their circumstances. A parent's death. A desertion. Some had committed a minor crime. Maybe they stole some apples. In those days, many children went to jail just for stealing a few lumps of coal.

"While getting ready for the trip, they all lived together for a short period in a building that was like a group home, only this one was twelve stories high and packed with children! Some were so skinny that their shoulder blades stuck out like wishbones, and most balked at being put into clothes that were tight-necked and scratchy as burlap.

"But not Lillian. Lillian loved all the attention.

"*Stand up straight.* She stood up straight.

"*Don't scratch.* She stopped scratching.

"*Smile. Curtsy when introduced. Lower your eyes in modesty.* Noted, noted, noted. Lillian practiced her 'Yes, ma'am's and 'No, sir's and did not even fuss when a cranky woman with a comb pulled and tore at the knots in her long, thick hair.

"Finally the big day arrived. Just before noon, a large group of children were led into a great, empty hall and lined up in rows. Each child held a suitcase. The boys were so clean in their short pants and cotton broadcloth shirts buttoned high around their necks. All the girls were wearing new dresses. Lillian studied the back of the thin, red-haired girl in front of her. She was holding the hand of a dark-haired little boy and had six perfect curls hanging like sausages around her head.

"In front of the room, the Reverend walked back and forth. 'A clean slate,' he kept repeating, each time with more force. He patted heads and straightened collars, and, when he finally stopped pacing and gestured for the children to start moving out, he was standing directly in front of Lillian.

"Well, that did it! Lillian decided that it wasn't by chance that the leader of this whole expedition stopped right in front of her. This was a sign! She must be the one who was most destined for a life that was wonderful and marvelous!

"When the lines of children started moving, Lillian followed the girl in front of her onto the streets of New York. People looked at them as they passed. Lillian tossed her freshly washed and combed hair. She flashed each stranger a smile. She was sure they were wondering: *Who is that immaculate child who walks in such a straight line? Where is she going? How I envy her!*

"All the way to the train station, Lillian dug her nails into the flesh of her thigh to keep from breaking into song. What a train ride it was to be!"

CHAPTER 20

The Knitting Lady shifted in her chair and continued. "There were fifty children accompanied by five adults who were leaving by train from New York City that day. The children had never seen anything like Grand Central Station. There were pillars of marble as thick and mottled as tree trunks. Steel posts rose a hundred feet high. Picture the long lines of track, the confusion and excitement of trains pulling out. Put yourself in the children's brand-new shoes. They covered their ears as train whistles blew. That's our train! All aboard! The children were hustled up the steps, the smallest ones tucked under arms like suitcases to be carried aboard.

"'Best day of my life,' one boy kept saying. And another: 'Hip, hip, hurrah for the Wild West!' The train lurched. Everyone squealed as it picked up speed.

"As I said earlier, the children had been told that it was going to be a long journey, but they didn't grasp the full meaning of that. Many had never set foot outside of their neighborhoods, so some thought *long* meant they were going to New Jersey, just across the river. One girl took to heart the Reverend's description. Pure air and all the food she could eat. *Why,* she thought, *this train must be going to heaven.*

"At first, there was so much energy. The antsy children couldn't sit still. The talky ones couldn't get their words out fast enough. But eventually, the rocking of the train, the grinding hum of the rail, wore them all down. One after another, the children took on a brain-dazed look, like baby birds who had been pushed from the nest for the first time."

"But not Lillian," I said. "She wouldn't look dazed."

"W-why not, Cal?"

"Because she wouldn't want anyone to know what she was feeling inside."

"Exactly! S-she was in a window seat, next to an agent, one of the adults who were paid to accompany the children. One of Lillian's hands was in the pocket of her dress and she was clasping something. Take a guess, what?"

"A snack!" Monica said. "That's what I would have taken. You know how I'm always hungry. And if I didn't eat on a train, I know I'd get train sick."

"N-no, not a snack. Here's a clue: It was something she wasn't supposed to have. Hold that clue awhile. It'll come to you. Many hours passed, and Lillian's head began to loll. She jerked herself awake, then drifted off again, slumping against the agent next to her. This woman in her dark blue suit removed Lillian's head from her shoulder, like it was a muddy thing. Then, she straightened her own small hat. I bet each of you would recognize the woman, how her eyes were always taking measure. That's right, Whitney, she was like a social worker of that time.

"So Lillian drifted in and out of sleep. When awake, she saw things out the window that a city girl would not have names for. Forests, silos, fallow fields. Once when she woke, the train was stopped at a station. She had never seen so much space or anything look as lonely as that one wooden building set against a backdrop of sky.

"Other times, Lillian slept right through the stops, only vaguely aware of movement and that the train always felt lighter. At some point, she realized why. At each stop, some of the children got off and the train moved on without them. It was always the children who had placards hanging around their necks."

"Placards?" I asked.

"Oh!" the Knitting Lady said. "I forgot to tell you all about the placards!" She demonstrated by wrapping a piece of yarn loosely around her neck. "The placards were pieces of cardboard that hung on string just like this. Before getting on the train, an agent hung placards on some of the children. Most of the babies—teeny, khaki-colored, scowling things—had numbers pinned to their bonnets. Lillian didn't get a number, but the girl in line in front of her—the red-haired girl with the six sausage-shaped curls—was number thirty-four."

Whitney shouted out: "Question! Was the redheaded girl special because she *had* a number? Or was Lillian special because she *didn't* have one?"

"Those are the s-same questions that were driving Lillian crazy."

Whitney went on, "And how about the dark-haired boy holding her hand? Did he have a tag?"

"There's no dark-haired boy in this story," Fern insisted.

Whitney said, "Oh, yes, there is. He's holding the hand of Miss Sausage Hair."

"G-good memory, Whitney. The dark-haired boy is her brother."

Fern broke in: "So Lillian had a brother?"

The Knitting Lady explained patiently, "No, the brother belonged to the red-haired girl. And no, he did not have a tag. Lillian could read, so she put her mind to figuring out what was written on the girl's placard. First, there was her name—*Rosie*—and then her age—*7. Red hair. Green eyes. Very quiet and hopeful.* There was something else written there—*Trenton, Mo.*—but Lillian couldn't make sense of it.

"It wasn't until the fourth day of the trip, after the train crossed a big river and pulled into yet another station, that the words *Trenton, Mo.,* made sense. Those were the same words that were written on the station platform. Lillian pressed her face against the window and watched as all of the children with 'Trenton, Mo.' on their placards exited the train.

"By this point in their travels, the children were a far cry from the clean and spotless children who had boarded in New York City. The older ones looked numb from being cooped up for so long, and you all know how toddlers can get just looking at dirt. Well, you never saw a toddler as wrinkled and stained as number 30! But a woman holding a sign with NUMBER 30 written on it stepped out of the crowd waiting on the platform. She rushed forward waving wildly and then scooped up number 30 like the child was a lottery prize. All around, similar scenes were taking place.

"I signed up for number 15!

"That cute little 21 is mine!

"In the middle of all the confusion, Rosie, number 34, was standing and looking as bewildered as if she had just been dropped, suitcase and all, right from outer space. Kaboom!

"A man wearing farmer's overalls and a woman wearing a faded flowered housedress stepped out of the crowd. They were holding a sign: 34. The man walked up to an agent, put out his hand, and they did one of those long, slow, serious pumping handshakes. The farmer pointed to

Rosie. The woman's hand reached out toward Rosie's hair, then pulled back suddenly as if she were too hot to touch.

"Lillian pulled on the sleeve of the agent sitting next to her. 'What's that man saying?'

"The woman bristled. 'Don't point! And don't pull! If you want to be picked, you best mind your manners.'

"Lillian didn't understand. 'Then why are they picking her? She's not doing a curtsy or smiling or anything good-mannered.'

"The agent's body made a sharp movement like she just experienced a twinge of heartburn. 'That girl doesn't have to do anything right. They asked for a red-haired, green-eyed seven-year-old girl, and the bill was filled. Just like they ordered her from the Sears Catalogue.'

"As Lillian watched, her eyes went soft with a feeling of embarrassment."

"Embarrassment?" I asked. "Why would she be embarrassed?"

"Th-that is the question, isn't it? Lillian did nothing wrong."

The Knitting Lady looked pointedly around the room, set her eyes on each of us in turn. When she got to Whitney, her eyes held a little longer.

"Because she figured something must be wrong with her," Whitney said.

"Why, Whitney? Explain why Lillian w-would think something was wrong with her."

"Because she wasn't picked," Whitney answered sharply. "Why else didn't she get picked? Because something is wrong with her."

It didn't make any sense to me why Whitney was acting so agitated. It was just a story. "It's just a story, Whitney," I said.

I waited for Whitney to snap something back, but for once, she didn't. She didn't seem angry at me in particular. She seemed angry at everyone and everything.

The Knitting Lady picked up her needles and started knitting as she spoke. "That's true, Cal. It's a story. But Whitney understands what Lillian was feeling. It's no different from today, is it? Certain children are adopted because they just happen to have a certain color hair or they are a certain age or sex."

Now I understood, and it *was* unfair! "Just because someone has red hair! What's the big deal about that? There's nothing wrong with Lillian."

The Knitting Lady was nodding. "But how do you think Lillian felt, sitting there behind a glass window, watching one child after another being claimed as if they were valuable jewels?"

"Really, really bad," Monica said. "I bet she started crying. I would. I feel like crying right now just thinking about it."

"But Lillian would never cry," I said. "I bet she had a face to put on just for moments like this one."

"B-but she felt like crying, certainly. At that moment, Lillian was struck by a fit of longing to see her mother's face. She had to see it, feel her mother's eyes passing over her with love and approval. But there was no mother. *I am alone,* she thought. *Really, really alone.*

"The train began moving again. There were not many children left aboard. Holding back tears, Lillian looked out and saw Rosie standing on the platform, a finger wedged between her lips, her hair like a flame on a slender white candle.

"In the front of the train, one of the other unclaimed children—the little dark-haired boy, Rosie's brother—started wailing."

"That makes me so mad, I want to punch someone," Whitney said. Her whole body was twitching. "Why didn't that farmer take Rosie *and* her brother? People should not be allowed to split up . . . split up— Amber, what shouldn't they be allowed to split up?"

"Siblings," Amber said quietly.

"I d-don't know the answer to your question, Whitney. That's the way it happened. Lillian thought Rosie was lucky, but how lucky was she? To be taken from her brother? For her brother to be taken from her?

"When the station was out of sight, the agent next to Lillian gave a shudder and fell asleep. Now it was safe for Lillian to reach into her pocket and take out her smuggled treasure."

"What treasure?" Fern asked.

"Yeah, I forgot about that," Monica put in. "Something in her pocket."

"Any g-guesses what it is? Cal?"

"I don't know."

"Amber?"

She did not hesitate. "The fancy French glasses."

"Correct! The l-lorgnette. And what do you suppose she did with the glasses, Amber?"

Amber closed her eyes and said, "Lillian ran her fingers over the pieces of glass."

"Yes," the Knitting Lady said, "and as she held the lorgnette, she felt herself being rejected by her neighbors in New York, her rich relatives, and now by the people of Trenton, Missouri. She felt the desertion of a father she never knew. She saw her mother's face fading feature by feature and knew that, one day, she would barely be able to remember her mother at all. Sadness, hurt, anger, and fear. For the next few hours, she wrestled with these feelings and pinned them down like they were wild animals. She tamed them into something else."

"What?" Fern asked.

"Vows. That d-day on the train, Lillian made three vows:

1. Nobody will ever hurt me again.
2. Someday, everyone will know my name.
3. My life will never be ordinary. It will be spectacular.

"In her window seat, she pulled her back up straight and sat aloof like some kind of untouchable queen. Lillian held her mother's lorgnette to her face. The scenery rushed by. She used this very last piece of her past to look forward into her future."

"And then?" I asked.

"And then . . . and then . . . for the next part of Lillian's story, there's always another day."

CHAPTER 21

"I have vows, too," Whitney said to me. Her face started twitching and winking, like it was being bombarded by small jolts of electricity. Whitney might as well have been wearing a neon sign that said, *I've got a secret!*

The Knitting Lady told us that this was enough storytelling for one day. "Go over to the park. Run off some steam."

We were out the door and halfway up the street when Whitney started looking around for intergalactic spies. Finding none, she decided it was safe to bring up her supersecret subject—her *only* subject. "My vow is to find her this month."

"Her?" Fern asked, and Monica rolled her eyes, and Fern said, "Oh, *her.*"

Whitney rubbed her palms together and laughed like a mad scientist in a bad horror movie. "I have all the necessary information in my hungry little hands."

When we got to Horace Mann Middle School, she insisted that we take a detour onto the deserted campus where she proceeded to point out a million things that I had no reason to care about. Over there was the door where she, *not I,* would enter on the first day of school. The portable on the right was the office where she, *not I,* would meet the principal. Under the large tree was where she, *not I,* would eat lunch every day.

After I got the complete and unnecessary tour of a school I cared nothing about, Whitney returned to her previous subject. "So, you're all taking off with me, right." It wasn't even a question. "You're all coming with me on this mission. Man-oh-man, it's gonna be great."

At least I could count on Monica to be a wimp. "The Knitting Lady will be mad!" she said, and I kept encouraging her. "How can you take off with your arm in a cast?" and "Think how tired you'll get!" and "Mrs. S. will have a fit when she finds out!" Monica kept nodding in agreement with me, but I also noticed how her eyes started darting back and forth to Whitney. Then the nodding stopped. Whitney didn't even say anything, she didn't have to. In the list of things that Monica was afraid of, getting on Whitney's bad side was high up there.

"Okay, count me in," Monica finally agreed.

Fern giggled and gave the thumbs-up sign, although I'm not really sure that she understood exactly what she was agreeing to do.

And of course Amber was with Whitney all the way.

"So where *is* your sister?" Monica asked. "Is it far? I

hope we don't have to walk far 'cause, you know, I don't like getting all sweaty and—"

Whitney broke in. Her expression was mysterious. "It's far. That's all I can say for now. The details will be revealed at the appropriate time."

Meanwhile, I was thinking: *Maybe, just maybe, the appropriate time will be NEVER. Yes, that would be exactly like Whitney. She was definitely the all-talk type. In any case, I will absolutely refuse to go because that is exactly the same as running away, which is exactly what the social worker ordered me not to do under any circumstances. Don't even consider it! And didn't Whitney herself say to hurl myself into hot lava before getting on the wrong side of Mrs. S.?*

I also thought: *Who are those girls who have been walking behind us for blocks? Why are they following us and pretending not to?*

When we got to the playground, the girls stood off from us in a huddle at the top of the climbing structure. There was a tall one who poked the skinny one who shook her head no. Then, a girl wearing a belly shirt pointed to a girl in a pink tank top who mouthed, *Not me*. Then they seemed to all turn at once to a girl with flippy hair, who shrugged like she had known all along that they would get around to her. She jumped on the fireman's pole, slid down, and walked toward us. She was trying to act like it was no big deal, but I noticed that she kept turning around and looking back to her friends for support. When she was right in front of Whitney, she flipped her flippy hair and said: "You go to Horace Mann, right?"

"Righto," Whitney said back.

"You all eat lunch together under the tree, right?"

"Righto."

"We thought so," she said. "We were wondering . . ." Another look back at her friends. "We've seen you around. We were wondering . . . like . . . who you are?"

"Whitney," Whitney answered.

"No. I mean, what are you?"

Whitney snapped, "What's that mean?"

"Hey, don't get mad. It's just that everyone wants to know. You live in that orange house. And you're always together, but you can't be sisters or cousins, right? I mean, you're so pale." She paused and pointed to me. "And she's so dark. . . ." Then she pointed to Amber, but changed her mind and pointed to Monica instead. "And she's so big. And you're all the same age, so you can't be sisters."

Whitney said quickly, "We're friends. Like you and your friends."

Flippy Hair dismissed that immediately. "No, that can't be it. Friends don't live in the same house." She turned and pointed to her friends who looked scared that we might bite. "We don't get it. We just don't get it."

"I have two questions," I asked the Knitting Lady as soon as I got back to the Pumpkin House. "What are we?"

"A tribe," she said. "Second question?"

"Did your hands get like that from knitting?"

She put down the yarn and spread her hands flat on her thighs. The veins were thick, and I had to stop myself from reaching out and pressing one of those plump worms. "I g-guess they are big and muscular compared to the pint-sized rest of me. But did I get them from knitting? Hmmm. That's hard to say. I've been knitting a long time. I remember when I first started, my hands would cramp up something fierce." She wiggled her fingers.

"Your hands used to hurt?" I exclaimed. "Mine hurt, too. I thought I was doing something wrong. So I'm not doing anything wrong?"

She gave me a funny look. "If I was going to tell the story of your life, know how I'd start it? *Cal Lavender worries way too much about doing something wrong.* You and Monica have a lot in common that way. Let's see what the Stitch Reader can see."

I handed my knitting to her, and she let out a long, approving whistle. I have to admit that my knitting was pretty impressive. Nobody else knit first thing in the morning and last thing at night like I did. My work had a lot of sun colors in it, yellows and golds, and was already three times as long as anybody else's.

"So what do you see in my knitting now?" I asked her. "Much looser, right?"

She pulled the material gently and watched it spring back into shape. "A nice, even h-hand. There's a calmness to it. Uh-oh. Here."

She had homed right in on one of my few mistakes. A couple of stitches had somehow gotten tangled together. "What were you thinking when you were working on this row?"

"Nothing. I wasn't thinking. I was just knitting. And listening to your story."

"What part of the story?"

"I don't know! How am I supposed to know? I don't remember!"

She didn't ask anything else. I slid my finger along the stitches, then pressed my fingertip gently into the point of the needle. I said, "Let's say that *for instance,* I did remember. Not that I do! But let's say that I did. What would it mean?"

"It means that right here"—she lifted my finger from the point and placed it on the twisted row—"right here, your mind was not at peace. Does that make sense?"

"Sure," I said, "*if* I could remember. Which I definitely cannot!"

Okay, so I could remember. I knew exactly what the Knitting Lady was saying when my hands lost their way. She was saying that Lillian *was watching her mother's face fade feature by feature.*

CHAPTER 22

Possible opening sentences for "The Cal Lavender Story" by Cal Lavender:

> Cal Lavender will never let her mother's face fade feature by feature.
> Cal Lavender worries way too much about doing something wrong.
> Cal Lavender vows that she won't let Whitney talk her into doing anything stupid.
> Cal Lavender vows she will be the best knitter the Knitting Lady has ever seen.

It was very strange, but I started seeing Lillian everywhere.

Whenever we were riding in the van, I sat in the back and studied the shape of Amber's head. I said to myself: *I bet Lillian's head was shaped like that.* When Monica acted fearful, when Fern seemed to be in another world, I knew that Lillian sometimes felt those ways, too, even though she would never show it.

When everyone was asleep, I looked out my window and saw the silhouettes of the spindly rosebushes on the patio. The shadows cast by the moonlight looked like her. I knew that if it was day and I was looking out this same window, clouds would drift by in the form of Lillian walking, Lillian dancing, Lillian making her vows.

CHAPTER 23

I had an important question that I could not get out of my mind. I found the Knitting Lady and everyone else in Talk Central. "Who's the best knitter in the Pumpkin House?" I asked.

"And don't do that thing that grown-ups always do!" Whitney put in. "Don't say that everyone is the best in her own way, blah-blah. Nobody falls for that kind of bull."

The Knitting Lady laughed. "I wouldn't do that."

Whitney pointed to Monica. "It can't be her because she won't even try knitting."

"I can't do it! I don't know how, and, anyway, it hurts my hands."

Then Monica pointed to Fern. "And it can't be her because she's always losing her knitting and starting over. Fern, have you ever finished anything?"

"I don't think so," Fern said.

"Who's the best then?" Whitney asked.

There was not even an "Ahhh" before the Knitting Lady answered. "That's easy. Amber."

Amber was peeking up through her bangs-that-aren't-there, as surprised as the rest of us to be named Miss Pumpkin House Knitter of the Year. It dawned on me that I had never seen any of Amber's finished work. Whitney burst out, "You've got to be kidding. Man alive, Amber is the *worst* knitter."

Monica agreed. "No offense, Amber, but you are."

Whitney addressed me: "Have you ever seen what she does?" Then she turned to the Knitting Lady. "Oh, you're joking. I get it now."

"I'm not j-joking. Amber, go get some of my favorites."

Amber came back with full hands and set them out on the coffee table. There were five small, doll-sized things. A little sweater. A yellow cap. A knitted pair of pants. Talk about the need to be *loose, loose.* The knitting was so tight, each item stood up on its own like a little piece of armor.

But tight was only the beginning of the problem. I picked up the little sweater. It had a nice pattern that must have been very hard to do without losing her peace of mind. It was pink and red, but with three sleeves and no opening for the head.

Every piece was like that! Absolutely perfect and perfectly wrong! The pants were joined at the cuffs so that you'd have to be shaped like a circle to wear them. The cap came to a sharp alien-head point. The dress was a complete and total success, but only if you happened to have six arms and a giraffe neck.

I said, "Nobody can wear these. Therefore, she can't be the best knitter."

Amber looked hurt. Her hands started rubbing the back of her neck. I also noticed that thin wisps of reddish-brown hair had begun to sprout all over her head. She looked like a newly hatched bird.

The Knitting Lady gently removed Amber's hands from her hair and made a cup of them. "My favorite," she said, indicating the dress in the center. "Totally impractical, Cal. But that's the beauty of it."

The beauty of it? Amber's knitting broke all the rules, or what I thought were the rules. How was I, Cal Lavender, supposed to become the best knitter if the rules changed for each person? I asked, "After Amber, then, who would you say is the best knitter?"

"I'm the fastest knitter," Whitney bragged.

"And the messiest," I pointed out.

"Well, la-de-dah!"

The Knitting Lady kicked off her shoes, bent over, and rubbed her feet. "Squabbling. Is that the only cure for boredom around here?"

"No, telling a story!" Whitney insisted. "That'll make us stop."

"Lillian!" Monica said.

"Where did we l-leave her?"

I had the answer. "Riding the train into her future."

"What does she have with her?"

"The lorgnette," Fern said, proud that she remembered.

"And what else does she h-have?"

We yelled out the first things that popped into our heads: *Shoes! Toothbrush! A suitcase!* It was Amber who said, "Vows."

"Th-that's the answer I was looking for. She's on the train and there's an important stop coming up. The agent next to Lillian told her to tidy herself up the best she could. *Straighten the bow on your dress. Put on a smile.*

" 'What happens if no one picks me?' Lillian asked.

" 'Someone will.' Only the way the agent said it, f-flatly without any enthusiasm or flattery, didn't give Lillian much hope.

" 'But what if they don't?' she asked.

" 'Then, you get put back on the train and returned to New York. And where would you be then? So don't make trouble.'

CHAPTER 24

"Ten children," the Knitting Lady continued, "all that were left of the original fifty, stepped off the train that afternoon. Girls in disheveled dresses looking as rumpled as used wrapping paper. Boys with greasy hair as though it had been ironed flat on their heads. The agents advised them to step lively, to appear energetic and self-reliant, but they mostly lumbered off like cattle, stiff in the joints, tired and bewildered from so many claustrophobic days on the train.

"Two teenage girls held hands. A tall boy protectively wrapped an arm around Rosie's little brother. Even arch-enemies stood close to each other, blinking through the haze and dust at the throng of strangers gathered to see them. Across the platform, a man with a peculiar way of walking stepped out of the crowd and headed their way.

"Lillian was the only one standing off by herself, her attention focused on some cattle grazing by the tracks. Were these the cows the Reverend had told her she would learn to milk? She felt a jolt of disappointment that they looked so dull and stupid.

"*So this is the Wild West,* she thought. She didn't know what she had expected.

"Oh, yes, she did! She had expected everything: things that were shiny and new, acres of satin and lace for dresses, trees blossoming with honey cakes. The train had left New York in the height of a sticky, choking summer, and she was now standing in something even worse. Nebraska heat can fry anybody's nerves to the flash point."

"Tell about the man!" Whitney demanded. "The one with the wacky walk."

"You r-really homed in on him. Good instincts. He's an important part of the story. Mr. R. M. Tankersley was a chicken farmer. The area was full of such gruff, barrel-chested men who had been toughened by work and weather.

"To look at him, Mr. R. M. Tankersley may have appeared to be a man without a lot of inner feelings. But he was a man who loved his wife so fully and deeply that he was ready to do anything for her, no matter how desperate and impractical.

"Several weeks earlier, Mr. Tankersley had spotted posters announcing the impending arrival of the children from New York City. Those posters got him thinking. Maybe, just maybe, one of the train children would be the key to solving his problem."

WANTED! HOMES FOR CHILDREN
A company of homeless children
from the East will be arriving.

These children are of various ages and of both sexes,
having been thrown friendless upon the world.
The citizens of this community are asked to assist
the agent, MISS CHARLOTTE FRY, in securing
good homes for them. Persons taking these
children must be approved by the local committee.
They must treat the children in every way
as a member of the family.

A VIEWING AND DISTRIBUTION WILL BE MADE AT THE OPERA HOUSE.

"For weeks now, there had been such notices posted
all around town. It seemed to be all the citizens could talk
about. *What kind of children are these? Did they have
immoral parents?* Even those who had no intention of taking in a child showed up at the train station to peek at the
unfortunates.

"In crowds, Mr. Tankersley was usually painfully shy.
He knew that about himself, so all morning before the
train arrived, he sat out by his chicken coops, taking long,
slow drinks of blueberry wine, a way of building up his
courage. And now he was walking across on the train platform, his mouth stained a deep, brownish-purple. Despite
the alcohol, his eyes held a sharp focus as he scanned the

children. He automatically ruled out the boys. A boy wouldn't do at all. So that left only five to choose from. *No, not that girl or that one either.* He looked over each in turn, making dissatisfied little clicks with his tongue. None could hold a candle to what he needed.

"Then he focused in on Lillian. She was wrong by a mile—wrong age, wrong coloring—but his eyes kept coming back to her. Perhaps he was drawn to the way she held herself apart from the others. In any case, he walked his peculiar walk right up and asked in her face, 'Girly, you have good eyes?'

"The man made Lillian feel turned upside down like a carnival ride. Despite all her practicing for just this moment, she was barely able to whisper a single word: 'Eyes?'

" 'Good eyes?' he responded.

" 'Good?'

"The man drew himself up. 'What's the matter with you, girl? You a parrot? What are you hiding in there? Open up now, let's see them teeth.' His hand, like a rough claw, latched on to her jaw. 'Come on, girly. My mind is set on this, but I can't afford no one whose dentaltry's not sound.'

"She felt a thick salty finger take a commanding sweep around her gums, over the bumpy surface of her tongue and the points of her canine teeth. When the finger ran over the gully of her right molar, she remembered vow number one. Which is . . ."

"No one will ever hurt me," I said.

"So Lillian bit down. Hard. The man let out a shocked, whooping yell. Our Lillian was furious. Mr. Tankersley, who was yelling, 'The little rascal bit me!' was furious, too. The crowd was furious. You could tell by all the stern chins jutting in Lillian's direction. The agent—Miss Charlotte Fry—rushed over. To Lillian, she hissed, 'Have you taken leave of your senses?'

"Then she turned to Mr. Tankersley and, without extending her hand, said: 'Miss Charlotte Fry, agent for these children. And you are?'

"'R. M. Tankersley. Anyone here can vouch for me.'

"'I'm sure they can.' Miss Charlotte Fry drew a deep breath, getting a clear whiff of alcohol. 'But there are procedures, sir. You can't walk up and take a child. That's why we're gathering in the Opera House. If you're still interested—'

"'I'm interested.' He was sucking on his finger. 'I'm interested.'

"Several men sidled up to Tankersley and tried in their awkward farmer ways to make light of the episode. Their wives felt very protective of Tankersley because of all his troubles at home. They turned their cold comments on Lillian:

"Shame on her!

"Took leave of her senses, all right!

"She is the homeliest, most unpromising girl in the whole lot.

"Incorrigible! It's the blood that tells.

"A few moments later, the children were led away from the station. They made quite a sight, walking single file past the feed and grain store, the library, the post office, the newspaper office, toward the Opera House. The townspeople, including R. M. Tankersley, followed in a pack behind them. He kept his eyes on the back of Lillian, the way her shoulders were still thin but square, the way they never slumped.

⌇

"Sitting on chairs on the stage of the Opera House, the girls kept their legs crossed daintily at the ankles as they had been coached; the boys had hats on their laps. At the podium, Mayor Clyde Shook gestured with the full length of his arm. 'Our great need today, fellow citizens, are strong hands and hearts willing to take in one of these homeless waifs. The Society that sent these children says that the lot of them has had good discipline. I personally felt the arm of this fine young man behind me. His eyes may be a little crossed, but he would be mighty useful on the farm.'

"'Mayor Shook! Mayor Shook! I have a question about these youngsters!'

"'Who is that yelling out? Ah, a Hazeltine. Margaret, why don't you pose your question loud enough so the balcony can hear you. Don't be shy!'

"The plain, round-faced woman stood and made a megaphone of her right fist, 'Here's my question. Let's say we're thinking it would be a nice gesture to open our doors to one of these orphans. But say, when we get the little fella home, well, people have different ways. What if the little fella can't undo his upbringing, if you see where I'm headed with this?'

"'That's a good question Margaret poses,' the mayor said. 'The lady sitting here to my right, Miss Charlotte Fry, gave me her solemn assurances that if you and your orphan don't get along, an official agent will come right on over to your place and take that child back.'

"'Is there a charge for any of this?'

"'No ma'am. Your child comes free on a ninety-day trial basis. Does that answer your questions, Margaret?'

"'Yes sir, it does. I already have five daughters at home, so I'll take that little fella over there, third one in. Bet he can handle chores and a half—especially after I fatten him up with my cooking.'

"Another voice came out of the crowd: 'Hold it there, Margaret. I had my eye on that one. Mayor Shook, not fair, just because—'

"'Hold on here, folks. We don't want to go pitting neighbor against neighbor. I believe Miss Charlotte Fry wants to say a few words.'

"The agent stood and walked to center stage. 'All this enthusiasm is very encouraging. But it is no light matter taking an unknown child into your home. There's been a committee appointed of your own townspeople to approve each match. And even when the committee approves a family, that does not end it. The child also has a say in the matter. Any child who doesn't want to go with a particular family does not have to go. And any child who wants to leave a family has that right. Any questions?'

"Fifty adult hands shot up, and one child's hand, Lillian's. The mayor showed the audience his own palms. 'Now, folks, why don't we just get started, and I'm betting that questions get resolved along the way. We might as well begin with the little fella that Margaret has her eye on. No catfights now, ladies. Young man, come forward.'

"The child in question was seated next to Lillian, and when he didn't budge, she gave him a good pinch. Still, the child didn't move. Only when the mayor himself came over—'Come on, son. No one's gonna bite you'—did the child finally stand. The mayor kept prodding, 'That's right, son, a few more steps into the spotlight, good boy. What's your name, son?'

"But before the child could answer, the Hazeltine

woman shouted, 'You wanna come home with me, little boy? The Hazeltines will give you your own pony.'

"Still the child didn't speak, which made the audience buzz with speculation.

"*Bet that boy has a screw loose!*

"*His ears must be clogged with New York dirt!*

"*Bet he speaks only one of those gutter foreign tongues, not a lick of English!*

"But the child was clearly neither deaf nor stupid. There was definitely a whole lot of something going on behind those eyes. When he finally gathered up what he had to say, his hands were balled into little fists.

"He shouted, 'I ain't no widdle boy! I'm a widdle girl!'

"Well, that caused a sensation! People gasped. Some started laughing so hard their eyes rolled to the top of their heads. Agent Fry frantically thumbed through a stack of papers, and only when she found the right one did she admit the mistake: 'He's right. I mean, *she's* right. He IS a girl! It says so right here.'

"The mayor asked, 'Young lady, what happened to your dress?'

" 'Can't tell,' the girl said.

" 'Don't be disobedient. You want one of these nice people to take you home?'

"The girl dropped her chin to the dimple of her neck. 'I went and—'

"'Speak up. We can't hear you.'

"'I said'—and now she was shouting—'I went and peed my dress. So Charlie over there slipped me these britches from his suitcase.'

"Well, that got everyone as giddy as confetti, and the mayor took advantage of the high spirits. 'No harm done, right, folks? This is one resourceful little gal. Spunky! Margaret, I suppose you'll pass. You got enough females at your place.'

"But Mrs. Hazeltine was already rushing down the aisle, squealing at the top of her lungs, 'Oh, isn't she the most precious? Of course I want her.'

"The girl in the boy clothes asked, 'Can I have a pony even if I am a girl?' And when Mrs. Hazeltine said, 'Of course, of course,' the child flung herself off the stage like a bouquet into the woman's open arms.

"The townspeople had certainly seen some very touching theatrical scenes performed on that stage. But never had they witnessed anything as all-around emotionally satisfying as what had just transpired. After that, there was one happy ending after another. The mayor announced: 'Eleven-year-old Chas F. Doesn't he have a fine head and face? Taken by Wilson Moore. Ten-year-old Mary C. Bet she was an exceptional baby, fat and pretty. Goes to C. H. Hawkins. Joseph P. Six years old, still speaks a little of that funny Irish language. Goes to Mrs. L. M. Leggett.' It was like musical chairs in reverse—one by one a child was taken away, leaving an empty chair behind.

"'Our next little lady,' the mayor said. 'It says here that she comes from a fine American family.'

"Lillian stepped to center stage into the circle of light and felt warmth wash over her. When she looked down at her arms, she almost didn't recognize them. She couldn't stop admiring how the spotlight gave her skin a milky glow like that of a marble statue.

"'An orphan like the others,' the mayor continued. 'But different from the others on the mother's side. This girl comes with a fine American pedigree, only her mother fell out of the good graces of her respectable family by a foolish act. I think you all know the kind of act I'm talking about without having to embarrass the ladies in attendance today. Under other circumstances, this girl would have been raised in the lap of luxury.'

"Now this was news to Lillian. What had been her mother's foolish act? And what was this *lap*? Lillian had never met anyone named Luxury. How could she have almost been raised in Luxury's lap?

"Lillian's thoughts were cut off by the sound of a woman's sharp, accusing voice ringing out from the audience: 'Pettygree or no pettygree. She sank her chomps into Tankersley.' Another voice hollered, 'Didn't offer no apology!'

"The mayor gave a fake laugh. 'All the more reason to open your hearts, folks.'

"But other voices drowned him out:

"*Incorrigible! Naughty! Shameful! Disrespectful!*

"*New York City manners! Should be locked up for what she done!*

"*Lock her up! Send her back!*

"With all the commotion, Lillian realized that she had to do something or she would be sent back to New York. Isn't that what the agent had told her? What could she do to redeem herself? How could she win them over, convince them that she was a special girl, a girl with vows and a future?

"The solution came to her. She walked over to the mayor, pulled on his shirtsleeve, and whispered something in his ear.

"'Folks! Folks! Listen here!' The mayor managed to get their attention. 'The little lady knows she did wrong, and she wants to make amends. She tells me that she's very good at singing and wants to provide a little entertainment.'

"He nodded in her direction. She walked to center stage. The audience grew quiet. Miss Charlotte Fry's neck strained forward. Lillian was nervous, all right. What if she forgot the words? What if they didn't like her? But then, her own past gave her all the encouragement she needed. The footlights and the velvet curtain reminded her of all the applause she had gotten on the streets of New York. Hadn't those people adored her! Aren't people all the same, New York or Nebraska? Won't these people love her, too?

"Her confidence swelled, and she began singing. She really gave it her all. Only this was not one of those nice hymns from church that Nebraska family people appreciate. It was a song that Lillian had learned on the streets—something lively and catchy about sailors and a woman who wears fancy underwear. Definitely not a song for a proper young lady.

"She did a dance, too, some fast-moving foot shuffling and twirling, and right before she got to the end, she swiveled her hips like a hoochy-coochy girl. When she curtsied, tiny droplets of sweat twinkled on the dark hairs of her arms. The shocked audience stared as if she had cast a spell. She heard a sharp, disapproving inhale of one hundred breaths. A cough. She heard the rustling of stiff clothing.

"And then there was not even a peep. Lillian stood in the spotlight frozen, like a girl in a field listening for a storm cloud to break. The only thunder was one pair of hands that started clapping and one voice, loud and thick with blueberry wine, saying, '*Dang!* That's good entertainment!'"

CHAPTER 25

"Hoochy-coochy girl!" Whitney imitated.

"She didn't go live with that Mr. Tankersley, did she?" I asked.

Fern asked Whitney, "What's a hoochy-coochy girl?"

Monica was chewing her nails. "I can't stand it if she went with that guy."

Fern again: "What guy?"

I repeated: "Tell me she didn't go with him."

"Oh, that guy!" Fern remembered.

"She did g-go. The committee routinely approved every single match, and Lillian didn't put up a fuss."

I couldn't believe it. Even Lillian, who would never fuss for no reason, wouldn't stand for this. "Why would she do that? What about her vows?"

Whitney was shaking her head sadly at me. "Man-oh-man, you think you know everything, but you don't know about kids like Lillian, kids like us."

"Why should I?" I sniffed. "I'm not really like you. My mother is—"

The Knitting Lady, who does not usually interrupt,

broke in. "Whitney, Cal is still new here. Tell her why Lillian would go with Mr. Tankersley."

"Let her figure it out herself!"

"A-Amber, can you explain?"

She began, "Where else could she—" Then Whitney couldn't stop herself, "Man-oh-man, Cal. Don't you get it? No one else wanted her even though she's the best kid in the bunch."

"Definitely the best," I said.

We agreed on that. Still, I was confused. Lillian had the guts to sing in front of an audience full of strangers. Lillian wasn't the type to be pushed around. So why would she go with smelly old Tankersley? There must have been plenty of other choices. There had to be. I explained my reasoning. "Lillian could have said to Miss Charlotte Fry, 'Excuse me, but I would rather go back home—'"

Whitney made an exceedingly rude raspberry sound. "What planet are you on? No one is waiting for her all lovey-dovey, 'Come home to me, precious baby jewel.' Face it, she's caught between a . . . a . . . Amber! What's she caught between?"

"A rock and a hard place," Amber answered.

Monica was explaining the latest turn in the story to Fern, who, as usual, was a few steps behind. "Lillian had so much courage! I would have been terrified to be up on that stage singing. Terrified! But not her."

"Yeah," Fern added. "She wasn't scared of anything. But she still had no other choice!"

"Right! Even Fern gets it," Whitney said. "Lillian's in the same boat as Basket Boy when someone came along and plucked him out of the reeds. What could he say? 'No thank you because I don't like the looks of you'?"

The Knitting Lady looked pleased. "Girls, I could not have put that better myself! Of course Lillian wasn't exactly weak in the knees with gratitude. But she knew she could handle whatever came. She reminded herself that she still had her vows in place. Going home with Mr. Tankersley wasn't a long-term thing. That's what she told herself. It was only a temporary stop on her way to her spectacular life."

When the Knitting Lady put it that way, it made sense to me. "Now I understand. Lillian didn't fuss because she knew this wasn't her real life."

"Th-that's exactly what she told herself, Cal. But this is as much a part of her story as anything else. It shaped who she was and what she would someday be. Lillian was too young to understand that yet. But everyone is always living her story."

So that's when she said it: *Everyone is always living her story.* And that's when I thought: *What kind of nutty philosophy is that? Who would buy it? Everyone? Always? Maybe Whitney and Amber belong here and maybe this is*

Monica and Fern's story, but not mine. But I let that particular subject drop and asked, "So, what happened next?"

The Knitting Lady raised an eyebrow.

"I know! I know!" Fern said, waving her arm in the air.

Of course, none of us could believe it. "*You* know?" Whitney asked suspiciously.

"Go on," Monica pressed.

Fern had a pleased look on her face. "What happens next is . . . we need to wait for another time."

"Exactly," the Knitting Lady said.

∽

That night before lights-out, Amber pulled out something from the top drawer in her dresser. It was one of those black-and-white notebooks that looks like it could start mooing any minute.

"What's that for?" I asked.

Amber opened to the first page and, in her pretty handwriting, wrote: *Life in the Pumpkin House. The main characters—Whitney, Cal, Amber.* Then she passed the book and a pen to Whitney.

"What do you want me to do? Nah-uh. I hate writing. This isn't school."

Amber took back the book and wrote: *But you have to. It's our story! We have to write it down.*

"Man-oh-man, okay, but only because I have to." She wrote: So what the heck am I supposed to write about? When she passed the book to me, I noticed that her penmanship was a lot like her knitting. As for my handwriting, it wasn't as pretty as Amber's, but more straight up and down. Teachers were always complimenting me because it's so easy to read. I wrote:

Mr. Tankersley gives me the creeps.

Whitney, did the Opera House remind you of something?

"What?" Whitney asked, then remembered that she was supposed to write. What??????

The Foster Kid Fashion Show.

"Yes!!!!! Man-oh-man, Amber, you're so right!" she said. "Makes me wanna barf just thinking about it. At least Lillian didn't have to keep changing into stupid clothes. They made me wear this stupid dress." In the book, Whitney wrote: Drawing of me in stupid dress

What's the Foster Kid Fashion Show?

Get down on your knees and pray that you never, ever have to be in one of those!!!! Whitney looked up from the book and said, "The time they made me be in it, I messed it up big time, so they never asked me again. If you do have to do it, make sure you mess up." She wrote: Fashion Show Advice—

Spill something or trip, then said, "The whole thing is so embarrassing, you'll want to crawl in a hole and die. You know it must be embarrassing because I'm not the embarrassed type."

But what is it???

I told you already!!! A fashion show!!!

???

A fashion show for kids who need foster homes or to be adopted.

They invite all the grown-ups who are thinking about adopting or taking in a foster kid. And then, they dress you in clothes that stores donate and you have to walk across a stage while everyone's watching.

I wouldn't like that! Cal Lavender doesn't like anyone staring at her!

They make you do it! It really sucks because you have a name tag and after the fashion show people who like the way you look come up and ask all sorts of personal questions. They pretend they're only making nice conversation, but you know their trying to decide whether they want to adopt you or someone else.

They're trying. It's not their trying. What kind of questions?

Like Whitney, how long have you been a foster kid? And Whitney, ha-ha, why are you so petite? That's the polite word for shrimp.

Then what happened?

I would have gotten adopted if I wanted to but people just pissed me off so I showed them my scar and that was that.

Some kids get new homes and some kids don't.

"That's unfair!" I blurted out. Then remembered to write, *That's unfair.*

"Amber's right," Whitney said. "We better write this stuff down so people will know our story." She wrote: *End of Part One of the hysterical document by Whitney, Amber and Cal.*

"Historical document," I corrected.

"Well, somebody better get hysterical over it!" Then Whitney slammed the cow notebook closed and stuffed it under her mattress. After that, she curled up around Ike Eisenhower the Fifth's home, like he was a real pet instead of a bug in a mayonnaise bottle.

I tried to sleep, but my mind kept spinning. *I won't be in a fashion show! I won't! And I wouldn't let Tankersley look at my teeth either!*

"Cal?" It was Amber. "Are you asleep yet?"

"Not yet," I said.

"Don't worry, Cal. I won't fall asleep. Not until you and Whitney do."

CHAPTER 26

Most average eleven-year-olds don't think very much about time. Unlike me, they haven't turned it around and around in their head and come to a very interesting conclusion: Time is strange. By this I mean that time can go both slow and fast at the *very same time*. Here's some examples:

Sometimes in the morning at the Pumpkin House, I would wake up groggy and reach for the familiar length of Betty's arm, and when I didn't feel it, I bolted upright. *Bam!* Time stopped.

Or at the most ordinary moments—like while I was brushing my teeth or knitting a row—Betty's face would materialize before me, hovering like one of those huge Thanksgiving Day parade balloons. *Now! Now! Now! I want Betty now!* At those moments, every second seemed like an hour. It was about three million times worse than sitting in class waiting for the bell to ring.

But time also had a way of flying by. I had to admit that, for not being my real life, things could sometimes get somewhat interesting around the Pumpkin House. For instance, one afternoon we went to the branch library, where I took it upon myself to introduce everyone to the Dewey decimal system. Personally, I don't know how anyone gets along without knowing the Dewey decimal system.

We also went to the park a lot, so much so that I began to think of it as Pumpkin House Park. I borrowed a bathing suit from Fern (same size as me), and we all went to the pool, even Monica who had to sit on a chair because of her arm cast. I didn't think she minded at all, because I assumed she was afraid of the water. She and the Knitting Lady sat together and laughed a lot.

The pool was as good as Whitney said it would be. There was a high dive *and* a big, mushroom-shaped canopy that sprayed water and made everyone screech. As anyone who knows Cal Lavender would suspect, I passed the swimming test the first time out.

One time, I was sitting out with Monica, and we were watching people go off the high dive. We watched one girl in particular. She was about fifteen and wearing a red one-piece with straps that crossed in the back. She paused a moment, then stretched her arms above her head. With a bounce, she dove, then she turned into a ball and spun in the air. Her body unfolded and became a straight arrow entering the water.

I was thinking that someday, somehow, I was going to know how to do that. But it surprised me when Monica—

always-scared-of-something Monica—said, "I want to know how that feels."

That was the first day that I really talked to Monica, and I learned all sorts of stuff that I never expected. We talked about things we wanted to do in life, and what seemed too scary and what seemed impossible. It was like discovering a whole new Monica! When the Knitting Lady said it was time to go home, it was already four o'clock. See? That's what I mean by time being weird and just racing by.

On Mondays, Wednesdays, and Fridays, it was my turn not to fall asleep until Amber and Whitney did. The other nights I got to fall asleep easier, just knowing that Amber was still awake.

One of the best times was the day we all went shopping. At first, I insisted that I didn't need any new clothes, since Betty was coming for me any minute. So why get things that I didn't need?

"I can just keep washing out what I've been wearing," I insisted.

But Whitney held her nose, and if Whitney was holding her nose, I realized I must be getting pretty ripe—and Cal Lavender is not the type of person who walks around being ripe—so I agreed to go. But just this once.

As I mentioned before, I was used to doing all my shopping at Sacred Heart Community Center where an eleven-year-old girl can walk in and pick out any kind of outfit she wants and it doesn't cost her one red cent. But the Knitting Lady insisted that it was time for me to have something brand-new. "J-just for you," she said. "Something that hasn't been worn by anyone else. You deserve that."

I left the store with new red sneakers and a blue gingham two-piece bathing suit (my first two-piece) and a pair of pajamas that I really didn't need but the Knitting Lady insisted that I get because I had never before seen pajamas with a *One Fish, Two Fish, Red Fish, Blue Fish* design. I know I read at an eighth-grade level, so that particular book is way too young for me. But it's fun to have things that remind you of when you were in first grade.

I also saw time passing in other ways, like the way my knitting kept growing and growing until it tumbled to the floor, all yellow and gold, like Rapunzel's hair. I had made up my mind that if I couldn't be the most interesting knitter like Amber or the fastest like Whitney, I would be the longest knitter. Soon, I was working on what the Knitting Lady dubbed The Longest Piece of Knitting That Has Ever Been Knitted at the Pumpkin House.

I noticed time passing in Amber's hair, too. She had stopped pulling at it so much, and now eyelashes were beginning to sprout on her lids and the bald patches on her scalp were slowly filling in. It had been a long time since Fern's eye was swollen. You couldn't even tell that it had ever been bruised. And then one day, Monica went to the doctor to get her cast off, and, believe it or not, she didn't cry or even act scared. She came out of the doctor's office with a big smile and an arm that was pathetic-looking, white and so much bonier than the rest of her. She seemed to be getting braver about other things, too. She actually tried one of my Infinitely Superior Lettuce, Tomato, Cucumber, Avocado, Mustard, and Mayonnaise Tortilla Roll-Ups.

We worked on our Cow Notebook historical document almost every day, and I saw time passing in the way the pages were filling up.

Monica says I don't have the guts to go find my sister. Ha! Monica the wimp saying I don't have guts! You have to plan something like this. I've been planning my head off.

Picture of Me planning my head off ———→

Monica's not such a wimp any-more. Anyway, there's no need to rush. You want to do this right, right?

Man-oh-man, we'd be gone by now if it wasn't for a certain something that I'm waiting for that's holding me back. Don't ask me what it is.

What is it?
Three guesses

The Knitting Lady's story. You don't want to leave before it's over.

Everyone would kill me if we left before the end, right?

Definitely! And who knows how long the story will go on?

What I didn't write was that I was hoping the story would go on forever. Or at least until Betty did whatever she had to do so that I could go back to my real life again.

༄

The next time I met with the social worker, I told her that I had been thinking very seriously about these so-called rules that Betty had to follow.

"Just what are these rules?" I asked.

Mrs. S. said it was very simple. There was just one rule really. Betty had to show that she was capable of taking care of me. "Instead of vice versa. You're the child and your mother is the adult. But you're the one who keeps taking care of her."

I thought: *What's the big deal? We get along fine—just fine—with me doing most of the taking-care-of. Rules are made for an average, ordinary family, but that's not us.*

I said, "Eleven and one month—no, two months now—is almost an adult."

Mrs. S. said, "Don't you believe it. Your mother has to start being the mother."

"But she's not like other mothers. How do you expect her to do that?"

Without looking up from my paperwork, the social worker said, "If your mother really loves you, she'll find a way to change and do what she's supposed to do. That's what a mother does."

"And if she doesn't?"

Mrs. S. didn't answer my question. But in the silence, I heard her answer: *It means she doesn't love you enough.*

∽

I tried to fall asleep that night, but couldn't. I needed an answer. I went looking for the Knitting Lady and found her in her bedroom.

"I have a for-instance question," I said.

The Knitting Lady yawned. "Don't mind my yawn. That's just age speaking. I'm always ready for a for-instance question. It gives the brain a chance to stretch. Go."

"Let's say that someone really wants to do something. It's a very important thing to do, and in their heart they want to do it. This thing that they want to do doesn't seem like a big deal. I mean, if you look around, you see that most people in the world have no trouble doing it. But for some reason, it's just hard for this person to do this thing because they're not the typical, average person and things that are no sweat for other people are really, really hard for them."

I paused to catch my breath and thought: *I'm making no sense at all.* I asked, "Am I making any sense at all?"

"Perfect sense. G-go on."

"I don't know what else to say. I just want to know if the person can do it or not."

"It depends."

"On what?" I felt my heart beating. "It depends on love, doesn't it? If the person loves enough, nothing will hold her back. And if she doesn't love enough, then she won't do what she should be doing. That's it, isn't it?" My voice got louder. "Isn't it?"

"Who said it's only a m-matter of love? Life is more complicated than that. For instance, Lillian's mother loved her, right? She loved her enough to give up everything. But love couldn't stop her from dying."

I shivered. "She left Lillian all alone."

"That's the way it seemed," the Knitting Lady said. "But that's because Lillian didn't know her own h-history."

"What history? She has no history! Her own family gave her away."

"That's not the h-history I'm talking about."

My words came out sharp and frustrated. "You keep talking about this history, how Lillian's a part of it, and Whitney and Amber, and me, too. But I don't know what you're getting at. I don't care. I just want Betty. If she loves me, she'll find a way."

I expected the Knitting Lady to launch into one of her

philosophical discussions, to go on and on about ancestors and things that I didn't want to hear about. I wouldn't listen to that! I waited for her to say the exact wrong thing so I could storm out of the room. She filled her mouth with air, and, for a second, I saw her skin the way it must have looked once, without the wrinkles of time. Then she blew out the air. There was a long, odd silence. She said nothing, nothing at all.

CHAPTER 27

First thing in the morning, the Knitting Lady called an emergency storytelling session. How can a story be an emergency? I pulled off my pajamas, folded them extra neatly, put on shorts and a top, then walked calmly down the stairs like I wasn't burning with curiosity, which I was, but Cal Lavender isn't about to let anyone know that she's burning with anything.

Whitney, of course, had no such restraint. She nearly pushed me over in her rush to get down. Monica and Fern were already in Talk Central, drowning their cornflakes in milk. Amber was in an armchair, her feet tucked under her bottom. She was knitting one of her creations with multi-colored yarn. Whitney flopped on the floor by my chair and, without asking, used my lap as a resting place for her stinky feet.

"If you don't mind," I said, lifting them and setting them back on the floor.

"What's the matter with you?"

I thought: *Why, nothing. Everything is just dandy. I've got a social worker who won't tell me about my own life, and Betty, who may or may not decide to become a mother—whatever that means, and where is Betty? And what happens if someone like smelly Tankersley decides that Cal Lavender is the exact type of girl he wants to take home? And please, please, please let Whitney forget about her plan to find her sister.*

"Nothing," I said. "Nothing is the matter. Everything is just great."

"Good!" Whitney said. "Because it's important that nothing's the matter with you. Because . . . you never know when big things may be happening. Big!"

I tried to avoid eye contact, but Whitney was bobbing all over the place, making sure that I couldn't escape her winking.

It was a big relief when the Knitting Lady put her finger to her lips, signaling us to be quiet. As far as I could tell, an emergency storytelling session was pretty much like a regular storytelling session, except that she started right in, no catching up or anything.

"L-Lillian was standing in the front yard of the Tankersley farmhouse. To a girl from a city, it all looked unreal, like a set in a snow globe before someone shakes it. In her mind, Lillian went over the things Mr. Tankersley had told her during the long, bumpy carriage ride: In the winter, they will get snow, plenty of it. Lillian will have her own room behind the alcove. Mrs. Tankersley has a sickness. Mr. Tankersley will teach Lillian how to candle an egg. Mrs. Tankersley has been sick for a while. Their closest neighbor is five miles away.

"Mr. Tankersley led her into the house. The front door squeaked and closed behind them with a slam. 'Let's go meet your new mother,' he said. 'But don't go making her laugh right away. It might set her heart palpitating.'

"When he opened the door to the dark bedroom, Lillian was hit with a closed-in smell, like the odor that rises from old water in a vase of rotting flowers. 'Ida,' he said. Then Mr. Tankersley made a big production of opening the curtains and shutters. When the light poured in, Lillian saw a new look on his face, something she never expected. The look was full of hope. Ida—his wife, Lillian's new mother—was in the bed, a woman as pale as chalk. The sight of her made Lillian shiver, like a cold finger had just run up her spine. The woman's eyes were oversized, like she was seeing horrible things that nobody else could see.

"Mr. Tankersley sat in the chair beside the bed and took the woman's hand in his. 'Ida, I brought you someone.' He turned to Lillian, gestured at her with his chin. 'Go on, then. Say hello to your mother.'

"Lillian remained in the doorway, looking at the specter in white propped against a heavy wooden headboard. She said, 'Hello.'

"'Hello, *Mother*,' he prompted. 'Call her that. Say, *Hello, Mother.*'

"Lillian cleared her throat with a cough. *Mother*? Call her Mother? This woman wasn't *anything* like her mother. This wasn't her life. But she said it anyway, 'Hello. Mother.'

"Mr. Tankersley nodded in approval. He kept nodding as if his movements were catching and his wife would be energized by them. 'Isn't that nice, Ida? Your new little girl has come to say hello.'

"More silence. But Mr. Tankersley continued as if his wife had spoken right up and a whole other side of the conversation had taken place. 'Your little girl is here now, Ida. Now and every day.' He turned back to Lillian. 'Come on now, you. Kiss your mother. Go on, closer.'

"Lillian took two steps. 'I can't. I can't,' she said.

"'Sure you can. It is your own sweet, dear mother waiting here for you.'

"'I can't,' she repeated. But then she did. The skin tasted dry and bitter.

"'You wanna say something to our little girl, Ida. She's waiting.'

"Nothing."

At this part, Fern spoke up. She was totally confused. "So, who's the lady in bed?"

"Man-oh-man, something's nutty with her," Whitney said.

"I'm not nutty!" Fern protested.

"Not you! The mother. I think she's sad," Monica said.

"S-sad? N-nutty? Any other ideas?"

"I think . . ."

"G-go ahead, Amber."

"I think her own daughter died. Lillian is supposed to be her substitute daughter."

"Whose daughter?" Fern asked.

It turned out that Amber was right. The Tankersleys had had a daughter who died, and Mr. Tankersley thought that a new girl would snap his wife out of being depressed. At this point, we were all feeling a little sorry for the Tankersleys. How could you not get depressed when you had a cute little daughter and that daughter got sick and then died in your arms? I, for one, was even hoping that Mrs. Tankersley jumped right out of bed and hugged Lillian and Lillian hugged her back and they all lived together happily in the farmhouse. I think we all liked that idea.

But the next part of the story made us change our minds. Whitney especially. Whew! It took the Knitting Lady several minutes to calm her down. When she heard that the Tankersleys gave Lillian the same name as their dead daughter—Faith—Whitney slammed her palm on a table. "I hate that! Man-oh-man, in my fifth—no! my ninth—foster home the mother kept calling me 'Patty.' Do I look like a Patty? No!"

"Is Patty the same as Faith?" Fern asked.

"No! Patty was some little kid who died. I felt bad because little kids aren't supposed to die. But man-oh-man, I got sick and tired of being Patty. I didn't die. I was plenty alive. It was *Patty, Patty, Patty.* So I ran away."

I would have done the same. Absolutely. Cal Lavender would never allow herself to be called anything other than Cal Lavender. So it was confusing to me that Lillian didn't seem to mind at all or at least she didn't show it. The Knitting Lady explained that she let the Tankersleys call her Faith, but she never, ever stopped thinking of herself as Lillian.

"Why?" I asked.

"B-because Lillian decided this wasn't her real life, so let those people call her what they wanted to call her."

That was something that I could definitely understand. But the name was just the start of Lillian's problems. Ida Tankersley never jumped out of bed and hugged her. The haunted look never disappeared from behind her eyes. Eventually, Mr. Tankersley lost hope, and, with it, he lost interest in Faith/Lillian. If the girl couldn't cure his wife, then, by golly, she was going to have to earn her keep. Faith/Lillian began taking on all the farmwife chores. She cooked the breakfast, did the cleaning, the laundry, prepared the dinner. She ended each day by giving Ida Tankersley's hair one hundred strokes of a brush.

Days, sometimes weeks went by, when Mr. Tankersley

said little more than a few words to her. *Do this! Get that job done by sundown!*

"No school for Lillian?" Monica asked.

"N-no school."

"No friends?" Fern asked.

"T-too much work for friends. Besides, they lived out in the middle of nowhere."

Whitney was still all worked up. "No cakes dripping with honey either. Or dresses made of . . . made of what, Amber?"

"Gingham," she answered.

"Yeah. Gingham! But was there butter to church?"

"Churn," I corrected.

"And quilts to make? Hell, yes. I bet it was Cleaning Madness around the clock. Enough chores to choke a . . . choke a what?"

"Choke a horse," Amber and I said together.

"Yeah, a horse," Whitney said.

Monica said, "I would pass out if I had to do all that work! Unfair!"

The Knitting Lady agreed. "Y-yes, unfair! But compared to some of the other children who had come west, Lillian had it only half bad. At least she had food to eat and a roof over her head."

It turned out that some of the so-called *nice* families had lied like a rug. Some children were taken to farms and worked half to death. If the children refused to work, or passed out from too much work, well, they didn't get anything to eat. Some were given only rags to wear, and some got hardly any food, even when they worked all day and into the night. In the worst situations, the children were treated worse than the farm animals.

"They were hit," Amber said softly.

"T-that's true. I know it's hard to hear something like that."

Monica put her hands over her ears. "I don't want to hear it."

"N-nobody likes to hear it, but it's important to remember. Some of those children were . . . *hit* is not a strong enough word. They were beaten. And not one of them—not the laziest or the most ornery—deserved it. Not one."

I couldn't stop myself from looking at Amber just then. I couldn't help but think about what I had read in her social-work file, how in some ways, Amber's life had been even sadder and more unfair than what was happening to Lillian. Amber caught me looking at her, but she didn't turn away. Her expression didn't change. I repeated the Knitting Lady's words: "Not one deserved it. Not one."

Monica and Fern had also gotten quiet, which made me wonder what was written in their files. I would probably never know exactly what brought them to the Pumpkin House. But I knew that bad things had happened to them, too.

Maybe the Knitting Lady could read minds as well as she could read stitches: "Now, Cal, don't you go feeling all s-sorry for these children. Don't start pitying them. No pity! Do you know why? Because the things that happen to us—the bad as well as the good—make us who and what we are."

At that, we had a million comments and questions.

So, what happened to the little girl who looked like a boy? Did she get a pony or not?

And the brother of the red-haired girl?

No, not the brother! I want to know about the red-haired girl!

And the girl who was exceptional.

Exceptional?

Baby Mary, fat and pretty.

"S-some were lucky, some weren't," the Knitting Lady said. "And each one of those children has a story as dramatic as Lillian's. But to tell them now, all at the same time? Whew, I'm afraid my storytelling ability isn't up to that task."

"So go on about Lillian," Whitney insisted.

The Knitting Lady told us that Lillian did have one farm chore that she actually liked. That was to candle the eggs. I didn't have a clue what that meant and neither did anyone else, so the Knitting Lady explained. In the old chicken-farm days, eggs were held up to a light to see if they were fertile or not fertile. Tankersley taught her how to turn the egg quickly to throw the yolk near the shell. She knew she had a fertile one when she spotted the blood vessels of the embryo fanning out like a huge red spider.

"Gross! Why would anyone like that job?" Monica asked.

"Any i-ideas?"

I had one: "Even though she knows this is not her real life, she tries to be the best in everything." I paused. The Knitting Lady nodded in encouragement. "I think Lillian made up her mind to become the best egg candler in the entire state of Nebraska. She may not be the most creative egg candler or the fastest egg candler, but she was the best all-around egg candler." I had more to say, but I ran out of breath.

"There was one more thing our Lillian excelled at," the Knitting Lady went on. "One day, she was cleaning out a shed and found an old typewriter. It was rusty and some of the keys didn't work, but she taught herself to type. Pretty soon, neighbors were bringing her things that needed typing up. Most often, they paid her in produce and livestock. Mr. Tankersley got quite a number of chickens that way. But sometimes, she was given cash and managed to squirrel away a bit before Tankersley took the bulk."

"She was saving up for something!" Monica said.

"Something important!" Fern added.

"E-even Lillian wasn't sure what she was saving for, but she saved and saved. One Saturday when she was in town doing errands, she came upon a poster in the window of the dry-goods store. A vaudeville show was coming to town, and to say that Lillian was excited is putting it mildly. Every cell in her body longed to see new things, glamorous things that she knew existed in the world. So the promise of a vaudeville show? To see performers all the way from New York and even Europe? There was no doubt where some of her life savings would go. Without telling Tankersley, Lillian bought a ticket and for weeks could think of nothing else."

The Knitting Lady shut her eyes, not squeezed tight all scrunchy, but softly like a curtain dropping. She placed one hand to her heart and rested it there. If you looked closely, you could see it moving up and down to her breathing. She was really digging deep this time. Nobody said anything. We all knew better than to rush the Knitting Lady while she was gathering up the threads of her story.

"The Opera House," she finally said. "The place where lives are changed."

CHAPTER 28

"The v-vaudeville show was everything Lillian had dreamed of, and more. There was Peg-Leg Bates, a man with a leg as wooden as a broom handle, who danced his heart out. A woman played a ukulele like it was on fire. A man ate lit matches like they were chewing gum. Lillian clapped and clapped until her hands were red and stinging.

"And now an act called 'Little Miss' was scheduled to close the show. The curtain opened to a stage that was still and empty. Lillian wasn't the only one to feel a flutter of disappointment. Where was the swelling music and the fabulous set? Where was the dramatic opening that grabbed your attention and held it like a vise grip?

"Just as everyone was getting restless, a girl walked into the center of a single spotlight. She was pretty enough, with golden curls to her shoulders and enormous, round blue eyes. Normally, vaudeville audiences couldn't get enough of children's acts. But after so many hours of excitement, the audience was expecting more than one girl in a fluffy pink tutu. After all, this was the act that would send them back to their dusty farms and ordinary lives for another year.

"A piano player made a few light tinkling notes. The girl rose on the balls of her feet and made short, mincing steps that carried her forward and backward. Her arms rose listlessly up and down from her sides. But it was more than her mediocre dance talent that was making the audience squirm in their seats. There was something about this girl that seemed unbearably sad beneath her smile, like she was carrying the weight of the world.

"This was not what the audience had come to the theater to see! They wanted to escape the troubles of the world, not see them written on the face of an untalented child. You could hear their opinion of Little Miss in the whispers that traveled along the rows of the theater like a game of Whisper Down the Lane. *She's not a talented miss. Sad little thing. Sad little miss.* The pianist tried to add a little pizzazz with a quick, light running scale of notes. But Little Miss remained stilted and worn. She ended her act with a weak curtsy. Her hand went to her mouth, and she blew meaningless kisses.

"There was a clap here and a clap there, but the audience couldn't wait to get out of the theater. I'm sure that many of those people were thinking, *Tsk, tsk, such a young child should be going home with a proper family, rather than embarrassing herself on stage all hours of the day and night.*

"Suddenly, from the back row, came a man's voice that

reverberated throughout the theater: 'It's Nellie! Nellie! Don't you know me?'

"Everything came to a stop. Antsy kids who had fled into the aisles looked like they were playing a game of Statues. Wives paused midsentence, their mouths in perfect circles of astonishment. Husbands pivoted in the direction of the man's voice, their free hands set on their foreheads like sailors trying to spot land.

"Still nothing moved, except the man, his face thin and pale with emotion. He stretched out both arms and declared, 'I saw her picture on the posters! I've been tracking her from town to town. Nothing will keep me from her.'

"On stage, Little Miss, hearing the man's cry, froze with one hand in the air where her kisses sat half blown away. She peered across the footlights and then came alive. 'Poppa! Poppa! You came back for me like you said you would. Poppa, take me home!'

"What a commotion! The father rushed forward like a madman. Halfway to the stage, three confused ushers put their shoulders together to block his path. Still, he managed to push through the trio of burly, red-faced men. That was the strength of this skinny father's will!

"Next, the theater company manager—Mr. H. W. Mergenthal himself!—came onto the stage, shaking his fist. His features were hard, his voice all business. 'This is an outrage!' he bellowed. 'We don't know this man. Who is he?'

"'*She* knows me!' the father shouted.

"With a squeal of 'My poppa!' Little Miss took a step closer, but the piano player jumped up, scooped her into his arms, and carried her offstage.

"'She's our little star!' the company manager insisted, his voice coarse and threatening. 'She's under contract to us.'

"The father shook off the ushers like they were nothing but flies. He challenged the manager: 'What contract is more important than the bond between child and parent?'

"In the audience, the farmers and shopkeepers, the women and children rose from their seats, all of one mind:

"'Give him his daughter! Let her have her father!'

"'No!' H. W. Mergenthal shouted.

"'Yes!' the audience demanded.

"Mayor Clyde Shook pushed his way to the front. Wrapping a thick arm around the father, the mayor, his voice thick with outrage, said, 'I've never seen this man in my life. But he deserves to have his own flesh and blood. What's right is right!'

"At that, H. W. Mergenthal's chin dropped to his chest, and, when he looked back up, the hardness had slid off his features. His voice had a choke in it. 'I am so ashamed. Greed got ahold of me. But you fine, honest townspeople have shown me the light. Business can never come before family. Nobody can stand in the way of parent and child.'

"The piano player returned hand in hand with Little Miss, and, oh, what a difference! Her smile dazzled way to the back of the balcony. And what a dance she performed! A dance of gratitude. Her final dance. She spun and soared. She was air itself. And when she was done, to the cheers of the audience, H. W. Mergenthal lifted her in his arms.

"And what of our Lillian? She was transfixed. From the moment Little Miss had cried out 'Poppa!' Lillian had barely moved a muscle. Her mind latched on to an idea. No, it was more than an idea; it was the culmination of all her vows, of what she knew to be her destiny. Barely able to breathe, she watched as the manager stepped to the edge of the stage and handed Little Miss—a vision in pink-and-white tulle—to the father she always knew would come. At that, Lillian gave a low, involuntary cry of recognition.

‿

"Sh-she knew what she had to do. That night, when the Tankersleys fell asleep, Lillian packed her belongings. She didn't take much, some clothes, a hat she always liked. Right, Amber. Your fingers are in two circles. Of course, she took the lorgnette.

"She loaded the carriage and started driving to the

city. It was a good thing there was a full moon because the road was normally pitch-black and full of shadows that warn a young girl: *Turn around and go home!* But that night, there was plenty of light for Lillian to say good-bye:

"*Good-bye to dusty roads that lead nowhere.*

"*Good-bye to cows that stare dumbly behind the fence.*

"*Good-bye to thick air that turns everyone old and wrinkled.*

Good-bye to people who never really knew me.

"Lillian took one more thing—her typewriter. She wasn't sure why. It was a heavy, clunky old thing, but she trusted her instincts and threw it into the wagon at the last minute."

Monica looked worried. "Wasn't she scared?"

"Of c-course. Nobody heads into a whole new future without being scared."

I had a thought: "But Lillian told herself that she wasn't scared, not one little bit. Everything was going to work out."

"Well, did it?" Fern asked me.

"How should I know? It's not my story." I asked the Knitting Lady, "So did it?"

"W-work out? Mull that question over for a while, all of you. Next time, I want to hear what you think."

CHAPTER 29

I, Cal Lavender, have something to say about moods.

Most ordinary eleven-year-old girls are mood factories, pumping out temper tantrums and hissy fits twenty-four hours a day. But not me. I don't have crying spells that come out of nowhere. I highly recommend this way of living because, from what I've observed, moods make you say and do enormously stupid things.

To tell the truth, grown-ups aren't always much better than kids. Mrs. S., the social worker, is a prime example. Someone with such an important job should not go from zero to a hundred on the ticked-off scale because of a few suggestions that I made at our next meeting:

SUGGESTION 1: Let's say, one sister is in a foster home and another sister is adopted. Shouldn't someone arrange things so those two sisters get to meet each other sometime?

SUGGESTION 2: Wouldn't it make her social-working job easier if Betty also lived in the Pumpkin House where I could help her do whatever it is she needs to do in order to pass the good-parent test?

These perfectly logical suggestions caused Mrs. S. to bristle. There were little drops of dried, white spit on the corners of her mouth, and they came flying off. "*Betty* has to cooperate," she insisted. "*Betty* has to put *your* needs before *her* needs."

What also surprised me was that the Knitting Lady could have moods, too. Sometimes, she would get flustered if she thought we were missing something important in her story. Once she got all weepy-eyed at something I said, but I'm not going to say what that was right now. Another time, I heard her go off like a siren—*Ooooooooh!*—when someone at the Department of Children's Services suggested moving Fern to a different group home for no real reason.

You would think that someone who had a finely developed knitting peace of mind wouldn't have moods. You would think! So that got me to reconsider my position. Maybe a mood or two isn't a terrible thing to have every once in a while. Maybe.

⸙

Man-oh-man, Cal, I can't believe you told Mrs. S. that she should help me find my sister.

I didn't name names. I didn't say Whitney's sister!

U think you know everything but you don't know how everyone knows everything about U here. It's like they're part dog's nose. U even <u>think</u> something against the rules and Mrs. S. gets wind of it! Man-oh-man, I know she will. You screwed things up!

I didn't screw anything up!

I had another dream.

About my sister? Yeah it had to be! What????

She wants Cal to help find her. It won't work without Cal.

Says who??

Amber's dream! See, I didn't screw things up!

You did! But don't blow a gasnet about it!

A gasnet?

A gasnet! A thing on a car that blows up.

??????

A gasket. It blows up when a car gets too hot.

I'm not too hot! Cal Lavender is never too hot!

Hahahahahahahahahahaha you're hot now. Cal is gasket hot!

That was when Whitney decided that we should have a test run before we really set off to find her sister. Considering it was Whitney's idea, it actually made sense. That night, we would wait until dark. Then, we would all climb out the window by my bed. I would check out the buses and map out a plan.

That's how I had things figured. If I went with them on the test run, they wouldn't need me when it came time for the real thing. Dream or no dream, I wouldn't have to go. I could stay in the Pumpkin House and be there when

Betty came to pick me up. That was my vow. I'd be back from the test run before anyone noticed we were gone. It was just practice.

⬭

One more thing. Here's what I said to the Knitting Lady the time she got all moody weepy-eyed. "I have Betty's eyebrows," I was telling her.

"They're nice, s-strong brows."

"Do people always get things from their mother?" I hesitated. "Like a stutter?" I had never asked about her stutter, but she didn't seem to mind at all.

"My mother didn't stutter, if that's what you're asking."

"I keep watching out for them," I said.

"For what?"

"For Betty's moods. If I have her eyebrows, one day I could have her moods, too."

"You w-worry about that?"

"They could sneak up on me. Sometimes..." I paused.

"Go on."

"Sometimes I wish I *would* get Betty's moods. Inherit them. All of them!"

"W-why on earth?"

"Because then I'd know."

205

"Know what?"

"Exactly how Betty feels."

That's when the Knitting Lady got the weepy look.

Anyway, that's all that I, Cal Lavender, have to say about moods for right now.

CHAPTER 30

The big night. As I mentioned before, it was Whitney's bright idea to make our getaway through the window above my bed.

"No way," Monica said.

"Go!" Whitney ordered me.

"Go where?" I was staring two stories straight down onto a slab of hard, neck-breaking concrete patio.

"Just go! Jeez-Louise, I thought you said you'd climbed out windows before."

"I did. Lots of times. Sometimes Betty didn't pay the landlord and we had to—"

Whitney gave me a sharp push. "Go, then!"

"Usually, there was a fire escape. I assumed you were going to have a ladder."

Whitney spoke in a mocking baby voice. "'I assumed you'd have a ladder.'"

I faced her with my hands on my hips. "I hate people imitating me!"

Whitney threw herself, dirty shoes and all, on my bed. "I got another idea. I saw this in a movie once. Did you ever see that movie, these two firemen—no, it was three firemen, and maybe it wasn't a movie, maybe it was a TV show—well, they were stuck on the roof of this building—and you can't believe the flames—well, the girl in the movie, she—"

I broke in. "Are we going or not, Whitney?"

"Jeez, of course, I was getting to that. Anyway, the two firemen held the bravest fireman by the ankles out the window and lowered him—"

Monica looked pale. "I'm not doing that. No way I'm doing that."

"Did I see that movie?" Fern said. "Can we go to a movie tonight?"

Whitney ignored both of them. "As I was saying, Cal and Amber can hold me by my feet and lower me head-first to the ground." She picked up the mayonnaise jar.

"What are you doing with that?" Fern asked.

"You think I'm going anywhere without Ike Eisen-hower the Fifth?" She tapped on the side of the jar. "Don't worry, Ike. I won't go anywhere without you!"

She had to be kidding. I said, "You have to be kidding!"

What happened next was so logical and so practical that it was something I would definitely have thought of myself if Amber didn't get there first. "Come on," she said.

Her head was poking halfway into the hallway,

looking left, then right. She went first, then Fern and Whitney. Monica seemed paralyzed, so I pushed her ahead of me. And just like that, all five of us—six if you count Ike—went slinking down the stairs and across the living room floor. I made sure the door stayed unlatched when it closed behind us.

"Piece of cake," Whitney said.

Outside, a thick, warm mist was falling. It wasn't much of a rain, just enough to wet down the sidewalk and release the smells of concrete. "Let's go, let's go," Whitney urged, then turned and started walking up the street. No, it wasn't walking. She was more like a dog pulling on a leash. Right behind her was Amber, wearing clothes the same color as her skin, a pale gray, like the world never stopped raining on her. Next were Monica and Fern with their arms looped around each other's shoulders.

I thought: *Maybe the entire Department of Children's Services knows exactly what we're up to and right now they're deciding that I've blown any chance to ever go back with Betty. That's it! I am definitely going to turn around and go back into the Pumpkin House.*

That's what my logical brain decided. But my feet started doing a very un–Cal Lavender type of thing. I followed the others. I noticed a mockingbird on a telephone wire, whirring and clicking deep in its throat. And then I noticed the sudden cry of a cat, the whoosh of a car tire, the hum of a streetlight. I have to admit that I felt a charge from all these night sounds, like being with Betty when she was in one of her all-night moods. I was flooded with a sense of freedom, like I'd been suffocating and hadn't even realized it.

I thought: *Lillian must have felt this way when she left the Tankersleys in the middle of the night. The feeling of being the only one awake when other people are asleep. It must have felt just like this, like anything and everything was possible, like a whole new life was waiting for her just up the road.*

I hunched my shoulders against the drizzle and kept walking. Nobody would understand this feeling. Nobody but Lillian. Nobody but Betty. Nobody but me.

When I finally caught up with the others, they were clustered around the bus stop. Whitney was up and down from the bench, tapping on Ike Eisenhower the Fifth's jar, jiggling her right leg, popping four sticks of gum into her mouth at once. "Man-oh-man," she said.

That's when I saw something in her expression that was as familiar to me as if I had just run my hands up and down my own face. "What?" I asked.

"Man-oh-man, Cal. You know! The Pumpkin House is the best place I've ever been. But there's nothing— nothing!—like blowing out of a foster home."

I checked the posted schedule. The last bus on this

particular route came at ten p.m., so next time, Whitney would have to get an earlier start. "This is the number 26," I explained. "It'll take you downtown. Do you want to go downtown?" (Notice how I cleverly said "take *you*," not "take *us*.")

When she didn't answer, I went on. "That's where all the buses leave from. You'll have to know which one to catch after the 26. Do you know which bus goes to your sister's neighborhood?"

Whitney pulled out her wad of gum and stuck it to the bottom of the bench. Then, she started working on an open bag of sunflower seeds. *Crack.* "How could I"—*crack, crack*—"know which bus to take?" *Crack.* "You're the bus genius."

"So what's your sister's address?"

Whitney spit out a shell by her feet. "It's a secret! I had to steal to get it."

"I can't tell you what bus to take if I don't know where she lives."

Whitney glanced around, checking for her usual spies. "You'll know," she said, "when you need to know."

And that was that. That was the full and complete story of our practice run to find Whitney's sister.

CHAPTER 31

At 11 a.m. What a slug! I'd never slept that late before, not even when I was up all night with Betty.

At 11:05 a.m. Amber was still asleep. I peeked into the next room. Fern and Monica were still snoring away. What time did we finally come back in? Late.

At 11:15 a.m. At first I thought that maybe the Knitting Lady was also still asleep. That's how quiet it was downstairs. Then I heard mumbling coming from Talk Central.

I must point out that Cal Lavender never eavesdrops. Eavesdropping is something that a Whitney type of person would stoop to do. Eavesdropping is not polite at all, so I would never eavesdrop. That said, in this particular situation, I just happened to be standing behind the half-open door, waiting for a break in the conversation. The conversation that I wasn't eavesdropping on went like this:

K.L. (Knitting Lady): If you get s-some vows in place, you can have anything you aim for.

W. (Whitney): Like what?

K.L.: Well, some people aim for a big job and some people aim for a big car and some people want big adventures.

W.: What did you want when you were my age?

K.L.: I guess I wanted love. Love as big as a van.

W.: I want . . . I know what I want but I'm not telling.

K.L.: Fair enough. But to get it, you have to make a decision.

W.: What kind of decision?

K.L.: You can keep wanting what you don't have. Or you can open your eyes and start seeing what you c-can have, what you already have.

W. *(anger in her voice)*. Just because I'm a foster kid, I'm not gonna settle. That's what some of those orphan-train kids did! But not Lillian!

K.L.: No, not Lillian.

W. *(mocking voice)*: What am I supposed to say? Oh thank you, thank you, because I wasn't stuck on a train in 1892 and worked to death! Man-oh-man!

K.L.: Not what I'm saying. I w-would never suggest being grateful for that.

W. *(her voice softer now)*: Then what? What are you saying? What do I have?

There was silence. I moved a little closer to the door opening. I wanted to see what they were doing in the silence. What was the look on Whitney's face? What was the Knitting Lady doing? Was she talking about Whitney's sister? That was it! That must be it! Or was it something else? What *did* Whitney already have?

The Knitting Lady spoke again. "Cal? Come on in. Better yet, go upstairs and wake the others. What sleepyheads! You'd think they were gallivanting about all night! I'm an old lady, you know, so I don't have forever to finish this story.

∽

"So, d-do you remember the question that I asked you to think about?"

Fern burst out, "I do! I remember! Did everything work out the way Lillian wanted it to?"

"G-good for you, Fern."

"See, I can remember things. I can."

"Who w-wants to take a stab at the answer? Monica?" She shook her head.

"C-Cal? Anyone?" She sighed. "No one. I guess you'll just have to wait and see.

∽

"From the front door of the Opera House, Lillian heard the grunts and pounding of men doing hard physical work. She hesitated. No! If she hesitated, she would never get what she wanted. So she stepped inside and looked around at the big men with paint and dust on their clothes and in their hair. One man was breaking apart the acrobats' trapeze. Two others strained to move a couch. Then, there he was!

"That early in the morning, H. W. Mergenthal certainly didn't look like the dazzling company manager of the night before. He held a clipboard, looking like a squat, tired, irritable middle-aged man. Lillian didn't want to lose her courage. So she carried all she owned in the world to the foot of the stage, dropped it by her ankles, and said, 'I'm here for the part.'

"One of the workers elbowed Mergenthal in the side. She heard him say, 'Wouldn't be a small town without at least one.'

"*Without at least one of what?* she wondered.

"The manager turned and took in everything about Lillian at once—her suitcase; her earnest, eager look; her cheap farm-girl clothes. 'So,' he said. 'You wanna join vaudeville.' His hands flipped up from the wrists like he was balancing two heavy trays. 'What's your act?'

"Lillian flashed him a smile that she had been rehearsing just for this moment: 'You are looking at Little Miss.'

"Mergenthal's lips tightened slightly like he just burped up something sour. 'Hey, kid, didn't you see the show? We have a Little Miss.'

215

"'It must be a terrible blow, her going back to her father and all,' she said. 'But your troubles are over. I can replace her.'

"As Lillian was talking, she didn't see the creeping smile of amusement that came over the great man's face. She didn't notice how the workers started nudging one another. But she did notice when a woman, very short and small-boned with close-cropped dark hair, came onto the stage from the wings and called out, 'Harry! When are we out of here?'

"H. W. Mergenthal held up a warning finger to the woman and said her name sharply—'Florence'—before turning back to Lillian. 'What's your name, hon?'

"'Lillian.'

"'Okay, Lily. Just how old are you?'

"She lied. 'Seventeen.'

"'Right,' he said, sarcastically. 'And I'm twenty-one.'

"'Sixteen, then.'

"He paused like he was going to argue again, then changed his mind. 'Okay, sixteen-year-old Lily of Nebraska. First of all, let me introduce you to Little Miss.'

"The dark-haired woman named Florence rolled her eyes, and Lillian noticed they were blue. Very blue. And very round. H. W. Mergenthal noticed that Lillian noticed.

"'Smart girl,' he said. 'Add a blond wig, the right makeup, and Florence can pass for fourteen, though she's a long way from that.' The woman gave him a light punch on his shoulder. 'It's all an act,' she explained flatly.

"Lillian repeated the words in her head: *An act. All an act.* Which meant that Little Miss had never really been taken from her family. Which meant that there really was no Little Miss. Which meant that . . . that . . . Lillian felt her future, her destiny, the very vows that had sustained her through those hard, cold Nebraska winters, begin to disintegrate around her. People would never know her name. Her life would never be spectacular.

"And there was something else. Something so important that Lillian did not even acknowledge it to herself. And don't say that you don't know. I know that each one of you knows."

Fern, of all people, began, "When she was watching Little Miss . . ." Monica continued, "Lillian thought that if her name was on a poster . . ." Whitney broke in, "And if she was famous and on stage . . ."

"Y-your turn, Amber."

"That someone would find her, too. Her father, maybe. Or one of those rich relatives."

"Understand, C-Cal? So what was it? What was that hope deep inside of Lillian?"

"That . . . that someone would rush to the front of the stage and take her back to her life, her real life. But Lillian didn't say that. She would never say that out loud!"

"Of c-course not! H. W. Mergenthal shrugged. 'Sorry, kid. We don't need a Little Miss.' He paused. He probably felt sorry for her. 'But you got spunk. There's always room for another spunky-kid act.'

"Lillian jumped on her second chance. 'I can sing,' she said, even though she had not sung in years.

"H. W. Mergenthal rubbed his cheek. 'Can't use another singer. How about spitting fire? A kid spitting fire would be something to see!' But when she shook her head, she noticed that the light in the man's eyes dimmed a little.

"*No!* she decided firmly. She can't get back in the carriage and return in shame and defeat to the Tankersley farm. Not when she had come this close—*this close!*—to fulfilling her vows. If the troupe would just take her along with them—take her to the next city and the next and the next—she would do anything. She didn't even have to be on stage. That was it! She could be useful in some other way. Think practical.

"H. W. Mergenthal started barking orders to the workers, moving upstage, downstage, stage left and right. When he got back to Lillian, he seemed surprised that she was still standing there. 'So . . . um, er, Lily, think of anything you can do?'

"'I can type,' she said. 'I'm the fastest typer you've ever seen.'"

"How fast?" Monica asked.

The Knitting Lady moved her fingers in imitation. "That's exactly what the theater manager wanted to know. At that point, Lillian could type fast enough to impress farmers, but it wasn't enough to suit the needs of the great H. W. Mergenthal. It would take Lillian hours and hours of practice to bring up her speed. She had to work on her accuracy, too. Typing and knitting have a lot in common. If you're fast but make a lot of mistakes, nobody has much use for that."

I shot a pointed look at Whitney, but she didn't seem to recognize the tie to her own particular knitting disasters. Rather, she was bombarding the Knitting Lady with opinions: "A few mistakes don't matter!" And, "Man-oh-man, she's not going to be a typer forever. Typing is too boring." And, "Skip typing and get to the next good part!"

The Knitting Lady got one of her knowing smiles. I imagine it was the same smile that the great H. W. Mergenthal got when he knew he had pulled a good one on the audience. "You w-wouldn't be saying that if you remembered."

Fern pounced. "What? Remember what? What?"

"Relax, Fern," Monica said. "No one remembers."

"I planted a h-hint, way back in the story."

We all turned to Amber, who had a blank look. Then, when everyone looked at me, I pointed out, "It couldn't have been a very good hint if not even Amber or I can remember. Maybe you need to plant your hints a little better."

"Cal, I w-will certainly take that suggestion to heart. Pulling all the pieces of a story together is not the easiest thing in the world, but I want to do my best. Let's forget the hint for now and go back to the theater. The workers put together a makeshift desk from some crates and placed Lillian's typewriter on top. She cracked her knuckles. 'What should I type?' she asked.

"Mergenthal flipped through his clipboard and pulled out a sheet filled with names, dates, and dollar amounts. 'See what you can do with this.'

"Her typewriter was an old Underwood model, the kind of machine you only see now in old movies. It must have weighed a ton and a half. And the noise! When Lillian started typing, you could hear that clickity-clackity-clack all the way to the balcony. H. W. Mergenthal circled Lillian, looking at her from every angle. Every once in a while, he snapped an order that she did her best to follow:

"'Straighten your back! No, not like someone just slapped you with a whip. More relaxed! Graceful. Sway a little.'

"'Make some fou-fou movements with your hands. And smile! Can't you smile?'

"Truthfully, the typing was taking so much of Lillian's concentration that she didn't even consider what she looked like. Besides, what did it matter if she was biting her lower lip and frowning so hard that a V formed between her eyebrows? Why on earth did she need to smile? But she straightened her back and smiled and swayed. She tried to imagine that she was playing a complicated piece of music on the piano instead of typing letters onto a cheap piece of white paper.

"'Good fou-fou,' Mergenthal said.

"Lillian thought: *He won't be saying that when he sees all the mistakes. He'll never hire me then.* She watched his face carefully as he ripped the paper from the roller and studied it with a lot of 'hmmmmm's' and 'uh-huh's.'

"'Gotta get faster,' he finally said. 'And can't have any mistakes. None! We'll aim for what? What sounds good— 99 percent? No, 99.9 percent accurate.'

"'I'll practice, sir, practice till my hands fall off—99.9 percent, sir!'

"Again, Mergenthal didn't comment. He kept looking at Lillian, and, without taking his eyes off her face, he yelled, 'Florence, bring your red case.'"

It was here that the Knitting Lady made an interesting comment. "Ten, eleven, twelve, thirteen are fascinating ages. One minute I can see the little girls you were, and the next I can see the women that you'll soon be. It doesn't take much. Just the trick of light hitting you one way or another."

I knew what the Knitting Lady was saying. For

example, Whitney looked one age in her body and another age in her face. Now that Amber's hair was growing back in, she didn't look like a sad little ten-year-old. I would have to say that she looked at least eleven."

"What about Lillian?" I asked. "Did she look older or younger than she was?"

"That's w-what I'm getting to. Inside the red case were the tools to make Lillian any age that they wanted her to be."

"Lipstick!" Whitney yelled. "Eye shadow, lip liner, eyeliner."

"The whole k-kit and caboodle. No Nebraska farm girl ever wore makeup, so Lillian didn't really know what was happening to her. The puffs of sweet-smelling p-powder on her skin and the feel of hands fussing with her hair, piling it into a great beehive on her head. When Florence was done, she stepped back to admire her work."

"I don't get it," Fern complained. "All that fuss to be some typing person?"

Amber said something softly, which the Knitting Lady asked her to repeat. "The Fastest Typer."

That was the big hint! I had one word in my mind so I said it: "Digits."

I knew the Knitting Lady heard me, but she had a faraway look. She was back in Nebraska with Lillian. "So, the great H. W. Mergenthal said, 'What do you think of this? Lovely Lily with her Delightfully Dexterous Digits.'"

"Oh!" Monica burst out. "I get it."

"Get what?" Fern shouted.

I wiggled my fingers, which made Whitney slap her palm on her forehead—"Oh!" Then, Fern also said, "Oh!" only I'm not sure if she really got it or just didn't want to feel left out.

"B-but Lillian shouted, 'No!' "

"What did she mean by *no*?" I asked.

"That's the same thing that H. W. Mergenthal asked. He was not a man used to having anyone say no to him.

"But Lillian stood her ground. She announced to everyone, 'No, not Lily. *Lillian. Lovely Lillian with her Delightfully Dexterous Digits!'* "

CHAPTER 32

Later that day, the Knitting Lady took us to the pool, which is one of the best places for avoiding conversations of a serious nature. Whitney kept trying to bring up her only topic—the search for her sister—but all I had to do was turn an underwater backward somersault or act like my ears were too clogged with water to hear a word. For a while, Whitney even distracted herself by insisting that we put our butts up against the warm-water jet to experience the magnificent sensation.

WHITNEY: It's just like one of those fancy Jack Uzi things. I'll bet my sister has one in her own personal bathtub.

FERN: One of what?

AMBER *(correcting)*: A Jacuzzi.

ME: *Performing dead man's float for forty-eight seconds, my all-time breath-holding record.*

MONICA: So when are we going to track her down? I'm not scared at all of going!

FERN: Going where?

MONICA: Fern!

FERN: Oh, going you know where.

MONICA: To find you know who.

FERN: Who?

ME: *Out of the pool, walking slowly to the deep end, cannonballing off the side.*

LIFEGUARD *(blowing whistle at me)*: No diving off the sides!

Whitney and the others kept appearing inches from where I landed. Wherever I swam, there they were.

WHITNEY: I'm just waiting for her to finish the story and then we'll go.

ME: *Sitting on the bottom of the pool, legs crossed.*

When I came up for air, I was cornered, wedged between the steps and a semicircle of Pumpkin House girls. Whitney was saying, "She's near the end of the story!"

I said, "You don't know that."

She said, "Of course I do," and I came back with "How do you know?"

"Well . . . ," Whitney hesitated. "Amber, how do I know?"

"Because," Amber said, "that's the way a story works. It starts one place and circles back to the beginning."

"We're back to digits," Whitney said, and then demonstrated by turning a somersault in the water.

"I'm freezing," I said. "I need to get out."

I hoisted myself onto the edge of the pool and grabbed my towel. "Gotta pee," I said. They wouldn't follow me if I had to pee.

They followed me. They waited outside the stall. Then they crowded around the sink while I washed my hands. I said, "She could be tricking us and not be anywhere near done with the story."

Fern edged close to the mirror, inspecting her nose for blackheads. "Why would she trick us?"

"Because . . . ," I said. "Because . . ." *Because I don't want the Knitting Lady to be near the end of her story, because if she is, it means that Whitney is going to demand that I run off to find her sister, and while I think that's just fine for her to do, because this* is *her life, I'm not about to put* my *whole life at risk.*

I said, "Whitney, don't you need another test run?"

"Naw on test run. You can lead the way when we take off."

I looked in the mirror. My eyebrow was buckled in the middle. I flashed on my most recent conversation with the social worker, who told me that Betty was showing signs of—*quote*—coming along—*unquote*. Mrs. S. sounded surprised beyond belief. The next thing she said—*So you better stay put!*—returned to haunt me.

I lifted my soapy hands to my face, brought them down again. "Not really," I said.

Behind me, Whitney was talking to my reflection. "What's that mean?"

"Not really what?" Fern asked.

"Not really . . ." There was no way to tiptoe around this. "I'm not going with you."

Fern stopped squeezing blackheads. Monica backed away and collapsed onto a bench. Amber's hand dashed to her mouth, then dropped back to her side.

Whitney stuck her finger in her ear. "Man-oh-man, my ear must be clogged with pool water. I swear I didn't hear right."

"It's not like you actually need me to go. I'm perfectly willing to provide you with the most detailed bus information possible."

"You're not going?" Fern started giggling, then turned to everyone else—"She's not going?"—and then back to me— "How can you not be going?"

Whitney didn't leave me a chance to explain. "Because, she still thinks Betty is going to show up any minute and whisk her away back—"

"—to my real life," I said. "The social worker said I could be going home any time now."

"She did not!" Whitney insisted.

"She said something like it. She said— How do you know what she said or didn't say?"

"I listened in. She didn't say that!"

I swirled around. "I hate eavesdroppers."

Whitney didn't miss a beat: "Liars who say they are going to do something but then don't are the scum of the earth."

"I never said I'd go with you."

"Scum of the earth!"

And then Monica said that I should think about Whitney instead of always thinking about myself, and Fern said, "Yeah," and Whitney said, "Don't you get it, Cal? This *is* your real life. You're one of us. Family. Sort of, in a way, kind of."

Some family.

"Look at me," I said. "Do I look like I'm listening to what any of you are saying?"

I leaned over the sink and washed all the soap off my face.

⟳

Why do you need me? You said I don't know anything.

Not about life in here, but out there you, Cal Lavender, your a woman of the world. We need a gliding light!

It's you're, not your. And guiding. You mean a guiding light.

No, you can glide us through the city. Wait! Now I

know why you don't want to go! Your jealous I have a sister and you don't.

You've got to be kidding.

It's okay, Cal! Don't be embarrassed. I know how it feels, but don't worry. I won't let you down. I'll share. We'll all be sisters. She'll be your sister too.

They worked hard on me, but I told them over and over: No! Finally it got through. "End of discussion!"

For days after that, war was declared in the Pumpkin House, and I was the enemy. On the stairs, Whitney just *happened* to stumble and push me into the banister. They made sure I was the last one to the van and locked the door until the Knitting Lady insisted that they open it. Monica kept appearing out of nowhere and asking, "What's up *your* butt?" Fern laughed hysterically every time she saw me. Even Amber. Her eyes kept darting away from me like I was an enormous embarrassment.

Then things escalated.

Someone put shaving cream on my toothbrush. Someone dumped Rice Krispies on my bed. Someone wrote a note telling me to call Betty but when I called the number, I got Dial-A-Prayer. Someone unraveled six inches of my knitting.

Don't think for a minute that any of this bothered me.

～

One day after lunch, I sneaked into the bedroom and slipped the Cow Notebook from under Whitney's mattress. I really didn't care what they were saying about me, but I figured I should see if Whitney was plotting anything dangerous. That was my right! I opened to the last page that had writing on it. It also happened to have Whitney's fingerprints in jam on the corners.

Hahahahahahahahaha! I knew it! I knew you'd look!

I slammed the book shut.

⌇

Then for days, no one tied my shoelaces together or threw my bathing suit out the window. No one made snotty remarks when we were in the grocery store or tried to trip me as I walked to the refrigerator. Whitney didn't stand over my juice, make a ball of spit, and let it drop in a long string into the glass.

They ignored me. I have to admit that they were exceptionally good at it. Your average, ordinary girls can't pull off the silent treatment for more than a day or two. Somebody eventually cracks. But they were better than most.

Don't think that any of this bothered me either.

⌇

After about four days into their stupid, silent grudge, I found myself feeling extremely strange. If Cal Lavender was a person prone to having moods, I would say that I woke up feeling sad and scared and angry and unhappy and lonely. For some reason, my eyes kept tearing up.

Maybe it was allergies.

I gathered up my knitting—congratulating myself once again on making the longest knitting project ever produced in the Pumpkin House even though certain jealous, petty people had unraveled some of it. I went downstairs.

Nobody but the Knitting Lady was around. Good. Everyone else was . . . I didn't care where they were.

The Knitting Lady took a quick look at me and stopped washing dishes. I followed her into Talk Central. "I'll stitch," I said. "But I have nothing to bitch about. Everything is just fine."

I knitted a row. The Knitting Lady finished her row, flipped her yarn, and started down the other side. She was humming—*hum, hum, hum*—I think it was one of those old-time songs that Lillian sang on the streets of New York.

This was better. I was definitely starting to feel less strange. I settled into my knitting. I was going home soon. Who cared about Whitney? Or Amber? Not me. Who cared if Monica or Fern ever talked to me again? Not Cal Lavender. I didn't care.

But then the stitches blurred up because my eyes were all full again. I set down the needles, gave them a little push. Half the length of my knitting tumbled to the floor.

"This is weird," I said.

The Knitting Lady handed me a tissue. I dabbed at the

puddles in the corner of my eyes. It was a good thing she didn't insist on having a heart-to-heart conversation because that was the last thing I wanted to have. She kept knitting and humming.

"I'm done with this," I said. I meant that I was done with the Kleenex. But as soon as I said it, I realized I was done with more than that. I was done with the teary eyes and feeling strange, with everyone and everything that had to do with the Pumpkin House.

"Done with your knitting?" she asked.

I was done with that, too. "It's long enough. Here!" I thrust the needles at her.

But she wouldn't take them. Rather, she bent with an old-lady groan and scooped up the section of my knitting that had fallen to the floor. "N-nice," she said. "But it's not finished yet."

"How will I know it's finished when I don't even know what it is?"

"Oh, d-don't worry about that. It'll be done when it's done. You can knit while I tell you more of the story. The others heard this part earlier this morning. You don't want them knowing something you don't know, right?"

I shook my head very quickly.

"That's very important. You girls all have to be on the same page. . . . Ready?"

I made one stitch and by the time I reached the end of the row, the Knitting Lady was bringing me up to date.

CHAPTER 33

No vaudeville performer ever put more effort into her act than Lillian did, the Knitting Lady told me. During the long train rides between cities, while waiting backstage during rehearsals, in lonely boardinghouses in the middle of the night, Lillian practiced.

To demonstrate, the Knitting Lady placed her needles at her side, sat up with exaggerated straight posture, and danced the pads of her fingers on her thighs. "Lillian drove herself mercilessly, like a great athlete trains," she said. "Day after day after day, no rest, no excuses until Lillian reached the world record. Twenty-five taps a second. *Thwack-thwack-thwack.* So fast that the sound came out as one long continuous *thwack.* And still, she kept practicing."

The Knitting Lady said that there were times when Lillian's head felt as though it would split like an egg from the intense concentration. Her hands sometimes cramped so badly that she couldn't even pick up a fork. But the physical pain was nothing compared to the voices in her head.

"You mean . . ." I made cuckoo circles by my temple.

"N-not *those* kinds of voices. The voices that say, *I can't. Someone like me—a kid who doesn't live with a mother and father—can't be the best. I can never make anything of myself.*"

"Lillian felt this way?"

"I know she did."

I disagreed. "I don't believe it. Lillian wasn't the type. She did everything so perfectly. Remember her vows? She was unstoppable. You said so in the story."

"An interesting p-point. But being unstoppable doesn't mean she had no doubts. It meant that she was willing to drive herself to perfection, to do anything to stem the flow of doubts. Do you understand?"

I hesitated. "I think . . . well, maybe it means that when Lillian was typing, she got all wrapped up in the typing like some people do when they're knitting or cleaning. She could forget everything else."

"L-like?"

"Like forgetting about her mother. And rich relatives who thought they were too good for her."

"All that. So you see that Lillian was two ways at once—both incredibly resourceful and independent. But also full of doubts and sadness—anger, too."

That was a confusing thought to me. "You mean she was living two different lives at the same time?"

The Knitting Lady closed her eyes in a that's-a-tough-question-to-answer kind of way. "I think you're asking something else."

"I am?"

"I think you're asking if Lillian ever got over losing her mother."

I felt those words deep in my ribs. "Did she?"

"No, she n-never forgot. But she eventually understood that accepting her new life didn't mean she was cheating on her old one. Do you know what I mean by that?"

I didn't, but in a way I did. I said, "Oh," because I couldn't think of anything else to say.

"Any m-more questions?" When I shook my head, she said, "Well, that's that. Now you're all up to date on the story."

∽

Whitney was the first to break the silent treatment.

I had gone over to the park by myself and saw them, a circle of my enemies around the teeter-totter, their backs to me, their heads bowed like they were praying. Then their heads bolted up, and Fern let loose with one of her nervous, high-pitched giggles. Whitney had a toothpick in her mouth. She moved it from one side to the other. "Oh, it's just *you*. I was scared it was *her*."

"Her who?"

"The Knitting Lady."

Monica looked at me suspiciously. "You didn't tell her anything, did you?"

"Of course not."

"Not that there's anything left to tell," Whitney said. And together, both Monica and Fern hissed in my direction, "Thanks to *you.*"

"Me? Why me?"

"Didn't you hear the big news?" Monica asked.

"What big news? Remember, nobody's talked to me in days."

Fern got all sad-looking. "It's all over—"

Whitney interrupted. "I'll tell her! It's my dream that's been smashed to . . . Amber, what's my dream been smashed to?"

"Smithereens," she answered.

Whitney's bottom lip was pushed out. "I've given up any hope whatsoever of tracking down my sister. So what do you think of *that,* party pooper?"

"Yeah, so what do you think of that?" Fern echoed.

"Man-oh-man, my all-time best thievery from a social worker, and for nothing!"

I still didn't understand. So I wasn't going with them. But excuse me, just because *I* wasn't going didn't mean that *they* couldn't go. I make a loud sound of exasperation and said, "Excuse me, but I don't see any chains around your ankles. What's stopping you?"

"Everything!" Whitney said, and I asked, "Like what?" and Whitney answered, "For one, Amber's dream. We can't go without you. For two, the directions."

This was still making no sense. "I'll write everything down. I'll draw a map."

"Man-oh-man, we'll be wandering all over from here to . . . to . . . where will we be wandering to, Amber?"

"Timbuktu," she said in her soft way.

I opened my mouth to say, *City buses don't run to Timbuktu,* but Whitney was holding up her hand like a traffic cop. "Stripped of my lifelong dream!"

"Gone!" Fern said. "Like that!" She tried to snap her fingers but no sound came out.

⤷

When people are being totally illogical, a logical person must step right up and take the situation in hand. All I had to do was get Whitney's sister's address, and, once I wrote out the directions, they would see it didn't take a bus genius to get around. They wouldn't need me.

I left them at the park and rushed back to the Pumpkin House, up the stairs, and locked the bedroom door behind me. I slipped my hand under Whitney's mattress where she kept the stolen papers.

Yuck! Double yuck! She kept a lot more under there than papers. But nothing—not half-eaten apples,

sunflower-seed shells, and other slimy, sticky things—
would stop me. I was up to my elbow, then my forearm,
and then I felt them.

Papers! I pulled out the stack. I figured I would have a
lot of reading to do. But then on page 2, I read something.
Then I reread what I thought I had just read, and then I
read it again.

If anyone had seen me just then, I know what they
would have seen. You know what a baby looks like when
she's startled, when she's overcome with a sensation like
she's falling?

That was me, Cal Lavender, who never gets surprised
by much, eyes all bugged out, arms outstretched, breathing
stilled. My whole body went rigid, like the whole world
had dropped away and nothing solid was left beneath me.

CHAPTER 34

I couldn't wait until they came back, so I rushed to the park. They were lined up on the swings. Perfect!

"I changed my mind. Count me in. Let's go tomorrow. Why wait?"

Whitney dragged her feet to stop swinging. "Um, er, why so soon?"

"Why not? Why keep your sister waiting any longer?"

Monica and Fern did the cheerleading for me: "Yeah, Whitney"—*giggle, giggle*—"why wait? . . . Let's do it! . . . Tomorrow. . . . For sure!"

I said, "You don't look very happy about it, Whitney."

She kept looking at me, trying to know what I knew, trying to know if I knew what she was thinking I might know but couldn't believe I knew.

"Whitney?" Monica asked. "You *are* happy, aren't you?"

"Happy? Of course, I'm happy. Why wouldn't I be happy? Man-oh-man, happy, happy, happy."

Cal Lavender isn't normally a revengeful type of person. But in this case, revenge was going to be very sweet.

～

Here's what I had read in Whitney's stolen file:

An eighteen-month-old girl was taken into protective custody by the county Department of Children's Services. Whitney S. is the only child of . . . I stopped there. Not wanting to jump to conclusions, I scanned the rest of the file, every word of it.

Here's what I most definitely did not read: Any mention of a sister—past, present, and certainly not future.

CHAPTER 35

Here's how I imagined things would go that night:

ME: It's time to go, Whitney. Tell me your sister's address.

WHITNEY: I can't. *(Whitney falling to the floor in a heap of guilt and remorse)* I can't because I lied! I lied, I tell you, I lied!

A CHORUS OF EVERYONE ELSE: You lied? How could you! Apologize to Cal.

WHITNEY *(at my feet)*: Cal, can you ever forgive me?

ME *(taking my time)*: I'll think about it.

～

Here's how things actually went that night:

ME: It's time to go, Whitney. Tell me your sister's address.

WHITNEY: Okay.

ME: Okay?

WHITNEY: Okay, but not here. Outside. Man-oh-man, let's get out of here already.

ME: But . . .

WHITNEY *(throwing herself on her stomach and crawling to the bedroom door as though she's an army man, checking to make sure the coast is clear)*: Let's go.

ME: But . . .

WHITNEY *(picking up Ike Eisenhower the Fifth and leading Monica and Fern down the stairs. Voice in a loud whisper)*: Cal! Let's go, Amber!

ME: But . . .

In any life story about Cal Lavender, it would definitely say that she is not the kind of person who gets roped into doing something she doesn't want to do. So why did I follow her down the stairs? I suppose I just wanted to see what Whitney was planning to do. What would she say when she couldn't produce this famous sister?

"Whitney, do we need one token or a pass?" We were standing at the bus stop, waiting for the number 26 to start our journey. I saw her mind scrambling before she answered.

"One token? You gotta be kidding, right? You think it's only one bus ride?"

"A pass then. It's good for all night."

Monica looked worried. "All night? You don't mean like *all* night, do you? I'll get too tired."

For weeks, everyone had been stashing away part of

their allowance, which they now turned over to me. I could tell that the driver of the number 26 wasn't thrilled when I gave him the clinking pile of pennies, nickels, dimes, and quarters. The look he gave me wasn't friendly at all. I assured him that it was the exact amount, but did he believe me? No. Not even when I told him that I was extremely good at math. He had to count every coin himself before handing over our passes.

The number 26 was a long, stop-and-go ride with people getting off and people getting on, and finally, we were there. Downtown. My home turf! Here's where time gets weird again. It seemed like I had been gone for years, yet at the same time it was all so familiar, like I hadn't been gone at all. There was the Thrifty Cuts beauty parlor, and the "Nothing More than 99 Cents" Discount Mart.

I led the way into the bus station and picked up a bus schedule. "So where to?"

"North," Whitney said with so much confidence that I thought for a minute that maybe I was wrong, maybe I had missed something in the file, maybe, in fact, there was a sister and we were on our way there right now. "We want the number 46B bus," I said. "That goes north."

We found the bus waiting and hopped on right before it pulled away from the station. And when we were as far north as we could go, I asked, "Where next?" and Whitney said, "West, all the way," so I checked the schedule and decided we should take the number 17.

By this time, it was getting pretty late and buses were running slow. We stood on a corner for twenty-five minutes waiting for the number 17 to show up. It was empty except for a couple of old, sad-looking guys. I kept waiting for the bus driver to ask what a bunch of ten- and eleven-year-old girls were doing on the number 17 bus at ten o'clock at night, but he never did.

"Can we go south from here?" Whitney asked me.

"If you'd just tell me where we need to go, I could—"

She ignored me and tapped the bus driver on the shoulder. "South?"

"Number 74, ladies," he answered. "Next stop, runs on the hour."

So we got off and we waited and we waited and when the number 74 finally pulled up, we got on, and Whitney handed me Ike Eisenhower the Fifth before grabbing the bus map from me. She ran her index finger from left to right.

"Whitney?" Monica asked.

"Shhhhh. I'm concentrating."

"Whitney?" Monica's skin was kind of green. "I'm getting bus sick. Are we almost there yet?"

Whitney didn't take her nose out of the schedule. "Jeez-Louise, if we were almost there, I would have done this alone months ago. I told you it was far."

So that's how it went. After the 74, we took the 37, the 68A, the 24, the 18, the 6 express (only the express part wasn't running at that time of the night, so there were about a million stops). At some point, everyone stopped talking to everyone else. Even Fern stopped giggling. We just stared out the windows like we were in some kind of public-transportation trance. We went north, east, south, southeast, and northwest until nobody had any idea of where we were.

Even I, the bus genius, was dazed, but I was certain of one thing. We had passed by the same places more than once. Definitely. I was sure of it. But did I bring that up? No!

I also didn't point out that we had taken the 43 north and then twenty minutes later hopped on the 43 south. I didn't say anything because by then I figured out what Whitney was up to. If she kept us moving, maybe we wouldn't figure out that she had no place to go. I said nothing because I knew that all I had to do was wait.

At the corner of Trescony and Langdon Streets, her time finally ran out.

"That's it," Monica announced, holding her stomach. "I'm not getting on another bus."

"Me either," Fern said.

We were in a neighborhood that looked vaguely familiar, but I guess most neighborhoods look like this one did. Houses all lined up with perfect squares of green lawn. Most of the windows were dark. Standing under a street lamp, I squinted at the schedule. "There aren't any more buses until morning."

That did it. Monica and Fern started whining like sick cows. They were starving! They were tired! They should have known better than to trust Whitney! "Cal, do something!" they pleaded.

"Do what?" I said, all innocence. "I could do something if Whitney would tell me the exact address. But Whitney won't do that, will you, Whitney?"

Monica turned on her—"Tell her!"—and Whitney looked so pathetic that I almost felt sorry for her. Only I didn't. I kept pushing. "Why won't Whitney tell me where her sister lives? Why, Whitney?"

"Because . . . ," Whitney was stammering. "Because . . ."

Then Amber, who had been her usual silent self all night, spoke up. "Because we're here. Right, Whitney?"

"Here?" I blurted out. "How do you know?"

Amber's voice was strong, her eyes steady on mine. "Because I dreamed it."

That gave Whitney enough time to wipe the thoroughly confused look off her face. "That's right. Man-oh-man, and you were ready to bail out on me, but here we are. I knew we'd make it, man-oh-man. We did it and now I'm here."

Monica suddenly looked much better. She started

doing this little jumping-up-and-down dance. Fern was clapping her hands and saying, "What now? What now?"

I noticed Whitney turned pleading eyes on Amber for help, but Amber's face remained blank.

I asked pointedly, "So which house? Where does this famous sister live?"

Whitney pointed to a house that looked like every other house, except for a small glow of light coming from a window by the side.

"Let's go!" Now Fern was also jumping up and down.

"No," Amber said. "She's got to go alone."

Whitney looked surprised. "I do? Right, I do." She took a few tentative steps, turned, lifted her hand to wave at us and give us a smile. It was a strange smile, which I suppose is the only smile she could have, considering that she was sneaking up to the house of total strangers and would eventually have to come back and confess the truth to us once and for all.

The way the streetlight was angled gave us a perfect view of Whitney's every move. She crossed the street, climbed over the picket fence, and pressed her body against the side of the house the way the police do in movies before they kick in the door of someone on the Most Wanted list. She edged closer and closer to the glowing light. Then she got down on hands and knees and crept until she was just under the window.

She peeked in, ducked her head below the sill, peeked in again. She stayed in that awkward, uncomfortable position for a long time.

Then, just when I thought Whitney would never come back and face us with the truth, she took a running start across the lawn and hopped the fence like it was nothing but air.

CHAPTER 36

"You should see it!" Whitney said. "Her room is like a palace."

"What color?" Fern wanted to know.

"Purple and orange! My favorites. There's a dog curled up on the floor and a kitten sleeping right on her pillow and a bird, one of those big expensive birds, a Starlight McDraw."

"Scarlet macaw," Amber said.

"Yeah, one of those, and she's got her own phone and I could see in her closet which is packed to the . . . what's it packed to, Amber?"

"Packed to the gills."

"With all sorts of stuff. The people who adopted her aren't cheapskates. She's got three pairs of skates, the expensive kind. And skis and a wall full of medals for gymnastics, which must mean she's the real bouncy type and takes after me."

"You're the younger sister," Monica pointed out. "So you take after her."

"We take after each other!"

Am I, Cal Lavender, the only one here who sees through this charade?

"And, man-oh-man, this next part you won't believe!"

Fern asked a breathless "What?"

"They came in right while I was looking. I ducked so they couldn't see me."

I couldn't help myself. "Who came in?"

"The parents! They look like movie stars, and they stood real close together."

"Like this?" Monica pulled Fern to her side.

"Closer! And they were holding hands and my sister was sound asleep in her big, fancy, everything-matches bed, like this." Whitney lay down on the bus-stop bench and pretended to be asleep. "They moved closer to my sister's bed."

"Like this?" Holding hands, Monica and Fern approached.

"And when they were standing right over her, the parents looked at each other and smiled. And then, the father reached over. Yeah, that's right, Monica, you're the father. And then, he tucked in my sister even though she was already perfectly tucked in!"

"Wow!" Monica said, and Fern sighed, closing her eyes to picture every detail.

Cal Lavender wasn't sucked in one little bit. I don't know what Whitney had been looking at all that time, but

I knew it wasn't a happy ending. I said, "Now we get to meet her, right? This is what we came for, right?"

I was very gratified to see Whitney's mouth tremble around the corners. I had her now. She was out of excuses. It was time for Cal Lavender to bring the truth to the surface. I faced the others. "I hate to break this to you, but Whitney's sister doesn't—"

Amber broke in, "She doesn't need Whitney anymore."

"That's not what I—"

Amber again, "That's why she wanted Whitney to come, to tell her that."

"The truth is—" I insisted.

"The truth is she wants Whitney to know that she's doing fine."

I whirled on her. "Amber, I can't believe you don't know that—"

"What?" She took me by the shoulders until she was looking directly into my face. "What? What truth do I need to know?"

And that's when I knew. I knew that she knew what I knew. I knew that Amber had known the truth about Whitney's sister for a long time, a very long time. Her eyes were daring me and at the same time, pleading with me. "Cal, what do I need to know?"

"That Whitney . . . that Whitney's sister . . ." My voice petered out.

Amber let go of my shoulders. "I know, Cal. I know that Whitney's sister doesn't need her. And Whitney doesn't really need her sister. Not anymore." She turned to Whitney. "Right, Whitney?"

"Why?" I said. I meant: *Why are you covering up for Whitney?* But Amber answered a different question. "Because Whitney has something else. Because you came all this way to help her. And Fern came. And Monica stopped being afraid and came. Whitney doesn't need a sister anymore because Whitney has us."

Being a stomach person, the truth of this hit me you know where. For once, Cal Lavender really didn't know what to say. So when Amber said, "Let's go home now," I didn't argue.

CHAPTER 37

After all those buses, we were only about a mile from the Pumpkin House. We walked in silence, our feet dragging, the streetlights turning us into long shadows. When we got there, the front door was locked. I had been the last one out, and I would never in a million years forget to leave the front door unlatched. That meant trouble.

For some reason, I didn't care. I don't know what anyone else was thinking, but I bet we were all thinking the same thing: *At least we're in trouble together.*

We decided to wait on the back patio. Morning would be here soon enough.

There was light from the full moon back there. I got a jolt seeing the Knitting Lady just sitting there, not trying to hide or anything, just sitting in a sweater, legs crossed, like it was the middle of a sunny afternoon and we were invited guests who had arrived on time for a party. What would she do now? Scold us? Lecture us? Ask for details and explanations?

"Sit," the Knitting Lady said, and pointed to a place next to her. Amber sat on her right, and then Whitney and the others formed a small circle. I was on her left.

"There's a l-little chill that's just coming up. Funny how it does that when it's close to morning."

She reached behind herself and pulled out a piece of knitting with familiar colors—all my yellows and golds. The needles were gone, and she had given it a smooth, finished edge. She handed one end to me and I held it as the other end was passed along. Each of us kept a section and draped it around our shoulders. The Knitting Lady must have known exactly when it was done because it was the perfect fit to cover all of us.

I glanced up. I imagined someone standing at my window and wondered how our group would appear to a stranger. There was an old lady looking a little older and more tired than usual. A girl whose black eye was gone without a trace. A girl whose once-broken arm was already as round and firm as the rest of her. A girl whose hair was almost fully grown in. A girl with a heart that no longer had a hole in it. There was me, looking like a perfectly ordinary eleven-year-old.

Now this is going to sound totally illogical, and by now it must be clear that Cal Lavender is never totally illogical without good reason. But there were others with us on the patio that night. A stranger at the window wouldn't have seen them, but I felt them.

I felt the presence of every girl who had ever passed through the Pumpkin House. Of Lillian and all those kids on the orphan train. I saw traces of them in Whitney, in Amber, in Monica and Fern. And, yes, in myself. We were all there that night, joined together in a tight, knitted circle.

I knew exactly what would happen next. The Knitting Lady had waited and waited until just the right moment. We needed to be ripe. None of us was surprised when she said, "Let's begin. Let's end. The final chapter.

CHAPTER 38

"L-Lillian wasn't even fifteen years old when she made her first professional stage appearance. She wore her hair piled on her head and dressed in a sparkling gown. Right before she started typing, she would always lift the lorgnette to her eyes and gaze out into the audience. It became one of her trademarks. For the first three months, the great H. W. Mergenthal kept Lovely Lillian with her Delightfully Dexterous Digits as the opening act, which was by far the worst spot to be. It took the audience forever to settle down. But she kept practicing and smiling and typing and swaying and eventually moved to fourth place on the bill, right before a new and very popular act called 'the Regurgitator.'"

I blurted out, "What kind of act is that?"

The Knitting Lady threw back her head and laughed: "So you know what *regurgitate* means!"

"Throw up," I said, and Whitney jumped in with more synonyms. "Puke, barf, upchuck, toss your cookies, lunch."

"That's the idea. This young man would swallow mouthfuls of kerosene and then regurgitate. You knew it was the real thing because he aimed at a flame, and that flame would whoosh up like an angry dragon."

"Whoa! Don't try that at home, kids!" Whitney laughed.

"It was Lillian's favorite act, and, at each show, she would stand in the wings transfixed. But it was more than the act that had caught Lillian's fancy. It was the Regurgitator himself. He was a very good-looking young man, with jet-black hair and a fake mustache, which gave him a foreign, mysterious look that audiences admired. The Regurgitator returned Lillian's attentions. He admired her spunk, her determination, and also the way she looked in those glamorous gowns. These two took one look at each other and sensed that they were two of a kind. They had an immediate understanding, much the way girls in the Pumpkin House have an understanding with one another, even though you don't always like to admit it. You see, the Regurgitator was also an orphan and a runaway, so he knew what it meant to feel alone in the world.

"It's an old story what happened next, and I think you're all mature enough to picture how it happened. It was only natural that these two young people started spending more time together, clinging to each other emotionally and physically during long train rides from town to town. Lillian became pregnant and gave birth to a baby girl. Does anyone remember Lillian's daughter's name?"

When no one answered, the Knitting Lady began

tossing out clues. "An all-night drive. Fruit trees in bloom. Throne? Little Raven?"

Black hair with purple streaks. Orphanage with plum trees. I remembered. "Brenda! The girl from the beginning of the story. The one who was dropped off at the orphanage. She threw the lorgnette on the ground when her mother drove away."

Whitney couldn't believe it. "Man-oh-man, *that* mother! That was Lillian?"

"It w-was."

"Even I remember!" Fern said. "I don't like that mother."

"Me either," Monica said. "She just dumped off her kid."

The Knitting Lady directed the next question to me: "I recall that you didn't much like her either at the beginning of the story. But now? What do you think of Lillian now?"

I didn't know *what* to think. "I don't like what she did to Brenda. I really don't like it! But at the same time, I can't *not* like Lillian. All the things that happened to her? All the things that she went through? I don't like her, but I *do*."

"You understand her now," the Knitting Lady said. "When you understand someone, when you see the path of her life, the choices she had to make, the things that stood in her way, the hurdles she leaped, things get more complicated. It's no longer . . . Amber, what is it no l-longer?"

"Cut and dried," she said.

"Black and white," I added.

"Exactly," Whitney said.

Fern was chewing on her knuckle. "I have a question. Did Lillian become a big star?"

The Knitting Lady put it simply: "No."

"Why not?" Monica asked. "She practiced and set the world record. She was the best!"

"S-sometimes, unfortunately, the best is not enough. That's not to say that Lillian ever stopped trying. She dragged her daughter, Brenda, across the country, but she never became the headliner she wanted to be."

"That's not fair," I pointed out.

"Since when is life always fair?"

I had no answer for that. I just listened as the Knitting Lady explained. "The problem was Lillian's timing. By the time Brenda was six, vaudeville was taking its last gasp of breath. Between the movies and radio, people were no longer so impressed by fast typing and fire-spitting. Like a lot of other performers, Lillian decided to go to California and try to make it as a movie star."

Whitney asked, "What happened to . . . to who, Amber?"

"The Regurgitator."

"Before B-Brenda was born, he joined another company."

I asked, "So the man who was driving when they dropped Brenda at the orphanage? That wasn't him?"

"Not her father, no." She paused to let that sink in and then told us that we were forgetting to ask the most important question.

"Why?" Whitney asked.

Amber said, "Why didn't she take Brenda to California, too?"

"That's the qu-question, all right."

For once, the Knitting Lady looked as confused as Fern usually looked. She swallowed hard. "This very question plagued Brenda her whole life. She never really stopped trying to find a satisfying answer. I can't believe it was simple selfishness on Lillian's part. No! I have to believe that she thought she was doing what was best for her child."

"But Brenda didn't like it!" I said. "She didn't like it one little bit."

The Knitting Lady asked if I thought Brenda missed all the excitement of her former life, all the moving about and the closeness she had with her mother.

I said, "Yes, ma'am. I know for a fact that she did."

"D-do you think there was anything that Brenda actually liked about living in the Home?"

"No," Monica said quickly.

"M-maybe just one thing?"

"Maybe," I said, "she liked being around kids her own age—but only if the kids weren't mean to her, which I hope they weren't. Were they?"

"K-kids are kids. Sometimes, they can be very hurtful, especially if they've been hurt themselves. But other times, they made Brenda feel very much at home."

"And worrying," Monica said. "I bet Brenda didn't miss worrying about her mother all the time."

"Safe," Amber said. "She liked feeling safe."

"All that!" the Knitting Lady said. "So that's it. The end of the story."

The end? I wasn't the only one who thought she heard wrong.

"The end?" Fern repeated. "Did I miss something?"

I thought: *This can't possibly be the end.*

So I said, "It would be a totally unfair thing to leave us hanging like that, especially after what we've been through tonight."

Whitney's head snapped from me to the Knitting Lady. "Don't ask what we've been through tonight. Just tell the end of the story."

"That's it. I'm d-done."

We all protested—"You're not!"—which made the Knitting Lady mutter that this was her story and she should certainly know when she was done telling it.

Monica said, "No story ends like that."

And then Whitney went, "It's not just your story any-more. It's our story now, and we know it's not finished."

"Your story?" the Knitting Lady asked. "Is it, now? Is it your story? If it's your story, then you should be able to finish it yourselves."

I didn't understand. "You mean make up the ending?"

The Knitting Lady held up a finger, the same finger she used to poke through the mistakes in my knitting. "You're all quite capable of completing the story because you have all the information you need to work it out. So wh-wh-wh-wh . . ."

She stopped, took a breath. "So what becomes of Brenda?"

"Did she ever get adopted?" Whitney asked.

"N-no."

"Did she ever see her mother again?"

"No. But she n-never forgot her."

"Did Brenda ever have kids?"

"At some p-point in her life, Brenda made up her mind that she would never be like other people. She went numb inside. She closed up like a—"

"Stop it," Amber said. "I don't like this part of the story. I don't want to hear any more."

The Knitting Lady pulled her closer, gathering her into a hug. "It doesn't mean that Brenda didn't have a family, only that hers was a different kind of family. Her whole adult life, Brenda surrounded herself with kids."

Now Amber's voice came in soft, eager—"She did?"—and Fern asked, "What kind of kids?"

"K-kids who like to hear stories."

"Like us?" Monica asked.

"Exactly l-like you."

I asked, "Why did she tell stories?"

"B-because the kids needed to hear them and Brenda needed to tell them. It was like she was chosen by something larger than herself. Oh, she had her doubts. She often wondered why someone so shy, someone who was always tripping and stumbling over her words, had somehow been picked to tell the stories."

"Tripping and stumbling?" I asked.

"Oh, d-didn't I mention that before? As a young girl, her stutter was quite pronounced and it embarrassed her. But at some point in her life, she stopped asking why she felt compelled to tell stories and just told them."

We all went quiet then. The first light of morning was coming into the backyard. It was spectacular, like sunrise over the Grand Canyon or some other place that a city girl such as myself had never seen in person, but that was the way I imagined it would be. Maybe there was something special in the air that morning to create such a sunrise. Or maybe it was a reflection of the light—*snap!*—that was going on inside each of us.

I asked, "This Brenda?"

"Y-yes, Cal?"

"This girl who lived in the Home? Who never saw her mother again? Who grew up and told stories?"

The Knitting Lady stood, stretched her arms over her head. Even with all the wrinkles, I could see what she must have looked like as a kid, her hair long and purple-black, hanging down in two ponytails. And even though everyone, even Fern, knew the answer, I asked the question anyway, just to finish the story in the proper way. "This girl Brenda? Is she you?"

The Knitting Lady gave a big yawn, but I could see teasing behind her eyes as she said:

"Now, girls, whatever gave you that idea?"

CHAPTER 39

Isn't this just the way life is?

For weeks and weeks, I had been waiting for the front door of the Pumpkin House to swing open, for Betty to sweep in and for my real life to begin again. So wouldn't you know it? Just when I had settled in and arrived at the conclusion that this particular life and these particular people were my real life as much as any other, the door *did* swing open. In walked Mrs. S. the social worker, who told me to pack my bags.

"You're going home," she said.

It happened just like that.

At the front door, they lined up to say good-bye. Monica had her arm looped around the shoulder of giggling Fern. "Man-oh-man," Whitney said. "Don't ever forget the girl who kicked heart disease's butt."

"And Ike Eisenhower the Fifth," I said.

I hugged Amber the hardest. She brushed away her new bangs, playfully, like a puppy.

Then the Knitting Lady was standing in front of me, no longer exactly eye to eye. I must have grown half an inch since that first day. When she handed me a set of knitting needles and a brand-new ball of yarn, I tried not to tear up because Cal Lavender is not the type to make a big whoop-de-do fuss about something as ordinary as a ball of pumpkin-colored yarn. But my eyes started burning a little, and it felt like warm little bugs moving down my cheeks. They rolled and rolled.

"Get out the windshield wipers," Whitney said, which embarrassed me at first, until I noticed that I wasn't the only one who needed those wipers.

The social worker drove. I sat in the back. I had a million questions, but I didn't ask them. Instead, I started knitting. I didn't know what I was making. I just trusted that when the yarn ran out I would have the exact pumpkin-colored thing that I needed.

When Betty saw me, she didn't say anything. Which, if you knew Betty, was a full-blown miracle. She cupped her hands on my shoulders and just looked at me in a way that made time and space disappear.

I remembered what the Knitting Lady had warned: Sometimes love isn't enough.

But sometimes it is.

Maybe now is where you're dying to hear about how I went on to live a very typical, average life. But I could never be a typical eleven-year-old—or twelve- or thirteen-year-old, for that matter.

True, Betty learned plenty about what it means to be the grown-up in the family. But Betty was still Betty. When she got the itch, we moved. I didn't always get to bed at a decent time or make it to school, but I still managed to learn more than the average kid.

If I ever do get around to writing my life story, it will say: *Cal Lavender had adventures you can't believe. Just ask her sometime.*

I never again saw Whitney and Amber, Monica and Fern, but I thought about them a lot. In a way, you can say that I never stopped thinking about them. I knew they were out there, thinking about me, too, about the Knitting Lady's story, pulling on the threads of our shared history to create their own life stories.

And I bet one thing. I bet that their stories are like mine in one way—anything but typical and ordinary. After all, that's what kids like us call life.

AUTHOR'S NOTE

The Knitting Lady's Guide to Making a Scarf

One of the best things about knitting is that you don't need much to get started—just two needles and a ball of yarn. Don't forget good lighting and your peace of mind.

I recommend starting with medium-weight yarn. It doesn't have to be expensive, but wool or a wool blend is good—it stretches and won't make your hands all sweaty. Use needles that are at least size 9. The bigger the needle, the faster the knitting goes, but don't get something that's too cumbersome for your hands. Plastic needles are good, but I like wooden needles best—they aren't slick and don't let stitches slide off when you aren't looking.

The first step is *casting on*, which creates the first row of stitches on one of the needles. This can be pretty intimidating for a beginner, so find someone to do this for you. (It's fun and you can learn it later.) Ask the person to cast on between 15 and 20 stitches for a scarf, depending on the width you like.

It's time to knit. Holding the needle with the stitches in your left hand, angle the point to the right. With your right hand, put the tip of the empty needle into the first stitch, from front to back, making an X with the tips.

Hold both needles at the X in your left hand. Using your right hand, loop the yarn from the ball up and away from you. Then bring the yarn toward you and down between the two needles. Whew! Got that? It sounds more complicated than it is.

Now, keeping tension on the wrapped yarn, bring the tip of the right needle (with the wrapped yarn) through the loop on the left needle to the front. Is the right needle now in front of the left one? You got it!

Almost done. Just slide the right needle up and away until the loop on the left needle drops off and you have a new stitch on the right. Congratulations! You just completed your first knit stitch.

Continue knitting until the left needle is empty and you have a row of gorgeous new stitches on the right needle. Switch sides now—move the needle with the stitches to your left hand—and start a new row. Keep going until your scarf is the length you like and ask someone to *bind off* for you. That's another fun thing you can learn once you become a whiz with the basic stitch.

As you knit, don't forget the Knitting Lady's mantra: *In through the front door / run around the back / peek through the window / off jumps Jack.*

If you want more ideas about knitting, like how to make a scarf with lots of colorful stripes and a fringe, check out my Web site: www.jillwolfson.com.

GOFISH

JILL WOLFSON

What did you want to be when you grew up?
I wanted to be so many different things. A dancer. A director. A teacher. The weather anchor on TV. A spy. A photographer. For about a week, I wanted to be a veterinarian. I couldn't make up my mind. Strangely enough, I entered college as a math and physics major—I was really good at puzzles—then graduated four years later with a degree in English and documentary film.

When did you realize you wanted to be a writer?
I think I was always destined to be some kind of artist or writer. When I was in elementary school, I used to hold camps for the younger kids on the street. I didn't charge much—3 cents an hour—so all the parents loved it and were happy to enroll their kids. It was the cheapest babysitting ever. Truthfully, it was mostly an opportunity for me to have a cast to perform shows that I wrote and directed. I loved being the big boss. The show I

remember most was a musical version of *The Little Mermaid* with my younger sister in the title role. It was awful, but everyone applauded anyway.

What's your first childhood memory?
I don't know if this is an actual memory or some story about my childhood that my parents told over and over until I think I remember it. In any case, I *think* I remember my bedtime ritual. I had a crib filled with dolls and stuffed animals and before I went to sleep, I had to line them up and kiss each one good night. Then, I held each doll's face between the bars of the crib and made my mom kiss each one. Obsessive-compulsive disorder or great bedtime stalling tactic? I still hate going to bed and sleep with a stuffed animal, Ducky, who might really be a platypus. It's up for debate.

What's your most embarrassing childhood memory?
Being stuck in a car in the Lincoln Tunnel in New York and needing to pee. Really, really, really needing to pee. When we finally got to a gas station, I dashed out of the car, but didn't make it through the parking lot. I just sat down on the cold concrete. Mortifying. After that, my family kept a pot in the car for such emergencies. Even more mortifying.

What was your worst subject in school?
History. I was more of a math type.

What was your first job?
Babysitting for a large, Catholic Italian family that lived a

few doors down from our row house. There were four daughters and the household was completely out of control, but I loved the chaos since my own household was so orderly (and boring, in my eyes). As someone who grew up Jewish, I was especially taken with how the family celebrated Easter. Each year, the parents bought a bunch of live ducklings and chicks that were dyed bright blue, hot pink, and purple like Easter eggs. Holy moly! Where was the Humane Society? When I think back on the spectacle of babysitting four kids and all those cruelly dyed baby animals running amuck, I shiver.

Where do you find inspiration for your writing?
"When you're writing, your story is everywhere." Who wrote that? Someone famous, I think. For me, that's the way it works. When I'm in the process of creating a story, I find material everywhere—in the way a stranger in a restaurant eats, an overheard snippet of conversation. Mostly, my inspiration comes from two sources: my own kids, and my memory of my own 11-year-old self.

Which of your characters is most like you?
There's a little of me in most of them. Like Whitney, I've been known to screw up words. Like Amber, I can be very shy. Like Cal, I can be totally controlled and controlling. And of course, everyone in my family has more knitted scarves, hats, and socks than they probably want.

Are you a morning person or a night owl?
Morning, by choice. Night owl, when insomnia hits.

What's your idea of the best meal ever?
I'm vegetarian and never met a vegetable I didn't like, except for parsnips. And rutabaga. And, okay, okra. So the best meal would be lots of grilled vegetables topping a fabulous homemade pizza. Lots of cheese.

Which do you like better: cats or dogs?
Dogs, but don't let my cat Shango read this.

What do you value most in your friends?
They inspire me to want to be the best person I can be. And they make me laugh. You can't be my friend if you don't make me laugh.

Where do you go for peace and quiet?
I live a few blocks from the Pacific Ocean, so I love putting on my wetsuit (the water is very cold) and paddling way out on my boogie board. Just the sound of gulls, far off waves against the shore, and my own breathing.

Who is your favorite fictional character?
The two that pop first into my mind: Scout in *To Kill a Mockingbird* and Ignatius J. Reilly in *A Confederacy of Dunces*.

What are you most afraid of?
Being afraid. That's what paralyzes me.

What time of the year do you like best?
I love the change of seasons, the excited anticipation of what's coming up, and the sweet, sad feeling of something going away.

What is your favorite TV show?
Sorry, don't have TV. I don't mean to sound all pretentious and high-minded, but here's how it came about. For a while, I was the only adult in a household of four teenagers (my own and two friends who needed a place to live). I got sick of the sound of TV day and night, and one day on a whim, I cancelled the cable. Surprisingly, no one seemed to mind. They just started watching the same few movies over and over again, notably *Mean Girls* and *Wayne's World*. "Foxy Lady," anyone?

If you were stranded on a desert island, who would you want for company?
Oh, my friends and I play this game all the time. Desert Island books. Desert Island music and meals. Of course, we always name each other first as Desert Island company, but then we stop the politeness and get serious. My choices always tend to be long dead; Mark Twain, Jane Austen, and the Buddha, for example. Plus, I'd invite any great woman surfer because since I'm on an island, the Buddha and I might as well ride the waves.

If you could travel in time, where would you go?
Way in the future to see if humans have finally figured things out.

What's the best advice you have ever received about writing?
One of the worst pieces of advice is to write about what you know. I think we should write about what we *want* to know.

What do you want readers to remember about your books?
That they really laughed or really cried.

What would you do if you ever stopped writing?
I'm kind of a grasshopper when it comes to interests and passions. Let's see, would I want to become a neurosurgeon or a beekeeper? It's a toss-up right this minute.

What do you like best about yourself?
That I analyze everything.

What is your worst habit?
That I analyze everything.

What do you consider to be your greatest accomplishment?
It's corny, but raising my two kids. They made it to college with no broken bones!

What do you wish you could do better?
Sing. I'm the kid in school that the teacher asked to just mouth the words. Very sad, since other than not being able to carry a tune, I would have made a great backup singer for a '60s soul group.

What would your readers be most surprised to learn about you?
That I was co-captain of the high school cheerleaders. I hang my head in embarrassment.

Keep reading for an excerpt from

Jill Wolfson's **Home, and Other Big, Fat Lies**,

available now in hardcover from Henry Holt.

EXCERPT

Let's say you're a kid who's small for her age and some other kids who are way overgrown decide it would be the most hilarious thing in the world to shove the new kid in the house into the clothes dryer and slam it closed. I can tell you how to get out of that dryer by kicking and screaming bloody murder so that the foster mom with the bald spot on the top of her head rescues you in front of the entire snickering ha-ha-ha-ha-ha-ha house full of kids.

I can also give you the complete rundown on the most common varieties of foster parents you're likely to run into. Like the look-on-the-bright-side ones who go on and on until your head is ready to explode like a potato in a microwave about how lucky you are that you weren't born a foster kid in 1846. Or the one I nicknamed Miss Satan because she was so evil, and I bet she's still alive because everyone knows you can't kill pure evil. Or the one who won't like you screaming bloody murder even when the family dog sticks its nose in your crotch and who says things like, "A little, bitty dog never hurt anyone."

Oh yeah, well, what about the Demon Dog from Hell?

Man-oh-man, I can tell you other things too. Important things you need for survival, not baby stuff.

Like how to jump down from and then shimmy back up to a second-story window.

And how to kick heart disease in the butt. Scary thought, right? But I have the scar right down the center of my chest to prove it.

I can tell you how to slip some *quote-unquote* souvenirs from a foster home into your pocket without anyone noticing a thing missing.

But there are a few things I don't know much about. I admit it. Trees are one. In the World of Whitney, that's just something I never needed to know, so why waste a bunch of words on it? In some places, the people have a hundred different words for something that's important to them. Like, in Alaska, the people have one word for wet snow—say, *oogabloga*—and a totally separate word for the big flaked kind of snow—like *moogablogo*.

For me, one word for tree has always been good enough, and that word is *tree.* There are small trees and big trees, trees that stay green all year and trees where the leaves fall off. Those are called *decidingus* trees because they all *decided* to let their leaves fall off for the winter. And there was the tree that I used for sneaking out of my sixth foster home because they duct-taped my bedroom door shut to keep me from being a *night howl*. That means I like wandering around and making lots of noise after dark.

That's about the whole sum total of it for trees and me.

So you can imagine how thrilled I was to be heading to Foster Home #12, where there was bound to be some real tree nuttiness going on. How did I know this? I saw a map of California, and way at the top there was no big ● (big city) or even a medium-sized • (medium-sized city). Where I was headed, the map was a blob of green with hardly any \\\\\\\ (roads). That meant trees, lots of them.

On a Sunday morning, the social worker from way up north came all the way south to the Land of Concrete to pick me up from my old foster home and take me to the new one. I was in the back seat of her official Department of Children's Services car. My pet pill bug, Ike Eisenhower the Sixth, was curled up in some leaves in a mayonnaise jar on my lap. I was working through a supersize bag of sunflower seeds—*crack*—spitting the shells out the window and sizing up my future.

Here's the way I saw it. There are two true, never-going-to-change facts of life for me. I'm going to die someday. And I am not going to last long in this new foster home. There's no getting around either one of them. *Crack.* Especially the second. *Crack.* No matter how things seem at first . . . *crack.* No matter how much the people tell me they want me around . . . *crack* . . . I'm going to get under their skin like a bad heat rash. Like a rubber band growing tighter and tighter around their throats. *Crack, crack, crack!*

"Can you stop it with those seeds?" the social worker blurted out.

"Nope," I said.

"It's been six hours and three hundred miles with that cracking."

"I need to be doing something with my hands. You don't want to see me without anything to do with my hands."

"Ugly, huh?"

"Very ugly."

By this time, we were out of San Jose, past Oakland, past Sacramento, all the way to where there were no more buildings, where the sky was no longer blue like a normal California sky. It looked like chocolate chip ice cream melted and schmooshed together. I rolled down the window and felt something like a damp rag slap across my face. That was the air. I stuck out my head even farther, all the way to the neck.

"In, please," the social worker said.

"Can't hear you," I lied.

I spotted a huge truck hauling logs that was coming at us from the opposite direction. I waved at the driver, then pulled down on a pretend cord, which everyone knows is the way to get a truck driver to sound the horn, unless the driver happens to be an old sourpuss, which this one was because all I could hear was wind banging on my eardrums. The truck got closer. I could see the driver's face now, and it wasn't smiling. It was screwed up, like I was a ghost.

"Get your head in!" the social worker was screaming. The driver blasted the horn, *really* blasted it. I cheered and waved. My ears were ringing. My eyes were tearing. Gravel was flying. Whoooo!

"Are you out of your mind?" the social worker screeched.

Man-oh-man, what was *her* problem? My nose didn't get knocked off or anything. She pulled to the side of the road, shut off the engine, and refused to drive any farther until I brought my head in and rolled up the window. "And lock the door," she ordered in a shaky voice.

That was the only major excitement for a while. After that, it was just trees to the right, left, ahead, and behind. It was a jungle out there, only not an interesting *jungle* jungle with monkeys and tigers and vines to swing from. This was just a lot of trees. There was a sign that said SCENIC HIGHWAY, and I wondered, What kind of idiot do they think I am? Of course it's scenic when everything looks like a postcard. Only it wasn't my kind of postcard. I like the ones where they paste an antelope and a jackrabbit together so you think there's really such an animal as a jackalope. Which I did for a while. I mean, why wouldn't I?

The social worker didn't take her eyes off the road, except to glance at me every ten seconds through the rearview mirror. "Girl with your kind of energy?" she said. "Good fresh air can work a miracle. This is where you belong, just the kind of home you need."

Who was she kidding? In social worker language, what she really meant was "Whitney, you've already been thrown out of or run away from every foster home in the world of civilization. That's why I have to drive you here to the middle of nowhere."

Home? I thought. One more place where *other* people belong, one more big, fat lie.

Frommer's®

THAILAND

13th Edition

By Ashley Niedringhaus

FrommerMedia LLC

FROMMER'S STAR RATINGS SYSTEM

Every hotel, restaurant, and attraction listed in this guide has been ranked for quality and value. Here's what the stars mean:

★　　　　　Recommended
★★　　　　Highly Recommended
★★★　　　A must! Don't miss!

AN IMPORTANT NOTE

The world is a dynamic place. Hotels change ownership, restaurants hike their prices, museums alter their opening hours, and busses and trains change their routings. And all of this can occur in the several months after our authors have visited, inspected, and written about, these hotels, restaurants, museums, and transportation services. Though we have made valiant efforts to keep all our information fresh and up-to-date, some few changes can inevitably occur in the periods before a revised edition of this guidebook is published. So please bear with us if a tiny number of the details in this book have changed. Please also note that we have no responsibility or liability for any inaccuracy or errors or omissions, or for inconvenience, loss, damage, or expenses suffered by anyone as a result of assertions in this guide.

A barefoot monk climbs
a temple staircase in
Chiang Mai.

CONTENTS

The island of Ko Phi Phi in Krabi Province (see p. 274).

A LOOK AT THAILAND

As you'll see in the pages that follow, there are few destinations on earth that can match Thailand for visual appeal. The country is, quite simply, a feast for the senses. Look in one direction to gleaming skyscrapers; gaze in another and a vermillion-and-gold peaked temple that hasn't changed in centuries will come into view; glance behind and you may see (and smell) a crowded street market, with *tuk tuks* zipping through, and locals happily munching on the planet's best street food. Travel a little and you'll be at the impossibly cerulean seashore, the blue of the waters interrupted by wind-sculpted karst outcroppings. Wander into the mountains and you'll find waterfalls, and electric green tea plantations, and hill tribes dressed in intricately handwoven fabrics. What follows in these pages is just a small taste of what this splendid country has to offer.

Pauline Frommer, Editorial Director

This royal sala was built in 1890 in the Phraya Nakhon cave for a visit by King Rama V (see p. 179). Because of a roof collapse, natural light can now enter the cave, and a small forest has grown inside it.

BANGKOK & CENTRAL THAILAND

The Moon Bar (see p.131), is one of the city's top nightspots—and we mean that literally.

ABOVE: A tuk-tuk ride is as much entertainment as it is transportation. But don't get taken for a ride on the cost (see p. 63 for advice). BELOW: A woman in traditional Thai dress demonstrates the art of silk weaving at Jim Thompson's House (see p. 109).

The 37 virtues needed to achieve enlightenment are embodied by the iron towers of Wat Ratchanatdaram and built in 1846. It was commissioned by King Rama III for his princess granddaughter (the name means "Niece's temple," see p. 113).

A monk shops for religious charms at the city's largest amulets market (p. 114).

Pantip Plaza is nerd heaven, a massive mall for tech (see p. 124).

One often sees traditional Thai dance at Erawan Shrine (p. 108); dancers are hired by worshippers as a thank you when prayers are answered.

Chatujak Market is one of the world's largest, covering some 27 acres. See p. 108.

Though its name means "milled rice," for the rice market that once was here, Khao San Road today is a hopping area, beloved by backpackers. See p. 132.

Damnoen Saduak Floating Market (p. 135).

At Wat Mahathat (p.114), an ancient statue peeks out from the tree roots that grew around it.

The Grand Palace (p. 106) is actually a complex of temples, gardens, halls, and other structures. Begun in 1782, it roughly follows the plan of the former palace in Ayutthaya.

A group of monks strolling at sunrise through the ancient capital of Ayutthaya (p. 283).

The King Narai Land Festival in Lopburi (p. 292). Paraders wear traditional Thai robes.

Legend has it that a Siamese soldier hid behind this giant Buddha statue, and scared away the invading Burmese troops by fooling them into thinking the statue was talking. It's at Wat Si Chum in Sukhothai (p. 301).

THE COAST & ISLANDS

Much of Ao Phang Nga National Park (p. 264) is in the Andaman Sea. The best way to see the park's limestone tower karst islands is by kayak.

Fire dancers at a party on the beach in Ko Samet (p. 150).

Trying out water jet boots in Ko Samui (p. 186).

Visitors should plan to be inside the Khao Luang Cave (p. 178) at around 10:30am. That's when shafts of light enter, giving it an ethereal cast.

A monkey eats a mango.

Some 40 jungly islands make up Ang Thong National Park (p. 208), most with limestone cliffs and pink sand beaches.

Khao Sok National Park (p. 185) holds southern Thailand's largest virgin rainforest, many caves to explore, and islands that jut upwards from a large lake.

Entertainment at a Full Moon Party on Ko Pha Ngan (p. 209).

Those who decide to vacation on Ko Phi Phi Don find hotels on Loh Dalam Beach (pictured, p. 274).

NORTHERN THAILAND

Known as the "roof of Thailand," Doi Inthanon National Park (p. 351) holds the highest peak in the country. About 3 km below it are these ceremonial pagodas and gardens, created in the late 1980's.

Try Chiang Mai's famed Khao Soi curry (p. 336).

Wat Rong Khun in Chiang Rai (p. 379).

A member of the Akha Hill Tribe.

A Lisu Hill Tribe child.

The Padong Tribe are known for their neck rings.

A member of the Hmong tribe. For info on all the hill tribes go to p. 52.

Women pick tea leaves at a plantation outside of Chiang Rai.

Floating lanterns light up the sky outside of Wat Phra Singh (p. 318) during the Yee Peng Festival.

From this viewpoint at Ban Doi Sa-ngo Chiangsaen one can look over the "Golden Triangle"—the area where Thailand, Laos, and Myanmar meet.

The Wat Ming Muang in Chiang Rai (p. 374) is more than 700 years old.

Women perform the so-called "Nail Dance" at Wat Phra That Hariphunchai in Lamphun (p. 350). In a corner of the compound are four footprints in stone, believe to have been left by the Buddha himself.

THE BEST OF THAILAND

From the temples of Wat Pho and The Grand Palace through to Thailand's Khao Yai and Doi Inthanon national parks and Ko Hong rock, to scuba diving in Ko Pha Ngan and the white, sandy beaches of Hua Hin, Thailand is a land of variety. The country has plenty to satisfy single travelers, couples, or families, from Bangkok's shopping and nightlife to adventure sports in the northern hills or a pampering spa at a beach resort. All topped off with the famous Thai hospitality: their smiles and irresistible, laid-back attitude.

CITIES, TOWNS & COAST   Begin in **Bangkok,** with its chaotic mix of ancient temples and modern glass towers, street markets and stylish shopping malls, tuk-tuks, and river taxis. Then head north to the venerable, walled city of **Chiang Mai** for a peek at the capital of the region once known as "the Kingdom of a Million Rice Fields," but leave at least a few days to sprawl on a beach.

COUNTRYSIDE   Go trekking or white-water rafting in the **northern hills** that are home to brightly dressed hill-tribes; cycle round the ancient cities of **Ayutthaya** and **Sukhothai** in the Central Plains; pick from over a hundred **national parks** to explore; or cruise along the **Andaman** or **Gulf coast** in search of stunning dive sites.

EATING & DRINKING   Thai cuisine is enough reason in itself to visit the country, and whether you crave the brow-mopping challenge of a fiery *tom yam* or an aromatic bowl of noodles in broth, you'll find it all here. Learn to eat like the Thais, squatting on low stools at street-side food stalls, but treat yourself at least once to a gourmet feast on starched tablecloths, served by waiters in traditional dress.

best AUTHENTIC EXPERIENCES

o **Chatting with monks:** Thai temples rank high on most travelers' hit lists, but many are surprised to find the experience can be an interactive one. Many monks are eager to practice their English; and some temples even have set times for "monk chats," open to visitors of all religious backgrounds for one-on-one talks. See p. 321.

o **Speaking Thai for the first time:** You'll stumble over your first dozen attempts at "sawasdee" (hello) or "khop khun" (thank you), and you might even confuse your "khun" (said by men) and your "ka" (said by women). But it won't matter once you notice how much your effort is appreciated. See p. 426 for a list of Thai phrases.

o **Bargaining:** Many Western visitors are shy about offering a lower price than advertised for goods, but bargaining is the norm in Thailand. Start by offering 50 to 70% of the item's stated price and increase your offer as the vendor decreases the sale price to reach an agreement, but don't haggle about just a few baht.

o **Riding in a tuk-tuk:** Thais do it out of necessity, while foreigners do it for the thrill of roaring round town in these screaming, open-sided, brightly decorated vehicles. Savvy drivers know there's money to be made from foreigners, so bargain to get a reasonable price. See p. 63.

o **Taking your first bite of street food:** Squat on a low stool, embrace the sweat dripping down your brow, and enjoy a street-side meal. Don't worry about language problems. Simply point to an appealing dish, settle down, and dig in. Once that unbeatable combination of perfectly balanced sweet, salty, bitter, and spicy hits your lips, it won't matter what language you speak because your mouth will be too full *to* speak. For tips on choosing clean street food vendors, see p. 94.

o **Watching Thai boxing (Muay Thai):** Half the fun of watching a *Muay Thai* match is the passion displayed by the peanut gallery. You'll probably watch the audience more than the boxers themselves, as they flail their fists in the air and scream encouragement for their chosen athlete. Join in the fun and root for the same fighter as the locals around you. See p. 50.

o **Tasting durian for the first time:** Thais call durian "the king of fruits." It is the single-most controversial fruit in Asia, and most hotels charge cleaning fees if you eat it in your room. To some, it smells like a pair of old socks or a dirty gym bag (hungry yet?) but the creamy taste and smooth texture is irresistible to many. Trying it is a rite of passage.

best FAMILY EXPERIENCES

o **Relaxing on a sandy beach:** If there's one thing that kids and adults can agree on is that there's nothing that says "vacation" quite as powerfully as a white-sand beach fronted by an emerald sea. The island of **Ko Chang** (p. 155) offers that, along with plenty of land- and sea-based of excursions and activates to keep everyone entertained.

o **Befriending restaurant staff:** In fact, you won't need to befriend them as they'll befriend your kids first, and they'll probably amuse the children while you enjoy your dinner in peace.

o **Visiting the Siam Museum:** Kids are often bored silly by museums, but Bangkok's Museum of Siam is not so much about ancient history as what it means to be a Thai, and as such is interesting to all ages. Its has tons of hands-on exhibits, plus chances to dress up in period costume and see how accurately one can fire a cannon. See p. 110.

○ **Visiting a floating market:** In bygone days, much of Thailand's commerce took place on canals, and floating vendors sold everything from farming implements to bowls of noodles. These vendors' skills have not been lost, and though floating markets such as the one at **Damnoen Saduak** (p. 135) are now geared mostly to tourists, a ride around the canals looking at the fruits and flowers on sale is a great adventure for kids.

○ **Watching wildlife:** And by that we mean doing so in one of Thailand's national parks. Specifically, tours of **Khao Yai National Park** (see p. 137) accommodate families with kids of all ages, and the knowledgeable guides will have the entire brood on the lookout for elephants and rare birds.

○ **Riding the Skytrain in Bangkok:** It was built to alleviate Bangkok's traffic problems, but it could just as easily have been designed to help visitors get to know Bangkok. Grab a window seat and watch the city sail by from 20m (65 ft.) above ground. See p. 60.

○ **Going eye to eye with a parrotfish:** Diving is one of the most popular activities in Thailand, but even snorkelers will be blown away by the colorful wonderland that lies just below the surface of the Andaman Sea and the Gulf of Thailand. The best place to learn to dive? Ko Tao (p. 217). A great spot for snorkeling? Ko Surin (p. 262).

THAILAND'S best MUSEUMS

○ **Hall of Opium (Chiang Rai):** The Golden Triangle in northern Thailand is no longer the drug-smuggling hotbed that it once was, but the fascination with the opium-growing days still blooms. Multimedia and sensory exhibits guide visitors through the wild history of kingpins, cartels, and the 5,000-year chronicle of poppy growing and opium trade in Thailand, Myanmar, and Laos. See p. 387.

○ **The Jim Thompson House (Bangkok):** A visit to the home of Thailand's most famous expat and the founding father of the Thai silk trade. Thompson cobbled this teak treasure from old homes around the region and reassembled it in Bangkok before he mysteriously disappeared in the Malaysian jungle in 1967. Wandering the gardens and taking a tour of the house is a charming way to spend an hour and a half. See p. 109.

○ **Bangkok Art & Cultural Centre (Bangkok):** The BACC lacks a permanent collection, which means there is always something new to see. The nine floors of display space bring a rotating showcase of exciting contemporary exhibits. Private collections and up-and-coming Asian artists are on regular rotation, and the cultural center is a nice place to do some last-minute shopping. See p. 107.

○ **Queen Sirikit Museum of Textiles (Bangkok):** The crowds at the Grand Palace can get overwhelming, which is why too many tourists, making a quick exit, miss this gem. It displays many of the queen's formal gowns from over the years, and offers visitors a greater understanding of the Thai silk industry and the craftsmanship that goes into making these exquisite dresses. Plus it's not nearly as crowded as the rest of the palace! See p. 106.

o **MAIIAM Contemporary Museum (Chiang Mai):** Chaing Mai is an art lovers' paradise, supporting a vibrant local community of artists and gallery owners. The city's artsy hub is the MAIIAM Contemporary Museum, which has traditional art galleries to as well as spaces for performance art, film screenings, educational talks, and fashion and design exhibits. See p. 323.

THAILAND'S best ARCHITECTURAL LANDMARKS

o **Wat Arun:** Close your eyes and conjure up an image of a Thai temples. No doubt something resembling this breathtaking riverside beaut will spring to mind. Sunrise is the best time to view the "Temple of Dawn," one of Bangkok's iconic sights. See p. 113.

o **Ayutthaya:** Just a hop and a skip from Bangkok, Ayutthaya is Thailand's most visited historical sight, and this former capital of the kingdom doesn't disappoint. Its crooked stupas and broken Buddha images evoke a long-lost era. Look for the stone carving of Buddha's face picturesquely ensnarled in the roots of a bodhi tree, as if designed to be that way all those years and years ago. See p. 283.

o **Sukhothai:** Capital of the first true Siamese kingdom, Sukhothai (meaning "the dawn of happiness") is an inspiring place to visit. Slender stupas pierce the sky, and graceful, jointless Buddhas are sculpted in mid-stride. If you can, time your visit to coincide with the Loy Krathong Festival, when the clock seems to rewind time almost 800 years. See p. 299.

o **The walls of old Chiang Mai:** Originally the capital of the Lanna Kingdom, Chiang Mai is steeped in over 700 years of history, and a stroll around its ancient city walls, gates, and moat gives a sense of how things used to be. For an extra challenge, see if you can track down the outer ring of earthen ramparts (*kamphaeng din*), some parts of which still exist. When you find them, slurp down a bowl of *khao soi* to celebrate. See p. 311.

THAILAND'S best BEACHES

o **Nai Thon Beach** (Phuket): Patong might be Phuket's best-known strip of sand, but Nai Thon gets this beach bum's vote for prettiest on the island (and there's some stiff competition!). It's a perfect, 500-m (1,640-ft.) arc of golden sand lapped by turquoise waters and protected by two rocky headlands. Oh, and I almost forgot the best thing about it—there's hardly anyone there. See p. 250.

o **Loh Dalam Beach** (Ko Phi Phi): The north-facing beach of Phi Phi Don's two back-to-back beaches forms a perfect horseshoe and is fringed by blinding white sands. It's very shallow, so not too good for swimming, but if you take a walk out in the bay as the sea recedes at low tide, you'll enter a wonderland of corals, sea urchins, and sea anemones, without even needing a mask and snorkel. See p. 274.

○ **Ao Nang** (Krabi): Though it's known to most people as a jumping-off pier for nearby Railay Beach, Ao Nang is much less crowded and has more options for dining and shopping, so is better suited to families. The beach itself is fine and safe for kids, but it's also easy to take boat trips to the many islands in Phang Nga Bay from here. See p. 268.

○ **Had Sai Khao** (White Sand Beach, Ko Chang): This west-facing beach, with its gorgeous powder-soft sand and fringe of palm trees, fits anyone's notion of paradise, particularly when there's a sinking sun setting the sky ablaze. There's a wide choice of places to stay and eat, and it's long enough to get away from the crowds. See p. 157.

THAILAND'S most COLORFUL FESTIVALS

○ **Songkran:** Thailand's traditional New Year festival lasts for a week or more, though it's officially only April 12 to 14. Often called the Water-Splashing Festival, it involves lots of playful fun with spray guns and buckets. Kids love it and it's worth planning a holiday around. See p. 40.

○ **Loy Krathong:** Thailand's second-biggest festival, usually in November, involves floating candle-lit *krathong* on rivers and waterways throughout the kingdom. Without a doubt the most visually beautiful of all Thai festivals, it marks the end of the rains and beginning of the cool season, a great time to be in Thailand. See p. 40.

○ **Phuket Vegetarian Festival:** The highlight of this eye popping spectacle is when devotees parade the streets with skewers, swords, and drill bits stuck through their cheeks. Don't attend if you'd be disturbed by such scenes; do attend if you've got a strong stomach and want to see some unforgettable sights. What does this have to do with going meat-free? Eating a clean diet and self-inflicted pain is a way of purifying the body. See p. 232.

○ **Chiang Mai Flower Festival:** Taking place in February, when the maximum number of flowers are in bloom in North Thailand, this festival features floats smothered with bright-colored and sweet-smelling blossoms, accompanied by proud representatives from local schools and businesses dressed in elaborate costumes. See p. 316.

THE best GIFTS TO BRING HOME

○ **Textiles:** Thai silk is of a consistently high quality, and different regions of the country are famed for different weaving styles and designs. Tailored items of clothing make great souvenirs, but don't overlook garments made of local cotton and hemp, which are more comfortable to wear in a hot climate.

o **Home decor:** Thai designs display a flair that is admired worldwide, and small, packable items of home decor make ideal gifts. A bamboo and *sa* paper lantern weighs next to nothing, a set of table mats in a striking design is similarly packable, as is a compact set of coasters.

o **Lacquerware:** Though the process of making lacquerware is long and laborious, the finished product is both distinctively Thai and very light to carry. Bowls and plates, trays, jewelry boxes, and decorative animals are just a few top picks.

o **Silverware:** Thai silverware, particularly that made by the northern hilltribes, is highly valued for its comparative purity and quality artistry. Common items include jewelry (earrings, pendants, and bracelets, and even belts) and embossed bowls showing scenes from Thai history.

o **Ceramics:** Like woodcarvings, ceramics are bad news when it comes to baggage allowance, but some items are so beautiful that you may be tempted to ship them home. Look out for vases, plates, and trays made of celadon, which has a distinctive pale-green color and a cracked glaze. Most store owners can arrange shipping or give directions to the nearest post office or DHL branch.

best SMALL-TOWN THAILAND EXPERIENCES

o **Looking down over Mae Hong Son from Wat Phra That Doi Kong Mu:** From this temple on a hill, the entire town of Mae Hong Son, including Jong Kham Lake and the Burmese-style temples on its shores, is spread below you. That is when the town isn't socked in by cloud; its nickname is *muang sam mork* ("City of three mists"). See p. 370.

o **Exploring Thailand's oldest town:** Lamphun, just south of Chiang Mai in the north, claims to be Thailand's oldest continually inhabited town. Wander around the largely intact city wall, pay your respects to the statue of city founder Queen Chamadhevi, and visit the temple named after her that has a stupas built in the Dharavati period, over 1,000 years ago. See p. 349.

o **Hiding out in Loei:** If you want to give tourists the slip, make a beeline for **Loei** (p. 397), a sleepy but friendly town in Isan without any big attractions but heaps of local charm. Beautiful scenery awaits along the Mekong Valley to Nong Khai (p. 398) route, or you can put on your hiking boots and trek to the top of Phu Kradung (p. 397), a great place to live out the laidback Thai attitude of *no worries* (*mai pen rai*).

o **Seeing the sun rise over a sea of mist:** It's only possible in the north and during the cool season, but it's a sight to remember—the sun emerging from a sea of mist in the valley below. Spectacular sights include the Mae Hong Son loop (p. 359) and from the summit of Doi Luang Chiang Dao (p. 353).

- **Monkeying around in Lopburi:** Situated just north of Ayutthaya, Lopburi was a favorite summer residence of former kings, particularly King Narai (r. 1656–88). It's worth visiting King Narai's Palace as well as Khmer-inspired Phra Prang Sam Yot, which is a favorite hang-out for the hordes of macaques that live here. See p. 292.

- **Crossing the bridge over the River Kwai at Kanchanaburi:** Before you cross the bridge on a special train to Hellfire Pass, pay your respects at the town's immaculately maintained Allied War Cemetery. You'll work out from the gravestones that many of those who died building the "Death Railway" were only teenagers. Take a tour of the Thailand–Burma Railway Center to learn more about what happened here. See p. 137.

- **Kicking back at Prachuap Khiri Khan:** Turquoise waters and limestone mountains in the distance are views typically only found in the Andaman Sea, but this little place south of Hua Hin offers all that and more. Wiggle your toes in the sand of local beaches, stuff yourself with seafood, and practice your Thai with the locals. See p. 181.

THAILAND'S best RESTAURANTS

- **Gaggan (Bangkok):** All hail the four-time winner of "Asia's Best Restaurant" by the organization World's 50 Best (Gaggan was ranked number 5 in the world in 2018). It's a quirky place to dine: the menu is presented as a series of emojis with each course representing the emotions of the symbol. It's also VERY hard to get in: Chef Gaggan Anand has announced he'll pack up and explore culinary ventures in Japan in 2020, so winning a reservation is like winning the lottery. See p. 91.

- **Jay Fai (Bangkok):** Hunched over a rudimentary wok in Old Town, Bangkok, the petite Jay Fai is still cooking her famous crab omelets and crab curry dishes well into her 7th decade. Known for wearing bug-eyed goggles, Jay Fai was a legend even before becoming the only street food vendor to earn a Michelin star in the inaugural 2018 guide. To the surprise of many, her prices haven't risen since. See p. 95.

- **Khao Soi Lam Duan Fah Ham (Chiang Mai):** *Khao soi*, a spicy, yellow Burmese-style curry with both fried and boiled noodles, is a beloved regional dish in the north of Thailand. One of the best local spots for this cheap and authentic dish is Khao Soi Lam Duan Fah Ham. In business for more than seven decades, it's been said they make more than 50 pounds of noodles a day. See p. 342.

- **Acqua (Phuket):** Under the watchful eye of Sardinia-born Alessandro Frau, Acqua brings to life a creative menu of seafood-based Italian dishes with European precision and cooking techniques. The wine list is the best outside of Bangkok, and top international suppliers bring in freshwater fish, smoked burrata, and perfectly ripe tomatoes. See p. 254.

o **Street food vendors:** Without open-air stalls, pushcarts, and roaming barbecue grills, Thailand wouldn't be what it is today. Dishes created in the open air are imbued with history and culture—and they'll likely be the best food you'll ever have while traveling. Someone once told me that to eat like a local is to be accepted like a local, and that, in its purest form, is my favorite thing about living in Thailand. See p. 94.

THAILAND'S best HOTELS

o **Mandarin Oriental (Bangkok):** This momentous property opened on the banks of the Chao Phraya in 1876 and has been a landmark ever since. The hotel's old-world glamour and Thai charm have attracted a host of dignitaries and celebrities over the years, including Somerset Maugham, Noel Coward, Princess Diana, Elizabeth Taylor, and David Beckham. See p. 68.

o **Dhara Dhevi (Chiang Mai):** Built to resemble an ancient Lanna-era kingdom, this 60-acre property comes complete with moats, walls, and gorgeous rooms outfitted in Thai silks and hill-tribe prints. After a night or two here, you'll feel like royalty. See p. 328.

o **Four Seasons Tented Camp Golden Triangle (Chiang Rai):** Trumpeting elephants call out from the jungle while the sun sets over neighboring Burma. This all-inclusive resort in the hills of northern Thailand offers spa treatments in a lush outdoor jungle setting, gourmet meals, and ethical interactions with playful pachyderms. See p. 388.

o **Soneva Kiri (Koh Kood):** Kick things off on the right (very luxurious) foot and take the 70-minute flight from Bangkok on the resort's eight-seater Cessna plane to Ko Mai Si, the hotel's private island. The pampering doesn't stop until you leave these spacious suites and their palm-lined beaches. Eat plenty of fresh-caught fish. See p. 164.

o **Supanniga Home Boutique Hideaway (Khon Kaen):** The hotel doubles as meditation retreat for local Thai monks, and that tranquil vibe extends to the villas, set on lush grounds and surrounded by mango trees. The on-property restaurant offers a menu of the owner's grandmother's recipes. Khon Kaen is the gateway to Isan, a province in the northeast part of Thailand. See p. 395.

o **The Nai Harn (Phuket):** The Nai Harn overlooks a near-perfect slice of sand with turquoise waters rolling in and yachts in the bay. The service is fantastic, the food is excellent, and there's a great spa and wine menu. Besides ownership of one of the yachts, what more could you want? See p. 239.

SUGGESTED ITINERARIES IN THAILAND

2

Thailand is often the first Asian country Western tourists visit. It's not hard to see why. This vast and treasure-filled nation is supremely affordable, with astonishingly delicious food on quite literally every street and people who are the most welcoming on the planet. In this laid-back country, though, it isn't always necessary to plan full days of museum-hopping, touring, and shopping, like one would in Paris or Rome. I urge even the most Type A of travelers to leave some room for spontaneity (Bangkok's infamous traffic will likely delay a few plans).

Most trips begin and end in Bangkok—the country's capital and commercial center—and travelers' itineraries often include some beach time mixed in with a bit of history and adventure. With well-timed, short domestic flights, the highlights can be seen in 10 to 14 days, but linger a bit and you'll better experience the country's rich history and a profound spirituality. The itineraries listed here should serve as inspiration for ways to spend your days, but they're also ripe for mixing and matching.

THE REGIONS IN BRIEF

The Thais compare their land to the shape of an elephant's head, seen in profile, facing the West, with the southern peninsula representing the dangling trunk. Thailand is roughly equidistant from China and India, and centuries of migration from southern China and trade with India brought influences from each of these Asian nations. Thailand borders Myanmar to the northwest, Laos to the northeast, Cambodia to the east, and Malaysia to the south. Its southwestern coast stretches along the Andaman Sea, its southern and southeastern coastlines perimeter the Gulf of Thailand, and every coast boasts a myriad of islands. Thailand covers roughly 514,000 sq. km (198,450 sq. miles)—about the size of France or California—and spans over 1,600km (over 1,000 miles) from north to south. It is divided into six geographic zones, within which there are 76 provinces.

Thailand

Chiang Saen
Chiang Rai
Chiang Khong
Fang
**GOLDEN
TRIANGLE**
Mae Hong
Son
Pai
**NORTHERN
HILLS**
LAOS
VIETNAM

Lamphun
Chiang Mai
Lampang
Nan
Yom
Mekong
Vientiane

BURMA
Mae
Sariang
Phrae
Wang
Nong Khai
Ban Chiang
Loei
Si Satchanalai
Uttaradit
Udon
Thani
Nakhon
Phanom
Sukhothai
Tak
Phitsanulok
Chi
Mae Sot
Kamphaeng
Phet
Ping
Phetchabun
Khon Kaen
ISAN

Nakhon Sawan
Phimai
Mun
Ubon
Ratchathani
Noi Noi
Khwaewae Noi
**CENTRAL
PLAINS**
Chao Phraya
Lopburi
Nakhon Ratchasima
(Khorat)
Surin

Nam Tok
Kanchanaburi
Ayutthaya
Sam Rong
Nakhom
Pathom
Bangkok
Chon Buri

*Andaman
Sea*
Cha-Am
Phetchaburi
Bangsaen
Hua Hin
Pattaya
Chanthaburi
CAMBODIA
Prachuap
Khiri Khan
Rayong
Ko Samet
**EASTERN
SEABOARD**
*Kra
Isthmus*
Ko Chang
Trat
Chumphon
Ko Tao
Ko Mak
Phnom Penh
Ranong
Ko Pha Ngan
Ko Kut

Ko Surin
**(Surin National
Marine Park)**
Ko Samui
VIETNAM
Khanom
Chao Lak
Phang Nga
Surat
Thani
**SOUTHERN
PENINSULA**
Nakhon
Si Thammarat
*Gulf of Thailand
(Gulf of Siam)*
Phuket
Krabi
*Ko
Phi Phi*

*Andaman
Sea*
Songkhla
Had Yai
Pattani
Ko Tarutao
(Tarutao National Park)
Narathiwat
MALAYSIA
Sungai Kolok

0   100 mi
0   100 km

BANGKOK Located on the banks of the Chao Phraya River—Thailand's principal waterway—Bangkok is more or less in the geographical heart of the country on both a north–south and east–west axis. It is home to more than 10% of the Thai population, as well as plenty of expats who bustle along with the commuter crowd, glad to be based in this crazy metropolis. Its congested streets and infamous gridlock can be frustrating, though its glittering temples, colorful markets, and carefree inhabitants can be endearing in equal measure.

THE EASTERN SEABOARD The coastline east of Bangkok—often referred to as the Eastern Gulf—is home to Pattaya, Rayong, and Trat. These are popular weekend destinations for Thai families and expats alike. For the best beaches, however, you'll need to hop on a boat to Ko Samet, Ko Chang, or Ko Kood, all of which offer resorts and spots to scuba.

THE SOUTHERN PENINSULA A long, narrow peninsula protrudes south to the Malaysian border with the Andaman Sea on the west and the Gulf of Thailand to the east. Due to the high number of popular destinations in the south, this guide divides the region into two chapters—one focusing on the east coast and another focusing on the west coast.

Off the Gulf coast, Ko Samui has gone from sleepy hideaway to a heaving tourist magnet, while Ko Pha Ngan and Ko Tao are following in its wake. Farther south, the three southernmost provinces of Yala, Narathiwat, and Pattani are home to a considerable Muslim population. Take extreme care in this region: Regular, violent attacks by insurgents target public markets as well as transport and Buddhist centers. Off the Andaman coast, the islands of Phuket, Ko Phi Phi, and Ko Lanta, as well as the peninsula of Krabi, boast the some of the country's loveliest beaches and pose no safety risks.

THE CENTRAL PLAINS Thailand's central plains are an extremely fertile region: Its abundant jasmine rice crops are exported worldwide. The main attractions of the area, however, are the atmospheric ruins at the historic cities of Sukhothai and Ayutthaya, both former capitals of the Kingdom of Siam. To the west of the central plains, Kanchanaburi, on the River Kwai, is the site of the infamous World War II "Death Railway," where an estimated 16,000 Allied prisoners of war and around 100,000 Asians died during its construction for the Japanese. Other significant towns in this region are Lopburi, a favorite haunt of former kings of Siam; Phitsanulok, a major crossroads in the northern plains; and Mae Sot, a remote outpost near the Myanmar border and jumping-off point for a trip to Ti Lor Su Waterfall, in the Umphang Wildlife Reserve.

NORTHERN THAILAND The north is a mountainous region and coolest from November to February when conditions are ideal for trekking to visit the region's brightly dressed hill-tribes. This is also elephant country, but now that logging is banned, many pachyderms are sources of entertainment for tourists at elephant camps. (More on that on p. 325.) The cool hills in the north are well suited for farming, particularly for strawberries, asparagus, peaches, and litchis. Today, agricultural programs and charities, such as the Mae Fah Luang Foundation, are retraining hill-tribe villagers whose main crop used to be opium poppies. Settlements around Doi Tung have implemented crop replacement schemes, propagating coffee and macadamia nuts.

The major towns in the north are Chiang Mai, Chiang Rai, Lampang, and Mae Hong Son. The best way to enjoy the region's scenic beauty is by taking a motorbike or car around the Mae Hong Son Loop; or, for those with less time, a quick trip to Thailand's highest point in Doi Inthanon National Park, or to the infamous Golden Triangle, where the borders of Thailand, Laos, and Myanmar meet.

ISAN The broad and relatively infertile northeast plateau that is Isan is the least developed region in Thailand. Bordered by the Mekong River, it separates the country from neighboring Laos, though the people of Isan share linguistic and cultural similarities with their neighbors. The region's attractions include the remains of a Bronze Age village at Ban Chiang, as well as significant Khmer ruins at Pimai and Phnom Rung, near Nakhorn Ratchasima, also known as Khorat. The greatest asset of the region for tourists is the easy-going lifestyle of the region and it's a perfect place to unwind along the banks of the mighty Mekong River.

THAILAND'S GREATEST HITS: A COUNTRY TOUR IN 10 DAYS

While more time is always better, in 10 days, you'll have enough time to hit the beach, buzz around Bangkok, and make it to the north for trekking. The tour outlined below is for travelers who want to take in the country's highlights. The flexibility of another 2 to 4 days will allow for a few more sights, like a day trip from Bangkok to Ayutthaya or island hopping down south. I've outlined a top-level plan here but keep reading for a more zoomed in guides to the different regions.

Days 1 and 2: Bangkok

Since jetlag likely has you up at odd hours, the bustling 24-hour flower market, known as **Pak Klong Talad** (p. 126), is where to head first (whenever "first" may be). The blooms are used to make ornate arrangements for weddings, funerals, temple offerings, and many hotels come here to outfit the lobby and guestrooms with fragrant flowers. Keep any eye out for women folding lotus blossoms and stringing jasmine to make temple offerings. If you have another day of waking up before dawn, use the early time to "make merit" and offer alms to the local monks for good fortune on your journey. With bare feet and saffron colored robes, the Thai monks walk the streets of the city in the early morning to collect food and donations. You'll likely be able to find them near your hotel around 6am, but check with the front desk about where to find fruit to donate.

After these early morning adventures, follow our Bangkok Day 1 and Day 2 itineraries as laid out on p. 14 and p. 15, for the daylight hours. Spend 1 night on a foodie deep-dive getting acquainted with the country's incredible street food. **Chinatown** is the best spot to try a host of dishes, and you can do this on your own or with a guide (see p. 89 for recommended tours). The other night could be more upmarket, dining at one of the city's foodie hotspots, like **80/20's** (p. 90)—80% of the designed-to-share menu comes from a nearby market.

Days 3 to 5: The Beach

Catch an early morning flight from Bangkok to **Krabi** (p. 266), a stunning beach destination. Like tropical neighbors Phuket and Ko Samui, the Krabi airport offers direct flights to Chiang Mai, which is your next destination in Thailand. Spend the days flitting between boat rides, donning a snorkel mask to see if you can find a sea turtle, eating your weight in seafood, and enjoying pampering massage treatments. Spa retreats, over-the-top villas with private pools, and low-key beach bungalows are available to suit every budget and travel style.

Days 6 to 9: Chiang Mai

A 90-minute flight will take you from Krabi to the Rose of the North, and you'll notice a palpable difference the moment you step off the airplane. *Money-saving tip:* Budget travelers should look to make a connection in Bangkok, which isn't as taxing as it sounds and which will lower the price significantly. You can easily make it to Chiang Mai in time for a late lunch with the connection. Just be mindful of booking tickets to and from the same airport in Bangkok.

When you land, check in to your hotel, grab a bowl of *khao soi* at **Khao Soi Lam Duan Fah Ham** (p. 342), stroll around the **Old City** (p. 313), browse the stalls at the famous **night market** (p. 345), and end the night listening to local music at a hot spot like the **North Gate Jazz Co-Op** (p. 349).

Fill the next day with a morning trip to the dazzling hillside temple of **Doi Suthep** (p. 320), where you ring the bells for good luck, and head out for an afternoon **cooking class** (p. 323 has my top picks) that will include a trip to a local market. If your cooking class is in the morning, head to Doi Suthep in the afternoon. It's beautiful all day long.

For Day 8, arrange an early pick-up at your hotel by the **Elephant Nature Park** (p. 46) for a full morning and afternoon of playtime with rescued elephants in a beautiful mountain setting. You'll feed them treats, learn about the herds, and observe them bathing. It's a beautiful day interacting with these majestic animals. Return and shower up at the hotel (elephants can be smelly!), then head to an open-air eating and shopping center called **One Nimman** (p. 341) for dinner and a drink.

On your last full day in Chiang Mai, it is time to do some serious retail therapy. Not only is the shopping in Chiang Mai is excellent, visiting the stores here affords a fascinating look into Thai culture, and the current state of its arts-and-crafts scene. Best place to go is Charoenrat Road where you'll find more than a dozen boutiques, including **Sop Moei Arts** (p. 343) for high-end hill-tribe handicrafts, **Vila Cini** (p. 347) for silk, and the **Elephant Parade House** (p. 344) for colorful elephant figurines. Grab lunch at **Ginger & Kafe** (p. 339) and browse their small boutique before leaving. If you still have time before your flight, you could continue shopping in town at **HQ Paper** (p. 344) and **Chiang Mai Cotton** (p. 346), or enjoy one last massage before the long flight home. With a few locations in town, you're likely close to a **Let's Relax** (p. 327).

Day 10: Bangkok

While there are a growing number of international flights departing from Chiang Mai, you'll likely catch a flight home from Bangkok. Spend your day lounging in Lumpini Park or doing some last-minute shopping. If you didn't make it to the weekends-only Chatuchak Market, plan to do that before flying out.

BANGKOK ITINERARIES

The Thai capital has a lot to offer but can be somewhat daunting, what with its chaotic traffic and hectic pace. The following itineraries should help cut down on time getting from one place to the next, as they explore one, or two, areas at a time. Tack these one-day itineraries onto the beginning—or the end—of any trip to Thailand, since you'll likely fly in and out of the capital city. If you're going to split it up: Spend time touring the city sites at the start of the journey and then use a day at the end to fill your suitcase with beautiful handicrafts, silk fashions, or souvenirs that you won't want to haul around the country.

Day 1: Bangkok's Riverside Sites

Start your tour of Bangkok at **Central Pier** (p. 61), next to Saphan Taksin BTS, where you can hop on a fast river taxi or the more comfortable wide-berth Chao Phraya Tourist Boat.

Heading north along the S-curve of the river, you can hop off to visit many of the city's historical sites. The first stop should be an early morning arrival at the famed **Wat Phra Kaew** (p. 104), the temple of the celebrated Emerald Buddha, and the **Grand Palace** ★★★ (p. 106). From there, it's a short walk to **Wat Po** ★★★ (p. 114) and the Giant Reclining Buddha.

Take a lunch break to rest your legs and eyes, or even get a massage at the on-site massage school at Wat Pho. Then carry on upstream to visit the **National Museum** ★★ (p. 110), where you can easily spend a couple of hours delving into this proud nation's past. If you've still got it in you, after visiting the museum, for a different type of sightseeing, wander north to Banglampoo and nose around **Khao San Road** (p. 132), the vibrant backpacker strip.

This is a lot to see in a day—but it does cover the city's unmissable sights and avoids traffic delays by using river transport. If you enjoy traveling on the river, you may want to end the day by taking a **dinner cruise** (see p. 69 for options), on which you can see the city by night.

Day 2: History, Shopping and Thai Massage

Start your second day in Bangkok at the **Jim Thompson House** ★★ (p. 109), the beautiful wooden home on stilts of the American who rejuvenated the Thai silk industry. It's in the heart of the city near the National Stadium BTS and offers a fascinating lens through which to look at the country's not-so-distant past.

The shimmering silks on display in the shop at Jim Thompson's should put you in the mood for a full-frontal attack on the city's shops: About a 10-minute walk from the Jim Thompson is **MBK Center** (p. 124), a multi-floor home to everything from funky fashion to phone accessories. Adjacent to the Siam BTS is **Siam Paragon** (p. 94), a center filled with super-luxury boutiques and a huge choice of restaurants. If you still haven't found that special something, continue to the funky, trendy stores found in the maze of lanes in **Siam Square** (p. 58).

Have lunch a mall food court either at Siam Paragon or MBK. Dining at MBK is the more affordable, local experience of the two. Thais love food courts, and the experience is much nicer than a food court in the West. Next, drop off your shopping bags at the hotel and head off to enjoy Thailand's famous massage. Thais believe regular massage is an essential part of a holistic well-being and foreign visitors are often shocked at how inexpensive treatments are (expect to pay $15 to $30 an hour). During Thai massage, a professional massage therapist will bend and stretch you, an experience many have compared to lazy man's yoga. **Health Land** (see p. 118) or **Asia Herb** (p. 118) are both major chains with top rate services.

You should be feeling as light as a feather after this, but you'll feel even lighter when you ride up to the 61st floor of the Banyan Tree Hotel, on Sathorn Road, to knock back a sundowner at **Moon Bar** (p. 131) while drinking in the city views in every direction. For dinner, if you want a sense of occasion, head around the corner to **Nahm** ★★ (p. 88)

Day 3: Chatuchak & Chinatown

If it is Friday or Saturday, take the BTS to Mo Chit for a morning of treasure hunting at the **Chatuchak Weekend Market** (p. 127). Plan to arrive before 10am to beat most of the crowds. You'll want to grab a coffee before arriving since the options at the market aren't great. But while the java is so-so, the snacking possibilities are endless, so come hungry. You'll need that fuel to power through the thousands of shops. When you've had enough of the stalls, heat or crowds, head back to the hotel for a cooling dip in the pool. If it isn't Saturday or Sunday, the market will be closed, so consider a morning stroll in leafy **Lumpini Park** (p. 120) where you can paddleboat and look for monitor lizards. **Soi Polo** (p. 95) is a short walk from Lumpini Park, and it's home to the best fried chicken in Bangkok. Head there for lunch.

Next on the itinerary for the day is Chinatown. **Wat Tramit** (p. 116) is home to a golden Buddha with a very high net worth, and you'll want to catch the sunset from the Golden Mount aka **Wat Saket** (p. 115). From there, it is time to eat. You won't have time to wait in the 4-hour line to get the famous crab omelet at **Jay Fai** (p. 95), and that's okay because **Krua Apsorn** (p. 96), right around the corner, makes a killer version that's just as good. Next, head to **Yaowarat Road** (p. 57) for more street eats and a great atmosphere. When you've had your fill, join the fray on **Soi Nana** (p. 131) where old is cool again, and 100-year-old shophouses (a tall, narrow home) are now great cocktail bars, like **Teens of Thailand** (p. 131) and **Tep Bar** (p. 132). There is enough here to keep you happy, and drinking, until the end of the night.

Day 4: Day Trip from Bangkok

The best option is to head for the ancient Thai capital of **Ayutthaya** ★★★ (p. 283) where 13th-century temples and ruins are on display, including a famous stone Buddha face ensnarled in a tree. It is a 90-minute drive from Bangkok and it's a lot of fun to rent bikes from a local vendor and tour the archeological site. If your trip to Southeast Asia includes a stop to see Angkor Wat in Siem Reap, Cambodia, the temples at Ayutthaya might feel redundant. If so, a trip to **Khao Yai National Park** ★ (p. 137), offers welcome greenery, local wineries, and a chance to see elephants in the wild. The journey to Khao Yai takes 1 hour and 50 minutes.

ANCIENT CAPITALS TOUR IN 1 WEEK

This 1-week itinerary, heading north from Bangkok, traces the nation's legacy back to its ancient seats of power. First, you'll head north to Ayutthaya—the capital of Siam until the late 18th century—and then you'll carry on via Phitsanulok to Sukhothai and Si Satchanalai, the birthplace of the Kingdom of Siam (it was here that Thai language, art, and architecture as we know it today began). Final stop is the ancient Lanna capital of Chiang Mai, which became a part of Siam/Thailand only in the early 20th century. The journey can be made by a combination of bus and train, though I'd recommend hiring a driver (see p. 408), which offers more comfort and flexibility.

Day 1: Bangkok to Ayutthaya

You can make the short trip north from Bangkok to Ayutthaya (see "Side Trips from Bangkok," in chapter 6) in about an hour and a half, leaving

Ancient Capitals Tours in 1 Week

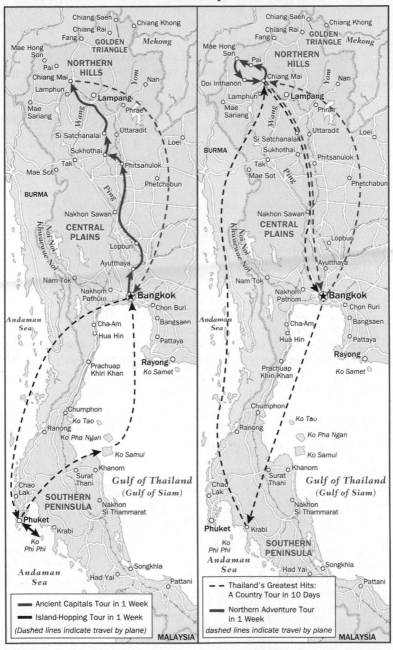

most of the day for sightseeing. The best way to see the sights and appreciate the expansiveness of the temples is to rent a bike, though driving is possible. Start pedaling for **Wat Phra Mahathat** ★★★ (p. 289), in the city center, which is the most striking of the Ayutthaya ruins, and **Wat Phra Si Sanphet** ★★ (p. 289), with its three slender stupas. If you have time, take a late-afternoon tour by longtail boat around the city island to see the more far-flung ruins. In the evening, dine at a **floating restaurant** on the riverside (p. 298). The ruins are illuminated in the evening, so a **night tour** (p. 287) is another option. Return to your Ayutthaya hotel.

Day 2: Bang Pa-In, Lopburi & Ayutthaya

Today, drive (or be driven) to two interesting destinations near Ayutthaya, allowing half a day for each site. **Bang Pa-In** (p. 292) was not an ancient Siamese capital, but was a royal retreat that was particularly popular in the reign of King Chulalongkorn (r. 1868–1910); the curious mix of Thai and Western colonial architecture makes a striking contrast Ayutthaya's ruins.

Grab a bowl of rice or noodles for a roadside lunch as you head north to **Lopburi** (p. 292), another favorite royal retreat in the era of King Narai. Visit **King Narai's Palace** (p. 293) and the museum on the grounds. Take a look at **Ban Vichayen** (p. 293), once home of King Narai's Western advisor, Constantine Phaulkon; and visit the town's mischievous macaques at **Phra Prang Sam Yot** (p. 293) before heading back to **Ayutthaya.**

Return to Ayutthaya for the night, grab a cold beer and take a stroll along **Naresuan Road Soi 2,** where you'll find street snacks, Western food, and live music.

Day 3: Phitsanulok

Check out early and drive to **Phitsanulok** (p. 294). Most of the day will be spent looking out over endless rice paddies during the 300-km (186-mile) journey. Check in at your hotel (p. 297), and then cross the river and stroll upstream to **Wat Yai** ★★ (p. 290), the town's only must-see attraction. In the evening, take a stroll back downstream beside the Nan River to the **Night Market** (p. 291); order some flying vegetables (a type of water spinach popular in Thai cooking) and have your camera ready to catch them being thrown some distance by the chef onto plates.

Day 4: Sukhothai

Drive to Sukhothai, check into your hotel and spend the rest of the day exploring **Sukhothai Historical Park** ★★★ (p. 299). As in Ayutthaya, it's fun to see the central area by rented bicycle, though for the furthest temples you'll need car or taxi. Start at the **Ramkhamhaeng National Museum** (p. 301) to get clued up on this remarkable site, and then head for the most important ruins at **Wat Phra Mahathat** ★★, **Wat Trap-hang Tong,** and **Wat Si Chum** (p. 289, 302, and 301).

Ask at your lodging if there is a **light and sound show** presentation at the historical park in the evening. If there is, it's a sight to remember; if not, it's on to dinner and drinks at the eccentric **Dream Café** ★ (p. 304).

Day 5: Si Satchanalai & Chiang Mai

Most of this day is spent wending your way north from the central plains into the northern hills, with a welcome break at the ruined temples of **Si Satchanalai** ★ (p. 297). The main temples to see here are **Wat Chang Lom** and **Wat Phra Si Ratana Mahathat** ★ (p. 305). On leaving the site, look out for another roadside lunch stop, and then sit back and watch the landscape become more dramatic as you make your way through the hills to **Chiang Mai** ★★★ (p. 311), capital of the north. This ancient but hip city has a great range of places to stay, so check out the listings (p. 327) to find somewhere that suits your budget.

You'll want to stretch your legs after a day in the car, so make for the **Night Bazaar** ★ (p. 345), and be prepared for furious bargaining as you shop for souvenirs. If hunger pangs overtake you while shopping, pop into **Anusarn Market** and follow your nose to the most appealing aroma. If you can wait, cross the river to **David's Kitchen** ★★ (p. 336), where you can enjoy their new wine bar, **Piccolo** (p. 349), after dinner for live music.

Day 6: Chiang Mai

For the last full day of this trip, you get to make a choice. If you'd like to get a sense of the city's long history, take a walk from the northeast corner to the southwest corner of Chiang Mai's Old City, winding through the back streets and taking in the principal temples: **Wat Chiang Man** ★, **Wat Chedi Luang** ★★★, and **Wat Phra Singh** ★★★ (p. 317 and 318). Stop off for lunch at either **Ruen Tamarind** ★ (p. 339) or **Huen Phen** ★★ (p. 340) along the way, and sit for a while in **Buak Had Park** at the end.

If, on the other hand, you've had enough history for one trip, you might like to spend the day learning how to prepare some tasty Thai dishes at the **Chiang Mai Thai Cookery School** ★ (p. 323). Other options include **boat trips** on the river, a visit to an **elephant camp** (p. 325) or a drive up Doi Suthep to visit the north's most famous temple—**Wat Phra That Doi Suthep** ★★★ (p. 320).

In the evening, wander around the Night Bazaar, engage in more drinking and dancing at the riverside bars, or pack your bags and take an early night.

Day 7: Chiang Mai to Bangkok

If you have time before your flight leaves, try to do some last-minute shopping in Chiang Mai or book one last massage. If there's no time, then bon voyage.

ISLAND-HOPPING TOUR IN 1 WEEK

This itinerary offers a glimpse at three of Thailand's most lauded beach destinations—Phuket, Ko Phi Phi, and Ko Samui. If you like what you see, you may be tempted to stay longer than suggested here—but don't overstay your visa!

Day 1: Bangkok to Phuket

A short flight and transfer from Bangkok will bring you to **Phuket** ★★ (p. 225), which has a range of accommodation from luxurious resorts to simple guesthouses. Make dinner reservations at **Suay** ★★ (p. 259) for a delicious taste of what southern Thailand has to offer. Enjoy a lazy meal and while plotting a week's island hopping.

Day 2: Phuket

Time for some serious rest and relaxation. Give yourself a day on the beach of your choice or by the pool, snacking from the pool bar or passing vendors on the beach.

In the evening, check out the street snack, raunchy bars, and discos along **Bangla Road** in the heart of Patong. The people-watching is phenomenal. Dinner at **Acqua** ★★★ (p. 254) is a much more highbrow way to spend the night, and the restaurant has the best wine list on the island.

Day 3: More of Phuket

Today you'll explore the island by car (and driver if necessary) and hit up the island's top beaches (p. 228), like Karon and Kamala. Stop off somewhere with scenic views, such as **On the Rock** ★★ on Karon Beach (p. 229), for a lazy lunch. From here head to the island's northeast to visit the **Phuket Elephant Sanctuary** (p. 237), the only reputable elephant sanctuary down south, where you can bathe and feed them.

As dusk falls, park up in **Phuket Town** and take a stroll around the colonnaded streets of Sino-Portuguese houses before dining at **Ka Jok See** ★★ (p. 257). If you're not ready for bed yet, head for **Dibuk House** (p. 261) for creative cocktails or **Catch Beach Club** (p. 261) for DJs and dancing on the sand.

Day 4: Day Trip to Ko Phi Phi

Just about every tour operator on Phuket runs day trips to **Ko Phi Phi** ★, so check the schedule of a few and sign up for one that appeals (there's not much difference one to the next).

During a boat ride of a couple of hours you'll see plenty of karst outcrops of the kind that typifies Phang Nga Bay. If it is open (parts have been closed for a few months each year to help with environmental protection), you'll probably be taken to **Phi Phi Leh** first (p. 274; it's the smaller, uninhabited island), where you'll have the chance to snorkel and explore Maya Bay, made famous by the movie *The Beach* (p. 274).

From here you'll go to **Phi Phi Don** (p. 274), which, depending on the season, might be heaving with vacationers. Lunch is usually included in these day trips, and a clamber up to the viewpoint over the back-to-back horseshoe bays brings a sight to treasure. Once back on Phuket, treat yourself to a meal to remember at **Acqua ★★★**, on Kalim Beach (p. 254).

Day 5: Phuket to Ko Samui

Hop a flight from Phuket to **Ko Samui ★★★** (p. 186), and you'll be able to compare the sand and sea color at Thailand's two most popular beach destinations. The fun begins at Samui airport, where you'll feel like you've landed in Disneyland in an open-air airport with perfectly manicured gardens.

If it's peace and quiet you're after, book into the **Six Senses ★★★** (p. 265), in the northeast corner of the island, where you can be sure nobody will disturb you except your personal butler. If you're more into partying, go for something in the heart of the action on Chaweng Beach.

Spend the rest of the day relaxing and settling into your resort, which will have plenty of activities on offer. Dine at your chosen resort as well, and get a sound night's sleep before the last full day of this tour.

Day 6: Ko Samui

There are two attractive options for today, from which you'll have to choose just one. The first is to hire a car (with driver if necessary) to explore the island's ring road. Along the way, you can take in such sights as phallic rocks, mummified monks, and waterfalls. The second alternative is to sign up for a tour of the **Ang Thong National Marine Park ★★** (p. 208), a cluster of rugged islands where you get to paddle a kayak through turquoise waters and scramble to the top of a hill for a breathtaking view.

However you spend the day, treat yourself to a celebratory meal in the evening at **Dining on the Rocks ★★★** (p. 202). If you still have energy, check out Chaweng's coolest bar, **CoCo Tam's** (p. 207), which is home to strong rum cocktails and the island's best fire show.

Day 7: Ko Samui to Bangkok

Put on your best white shirt to show off your suntan, take a cab to the airport, and zip back to Bangkok.

NORTHERN ADVENTURE TOUR IN 1 WEEK

With a distinct (and delicious) regional cuisine, fantastic temples, ethical elephant camps, and cooler temperatures, Northern Thailand is one of the most appealing parts of the country. Here's a good way to get to see a huge tract of the northern hills, as well as the ancient temples of Chiang Mai. You'll follow the Mae Hong Son Loop out to the northwest border with Myanmar. On the return leg, the route detours from the Loop to the highest point in Thailand, where you might even need a jacket.

Day 1: Bangkok to Chiang Mai

After a flight or an overnight train journey from Bangkok, arrive in Chiang Mai. Follow any of the Chiang Mai suggested in "Thailand's Greatest Hits."

Day 2: Chiang Mai to Pai

Book a car and driver or strike out on your own for 5 days, during which you will explore the north. Route 107 branches left at Mae Malai onto Route 1095. The road follows 762 switchbacks over an attractive range of hills before arriving at **Pai ★** (p. 360). Once a hippie hangout, Pai still has an easy-going vibe with opportunities to explore the leafy countryside. Check into the gorgeous **Belle Villa ★★** (p. 365) outside of town. If you need some exercise, walk up to **Wat Phra That Mae Yen** (p. 363), on a small hill to the east of town. In the evening, enjoy a tasty Thai meal (p. 365), and then check out the live music in the surrounding area.

Day 3: Pai to Mae Hong Son

It takes about half a day to negotiate the steep, narrow road through the mountains to **Mae Hong Son ★** (p. 359), and the journey is a full day after you make a recommended stop off to explore **Spirit Cave ★** (p. 367), located near Soppong.

In Mae Hong Son, check into the **Imperial ★★** or **Fern Resort ★★★** (p. 371), and then take a stroll around **Jong Kham Lake** and grab a few pictures of the Burmese-style temples of **Wat Jong Kham** and **Wat Jong Klang** (p. 370). Dine at **Fern Restaurant ★★** (p. 372) and get an early night, as tomorrow is a long day's drive.

Day 4: Mae Hong Son to Doi Inthanon

Today's journey starts out on the southern (and longest) part of the Mae Hong Son Loop, passing through Khun Yuam and Mae Sariang before branching off to Thailand's highest peak—**Doi Inthanon.** The long journey doesn't leave much time for sightseeing, but it's a good idea to take frequent, short breaks to stretch your legs. One such stop could be at the **World War II Museum,** in **Khun Yuam** (p. 373), while the **Riverhouse Resort,** in **Mae Sariang** (p. 374), is a good choice for lunch. About 80km (50 miles) east of Mae Sariang, turn left onto Route 1088, and then at the small town of **Mae Chaem,** turn right and climb to the peak of **Doi Inthanon ★★★** (p. 351). Stay in the log cabins at the national park headquarters, and eat at the neighboring cafe.

Day 5: Doi Inthanon to Chiang Mai

It takes only a couple of hours to drive from the summit of Doi Inthanon to Chiang Mai, so you can spend the morning exploring the upper reaches of the mountain, where it's much cooler than down in the valley. Walk the **Ang Khang Nature Trail** (p. 352), near the park headquarters, and notice the wealth of plant and bird life. On the way down, stop at the **Wachirathan and Sirithan Falls** for some photos, and at the **Mae Klang Falls** for a grilled chicken and sticky rice lunch on the fly.

Once back in Chiang Mai, unwind with a spa session, either at your hotel or at **Oasis Spa ★** (p. 326), in the town center.

For dinner, track down the stylish **David's Kitchen ★★** (p. 336) or eat your way through the food sections at the night market.

Day 6: Around Chiang Mai

Head straight up the city's guardian mountain to **Wat Phra That Doi Suthep ★★★** (p. 320), where you can listen to bells tinkling in the breeze and look down on the city sitting in the valley below. The classic image at this temple is of the gleaming stupa that stands in a marble courtyard at the heart of the complex.

At the base of the mountain, turn left onto the Superhighway, which sweeps around the north of the city, and look out for the turn to **Sankampaeng** (p. 347) along Route 1006. After breaking for lunch at **Fujian ★★★** (p. 338), keep driving east, stopping at any showroom or workshop that catches your eye. These present good opportunities not only for interesting photographs but souvenir shopping too.

You can complete your shopping in the evening at the **Night Bazaar ★** (p. 345), where you'll find everything from a 50¢ hill-tribe doll to a $5,000 antique.

Day 7: Chiang Mai to Bangkok

If you find that all your shopping won't fit into your bags, hurry to the post office and mail a box of goods back home. After that, head for the airport and wave goodbye to the friendly folks of northern Thailand.

THAILAND IN CONTEXT

*S*anuk mai? (Is it fun?) is a question frequently asked in Thailand, and the choice of question says a lot about the priorities of this fun-loving place. For Thais, anything that is not sanuk (fun) is not worth doing, so a positive response to the query (*"Sanuk, krup"* for men or *"Sanuk, ka"* for women) is bound to be met with a beaming smile, showing pleasure that outsiders are able to enjoy the Thai lifestyle.

The idea of fun permeates the culture, from slurping roadside noodles to finding creative and hair-raising ways to beat the traffic, or messaging friends animated emojis. So, while Thailand is no longer as undiscovered or as cheap as it was a decade ago, the magnetic attraction of its sparkling temples, idyllic beaches, mountain trails, fiery cuisine, and market culture is as strong as ever. Welcome to Thailand. Ready to have some fun?

THAILAND TODAY

Most of Thailand's 68 million people live in the countryside or in rural villages, where they earn a living in agriculture, predominantly by rice farming. However, as in many developing nations, there is a constant drift of people from the country to the city, and Bangkok, the nation's capital, is now home to over 8 million. The city's inhabitants are divided between wealthy Thais, often of Chinese ancestry, who are educated and hold formidable positions, and mostly low-income earners who came from the rural hinterland (termed "upcountry" by Thais). Hierarchy, or class, is an important distinction to Thais, who, like many of the region's nations, follow a loose version of India's caste system. Interestingly, as a foreigner, you are generally awarded a position of stature, regardless of your social standing back home, just as long you don't flout Thai etiquette (see "Thai Etiquette," p. 410).

So, who exactly are the Thai people? It's hard to say. There really are no historically "ethnic" Thais, but understanding some of Thailand's history helps to understand how it operates in the present day. Today's Thais emerged from waves of various immigrants going back around ten centuries. Central Thailand is a true mix of people; however, southern Thais have a closer ancestral affinity with Malays, while Thais in the north are more closely related to the Chinese, Laotians, and Burmese. The north is also home to small groups of Akha, Lisu, Lahu, Hmong, and Yao (p. 356)—brightly dressed hill-tribes who migrated south from China and Tibet during the past century. In the northeast province of Isan, Laotian influence prevails. The remaining population is divided between Chinese and Indians, Malays, Karens, Khmer, and Mons.

Despite this ethnic diversity, when it comes to religion, over 95% of Thailand's inhabitants are Buddhist, and there are over 40,000 temples scattered around the country—which might explain why many visitors feel some sort of temple fatigue. There are small pockets of Christians, particularly in the north, where missionaries have had limited success in converting hill-tribes. Muslim communities tend to be concentrated in the south, where unpredictable attacks by separatists on schools and government buildings have made the southern provinces off-limits to tourists for some years now.

Unlike its neighbors, Thailand was never colonized, a fact which has helped to keep its rich culture undiluted and has undoubtedly contributed to the country becoming Southeast Asia's most popular tourist destination. The 32 million or so visitors who arrive every year have made tourism the nation's biggest earner, an honor held not so long ago by rice, the staple food of the region. Thailand has a high number of return visitors, though exactly what endears them to the place varies according to individual taste. For some it's the glittering temples, for others it's a laid-back resort overlooking a tranquil beach, while for others it's the chance to go on a shopping spree or to study meditation or Thai cooking. For many, the most memorable moments are encounters with the Thai people, who are generally warm and welcoming; delighting in foreigners who take an interest in their heritage, language, food, and customs. Above all, the Thai people have an incredible sense of humor—a light-hearted spirit and a hearty chuckle go a long way toward making friends.

Given the vagaries of Thai politics (more on that below) and unpredictable weather patterns, it is difficult to foresee what is in store for the country, but the Thais' enduring resilience has held firm through these ups and downs.

THE MAKING OF THAILAND

EARLY HISTORY Archaeologists believe that Thailand was a major thoroughfare for *Homo erectus* en route from Africa to China and other parts of Asia. Stone tools, dating back some 700,000 years, have been excavated around Lampang in northern Thailand. Cave paintings, found throughout the country, are believed to originate as early as 2,000 B.C.; these show people dancing and hunting, as well as domesticated and wild animals in grass-like settings that appear to be rice paddies. Human remains have been excavated at many sites, the most famous of which, **Ban Chiang,** in the northeastern province of Udon Thani (p. 395), contained copper and bronze items dating back to 2,500 B.C., said to be the earliest examples of the Bronze Age in Thailand.

It is generally thought that many of the peoples of Southeast Asia migrated south from areas in both central and southern China. These people, known as the *Tai*, settled in what are now Vietnam, Laos, and Thailand, and shared a similar culture and language. Their descendants are the core bloodline of the Thai people of today. The early Tais lived in lowland valleys in groups of villages called *muang* that were ruled over by a *chao* or feudal lord. They lived in stilted houses, making a living from subsistence agriculture; in fact, little has changed in rural areas, and travelers can still witness this bucolic lifestyle.

THE DVARAVATI (MON) PERIOD From the 6th century, Southeast Asia underwent a gradual period of Indianization. Merchants and missionaries from India introduced Brahmanism and Buddhism to the region, as well as Indian political and social values—and art and architectural preferences. Many Tai groups adopted Buddhism, combining its doctrine with their own animistic beliefs. But the true significance of India's impact can be seen in the rise of two of the greatest Southeast Asian civilizations—the Mon and Khmer.

The **Mon** were the earliest known inhabitants of lower Burma, and it was they who introduced writing to the country as well as Buddhism. Around the 6th century A.D., their sphere of influence expanded, and they established Theravada Buddhism in Thailand. Mon settlements can be found at Lamphun, near Chiang Mai; Lopburi; Nakhon Pathom; Nakhorn Ratchasima (also called Khorat); and into Cambodia and northern Laos. Sadly, this once-proud race is now struggling to retain their culture in Myanmar in the face of military oppression, though many have fled to Thailand and live, mostly in refugee camps, near the border west of Kanchanaburi.

THE KHMERS By the early 9th-century A.D., the **Khmer Empire** had risen to power in Cambodia and spread deep into modern-day Thailand with might that often draws comparisons to the Roman Empire. With each conquering reign, magnificent Khmer temples honoring Hindu deities were constructed in outposts, thus expanding the Cambodian presence in the empire. Brahmanism, having been brought to Cambodia with traders from southern India, influenced not only Khmer religion and temple design (with the distinct corncob-shaped *prang*, or tower) but also government administration and social order. Conquering or forcing villages into their control, the Khmers placed their own leaders in important centers and supplied them with Khmer administrative officers. The empire was extremely hierarchical, with the king exerting supreme power and ruling from his capital.

Angkor, Cambodia's great ancient temple city, was built during the reign of Suryavarman II. It is believed the temples of **Pimai** (p. 393) and **Phanom Rung** (p. 402), in the Isan province, predated the Khmers' capital temple complex, thus influencing its style. For visitors who have not been to Angkor Wat in Cambodia, a trip to these beautifully restored temples is a memorable experience, and for admirers of Khmer architecture, they are unmissable.

The last great Khmer ruler, **Jayavarman VII** (1181–1219), extended the empire to its farthest limits—north to Vientiane in Laos, west to Myanmar (Burma), and down to the Malay peninsula. It was he who finally shifted

THAILAND IN CONTEXT   The Making of Thailand

Khmer ideology away from Hindu-based religion toward Buddhism, which inspired him to build extensive highways (portions of which are still evident today), rest houses for travelers and hospitals in the outer provinces. Jayavarman VII's death in 1220 marks Thailand's final break from Khmer rule. The last known Khmer settlement in Thailand is at **Wat Kamphaeng Laeng** in Phetchaburi (p. 179).

THE LANNA KINGDOM: THE NORTHERN TAIS By A.D. 1,000, the last of the Tai immigrants had traveled south from China to settle in northern Thailand. In 1239, a leader was born in Chiang Saen who would conquer and unite the northern Tai villages and create a great kingdom, which came to be known as Lanna, or "a million rice fields." Born to the king of Chiang Saen and a southern Chinese princess, **Mengrai** ascended the throne in 1259 and established the first capital of his new kingdom at Chiang Rai in 1263. He then conquered and assimilated what remained of Mon and Khmer settlements in northern Thailand, and, in 1296, shifted his base of power to **Chiang Mai** (p. 311), which translates as "New City."

The Lanna Empire would strengthen and ebb over the following centuries; at its height, in the late 15th century, it extended into Myanmar; Luang Prabang, in Laos; and Yunnan province, in China. Lanna society mixed animistic beliefs with Mon Buddhism. The Lanna era saw the rise of a scholarly Buddhism with strict adherence to orthodox doctrines. Its kings were advised by a combination of monks and astrologers and ruled over a well-organized bureaucracy.

SUKHOTHAI: THE DAWN OF SIAMESE CIVILIZATION While Mengrai was busy building Lanna, a small southern kingdom was simultaneously growing in power. A tiny kingdom based in Sukhothai remained in obscurity until the rise of founding father King Indraditya's second son, Ram, who helped to defeat an invasion from neighboring Mae Sot, on the Burmese border. He proved a powerful force, winning the respect of his people, and upon his coronation in 1279, **Ramkhamhaeng,** or "Ram the Bold," set the scene for what is recognized as the first truly Siamese civilization. This era is among the most artistically important in Thailand and is considered a cultural awakening.

In contrast to the Khmers' authoritarian approach, Ramkhamhaeng established himself as an accessible king. It is told he had a bell outside his palace for any subject to ring in the event of a grievance. The king himself would come to hear the dispute and would make a just ruling on the spot. He was seen as a fatherly and fair ruler who allowed his subjects immense freedoms. His kingdom expanded rapidly, it seems; through voluntary subjugation, it reached as far west as Pegu in Myanmar, north to the Laotian cities of Luang Prabang and Vientiane, and south beyond Nakhon Si Thammarat, to include portions of present-day Malaysia.

After centuries of divergent influences from external powers, we see for the first time an emerging culture that is uniquely Siamese. A patron of the arts, King Ramkhamhaeng commissioned many great Buddha images. While few sculptures from his reign remain today, those that do survive display a cultivated creativity. For the first time, physical features of the Buddha are Siamese in manner. Images have graceful, sinuous limbs and robes, insinuating a radiant and flowing motion; examples can be seen today in the **Sukhothai Historical Park** (p. 299). Ramkhamhaeng initiated the many splendid architectural achievements of Sukhothai and nearby **Si Satchanalai** (p. 299). He is also credited with developing the modern Thai written language, derived from Khmer and Mon examples of an archaic South Indian script. Upon Ramkhamhaeng's death in 1298, he was succeeded by kings who would devote their attentions to religion rather than affairs of state. During the 14th century, Sukhothai's brilliant spark faded almost as quickly as it had ignited.

AYUTTHAYA: SIAM ENTERS THE GLOBAL SCENE   In the decades that followed, the nation faltered with no figurehead, until the arrival of U Thong—the son of a wealthy Chinese merchant family. Crowning himself **Ramathibodi,** he set up a capital at **Ayutthaya,** on the banks of the Lopburi River (p. 286). From there, he set out to conquer what was left of the Khmer outposts, eventually engulfing the remains of Sukhothai. The new kingdom combined the strengths of its population—Tai military manpower and labor, Khmer bureaucratic sensibilities, and Chinese commercial talents—to create a strong empire. Ayutthaya differed greatly from its predecessor. Following Khmer models, the king rose above his subjects atop a huge pyramid-shaped administration. He was surrounded by a divine order of Buddhist monks and Brahman sanctities. During the early period of development, Ayutthaya rulers created strictly defined laws, caste systems, and labor units. Foreign traders from China, Japan, and Arabia were required to sell the first pick of their wares to the king for favorable prices. Leading trade this way, the kingdom was buttressed by great riches. Along the river, a huge fortified city was built with temples that equaled those in Sukhothai. This was the **Kingdom of Siam** that the first Europeans, the Portuguese, encountered in 1511.

But peace and prosperity would be disrupted with the coming Burmese invasion that would take Chiang Mai (part of the Lanna kingdom) in 1557, and finally Ayutthaya in 1569. The Lanna kingdom that King Mengrai and his successors built was never to regain its former glory. Fortunately, Ayutthaya had a better fate with the rise of one of the greatest leaders in Thai history. **Prince Naresuan,** born in 1555, was the son of the puppet Tai king—placed in Ayutthaya by the Burmese. Although Naresuan was a direct descendent of Sukhothai leaders, it was his early battle accomplishments that distinguished him as a ruler. Having spent many years in Burmese captivity, he returned to Ayutthaya to raise armies to challenge the Burmese. His small militias proved inadequate, but in a historic battle scene in 1593, Naresuan, atop an elephant, challenged the Burmese crown prince and defeated him with a single blow.

With the Tais back in control, Ayutthaya continued through the following 2 centuries in grand style. Foreign traders—Portuguese, Dutch, Arab, Chinese, Japanese, and English—not set up companies and missions, but some also attained positions of power within the administration. Despite numerous internal conflicts over succession and struggles between foreign powers for court influence, the kingdom managed to proceed steadily. While its Southeast Asian neighbors were falling under colonial rule, the court of Siam was extremely successful in retaining its own sovereignty. It has the distinction of being the only Southeast Asian nation never to have been colonized—a point of great pride for Thais today.

The final demise of Ayutthaya would be brought about by two more Burmese invasions. The first, in 1760, was led by **King Alaunghpaya,** who would fail, retreating after he was shot by one of his own cannons. But 6 years later, two Burmese contingents, one from the north and one from the south, would besiege the city. The Burmese pillaged and plundered the kingdom, capturing fortunes and laborers for the return to Burma. The Thai people still hold a bitter grudge against the Burmese for these atrocities.

THE RISE OF BANGKOK: THE CHAKRI DYNASTY The fall of Ayutthaya forced the Siamese to move their capital. **Taksin,** a provincial governor of Tak in the northern central plains, rose to power on military excellence and charisma. Taksin was crowned king in 1768 and moved the capital to **Thonburi** (p. 58), an already well-established settlement on the western bank of the Chao Phraya River, now a suburb of modern Bangkok. Within 3 years he'd reunited the land from the previous kingdom, but his rule would not last. Over time he was able to successfully propagate the false notion that he was in fact divinely appointed as ruler. Legend tells that Taksin suffered from paranoia and his claims to divinity offended many, including the monastic order. His own wife, children, and monks were purported to have been murdered on his orders. Regional powers acted fast. He was swiftly kidnapped, placed in a velvet sack, and beaten to death with a sandalwood club—so no royal blood touched the soil. He was then buried secretly in his own capital. These same regional powers turned to the brothers Chakri and Surasi, great army generals (*phraya*), who had recaptured the north from Burma, to lead the land. In 1782, Phraya Chakri ascended the throne as **King Rama I,** founder of today's Chakri dynasty.

The Thai capital was relocated by King Rama I across the Chao Phraya River to the settlement of **Bangkok** (p. 54), where he built the Grand Palace, royal homes, administrative buildings, and great temples such as Wat Phra Kaew. Immigrant Chinese, who previously occupied the space, were moved from the riverside location to Yaowarat, where they remain today. The city teemed with canals as the river played a central role in trade and commerce. Siam was now a true confluence of cultures, no longer limited to the Tai, Mon, and Khmer descendants of former powers. Despite military threats from all directions, the kingdom continued to grow through a succession of kings from the new royal bloodline. Rama I, and his successors, expanded the kingdom to the borders of present-day Thailand and beyond. Foreign relations in the modern sense were developed during this early era with formal ties to European powers.

King Mongkut, Rama IV (r. 1851–68) had a unique upbringing. During 27 years as a monk (joining the monkhood at some stage of their life is a tradition all Thai men are expected to follow, even today), he developed an avid curiosity, which, throughout his reign, led to enormous innovation, dynamism, and appreciation for the West. It was King Mongkut who employed Anna Leonowens (who was the inspiration behind the character Anna, in *The King and I*) as an English tutor for his children. Her account of court life is still considered grossly inaccurate and offensive by Thais; indeed, anyone found with copies of the book, or the movies—all of which are banned—can be tried for *lèse-majesté*.

Mongkut's eldest son, **King Chulalongkorn, Rama V** (r. 1868–1910), led Siam into the 20th century as an independent nation, by establishing an effective civil service, formalizing global relations, and introducing industrialization. It was during his reign that all of Siam's neighbors fell under the colonial yoke, while Chulalongkorn managed to play the European powers off against each other and thus maintain Siam's independence.

THAILAND IN THE 20TH & 21ST CENTURIES The reign of **King Prajadhipok, Rama VII** (r. 1925–35), saw the growth of the urban middle class, and the increasing discontent of a powerful elite. By the beginning of his reign, economic failings and bureaucratic bickering weakened the position of the monarchy, which was severely affected by the Great Depression. In 1932, a group of midlevel officials instigated a coup d'état. Prajadhipok abdicated in 1935 marking the end of an absolute monarchy in Thailand.

Thailand's ninth king and the one most Westerners are familiar with, was **Bhumibol Adulyadej, Rama IX.** He played an active role in stabilizing the nation, acting as a figurehead from 1946 until his passing in October 2016, holding the title world's longest reigning monarch. A compassionate man, he commanded (and still does posthumously) enormous loyalty from the Thai people by promoting cultural traditions and supporting rural reforms, especially among the poor. Today, many Thais still refer to him as "father" and his December 5th birthday marks a national celebration of Father's Day. Rama IX was followed by his son, **Maha Vajiralongkorn, Rama X.** He is a complicated figure who has been married and divorced three times; much of his adult life has been spent living in Europe. During his father's illness, he took over many of the royal duties and the transition of power was smooth.

The push for democracy still labors on today. The country's original constitution, written in 1932, was more a tool for leaders to manipulate than a political blueprint. Over the following decades, government leadership changed hands fast and frequently. The army has always had an imposing influence, most likely the result of its ties to the common people as well as its strong unity. In 1939, the nation adopted the name "Thailand"—land of the free.

During World War II, the fledgling democracy was stalled in the face of the Japanese invasion in 1941. Thailand speedily submitted, choosing collaboration over conflict, even going so far as to declare war against the Allied powers. But at the war's end, no punitive measures were taken against Thailand, thanks to the Free Thai Movement organized by Ambassador Seni Pramoj in

Washington, D.C., who had placed the declaration of war in his desk drawer rather than delivering it.

Thailand avoided direct involvement in the Vietnam War but assisted the Americans by providing runways for their B-52s and storage for the toxic defoliant Agent Orange. In turn, it benefited enormously from U.S. military-built infrastructure. The United States pumped billions into the Thai economy, bringing riches to many but further impoverishing the rural poor, who were hit hard by the resulting inflation. Communism became an increasingly attractive political philosophy to the poor as well as to liberal-minded students and intellectuals. A full-scale insurrection seemed imminent, and this naturally fueled further political repression by the military rulers.

In June 1973, thousands of Thai students demonstrated in the streets, demanding a new constitution, one with democratic principles. Tensions grew until October, when armed forces attacked a demonstration at Thammasat University in Bangkok, killing 69 students and wounding 800, paralyzing the capital with terror.

The constitution was restored, and a new government was elected. Many were still unhappy the protests persisted for 3 years until the army seized control in an effort to impose order, and another brief experiment with democracy was at an end. **Thanin Kraivichien** was installed as prime minister of a new right-wing government, which suspended freedom of speech and the press, further polarizing Thai society.

In 1980, **Prem Tinsulanonda** became prime minister, and during the following 8 years he managed to bring remarkable political and economic stability to Thailand. The Thai economy grew steadily through the 1980s, fueled by Japanese investment and the departure of Chinese funds from Hong Kong.

Things changed dramatically in July 1997, when Thailand became the first victim of the Asian Economic Crisis. Virtually overnight, the baht lost 20% of its value, followed by similar downturns in money markets throughout other major Asian nations.

In January 2001, the Thai people elected Populist candidate **Thaksin Shinawatra.** A self-made telecom tycoon, ex-police officer, and member of one of the nation's wealthiest families, Thaksin came into office promising economic restructuring and an end to widespread corruption and cronyism. Thaksin's popularity grew from aggressive reforms that brought the country out of debt. In November 2003, Thailand paid back its $12 billion loan to the International Monetary Fund, money borrowed during the 1997 currency crisis. The prime minister also waged a "War on Poverty and Dark Influence," cracking down on mafia activity and bribery; however, his tactics were often heavy-handed and wholly ignored human rights. Most glaringly, he is held responsible for the on-the-spot killing of suspected drug traffickers (estimates claim that as many as 3,000 people were shot dead with no legal process during his administration). Similarly, Thaksin's aggressive response to Muslim unrest in the far south came under international criticism.

In September 2006, the Royal Thai army, backed by the King, staged a bloodless coup d'état and Thaksin was ousted overnight. During 2007, under the military junta, democratic reforms were stalled, press freedoms were curbed, and Thaksin and his family were convicted in absentia for fraud.

THAILAND–PRESENT DAY Recent years have been characterized by the conflict between the People's Alliance for Democracy (PAD), better known as the "yellow shirts," and the similar-sounding United Front for Democracy against Dictatorship (UDD), or the "red shirts"—supporters of Thaksin. In the most recent general election of July 2011, **Yingluck Shinawatra** (Thaksin's sister) of the Pheua Thai Party was voted into power as Thailand's first female prime minister. During her time as prime minister, she couldn't shake the belief that many Thais shared: Her brother was pulling strings from afar and joining political meetings via Skype.

Yingluck made two disastrous decisions during her 3 years in office. First, she created a rice-pledging scheme to boost the economies of the local farmers. Essentially, the plan was for farmers to sell the crop to the government at above market rates, which would force the global price of rice to rise. This backfired when India, which was watching all this from afar, lifted its ban on rice exports, and flooded the international food market. Rice prices in Thailand sank, as did the economy. The other controversial move was to introduce a bill that would pardon a long list of politicians, including her brother. Protests began in October 2013, and heavily impacted life in Bangkok; naysayers occupied Lumpini Park for months. Finally, in January 2014, Yingluck declared a state of emergency. Amid heavy boycotts, she and nine of her ministers were forced out by the courts on May 7, 2014. Just over 2 weeks later, the military launched a coup and took over Thailand for the 12th time since the absolute monarchy ended in 1932. To this day over 4 years later, the junta is still ruling.

In August 2014, the former Commander-in-Chief of the Royal Thai Army Prayut Chan-o-cha became the 29th prime minister. Almost 1 year later, on August 17, 2015, a bomb exploded at Bangkok's Erawan Shrine killing 20 people, mostly Chinese tourists. Two suspects were captured, but little was or has been released about them. Thailand was dealt another devastating blow when the beloved Rama IX died on October 13, 2016, after years of declining health. In the year following his death, 10,000 mourners a day came to view his coffin at the Grand Palace, and the country entered a year-long state of mourning, with most people choosing to wear black for several months or a full year. An elaborate, multiday state funeral was held at the Grand Place in October 2017 and the year of mourning ended.

As for Prime Minister Prayut Chan-o-cha he has ruled with a heavy hand, quashing press freedoms and protests, and jailing political opponents. Though a new military drafted constitution was signed in April of 2017, one designed to set the country on a path towards elections and restore democracy, as we go to press elections have yet to occur and have been rescheduled several times. Despite a wild and sometimes unstable political history, Thailand is a safe place to live and visit, and political flare ups tend to happen behind closed doors.

RELIGION IN THAILAND

Thai culture cannot be fully appreciated without some understanding of Buddhism, which is practiced by 95% of the population. The Buddha was a great Indian sage who lived in the 6th-century B.C. He was born **Siddhartha Gautama,** a prince who was carefully sheltered from the outside world. When he ventured beyond the palace walls, he encountered an old man, a sick man, a corpse, and a wandering monk. He concluded that a never-ending cycle of suffering and relief exists everywhere. Sensing that the pleasures of the physical world were impermanent and the cause of pain, he shed his noble life and went into the forest to live as a solitary ascetic. Nearing starvation, however, he soon realized this was not the path to happiness, so he turned instead to the "Middle Way," a more moderate practice of meditation, compassion, and understanding. One night, while meditating under a Bodhi tree after being tormented by Mara, the goddess of death, Siddhartha Gautama became enlightened. With his mind free of delusion, he gained insight into the nature of the universe and viewed the world without defilement, craving, or attachment but as unified and complete. He explained his newfound ideology, **The Dhamma,** to his first five disciples, at Deer Park in India, in a sermon now known as "The Discourse on Setting into Motion the Wheel of the Law."

After the death of Buddha, two schools were formed. The oldest, **Theravada** (Doctrine of the Elders), is sometimes referred to, less accurately, as Hinayana (the Lesser Vehicle). This school of thought prevails in Sri Lanka, Myanmar, Thailand, Laos, and Cambodia. It focuses on the enlightenment of the individual with emphasis on the monastic community and the monks who achieve nirvana in this lifetime. The other methodology, **Mahayana** (the Greater Vehicle), is practiced in China, Korea, and Japan, and subscribes to a notion of all of mankind attaining enlightenment at the same time.

The basic document of Thai, or Theravada, Buddhism is the **Pali canon,** which was documented in writing for the first time in the 1st century A.D. The doctrine is essentially an ethical and psychological system in which no deity plays a role in the mystical search for the intuitive realization of the *oneness* of the universe. While it is a religion without a god, Theravada traditions follow a certain hierarchy based on age among monks and practitioners. The practice requires individuals to find truth for themselves through an inward-looking practice cultivated by meditation and self-examination. Although interpretation varies, the Buddha's final words are said to be "strive on with diligence."

If there is no deity to worship, then what, you might ask, are people doing in temples prostrating themselves before images or statues of the Buddha? Worshipers bow three times before the image: Once for the Buddha himself, once for the *sangha* (the order of monks), and once for the *dhamma* (truth). Prostrations at the temple are also a way to honor Buddhist teachers and those who pass on the tradition, to show respect for the Buddha's meditative repose and equanimity, and to offer reverence for relics (most temples house important artifacts, especially in the stupa).

Buddhism has one aim only: To abolish suffering. Buddhist practice offers a path to rid oneself of the causes of suffering, which are desire, malice, and delusion. Practitioners eliminate craving and ill will by exercising self-restraint and showing kindness to all sentient beings. Monks and members of the Buddhist Sangha, or community, are revered as those most diligently working toward enlightenment and the attainment of wisdom.

Other aspects of the philosophy include the law of karma, whereby every action has an effect and the energy of past action, good or evil, continues forever and is "reborn." Consequently, *tam bun* (merit making)—basically performing any act of kindness no matter how small—is taken very seriously.

Merit can be gained by entering the monkhood, which most Thai males do for a few days or months to study Buddhist scriptures and practice meditation. But these days it can equally be gained by transferring frequent flyer points to a charity or feeding a street dog.

When monks in Thailand go on their **alms** round each dawn, they are not seen as begging, but as giving Buddhist devotees an opportunity to make merit. When making merit, it is the motive that is important—the intention in the mind at the time of action—which determines the karmic outcome, not the action itself. Buddhism calls for self-reliance; the individual embarks alone on the Noble Eightfold Path to Nirvana with the aim "to cease to do evil, learn to do good, cleanse your own heart."

Opportunities to study Buddhism or practice meditation in Thailand with an English-speaking teacher are limited, though some programs are designed particularly for foreigners, such as at **Wat Suan Mokkh** in Chaiya (p. 184) and **Wat Rampoeng** in Chiang Mai (p. 324).

Most Chinese and Vietnamese living in Thailand follow Mahayana Buddhism, and several temples and monasteries in the country support this tradition as well.

ART & ARCHITECTURE

The **Sukhothai period** (13th–14th c.) is regarded as a period of notable achievement in Thai culture, with big advancements made in art and architecture. One of the lasting legacies of the Sukhothai period is its sculpture, characterized by the graceful aquiline-nosed Buddha either sitting in meditation or, more strikingly, walking contemplatively. These Buddha-figures are considered to be some of the most beautiful representations ever produced of this genre. The city of Sukhothai itself is said to be an expansion of the decorative style typified by Khmer works. With the inclusion of Chinese wood-building techniques, polychromatic schemes, and elegant lines from Japanese-influenced carvings, the *wat,* or temple—with its murals, Buddha sculptures, and spacious design—is defined as the first "pure" Thai Buddhist style. During this period came the mainstays of Thai temple architecture: The *chedi* (stupa), *bot, viharn, prang, mondop,* and *prasat.*

The dome-shaped *chedi*—better known in the West as stupa—is the most highly regarded edifice here. It was originally used to enshrine relics of the

Buddha but later included holy men and kings. A stupa consists of a dome or tumulus, constructed atop a round base (drum), and enveloped by a cubical chair, representing the seated Buddha, over which is the *chatra* (umbrella) in one or several (usually nine) tiers.

The *bot* (*ubosoth* or *uposatha*) is the ordination hall, which is generally off-limits to women. It consists of either one large nave or a nave with lateral aisles built on a rectangular design with Buddha images mounted on a raised platform. At the end of each ridge of the roof are graceful finials, called *chofa* (meaning "sky tassel"), which are reminiscent of animal horns but are thought to represent celestial geese or the **Garuda** (a mythological animal ridden by the god Shiva). The triangular gables are adorned with gilded wooden ornamentation and glass mosaics.

The *viharn* (*vihaan* or *vihara*) is the assembly hall where the abbot conducts sermons. The design is similar to that of the *bot*, and the hall is also used to house Buddha images, but it is generally a larger building. The *prang,* which originated with the corncob tower of the Khmer temple, is a form of stupa that can be seen in many temples at Sukhothai and Ayutthaya. The *mondop* may be made of wood or brick. On a square pillared base, the pyramidal roof is formed by a series of receding stories, enriched with elaborate decoration, and tapering off to a pinnacle. It may be used to enshrine holy objects, or as a library for religious ceremonial objects, as it does at Wat Phra Kaew (p. 104) in Bangkok.

The *prasat* (castle) is a direct stylistic descendent of the Khmer temple, with its round-topped spire and Greek-cross layout. At the center is a square sanctuary with a domed *sikhara* (tower) and four porchlike antechambers that project from the main building, giving the whole temple a multileveled contour. The *prasat* serves either as the royal throne hall or as a shrine for venerated objects, such as the *prasat* of Wat Phra Kaew in Bangkok, which enshrines the statues of the kings of the present dynasty.

Less recognized architectural structures include the *ho trai* (library), which houses palm-leaf books; the *sala,* an open pavilion used for resting; and the *ho rakhang,* the Thai belfry.

The Ayutthaya and Bangkok periods further cultivated the Sukhothai style by refining materials and design. The **Ayutthaya period** saw a Khmer revival when Ayutthayan kings built a number of neo-Khmer-style temples and edifices. The art and architecture evident in early Bangkok allude to the dominant styles of the former capital. After the demise of Ayutthaya in the 18th century, the capital was established briefly at Thonburi before being moved across the Chao Phraya River to Bangkok, where replicas of some of Ayutthaya's most distinctive buildings were constructed. Khmer, Chinese, northern Thai, and Western elements were fused to create temples and palaces in what is now known as the **Rattanakosin style,** of which the key features are height and lightness, best exemplified at Wat Phra Kaew and the Grand Palace (p. 106) in Bangkok.

During the latter days of the Ayutthaya period, Jesuit missionaries and French merchants brought with them distinctly baroque fashions. Although

Thailand was initially reluctant to foster relations with the West, these European influences eventually became evident in architecture. **Neoclassical devices** were increasingly apparent, notably in the Marble Temple (p. 113), in Bangkok, which was started by King Chulalongkorn in 1900 and designed by his half-brother, Prince Naris. Thanks to a number of Italian engineers, Art Deco became an important style in Bangkok and is seen in the arched Hua Lampong Rail Station. The style is so ubiquitous that many writers use the term **Thai Deco** to describe certain buildings.

Today's Bangkok is almost indistinguishable from other Asian capitals; a mix of Thai classical, modernist, neo-Greco, Bauhaus, and Chinese shop-house styles all meld into a unique, urban mishmash. Sadly, vernacular styles, such as old Thai wooden houses, were largely cleared decades ago and the *klongs* (canals) filled to give way to high-rise offices and apartments. Today, efforts are being made by a new generation of educated Thais to bring architectural integrity to the city. From 100-year-old shophouses that are now hotels to World War II-era warehouses converted to creative spaces, this is one of the most exciting times for blooming creativity with a heavy hand for preservation.

EATING & DRINKING

Food is one of the true joys of Thailand. If you are not familiar with Thai cuisine, imagine the best of Asian food ingredients—fragrant spices, sweet coconut or citrus, ripe red and green chilies—combined with sophistication. You can find all styles of Thai (and international) cooking in Bangkok, from southern fiery curries to smooth northern cuisine. Basic ingredients range from shellfish, fresh fruits, vegetables—asparagus, beansprouts, morning glory (water spinach), baby eggplant, bamboo shoots, and countless types of mushrooms—and spices, including lemongrass, mint, chili, garlic, and cilantro (coriander). Thai cooking also incorporates coconut milk, curry paste, peanuts, and a large variety of noodles and rice.

Among the popular dishes you'll find are *tom yum goong,* a Thai hot-and-sour shrimp soup; *satay,* charcoal-broiled chicken, beef, or pork strips skewered on a bamboo stick and dipped in a peanut-coconut sauce; spring rolls (similar to egg rolls but thinner); *larb,* a spicy chicken or ground-beef salad with mint-and-lime flavoring; spicy salads, made with a breadth of ingredients, but most have a fiery dressing made with onion, chili pepper, lime juice, and fish sauce; pad Thai, rice noodles fried with shrimp, eggs, peanuts, and fresh beansprouts; *khao soi,* a northern-style Burmese soup with light yellow curry and layers of crispy and soft noodles; a wide range of explosive curries; and *tod man pla,* fried fish cakes with a sweet dipping sauce.

Seafood is a great treat in Thailand and is served at a fraction of the cost one would pay elsewhere. In the south, Phuket lobster (a giant langoustine) has no pincers and a firm trunk and is generally different from the coldwater variety you'll get in Maine or Brittany.

A word of caution: Thais enjoy incredibly spicy food, much hotter than is tolerated in even the most piquant Western cuisine. Protect your palate by saying *"Mai khin phet,"* meaning "I do not take it spicy." Also note that most Thai and Chinese food, particularly in the cheaper restaurants and food stalls, is cooked with a lot of MSG (known locally as *phong churot*), and it's almost impossible to avoid. If you don't want MSG, say *"mai sai phong churot."* However, if you're dining in restaurants where foreign clientele are regulars, the kitchen usually will have made allowances for this.

Thailand's Amazing Fruit

Familiar fruits are pineapple (sometimes served with salt and chili powder), mangoes, bananas, guava, papaya, coconut, and watermelon. Less familiar options are durian (in season during May and June, this Thai favorite smells like old socks); mangosteen (a purplish, hard-skinned fruit with delicate, white segments that melt in the mouth but stain your hands and clothes, and is available Apr–Sept); and jackfruit (large and green with a thick, thorny skin that envelops tangy-flavored flesh and is available in June and July). The pink litchi, which ripens in April, and the smaller tan-skinned longan, which comes in season in July, have very sweet white flesh. Other unusual fruits include tamarind (a sour, pulpy seed in a pod that you can eat fresh or candied); rambutan (small, red, and hairy with transparent sweet flesh clustered around a woody seed, available May–July); and pomelo (similar to a sweet and thirst-quenching grapefruit, available Aug–Nov). Some of these fruits are served as salads; pomelo and raw green papaya salads, for example, are excellent.

All-Day Eating

Thais take eating very seriously and love to snack nonstop. Business lunches consist of several dishes, and some hotels offer blowout buffets at very reasonable prices. That being said, most casual diners settle for a one-course rice or noodle dish at lunchtime. Most restaurants throughout the country offer lunch from 11am to 1pm; in Bangkok, street eateries, markets, and food stalls are packed during this busy time.

Thais usually stop at one of the country's many street-side food stalls for a large bowl of noodle soup (served with meat, fish, or poultry), or dine at a department store food court where they can buy snacks from many different vendors and have a seat in an air-conditioned environment. A note on etiquette: You won't see Thais walking down the street munching. Sit while you eat.

Dinner is the main meal, and for a Thai family this usually consists of a soup *(gaeng jued);* a curried dish *(gaeng phet);* a steamed, fried, stir-fried, or grilled dish *(nueng, thod, paad,* or *yaang);* a side dish of salad or condiments *(krueang kiang);* steamed rice *(khao nueng);* and some fruit *(ponlamai).* Thais always share a variety of dishes (balanced as sweet, salty, sour, bitter, and spicy).

All dishes are served together and are sampled by diners in no particular order. Thai cuisine has no concept of "courses," and dishes come when they are hot and ready, which means some people at the table are served well before others. Restaurants that cater to foreigners generally manage the coursing system a bit better, but it's not always a guarantee that appetizers arrive first.

Eating Tips

To give an idea of how much it will cost to fill up on local food or try fancy spots, restaurants are divided into categories: **Expensive** means that a meal for one without drinks will probably cost more than 1,000B; in **moderate** places, expect to pay from 999B to 500B; **inexpensive** means you'll pay less than 500B per person—often as little as 40B a plate!

Smart dining tip 1: Mondays in The Kingdom are street cleaning days, so in most areas, you won't find any street food. Push-carts with fruit are around, but it's generally wise to plan your street meals for the other 6 days of the week.

Smart dining tip 2: Especially if you plan to eat lots of street food—and you should!—you should learn a few key protein words in Thai (see chapter 15). When in doubt: Look around the stall. Many vendors will use cartoon animals in their sign to indicate what they're selling or will have a small child's toy in the shape of, let's say a chicken if that's what they sell.

Smart dining tip 3: Thais are practical about table manners when dining casually. If something is best eaten with the hands, then eat with your hands. If there are seeds or bones, pick them out of your mouth and put them into a tissue. Most meals are served family-style, and it's a big no-no, not to mention unsanitary, to use your personal spoon to take food from the communal plates.

Smart dining tip 4: Most meals are a bit of East meets West: Single-serve noodle soups are eaten with chopsticks and a Chinese spoon; rice dishes are eaten with a spoon and fork. Hold the spoon in your right hand and use the fork in the left to load the spoon for delivery.

Drinking Culture

Liquor and beer are available from 11am to 2pm and 5pm to midnight at 7-Eleven stores and supermarkets. Most bars serve alcohol until around 1am and everyone shuts down sales of alcohol on Buddhist holidays. Thailand

HOW TO IDENTIFY clean STREET STALLS

The Thai government periodically checks street vendors for cleanliness, awarding those who pass a green and blue sign that says, "Clean Food Good Taste." There is no need to bypass a stall that doesn't have this emblem. This inspection isn't closely regulated and bribes are common. Instead, use common sense. The first indicator of a clean place is a crowd of people, ensuring that each dish will be made fresh to order and not sitting out in the elements. Next, avoid consuming raw fish and remember that most stalls sell a single dish, so they need to select the best ingredients to gain a competitive edge. Street food vendors listed in this book are well-established and have a long-standing reputation for cleanliness. If you're still hesitant, book a tour with one of the reputable guides listed in Bangkok (p. 89) or Chiang Mai (p. 323).

brews several beers; the best known is Singha, though Leo and Chang are popular brands. Imported beers, such as Heineken, are also widely available. Despite sky-high taxes that drive up the price, wine is becoming a favorite among the country's middle class. While not award-winning or all that tasty, local Thai and regional vintages are increasing in quality and popularity.

Mekong and Sang Som are two of the more popular local "whiskeys," even though the latter is more like rum (fermented from sugarcane). "Whiskey" is a bit of a blanket term that covers most dark spirits. Thai whiskeys are nowhere near as nice or smooth as American or Scottish counterparts.

WHEN TO GO

The high season for tourism is mid-October through mid-February. Prices skyrocket and hotels fill up then, particularly around Christmas and New Year, so make advanced reservations. Off-season weather, however, is not intolerable, and some travelers report joyfully trading the crowded beaches and elevated prices of high season for a rain shower or two.

Thailand has two distinct climate zones: **Tropical** in the south and **tropical savanna** in the north. **Hot season** lasts from March to May, with temperatures averaging in the upper 90s Fahrenheit (mid-30s Celsius), with April being the hottest month. Expect sporadic rains and avoid the north in March. In recent years, dense haze has blocked views and caused respiratory problems.

Rainy season often begins in June and lasts until late October or even mid-November. The average temperature is 84°F (29°C) with 90% humidity. While the rainy season brings heavy downpours, it is rare to see an all-day episode. From June to September, daily showers usually come in the late afternoon or evening for 2 to 3 hours. Trekking in the north is not recommended during this time due to slippery conditions and icky leeches.

Cool season is from November to February with temperatures from 70s°F to low 80s°F (26°C–29°C), with infrequent showers. Daily temperatures can drop as low as 60°F (16°C) in Chiang Mai and 41°F (5°C) in the hills; one or two nights may even see frost.

The **Southern Thai Peninsula** has intermittent showers year-round and daily downpours during the rainy season (temperatures average in the low 80s Fahrenheit/30s Celsius). Phuket's high seasons runs from November to April. Ko Samui's best weather lasts from about December to February, though it's usually very pleasant until October when tropical storms arrive. If your heart is set on diving, do diligent research (or call PADI) before booking. And remember: The knowledge of local operators or hotel concierge teams almost always supersedes that of Google.

Calendar of Events

The annual water war known as Songkran gets all the glory but there are a host of other religious and secular events not to miss, like a vegetarian festival that gets surprisingly gruesome, incredible Chinese New Year parades, and the peaceful and restorative tradition of Loy Krathong. Many of Thailand's holidays are based on the Thai lunar calendar, falling on the full moon of each month; check with the Tourism Authority of Thailand (TAT; www.tat.or.th) for the current year's schedule. Chapter 12, "Chiang Mai," includes a list of festivals and events specific to the north.

On National and Buddhist holidays and polling days, government offices, banks, small shops, and offices—as well as some restaurants and bars—usually close. Public transport still runs on holidays, though.

JANUARY TO MARCH

Thailand celebrates New Year's Day the same as the rest of the world. At the end of January or early February, **Chinese New Year** is celebrated vivid parades, firecrackers, and Lion Dances associated with this holiday. Things get most raucous on Bangkok's Yaowarat Road, in the heart of Chinatown. The **Flower Festival** in Chiang Mai takes place the first week of February, which is a beautiful time (it's when the north is in bloom), springing to life with parades, floats decorated with flowers, and beauty contests. In **late February** or **early March** (the full moon for the third lunar cycle) is **Makha Bucha Day,** one of three holy days. This one celebrating a spontaneous gathering of 1,250 disciples to hear the Buddha preach. At all Bucha festivals, Thais walk mindfully three times round the stupa at their local temple carrying flowers, candles, and incense as offerings. Foreigners are welcome to join in.

APRIL

Songkran is the New Year according to the Thai calendar, and it's an event that begins officially on April 13 and lasts 3 days. After honoring local monks and family elders, folks hit the streets for massive water fights. Be warned—foreigners are the Thais' favorite target. Cellphones, cameras, and valuables should be kept in Ziploc bags. Wear thin, quick-drying clothes, expect to get wet, and have a good attitude about this crazy Thai experience!

MAY

National Labor Day falls on the 1st. **Visakha Bucha Day,** marking the birth, enlightenment, and death of the Buddha, falls around mid- to late **May,** depending on the lunar calendar.

JULY

Thais celebrate **Buddhist Lent** immediately following **Asarnha Bucha Day,** a holy day to commemorated Buddha's first sermon. Occurring in mid-July (depending on the lunar calendar), the day signals the beginning of the rains' retreat and the 3-month period of meditation for all Buddhist monks. It is a common time for laymen to enter the monkhood for a period.

AUGUST

August 12 honors the birthday of HM Queen Sirikit and is also **Mother's Day.**

OCTOBER

On **October 23, Chulalongkorn Day,** marks the death of Rama V, who is remembered and celebrated. A 9-day **vegetarian festival** is to promote mind and body purification is observed countrywide but nowhere quite as wild as Phuket. On the island, people bring themselves into a trance-like state that enables fire walking and extreme body piercings, like stabbing swords through their cheeks.

NOVEMBER

Loy Krathong, in late October or November, is Thailand's most beloved festival, although it's not usually a public holiday. After dark, handmade banana-leaf vessels are launched down rivers, and lanterns are hoisted into the sky to symbolize the release of sins. The most spectacular celebrations are in Sukhothai and Chiang Mai. Watch out for fireworks and firecrackers in the street in the build-up to this festival. Troublesome monkeys in Lopburi are treated to a banquet of food in the fourth week—all in the name of making merit.

DECEMBER

December 5 marks the birthday of the late King Bhumibol and is also **Father's Day. King's Cup Regatta** in Phuket sees competitors racing yachts, in this exciting international event, which takes place the second week of December.

RESPONSIBLE TRAVEL

Choosing a responsible tour operator is not easy, as just about all of them these days use the buzzword "eco-tourism" in their sales pitches. Ask them exactly what they are doing to reduce their carbon footprint and to benefit the local community in the areas that their tours visit. We've listed several in this guide, and you can also contact the **Thai Ecotourism and Adventure Travel Association** (www.teata.or.th).

Some hotel groups, such as the **Banyan Tree** and **Four Seasons,** have made huge efforts over the past decade to implement sustainable projects, including a pledge to reduce their carbon footprint in all their resorts by 10% each year.

In more than 120 national parks, visitors can see the local wildlife species in residence, as well as appreciate the delicate balance of each habitat. The more popular parks have clearly displayed interpretation facilities at their visitor centers, as well as trails with bridges and catwalks, and markers explaining the important elements of the environment and its inhabitants. They also provide log-cabin-style bungalow accommodation, plus tents and supplies for campers. Get in touch with the **Department of National Parks** at ⓒ **02562-0760,** or visit its website (http://web3.dnp.go.th/parkreserve/nationalpark.asp?lg=2), where you can find info about the parks and also make online reservations.

Unfortunately, Thailand is way behind much of the world in general eco-awareness; conflicts between economic and ecological interests generally work out in favor of the former. Environmental problems include deforestation, air and water pollution, a massive addiction to single-use plastic, flooding, habitat loss, and consequent species loss. Among the mammals in danger of extinction in Thailand are tigers, leopards, and elephants. For information on ethical elephant camps and the plight of the tigers, see Chapter 4.

Fortunately, thanks to efforts by NGOs like the World Wildlife Fund, Thai authorities are also finally taking tiny steps to preserve the nature and wildlife, from swamp jungles in the south, to mountain forests in the north, to the many marine parks in the Gulf of Thailand and the Andaman Sea.

Another step in the right direction: **Koh Phi Phi** was closed off to tourists in 2018 indefinitely to give the natural habitats a break from an unending stream of visitors and boats. All tour operators should be well-versed in seasonal and government-imposed closings.

ACTIVE TRIP PLANNER

4

From oceans teeming with colorful fish to view with a diving mask, to corner-hugging motorcycle trips, to fast-moving zip lines through lush canopies, Thailand is bursting with active pursuits. It also offers meditation courses, cooking classes, and pampering four-hand massages. But we deal with those softer activities in the destination chapters. As for this chapter? Thrill seekers only, please.

The great thing about all the adventures that follow is that they presume no previous training, and tour outfitters can offer exciting experiences that are well planned and safe for everyone, from beginners to experts. This chapter gives an overview of the many options available—along with some recommendations for tour operators—but refer to the specific destination chapters throughout this book for further details, dive sites, trailheads, and boxing rings.

ORGANIZED ADVENTURE TRIPS

As you read through this guide, you'll realize we're big fans of independent exploration and discovery. But when it comes to adventure travel, there are advantages to planning a trip through a tour operator, whether it's one based in Thailand or an international operator with a specialty in your preferred activity.

The most significant advantage is time. If you have 2 weeks to spend in Thailand, you'll want to fill your days. That's where organized tours can help, by transporting you swiftly to the locations where the fun happens, and planning everything else (accommodations, dining and more). Equipment is another important consideration; why take a mountain bike or heavy diving gear halfway around the world when you can rent it locally at very reasonable rates?

Below is a vetted list of both Thai and international tour operators—with special attention given to companies that promote sustainability—to help with your trip planning. Some travelers prefer to sign up with international operators that have established a reputation for providing a smooth experience for their clients, though such tours usually come with a hefty price tag attached. Tours offered by Thai-based tour operators have prices that are significantly lower, in some cases up to half of what you might pay an international tour operator.

Multi-Sport Tour Operators

Smiling Albino ★★★ (www.smilingalbino.com; ℰ **02107-2541**) is Pan-Asian, expat-run but Bangkok-based, offering trips that combine daily heart-pumping activities with hefty doses of culture and activities. The country-wide Trek and Trail trip, for example, has guests biking, hiking, and seeing some of the country's most important sites.

Active Thailand ★★ (www.activethailand.com; ℰ **05385-0160**), based in Northern Thailand, is a top choice for travelers who want to add a few days—but not 2 full weeks—of kayaking, hiking, biking, white-water rafting, or zip lining onto their itineraries.

Intrepid Travel ★★ (www.intrepidtravel.com) is a massive multinational company based in Australia. It features a range of tours for travelers yearning to get off the beaten track, lasting from 8 to 22 days. Their active tours in Thailand combine trekking, cycling, and kayaking.

World Spree ★★★ (www.worldspree.com; ℰ **866/652-5656**) is usually the price leader to Asia, and Thailand is no exception. It offers great value trips throughout the year, some just to Thailand, others that mix a visit here with Cambodia or Laos. And unlike many other Asia specialists, World Spree never includes bogus "shopping experiences" (where travelers are steered into stores where the tour company gets a kickback). Expect top quality guides and accommodations for a lower-than-usual price.

ACTIVITIES A TO Z

Biking

Given Thailand's climate and well-developed road network, biking tours provide an ideal way to discover the country. Several companies offer tours throughout the kingdom, from beach destinations like Phuket, to the lush paddies of the central plains, and rugged highlands of the north.

Some cycling fanatics even take their own bikes with them to ensure their preference for make and models, but we don't think that's necessary. Regional outfitters have bikes to suit a variety of skill levels, road conditions and tastes. Organized cycling tours plan safe itineraries, ensuring that all cycling will be along *sois* and country roads where participants can focus on the delightful surroundings rather than other vehicles on the road. Knowledgeable guides and experienced mechanics accompany tours.

TOUR OPERATORS

Backroads ★★ (www.backroads.com; ℰ **1-800-462-2848** in the U.S.) is a multinational outfit that offers immersive and athletic trips. Their bicycle trips in the Golden Triangle appeal equally to culture vultures and pedal pushers. Itineraries wind through verdant rice fields and along the Mekong River with stops at local villages, temples, and famous street food vendors along the way.

This is a top outfitter for families, as well, with doable trips for cyclists of all ages and levels of fitness.

Grasshopper Adventures ★★★ (www.grasshopperadventures.com; *©* **02280-0832** in Bangkok) is a premier outfitter for biking in Thailand and throughout the rest of Asia. Along with half-day rides (like their popular street food and biking tours in Chiang Mai and Bangkok), Grasshopper has 1-week, 10-day, and 2-week itineraries in all parts of the country, as well as combo trips that go to both Thailand and Cambodia.

Spice Roads ★★★ (www.spiceroads.com; *©* **02712-5305** in Bangkok) is a slightly smaller company than Backroads but not by much, offering cycling tours throughout Southeast Asia. The significant difference between the two is that Spice Roads is based in Bangkok, giving it a good store of local knowledge. It offers a broad range of tours, covering the entire country and lasting between 1 day and 2 weeks.

Diving & Snorkeling

Diving is the most popular type of active vacation in Thailand. Every year thousands of visitors get their PADI (recognized scuba diving qualification) certification here while thousands more divers, the experienced ones, come for fun dives, and even reef restoration volunteer trips. Hundreds of species of coral and reefs grace the waters of the Andaman Sea and the Gulf of Thailand, along with as many species of fish, crustaceans, sea turtles, manta rays, and even whale sharks.

Scuba diving comes in several "flavors" in Thailand. From Ko Tao or Phuket (see chapters 8 and 9), experienced divers can take daytrips that includes two or three dives. Long-term scuba trips are also doable, on live-aboard boats that run seasonally. And scuba training and certification packages are common; it usually takes about 5 days to get certified. Always check that an operator has PADI-certified dive masters and that their boats have the full complement of certificates of approval issued by international marine safety organizations. For more information on diving, see chapter 8 and 9.

Since many reefs are close to the surface Thailand is a vibrant scene for snorkelers, too, especially such places as the Surin Islands in the Andaman Sea. Pretty much every beach has independent operators or guesthouses that rent snorkels, masks, and fins for the day; in addition, beach hotels offer brochures for boat operators that take groups of snorkelers to well-known reefs, sometimes off neighboring islands.

DIVE OPERATORS

See p. 236 for recommended outfits in Phuket, p. 204 for operators on Ko Samui, and p. 221 for dive schools on Ko Tao.

Elephant Handling

Elephants have a complicated history in Thailand. For thousands of years, Asian elephants—which are significantly smaller than their African counterparts—were used to haul logs, clear forests, and transport the royal family. When the Thai government banned logging in 1989, it abruptly left thousands

THAILAND'S top 10 NATIONAL PARKS

With well over a hundred national parks scattered around the kingdom, picking a favorite is as challenging as choosing a favorite Thai dish. So, fine, if you twist my arm: Similan and a curry dish called khao soi. But wait . . . maybe it's Khao Yai and a spicy plate of *larb*. Impossible to pick one, here is a top 10 list to help with the decision-making process. No matter where you go, it will these national treasures will provide a deeper appreciation for the country's diverse plant and animal life.

Ang Thong   A swell day trip from Ko Samui, this archipelago of limestone islands in the Gulf of Thailand features pristine beaches, hidden lagoons, and sweeping views. See p. 208 for more.

Doi Inthanon   Home to Thailand's highest mountain, Doi Inthanon (2,565 m/8,415 ft.) is a favorite haunt of bird watchers because of the huge variety of birds that live or visit here. Nature trails near the summit pass through some dramatic terrain. See p. 351 for more.

Erawan   If you visit Kanchanaburi, don't miss this park, which has the country's most beautiful waterfall, tumbling over seven tiers, and Prathat Cave with its impressive stalagmites and stalactites. See p. 137 for more.

Kaeng Krachan   Occupying nearly 3,000 sq. km (1,158 sq. miles) of forest in Petchburi Province, this is Thailand's biggest national park and provides shelter

for elephants, sambar deer, and gibbons, among other species. See below for more.

Khao Sok   Easily reached from Phuket or Krabi; this park is very popular for kayaking trips on the lake and treks to look for sun bears, gaurs, hornbills, and pheasants. See p. 185 for more.

Khao Yai   Located just a few hours' drive northeast of Bangkok, Khao Yai was Thailand's first national park (established 1962) and is still the best bet for seeing a variety of wildlife. See p. 137 for more.

Ko Chang   Thailand's second-largest island, Ko Chang ("Elephant Island") is just one of 50 islands in the eastern Gulf under national park protection; it boasts some of the country's best beaches and dive sites. See p. 155 for more.

Phu Kradung   Situated in Thailand's northeast, this pine-capped plateau is only accessible by a tough trek, though you can hire a porter to carry your gear up. See p. 397 for more.

Sam Roi Yot   "Three hundred peaks" park is just south of Hua Hin; it's peppered with limestone hills (thus the name) and has some great viewpoints, a beautiful pavilion in Phraya Nakhon Cave, and lots of wading birds. See p. 179 for more.

Similan   Whether you're a diver or snorkeler, you can't fail to be impressed by the countless varieties of corals and colorful fish surrounding these nine islands in the Andaman Sea. See p. 45 for more.

of elephant handlers (known as *mahouts*) without a source of income but with the responsibility, still, of a huge animal to look after and feed. Elephants eat about 10% of their body weight a day, so feeding them quickly became a financial burden too heavy for most *mahouts* to bear. This opened the floodgates for using elephants for tourism, and former logging herds were moved to Chiang Mai. Once in the north, many were "taught" to perform circus tricks. Domesticating an elephant so that it can juggle soccer balls or use a paintbrush and canvas to make art frequently involve ruthless practices, practices that have come under intense criticism from animal welfare activists. A number of elephants also carry tourists on mounted platforms affixed to their backs, an equally cruel practice. If riding is offered at a camp, bareback riding, where you'll sit on the elephants' shoulders, is much kinder to the animal. That being said, some insist that rides should be eliminated entirely.

So should you avoid elephant camps, and elephant experiences? Not necessarily. The conservation-focused team at the Golden Triangle Asian Elephant Foundation (GTAEF), which works in partnership with the Anantara Golden Triangle (p. 388) and the Four Seasons Tented Camp (p. 388), make the claim that since there is no government support for former working elephants, mass tourism is the only way to guarantee these creatures are looked after and fed. In the spirit of supporting the well-being and livelihood of Thailand's pachyderms, and getting a pretty cool selfie in the process, here are a few safe, conservation-focused camps. These camps are places where you can enjoy a positive, educational day with these gentle giants without worry or feeling like you're part of the problem.

ELEPHANT CAMPS

Elephant Nature Park ★★★ (www.elephantnaturepark.org; ℂ **053810-8754**), some 60km outside of Chiang Mai, is home to former logging and circus elephants, and one of the first sanctuaries for rescued elephants in Thailand. Visitors spend the day wandering the grounds with a *mahout* and helping them wash and feed the elephants. Seeing the elephants roam freely and interact with each other will make your heart feel good.

Patara Elephant Farm ★★ (www.pataraelephantfarm.com; ℂ **08199-22551** in Chiang Mai) runs an "elephant owner for a day" program where guests learn to care for the elephant by performing health checks (you'll learn lots about elephant poop), exercising the beasts, and feeding, and bathing them. Programs are full- and half-day; bareback riding is optional. Professional photos are included so that you can focus on your pachyderm.

Phuket Elephant Sanctuary ★★ (www.phuketelephantsanctuary.org; ℂ **07652-9099**) is the only elephant experience outside of Chiang Mai that we recommend. Guests watch with joy as formerly abused elephants play freely in the freshwater lagoons, and help feed them bananas and pineapples. Famous animal rights activists, like Leonardo DiCaprio, have visited this sanctuary. But be careful, several unethical companies have started marketing themselves as the Phuket Elephant Sanctuary. Make sure you're at the original.

Golfing

Thailand is a paradise for golfers, with courses scattered around the kingdom, many designed by top course architects. Add the warm climate and very reasonable fees, and you have an activity that attracts golfers from all over the world, but particularly from Japan and Korea (they descend on the country in planeloads, hauling their golf bags through customs). However, it's not necessary to cart your gear with you as all courses will rent clubs, shoes and all the accessories you'll need for a reasonable fee. Caddies and golf carts are also very affordable.

THE PLIGHT OF THAILAND'S tigers

Unfortunately, Thailand is not a haven for wild or semi-wild animals, and, more often than not, animal interactions come at the expense of the animal. Only adding to the problems is the fact that the government offers little-to-no oversight or regulation. The two creatures that pay the highest price are tigers and elephants. A May 2016 raid, and subsequent expose by *National Geographic* on the famous Tiger Temple, was an eye-opening event for many Thais, who had long turned a blind eye to animal abuse in the name of tourism dollars. The tigers were drugged, held in terrible conditions, malnourished, beaten, and raised for trade on the black market. (*National Geographic* reported the temple annually made US$3 million in its heyday.) Tourists would visit the temple to take photos laying down with the big cats or daringly putting their head between the jaws of the sedated animals. When the temple, which ran under the guise of a monastery, was raided there were 40 tiger cubs found dead in the temple's freezer, along with dozens of malnourished adult tigers. Fast forward 2 years and the group that ran the Tiger Temple has obtained legal status to run it as a zoo, and have plans to reopen. This guidebook series, and its author, does not endorse or recommend any outfitters that provide, encourage, or support interactions with tigers. We hope you'll join us.

If you're interested in more than just a single round, **Golfasian** (www.golf asian.com; © **02714-8470**) is a well-established tour operator with connections at courses around the country. From booking tee times and caddies to planning weeklong golfing retreats with hotels and transportation, they're pros through and through. See individual chapters for the pick of the courses in that region.

Kayaking

Like cycling, kayaking is an eco-friendly activity that causes minimum impact on the environment while providing healthy exercise and magical perspectives of Thailand's varied landscapes. The most popular area to practice this easy sport, which most beginners get the hang of very quickly, is around **Phang Nga Bay** (p. 235) near Phuket, where limestone outcrops rear up out of the tranquil waters. If you sign up for a tour with an experienced outfitter, they will time the visit for low tide allowing you to paddle through shallow caves into hidden lagoons (called *hong*, or "room" in Thai) that display a pristine beauty. Other popular areas for kayaking are Cheow Lan Lake in **Khao Sok National Park** (p. 185), as well as the marine national parks of **the Ang Thong Islands** (near Ko Samui) and Ko Tarutao in the Andaman Sea near the Malaysian border). Guided tours of Chiang Mai's Mae Ping River can be arranged, as well as white-knuckle kayaking trips on powerful rapids. Many organized adventure tours include kayaking on their itineraries, but for a specialist, contact one of the companies below.

TOUR OPERATORS

Siam River Adventures (www.siamrivers.com; ✆ **089515-1917** in Chiang Mai) offers a range of active trips, including white-water rafting and mountain biking. Most intriguing are their 1- to 5-day white-water kayak tours, many of which come with instruction.

Paddle Asia (www.paddleasia.com; ✆ cell: **081893-6558** in Phuket) is the best company to contact for a customized kayaking tour lasting several days. Their most popular destinations are Khao Sok National Park and the Tarutao Islands.

John Gray's Sea Canoe ★ (www.johngray-seacanoe.com; ✆ **07625-4505** in Phuket) is a highly respected outfitter that specializes in tours of Phang Nga Bay that combine kayaking with a seafood supper under the stars.

Kitesurfing & Windsurfing

Windsurfing has long been popular in Thailand, particularly at such beach destinations as Pattaya, Phuket, and Ko Samui. It continues to be so, though these days it is somewhat eclipsed by the more demanding, more exciting, sport of kitesurfing, often referred to as kiteboarding. As well as at the main beach destinations, this sport can be studied and practiced at Ko Pha Ngan, Hua Hin, Chumphon, and Pranburi (south of Hua Hin). It takes a while to pick up the skills necessary to get airborne, but once you're up there, it all seems worth it. Of course, on windless days it's hopeless; check out Kiteboarding Asia's website for month-by-month wind conditions in each of their locations. A 3-day beginners' course costs around 11,000B.

TOUR OPERATOR

Kiteboarding Asia (www.kiteboardingasia.com; ✆ cell: **08159-14594**) is our pick for this sport, certified by the International Kiteboarding Association (IKO) and offering a variety of courses as well as equipment rental. They have eight schools in Thailand.

Motorcycling

One of the best ways to explore Thailand, especially the mountainous north, is on a motorcycle, and the availability of inexpensive bike rentals tempt many to hit the high road. However, I'd advise not to take to the open road without some previous experience—especially if you're looking to ride something more substantial than a "twist-and-go" scooter.

Laws are pretty relaxed about renting bigger bikes without checking for a proper motorcycle license issued by the home country. That's okay if you've got the preverbal miles on your tires, but be a defensive driver as you'll likely encounter other foreigners who have bit off more than they're capable of handling.

Be sure to check the tire treads on bikes and take photos of any knicks or dings before driving off. Also, don't be alarmed if the rental place holds on to your passport during the rental period; it's a common practice. You can get lots of good advice for independent travel, including maps and recommended shops, from **Golden Triangle Rider** (www.gt-rider.com). Even then, it's wise to consider joining an organized bike tour with one of the companies below.

TOUR OPERATORS

Big Bike Tours (www.bigbiketours.net; ℭ **080127-2595** in Chiang Mai) offers on-road and off-road tours that span the country. Tours are fully-inclusive. Top of the line gear and bikes, like BMW and Kawasaki, are standard issue.

Asian Motorcycle Adventures (www.asianbiketour.com; ℭ **080493-1012** in Chiang Mai) runs 10-day loop tours from Chiang Mai to Mae Hong Son, Nan, and the Golden Triangle, including riding up Doi Inthanon, Thailand's tallest mountain.

Rock Climbing

Rock climbing has exploded in popularity in Thailand during the last 2 decades, and many choose to visit the country specifically to practice this thrilling sport. The cliffs around Krabi, particularly at Railay Beach (p. 268 for information on routes, guides, and gear), attract thousands of climbers, though there are also good bolted routes on Ko Phi Phi and around Chiang Mai. Stamina and balance are required for this activity (and, it goes without saying, a good head for heights). Equipment rental and tuition is much cheaper than for many other extreme sports, with daylong introductory courses averaging 2,000B.

ROCK-CLIMBING SCHOOLS

Basecamp Tonsai (http://basecamptonsai.com; ℭ **081149-9745** in Krabi) is one of the most popular and professional schools on the rock-climbing Mecca that is Railay Beach. They also have the best program for deep-water soloing, a form of independent rock climbing without ropes or harnesses. Courses are charted above the water so that when a climber is tired or falls, he or she splashes to safety.

Chiang Mai Rock Climbing Adventures (www.thailandclimbing.com; ℭ **05320-7102**) has a 3-day introductory course for beginners and takes more experienced climbers to the top of Crazy Horse Buttress, a famously challenging climb, where climbers test their skills on the crag's single- and multi-pitch rope courses.

Surfing

Dreams of hanging ten on an epic wave in Southeast Asia should be reserved for the beaches in Bali. But Thailand has a few key spots with barrel waves and other nice challenges. Monsoon season in Phuket (June to September) produces the best waves. On Phuket, Kata Beach is home to an annual surfing competition, and Kalim beach, on the north side of Patong, are reliable surfing beaches.

SURF SCHOOL

Phuket Surfing (www.phuketsurfing.com; ℭ **089874-9147**) offers a wide range of packages from hourly lessons (1,200B) to a 5-day/10-hours of lessons deal (8,000B). The shop rents all gear, including boogie boards and SUP kayaks. Their website is a good source for weather reports on the latest break wave heights.

Thai Boxing (Muay Thai)

Thailand's national sport of Muay Thai is known as the art of eight limbs, and many find it an enjoyable challenge to learn. Lessons in this fast-moving, full-body sport are available at camps around the country. Some lesson locations are super glam, like the open-air ring overlooking the ocean at the Four Seasons Resort in Ko Samui (p. 186), and often include special post-workout massages designed to heal the aches and pains associated with a round in the ring. More serious gladiators spend a week or two at an intensive training camp with Muay Thai masters. Returning home with body hardened by high-intensity workouts and sun-kissed by the sun could be the ultimate souvenir.

TRAINING CAMP

In addition to these listings, we have recommended training centers in individual destination chapters.

Lanna Muay Thai (www.facebook.com/Lanna-MuayThai-135464199806574; © 05389-2102 in Chiang Mai) is a familiar name among top boxers in Thailand, and the camp has turned out many competent, foreign kickboxers over the years. Training can be booked for a range of times like by the day (450B) or month (8,800B).

Jaroenthong Muay Thai Gym (www.jaroenthongmuaythaikhaosan.com; © 02629-2313) is an acclaimed gym with two locations in Bangkok. The facilities are top of the line, regularly updated, and the instructors speak English; drop-in sessions start at 600B.

Additionally, the website **www.muaythaicampsthailand.com** offers details, opinions, and pricing on short- and long-term training centers around Thailand.

Trekking

Thailand's mountainous jungle terrain in the north is catnip for trekkers, with a network of trails that vary in difficulty from easy to difficult. There are hundreds of agencies that offer trekking tours in Chiang Mai, and some of them claim to visit "untouristed areas," though this is highly unlikely, as nearly every corner of the region has been uncovered in the last 2 decades. Nevertheless, it is possible to find a trek that takes you through several hill-tribe villages and some delightful countryside. Choose your operator carefully (see p. 324) and seek out community-based projects, where the local people reap real benefits from your visit.

Treks can last 1 to 5 nights and average 3 to 4 hours per day of walking on jungle paths. All tours provide local guides to accompany groups, and accommodation along the routes vary from setting up camp to local homestays to simple hotels. Some trips break up the walking and hiking with elephant encounters, trips in four-wheel-drive jeeps, or light rafting on flat bamboo rafts. Chiang Mai (see chapter 11) has the most trekking firms, but Chiang

ACTIVE TRIP PLANNER | Activities A to Z

Rai, Pai, and Mae Hong Son (see chapter 12, "Exploring the Northern Hills") also have their share of companies.

TREKKING TOUR OPERATORS

Mirror Foundation ★★ (www.themirrorfoundation.org; ℂ **05373-7412** in Chiang Rai) is an NGO that provides sustainable, private tours with the goal of bettering the lives of hill tribe families. Tours are booked via the group's trekking website, while volunteer programs, like teaching English to hill tribe children, are organized through the foundation's website.

Population & Community Development Association (PDA) ★★ (www. pdacr.org; ℂ **05374-008** in Chiang Rai) has great programs that are above the line on ethics and service. Treks are led, managed, and organized by the experts who curate the Hilltribe Museum & Education Center (p. 378), so there is a large emphasis placed on interacting with (not just staring at) rural tribes. Homestays, meals, and more are organized to foster engagement and tour fees flow directly into the pockets of the locals.

Trekking Collective ★ (www.trekkingcollective.com; ℂ **05320-8340** in Chiang Mai) specializes in customized trips planned around clients' interests, be it bird-watching, hiking Chiang Mai's mountains, or learning about the local flora and fauna.

White-Water Rafting

River rafting is very popular in North Thailand between July and March, with peak rafting season coinciding with the July to October rainy season. Rainy season brings rivers swollen with mountain water, but flash-flooding is common during this time, so you'll want to make sure that safety measures are taken seriously. It's possible to take rafting trips of just a few hours, but it's much more fun to make a 2-day trip, and overnight in jungle camps. Rapids are generally class III and IV but are big enough to be loads of fun.

Thai Adventure Rafting (www.thairafting.com; ℂ **05369-9111** in Pai) started off the craze long ago and still run exciting 2-day trips along the Pai River with excursions to hot springs and waterfalls.

Siam River Adventures (www.siamrivers.com; ℂ **08951-51917** in Chiang Mai) runs single and multiday rafting trips on the Mae Taeng River, which has class III rapids.

Watching Wildlife

Just a century ago, the jungles of Thailand were so thick with wildlife that people didn't dare travel alone for fear of attack by tigers, snakes, and other predators. These days it's just the opposite—naturalists sit in hides for days on end in the hope of glimpsing some of the country's few remaining exotic species. As the country's forests have been systematically stripped, the habitat of many animals has disappeared, so the animals have gone as well.

The country's first national parks were established in the 1960s in an attempt to offer some shelter for species in decline, and to date, there are over a hundred parks scattered all over the country. These are inevitably the best

BEING A sensitive TREKKER

Thailand's hill tribes are migratory descendants from Myanmar, China, and Tibet, and, traditionally, call villages in the mountainous regions of Northern Thailand home. Today, these groups of people are some of the most marginalized in Thailand and several factors, like a lack of reliable documentation and Thai bureaucracy, make it difficult for them to find a path to citizenship or traditional paths for work. Members of hill-tribe communities are often called *Chao Khao*, which translates to "mountain people." As a way of earning money, these villages welcome visitors to learn about their centuries-old way of life, and some camps subsist entirely on tourist dollars.

Many travelers are drawn to the hill-tribe villages in search of a "primitive" culture, unspoiled by modernization—and tour and trekking operators in the region are quick to exploit this. Companies advertise treks as non-touristic, authentic, or eco-tours in an effort to set themselves apart from tacky tourist operations or staged cultural experiences. Do not be misled: There are no villages here that are untouched by foreign curiosity. In the worst cases, as with the camps of "long-neck" (Padaung tribe) from Myanmar, they have become Disneyland-like human zoos, with fees paid to individuals for photographs and zero long-term sustainability.

This shouldn't discourage anyone from joining a trek or tour; just be aware and avoid any bogus claims. It is also advisable to leave any preconceptions of "primitive" people to 19th-century anthropological journals; rather, come to learn how these cultures grapple with complex economic and social pressures to maintain their unique identities—and learn what makes each tribe unique. (For a breakdown of the different tribes in Northern Thailand, see p. 356.) As a general rule, the further away from Chiang Mai or Chiang Rai you go, the more authentic the experience will be.

Awareness of the impact of tourists is also important: Practice cultural sensitivity, ask before taking photos, and ask your guide how to say "hello" or "thank you" in the local dialect. With this as a mission, visitors can have an experience that is quite authentic and, refreshingly, has little to do with preconceptions and expectations.

Other ways to sustainably support the hill-tribe communities and to make sure your baht reaches the local people is to do a homestay or buy traditional handicrafts at authorized stores (see shopping in Chiang Mai, p. 343). If you're traveling through Chiang Rai, a good place to visit before touring a hill tribe is the **Hilltribe Museum & Education Center** (p. 378 for more information). The informative museum is run by the **Population & Community Development Association** (PDA; www.pdacr.org), and the group's sustainable treks are highly recommended.

places to go looking for wildlife, though in many parks visitors are unlikely to see much more than a few birds and butterflies, ants, and spiders. One notable exception is **Khao Yai National Park ★** (p. 137), where visitors accompanied by a guide are almost guaranteed to see hornbills, gibbons, elephants, and deer in a single day. Other national parks, where you can enjoy the country's flora and fauna are **Doi Inthanon,** which contains Thailand's highest mountain, and **Kaeng Krachan,** the country's biggest park in Petchaburi Province.

During the summer months of June, July and August, day trips from Bangkok can be arranged by **Wild Encounter Thailand** (www.wildencounter thailand.com) to see Thailand's Bryde's whales, a large whale closely related to the blue and humpback whale. They feed on small fish in the Gulf of Thailand and rise from the water in a vertical position with their mouth agape. This feeding technique makes for great visibility in spotting the whales, and it's a fun day on the water.

TOUR OPERATORS

Khao Yai Nature Life (www.khaoyainaturelifetours.com; ℭ **081827-8391**) offers overnight and day trips to explore the nature of the national park. This is the top outfit for bird-watching in the park.

Green Trails (www.green-trails.com; ℭ **05327-8517** in Chiang Mai) operates 2- and 3-day tours in several national parks, including Khao Sok and Khao Yai.

Zip Lining

There's no rush like soaring through the canopies of the Thai jungle on a zip line. Flying from platform to platform with the wind in your face is a freeing feeling. And besides a weight restriction, most operators limit riders to 275 pounds, and being at least a meter tall (3.2-feet), this is an action-packed activity suitable for almost everyone. Chiang Mai is the best place to wiz around, but outfitters are available in tropical destinations like Ko Samui, too.

TOUR OPERATOR

Flight of the Gibbon ★★★ (www.flightofthegibbon.com; ℭ **05301-0660** in Chiang Mai) is Thailand's original zip-line company, and their outstanding reputation for fun and safety makes them the best in the country. Operating about an hour outside of Chiang Mai, day trips are available, as well as multiday tours that include village homestays, rock climbing, and ethical elephant encounters. The brand's commitment to sustainable efforts, like animal rehabilitation and reforesting, is a shining example to others in The Kingdom.

SETTLING INTO BANGKOK

With a population of almost 9 million in a country of 68 million, Thailand's capital teems with humanity. As the cultural heart of the kingdom, the city keeps many traditions still visibly intact—yet Bangkok is at the same time a rapidly changing city. For some, it is a quick pit stop to see gilded temples before flying south; for others, Bangkok is a hedonistic, cocktail-laced escape from reality. Whatever your reasons for visiting, come to Bangkok with a passion for discovery because there is always something new to learn, eat, or try here.

5

Founded when King Rama I moved the city across the river from Thonburi in 1782, Bangkok is not a particularly ancient capital, but rather, as we implied above, a cool mix of modernity and tradition. Saffron-robed monks mingle in the *sois* (streets) with Starbucks-drinking, cellphone-wielding business types and the bouffant hair socialites colloquially known as *hi-so*. Luxurious, glass-clad condos brazenly penetrate the skyscape, juxtaposed with glittering *wats* (temples), ramshackle colonial edifices, and tin-roofed slums teetering along putrid canals. Compared to Hong Kong and Singapore, the city is way behind in development, and locals aren't as fluent in English as in these other Asian powerhouses.

The culture here is so gloriously rich, though, that exploring Bangkok, and eating its glorious food, should be a highlight of any trip to Thailand. Rivaled only by Chiang Mai in the north, Bangkok is also a swell place to shop, for everything from brand name luxury items (and, of course, knock-offs that won't last a week) to fine local handicrafts, silk, and jewels. And when it comes to nightlife, the endless array of night markets, bars, and clubs could make for a (potentially) sleepless night. More on that in the next chapter.

ESSENTIALS

Arriving

BY PLANE

Bangkok's **Suvarnabhumi International Airport** (airport code BKK) is the main hub for all international travelers arriving in Thailand; it also handles domestic flights in and out of the capital.

Referred to as "Krung Thep" by Thais, meaning "The City of Angels," the official name of Bangkok is a proud description of Bangkok's royal legacy—and the world's longest: Krungthepmahanakhon Amonrattanakosin Mahintharayutthaya Mahadilokphop Noppharatratchathaniburirom Udomratchaniwetmahasathan Amonphimanawatansthit Sakkathattiyawitsanukamprasit. Now try saying that five times fast.

Pronounced nothing like it looks, the correct way to say the same is "su-wanna-poom", and it's 30km (18 miles) southeast of the city. Suvarnabhumi offers a wide range of services, including luggage storage, currency exchange, banks, a branch of the British pharmacy Boots, ATMs, a post office, medical clinics, Wi-Fi, and telephones. Dining choices within the airport are so-so, and options are mostly the likes of Burger King or British pub-style spots for a pre-flight drink. For a quick meal and the airport's best cup of coffee, stop by a Dean & DeLuca. Before security near gate 8 is **Magic Food Point,** a 24-hour food court with cheap eats and the most authentic Thai food at the airport. 7-Eleven is a good place to stock up on snacks and gum before security. Within the airport complex, just a couple of minutes from the terminal exit, is **Novotel Suvarnabhumi Airport** (www.novotel.com), a four-star hotel. For more detailed information on Suvarnabhumi, see **https://airport thai.co.th/en.**

Bangkok's former international airport, **Don Muang** (airport code DMK) is 24km (15 miles) north of the heart of the city, and this is where most domestic flights (but certainly not all) and regional budget flights operate in Bangkok. It got a facelift in 2016/2017, and it's a clean, easy-to-navigate facility with cafes, international chains like Starbucks and ATMs. **Amari Don Muang Airport Hotel** (www.amari.com/donmuang) is opposite the airport and accessed via a sky bridge or a shuttle bus. For more details on Don Muang, see **www.donmuangairportonline.com**. There is a free shuttle bus that connects the two airports available 5am to midnight.

GETTING TO & FROM THE AIRPORTS From both Suvarnabhumi and Don Muang, it takes 30 to 90 minutes to drive to the city center, depending on traffic and if it is raining, which inexplicably doubles the commute time. Inexpensive and readily available, **taxis** are the best way to get to or from the city (and may be the cheapest way; see below for more on that). Taxis only take cash, so make sure you have smaller notes, like 20B, 50B or 100B, since 1,000B bills are hard to break. At Suvarnabhumi taxi counters, there are specific lines for van taxis, so look out for those if you're with a group or have extra baggage. Take a ticket from the automated machine, which will direct you to a corresponding number where you'll meet your assigned cab driver. From either airport, a trip downtown should cost about 300B, plus expressway tolls. Some drivers will ask for cash at the tolls, while others will add it on to the bill upon arriving at the destination.

If arriving at Suvarnabhumi during rush hour, consider taking the **Airport Rail Link** to the city center. The express train takes 15 minutes to **Makkasan Terminal,** near the Phetchaburi MRT station, and costs 90B. A local line takes 30 minutes to cover the same journey for 45B and arrives at the Phaya Thai BTS. Trains depart every 15 minutes from 6am to midnight. At first blush, this may seem like the most appealing option considering the price and transit time. But Bangkok's local transit systems, the BTS and MRT (more on p. 60), are tricky to navigate with luggage and cover only a fraction of the city's grid, so you'll very likely need a cab to reach your hotel from the station anyway (meaning the end price could be the same).

Private limousine services such as AOT offer air-conditioned sedans and drivers from both airports. Look for the booth in arrivals. Trips start at 1,000B. Advanced booking is not necessary.

Airport Express buses were terminated when the rail link launched, and local bus services are really only for people who know their way around. For these, you will need to get on a free shuttle, located at level 2 or 4, going to the **Public Transportation Center.** From there, buses costing around 42B cover 12 city routes, including major BTS stops and the Southern Bus Terminal.

BY TRAIN

Trains to and from the capital stop at **Hua Lampong Station** (⑦ 02220-4334), east of Yaowarat (Chinatown). Lying at a major intersection of Rama IV and Krung Kasem roads, it's notoriously gridlocked during morning and evening rush hours, so allow 40 minutes extra for traffic delays. Better yet, take the MRT to Hualamphong; it's across the road from the station.

BY BUS

Bangkok has three major bus stations, each serving a different part of the country. All air-conditioned public buses to the West and the Southern Peninsula arrive and depart from the **Southern Bus Terminal** (⑦ 02422-4444), on Putthamonthon Soi 1, west of the river, over the Phra Pinklao Bridge from the Democracy Monument. Service to the East Coast (including Pattaya) arrives and departs from the **Eastern Bus Terminal,** also known as **Ekkamai** (⑦ **02391-2504**), on Sukhumvit Road opposite Soi 63 (Ekkamai BTS). Buses to the north arrive and leave from the **Northern Bus Terminal,** aka **Mo Chit** (⑦ **02936-2841**), Kampaengphet 2 Rd., near the **Chatuchak Weekend Market,** and a short taxi ride from Mo Chit BTS or Chatuchak MRT station.

Visitor Information

The **Tourism Authority of Thailand** (TAT; www.tourismthailand.org) offers general information regarding travel in Bangkok and upcountry, and has a useful hotline (⑦ **1672**) reachable from anywhere in the kingdom; it's open daily 8am to 8pm. Ironically, TAT's offices are not always conveniently located for foreigners. Their main office is off the beaten track, at 1600 Phetchaburi Rd. (⑦ **02250-5500**). TAT produces an enormous number of glossy tourist brochures, including some for Bangkok; but beware, many are outdated.

Instead, Bangkok's free magazines, available in hotel lobbies, are more current. Look for *BK Magazine* (www.bk.asia-city.com); it's a fun, free weekly with info on the capital's events. English-language daily newspapers *Bangkok Post* (www.bangkokpost.com) and *The Nation* (www.nationmultimedia.com) have sections devoted to Bangkok must-sees.

City Layout

Nineteenth-century photographs of Bangkok portray the busy life on the **Chao Phraya River,** where a ragtag range of vessels—from humble rowboats to sailing ships—crowded the busy port. This was the original gateway for early foreign visitors who traveled upriver from the Gulf of Siam. Rama I (r. 1782–1809), upon moving the capital city from Thonburi on the west bank to Bangkok on the east, dug a series of canals fanning out from the river. For strategic reasons, the canals replicated the moat system used at Ayutthaya, Siam's previous capital, in the hopes of protecting the city from invasion. The city waterways represented the primordial oceans that surrounded the Buddhist heavens. A small artificial island was cut into the land along the riverbank and became the site for the Grand Palace, Wat Phra Kaew (the Temple of the Emerald Buddha), and Wat Po. To this day, this quarter is referred to as **Ko** (Thai for island) **Rattanakosin.** This is the historical center of the city and the main tourist destination for day trips.

The canals, or *klongs,* continued eastward from Rattanakosin as the city's population grew. Chinese and Indian merchants formed settlements alongside the river to the southeast of the island. The mercantile district of **Yaowarat** (Chinatown) is a maze of busy back alleys. Its main thoroughfare, Charoen Krung Road, snakes southward, following the shape of the river. On the eastern edge of Chinatown, you'll find the arched **Hua Lampong Railway Station,** a marvelous example of fanciful Italian engineering that dates back to 1916.

Just beyond Yaowarat, along the river, lies **Bangrak** district, where foreign interests built European-style residences, trading houses, churches, and a crumbling colonial Customs House. **The Mandarin Oriental Hotel,** the Grande Dame of Bangkok built in 1876, sits among them, one of the few great heritage properties left in town. Bangrak's main thoroughfares, Surawong Road, Silom Road, and Sathorn Road, originate at Charoen Krung, running parallel to Rama IV Road. Within Bangrak, you'll find many hotels and high-rises, restaurants, art galleries, and pubs, as well as the sleazy nightlife at Patpong or glitzy gay clubs in Silom Soi 4.

Back to Rattanakosin, as you head upriver, you'll hit **Banglampoo,** home to Bangkok's National Museum, Wat Suthat, the Giant Swing, and Klong Phu Khao Thong (Golden Mount). Its central point is **Democracy Monument,** a traffic circle where the wide Ratchadamnoen Klong Road intersects Dinso Road. Around the corner is Khao San Road, which was once solely a backpacker hangout. It's still clinging onto its hippie past with its budget accommodation, inexpensive restaurants, lots of tour agents, and youthful nightlife—but is also heading into the mainstream. Starbucks and Burger King are muscling in, and the neighborhood is losing some of its funky vibe.

Farther north of Banglampoo is leafy **Dusit,** home to Wat Benchamabophit, Vimanmek Palace, parks and the opulent **Siam Hotel.**

As Bangkok spread on the east shore of the river, **Thonburi,** the former site of the capital across the river, remained in relative isolation. While Bangkok was quick to fill in canals, ushering in the age of the automobile, residential Thonburi's canals remained, and a longtail boat ride through the area is a high point of any trip. Thai riverside homes, both traditional and new, and neighborhood businesses reveal glimpses of life as it might have been 200 years ago. Access to Thonburi's **Bangkok's Southern Bus Terminal** is via the Phra Pinklao Bridge from Banglampoo.

Back on the other side of the river, Bangkok grew and fanned eastward. From Ko Rattanakosin, beyond Bangrak, lies **Pathumwan.** American Thai silk connoisseur **Jim Thompson** lived in Thailand for more than 20 years from the 1940s until the 1960s, and his stunning house, located opposite the National Stadium, is open to visitors daily. Nearby is busy **Siam Square,** with its myriad boutiques and huge shopping malls. This area's hotels, cafes, and nightclubs attract scores of local teenagers and students. Beyond Pathumwan, **Wireless (Witthayu) Road** runs north to south, between **Rama IV Road** (at the edge of Bangrak) and **Rama I Road** (at the edge of Pathumwan). Here, the huge European embassies and the U.S. Embassy complex stand just meters from leafy **Lumpini Park** and a clutch of five-star hotels and chic shopping centers such as **Central Embassy** and **Central Chidlom.**

From Siam Square, **Sukhumvit Road** extends due east, its length traced by the BTS. Many expatriates live along the small side streets, or *sois*, that branch out from Sukhumvit. Tourist restaurants and big malls line the streets, with luxury hotels set alongside inexpensive hotels and hostels, fine restaurants and cheap local eats joints, as well as clothing stores and street-side bazaars. Easterly situated Sukhumvit is connected by the overhead BTS, which swiftly brings guests to **Phrom Phong** and **Thonglor** (aka Sukhumvit Soi 55 and spelled Thong Lo on the BTS line). Both neighborhoods are a hotbed of fine cocktail bars and outstanding Western restaurants. **Bangkok's Eastern Bus Terminal** is at Ekkamai BTS, on Sukhumvit Soi 63.

FINDING AN ADDRESS   Note that even-numbered addresses are on one side of the street and odd-numbered ones the opposite, but they are not always close to each other. So, 123 and 124 Silom Rd. will be on opposite sides of the street, but possibly 300m (nearly 1,000 ft.) or even farther apart. Most addresses are subdivided by a slash, as in 123/4 Silom Rd., which indicates that a particular plot has been subdivided into several buildings. Some addresses also include a dash, which means that the building itself occupies several plots. You'll find the term *thanon* frequently in addresses (sometimes abbreviated to Th.); it means "street" in Thai. *Soi* is a lane off a major street and is either numbered or named. If you are looking for "45 Sukhumvit Soi 23," it means plot 45, on Soi 23, off Sukhumvit Road. On Sukhumvit Road, even-numbered *sois* will be on the south side and odd-numbered *sois* on the north side.

For a **detailed street map** (beyond the one on your phone), **Asia Books** (www.asiabooks.com) is the best shop for maps on Bangkok and beyond. You'll find them at nearly every mall and at airports around the country. TAT offices offer local maps.

Neighborhoods in Brief

Unlike other cities, Bangkok's neighborhoods are hard to define, and they blur together in the maze of chaotic sois (side streets). Generally, when giving directions to a taxi driver, you'll want to tell the closest intersection or the name of the nearest BTS or MRT station near your destination. This will be much more successful than spouting off a name of a neighborhood.

Riverside & Thonburi Bangkok's grandest riverside hotels are all clustered near Saphan Taksin. You'll find wholesale silver, jewelry, and antique stores along Charoen Krung Road and Soi Oriental. Farther upstream, colonial buildings and churches give these old districts a certain charm. Across the river in **Thonburi,** you can discover Thai dance shows and theater, as well as low-cost riverside diners and watery markets.

Chinatown Also along the riverside, just south of the Grand Palace and Banglampoo, Chinatown is a frenetic maze of gold shops, market lanes, and old trading warehouses. It is an atmospheric home to indie nightlife and the best street food in the city.

Banglampoo and Dusit Home to the Grand Palace, this area lies within the area known as Ko Rattanakosin. It contains the city's most important historical sites, including the Grand Palace, Wat Phra Kaew, and Wat Po, as well as the Vimanmek Palace Museum. Within the area are numerous historic wats (temples), the National Museum, and the National Theater and Library. Khao San Road is the city's backpacker district and there are many budget guesthouses here. The only drawback here is that it's a real trek to get to the BTS or MRT.

Sathorn, Silom and Bangrak This area likes to think of itself as the Central Business District, though its "downtown" label is debatable. It is bound by Rama IV Road on the north, Yaowarat (Chinatown) on the northwest, and Charoen Krung Road due west, while Silom and Surawong roads run through its center. Many banks, businesses, and embassies have offices in this area, but it is also a good choice for travelers, with malls, reasonably priced restaurants, hotels, and (not so ideal) the seamier Patpong red-light area.

Siam, Ratchathewi & Phloenchit Sukhumvit Road, better known as Rama I Road at its western end, this main east–west thoroughfare is straddled overhead by the BTS. After crossing Ratchadamri Road (at the Erawan Shrine), it then becomes Ploenchit Road and runs directly east, crossing Wireless (Witthayu) Road at Chit Lom BTS (near the CentralWorld department store). It finally becomes Sukhumvit Road at the mouth of the airport freeway. Hotels, shopping complexes, office buildings, and some smaller embassies serve a thriving expat community here. Though rather far from the historic sites, it's a convenient and fun spot for those interested in shopping and nightlife.

Lower Sukhumvit: Nana to Ekkamai At the BTS stop by the same name, the neighborhood of Nana is home to some pretty naughty nightlife and outstanding Arab food. Follow the BTS to reach Asok, where Terminal 21 is a funky mall with a cool market vibe. Below the Asok BTS is a chaotic intersection with lanes of cars, buses, and motorbikes converging into a state of organized chaos. The next two stops are Phrom Phong and Thonglor; both are upscale neighborhoods with large Japanese and Western expats populations. The bar scene is outstanding here, and mixologists shake, stir, and pour strong cocktails in these parts. Reach Ekkamai, which is as far out most tourists will ever find themselves, for a laid-back neighborhood vibe, perky cafes, and a few notable art galleries.

GETTING AROUND

Bangkok's notoriously awful traffic can make even a local monk go a bit crazy, and you've likely heard horror stories of the legendary gridlock. But don't let that slow your roll. There are varied ways of getting around the city, including an air-conditioned subway, crazy-cheap taxis, buzzy canal boats, and even motorcycle taxis. Have some patience, remember to pace yourself, and, like the Thais around you, keep a smile on your face. Access to the town's modern and effective public transport is often a key factor in visitors' choice of accommodation so you'll find a map of the Bangkok metro lines on the inside cover of this book.

BY BTS   The **Bangkok Transit System (BTS)** is called "*rot fai fa*" by Thais, which translates as "skytrain"—an apt description. It opened in 1999 and is the best way to get around Bangkok. Majorly lacking in elevators—only 13 of the 36 stations have them—or even escalators, it unsuitable for the physically challenged. Coverage is limited to only a fraction of the city, though several extensions are in the works for the coming years. The current lines tick most of the major tourist areas, with the notable exception of historical sites like the Grand Palace. The air-conditioned train system provides good access to Bangkok's commercial centers. There are two lines: Silom and Sukhumvit and they interchange at the bustling Siam station.

Single-journey tickets cost 16B to 44B depending on distance. For single trips, it's fairly straightforward to buy tickets at the vending machines that have place names spelled phonetically in English. **Tip**: Select your destination's value before dropping coins into the machine, or else they'll be spit right out. Vending machines **only take coins** (no bills or credit cards), but you can get small change at the ticket booth as needed. Sometimes these lines can be obnoxiously long, so carry coins to avoid waiting. All ticket types (some you tap, others you swipe) let you through the turnstile and are required for exit, so be sure to hang on to them. Grab a **one-day pass** for 140B which is a time-saver and ideal if you plan to take five or more one-way journeys. Purchase a pass at any BTS ticket booth. The plastic SmartPass, known as a **Rabbit Card,** can be topped up as you go but this is only useful for travelers staying in Bangkok for a week or more who plan to ride the train multiple times per day. There is a 30B non-refundable fee for the card; buy it at any ticket booth.

At press time, the BTS expansion east from Bearing to Samut Prakan was still under construction. Most media outlets are reporting that it will not be done until late 2019.

Children ride for free. But confusingly, a child ticket is defined by the height of the child (90cm or 2-ft 9-in) instead of their age.

Hours of operation are daily between 5:15am and midnight. For route details, maps, and further ticket info, check **www.bts.co.th**.

BY SUBWAY   Bangkok's **Mass Rapid Transit (MRT)** has 18 stations. Beginning near the Hua Lampong Train Station, the MRT heads southeast past Lumphini Park before turning north, up to Lad Phrao, and then makes a wiggle westward near the Chatuchak Weekend Market before the terminus at Bang Sue. Ticket prices vary by distance and cost 16B to 42B, and the system uses small plastic tokens, which are swiped over a sensor to enter and deposited at the turn style on the way out. A **1-day pass** costs 120B and a **3-day pass** (must be consecutive days) is 230B. However, most tourists will only ride the MRT once or twice in a 3-day stay (likely if and when they chose to go to Chinatown), so the pass is often not worth buying. Vending machines accept coins and 20B, 50B and 100B bills, and this newer system is a bit more user-friendly than the BTS.

Plans are underway to double the MRT's coverage, including much-needed stops in the tourist throngs in Ko Rattanakosin.

Hours of operation are daily between 6am and midnight. The official website (www.bemplc.co.th) isn't very useful, so see a ticketing agent for questions.

The Skytrain and MRT are two separate entities, and while there have been talks of creating a universal card that works with both systems, it currently isn't available. The BTS and MRT share three connection points: Sala Daeng and Silom, Asok and Sukhumvit, and Mo Chit and Chatuchak.

BY PUBLIC RIVERBOATS   Efficient, wallet-friendly, and scenic, but not so comfortable, the public riverboats on the Chao Phraya are a great way to get around the sites in the city center and are a remarkable window into local life. Most sightseers will board at Central Pier, down the steps from the Saphan Taksin BTS. The major stops going upstream from Saphan Taksin are Tha Ratchawong (for Chinatown), Tha Thien (near Wat Po), and Tha Chang (near the Temple of the Emerald Buddha). Purchase tickets on board or from ticket offices at the piers.

The tourist boats operated by the **Chao Phraya Express** (www.chaophraya expressboat.com) offer the most relaxed way to travel along this busy river. These steady, wide-bodied vessels are huge, have plenty of seats and make regular stops along the river. Microphone-equipped guides offer short historical snippets in English about the sites you pass. **Short trips** start at 13B, but you can also buy an **all-day pass,** which includes a map showing all piers and nearby attractions, for 150B. This allows you to hop off and on at will. The pass eliminates fumbling for change, which has its benefits, but if you only plan to ride the ferry once or twice a day, it isn't worth it.

Cross-river ferries are small ferries that run only from the east bank to the west, so they're useful for getting to such places as Wat Arun or Klong San Market. They cost about 3B each way.

BY CANAL BOAT   Travel by a canal boating is about as local as transportation can get in Bangkok. It's a fun if somewhat odorous way to beat rush-hour traffic, allowing you to cross Bangkok from a starting point close to the Grand Palace and trek across to Sukhumvit through the commercial heart of the city. A narrow, dirty canal, Klong Saen Saep, runs the length of Phetchaburi Road, with stops in central Bangkok (and all the way to Thonglor, after a

Bangkok's Canals

The key to Bangkok's rise lies in the Chao Phraya River, which courses through its center, feeding a complex network of canals and locks that, until relatively recently, were the focus of city life. Lying just a few miles from the Gulf of Thailand, the river was a major conduit for trade, and the main reason behind its rapid growth. Today, not much has changed: Small yellow tugs pull great black barges filled with rice, coal, or sand up and down the river. These waterways fast became the aquatic boulevards and avenues of this low-lying, swampy city. Apart from structures built for royalty, ordinary Bangkok residents lived on water, in bamboo raft homes, or on boats. As

foreign diplomats, missionaries, and writers traveled to Bangkok, they drew parallels with the Italian city of Venice and renamed it the "Venice of the East." Not until the early 1800s were non-royal houses built on dry land.

Due to the health hazards posed by these open klongs, and the gradual need for more stable land with the advent of vehicular transport, many of the canals were paved over in the last century. By the late 1970s, most of the city's paddy fields had disappeared. In fact, much of today's Bangkok has been reclaimed from former marshland. Fears are growing as global warming raises sea levels and the effects of seasonal flooding on the city are becoming more drastic.

change at Krung Kasem Road). These long, low boats are designed to fit under bridges and have tarps that are raised and lowered by pulleys to protect passengers from any toxic splashes. Rides start at just 14B. Board the boats just north of Wat Mahathat. These canal buses really zip along and churn up a stink, but they offer a unique perspective on the last vestiges of what was once called the "Venice of the East," and taking one gets you through central Bangkok without having to inhale noxious bus fumes or endure motionless traffic.

BY CHARTERED LONGTAIL BOAT   Private boats are a great way to see the busy riverside area and to tour the narrow *khlongs* (canals) of neighboring Thonburi. Boat charters are available at any pier and the most common point of departure is the Saphan Taskin Pier. It won't take long for a man with a sign to approach you offering to coordinate a boat ride. Trips of varying length cost up to 1,000B per hour, per boat (1–6 people)—though drivers will try to get more so get ready to haggle. Be specific about destinations and times before you agree or board a boat.

BY PUBLIC BUS   Bangkok buses are very cheap but ply a confusing network and **they're not user-friendly** in terms of helpful ticket takers, or simply marked routes and stops. If you want to try them, blue buses are air-conditioned, and cheaper red or green ones are non-air-conditioned—and best described as fume-filled tin cans. Fares are inexpensive, between 5B and 30B, and you'll flag down the bus like you would a taxi. Bus drivers make rolling stops to let passengers on and off, making for a wild ride.

BY TAXI   Taxis are everywhere in this city and they are very affordable. Just flag them down (you can hail taxis along any road at any time, or join lines in front of hotels and shopping malls), and insist that drivers use the meter. At night, taxis will try to fleece passengers with demands for an extortionately high flat fare. You can choose to let these sharks be or remember that 150B or 200B isn't all that much (around $6) and agree to a fixed price for the sake of convenience.

Taxis charge a 35B flag fare which covers the first minute; thereafter, it is about 5B per kilometer. Most Thai drivers do not speak English or, surprisingly, read maps, so have your hotel concierge write out any destination in Thai.

Vacant taxis have a glowing red light on the lower passenger side dash. If a taxi pulls over without their light illuminated, they'll want to discuss a fixed rate. Simply wave them along if you don't want to negotiate.

Drivers rarely carry change. The best you will get is change from 100B notes, but drivers habitually claim that they have no change in the hope of getting a bit extra. Tipping is not necessary, but a 10B coin or 20B bill for a longer journey is appreciated.

BY CAR & DRIVER You'd have to be a bit mad to drive yourself around Bangkok as a tourist. Generally anarchic traffic, seas of cavalier motorbikes recklessly breaking every rule, and aggressive tactics by cabbies and truck drivers are the norm—not to mention limited parking. If you're in search of your own wheels, it is best to hire a car with a driver. Reputable companies provide sedans or minivans with drivers who know the city well, some of whom speak English. The best hotels provide luxury vehicles with an English-speaking driver or can assist in helping you book one. Major rental companies, like **Avis** (www.avisthailand.com; ✆ **02251-1131**) or **Hertz** (www.hertzthailand.com; ✆ **02266-4666**), offer chauffeured cars with an English-speaking driver or guide. These are about 1,000B an hour.

BY TUK-TUK As much a national symbol as the elephant, the tuk-tuk (named for the sound) is a small three-wheeled, open-sided vehicle powered by a motorcycle engine. It is noisy and smelly but its an adventurous rite of passage for first-time visitors to Thailand. They're not recommended for long hauls or during rush hour—if you get stuck behind a bus or truck you'll be dealing with unpleasant exhaust fumes. Negotiate all tuk-tuk fares with the driver; they will almost always be higher than the taxi fare to the same destination. Bargain with them, but know that you'll always pay way more than locals.

Look out: Tuk-tuk drivers are notorious for trying to talk travelers into shopping trips. They will offer you a very low fare but then dump you at small, out-of-the-way gem and silk emporiums, and overpriced tourist restaurants or brothels. Insist on being taken to where you want to go or find another ride.

BY MOTORCYCLE TAXI On every street corner, packs of drivers in orange colored, numbered vests standby to shuttle passengers around the city on the back of a motorcycle. Though they get you around fast when you're in a hurry (weaving through traffic jams, driving on sidewalks, and speeding down one-way streets the wrong way), they're also unsafe. Use them strictly for short distances (they're popular for short hops to the end of a long *soi*, or side street). They charge from 20B for a few blocks to 60B for greater distances. Hold on tight, watch your handbags, and keep your knees tucked in. Watch in awe as resident locals text, snack, or even read a book while the driver weaves in and out of traffic. Ladies wearing dresses or skirts are commonly seen riding sidesaddle, brazenly snapping selfies along the way.

ON FOOT Bangkok has some of the most vibrant streets in all of Asia. However, in general, Bangkok is not a pedestrian-friendly city, though improvements in the city center include the construction of skywalks. Bangkok sidewalks are a gauntlet of buckled tiles, loose manhole coverings, and tangled (live) wires. The city also suffers greatly from flooding and it would be tragically gross to wear open shoes in monsoon season. In addition, Bangkok's pedestrian traffic—particularly in the overcrowded BTS and at rush hour—moves at a painfully slow amble. It's best to go with the flow; otherwise, you'll only aggravate yourself. When crossing busier streets, look for pedestrian flyovers, or, if you have to cross at street level, find others who are crossing and follow them when they head out into traffic. Unlike in Western countries, crossing lights only serve as suggestions—drivers rarely stop to allow pedestrians to cross. A honking driver is a courtesy alert to let you know they won't be stopping as they come your way!

[FastFACTS] BANGKOK

ATMs ATMs are everywhere in Bangkok and those associated with Thai banks will take Visa, MasterCard, and other international cards.

Banks Many international banks also maintain offices in Bangkok, including **Bank of America,** 87/2 CRC Tower, Wireless Rd. (© 02305-2800); **JP Morgan Chase,** 20 Sathorn Nua Rd., (© 02684-2000); **Citibank,** 82 Sathorn Rd. (© 02232-2000). However, even if your bank has a branch in Thailand, your home account is considered foreign here and conducting personal banking will require special arrangements before leaving home.

Business Hours Government offices (including branch post offices) are open Monday to Friday 8:30am to 4:30pm, with a lunch break between noon and 1pm. Businesses are generally open 8am to 5pm. Small shops often stay open from 8am until 7pm or later, all week. Department stores are generally open 10:30am to 9pm.

Dentists Major hospitals offer dental services and there are clinics dotted around Sukhumvit and Silom roads in surprising frequency. Expat-centric Thonglor (Sukhumvit Soi 55) has several top operations, especially the upmarket **Thonglor Dental Hospital** (www.thonglordentalhospital. com; © 02382-0044). Pricing is commonly posted outside the building and major work, like a root canal, is much more affordable than in Western counties. In recent years, medical and dental tourism has been on the rise in Thailand.

Embassies & Consulates Your embassy in Thailand can (to an extent) assist you with medical and legal matters. Contact them immediately if there is a medical emergency, if you've lost your travel documents, or if you need urgent legal advice. The following is a list of major foreign representatives in Bangkok: **Australian Embassy,** 37 South Sathorn Rd. (© 02344-6300); **British Embassy,** 14 Wireless Rd. (© 02305-8333); **Canadian Embassy,** 15th Floor, Abdulrahim Place, 990 Rama IV Rd. (© 02636-0540); **New Zealand Embassy,** 14th Floor, M Thai Tower, All

Seasons Place, 87 Wireless Rd. (℗ **02254-2530**); and the **Embassy of the United States of America,** 95 Wireless Rd. (℗ **02205-4000**).

Emergencies In any emergency, first call **Bangkok's Tourist Police,** who can be reached at a direct-dial four-digit number, ℗ **1155,** or at ℗ **02678-6800.** Someone at both numbers will speak English. In case of **fire,** call ℗ **199** or **191,** both of which are direct-dial numbers. Individual, private hospitals handle **ambulance services;** see "Hospitals," below, or call your hotel's front desk.

Hospitals All hospitals listed here offer 24-hour emergency service. Make sure you have adequate travel insurance before you leave home. Major credit cards are accepted. **Bumrungrad Hospital,** 33 Soi 3, Sukhumvit Rd. (www.bumrungrad.com; ℗ **02667-1000**), has respected—but

costly—health practitioners and is the destination of choice in Bangkok for cosmetic surgery and (comparatively) affordable procedures. **BNH Hospital** at 9 Convent Rd., between Silom and Sathorn roads (www.bnhhospital.com; ℗ **02686-2700**), is extremely central; **Samitivej Hospital,** at 133 Sukhumvit Soi 49 (www.samitivej hospitals.com; ℗ **02711-8000**), is recommended for dentistry for young children, and for its maternity and infant wards.

Internet & Wi-Fi Cafes such as Starbucks offering free Wi-Fi are everywhere, especially along Sukhumvit and Khao San roads. Internet cafes are a dying breed but are common in backpacker-specific areas like near Khao San Road. Almost all hotels in Bangkok have free Wi-Fi.

Pharmacies Bangkok has many local pharmacies

that are safe for visitors to use. Hours vary location to location, but generally are 9am to 6pm. Another option is to visit a doctor and get prescribed drugs at a hospital or pick them up at an international store such as Watson's or Boots.

Safety In general, Bangkok is a relatively safe city, but be aware—especially on public transport—of pickpockets. Do not incite trouble; avoid public disagreements and hostility (especially with locals), and steer clear of gambling-related activities. If traveling alone at night, be alert, as you would in any city, and rely on your gut instincts; if you get a bad feeling about a place or situation, remove yourself from the scene. A Thai temper is virtually unheard of, but on rare (normally booze-filled) occasions, it can cause confrontations.

WHERE TO STAY

Bangkok offers fantastic value for money but remember that unless otherwise noted, hotel rates are subject to a **7% government value-added tax** and a **10% service charge.** In the high season (mid-Oct to mid-Feb), make reservations in advance, particularly over Christmas and New Year's Eve.

At the Airports

Hotels at **Don Muang** and **Suvarnabhumi International** airports are useful if you have a very-early-morning flight. **Amari Don Muang Airport Hotel** (www.amari.com; ℗ **02566-1020**) is linked by a bridge to the terminal and comes with a pool. Expect standard rooms from 2,500B. **Novotel Suvarnabhumi Airport** (www.novotel.com; ℗ **02131-1111**) has no set check-in time, meaning you can stay for 24 hours from whenever you arrive. It is just 5 minutes away from the airport on a free shuttle and offers four restaurants, plus a business center, Wi-Fi, and fitness facilities. Rates run from around 5,500B per room.

Bangkok Hotels

5

SETTLING INTO BANGKOK | Where to Stay

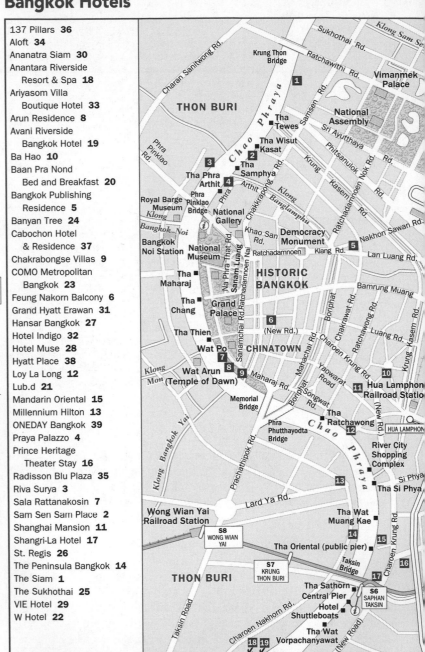

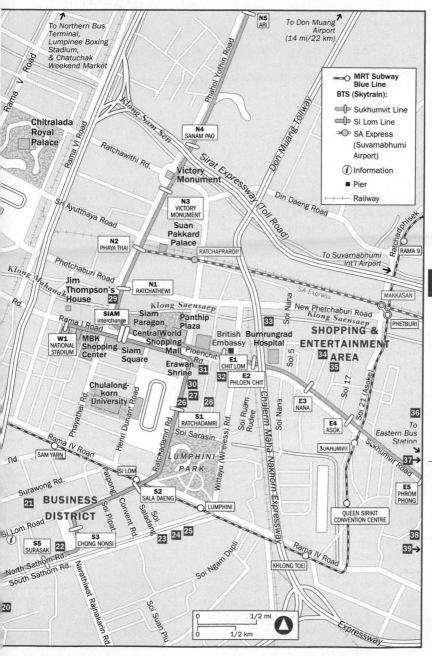

To Northern Bus
Terminal,
Lumpinee Boxing
Stadium,
& Chatuchak
Weekend Market

To Don Muang
Airport
(14 mi/22 km)

N5
ARI

**MRT Subway
Blue Line**
BTS (Skytrain):
Sukhumvit Line
Si Lom Line
SA Express
(Suvarnabhumi
Airport)
(i) Information
■ Pier
Railway

Rama V Road

Rama VI Rd.

Chitralada
Royal
Palace

Ratchawithi Rd.

Klong Sam Sen

N4
SANAM PAO

Sirat Expressway (Toll Road)

Don Muang Tollway

Din Daeng Road

Ratchadphisek

RAMA 9

Victory
Monument

Sri Ayutthaya Road

N3
VICTORY
MONUMENT

Suan
Pakkard
Palace

N2
PHAYA THAI

RATCHAPRAROP

To Suvarnabhumi
Int'l Airport →

MAKKASAN

Phetchaburi Road

Klong Mahanak

Rd.

Jim
Thompson's
House

29

N1
RATCHATHEWI

SA Express

New Phetchaburi Road

Klong Saensaep

PHETBURI

Klong Saensaep

Siam
Paragon

Panthip
Plaza

British
Embassy

Bumrungrad
Hospital

33

SHOPPING &
ENTERTAINMENT
AREA

SIAM
interchange

Soi Nana

Soi 5

34

35

Rama I Road

W1
NATIONAL
STADIUM

MBK
Shopping
Center

CentralWorld
Shopping
Mall

Siam
Square

Ploenchit
Rd.

E1
CHIT LOM

Erawan
Shrine

31

32

E2
PHLOEN CHIT

Soi Ruam
Rudee

Soi Nana

Soi 17

Soi 21 (Asoke)

36

To
Eastern Bus
Station

Sukhumvit Road

Chulalong-
korn
University

Phayathai Rd.

Henri Dunant Road

30

27

28

E3
NANA

E4
ASOK

SUKHUMVIT

37 →

26

S1
RATCHADAMRI

Soi Sarasin

E5
PHROM
PHONG

Rama IV Road

SAM YARN

Ratchadamri Rd.

LUMPHINI
PARK

Wittayu (Wireless) Rd.

Chalerm Maha Nakhorn Expressway

QUEEN SIRIKIT
CONVENTION CENTRE

38

39 →

SI LOM

S2
SALA DAENG

LUMPHINI

Surawong Rd.

BUSINESS
DISTRICT

21

Si Lom Road

S5
SURASAK

22

S3
CHONG NONSI

23

24

25

Patpong

Soi Pipat

Convent Rd.

Soi
Saladang

KHLONG TOEI

Rama IV Road

(i)

North Sathorn Rd.

South Sathorn Rd.

Narathiwat Rajnakarin Rd.

Soi Ngam Dupli

Soi Suan Plu

Expressway

20

0   1/2 mi
0   1/2 km

Riverside & Thonburi

A whole range of riverside hotels exists, including some of the top hotels in the city. Almost all price points boast great views and most operate free shuttle boats along the teeming Chao Phraya River, which makes them handy for shoppers, diners, spa-goers, and anyone needing the BTS. The finest don't come cheap, but, in recent years, plenty of new and reasonable midrange choices have opened. If you're short on time, consider booking a hotel in this area because you'll be near must-see sights, like the Grand Palace, Wat Pho, and Chinatown.

EXPENSIVE

Mandarin Oriental ★★★ The Oriental is the one hotel everyone has heard of before they come to Bangkok; the city's oldest hotel has been frequented by Thai royalty and glitterati, as well as a long roster of sports and film stars. Established in 1876, the Mandarin Oriental has evolved into a chic, contemporary venue known for its exceptional service. (How good? There are concierges stationed on most floors, so that guests can have any needs met without having to go down to the lobby). And though it's facing some stiff competition from recently opened luxury hotels, this venerable player just seems to get better. Over the years it has added a couple of swimming pools, a new wing, a venue for dinner shows, and a superb spa. The oldest part of the hotel, the Garden Wing and Author's Lounge, has been beautifully preserved. As you'd expect, rooms are sumptuously furnished, with deep, soft couches, fine wooden cabinets, lacquerware bowls, ceramic vases, and fresh-cut flowers. In fact, it's easy to imagine Joseph Conrad sitting in a corner penning one of his exciting tales, as he once did. There are modern touches aplenty though. For example, the bathroom mirrors have a heated panel behind part of them so they stay unfogged while steam from the shower wafts through the room (a plus for shavers). Several of its nine restaurants are among the city's top dining venues. Even if you don't stay here, stop by for a meal or a cocktail with live jazz.

48 Oriental Ave. (Charoen Krung Soi 41). www.mandarinoriental.com/bangkok. ⓒ **02659-9000.** 366 units. 19,000B–21,000B double, more for deluxe categories and suites. Saphan Taksin BTS. **Amenities:** 8 restaurants; lounge; bar; 2 outdoor pools; health club; spa; room service; babysitting; ferry shuttle service; Wi-Fi (free).

The Peninsula Bangkok ★★★ Though taller and sleeker than the Mandarin Oriental, which it faces across the Chao Phraya River, the Peninsula lives somewhat in the shadow of its illustrious neighbor. Yet when you compare all aspects of each, the Peninsula comes out very favorably. Rooms are generally bigger, and views, especially from the upper floors, are far superior. Furnishings are a perfect blend of traditional Thai and high-tech gadgetry, such as remote-controlled curtains. The bathrooms with marble counters are so stylish you'll want to stay in there all day, but then you'd miss the chance to visit the spa, set in a lovely colonial-style villa, and all the other wonderful facilities like the top-floor lounge bar and superb restaurants. Converted

Where to Stay

SETTLING INTO BANGKOK

wooden rice boats shuttle guests across the river, where all the action of Bangkok awaits.

333 Charoen Nakhorn Rd. www.bangkok.peninsula.com. ℂ 02861-2888. 370 units. 8000B–11,300B basic double, more for upgraded rooms and suites. Saphan Taksin BTS. **Amenities:** 4 restaurants; 2 bars; pool; tennis court; health club; spa; room service; babysitting; Wi-Fi (free).

Shangri-La Hotel ★ The big, brassy Shangri-La, on the banks of the Chao Phraya, boasts sprawling grounds and a jungle of tropical plants and flowers surrounding the resort-style pool. Rooms are in two connecting wings, both with river views; the newer Krung Thep Wing has slightly smarter rooms, and guests in suites have access to a private pool and dedicated concierge. All rooms—a whopping 802 of them—have teak furniture, larger-than-most bathrooms, and tasteful Thai touches. The views are better from the higher-floor deluxe rooms; some have either a balcony or a small sitting room, making them closer to junior suites—and a good value. The location is great but the level of service is average, leaving guests to feel lost in the shuffle of a rotating schedule of big gala events and huge conferences. The hotel's greatest flaw is that, when compared to legacy properties like the Mandarin Oriental, it fails to really shine.

89 Soi Wat Suan Plu, Charoen Krung Rd. (adjacent to Sathorn Bridge). www.shangri-la. com. ℂ 02236-7777. 802 units. From 8,000B–9,500B double; from 9,500B executive suite including breakfast. Saphan Taksin BTS. **Amenities:** 5 restaurants (including a floating one); 2 bars; outdoor pool; tennis court; health club; spa; room service; Wi-Fi (free).

MODERATE

Anantara Riverside Resort & Spa ★★ The Anantara Riverside is ideal if you want to explore Bangkok and, at the same time, escape it. On the western banks of the Chao Phraya River and a few miles downstream from the heart of old Bangkok, this sprawling resort feels like it's a world apart from the madness of the city. In fact, it can only be accessed by shuttle boat or taxi. The three wings of the hotel surround a large landscaped pool area with lily ponds and fountains. Children get the royal treatment here with a kids' club, kiddie pool, and special activities programs. Recreation, dining, and drinking choices are many, including such familiar restaurants as Trader Vic's and Benihana, as well a well-liked riverside terrace restaurant and a solid spa. As for the rooms, they are classically decorated (hardwood floors, lot of Thai silks, padded headboards on the beds), with river views from the balconies, and large bathrooms. Our favorite perk? Guests receive an international smartphone to use for free local and international calls, maps and more. By the way, dinner cruises on Manohra boats leave from here, so that's one of your evenings in Bangkok taken care of.

257/1-3 Charoen Nakhon Rd. www.bangkok-riverside.anantara.com. ℂ 02476-0022. 396 units. 4690B–9000B double inclusive of breakfast, more for upgraded rooms and suites. Ferry to Central Pier. **Amenities:** 6 restaurants; 3 bars; outdoor pool; 2 tennis courts; fitness center; spa; room service; babysitting; Wi-Fi (free).

Arun Residence ★ This cute hideaway, set in a former Sino-Portuguese home, was the first in a long line of boutique hotels to pop up along the riverside nearly a decade ago. Its rooms are all split level if a touch small, and some of the furnishings are showing wear-and-tear, but most guests are so taken with the spectacular views across the river to the eponymous *wat* (temple) they don't much care. It's suited to those who want to be in the thick of old Bangkok, as it's close to major sites (though public transport isn't on your doorstep). Onsite restaurant The Deck is a swell place to grab a drink and watch the sun dip behind the iconic landmark, though we don't recommend the food. *One warning*: no elevator means this isn't an appropriate choice for guests with mobility impairments.

36–38 Soi Pratoo Nok Yoong, Maharat Rd. www.arunresidence.com. ⓒ **02221-9158.** 6 units. 3,200B–4,200B double inclusive of breakfast, more for suites. Hua Lamphong MRT. **Amenities:** Restaurant; bar; Wi-Fi (free).

Avani Riverside Bangkok Hotel ★★ Everything about this towering hotel—from the swanky rooftop pool to modern rooms—feels a little bit hipper than usual, making it an ideal spot for travelers caught between the backpacker stage of life and the "need a kid-friendly hotel" stage. Rooms have photogenic views (all 248 facing the river), heavenly beds, fast Internet, and in-room technology like a free and fully loaded smartphone for guests. But the most exciting part of the hotel is the rooftop pool, which is one of the best in town. Forget your troubles as you sip a lychee martini while the infinity pool laps over the edge 26 floors above it all.

257 Charoennakorn Rd. ⓒ **02431-9100.** 248 units. 6000B–8400B double room; from 11,235B suite. Ferry to Saphan Taksin BTS. **Amenities:** 4 Restaurant; bar; fitness center; spa; Wi-Fi (free).

Chakrabongse Villas ★★★ Want to feel like royalty in Bangkok? Book a room at this riverside boutique that was Prince Chakrabongse's retreat from palace life, starting in 1908. Today, the villas, rooms (just seven of them), and lush gardens have been converted into an antique-laden hotel that is managed by the prince's granddaughter, Narisa. Decor varies from room to room; some have four-poster beds, others have canopied beds, some have wood-paneled walls, while others are decorated in pastel shades. The Chinese Suite, designed in homage to the nearby Chinatown, is exquisitely decorated with a spiral staircase leading to the second floor. Possibly even more evocative is the Thai House Suite, a 19th-century teak house brought from historic Ayutthaya. Service is impeccable and there's a pool and restaurant serving Royal Thai cuisine. They also have a river launch, canoes, and bikes for guests' use.

396 Maharaj Rd. www.chakrabongsevillas.com. ⓒ **02222-1290.** 7 units. 6000B–8900B double room, more for suites. Hua Lamphong MRT. **Amenities:** Restaurant; boat trips; loaner bikes and canoes; Wi-Fi (free).

Millennium Hilton ★★ The resurgence of the area surrounding this hotel, pioneered by indie art galleries and the creative hub of the Jam Factory, has been a boost for the Millennium Hilton. And its guests. Now that there's items of interest in the immediate vicinity there's even more reason to stay at this sky high beaut, towering 32 stories over the west bank of the Chao Phraya River. At its top, the Three Sixty Lounge, and infinity pool with a white sand sundeck, are particularly ace spots for watching the sunset and the sprawl of Bangkok and its bustling river life. Rooms and suites, all spacious, underwent a renovation in 2018, so they're spiffier than ever, if still quite corporate looking. Big thumbs up, though, for oversized windows which flood guestrooms with light, and the Jacuzzi tubs in the marble bathrooms. On-site are several restaurants, but you can do better. When it's time for sightseeing, a free shuttle boat is on hand to take guests across the river to the Saphan Taksin BTS, Asiatique or the River City shopping center.

123 Charoennakorn Rd. www.bangkok.hilton.com. © **02442-2000.** 533 units. 3,600B–4,700B double, more for suites. Free shuttle boat from Saphan Taksin BTS. **Amenities:** 4 restaurants; 2 bars; outdoor pool; health club; spa; babysitting; café; Wi-Fi (free).

Praya Palazzo ★★ This handsome Italianate mansion on the banks of the Chao Phraya River was constructed in 1923, and has been lovingly restored. Its 17 rooms and suites are all individually designed with period furnishings; they ooze character. Located on the west bank of the river opposite Phra Arthit Pier, the Palazzo is ideal for exploring the sights on Rattanakosin Island as well as the nightlife around Banglampoo. However, the hotel is only accessible by boat, which helps to enhance the sense of privacy, but also means guests are slightly limited in travel. I say "slightly" because guests have the use of a private boat, and are given a cellphone to call it when needed. On property, a small swimming pool and lush gardens surround the two-story building, and the Praya Dining restaurant serves some of the best Thai cuisine in the city. A small library and a gallery are beside the dining room, where guests can read the intriguing story of the mansion's history and painstaking renovation.

757/1 Somdej Prapinklao Soi 2. www.prayapalazzo.com. © **02883-2998.** 17 units. 3,500B–4,000B double. Phra Arthit pier. **Amenities:** Restaurant; bar; outdoor pool; room service; free boat shuttle; Wi-Fi (free).

Sala Rattanakosin ★★ This riverside retreat is the ultimate "room with a view": the hotel is right across the river from Wat Arun (p. 113), and many guests count watching the temple go from the glow of sunset to nighttime spotlights as a highpoint of their stay. That spectacular evening "show" is seen through (most) guestrooms' dramatic floor-to-ceiling windows (the view from the rooftop bar is pretty sweet, too). And to keep the focus on those views, rooms are chicly minimalist, with black-and-white color schemes, platform beds, free-standing tubs, and large bathrooms. If jet lag strikes, wake up early to offer alms to the local monks in saffron robes on the streets just outside.

39 Soi Thatian, Maharat Rd. www.salahospitality.com/rattanakosin. © **02622-1388.** 15 units. 3000B–5000B double, including breakfast; 12,900B suite. Hua Lamphong MRT. **Amenities:** Restaurant; bar; Wi-Fi (free).

Chinatown

Yaowarat (Chinatown) is a trip back in time, and it feels like not much has changed since this neighborhood laid down roots 1782, which is part of the charm of choosing a hotel in this part of town. There aren't a ton of choices, and what is available falls into one of two categories: Characterless monstrosities that host a revolving door of tour bus groups, or smaller boutiques (without all the bells and whistles of the larger resorts described above). But this atmospheric neighborhood is rich in street food, hip gin bars, and old-world charm.

MODERATE

Ba Hao ★   There are only two rooms at this four-story shophouse (a tall and narrow building) in Chinatown. Yep, only two. That can make reservations hard to get, but this space is so unique, and the neighborhood so interesting, it is worth a try. The ground level of the 60-year-old structure is a bar of the same name, serving cocktails, beer, and Chinese comfort classics (the duck wontons are amazing). For lodging guests, a shared living room with leather sofas, Eames chairs, and coffee stations occupies the second floor. The third floor is the Maitri Chit room, an open-plan suite with brassy accents, a working desk, subway tiles, plants, and great light. The fourth and final floor follows a similar layout and style but has the added perks of a balcony and a view of Wat Trimit. The bar-hotel shares its road with Teens of Thailand (p. 131), a happening gin bar, so it can be a touch noisy when the drinking crowd heads home.

8 Soi Nana. www.ba-hao.com (booking is completed on the Airbnb platform). ℂ **081454-4959.** 2 units. 3,100B and 3,700B inclusive of breakfast. Hua Lamphong MRT. **Amenities:** Restaurant; Wi-Fi (free).

Loy La Long ★★   Set in a 100-year-old wooden house, Loy La Long is loaded with personality and charm. Rooms are identified and sold on the website by color scheme, with green being the most stylish (leafy print wallpaper, a free-standing brass tub in the bathroom, platform bed). But all are fun, featuring lots of wood, quirky art, and river views. The entire space feels ultra-private, and is: to reach the entrance to the hotel, guests walk through a local temple. Best part about staying here? Ending the day relaxing in a wooden rocking chair, drink in hand, watching the boats on the river drift by.

1620/2 Songwat Rd. (inside Wat Patumkongka). www.loylalong.com. ℂ **02639-1390.** 6 units. 2,700B to 4,900B double inclusive of breakfast. Hua Lamphong MRT. **Amenities:** Restaurant; Wi-Fi (free).

INEXPENSIVE

Feung Nakorn Balcony ★   Located on Feung Nakorn Road, one the first roads in Bangkok, the neighborhood feels like not much has changed, which is a great reason for booking a room here. Bright and cheery rooms in this former elementary school accommodate a variety of budget-conscious travelers, offering four suites, 30 standard rooms, and four shared bunk-style rooms. A lovely garden setting, koi fish pond, and laid-back bar-restaurant add to the experience. Old Bangkok is on the hotel's doorstep along with incredible street food, temples tucked away down small lanes, and some of the city's trendiest bars around the corner on Soi Nana.

29 Soi Fueang Thong, Fueang Nakhon Rd. www.feungnakorn.com. © **02622-1100.** 42 units. From 700B dorm; from 1,650B room; from 2,100B suite inclusive of breakfast. Hua Lamphong MRT. **Amenities:** 1 restaurant; bar; Wi-Fi (free).

Shanghai Mansion ★★ With an open-air entrance spilling right into the heart of busting Yaowarat, this hotel is a small but shining example of a rise in character-filled boutique hotels springing up around town. This former Chinese opera house exudes Chinatown kitsch and 1930s Shanghai vibes. The lobby and rooms are adorned with lots of red, silks, lanterns, birdcages, Chinese porcelain, koi fishponds, and prints of beautiful girls dressed in cheongsam. The small-sized rooms (and slightly larger suites) keep the theme going, with vivid pink, green, and red silks, and Chinese lattice-frame beds, all evoking Old Shanghai. The hotel offers few perks, such as delicious Chinese high tea and free Wi-Fi, but its atmosphere far outstrips its better-equipped but characterless neighbors.

479 Yaowarat Rd. www.shanghaimansion.com. © **02221-2121.** 76 units. From 1,450B double; from 2,8000B suite. Hua Lamphong MRT. **Amenities:** Restaurant; room service; Wi-Fi (free).

Sathorn, Silom & Bangrak

If Bangkok were to have one single business district (it actually has many), this would be it. The area's main throughways are Surawong and Silom roads and parallel to them is the busy eight-lane Sathorn Road, off which you'll find the city's more prominent embassies, top hotels, police, and immigration HQs. The major problem with this area is that it snarls up with static traffic every evening; we suggest using trains to the Lumphini MRT stop at the top of Sathorn Road to avoid the gridlock. Plus, there's plenty of activities bars, and restaurants within walking distance of the following hotels.

EXPENSIVE

The Sukhothai ★★★ This hip hotel is a maze of low pavilions, pools, and courtyards, deftly combining crisp, contemporary lines with Thai objets d'art, Thai silks, and rich tones. Colonnaded corridors surround lotus pools adorned with brick *chedis;* the terra-cotta friezes and the celadon ceramics all have motifs borrowed from its namesake city. Expansive guestrooms boast fine silk walls, mellow teak furniture, and rustic floor tiles; all have double bathrooms with oversized bathtubs, a separate shower, and toilet. The hotel's Thai restaurant, Celadon, serves exquisite (if only lightly fiery) fare in a special occasion setting, while the Colonnade is considered the most indulgent brunch spot in the city. Sathorn's notorious gridlock make the location tough, but public transportation is within walking distance.

13/3 South Sathorn Rd. www.sukhothai.com. © **02344-8888.** 210 units. 7,000B–10,500B double; 11,500B–14,500B suites. Lumphini MRT. **Amenities:** 6 restaurants; bar; lounge; outdoor pool; tennis court; health club; spa; room service; babysitting; Wi-Fi (free).

W Hotel ★★★   This buzzy hotel is very conveniently located, just steps from a BTS station. Forget typical hotel lingo, because here self-fulfilling room categories are Marvelous, Wonderful, Spectacular, and even Extreme Wow (an over-the-top suite). Accent pillows on the hotel's heavenly beds are oversized Thai boxing gloves; the rooms are filled with other contemporary, graphic takes on traditional Thai designs. A lobby DJ makes the check in experience a blast and the W hosts a legendary Songkran pool party in April.

106 North Sathorn Rd. www.whotelbangkok.com. ✆ **02344-4000**. 403 units. From 9000B double; from 10,600B suite. Chong Nonsi BTS. **Amenities:** 2 restaurants; 2 bars; outdoor pool; spa; fitness center; pets allowed; room service; Wi-Fi (free).

MODERATE

Banyan Tree ★★   This immense luxury skyscraper hotel provides exceptional panoramas, a plethora of trendy dining venues, and a chic spa with spacious treatment rooms (including segregated wet-rooms for thalassotherapy treatments). Vertigo is the most popular of the upscale dining options, an alfresco venue on the vertiginous roof—though the views are better than the food. A must-do for hotel guests and city dwellers is to raise a glass to the good life under the stars at Moon Bar (p. 131), which is the best rooftop bar in the city. Given its stellar reputation in Asia, the hotel is popular with Asian families who take to its sleek, if not particularly Thai, good looks (expect lots of pillows, shiny woods, cutting edge bathrooms fixtures, and curvy furniture). Mention the Thai Wah building right out in front to ensure your taxi doesn't miss the theatrical torch-lit entrance; it's on busy one-way Sathorn. Stretch your legs or go for a picnic in nearby Lumpini Park.

21/100 S. Sathorn Rd. www.banyantree.com. ✆ **02679-1200**. 327 units. From 5,800B deluxe suite; from 8,300B suite. Lumphini MRT. **Amenities:** 6 restaurants; 4 bars; lounge; outdoor pool; health club; spa; room service; Wi-Fi (free).

COMO Metropolitan Bangkok ★★   Those pursuing a healthy lifestyle can do so with ease at the COMO Metropolitan. Every morning starts with a complimentary yoga class led by top instructors (there's also a mat in every room for those who prefer to practice on their own); on-site Glow restaurant serves a fruit- and veggie rich breakfast; the gym and pool are massive and well-equipped; and you're guaranteed a good nights' sleep, as the beds are topnotch, and the hotel is blissfully quiet (despite being hemmed in by a cluster of towers on busy Sathorn Road). We also must recommend the signature Shambala massage at the spa. And if all this is sounding a bit too wholesome, indulge in a cocktail in the Met Bar (exclusively for hotel guests and members, with DJs spinning eclectic lounge sounds) and then dine on-site at Nahm (p. 88), one of the most coveted restaurant reservations in the city. Staff are extremely friendly and helpful, and the rooms, if not memorable looking, are well-equipped and immaculate.

27 South Sathorn Rd. www.comohotels.com/metropolitanbangkok. ✆ **02625-3333**. 171 units. From 4,600B double, 11,500B suite. Lumphini MRT. **Amenities:** 2 restaurants; bar; outdoor pool; fitness center; spa; room service; Wi-Fi (free).

INEXPENSIVE

Baan Pra Nond Bed and Breakfast ★★ One of the few B&Bs in Bangkok, this 70-year-old house belonged to a former Supreme Court judge (*baan* means house, *pra* is a title given to high-ranking officials in Thailand, Nond was the judge's nickname). It was built for the astonishingly low cost of 8,000B all those years ago. Today, his family operates the canary yellow Thai-Colonial guesthouse with pride. The nine rooms are quaint and filled with old-fashioned furnishings (a big wooden armoire here, a canopy bed there), but with all the modern amenities today's travelers have come to expect. Light-filled, breezy common spaces are ideally suited for curling up with a good book; an artful portrait of the judge watches over one of the living rooms. The only downside: the house is smack-dab between two major roads, so it can get noisy. But the location is ripe for riverside exploration as it is steps away from the Saphan Taksin pier and BTS stop.

18/1 Charoen Rat Rd. www.baanpranond.com. ℭ **02212-2242.** 9 units. From 1,800B double including breakfast. Surasak BTS. **Amenities:** Outdoor pool; Wi-Fi (free).

Lub.d ★★ Meaning "sleep well" in Thai, Lub.d is a sociable hostel for backpackers who want a base in the center of the city. It offers a variety of accommodations, from eight-bed dorms with shared washrooms to private rooms with en-suite bathrooms. Furnishings are basic, but not without style, and functional, and all dorm beds have a reading light, power, and personal locker to store gear. Rooms are air-conditioned and there's a big communal room, as well as a small theater for watching movies. This original branch is well located on a side street off Silom Road, and there are other locations in Siam Square (Bangkok), Phuket, and Ko Samui (see website for details).

4 Decho Rd. www.lubd.com. ℭ **02634-7999.** 36 units. 300B eight-person dorm; 900B (shared washroom) or 1300B (private washroom) double. Chong Nonsi BTS. **Amenities:** Bar; café; lockers (in dorms), Wi-Fi (free).

Prince Heritage Theater Stay ★★ Bangkok has a rocky history of preserving historic buildings, especially theaters. Thankfully, this 100-year-old theater (which started as a casino, with an infamous all-male opera troupe) reopened in 2018 as a stylish, affordable place to bed down for a few nights. It has a range of room types: private suites, family rooms with shared bathrooms and communal rooms with different bed configurations (some are for women only). The latter are a little less "hostel-like" than usual, thanks to curtained-off mini-rooms in some, and pod-type lodgings in others. And because of high ceilings, lots of light, and nicer-than-most bathrooms, all digs are very pleasant. The "box office" area is now a vibrant living room with quirky décor, a bar and film screenings. The staff is topnotch. The hotel is steps from famous street food stalls, like Jok Prince, *the* place for a congee breakfast.

441/1 Charoenkrung Rd. (Siwiang). www.princeheritage.com ℭ **02090-2858.** 4 suites, 2 shared duplexes with 6 beds, 2 bunk rooms. From 500B bunk; 4,200B suite. Saphan Taksin BTS. **Amenities:** Bar/café; Wi-Fi (free).

Siam, Phloenchit, & Ratchadamri

Accessed along its entire length by the convenient BTS, Sukhumvit Road is the heart of commercial Bangkok. Here you'll find many of the town's finest malls and restaurants, as well as busy street-side shopping and dining stalls. Many businesses line this endless thoroughfare, and the small lanes, or *sois*, are crammed with bars and clubs. There are a few good budget choices (which are much better than those on busy and inconvenient Khao San Road), and direct access to the BTS means you can get anywhere you need to go in town at any time of day—which is a bonus when gridlock strikes.

Note: Siam (pronounced *See-yam*) BTS lies at the heart of the Rajadaprasong shopping area. Covered walkways link it to a number of Bangkok's larger and swankier malls, but there are few elevators for wheelchairs or baby strollers.

EXPENSIVE

Ananatra Siam ★★★　The Anantara Siam (formerly the Four Seasons) is a smart, well-appointed low-rise property. The entrance and lobby are majestic, with a sweeping staircase adorned with giant Thai murals and detailed gold paintwork on the high ceilings. The impeccable service begins at the threshold, and an air of luxury pervades. Rooms are oversized, featuring handsome color schemes (neutrals with jewel-toned accents), plush carpeted dressing areas, and large bathrooms. Cabana Rooms face the large pool and terrace area, which is filled with palms, lotus ponds, and tropical greenery. The dining is exemplary, especially **Biscotti** (p. 92). The concierge service is smart, well-connected, and practically predicts daily needs.

155 Ratchadamri Rd. www.anantara.com/siam-bangkok. ℂ **02126-8866.** 354 units. From 7,000B double; 22,000B suite. Ratchadamri BTS. **Amenities:** 5 restaurants; outdoor pool; health club; spa; room service; babysitting; Wi-Fi (free).

Hansar Bangkok ★★　This eye-catching tower tucked off Ratchadamri Road (just a few steps from the BTS station) provides superb all-suite accommodations. Digs are huge, ranging from 59–125 sq. m (635–1,346 sq. ft.), and those on upper floors have sweeping city views. They're equipped with all kinds of luxuries, from massive TVs to freestanding terrazzo bathtubs to high-end mattresses for the king-sized beds. Even without a traditional front desk setup, service is excellent. The location couldn't be better: just steps from a BTS station, with the Anantra Siam (see above) in front of it, blocking the noise from a busy road. Add the hotel's good-sized pool, the Luxsa Spa, and three classy dining options, and you've got a Bangkok base with comprehensive comforts.

3 Soi Mahadlekluang, 2 Ratchadamri Rd. www.hansarbangkok.com. ℂ **02209-1234.** 94 units. 6,000B–40,000B suites. Ratchadamri BTS. **Amenities:** 3 restaurants; bar; outdoor pool; spa; health club; room service; complementary minibar, Wi-Fi (free).

St. Regis ★★★　With a prime downtown location, this swish, luxury hotel has a fantastic view overlooking the Royal Bangkok Sports Club, and it's right next to the BTS station, making it very easy to get around. All rooms are a good size, with floor-to-ceiling windows, and sumptuously equipped with king-sized beds with upholstered headboards. The 15th floor is given over to health and wellness, with a truly incredible pool, fitness center, and gorgeous spa with 15 treatment rooms. Enjoy elegant Italian dishes at **JoJo** ★ or sushi and creative cocktails at **Zuma** ★★; both restaurants are just off the lobby.

159 Ratchadamri Rd., www.starwoodhotels.com/stregis. ℭ **02207-7777.** 228 units. 8,000B–15,000B double; 12,500B–70,000B suites. Ratchadamri BTS. **Amenities:** 2 restaurants; 3 bars; outdoor pool; health club; spa; concierge. Wi-Fi (5 mbps free; premium Wi-Fi 400B per day).

MODERATE

Ariyasom Villa Boutique Hotel ★★★   Thanks to a relatively hidden location down Sukhumvit Soi 1, but not so hard a cabbie will never find it, Ariyasom Villa flies relatively under the radar. A prominent engineer built the home between 1941 and 1942, and today his landscape architect granddaughter and her architect husband look after the place. With ownership pedigrees like that, it comes as no surprise this place is a manicured gem with lush gardens, a small pool, meditation space, and one of the top vegetarian restaurants in town. Rooms have teak wood flooring, sofas, Thai silk curtains, and comfortable beds. The name translates to the sanctuary of the enlightened, which is exactly what you'll be after just a night or two here.

65 Sukhumvit Soi 1. www.ariyasom.com. ℭ **02254-8880.** 24 units. From 5,650B double. Phloen Chit BTS. **Amenities:** 1 restaurant; outdoor pool; spa; Wi-Fi (free).

Grand Hyatt Erawan ★★   Where, in the 1970s, the former Erawan Hotel famously stood, the hulking Grand Hyatt now stands. It enjoys an ideal central location, amidst glittery temples, mega malls, and crazy-busy intersections, with the BTS whizzing by above. The hotel's design epitomizes glamour and exuberance with giant columns and staircases filling the open lobby. Spacious rooms are decked out in delightful silks, celadon ceramics, pseudo-antique furnishings, and parquet floors, and the suites are some of the largest in the city. The bathrooms are equally generous, and city views abound. The excellent spa occupies an entire floor, and the hotel's tearoom (p. 93) is a legendary institution. Join the host of well-wishes shaking joss sticks at neighboring Erawan Shrine (p. 108).

494 Ratchadamri Rd. (corner of Rama I Rd.). www.bangkok.grand.hyatt.com. ℭ **800/ 492-8804.** 380 units. 6,100B–9,300B double; from 13,100B suite. Phloen Chit BTS. **Amenities:** 4 restaurants; lounge; outdoor pool; tennis court; health club; spa; room service; babysitting; Wi-Fi (free).

Hotel Indigo ★★   Hotel Indigo is a fun and funky foil to the more traditional hotels in the neighborhood. A non-working pedal rickshaw takes up prominent real estate in the lobby, colorful furnishings are in the rooms, and antique radios are a nod to the location on Wireless Road, which means radio in Thai. Rooms are modern with sleek bathrooms. Most have views of the nearby embassies, and the hotel is equidistant from Lumpini Park and a BTS stop.

81 Wireless Rd. www.ihg.com. ℭ **02207-4999.** 192 units. From 3,999B double; from 16,000B suite inclusive of breakfast. Phloen Chit BTS. **Amenities:** 1 restaurant; bar; outdoor pool; small health club; room service; Wi-Fi (free).

Hotel Muse ★★ Thailand's late-19th century golden era is brought to life here, in a hotel that mixes European elegance and Asian motifs. Rooms and common spaces are moody, dark, and decadent, with textured wallpaper, claw-foot bathtubs, and sexy gold-and-brown color schemes. As for the location, it's ideal for those looking to shop until they drop. On the rooftop is a Prohibition-style speakeasy that's definitely worth a visit, as is the hotel's deeply pampering spa.

55/555 Langsuan Rd. www.hotelmusebangkok.com. ℂ **02630-4000.** 174 units. From 4,500B double; from 12,515B suite. Ratchadamri BTS. **Amenities:** 3 restaurants; bar; lounge; outdoor pool; small health club; spa; room service; Wi-Fi (free).

VIE Hotel ★★ A stone's throw away from the Jim Thompson house (and Bangkok's top luxury malls), the Thai silks in the rooms here are in homage to the hotel's famous neighbor and the country's most famous textile. *Mon khwan* pillows (a sturdy triangle shaped pillow designed for reclining) adorn the beds and wood accents, floor-to-ceiling windows, and high ceilings increase the classiness quotient. On the roof is a swish pool with a glass wall that overlooks the bustling city below. Service is flawless.

177/39-40 Phaya Thai Rd. www.viehotelbangkok.com. ℂ **02309-3939.** 154 units. From 3,900B double. Ratchadamri BTS. **Amenities:** 2 restaurants; bar; outdoor pool; health club; spa; room service; Wi-Fi (free).

Banglampoo & Dusit

This is a fast-gentrifying area but it still caters to a core clientele of budget backpackers, aging hippies, and young Thai tourists. Cheap eats and funky fashions abound and these neighborhoods are close to such sights as the Grand Palace and National Museum, but a long way from the Skytrain and subway, so getting around to other parts of the city from here is a bit of a problem. Most tourists hop on a river taxi from Phra Arthit pier to Saphan Taksin BTS.

EXPENSIVE

The Siam ★★★ It is a toss-up between The Siam and the Mandarin Oriental for the title of Bangkok's best hotel. American-born and Bangkok-based architect Bill Bensley designed this Art Deco beauty, and The Siam is the crown jewel in his hotel collection, which also includes the Four Seasons Tented Camp (p. 388) in Chiang Rai. The hotel is decorated with antiques, art, and *objets* from the musically inclined Thai family that owns the hotel—one of the sons is a Thai rock star. Well-appointed rooms mix Art Deco with Asian touches, and they're effortlessly chic. Connie's Cottage is a two-story teak house that belonged to a friend of Jim Thompson; pool villas are free-standing houses with a private pool. Be sure to explore some of the hotel's secret hideouts, like a screening room, record room, library, and Muay Thai ring. The spa is outrageously opulent, and private butlers make any request possible, including organizing ceremonies for sacred tattooing in the hotel's dedicated *Sak Yant* studio. The hotel is miles from any form of public transportation, but a stylish boat makes the 30-minute commute to the main riverside attractions an elegant affair. Smartphones with a useful chat function allow guests to connect with their butler at all times.

3/2 Thanon Khao, Vachirapayabal. www.thesiamhotel.com. © **02206-6999.** 39 units. From 21,000B for a suite. Take the hotel's boat from the pier by the Saphan Taksin BTS. **Amenities:** 2 restaurants; bar; outdoor pool; health club (with Muay Thai gym); tattoo parlor; hair & nail salon; spa; Wi-Fi (free).

MODERATE

Bangkok Publishing Residence ★★ The Bangkok Publishing Residence is part hotel and part museum, a combination that is totally charming. It was once a (yup, you guessed it) publishing house that produced local Thai magazines. Today, the 1960s shophouse exterior remains but the dividing walls have been removed, and the careful restoration of the historic building took 7 years. Antique furniture and timeworn floors give it a retro feel, but Bluetooth speakers and Nespresso machines make for a comfortably modern stay. The common spaces include a dramatic atrium, shelves of back issue magazines, typesetting tools, old typewriters, and family collectibles. The hotel is a 10-minute walk to Khao San Rd.

31-33-35-37-37/1 Lan Luang Rd. www.bpresidence.com. © **02282-0288.** 8 units. From 3,600B double including breakfast. Taxi from Hua Lamphong MRT. **Amenities:** Restaurant; outdoor Jacuzzi; Wi-Fi (free).

Riva Surya ★ Riva Surya has a lot going for it, but its biggest charm is what it isn't—super expensive. In a part of town dominated by 20,000B a night hotels, or dinky and dirty dorm rooms, this moderately priced hotel fills a need nicely. Rooms won't win any style awards, but that doesn't mean they're sore on the eyes. Instead, crisp white bedding, simple art, a desk chair, and side lamps fill out the digs, all of which have private balconies. Bathrooms have high-pressure showerheads and room to move around comfortably. Grab a drink at the riverside pool and watch the longtail boats zoom by or check out the indie nightlife on the hip Phra Arthit Road.

23 Phra Arthit Rd. www.nexthotels.com/hotel/riva-surya-bangkok. © **02633-5000.** 68 units. 3,025B to 4,690B double. Taxi from Hua Lamphong MRT. **Amenities:** Restaurant; bar; outdoor pool; health club; room service; parking (free); Wi-Fi (free).

INEXPENSIVE

Sam Sen Sam Place ★ I encountered some truly awful hostels while researching this book, particularly in this neighborhood. But at Sam Sen Sam Place, guests can get up close to all the Khao San Road action without the grit . . . or shared quarters. Occupying a 100-year-old Thai house on a quiet lane, this place offers a stay that feels like one is bedding down at a friend's home. Rooms are very clean, offering firm mattresses (a signature in Asia) and strong air-conditioning or powerful fans. A complimentary breakfast is part of the deal. A major perk: the hotel's lovely and relaxing garden.

48 Samsen Rd., Samsen Soi 3. www.samsensam.com. © **02628-7067.** 30 units. 565B for non-A/C room with fan and shared bathroom, 969B for a double with private bathroom and A/C. Prices inclusive of breakfast. Taxi from Hua Lamphong MRT. **Amenities:** Restaurant; Wi-Fi (free).

Lower Sukhumvit: Nana to Ekkamai

Access to the BTS, luxury malls, and an overwhelming number of cocktail bars, rooftops, and hip places to eat and drink make this is an appealing spot for shoppers, partiers and foodies. They'll find boutiques packed with character as well as highly affordable hotels and hostels.

EXPENSIVE

137 Pillars Bangkok Suites and Residences ★★★ From the moment the uniformed doorman opens the door, until the hotel's London-style cab takes you to the airport, prepare to be treated to some of the most kindly, detail-oriented service in the city. The hotel is the sister property of the luxurious 137 Pillars House in Chiang Mai (p. 328), and it opened its doors in 2017, revealing 34 luxurious suites named after the great royal periods in Thai history. Expressive artwork, huge closets, high thread count sheets, marble bathrooms, circular tubs, impressive balconies, and city views are just some of the perks. A drool-worthy rooftop pool and 24-hour butler service complete the picture. Residences come with kitchenettes and are configured into studios, one-bedrooms, and two-bedrooms. The extra space and kitchen make this lodging ideally suited for families.

38 Sukhumvit Soi 39. www.137pillarshotels.com. ℭ **02079-7137.** 34 units. From 4,900B for studio suite; from 21,000B suite. Phrom Phong BTS. **Amenities:** 2 restaurants; bar; outdoor pool; health club; spa; Wi-Fi (free).

MODERATE

Aloft ★★ Boldly colorful rooms here are high-tech—and have more than enough outlets to keep you charged 24/7. Each has a huge TV, tons of natural light, working desks, and speedy Wi-Fi. Mix business with pleasure in the club-like lobby. Its soundtrack of upbeat music will have you ready to dance, which you'll want to do on Soi 11, a party street at the doorstep of the hotel. Points collectors note: Aloft is part of the Starwood chain.

35 Sukhumvit Soi 11. www.aloftbangkoksukhumvit11.com. ℭ **02207-7000.** 297 units. From 2,859B double; from 7,199B suite. Nana BTS. **Amenities:** 2 restaurants; bar; outdoor pool; health club; Wi-Fi (free).

Cabochon Hotel & Residence ★★ Unlike several of the other century-old buildings that have been converted to hotels, the Cabochon only *looks* old (it was built in 2012). It's lobby décor, a mix of plush couches, old French magazines, African taxidermy, airplane figures, and bright butterflies frozen in time under a glass cloche also gives it that "old timey air". If you didn't know better, you'd think you were in the atmospheric, ultra-stylish home of a 1920's-era collector. Rooms are nice, too, if not quite as evocative, cleanly designed with bright white walls, tufted headboards and retro-fitted shower heads. Swim laps in the rooftop pool, nosh on Thai-Laos cuisine at the outstanding **Thai Lao Yeh ★★**, or enjoy being steps away from nightlife-heavy Thonglor. Cabochon means polished gem, by the way, which is quite apt for this charming boutique.

14/29 Sukhumvit Soi 45. www.cabochonhotel.com. ℭ **02259-2871.** 8 units. From 5,200B double inclusive of breakfast. Phrom Phong BTS. **Amenities:** Restaurant; bar; outdoor pool; Wi-Fi (free).

Hyatt Place ★   Cost-effective pricing is made possible by the hotel's policy of catering to the "self-reliant" traveler, so there aren't porters to bring bags to the room, guests can check-in online, and there are grab-n-go meals in place of room service. Nothing is missing, however, from the sleek contemporary guestrooms; they have lots of room to unpack, dedicated working space, and clean-lined bathrooms. The rooftop bar, **Aire,** is among the most affordable in the city, with signature drinks capped at 280B—a welcome reprieve in a city where alfresco drinking reaches the sky-high prices (500B or more per cocktail in some joints).

22/5 Sukhumvit Soi 24. https://bangkoksukhumvit.place.hyatt.com/en/hotel/home. html. ℂ **02055-1234.** 222 units. From 2,500B double. Phrom Phong BTS. **Amenities:** Restaurant; café; rooftop bar; outdoor pool; health club; Wi-Fi (free).

Radisson Blu Plaza ★★   Set just off busy Sukhumvit Road, the Radisson Blu is conveniently located near the BTS and sandwiched between the hip Terminal 21 and the upscale EmQuartier. Spacious rooms feel more like mini apartments, and they have upholstered headboards, city views, and free-standing tubs. Zip up to the 30th floor where you'll find **Brewski,** an ultra-relaxed rooftop bar with more than 100 selections of craft beer.

489 Sukhumvit Rd. www.radissonblu.com. ℂ **02302-3333.** 290 units. From 3,570B double; from 5,000B suite. Asok BTS. **Amenities:** 3 restaurants; bar; outdoor pool; health club; spa; Wi-Fi (free).

INEXPENSIVE

ONEDAY Bangkok ★★   Start-up entrepreneurs, bloggers on the road, and travelers looking for a sense of community will make fast friends at this upscale hostel-slash-co-working space. It has room types to appeal to every type of traveler. Some opt for a private with (or without) an en-suite bathroom, others mingle with fellow explorers in shared accommodations of either two-, four-, six-, or eight-bed rooms. Bunks come with private curtains, personal reading lights, and a bedside pocket. All rooms have a safety box, and custom furniture made by local craftsmen. The Wi-Fi is blazing fast (it is a co-working space, after all) and the hostel shares lobby space with Casa Lapin, one of the best coffee shops in town.

51 Sukhumvit Soi 26. www.onedaybkk.com. ℂ **02108-8855.** 31 units. From 380B for 8-bed dorm; from 2,500B for private room. Phrom Phong BTS. **Amenities:** Restaurant; cafe; shared kitchen; small theater; Wi-Fi (free).

WHERE TO EAT

With pushcarts carrying ice-packed fruit, middle-aged women mashing chilies for papaya salad, and hot coal grills ready to sear satay on nearly every corner, visitors do not go hungry in the Big Mango. Eating your way across the capital is one of the great joys of any trip to Thailand and a rite of passage for international gourmands. One of the great Bangkok experience is slurping bowls of 35B noodles at a street stand one night and dining at a wallet-melting, world-class restaurant the next.

Bangkok Restaurants

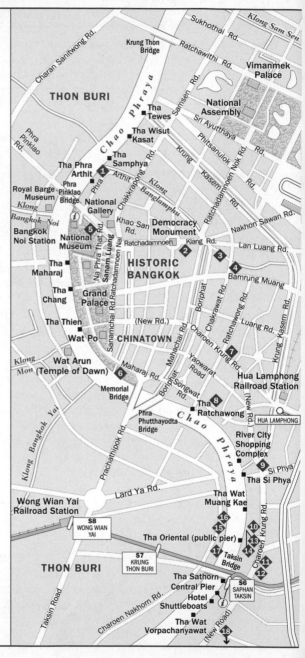

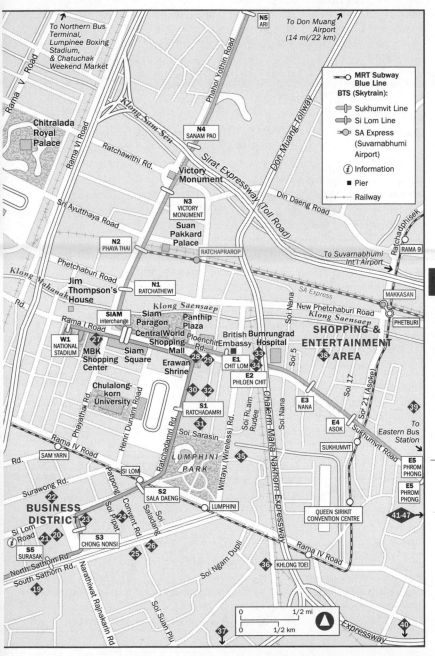

On the whole, menu costs are comparatively reasonable. You'll be able to eat well for around 1,000B for two, even at some of the town's better restaurants. If you order wine, Thai taxes on good vintages mean you may double that figure, though. Meals eaten on the street will be even cheaper. For our advice on how to choose a clean street food stall, see p. 94. We also recommend **food stall tours** on page 89. And if you'd like to learn how to **cook** authentic Thai food yourself while in Bangkok, please see p. 117.

Riverside & Thonburi

EXPENSIVE

China House ★★ CANTONESE   The opulent colonial-style house on the grounds of the Mandarin Oriental Hotel harkens back to the roaring 1930s Shanghai with dark woods, low lights, and splashes of color accenting the space. The unlimited dim sum buffet Tuesday to Friday fills the house during lunchtime, and bamboo baskets of the bite-size treats arrive in unending fashion until everyone is good and full. Weekends are popular with hungry families looking for a weekend brunch spot. But it's the perfect Peking duck wrapped in paper-thin pancakes that really steals the show, and it would be a shame to leave without ordering the signature dish.

The Mandarin Oriental Hotel, 48 Oriental Ave. © **02659-9000.** www.mandarinoriental. com/bangkok. Reservations recommended. Tues–Sun 11:30am–2:30pm and 6–10:30pm. Main courses 950B–2,900B. Set lunches from 888B; set dinners from 1,800B.

Mei Jiang ★★★ CHINESE   In the plush lower level of the Peninsula sits a Chinese restaurant that serves fresh, unfussy Cantonese dim sum and superbly authentic regional specialties from the Chinese provinces of Guangzhou, Fujian, and Sichuan. It also has such Northern classics as succulent Beijing Duck, eaten with warm pancakes, sweet plum sauce, cucumber, and shallots. Elegantly simple Chinese decor and delightful private rooms give it an edge over the city's other—more showy—Chinese restaurants. As the dim sum selection attests, this place is all about quality. The head-spinningly broad menu includes Chinese delicacies such as lobster and Australian abalone. Save room at the end of the meal for sesame dumplings and ginkgo nuts in ginger tea.

The Peninsula, Bangkok, 333 Charoen Nakhorn Rd. www.peninsula.com/bangkok. © **02861-2888.** Reservations recommended. Main courses 680B–3,400B. Daily 11:30am–2:30pm and 6–10:30pm. Short ferry from Hotel Shuttle Boat Pier (next to Saphan Taksin BTS).

Le Normandie ★★★ FRENCH   Since 1958, The Le Normandie has been the apex of formal dining in Thailand. The ultra-elegant restaurant, atop the renowned Mandarin Oriental, offers panoramic views of Thonburi and the Chao Phraya River. The dining room glistens, from place settings to chandeliers, and the warm tones of the butter-yellow silks impart a delicious glow. Perfectly manicured flora and fauna fill the room with fragrance and color. Some of the world's highest-ranked master chefs have made guest appearances here, adding their unique touches to the various menus, all of which change regularly. In 2018, under the guidance of chef Arnaud Dunand-Sauthier, Le

Normandie was awarded two Michelin stars. The five- or seven-course set menus showcase the talents of the kitchen with signatures like sea urchin and potato foam with champagne sauce. The service, as you might expect in such an establishment, is impeccable with no detail overlooked. If you want to indulge your sweet tooth, ask to look at the dessert trolley—it overflows with appealing options. Wines of every caliber pepper the extensive wine list.

The Mandarin Oriental Hotel, 48 Oriental Ave. www.mandarinoriental.com/bangkok. ℅ **02659-9000.** Reservations required at least 1 week in advance. Jacket required for men, no jeans or sports shoes. Main courses 2,450B–7,200B. Degustation menus 5,200 for 6 courses, 6,200 for 8 courses; less at lunch. Mon–Sat noon–2pm and 7–10pm. Ferry to Central Pier or Saphan Taksin BTS.

Sala Rim Nam ★★ THAI   The Oriental Hotel is the force behind this riverside Thai restaurant with its glittering interior, impeccable standards of cuisine, and commendable entertainment. The location is across the river from the main hotel, and the ferryboat ride is quite lovely. The set menu is an extensive degustation menu of Thai favorites. Nothing is too heavy and spice levels are carefully adjusted to suit individual tolerances and preferences. Guests can choose between sitting Thai-style on floor pillows or using the plush Western-style seating, from where they watch classical Thai dancers, in full regalia, perform ancient Thai legends and rousing drum-frenzied folk dances. Opt for the free shuttle boat that leaves the hotel's pier regularly, or take the BTS to Saphan Taksin and follow the signs to the Hotel Shuttle Boat Pier, just next to Central Pier. These shows are often unrehearsed, but the performances here are lovely and authentic.

The Oriental, Bangkok (on Charoen Nakhorn Rd., on the Thonburi side of the Chao Phraya River). www.mandarinoriental.com/bangkok. ℅ **02437-3080.** Dress code: Smart/casual. Lunch buffet 850B, dinner set menu 1,800B and 2,450B. Daily noon–2:30pm and 7–10:30pm, performance 8:15pm–9:30pm. Saphan Taksin BTS.

MODERATE

Never Ending Summer ★★ THAI   On the Thonburi side of the river is this funky, converted warehouse serving sophisticated, modern takes on Thai food. Duangrit Bunnag, Bangkok's best-known architect, of Jam Factory and Warehouse 30 (p. 121) fame, designed the space. He carefully preserved much of the original structure, adding industrial lighting, plants, and an open kitchen. The surprising pairing of cubed watermelon with dried fish flakes shines as does the braised pork belly with duck eggs. Cocktails are innovative and designed to pair well with the food. *Tip:* Plates are massive, so to keep prices in the moderate category, share them.

In The Jam Factory, 41/5 Charoen Nakhon Rd. Reservations recommended. ℅ **02861-0953.** Main courses 250B–500B. Mon–Fri 11am–2:30pm and 4–9:30pm, Sat–Sun 11am–9:30pm. Krung Thon Buri BTS.

Supanniga Eating Room ★★ THAI   The original branch was in Isan at the Supanniga Home in Khon Kaen (p. 395) but this family-run business has created a mini empire in Bangkok. Hungry foreigners and discerning locals wax poetically about the salty-sour fish cakes, cabbage in fish sauce, and the fermented sausages. The rest of the menu brings together the owner's grandmother's southern-style recipes from Trat, and family favorite dishes from Isan. The décor of this branch echoes that of the other locations: a casual space that feels like dining in the home of a friend.

392/25-26 Maharat Rd. http://supannigaeatingroom.com. © **02015-4224.** Mains 150B–300B. Daily 11:30am–10:30pm. Saphan Taksin BTS.

INEXPENSIVE

Jok Prince ★★ THAI   Why not start your day with a classic Asian breakfasts? Congee (rice porridge), is the most popular breakfast food in Thailand and most agree that Jok Price sells the best bowl in town. It's a small shop, down an alley near the Prince Theater. Once you arrive, order a bowl with minced pork balls, and top it off with either a raw egg or century egg (a preserved egg). The congee is smooth with a touch of smoky flavor (known as *wok hei*). Jok Prince serves congee all day long and into the night.

139 Charoen Krung Rd. © **089795-2629.** Daily 6–10am and 5–11pm. Mains 35B–100B. Saphan Taksin BTS.

Sathorn, Silom & Bangrak
EXPENSIVE

Eat Me ★★ ASIAN FUSION   An art gallery/restaurant hybrid, showing the works of local painters and photographers, the cheekily-named Eat Me turned 20 in 2018. It still has its rough-hewn chic looks, all exposed industrial beams, dark wood, and indirect lighting on the walls of the ever-changing exhibition space. As importantly, the menu remains strong, featuring such delicious fusion dishes as Tasmanian salmon tartare and spicy lemongrass chicken. Other lures include the late closing time (good news for night owls), the respectable wine list, and the fantastic desserts, such as sticky date pudding and lemongrass crème brûlée, brilliant culinary inspirations from the Aussie-Thai owners. *Tip:* The main air-conditioned room is a better bet than the mosquito-infested balcony overlooking the small courtyard.

1/6 Soi Pipat 2, off Soi Convent. © **02238-0931.** www.eatmerestaurant.com. Reservations recommended. Main courses 920B–4,990B. Daily 3pm–1am. Chong Nonsi BTS.

Le Du ★★★ THAI   After working in some of New York City's top restaurants (Eleven Madison Park and Jean-Georges), Chef Thitid "Ton" Thassanakajohn returned to his native Thailand in 2015 and proceeded to shake up the fine dining industry. His innovations cover everything from ambiance (the restaurant's bright white and ultra-minimalist décor keeps the focus on the grub, as does the action at the open kitchen) to the food, which often features ingredients rarely seen outside of Thailand (blue swimming crab and ant larvae were options on two recent menus). "Le Du" in Thai is a synonym for "season" and Ton and his team frequently change the 4- and 6-course tasting menus to feature seasonal produce, alongside local fish and quality cuts of meat. Chef Ton is a judge on Thailand's version of Top Chef so reservations can be hard to get. He's also a Master Sommelier and keeps a watchful eye of the wine list; he's quick to offer personal suggestions to patrons.

399/3 Silom Soi 7. www.ledubkk.com ℭ **092919-9969.** Four-course tasting menu 1690B, 6-course menu 2990B. Mon–Sat 6–10pm. Chong Nonsi BTS.

Sühring ★★★ GERMAN Before identical German twins Thomas and Mathias Sühring (lovingly known as 'The Twins') came around, German fare in Bangkok was represented only by the sub-par schnitzel served at beer pubs on Silom Road. Today, The Twins are introducing an elevated version of that cuisine, playful lighter dishes that make use of high-quality produce and artful plating. Delicious *spätzle* (a German pasta) is a highlight, as is a dish called "heaven and earth" that combines potatoes, black pudding, and green apple. A la carte menus are offered Monday through Thursday. On weekends only the eight- or 12-course tasting menu are available: "Klassikier" showcases classic favorites while "Erlebnis" mixes classics with more creative interpretations. Meals are served in a handsome townhouse. The wine list is outstanding.

10 Yen Akat Soi 3. http://restaurantsuhring.com. ℭ **02287-1799.** Tasting menus 3,400B–4,400B. Daily 5:30–9:30pm. Chong Nonsi BTS.

MODERATE

Baan Khanitha ★ THAI Our favorite location is on busy Sathorn Road but Baan Khanitha now has three off-shoots around Bangkok. It offers authentic Thai in a comfortable, classy atmosphere. For starters, choose the *yam som o*, a tangy salad with pomelo, shrimps, and chicken. Then graduate to a curry, from spicy red to mellow yellow and green; light salads; or fresh seafood, prepared as you like it. An indication of the authentic nature of the food here is that most customers are Thai, a rarity for upscale Thai eateries in Bangkok, and these restaurants are always packed.

www.baan-khanitha.com. 69 S. Sathorn Rd. (ℭ **02675-4200**) and 36/1 Sukhumvit Soi 23. (ℭ **02258-4128**). Main courses 400B–900B. Daily 11am–11pm. Sala Daeng BTS or Lumphini MRT stations (for Sathorn); Asok BTS or Sukhumvit MRT stations (for Sukhumvit 23).

Bunker ★★ AMERICAN Bunker's cuisine doesn't fit into just one category. The Filipino-American chef Arnie Marcella grew up in New York, worked in kitchens in Mexico, Italy, and New York City before falling hard for Bangkok and Thai food and deciding to move here. Dishes are an East-meets-West mash-up with a strong emphasis on organic ingredients often sourced from local producers. The menu frequently changes to make use of the freshest ingredients, but showstoppers from a recent meal included the cashew, broccoli, and pesto salad, pork spare ribs with Asian slaw, and the roast duck with smoked mushrooms and a runny egg. Bunker is hidden behind a concrete wall and the interior, spread over three floors, chicly combines mustard pops of color with a backdrop of smooth polished stone with copper accents.

118/2 Soi Suksa (Sathorn 12). http://bunkerbkk.com. ℭ **02234-7749.** Main courses 450B–980B. Daily 5:30–11pm. Chong Nonsi BTS.

5

SETTLING INTO BANGKOK | Where to Eat

Blue Elephant ★★ ROYAL THAI Long-known and respected for its cooking school (p. 117), Blue Elephant attracts diners looking for a taste of Royal Thai cuisine. That includes signature dishes of salmon *larb*; *mieng kham,* the classic betel leaf appetizer from the north; foie gras accompanied by a tart, tamarind sauce; Thai green curry made with black-skinned chicken; and more (there are also vegetarian options aplenty). Though the spiciness of some dishes has been tempered for foreign diners, others still pack a powerful, authentic kick. The wine list contains Thai and international bottles, some of which carry the restaurant's label. Set in an expertly renovated colonial house, the restaurant is elegant enough for special occasion meals.

233 South Sathorn Rd. www.blueelephant.com/bangkok. ☏ **02673-9353.** Reservations recommended. Dress code: smart/casual. Main courses 450B–800B. Daily 11:30am–2:30pm and 6:30–10:30pm. Surasak BTS.

Issaya Siamese Club ★ THAI Celebrity chef Ian Kittichai has his hands in more than a dozen projects across Thailand, including regular appearances on the *Iron Chef* series, but Issaya Siamese Club is his flagship restaurant. Kittichai's culinary education began at a young age when he would accompany his mother to a local market at 3am to help select quality ingredients for her curries. When he returned home from school, he would push a cart through the streets of Bangkok selling his mother's homemade curry. Issaya is a 1920s villa with heaps of brightly patterned fabrics and colorful walls. Dishes of note include the banana blossom and palm heart salad and a massaman lamb shank. The pastry chef is one of the best in the biz (the jasmine flower panna cotta is incredible). *Tip:* The restaurant is lost in a maze of small lanes so ask your hotel to give clear directions to the cab driver.

4 Soi Sri Aksorn, Chua Ploeng Rd., Sathorn. www.issaya.com. ☏ **026729-0401.** Reservations recommended. Main courses 380B–2,900B. Set lunches from 880B; set dinners from 1,800B. Daily 11:30am–3pm and 6–10:30pm. Khlong Toei MRT.

Nahm ★★★ THAI Austrian chef David Thompson made a name for himself dishing out authentic Thai flavors in London before settling in Bangkok. At the time, Thompson was the first *farang* (Westerner) to attempt to woo local palates with ancient Thai recipes. Thompson was meticulous in his research of this history of long-lost Thai dishes and used textbooks from the Royal Court to aid his study. Curries, stir-fries, salads, and soups use hard-to-find ingredients, like fiddlehead ferns, to create complex and balanced dishes that are worthy of all the praise Nahm has received. Though Thompson stepped down in mid-2018, chef Pim Techamuanvivit is continuing his work, and still using his recipes, to create set menus that showcase the intricacies of the cuisine with perfect execution from the staff. The only "miss" is the outdoor terrace next to the hotel pool. Watching guests swim laps during service is a surefire way to kill the mood, so always choose to sit inside.

In the COMO Metropolitan Hotel, 27 South Sathorn Rd. www.comohotels.com. ☏ **02 625-3388.** Reservations recommended. Main courses 640B–980B. Mon–Fri noon–2pm and 6:30–10:15pm, Sat–Sun 6:30–10:15pm. Chong Nonsi BTS or Lumpini MRT.

street food **TOURS**

Sampling street food is a highlight of any visit to Bangkok. To ensure you try the top plates, and do so in a safe fashion, consider one of the following tours:

Taste of Thailand (www.tasteofthailand foodtours.org; *(C)* **091571-7701**; tours from 1,450B) covers a wide breath of options, including a tuk-tuk tour through Old Town, and a Chinatown tour.

Bangkok Food Tours (www.bangkok foodtours.com; *(C)* **095943-9222**; tours from 1,150B) primarily operates in Chinatown but can cover Bangrak and local markets based on demand. Niche tours include bar hopping, bazaar food tours, and a biking and eating combo called "Bites and Bikes."

Chili Paste Tours (www.foodtours bangkok.com; *(C)* **0851436779**; tours from 2,000B) hires knowledgeable guides who speak eloquently about culture, food, and history, and how they connect. The company can arrange cooking classes as well.

A word on street food: In mid-2017, to the horror of just about everyone in Thailand (and gluttons around the world), the Bangkok Metropolitan Authority (BMA) quietly announced plans to ban Bangkok's street food vendors. The logic, they claimed, was the make the city more pedestrian-friendly. Backlash was swift and severe, and the TAT, Ministry of Foreign Affairs, and BMA softened their stance within days. However, the citywide cleanup did shutter the street food vendors on Sukhumvit Soi 55. Thankfully there have been no other clampdowns. But the estimated 20,000 street food vendors still live in trepidation, waiting to see what the government will do.

Somboon Seafood ★ SEAFOOD   This hectic seafood hall doesn't offer much style but it delivers fish so fresh it will usually be still swimming when you arrive. Though it's packed nightly, you'll still be able to find a table because the place is so huge. The staff is extremely friendly—between them and the illustrated menu, you'll have no problem picking out the best dishes. Peruse the large aquariums outside to see all the live seafood options such as shrimp, lobsters, and crabs. The house specialty, chili crab curry, is especially tasty, as is the *tom yum goong* soup (spiced to individual taste).

169/7–11 Surawong Rd. (just across from the Peugeot building). www.somboon seafood.com. *(C)* **02233-3104**. Main courses 190B–650B; seafood at market prices (about 800B for two diners). No credit cards. Daily 4–11:30pm. Chong Nonsi BTS.

INEXPENSIVE

Guay Jub Mister Joe ★★ THAI   I'd recommend coming here early in any trip to Bangkok because once you tried the signature dish of *guay jub* (often spelled *kuay jap*) you're likely to want to have it again before flying home. It's pork belly with tender meat and what just may be the crispiest pork skin in Thailand. One can order an entrée portion of just the pork with a thick soy sauce for dipping, but even on a hot Bangkok day, it's best in a bowl of soup with a peppery broth and rolled noodles. English menus are available, and you can order them to "put in all ingredients"—which means offal and entrails—or try it without; either way, a bowl costs 60B. Weekends are very busy.

46 Soi Chan 44, Bang Kho Laem. *(C)* **02213-3007**. Main course 60B. Daily 8am–4:30pm. Saphan Taksin BTS.

Muslim Restaurant ★★ THAI/INDIAN   Like the simple moniker it goes by, this restaurant doesn't appear to be much from the outside (or inside, for that matter), and very little has changed since it open more than 70 years ago. But if you park yourself in one of the classic wooden booths along the wall (they date back to the restaurant's opening) you'll be presented with a lovingly prepared, scrumptious feast. Recommended dishes are the *mataba gai,* or stuffed roti with chicken, crispy samosa, and the goat biryani with mint and cilantro.
1354-1356 Charoen Krung 42. ℂ **02234-1876.** Main courses 60–200B. Mon–Fri 7am–5pm, Sat–Sun 7am–3pm. Saphan Taksin BTS.

Prachak Pet Yang ★★ THAI   *Pet yang* in Thai means roasted duck—the big reason to head to this institution in Bangrak. The recipe and preparation methods haven't changed since the shop opened in 1909; a fourth generation of the original family still runs the place. The ever-so-slightly salty duck comes with a counterbalancing sweet sauce. It's so tender it practically melts the moment the breast meat hits your tongue, while the skin retains a perfect level of crispiness. Heaven.
1415 Thanon Charoen Krung, Silom, Bangrak. ℂ **02236-4830.** Full meal around 100B. Daily 8am–8:30pm. Saphan Taksin BTS.

Taling Pling ★ THAI   I've just one word for this friendly low-end Thai diner: Go! It's packed with office workers at lunchtime, so try for a table after 1pm or in the evening. Rustic wooden decor and delightful old photographs adorn the walls. Menus come with pictures of the dishes to aid foreigners, but the taste is thoroughly Thai and the low prices reflect this. Try the dry, fluffy catfish salad or the spicy green curry with beef. For those who really want to taste local flavors, the roast duck *panaeng* is recommended. Chicken in *pandanus* leaf and Thai fish cakes appease those whose palates prefer it less spicy. There are other branches on the third floor of CentralWorld department store (Chit Lom BTS), the ground floor of Siam Paragon (Siam BTS), and two further from the city center on Rama III and at Central Plaza Ladprao.
60 Pan Rd. (midway down the *soi,* connecting Silom and Sathorn rds.). http://talingpling.com. ℂ **02236-4830.** Main courses from 150B. Daily 11am–10pm. Surasak BTS.

Chinatown
MODERATE
80/20 ★★ THAI   The fraction in the name implies the percentage of ingredients (80) that are sourced locally. The offerings here marry Thai and Western ingredients all under the watchful eye of a young team of thirtysomething chefs. The menu rotates faster than a buzzing tuk-tuk but standouts and regular staples include a "catch of the day" cooked in banana leaf, steaks with bone marrow gnocchi, and plenty of dishes that employ the kitchen's signature fermentation techniques. The restaurant's Japanese pastry chef is one of the best in town, so save room for something sweet. The vibe is a little hipster yet relaxed and the service is smooth and friendly.
1052-1054 Charoen Krung Soi 26. www.facebook.com/8020bkk. ℂ **099118-2200.** 250B–500B main dishes. Wed–Sun 6pm–midnight. Hua Lamphong MRT.

Eiah-Sae ★ CAFE The doors to this Chinese tea and coffee shop first opened in 1927, and today it's one of the last places in town to serve traditional Thai-style coffee made with condensed milk. Their selections of Asian teas, both hot and cold, will save some calories and are far less sweet. For a snack with your caffeine, homemade bread is grilled over charcoal and topped with a creamy egg custard flavored with coconut or pandan leaf. You'd never know it today, but the lane where Eiah-Sae sits was home to the world's largest opium den until it closed in 1954. The only way to get a high here today is by drinking too many cups of coffee.

101-103 Padsai Rd. ℂ **02221-0549.** Drinks 25B. Mon–Sat 4am–8pm. Hua Lamphong MRT.

Nai Mong Hoi Tod ★ THAI In Thai, *hoi tod* means oyster or shellfish omelet; however, the famed *hoi tod* at this Chinatown institution is more like a crispy pancake than a traditional egg omelet. The fillings are oysters or mussels, which are then fried with egg and a sticky rice-flour batter to create a delicious meal. To help sop up the oil, the pancake sits atop a serving of beansprouts. There is no English menu, but foreign patrons are common, so you'll be able to point and smile your way through a successful order. Pull up a red plastic stool outside and take in the full atmosphere of Chinatown or sit inside at a metal table and watch the cooks in action.

539 Phlapphla Chai Rd. ℂ **89773-3133.** Mains 70B. Daily 11am–9pm. Hua Lamphong MRT.

Siam, Phloenchit & Ratchadamri
EXPENSIVE

Gaggan ★★★ INTERNATIONAL Welcome to the best restaurant in Asia. I can cite heaps of awards to back that assessment up. Gaggan was described as 'progressive Indian' when it splashed onto the scene in 2010. Today, it's harder to pin down, beyond saying that it is a culinary playground for chef Gaggan Anand's fertile imagination. In its current iteration, diners are presented a wordless, one-page menu with 25 emojis, each depicting a different course. Beautifully plated plates follow, each illuminating that cryptic menu. So the 'tongue' emoji corresponds to a dish that diners must lick off the plate while Kiss's "Lick it Up" plays over the restaurant's speakers. The food often makes use of the techniques of "molecular gastronomy," and sometimes takes its flavor profile from Indian fare. The bottom line: it's a lot of fun, but also very pampering: the high staff-to-guest ratio ensures smooth, polished service. On the drinks front, the sommeliers have a penchant for natural and organic wines. As a foil to the wacky menu is the restaurant's setting in a classic, white-washed wooden colonial house on a quiet lane.

68/1 Soi Langsuan, Ploenchit Rd. http://eatatgaggan.com. ℂ **02652-1700.** Reservations required. Set menu 6,500B. Mon–Sat seatings at 6pm and 9:30pm. Chit Lom BTS.

Ginza Sushi Ichi ★★★ SUSHI Fish is flown in daily from Tokyo's Tsukiji Market which makes this one of the most authentic places for sushi in town. The fact that the restaurant is on the ground floor location of a shopping mall

sweet spots AROUND TOWN

- **Hazel's Ice Cream Parlor & Fine Dining** (171 Chakkrapatiphong Rd., www.facebook.com/hazelsparlor) serves alcohol-infused shakes and ice creams, like bourbon vanilla and absinthe cream. There are plenty of non-boozy flavors, too, making this a fun stop for families. The 1950s building was a former publishing house, and the printing press still works.

- **Mont Nomsod** (www.mont-nomsod.com; 3 branches in Bangkok (most centrally located at MBK and 1 in Chiang Mai) sells homemade white toast cut into thick slices with spreads of coconut-egg custard and corn soup. The shop started as a humble street food stand in 1964.

- **Boonsap Thai Desserts** (1478 Charoen Krung Rd.; www.boonsap.com; ℃ 02234-4086) is a family-run shop that has been making their famous Thai sweets, like their legendary sticky rice with coconut custard, since the 1940s. Packages of take-away sweets make lovely gifts for loved ones back home.

- **Mae Varee** (1 Sukhumvit Soi 55; around the corner from the Thonglor BTS) sells grab-and-go orders of mango sticky rice. A perfectly cooked gluttonous rice (white color) is standard, but the green rice (made with pandan) and the black rice (made with whole grain sticky rice) are also delicious choices. Top the dish with a salty-sweet coconut cream and crisp mung beans. Mango season in Thailand is April to June but Mae Varee stocks sweet mangos year-round.

also gives the operation Japanese cred. Two dining rooms offer an intimate dining experience, and the sushi chefs are expert and charming. Menus are based on the daily catch, so vary greatly, but lunch menus always offer good value. This is the Bangkok branch of a celebrated Tokyo-based restaurant.

In the Erawan Mall, 494 Ploenchit Rd, ground floor. http://ginza-sushiichi.jp/english/shop/bangkok.html. ℃ **02250-0014.** Lunch from 1,800B, Dinner from 5,000B. Tues–Sun noon–2pm and 6–9pm. Chit Lom BTS.

MODERATE

Biscotti ★★ ITALIAN   This must be Bangkok's most stylish and consistently praised Italian restaurant. Its open kitchen, polished wood floors, and long tables give it a modern sophistication that few Italian restaurants in Bangkok can match. Equally unmatched are its cuisine and top-class service, which don't come with too hefty a price tag. Enjoy green asparagus, with truffles and mushrooms, a classic plate of cold cuts, a range of wood-fired pizzas, and an unending list of antipasti, not to mention homemade pastas and risottos. Also a specialty: very fresh fish dishes. Save space for one of the irresistible desserts, and accompany the meal with one of the first-rate wines.

In Anantara Siam hotel, 155 Ratchadamri Rd. www.anantara.com. ℃ **02126-8866.** Reservations recommended. Dress code: Smart/casual. Main courses 530B–980B. Daily 11:30am–2:30pm and 6–10:30pm. Ratchadamri BTS.

The Smokin' Pug ★★ BARBECUE   American husband-and-wife expats honed their barbecue craft in China before making a splash in Bangkok in 2015. A jam-packed location on Surawong was their home for 2 years before they moved into this more spacious setting on Langsuan. Baby back pork ribs arrive seasoned with a special sauce, and they fall off the bone with a prod of the fork. The tender pulled pork is piled high on a freshly baked bun. A host of homemade sauces have masking tape labels, just like they would in the U.S., and add a great flavor. The owners seem to know every patron by name and few places in town have a devoted following as "The Pug" does.

105 Langsuan Rd. www.smokinpugbbq.com. ℭ **02861-2888.** Main courses 380B–2,900B. Main dishes 350B–895B. Wed–Sat 5–11pm, Sun 5–10pm. Chit Lom BTS.

INEXPENSIVE

Din Tai Fung ★★ CHINESE   With branches dotted across the city, you'll never be too far from a basket of these lauded Taiwanese soup dumplings (known as *xiao long bao*). The pleated dumplings (we love the pork ones) come filled with a hot, brothy soup. To eat them, carefully lift the dumpling at the knot with chopsticks while supporting the bottom with the spoon. Bring the dumping to your mouth and bite a small hole with your teeth; slurp out the soup; dunk the dumpling into a soy-vinegar mix and eat it in one bite. Add orders of yam spring rolls, crab fried rice, and spicy wonton soup but make sure to leave space for plenty of *xiao long bao*. Cooking classes are available.

In CentralWorld shopping mall, at 999/9 Rama I Rd. www.dintaifung.com. ℭ **02646-1282.** Mains 150B–400B. Daily 11am–10pm. Chit Lom BTS.

Eathai ★★ THAI   Designed to resemble a traditional market, the cooking stations are quartered off into zones representing different areas of Thailand. Collectively they offer something for everyone. Upon entering, you'll get a card to use for purchases at the food stalls and or for purchasing pre-packaged goods, and pay the balance when you're ready to exit. If the weather isn't too hot, this is a great place to stock up on picnic provisions for an al fresco lunch in nearby Lumpini Park (p. 120). Simple Thai salads, whole sea bass steamed with herbs, fried omelets, and pad Thai with jumbo prawns are all satisfying choices.

Central Embassy shopping mall, at 1031 Ploenchit Rd. www.centralembassy.com. ℭ **02160-59912.** Main courses 40B–150B. Mon–Fri 11:30am–10pm, Sat–Sun noon–10pm. Phloen Chit BTS.

Erawan Tea Room ★★ THAI   This charming tea room at the Grand Hyatt makes for an ideal mid-day break from shopping. The Thai afternoon set is a delicious way to sample a selection of savory Thai snacks, like fried rice, som tum salad, chicken satay, and traditional soups and curries. Jams, cakes, and teas from across Asia are also on the menu for a more traditional afternoon tea experience. The dining room features classic teakwood furniture, oversized chairs, and panoramic views overlook of the nearby Erawan Shrine.

In the Grand Hyatt Hotel, 494 Rajdamri Rd. www.bangkok-grand.hyatt.com. ℭ **02254-1234.** High tea from 600B. Daily 10am–10pm. Chit Lom BTS.

MBK Food Island ★ THAI   For a casual, inexpensive option in the center of town, stop by the sixth floor of this market-style mall that's tops for tech and souvenirs. As well, Thai, Indian, and dedicated vegetarian stands abound offering tasty choices in a clean setting. Many vendors serve their food

BANGKOK'S street eats & food courts

As in most areas of Thailand, the city's many night bazaars and hawker stalls are where you'll find the best eats. But those who are nervous of getting sick or who are not inclined toward culinary adventures would do well to hire a foodie tour guide (p. 89) or stick to the many food courts, usually located inside shopping malls. Here, young Thais enjoy cheap meals in the luxury of air-conditioning; they can get packed with office workers at lunchtime. In almost all the food courts, you need to buy coupons first, exchange them for the dishes you order, and cash in any you don't use afterward. (150B per person should be enough to ensure you're not lining back up to get more coupons.) In addition to the ones reviewed below, other notable food courts include The Emporium, MBK (p. 124), Central Embassy's Eathai (p. 93), and CentralWorld's Loft concept. All are usually located on the top floor or basement of stores and resemble simple self-service cafeterias.

The city's small, open-air joints and markets are also popular for snacks and quick lunches; they open Tuesday to Sunday from dawn until late (Monday is street cleaning day in Bangkok and many chose this as their day off). Eating right next to smoke-belching buses may not be your idea of gastronomic heaven, but as often you'll be surrounded by the pungent aromas of garlic, chili, and barbecued meats, making it a totally unmissable Thai experience.

Chinatown This is the granddaddy of all street food areas and Bangkokians come from every neighborhood and brave horrendous traffic just to eat along Yaowarat Road after dark. "Witching hour" is around 5pm when the neighborhood's gold shops shutter their doors, market vendors begin to tidy up, and street carts emerge from storage. Street stands in this area are not reliable (in terms of opening and closing times), with hours that change like the wind. But even if your first choice is closed for the night, there will be a host of other options nearby.

Khao San Road Area You'll find street stands serving both Thai and Western foods on Phra Arthit Road, cutting through Soi Rambutri and heading toward Khao San Road. Look out for BBQ fish served hot off the coals, Chinese congee (johk), pad thai, and sizzling satays. These open-air food stalls extend to the busy Rambutri Road (parallel to Khao San Rd.), with many serving late into the night.

Siam Paragon Food Court Right at Siam BTS, this glitzy megamall doesn't just cater to big-brand boutique shoppers; downstairs, it has a host of low-cost eateries, pastry shops, and ice-cream parlors, as well as upmarket restaurants. The cheaper food stalls have just about every type of fare, including Thai, Indian, Japanese, and Vietnamese.

Surawong & Silom Roads Every day except Mondays, the length of upper Surawong Road (the end closest to Rama IV Rd.) is a cluster of snack stalls and fruit vendors that spill into adjoining Thaniya Plaza. In places such as Soi Convent off Silom Road, you'll find stalls selling crab and shrimp, noodles, fried vegetarian patties, and delicious boiled chicken on rice. Suan Plu Soi 8 is a bustling home to street food and Silom Soi 20 serves takeaway meals in the pre-work hours of 6 to 9am.

Note: There are number of great markets in Bangkok—beyond the food-specific ones listed in this chapter—that offer outstanding food and shopping options. Those are peppered throughout the next chapter, so keep reading.

buffet-style, allowing diners to point to what they want. Classics like *pad Thai*, beef noodles, and *grapow gai,* Thai basil chicken are standout options.

8th floor of MBK Center, at 444 Phayathai Rd. http://mbkfoodisland.com. ℃ **02620-9814.** Mains 40–100B. Daily 10am–9pm. National Stadium BTS.

Polo Fried Chicken ★★ THAI   Spend an afternoon walking around the streets of Bangkok and you'll see many woks bubbling with cracking-hot oil and trays of crisply fried chicken cooling on racks. Thai people love their fried chicken (but don't we all?) and the best place for it is this open-air shop near Lumpini Park on a street called Soi Polo. The owners double fry the chicken and add garlic, which makes these birds irresistible. The crispy skin is crunchy without being overcooked, and the meat retains a perfect level of tender juiciness. Other Isan treats, like *som tom* and sticky rice, are available as well.

137/1-2 Soi Polo. ℃ **02252-2252.** 200B for a whole chicken. Daily 7am–10pm. Phloen Chit BTS.

Banglampoo & Dusit
MODERATE

Jay Fai ★★ THAI   This is Bangkok's only street hawker to have received a star from the famed Michelin inspectors. But even before they bestowed that honor in 2018, this rudimentary shophouse (next to Thipsamai Phad Thai) was legendary. It is operated by Jay Fai who is now in her 70s; she is the adorable Thai woman hunched over the blistering woks. (Her signature goggles are to protect her eyes from the splashing oil.) Fai's father started the shop when she was just a young tot and she carries on the family business, and recipes, today. The *pat kee mow* (drunkard's noodles) and the crab omelet are her signature dishes, and they are terrific. Reservations are essential, but even with them you'll likely still wait an hour once you arrive, so plan accordingly.

327 Mahachai Rd. (at intersection with Samranrat Road). ℃ **02223-9384.** Main dishes 400B–1,000B. Mon–Sat 3pm–2am. Hua Lamphong MRT.

INEXPENSIVE

Err ★★ THAI   Sitting in the shadow of Wat Pho is this casual spin-off of Thonglor's fancy Bo.Lan (p. 97). The meticulous research and creativity of that restaurant is present and accounted for here in the food; it's also pleasant place to cool one's heals after touring the Grand Palace and major temples. The menu elevates down-to-earth fare, like stir-fried morning glory and *pad krapao,* and surprises with plates that are wholly original, like jasmine rice cured fish or sour green mango in fish sauce. The experience is capped off by the shabby chic setting with its 1960s Thai advertisements and hand-drawn art on the exposed brick walls.

394/35 Maharaj Rd. www.errbkk.com. ℃ **02622-22912.** Reservations recommended. Main courses 135B–380B. Tues–Sun 11am–10pm. Ferry to Ta Tien pier.

Hemlock ★ THAI   This place is extremely popular with Thai students, partly because of the very cheap prices and partly for the large number of vegetarian options on the menu. The walls are plain white with small, abstract artworks, and there's a piano in the corner that sometimes provides gentle background music for diners in the evening. It's quite small and can get crowded at times (reserve ahead to be sure of a table), and when it's busy, service tends to be a bit slow, but the food quality is consistently good. Try the miang, a tasty snack with nuts, garlic, ginger, and other crunchy morsels wrapped in leaves. The banana flower salad is also great.

56 Phra Arthit Rd., Banglampoo. ℂ **02282-7507**. Reservations recommended. Main courses from 80B. Mon–Sat 4pm–11pm. Ferry to Phra Arthit Pier.

Krua Apsorn ★★★ THAI   Under harsh, cafeteria-style lighting, and glowing white-tiled walls, is a shining star. Krua Apsorn is no secret, thanks to years of patronage from the Thai royal family and glowing media reviews, but even with its lines (they move fast) it's worth the wait. Over the years, I've eaten my way through the menu and everything is really delicious, but many come just for the crab omelet, which is generously stuffed with jumbo lump crab. Stir-fried crab with yellow chili, green curry with fish balls, and *tom yum* shrimp are also renowned. The Krua Apsorn empire has five other locations around town and the one on Samsen Road is the original.

169 Dinso Rd. www.kruaapsorn.com. ℂ **02668-8788**. Mains 50B–200B. Mon–Sat 10:30am–8pm. Hua Lamphong MRT.

Rarb ★★ THAI   Killer cocktails and one of the best plates of *larb moo* (a minced pork salad) make this tiny spot a must-try. At the helm is Karn Liang-srisuk, a name locals will recognize from his time at the legendary burger spot **Escapades,** which is across the street. The single page, handwritten menu focuses on meat-centric dishes and Isan comfort food, like a pork rib soup and fried rice, but the *larb* is the signature dish. Wash it all down with one of the brilliant R-rated cocktails (they have names that would make your mother—and the King of Thailand—blush).

49 Phra Athit Rd. ℂ **081406-3773**. Mains 40B–150B. Tues–Sun 5–midnight. Hua Lamphong MRT.

Thipsamai Phad Thai ★ THAI   Many visitors are surprised to find how different *pad Thai* tastes in Thailand from plates they've tried back home. For the iconic version of the dish, head to this indoor-outdoor shop on Maha Chai Road. Long lines make it easy to spot (they moves fast). Here, for their so-called "Superb" version (there are several different mixes on offer, each with

---

Anyone for Cricket?

Snack stands along Sukhumvit Road (also Khao San Rd.) sell all sorts of fried insects. Grasshoppers, beetles that look like cockroaches, scorpions, ants, and grubs are all favorite snacks for folks from Isan, in the northeast, where bugs are deliberately cultivated for the dining table and are an important source of protein in the region. How do these insects taste? Crickets are a bit like popcorn, and the beetles are something like—hate to say it—crispy chicken. Even if you don't indulge, it's a great photo opportunity.

a different name) chefs combine noodles, fish oil, shrimp, crab, mango, and prawns to create an intensely flavorful and complex meal. Open late!

313-315 Maha Chai Rd. © **02226-6666.** Mains 60B–200B. Daily 5pm–2am. Hua Lamphong MRT.

Lower Sukhumvit: Nana to Ekkamai

EXPENSIVE

Bo.Lan ★★ ROYAL THAI   Bo.Lan was founded by a husband and wife team, Thai-born chef Duangporn 'Bo' Songvisava and Australian-born chef Dylan 'Lan' Jones, who met while working at a top Thai restaurant in London. The menu comes from the pair's love of this cuisine and country. Ingredients are locally sourced and sustainable, with the restaurant working hard to achieve its zero carbon goal. And recipes were arrived at after much study of ancient cookbooks, to better represent Royal Thai cuisine. That means that the spice levels here are authentic and send even locals reaching for water. It's important to dine with someone who shares your spice tolerance because the set menus (à la carte menus are available only at lunch) are designed to share. The glamorous villa setting makes dinner at Bo.Lan a treat for any visitor to The Kingdom.

24 Soi Sukhumvit 53. www.bolan.co.th. © **02260-2961.** Set menus from 2680B. Tues–Fri 6–10:30pm, Sat–Sun noon–2:30pm and 6–10:30pm. Thong Lor BTS.

Upstairs at Mikkeller ★★ AMERICAN   At this 20-seater restaurant atop the Mikkeller beer bar, a 10-course set menu is expertly paired with craft beers from the famed Danish brewhouse. A rotating cast of dishes highlights gourmet American food (the work of chef Dan Bark, formerly of the popular Grace Restaurant in Chicago), like carrots with pomelo and fennel, roasted duck with beats, black garlic, and pumpkin, and a Wagyu beef served with truffle. In true Danish fashion, the dining room is minimally decorated, predominately white in color, and a touch Mid-Century Modern. Downstairs the bar has craft beers on tap and opens to a lush garden making it a perfect place for a nightcap.

26 Ekkamai soi 10 Yaek 2Ekamai Rd. http://mikkeller.dk. © **091713-9034.** Set menu 3300B. Wed–Sat 6–10pm. Ekkamai BTS.

MODERATE

Charcoal Tandoor Grill & Mixology ★★ INDIAN   As you can guess from the name, cocktails and grilled meats are the stars here. The latter are seared to perfection in a custom-built tandoor oven, which is kept going overnight so that such side dishes as *dal* (lentil stew) can be cooked for a good 12-hours before they hit the plate. New Zealand lamb chops, too, are coddled for hours, marinated overnight in chili, cumin, vinegar, ginger, and garlic. The menu has cocktail pairing suggestions (the New Delhi Duty-Free tipple arriving tableside in a duty-free bag with an Indian passport). The atmosphere is just as evocative as the food, with spice jars behind lattice screens, copper mugs sourced from New Delhi markets, reclaimed rough wood walls, and red-and-white checked aprons for each guest to keep the mess at bay. In the bathroom, the sounds (but thankfully not smells) of New Delhi are on the speakers at full volume.

Fraser Suites Sukhumvit, 5th Floor, 38/8 Sukhumvit Rd. Soi 11. http://charcoalbkk.com. © **02038-5112.** Mains 280B–500B. Mon–Sat 6pm–midnight; Sun noon–3pm and 6pm–midnight. Nana BTS.

The Commons ★★ INTERNATIONAL   Searching for a meal but not quite sure what you want? Head to The Commons, a market-style space in trendy Thonglor. There are innumerable options here, from Thai food at Soul Food 555, to wood-fired pizzas at Peppina, Tex-Mex at Barrio Bonito, or Bangkok's best burger at Daniel Thaiger. Craft beer and wine are available, too, and the space hosts live musicians for jazz sessions and acoustic covers of Western classics. It's fun and just a wee bit hipster.

335 Soi Thonglor Soi 17. www.thecommonsbkk.com. © **02712-5400.** Mains from 250B–500B. Daily 8am–1am. Thong Lo BTS.

Khua Kling Pak Sod ★★ THAI   The one thing you need to know before heading to Khua Kling Pak Sod is that the food is unapologetically spicy. And not just reach-for-another-glass-of-water spicy but five-alarm hot, which, according to the owner, is just how southern Thai food should be. With taste buds property prepared, try the dry curry with pork, stewed pork in sweet sauce, yellow curry, and fried rice with dried shrimp. The décor is a bit homely, but the food makes up for it in spades. There are four branches across town, but listed here is the location near the Thong Lo BTS.

98/1 Sukhumvit Soi 53 Alley. www.khuaklingpaksod.com. © **02185-3977.** Main courses 180B–480B. Daily 11am–2:30pm and 5:30–9:30pm. Thong Lo BTS.

Seafood Market ★ SEAFOOD   This place is very fun despite being touristy. Their motto is "If it swims, we have it," and they aren't exaggerating. Diners enter the giant hangar of a fish market, and, before sitting down, head to the seafood counters to pick supper, either live or on ice, all priced by the kilo. They then choose how they'd like their seafood cooked and what sauces they'd prefer. (Waiters can help with fish and sauce suggestions). The seafood is market price, and the fish incredibly fresh.

89 Sukhumvit Soi 24 (Soi Kasami). www.seafood.co.th. © **02261-2071.** Reservations recommended for weekend dinners. Market prices. Daily 11:30am–midnight. Phrom Phong BTS.

Somtum Der ★★ THAI   Posh places where one can sample Isan classics aren't a new concept in Bangkok, but few are as pleasing Somtum Der. The first branch is in Sala Daeng but we prefer the laid-back vibe of the Thonglor outpost (it's a nice casual spot in a fancy neighborhood). Kick off the meal with an order or two of fried chicken; it's the house specialty. Nearly a dozen takes on *som tum,* the famous spicy papaya salad, are on offer as well, with including a delish freshwater crab version. *Larb,* a minced pork salad, is another top pick. The restaurant prides itself on using local recipes, which mean the spice levels are authentic, too, so order *mai phet* ("not spicy") if a milder taste is preferred.

351/2 Sukhumvit Soi 55 (Thong Lor Soi 17). ℭ **02046-4904.** www.sumtumder.com. Main courses 100B–250B. Daily 11am–2:30pm and 4:30–10:30pm.

Sri Trat ★★ THAI   Dishes from Thailand's eastern seaboard—in particular Trat province—are rarely found in Bangkok, which is a shame, but a good reason to head here. Eastern Thai food uses an abundance of seafood, lots of fresh fruit and tends toward flavors on the sweet and herbal side of the scale. The phonebook-size menu has nearly 20 pages of dishes, most of which were developed by the owner's mother; that's her depicted in the large mural. Our favorites include a veggie-laden whole mud crab *(lon pu kai)* chili dip, and the complex massaman curry with young durian fruit. The cheerful staff is happy to make recommendations if you're indecisive.

90 Sukhumvit 33. ℭ **02088-0968.** Main courses 200B–350B. Wed–Mon noon–3pm and 6–11pm. Phrom Phong BTS.

Toby's ★ INTERNATIONAL   With flat whites and avocado toasts coming from the kitchen and the breezy, light wood and whitewashed walls, you'd be forgiven for thinking you'd gone for brunch in Sydney. You'll have to fight crowds on the weekends (brunch reservations are recommended), but when you settle in, your patience is rewarded with crispy French toast, house-cured salmon over poached eggs, cold-pressed juices, zucchini and corn fritters, and perfectly crunchy bacon. Toby's has a dinner menu, too, but there are better places in town to blow your baht on spaghetti and Western dishes.

75 Soi Sukhumvit Soi 38. www.facebook.com/tobysk38. ℭ **02712-1774.** Mains 200B–350B. Tues–Sun 9am–10:30pm. Thong Lo BTS.

INEXPENSIVE

Soul Food Mahanakorn ★★ THAI   Many expats bring first-time guests to Soul Food Mahanakorn because its reliably good Thai dishes cover a range of options and the drinks are innovative and strong. On the food front, that means creative spins on traditional street food. Standout dishes include the Chiang Mai classic *khao soi* (a Burmese-style curry with egg noodles), a banana flower salad, duck larb, and the tiger prawn satay. The owners offers more playful dishes, like a pulled pork *khao soi* burger, just down the road at The Commons (p. 98) and recently set up camp in Hong Kong.

56/10 Sukhumvit Soi 55. www.soulfoodmahanakorn.com. ℭ **02714-7708.** Main courses 220B–280B. Mon–Fri 5:30pm–midnight, Sat–Sun 11:30am–3pm and 5:30pm–midnight. BTS Thong Lo.

EXPLORING BANGKOK

First-time visitors are often amazed by central Bangkok's glittering modernity, and at the same time, delighted by the treasures found on its ramshackle back streets. It is very easy to stumble across hidden markets or large ones such as Chatuchuk, museums, or spectacular temples. This chapter presents the city's main highlights.

THINGS TO DO The **Grand Palace** and **Wat Phra Kaew** (the **Emerald Buddha Temple**), a compound packed with striking architecture and dazzling decoration, is far and away the most important sight, not just in Bangkok, but in the entire country. A **longtail boat ride** along the Chao Phraya River and narrow canals of Thonburi opens a window on the lives of the city's inhabitants, and a visit to any of the city's mega-malls shows how its inhabitants have embraced the Western love of **shopping.**

SHOPPING Bangkok is a shopaholic's paradise, boasting some of Southeast Asia's biggest malls stocked with every type of designer product, as well as street markets that buzz with activity. Depending on your mood, you can stroll in air-conditioned comfort round one of the malls in **Siam Square,** or test your bargaining skills at the mother of all markets: **Chatuchak Weekend Market.**

ENTERTAINMENT & NIGHTLIFE While the city is famed for its raunchy **go-go bars,** especially on **Patpong,** there are plenty of other ways to have a good time after dark. From graceful renditions of **traditional dances** to in-your-face, cheeky **ladyboy cabarets,** from over-the-top **clubs** like the **Sing Sing Theater** to laid-back **jazz venues** such as the **Bamboo Bar,** the city has something to suit all tastes. Oh, and did we mention world-class cocktail bars?

BANGKOK'S WATERWAYS

The key to Bangkok's rise lies in the Chao Phraya River, which courses stealthily through its center, feeding a complex network of canals and locks that, until relatively recently, were the focus of city life. Lying just a few miles from the Gulf of Thailand, the river was a major conduit for trade and the main reason behind its rapid growth. Today, nothing much has changed: Great black barges filled with rice, coal, or sand are towed up and down the river by small yellow tugs; at any time of the day you might spot gray Royal

Naval vessels, or Port Authority police, stout wooden sampans, and even blue barges stacked with Pepsi-Cola bottles, all plying these waters.

In the late 18th century, Thailand's first monarch of the Chakri dynasty, Rama I, moved the capital eastward from Thonburi (a suburb of today's Bangkok) across the river to the district that became known as Rattanakosin Island, so-called due to the human-made canals that surrounded this entire area. Like medieval moats, these canals (*klongs*) acted as a defensive barrier. Other canals were soon added, channeling the waters of the Chao Phraya into peripheral communities, feeding fish ponds or rice paddies, and nurturing the city's many tropical fruit orchards. These waterways fast became the aquatic boulevards of this low-lying, swampy city. Apart from structures built for royalty, ordinary Bangkok residents lived on water, in bamboo raft homes, or on boats. As foreign diplomats, missionaries, and writers traveled to Bangkok, they drew parallels with the Italian city of Venice and renamed it the "Venice of the East." Not until the early 1800s were non-royal houses built on dry land.

Due to the health hazards posed by these open *klongs*, and the gradual need for more stable land with the advent of vehicular transport, many of the canals were paved over in the last century. By the late 1970s, most of the city's paddy fields had disappeared. In fact, much of today's Bangkok sits on from former marshland. Fears are growing as global warming raises sea levels and the effects of seasonal flooding on the city are becoming more drastic.

For a glimpse of traditional Thai life, schedule a few hours to explore the waterways. You'll see people using the river to bathe, fish, wash their clothes, and occasionally brush their teeth at the water's edge (not recommended). Floating kitchens occupy small, motorized canoes from which the pilot-cum-chef serves rice and noodles to the occupants on other boats. Ramshackle huts on stilts adorned with 100-year-old fretwork tumble down into *klongs;* while at low tide, the rib cages of sunken ships appear out of the oozing mud.

Opportunities abound for exploring Bangkok's small *klong* networks and river arteries. The most frequently seen boat on the river is the **longtail,** a needle-shaped craft driven by a raucous outboard engine and covered in a striped awning. These act as river taxis for tourists and locals alike. Private longtails congregate at **Maharaj, Chang,** and **Si Phya** public piers and **River City.** Test your haggling skills and charter a longtail yourself for about 1,000B an hour—be sure to agree on the charge before you get in the boat.

Otherwise, if you head to the riverside exit of Saphan Taksin BTS, there's also an official kiosk down on the riverfront, with tickets for the hop-on, hop-off **Chao Phraya Express** (http://chaophrayatouristboat.com). It runs every half-hour, daily from 9:30am to 4pm (tickets 50B for single-journey and 180B day pass), and is a more comfortable option than the (more cramped) longtails or tatty wooden express boats that act as the city's river taxis.

However you tour the *klongs*, take time to explore **Klong Bangkok Noi** and **Klong Bangkok Yai.** Also stop at the **Royal Barge Museum** (p. 111), a wonderful riverside hangar crammed with long, narrow vessels covered in gilt carvings, brought out only to commemorate rare events such as a milestone in the monarch's reign or the visit of a dignitary. Tour operators offer half-day

EXPLORING BANGKOK | Bangkok's Waterways

Erawan Shrine **20**
The Grand Palace **12**
Jim Thompson's House **18**
Lumpinee Boxing Stadium **32**
Museum of Siam **14**
The National Museum **6**
Patravadi Theater **11**
Queen Sirikit Convention Center **25**
Ratchadamnoen Boxing Stadium **3**
Red Cross Snake Farm **31**
Royal Barge Museum **4**
Siam Society **24**
Vimanmek Teak Mansion **1**
Wang Suan Pakkard **19**
Wat Arun (Temple of Dawn) **15**
Wat Benchamabophit Marble Temple) **2**
Wat Mahathat (Temple of the Great Relic) **7**
Wat Phra Kaew (Emerald Buddha Temple) **10**
Wat Po **13**
Wat Saket (The Golden Mount) **8**
Wat Suthat and the Giant Swing **9**
Wat Traimit (The Golden Buddha) **17**

MARKETS

Khao San Road **5**
Khlong Toey Market **26**
Pak Klong Flower Market **16**
Patpong Night Market **30**
Suan Lum Night Market **27**

EMBASSIES

American Embassy **23**
Australian Embassy **28**
British Embassy **21**
Canadian Embassy **29**
New Zealand Embassy **22**

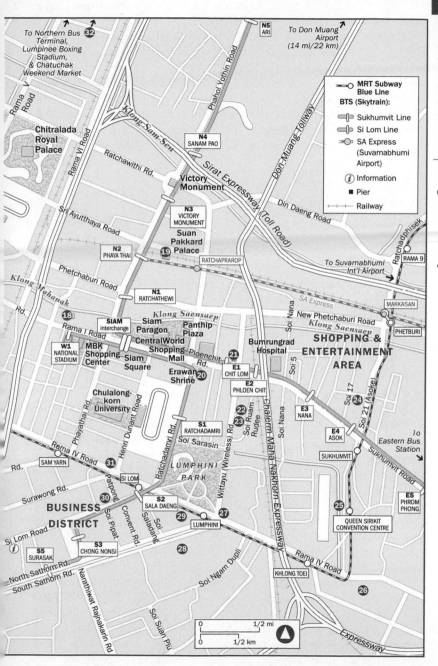

tours that include a visit to the Royal Barges Museum and cost about 850B per person, including an English-speaking guide: contact **Thai River Cruise** (www.thairivercruise.com; © **02476-5207**).

Many visitors are disappointed by the touristy **floating market** at **Damnoen Saduak** (p. 135), about 105km (65 miles) southwest of Bangkok, in Ratchaburi Province, though there's no denying it's a photogenic spectacle. A more authentic experience is to head either to the nearby **Amphawa Floating Market** or upstream along the Chao Phraya to picturesque **Ko Kret;** see "Side Trips from Bangkok," later in this chapter. Unlike Damnoen Saduak, which is at its best in the early morning so requires a pre-dawn start, the market at Amphawa buzzes between noon and 8pm, though it's only at weekends.

TOP ATTRACTIONS
Wat Phra Kaew & the Grand Palace

The number one destination in Bangkok is also one of the most imposing and visually fascinating. If you arrive at 8:30am, when the gates first open, you'll be able to snap people-free photos; also remember that it closes at 3:30 pm, so don't show up any later than 3pm. Though it's seen by thousands of tourists, who arrive at the gates in busloads, its immensity still dwarfs the throngs. After passing muster with the fashion police at the main gate and lining up for your ticket (keep it safe for admission to other sites), you'll be directed to the entrance to Wat Phra Kaew (the Emerald Buddha temple). Note that strict dress codes apply to visiting these sites, so be sure to wear appropriate attire; remember, shoes must be removed in places of worship (so slip-ons are a good idea), and you won't be allowed into any royal or religious site if you're exposing your shoulders or dressed in skirts/shorts above the knee. *Note:* Pay no attention to anyone who tells you the palace is closed for a religious holiday or because the king is there; it's a common scam.

Wat Phra Kaew ★★★ TEMPLE   This is the most revered temple in the kingdom, named for the petite jadeite (not emerald) statue that sits atop a huge gold altar in the main hall, or *bot*. The Buddha image is clothed in seasonal robes, changed three times a year to correspond to the summer, winter, and rainy months. The changing of the robes is an important ritual, performed by the high-ranking members of the royal family, who also sprinkles water over the monks and well-wishers to bring good fortune. The statue is the subject of much devotion among Thais; bizarrely, it is also the religious icon to which politicians (accused of corruption) swear innocence. The magically empowered statue was rumored to have been made in Northern Thailand in the 15th century, before being installed at a temple in Laos, only to be taken back by the Thais and brought to the capital around 1780—a sore subject between the nations.

As you enter the site, one of the first things you see is a stone statue of a hermit, considered a patron of medicine, before which relatives of the infirm pay homage and make offerings. The inside walls of the compound are decorated with murals depicting the entire *Ramakien*, a Thai epic, painted during

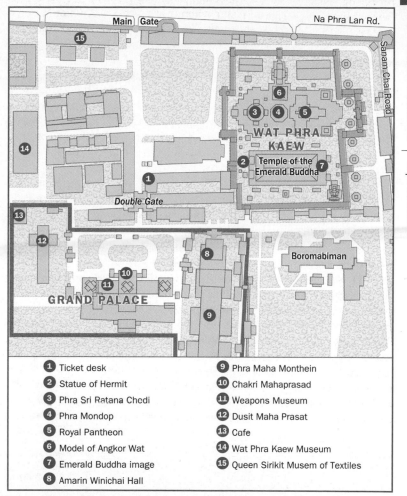

Main Gate · Na Phra Lan Rd.

WAT PHRA KAEW

Temple of the Emerald Buddha

Double Gate

Boromabiman

GRAND PALACE

1 Ticket desk	**9** Phra Maha Monthein
2 Statue of Hermit	**10** Chakri Mahaprasad
3 Phra Sri Ratana Chedi	**11** Weapons Museum
4 Phra Mondop	**12** Dusit Maha Prasat
5 Royal Pantheon	**13** Cafe
6 Model of Angkor Wat	**14** Wat Phra Kaew Museum
7 Emerald Buddha image	**15** Queen Sirikit Musem of Textiles
8 Amarin Winichai Hall	

the reign of Rama I in the 16th century and regularly restored. Its 178 scenes begin at the north gate and continue clockwise, and since it's an unfolding story, it's worth taking a separate tour of the cloisters after viewing the striking monuments housed in the complex.

Following around to the left, visitors are faced with three much-photographed structures: The first, to the west, is **Phra Sri Rattana Chedi,** a dazzling gold, slender, Sri Lankan-style stupa in the shape of an inverted cone; second, in the middle, is the library, or **Phra Mondop,** built in Thai style by Rama I, famed for its mother-of-pearl doors, bookcases containing the *Tripitaka* (sacred Buddhist manuscripts), human and dragon-headed *nagas* (snakes), and statues of Chakri kings; and third, to the east, is the **Royal**

Pantheon, built in Khmer style during the 19th century—it's open to the public in October for one day to commemorate the founding of the Chakri dynasty. To the immediate north of the library is a model of **Angkor Wat,** the most sacred of all Cambodian shrines. The model was constructed by King Mongkut (r. 1851–68) as a reminder that the neighboring state was once under the dominion of Thailand.

From here you can enter the central shrine, or *bot*, where the **Emerald Buddha** is housed on a tall pedestal. There's always a crush of people around the entrance, but try to take note of the exquisite inlaid mother-of-pearl work on the door panels. Late-Ayutthaya-style murals depicting the life of the Buddha decorate the interior walls; the images flow counterclockwise and end with the most important stage: Enlightenment. The surrounding portico of the *bot* is an example of masterful Thai craftsmanship.

As you leave the cloisters of Wat Phra Kaew and move into the grounds of **The Grand Palace ★★★**, it's easy to see that the buildings here were greatly influenced by Western architecture, including Italian, French, and British motifs. The royal family moved from this royal residence to the nearby Chitlada Palace after the death of King Ananda in 1946. Behind an intricately carved gate stands the **Phra Maha Monthien,** a complex of buildings, of which only the **Amarin Winichai Hall** is open to the public—it contains two elaborate thrones and is used officially only for coronations. Immediately west of this is the **Chakri Mahaprasad,** The Grand Palace Hall; built by British architects in 1888 as a royal residence for Rama IV to commemorate the centennial of the Chakri dynasty, it features an unusually florid mix of Italian and Thai influences. The Thai-temple-style roof rests physically (and symbolically) on top of an otherwise European building. The only part of this building open to the public is the small weapons museum, with entrances on either side of the main entrance, which displays a collection of spears, swords, and guns.

To the west of the Chakri Mahaprasad is the **Dusit Maha Prasat,** an audience hall built by Rama I that is now used officially only for royal funerals. Inside is a splendid throne inlaid with mother-of-pearl. On each of the four corners of the roof is a *garuda* (the half-human, half-bird steed of the God Rama, an avatar of the Hindu god Vishnu). The *garuda* symbolizes the king, who is considered a reincarnation of King Rama. This is the most photographed building in the Grand Palace; it is something of an icon of Thai architecture.

Beyond the Dusit Maha Prasat is a small cafe where you can find some refreshment, and, finally, the **Wat Phra Kaew Museum** houses some unusual exhibits, including elephant bones and costumes once used to adorn the Emerald Buddha.

On the Palace grounds is the **Queen Sirikit Museum of Textiles.** It displays a variety of Thailand's famously intricate woven textiles. However, it is often overlooked by tourists quick to leave the place, which is a shame, because the museum's exhibition of gowns worn by H.M. the Queen are breathtaking, and there's a detailed display that explains how the complex process of making Thai silk. Even if the dresses don't pique your interest, the museum's air conditioning offers sweet relief from Thailand's unrelenting heat and the gift shop is particularly lovely.

East of the river, on Na Phra Lan Rd., near Sanam Luang. www.palaces.thai.net. © **02224-1833.** Admission 400B. Price includes Wat Phra Kaew and the Grand Palace, as well as admission to the Vimanmek Palace (in Dusit Park). Daily 8:30am–3:30pm; most individual buildings closed to the public except on special days proclaimed by the King. Take the Chao Phraya Express Boat to Tha Chang pier, then walk due east, then south.

Bangkok Art & Culture Centre ★★★ GALLERY   This huge edifice, opposite the Siam Discovery Center, provides a showcase for Thai arts, music, theater, film, and design. The center doesn't have a permanent collection, which means there are always new exhibitions or cultural events taking place, so check the website before visiting to see what's on. Besides promoting the arts, the venue is a platform for cultural exchange with an emphasis on collaborations between students here and abroad. With over 3,000 sq. m (32,292 sq. ft.) of exhibition space, this is a premier home for contemporary arts.

Corner of Rama I and Phaya Thai Rds. www.bacc.or.th. © **02214-6630-8.** Free admission apart from special concerts and events. Tues–Sat 10am–9pm. National Stadium BTS.

Bangkok Doll Museum ★ MUSEUM   Founded in 1956 by Khunying Tongkorn Chandavimol, a Thai woman who trained at a prestigious doll-making school in Japan, the Bangkok Doll Museum showcases nearly 500 handcrafted dolls. Many of the figurines depict Thai culture and its people, from hill-tribe and ethnic groups in ornamental dress to Thai classical dancers in costumes that were designed after extensive research to ensure their historical accuracy. An additional collection displays dolls dressed in traditional clothing from countries around the world. It can be tricky to find the museum so have your taxi call to get directions.

85 Soi Mo Leng, Ratchaprarop Rd. www.bangkokdolls.com. © **022453008.** Free. Tues–Sat 8am–5pm. Victory Monument BTS.

Bangkok Forensic Museum ★ MUSEUM   Commonly referred to as the Siriraj Medical Museum or the Museum of Death, this forensic hub is not for the faint of heart. Displays showcase death and their causes. Bloodied murder weapons are in glass cases (some are expected, like bullets and knives; others, like a dildo, used to beat a woman to death, not so much). The most stomach-churning display are the human bodies, the centerpiece being the preserved body of Si Ouey, Thailand's most infamous serial killer who took the lives of more than 30 children in the 1950s. In an adjacent room, containers holding fetuses suspended in a murky formaldehyde that had various birth defects. Cancerous cells and body parts, skeletons, and more are all part of this macabre museum. The museum is on the 2nd floor of the Adulyadejvikrom building at Siriraj Hospital.

2 Wangang Rd., Bangkok Noi. www.sirirajmuseum.com. ℂ **024192601.** 200B. Wed–Mon 10am–5pm.

Children's Discovery Museum ★ MUSEUM   Bangkok isn't known for being particularly child-friendly and there a lack of spots specifically geared towards entertaining kids. But out near the Chatuchak Weekend Market (p. 127) is an attraction just for the 2-to-12 set. The highlights for most children are the dinosaur discovery section, where bones are buried in the sand for young archeologists to excavate and reassemble, and an outdoor splash pad and water playground with jets and fountains. A handful of exhibits were closed during our last visit and, mystifyingly, some sections had signs asking kids not to touch. But even with a few missteps, the free museum is worth checking out—especially when timed with a weekend trip to the neighboring market.

Queen Sirikit Park, Kamphaeng Phet 4. No website. ℂ **022724500.** Free. Tues–Sun 10am–4pm. Mo Chit BTS.

Erawan Shrine ★★ RELIGIOUS SITE   The Erawan Shrine is not old, but it is an interesting testament to the belief in spirits in Thai society. Built in 1956, next to what is now the Grand Hyatt Erawan, it stands defiantly at the center of a busy corner plot and in the shadow of the BTS. In a sumptuous spirit house at the center of this yard, a gilded statue of the four-faced Hindu god of creation, Brahma, named Phra Phrom in Thai, is enshrined. Construction of the shrine is believed to have put a stop to a spate of deaths of workers constructing the hotel site, and due to such mystic powers, it is today one of the most revered spots in the kingdom. Worshipers wafting bunches of incense and praying for success in love crowd the area. Even taxi drivers raise their hands from the steering wheel to give a *wai* as they pass by.

But the shrine as a long history of misfortune: In 2006, a Thai man with a history of mental illness decided to take an axe to the statue. As a painful testament to the depth of Thais' devotion to the spirits (and a pitiful lesson in human rights), the onlookers turned on him and beat him to death in broad daylight. In 2010, the Ratchaprasong intersection, where the shrine is located, was ground zero for Red Shirt protesters (for more on that, see p. 32) and again during another coup in 2012. The most tragic example of the shrine's misfortune came August 17, 2015, when a bomb exploded killing 20 and injuring more than 120 others, an act decried as terrorism by the Thai government. The shrine suffered minor damage and reopened a few days later.

On the corner of Rama I and Ratchadamri Rd. (next to the Grand Hyatt Erawan). No entrance fee. Daily dawn–8pm. Phloen Chit BTS.

Jim Thompson's House ★★★ HISTORIC HOME   American architect Jim Thompson settled in Bangkok after World War II, where he worked for the CIA and became fascinated by Thai culture and artifacts. He dedicated himself to reviving Thailand's ebbing silk industry, bringing in new dyes to create the bright pinks, yellows, and turquoises we see sold today and selling them to fashion houses in Paris and New York City. It was Jim Thompson silks that were used by costumier Irene Sharaff for the Oscar-winning movie *The King & I*, starring Yul Brynner. Mr. Thompson mysteriously disappeared in 1967 while vacationing in the Cameron Highlands of Malaysia and, despite extensive investigations, his disappearance remains unsolved. But that doesn't stop the speculation, and common theories suggest his anti-American viewpoints didn't sit well with the CIA while others blame a hungry tiger or communist spies.

All visitors join a guided tour of the house, which contains a splendid collection of Khmer sculpture, Chinese porcelain, and Burmese carvings and scroll paintings. The walls lean slightly inward to help stabilize the structure; the original houses used stilts without foundations. The residence is composed of a cluster of six teak and *theng* (a wood harder than teak) houses from central Thailand, which were rebuilt—with a few Western facilities—in a lovely garden, next to what is today murky *klong* teaming with life. No doubt it would have been magnificent 50 years ago. Thompson's art collection remains in the house today and includes rare porcelain from neighboring countries.

The attractions here include a relaxing cafe, a gallery space with a revolving collection of local artists' works, and a shop featuring silk shirts, neckties, homewares, bags, and scarves.

Dedicated shoppers and fans of the brand will want to take the BTS to the Bang Chak BTS stop for more shopping at the multi-story **Jim Thompson Outlet** (153 Sukhumvit Soi 93; www.jimthompson.com; ✆ **02700-2000**).

Snake Sightings

Lovers of all things reptilian can witness a sight rarely encountered anywhere else. The **Queen Saovabha Memorial Institute** in partnership with the Thai Red Cross has a **snake farm**, at 1871 Rama IV Rd. (✆ **02252-0161**), in the heart of Bangkok. Don't expect a bucolic "farm" setting; in fact, this is nothing more than a cluster of pretty colonial buildings, in the heart of the city, that provides a research institute for the study of venomous snakes. Established in 1923, this was the second facility of its type in the world. For a fee of 200B (50B for kids), you can see slide shows and snake-handling demonstra-tions weekdays at 11am and 2:30pm, and on weekends and holidays at 11am. You can also watch the handlers work with deadly cobras and (equally poison-ous) banded kraits, with demonstrations of venom milking. Later, the venom is injected into horses, which produce anti-venin for the treatment of snakebites in humans. The Red Cross Snake Farm sells medical guides and will also inoculate you against such maladies as typhoid, cholera, and smallpox, in their clinic. The institute is open daily Monday to Friday 9:30am to 3:30pm, Saturday and Sunday 9:30am to 1pm. It's a short walk from Sala Daeng BTS station.

Bolts of silks, cotton prints, and ready-made items are available for purchase, some at a discount.

6 Soi Kasemsan 2. www.jimthompsonhouse.com. ℂ **02216-7368.** Admission 150B adults; 100B children. Daily 9am–5pm; mandatory tours start every 20 minutes. On a small *soi* off Rama I Rd., near the National Stadium BTS.

Museum of Siam ★★ MUSEUM One of Bangkok's most engaging museums, the Museum of Siam is conveniently located in a grand old colonial building just a short walk from the Grand Palace and Wat Po. It is worth visiting while you're in this part of town, especially if you have kids with you, as there are many hands-on exhibits. To begin, visitors are shown a short video contrasting the lives of traditional and modern Thais, and then over the three floors of displays, the museum attempts to answer the question "What is Thainess?" by looking at key aspects of the country's evolution. There are rooms dedicated to the importance of rice and bamboo in Thai culture, and there's also a chance to practice your cannon-firing skills, dress up in Edwardian clothes for a period snapshot or pose as a street food vendor making a delicious meal. Equally engaging for children and adults.

4 Sanam Chai Rd. ℂ **02225-2777.** Admission 300B, free for children 14 and under and seniors 60 and over. Tues–Sun 10am–6pm. Express boat to Tha Thien, walk east to Sanamchai Rd, then 1 block south.

The National Museum ★★★ MUSEUM If you only visit one museum in Bangkok, it should be this one, as it is the main collection of the country's art and archaeology.

The building housing the museum was built as part of the Grand Palace complex when the capital of Siam was moved from Thonburi to Bangkok in 1782. Originally the palace of Rama I's brother, the deputy king and appointed successor, it was called the Wang Na ("Palace at the Front"). The position of the princely successor was eventually abolished, and Rama V had the palace converted into a museum in 1884. Thammasat University, the College of Dramatic Arts, and the National Theater were also built on the royal grounds, along with additional museum buildings.

To see the entire collection, take a map at the ticket office and give yourself a few hours; if you prefer not to wander, catch one of the English-language free guided tours on Wednesday or Thursday, beginning at 9:30am. Without a guide, you should start with the recently renovated **Thai History and the Prehistoric Galleries** in the first building. If you're short of time, proceed to the **Red House** behind it, a traditional 18th-century Thai building that was originally the living quarters of Princess Sri Sudarak, sister of King Rama I. It contains many personal effects originally owned by the princess.

Another essential stop is the **Buddhaisawan Chapel,** built in 1795 to house one of Thailand's most revered Buddha images, brought here from its original home in Chiang Mai. The chapel is an exquisite example of Buddhist temple architecture.

From the chapel, work your way back through the main building of the royal palace to see the gold jewelry, some from the royal collections, and the

Thai ceramics, including many pieces in the five-color *Bencharong* style. The **Old Transportation Room** contains ivory carvings, elephant chairs, and royal palanquins. There are also rooms full of all kinds of memorabilia: royal emblems and insignia, stone and wood carvings, costumes, textiles, musical instruments, and Buddhist religious artifacts. At the rear of the museum compound, look for fine art and sculpture.

The museum seems to be in a somewhat constant state of construction, and some exhibits might not be open. Call ahead to check if there is a particular room or display you're keen to see.

Na Phra That Rd. (✆ **02224-1333**. Admission 200B. Wed–Sun 9am–4pm. Free English-language tours Wed–Thurs 9:30am. Chao Phraya Express Boat to Tha Chang pier; about 1km/⅔ mile north of the Grand Palace.

Royal Barge Museum ★★ MUSEUM   Thailand must be the only country in the world to have a museum dedicated to its royal barges, and though it's not a big collection, it's very impressive. The awe-inspiring level of detail and decoration of each barge reflect an extraordinary skill on the part of the barge builders. The largest boats measures over 46m (151 ft.) and are occasionally used by the royal family during state occasions or for religious ceremonies. The king's barge, the *Suphannahong*, has a swanlike neck and central chamber; the boat itself is decorated with scarlet and gold carvings of fearsome mythological beasts.

Located on the Thonburi side of the river, the museum is not easy to get to under your own steam, so it's best to make it part of a longboat canal tour. As it's all located under one huge roof, around half an hour should suffice for a visit. If you can't make it to the royal barges, there is a smaller display of vessels at the National Museum (see above).

On the west bank of the river, on Klong Bangkok Noi (canal), north of the Phra Pinklao Bridge. (✆ **02424-0004**. Admission 100B adults, 100B extra for cameras, 200B for video. Daily 9am–5pm. Taxi or cross-river ferry from Tha Phra Arthit.

Siam Society and Kamthieng House ★★ CULTURAL INSTITUTION   The 19th-century **Kamthieng House,** on the grounds of the Siam Society Headquarters, was a rice farmer's teak house, transplanted from the banks of Chiang Mai's Ping River. Ethnographic objects from the everyday life of that era make up the bulk of the collection. Many agricultural and domestic items, including woven fish baskets and terra-cotta pots, are on display, and there's an intriguing exhibit on the Chao Vieng, or city dwellers, from the northern Lanna Thai kingdom.

Walking through the small but lush grounds—they're landscaped like a northern Thai garden—offers respite from the frenetic Asok intersection, just behind the hedge. Check the website for music concerts, lectures in English, and study tours given by experts.

131 Soi Asok (north of Sukhumvit on Soi 21). www.siam-society.org.(✆ **02661-6470**. Admission 100B adults, free children. Tues–Sat 9am–5pm. 10-min. walk from Asok BTS station.

Suan Pakkad Palace Museum ★★ PALACE   Wang Suan Pakkad ("Palace of the Lettuce Garden") is one of Bangkok's most delightful retreats.

This serene oasis was the home of Princess Chumbhon of Nakhon Sawan, an avid art collector and one of the country's most dedicated archaeologists; she partly financed the excavations at Ban Chiang I in 1967. In 1952, these five 19th-century teak houses were moved from Chiang Mai and rebuilt in a lushly landscaped garden on a private *klong*, separated by a high wall from the tumult of Bangkok's streets. The **Lacquer Pavilion** (moved here in 1958) came from a monastery and was a birthday present from the prince to the princess.

The collection here is diverse, with Khmer sculpture, ivory boxes, and some marvelous prints by European artists depicting images of Siam before the country opened to the Western world. There is an entire room of objects from the Ban Chiang site, including pottery and jewelry which date back to the Bronze Age. Look out for a superb Buddha head, from Ayutthaya, and an example of a royal barge, outside in a shed in the garden. Be sure to ask to see the pavilion housing the princess's collection of Thai and Chinese ceramics. The gift shop at Wang Suan Pakkad offers reasonably priced reproductions.

352 Sri Ayutthaya Rd. (btw. Phayathai and Ratchaprarop rds.). www.suanpakkad.com. ©02245-4934. Admission 100B adults, 50B children, including material for a self-guided tour of grounds and collections. Daily 9am–4pm. 10-min. walk from Phaya Thai BTS.

Vimanmek Teak Mansion ★★ MUSEUM *Note: At the time of publication, the hall was closed for renovations. Check to see if reopened before heading here.* Your ticket to the Grand Palace will also get you in to visit King Chulalongkorn's stunning golden teakwood mansion, often called Vimanmek Palace, situated in delightful Dusit Palace Park. Built in 1868, this mansion once stood on the small island of Ko Si Chang and was restored in 1982 for Bangkok's bicentennial. It's now a private museum with a collection of the royal family's memorabilia. English-speaking guides (every 30 minutes from 9:45am to 3:15pm) offer hour-long tours that take visitors through a number of the 80 exquisite apartments and rooms. Also in Dusit Park is the original **Abhisek Dusit Throne Hall,** originally built for Rama V in 1904. Today, it houses a display of Thai handicrafts, and buildings displaying photographs, clocks, fabrics, royal carriages, and other regalia.

193/2 Ratchawithi Rd., Dusit Palace Park (opposite the Dusit Zoo). © **02628-6300.** Admission 100B; free if you purchase a joint ticket for the Grand Palace. Daily 9:30am–4pm (last ticket 3:15pm). Taxi from Tha Thien pier.

TEMPLES (WATS)

Bangkok's many temples are each unique and inspiring. If you can see only a few, pay attention to the star ratings and hit the highlights (Wat Phra Kaew is listed earlier in the chapter due to its location within the Grand Palace compound and Wat Po is right next door). But while the big temples of Bangkok are must-see sites, don't pass up smaller neighborhood temples, which are ideal places to learn about Buddhism from local monks looking to practice their English. Early morning is a good time to visit temples: the air is cool, monks busy themselves with morning activities, and the complexes are generally less crowded.

Thai people make regular offerings to temples and monasteries as an act of merit-making. Supporting the *sangha*, or monkhood, brings one closer to Buddhist ideals and increases the likelihood of a better life beyond this one. Many shops near temples sell saffron-colored pails filled with everyday supplies such as toothbrushes, soap, and other common necessities, and Thais bring these and other gifts as offerings to Buddhist mendicants as a way of gaining good graces. If you get up very early, you may even see a morning alms collection by (usually barefoot) monks carrying their bowls around the neighborhood. Depending on the neighborhood, morning alms typically takes place around sunrise but check with your hotel's front desk for exact times and ideal locations for each neighborhood.

Small monetary contributions (the amount is up to you) are welcome at any temple, though the better-known temples already charge an admission fee. Devotions at a temple involve bowing three times, placing the forehead on the ground at the foot of the Buddha, and lighting candles and incense and chanting. Tourists are welcome to participate, but they are asked to pay particular attention to proper dress—take off your shoes and avoid baring your shoulders, thighs, upper arms, or back. If you kneel or sit to pay your respects, take care not to point your feet toward the Buddha images.

Wat Arun (Temple of Dawn) ★★★ TEMPLE   Formerly known as Wat Jaeng, the 79-m (260-ft.) high, Khmer-inspired tower was renamed the "Temple of Dawn," by King Thaksin, Bangkok's founder. He was keen to signal the rise of a new kingdom after Ayutthaya collapsed, and so borrowed the name—which means dawn—from the Hindu God, Aruna. Fittingly, it's at its most wondrous as the sun rises and sets.

The original tower was only 15m (49 ft.) high but was expanded during the rule of Rama III (1824–51) to its current height of 76m (250 ft.). At the request of the King, locals donated floral and decorative motifs made of ceramic shards and today they adorn the exterior. At the base of the complex are Chinese stone statues, once used as ballast in trading ships, which were gifts from Chinese merchants.

You can climb the central *prang*, but be warned: The steps are treacherously narrow and steep—and even more precarious coming down—so make use of the rail at the side. If you go up, notice the Hindu gods atop the three-headed elephants. The view of the river, Wat Po, and Grand Palace is well worth the climb. Be sure to walk to the back of the tower to the monks' living quarters, a tranquil world far from the bustle of Bangkok's busy streets. The gilded Buddha statues in formation make for great photos.

West bank of the Chao Phraya, opposite Tha Thien Pier. www.watarun.net. Admission 50B. Daily 9am–5:30pm. Take a water taxi from Tha Tien Pier (near Wat Po), or cross the Phra Pinklao Bridge and follow the river south on Arun Amarin Rd.

Wat Benchamabophit (the Marble Temple) ★ TEMPLE   Wat Benchamabophit, also known as the Marble Temple, was designed during the rule of Rama V and built in the early part of the 20th century. It is the most modern, and one of the most beautiful, of Bangkok's royal *wats*. Unlike the older

complexes, there's no truly monumental *viharn* or *chedi* dominating the grounds. Many smaller buildings reflect a melding of European materials and designs with traditional Thai religious architecture. Even the courtyards feature polished white marble. Walk inside the compound, beyond the main *bot*, to view the many Buddha images that adopt a wide variety of postures. During early mornings, monks chant in the main chapel, sometimes so intensely that it seems as if the temple is going to lift off.

Sri Ayutthaya Rd. (south of the Assembly Building, near Chitralada Palace). Admission 20B. Daily 8am–5pm. Taxi from Phaya Thai BTS.

Wat Mahathat (Temple of the Great Relic) ★ HISTORIC SITE

Built to house a relic of the Buddha, Wat Mahathat is one of Bangkok's oldest shrines and the headquarters for Thailand's largest monastic order. It's also the Center for Vipassana Meditation, at the city's Buddhist University, which offers some programs in English. (See p. 119 for information about courses.) Not many tourists stop at this temple, so you'll often find the young monks here eager to engage you in conversation.

Adjacent to it, between Maharaj Road and the river, is the city's biggest **amulet market,** where locals sell a fantastic array of religious amulets, charms, and talismans. Each amulet brings a specific kind of luck—to get the girl, to pass your exams, to keep bugs out of your rice stock, or to ward off your mother-in-law. (The newer amulet market is part of Wat Ratchanada, off the intersection of Mahachai and Ratchadamnoen Klang roads, across from Wat Saket.) See p. 115 for more.

Na Phra That Rd. (near Sanam Luang Park, btw. the Grand Palace and the National Museum). ✆ **02222-6011** (meditation center). Donations welcome. Daily 9am–5pm. Water taxi to Maharaj pier.

Wat Po ★★★ TEMPLE

Wat Po is among the most photogenic of all the *wats* in Bangkok; it's also one of the most active. Known as the Temple of the Reclining Buddha, Wat Po was built by Rama I in the 16th century and is the oldest and largest Buddhist temple in Bangkok. The compound is immediately south of the Grand Palace, but it takes 15 (often hot) minutes to walk from one to the other. The huge compound contains many important monuments, and the block to the south of Chetuphon Road is where monks reside.

Most people go straight to the enormous **Reclining Buddha** in the northwestern corner of the compound section. It is more than 43m (141 ft.) long and 15m (49 ft.) high, and was built during the mid-19th-century reign of Rama III. The statue is brick, covered with layers of plaster and gold leaf; the feet are inlaid with mother-of-pearl illustrations of 108 auspicious *laksanas* (characteristics) of the Buddha.

Outside, the grounds contain 91 *chedis* (stupas or mounds), four *viharns* (halls), and a *bot* (the central shrine in a Buddhist temple). Most impressive, aside from the Reclining Buddha, are the four main *chedis* dedicated to the first four Chakri kings and, nearby, the library.

The temple is considered Thailand's first public university. Long before the advent of literacy or books, many of its murals and sculptures were used to illustrate and instruct scholars on the basic principles of religion, science, and literature. Visitors still drop 1-satang coins in 108 bronze bowls—corresponding to the 108 auspicious characteristics of the Buddha—for good fortune, and to help the monks keep up the *wat*.

Wat Po is also home to one of the earliest Thai massage schools and you can learn about the traditional methods and medicine at the **Traditional Medical Practitioners Association Center,** an open-air hall to the rear of the *wat*. True Thai massage, such as that taught here, involves chiropractic manipulation and acupressure, as well as stretching, stroking, and kneading. Massage courses are available (9,500B for 30 hours), but many students prefer schools with tutors who speak more proficient English. There are also a few astrologers and palm readers available for consultation, though foreign visitors are bound to encounter language difficulties.

Maharaj Rd., near the river (about 1km/⅔ mile south of the Grand Palace). ⓒ **02226-0335.** Admission 100B. Daily 8am–5pm; Massage school ⓒ **02622-3551;** massages offered until 6pm. A short walk or taxi from Tha Thien pier.

Wat Saket (The Golden Mount) ★★ TEMPLE   Wat Saket is easily recognized by its golden *chedi*, atop a fortresslike hill near busy Ratchadamnoen Road in Banglampoo. King Rama I restored the *wat*, and 30,000 bodies were brought here during a plague in the reign of Rama II (r. 1809–24). The hill, which is almost 80m (262 ft.) high, is an artificial construction, begun during the reign of Rama III (r. 1824–51). Rama V built the golden *chedi* in the late 19th century to house a relic of Buddha, given to him by the British. The concrete walls were added during World War II to keep the structure from collapsing.

The Golden Mount is best known for its vistas of Ratanakosin Island and the rooftops of Bangkok and is beautifully lit at night. Every late October to mid-November (for 9 days around the full moon), Wat Saket hosts Bangkok's most important temple fair, when red cloth wraps the Golden Mount and a carnival erupts around it, with food, trinket stalls, and theatrical performances. One of my favorite ways to start the evening is to watch the sunset at Wat Saket before hailing a tuk-tuk to Chinatown for dinner or drinks.

Ratchadamnoen Klang and Boripihat roads. Entrance to the *wat* is free; admission to the Golden Mount is 10B. Donations welcome. Daily 7:30am–5:30pm. Taxi from Hua Lamphong MRT.

Wat Suthat & the Giant Swing ★ TEMPLE   This temple is among the oldest and largest in Bangkok, and author Somerset Maugham declared its roofline the most beautiful. Rama I started the construction and Rama III finished it; Rama II carved the panels for the *viharn* doors. It houses the handsome 14th-century **Phra Buddha Shakyamuni,** a Buddha image that was brought from Sukhothai. The ashes of King Rama VIII, Ananda Mahidol, brother of the current king, are contained in its base. The wall paintings for which it is known were created during Rama III's reign.

Outside the *viharn* stand many Chinese pagodas, bronze horses, and figures of Chinese soldiers. The most important religious association, however, is with the Brahman priests who officiate at important state ceremonies, and there are two Hindu shrines nearby. The huge teak arch—also carved by Rama II—in front is all that remains of an original giant swing, which was used until 1932 to celebrate and thank Shiva for a bountiful rice harvest, and to ask for the god's blessing on the next. The Minister of Rice, accompanied by hundreds of Brahman holy men, would lead a parade around the city walls to the temple precinct. Teams of men would ride the swing on arcs as high as 25m (82 ft.) in the air, trying to grab a bag of silver coins with their teeth. Due to injuries and deaths, the dangerous swing ceremony is no more, but the thanksgiving festival in mid-December, after the rice harvest, still continues.

Sao Chingcha Square (near the intersection of Bamrung Mueang and Thi Thong rds.). ℂ **02224-9845.** Admission 20B. Daily 9am–9pm. Taxi from Hua Lamphong MRT.

Wat Traimit (The Golden Buddha) ★★★ TEMPLE Wat Traimit, thought to date from the 13th century, would hardly rate a second glance if not for its astonishing Buddha image, which is nearly 3m (9¾ ft.) high, weighs over 5.5 tons, and is believed to be cast of solid gold. It was discovered by accident in 1957 when, covered by a plaster image, it fell from a crane during a move. The impact shattered the outer shell, revealing the shining gold beneath. This powerful image is truly dazzling and is thought date back to the Sukhothai period. Most scholars believe the Buddha was covered with plaster to hide its true wealth from Burmese invaders. Pieces of the stucco are also on display at the site.

It's worth paying an additional 40B at the ticket counter to enter the **Yaowarat Chinatown Heritage Center** (Tues–Sun 8am–5pm; 3rd floor of the temple complex) to learn about the rich history of Bangkok's Chinatown and the people who call this fascinating neighborhood home.

Traimit Rd. (west of Hua Lamphong Station, just west of the intersection of Krung Kasem and Rama IV rds.). Admission 20B. Donations welcome. Daily 9am–5pm. Walk southwest on Traimit Rd., look for a school on the right with a playground; the wat is up a flight of stairs overlooking the school. 2-min. walk from Hua Lamphong MRT.

CULTURAL & WELLNESS PURSUITS

Culture is all around you in Thailand—and there are ample opportunities to take part in the daily activities, festivals, ceremonies, events, and practices that weave the fabric of this society. The best part of Thai festivals is that, whether getting soaked by buckets of water at Songkran or watching candlelit floats drift downstream at Loy Krathong, foreign visitors are usually invited to join in. Thais are very proud of their cultural heritage, and opportunities abound to learn and participate. Keep an eye on free magazines, such as *BK Magazine* (http://bk.asia-city.com), or local newspapers, *The Nation* (www.nationmulti media.com) and *Bangkok Post* (www.bangkokpost.com), for major events during your stay. The **TAT** (www.tourismthailand.org; ℂ **1672**), doesn't have their finger on the pulse of the city quite like the local press.

Thai Boxing

Muay Thai, or Thai boxing, is Thailand's national sport, and a visit to either of the two venues in Bangkok, or in towns all over Thailand, displays a very different side to the usually gentle Thai culture. The mystical pre-match rituals live musical performances, and, of course, the frenetic gambling with bets placed by fast-moving hand gestures, appeal to fans of this raw, and often bloody, spectacle. In Bangkok, catch fights nightly at either of two stadiums. The **Ratchadamnoen Stadium** (Ratchadamnoen Nok Ave.; www.rajadamnern. com; ✆ **02281-4205**) hosts fights on Monday, Wednesday, Thursday, and Sunday, while the **Lumpinee Boxing Stadium,** north of Bangkok on Ramintra Road (www.lumpineemuaythai.com; ✆ **02282-3141**), has bouts on Tuesday, Friday, and Saturday. Tickets are sold by class, with ringside tickets starting around 2,500B; perfect for those who want to get up close to the action. Second class tickets are 1,500B and offer good views and a fun crowd. Mingle with gamblers wielding multiple cell phones and screaming and shouting in from the third-class seats (1,000B or less).

Keen to try some kicks and punches yourself? Learn the *art of eight limbs* at **Jaroenthong Muay Thai Gym** (www.jaroenthongmuaythaikhaosan.com; ✆ **02629-2313**). It's an acclaimed gym with two locations in Bangkok, including a new facility near Khao San Road; drop-in sessions start at 600B. Additionally, the website **www.muaythaicampsthailand.com** offers details on training centers around Thailand.

Thai Cooking Classes

Should you find yourself captivated by the complexity of Thai food consider a lesson in Thai cooking. Bangkok has excellent options for both beginners and advanced cooks. Here are a few of our favorites to add to your travel itinerary.

o **Silom Thai Cooking School** (68 Trok Walai Alley; www.bangkokthai. cooking.com; ✆ **084726-5669;** classes from 900B) squeezes in a market trip to stock up on produce with instructions, techniques, and tips for preparing six dishes. Familiar dishes are on the menu so get ready to master the perfect fried rice, pad Thai, and green curry. The open-air classroom is relaxed and the teachers are engaging and energetic. Morning and afternoon sessions are available.

o **Oriental Thai Cooking School** ★★ (www.mandarinoriental.com; 48 Oriental Avenue; ✆ **02659-9000**; classes from 4,000B) opened its doors at the Mandarin Oriental Hotel in 1986 and was the first cooking class in Bangkok. Courses cover four dishes and they're led by the charismatic chef Narain Kiattiyotcharoen. Like the hotel, the class and setting is five-star and ends with lunch presented at the beautiful Sala Rim Naam restaurant. The one drawback is that cooking is done in groups of three, so advanced cooks might find sharing a wok to be tedious. Weekend sessions include a market visit.

o **Blue Elephant Thai Cooking School** ★★★ (www.blueelephant.cooking school.com; 233 South Sathorn Rd.; ✆ **02673-9353;** classes from 3,300B) is the most impressive culinary class in town. Programs are jam-packed with information and there is a particular emphasis on royal Thai cuisine. Morning sessions include a market trip while the afternoon lessons spend a bit more time explaining different types of Thai ingredients. Classes are fast-moving and students work at individual stations.

o **Bangkok Bold Cooking Studio** ★★ (www.bangkokbold.com; 257 Charoen Nakhon Rd.; ✆ **0988290-4310**; classes from 2,500B). The restaurant by the same name is run by culinary heavyweights whose resumes include stints at Nahm (p. 88) and the Four Seasons, so classes here are a bit more advanced (but beginner sessions are available). The charming Old Town setting makes this a popular choice for guests staying near the river.

o **Cooking with Poo & Friends** (www.cookingwithpoo; ✆ **080434-8686**) runs cooking classes that include market tours. Chef Poo, the owner of an unfortunate nickname for someone in the food industry, grew up in the slums near the Klong Toey market and holds classes (1,500B per person) in her old neighborhood; class fees include transportation.

Thai Massage

A traditional Thai massage involves manipulating your limbs to stretch each muscle and then applying acupressure to loosen up tension and start energy flowing. Your body will be twisted, pulled, and sometimes pounded in the process. Some call it the 'lazy man's yoga' for all the bending and twisting that happens, and you just might be a little sore the next day.

For Thai massage to be beneficial, it should be fairly rigorous and at times it can be punishing: If the therapist is loath to use pressure from the start, you'll want to ask for more to experience the authentic massage. If you chose a street-side spa, choose one away from tourist areas—such as Khao San, Sukhumvit, or Silom roads, where Thais are patrons. *Note:* Many massage parlors on Silom and Sukhumvit roads are fronts for brothels, where (male) tourists will be propositioned for a variety of sexual favors.

There are countless spas and massage parlors around Bangkok; many offer good services at very reasonable rates. There are several reliable chains around town, each offering multiple branches, so you'll never be too far from a relaxing treatment. For your baht and body, try **Health Land** (www.healthlandspa.com for locations), an affordable and reliable chain of spas that efficiently operates a bit like a spa production line; they're best-known for their Thai massage. Another great option is **Asia Herb** (www.asiaherb.com for locations), which has packages that include time in a steam room and facials, or **Let's Relax** (www.letsrelax.com for locations) the most atmospheric of the chains with staff who typically speak fluent English. A quieter option is **The Touch** (www.thetouch1.com for locations), a small spa with two locations on Soi Ruamrudee. It offers excellent foot massages as well as authentic Thai massage.

Wat Po (p. 114) is touted as the best place to learn Thai massage. But the setting is pretty bare-bones and the women rubbing your sore muscles can be quite chatty with each other. For something more elevated and traditional (and quiet!)

check out **Divana Spa ★★** (www.divanaspa.com for locations; ☎ **02661-6784-5**), a well-respected venue for massages, facials, and anti-aging treatments. For all-out pampering, Bangkok's finest spas are almost always those in the most respected hotels, where time and money go into training and language skills. **The Elemis Spa ★★★** (www.elemisspabangkok.com; ☎ **02207-7779**) at the **St Regis Hotel** (p. 76) at 159 Ratchadamri Rd. and the **Oriental Spa ★★★** at the **Mandarin Oriental** (p. 68; www.mandarinoriental.com/bangkok/spa; ☎ **02659-9000**) at 48 Oriental Avenue are two of the finest, but they come with a hefty price tags—you're paying for expertise that leaves your muscles soothed, gets your blood flowing, and gives you a feeling of unparalleled well-being.

A word of warning: Budget spas that use untrained staff with no English skills make for not just an unpleasant experience, but a potentially painful one. If your masseuse doesn't understand a word of English, or there is no one to help translate your needs or aspects of your current health, such as sunburn, you might be taking a risk. Generally, places that offer "ancient" or "traditional" Thai massage have well-trained masseurs and masseuses who offer no extras, but if you are asked to pick a number from a group of dolled-up masseuses sitting behind a glass barrier, you can be sure the term "massage" is a euphemism for paid sex. Your chosen masseuse will then inform you of the "extras" available and the going rates.

Meditation

The House of Dhamma at 26/9 Lardprao Soi 15 (www.houseofdhamma.com; ☎ **02511-0439**) and **Wat Mahathat** (see p. 114) serve as meditation centers for overseas students of Buddhism. The latter is one of Thailand's largest Buddhist Universities and has become a popular center for meditation lessons, with English-speaking monks overseeing students of *Vipassana*, also called Insight Meditation. Daily instruction is available; call ahead (☎ **02222-6011**) to get the schedule and to make an appointment. Both offer good introductions to basic techniques.

Horse Racing

The prestigious **Royal Bangkok Sports Club** (www.rbsc.org; ☎ **02652-5000**) holds horse-racing events that are open to the paying public every second Sunday of the month; check the website for dates. The grounds occupy a prime spot on Henri Dunant Road, opposite Chulalongkorn University, north of Rama IV Road. Nominal admission fees and minimum bets apply.

Thai Language Classes

So you've learned your "Sawadee-khrup" or "Sawadee-kha," but want to take it a little further? Thais are very gracious and welcoming with foreigners butchering their language (the tones make you pronounce the most mundane phrases in laughable ways), but there are few good schools in Bangkok to help you get the pronunciations right. An exception is the superlative **American University Alumni Language Center** (179 Ratchadamri Rd.; www.aua thailand.org; ☎ **02252-8170**).

STAYING ACTIVE

Exercising in the Park

Lumphini Park and **Benjakiti Park** are the best places in town for logging some laps. Lumphini Park in central Bangkok (between Rama IV, Wireless Road, Ratchadamri Road, Sarasin) is the largest park in town, and justifiable comparisons link New York's Central Park and Lumpini Park. In addition to a jogging track, there's a large lake for paddle boating, playgrounds, and locals practicing tai chi in the early morning and aerobics in the evening. On Sundays in the cooler months (which corresponds with high tourist season), the Bangkok Symphony Orchestra (www.bangkoksymphony.org for schedules) offers free outdoor concerts. Large monitor lizards roam near the pod; they're generally harmless but don't get too close taking a photo or try and touch them.

A national tobacco monopoly once occupied Benjakiti Park (near the Queen Sirikit MRT or the Akoke BTS). Today, it's where early-morning joggers, nannies and their charges, and cyclists come for some fresh air. While the facilities aren't quite as nice as Lumpini Park, there are bikes rentals (40B per hour) and a 2km track. In either park, everything momentarily comes to a halt when the national anthem plays over loudspeakers at 8am and 6pm.

Fitness

All the finest five-star properties in town boast quality health clubs complete with personal trainers and top equipment. In addition, **Virgin Active** (www.virginactive.co.th for locations) has swanky, state-of-the-art clubs conveniently located around town. If you'll be in town for more than a few days, **GuavaPass** (www.guavapass.com) lets members book high-end boutique fitness classes (like spinning, cross fit, hot yoga, or Pilates reformer lessons) at studios all across town. Multi-class packages starting at 899B.

Golf

Various golf courses lie close to the city, a number of which are championship quality. **Thai Golfer** (www.thaigolfer.com) is *the* resource for reviews and up-to-date pricing for courses around the country.

o **Thai Country Club** ★★ (www.thaicountryclub.com; ℂ **03857-0234**), run by the Peninsula Hotel, is praised for its consistent greens and sumptuous clubhouse. This stunning 18-hole course lies just 45 minutes southeast of Bangkok. The following fees refer to low/high season rates: Greens fees are 3,650B–5,500B on weekdays, 4,850B–6,500B on weekends.

o **Pinehurst Golf & Country Club** (www.pinehurst.co.th; ℂ **02516-8679**), located in Pathum Thani, is a popular 27-hole course that served as the venue for the 1992 Johnnie Walker Classic. Greens fees for 18-holes are 2,000B on weekdays, 2,700B on weekends.

Yoga

Apart from the many hotels in town that schedule regular yoga classes, some downtown studios may offer special packages for visitors on extended stays.

Expect to pay 1,000B and up per class. One such studio is **Absolute You** (www.absoluteyou.com) with more than a dozen locations around town, including one in Amarin Plaza, close to the Grand Hyatt Erawan, on Ploenchit Road. There are numerous daily classes and schedules are posted on the website. (The studio also offers Pilates, spinning, and personal training.)

Yoga Elements Studio (www.yogaelements.com; ✆ 02255-9552), on the 7th floor at 185 Dhammalert Building, just behind Central Chidlom department store, is another a well-respected place for yoga, with a focus on *vinyasa* and *ashtanga* practice.

SHOPPING

Bangkok pulls in shoppers from all over the world, clamoring to find bargains at the endless street-side stalls, world-famous markets, or ultrachic, brand-name boutiques. Shopping is a real adventure in Bangkok. The big markets are a visual onslaught (don't miss the Weekend Market; see p. 127), and there are upmarket gift and antiques dealers as well as small souvenir stalls scattered about town. Below is a breakdown of where to shop around town. Another useful resource is Nancy Chandler's *Map of Bangkok*, which is available at bookstores throughout the city for 275B and has detailed insets of places such as Chinatown and the sprawling downtown.

Where to Shop
RIVERSIDE & BEYOND
Charoen Krung Road is full of goodies: antiques stores, jewelry wholesalers, and funky little galleries. Keep your eyes open, and you might stumble on a gem as you browse shop windows, especially at such places as **Lek Gallery,** at number 1124–1134 (www.facebook.com/pages/Lek-Gallery; ✆ 02639-5871), near Soi 30, which has attractive decorative items such as table lamps and some fine antique furniture. On that same soi, look out for **Warehouse 30 ★★** (www.facebook.com/thewarehouse30), a string of World War II-era warehouses reimagined by Duangrit Bunnag, Thailand's most famous architect. The shops offer something for everyone: co-working spaces, cafes, home décor, fashion, and art by Thai designers. **P. Tendercool** (across from Warehouse 30; www.ptendercool.com) is a bespoke furniture studio that makes exquisite tables and chairs. The art and antiques shops at the low-rise mall known as **River City** (www.rivercity.co.th; ✆ 02237-0077), on Charoen Krung Soi 38, have a great selection of porcelain, wood carvings, jewelry, and silk, but some outlets are overpriced (avoid the tailoring shops here, as the low standards of craftsmanship do not warrant the big bucks). If you're in the market for antiques, you need to know your stuff, as there are many fakes on sale.

The streets around the Mandarin Oriental are rich with family-run boutiques and make for a nice afternoon of wandering and window shopping. Start inside the hotel where you'll find exquisite one-off jewelry pieces at **Lotus Arts de Vivre** (www.lotusartsdevivre.com) and a **Jim Thompson** (www.jimthompson.com) shop for splendid silks. Outside and around the corner is the famed **O.P. Place** ★★ (www.opthai.com; ✆ **02266-0186**) with a heap of high-end shopping venues, from stores selling expensive designer luggage to jet-setter jewelry stores and amazing antiques, carpets, and fine silver tableware (much of which is Tiffany-like quality). Several of the shops, like **Ashwood Gallery** (3rd floor), sell museum-like pieces that are pre-certified by the Fine Arts Department, so you know you're getting the real deal. **Thai Home Industries** (35 Soi 40) sells upscale Thai goods, like baskets, mother-of-pearl napkin rings, knives, and temple bells. **T.R. Gift Shop Limited** (2-4 Soi 40) specializes in hammered stainless steel homegoods, like trays, water pitchers, candlesticks, silverware, and more; much of it is reminiscent of American designer Michael Aram's work. If you'd prefer bronze to stainless steel, **Siam Bronze** (www.siambronze.com; 1250 Charoen Krung) is one of the country's original producers of shiny woks, silverware, and more.

SUKHUMVIT ROAD

This area bursts with shops from one end to the other and Bangkok's biggest shopping malls (see below) have addresses on this road. For fine silk, stop in at **Almeta** (p. 129), a rival to the Jim Thompson brand.

SILOM, SATHORN & SURAWONG ROADS

Tucked away in the basement level of the MahaNakorn CUBE (96 Naradhiwas; www.donsfootwear.com; ✆ **092264-9647**) is **Don's Footwear**, a bespoke men's shoemaker. A 3-D scanner is used to ensure an ideal fit and 15 styles, from casual loafers to wingtips, are available; they also have a great shoeshine. The **Patpong Night Market** (p. 127), which runs between Silom and Surawong roads, sells traditional souvenir tchotchkes and counterfeit goods.

What to Buy
ANTIQUES

Buying antiques to take out of Thailand is tricky. Authentic antiques are more than 200 years old (they must date from the beginning of the Chakri dynasty in Bangkok), but these days most items are good reproductions that have been professionally "distressed"—even the Certificate of Authenticity can be a forgery. If you do find something real, remember that the Thai government has an interest in keeping authentic antiquities and sacred items in the country, and will require special permission for export.

By law, Buddha images are prohibited from export, except for religious or educational purposes; even in these instances, you'll still have to obtain approval from the **Department of Fine Arts** to remove them from Thailand. This rule is little enforced, though, and the concern is more for antique Buddhas than the cheap replicas you'll find in tourist markets. (Details on how to contact the Department of Fine Arts is on p. 420.)

Almost all the reputable antiques stores in Bangkok are along the endless **Charoen Krung Road** (centered along the section on either side of the post office), but many of these have shamelessly high prices aimed at wealthier tourists, and most items are Chinese, not Thai. **River City** and **O.P. Place** are both convenient places to hunt for art and antiques, as you can hit several stores within an hour, but neither quality nor authenticity is guaranteed.

BOOKSTORES
You'll find a number of bookstores offering a wide variety of English-language books. The two chains with the best choice are **Asia Books** and **Kinokuniya.** Asia Books is a local chain that specializes in regional titles and some overseas publishers. Its main branch is at 221 Sukhumvit Rd., between *sois* 15 and 17 (www.asiabooks.com; ℂ **02252-7277**). Outlets with a large inventory are at the following locations: **The Emporium** on Sukhumvit at Soi 22, **Siam Paragon,** on level 2, and **CentralWorld,** sixth floor.

The eclectic **Kinokuniya** (www.thailand.kinokuniya.com) has three stores in Bangkok, at **The Emporium** on Sukhumvit Road Soi 22, at **Siam Paragon,** and on the sixth floor of the **Isetan department** store at **CentralWorld** (ℂ **02255-9834**). This is Bangkok's best bookstore chain.

For secondhand books, try **Dasa Books,** 714/4 Sukhumvit (near **The Emporium,** between *sois* 26 and 28; www.dasabookcafe.com; ℂ **02661-2993**). It's a great place to grab a coffee and browse for long-lost titles, or exchange old novels free of charge. If you're in search of something specific, their stock list is regularly updated and available online.

DEPARTMENT STORES & SHOPPING PLAZAS
Bangkok's downtown looks more and more like urban Tokyo these days. The size and opulence of Bangkok's many malls and shopping areas are often a shock to those who imagine Bangkok to be an exotic, impoverished destination. Sipping cappuccino at a Starbucks overlooking a busy city street may not be what you've come to Asia to do, but to many, it is a comfort (especially after long trips in more rugged parts of the kingdom). The truth is that malls are focused on today's consumer-obsessed Thai youth; these hallowed halls of materialism are (sadly) much closer to the pulse of the nation than the many temples foreign visitors are keen to experience. Malls are where wealthy Thais hang out, meet friends, dine, and shop. I've listed some malls under "Where to Buy" above; below are some more highlights:

o **CentralWorld** (www.centralworld.co.th; ℂ **02635-1111**), on the corner of Rama I and Rachadamri roads contains Zen and Isetan stores, a fab food hall and a bevy of cinemas. Local designers sit alongside large branches of international brands like Uniqlo and Zara. Open daily 10am to 9pm. The Chit Lom and Siam BTS stations are both nearby.

o **Emporium** (www.emporium.co.th; ℂ **02269-1000**), stands proudly on the corner of Sukhumvit Soi 24. Bangkok's first luxury shopping mall, it underwent a renovation a few years ago, making it hip and cool again. The food hall is one of the best of any of the malls. Open daily 10am to 10pm. It's connected to Phrom Phong BTS.

o **EmQuartier** (693-695 Sukhumvit Rd.; www.emquartier.co.th/en; ℂ **02269-1000**) is a swanky new mall where Bangkok's elite come to see and be seen. The second-floor Quartor sections is devoted to local Thai designers and more than 50 restaurants are gathered in what's call the Helix section. Don't miss **Another Story** (4th floor of the Helux) where more than 150 international brands are on display in this fun "concept store." The mall is open daily 10am to 10pm. It's connected to Phrom Phong BTS.

o **Terminal 21** (www.terminal21.co.th) on Sukhumvit Soi 21 has city-themed floors, like Paris and Toyko, that offer everything from trendy Asian skincare to funky shoe stores. Thai teens love the knick-knack shops and the ample selfie opportunities. Open daily 10am to 10pm and near the Asok BTS.

o **MBK (Mah Boon Krong;** www.mbk-center.co.th; © **02620-9000**) lies at the intersection of Rama 1 and Phayathai. This massive megamall is a cross between a street market and a shopping mall and it's easy to get lost here. The Japanese **Tokyu Department Store** sells bargain-priced local fashions and accessories. There is an entire floor dedicated to technology, like fixing broken iPhone screens to selling outrageous cell phone covers. The food court is legendary for delicious, cheap eats. Open daily 10am to 10pm. Take the BTS to the National Stadium.

o **Pantip Plaza** (http://pantipplaza.com; © **02793-7777**), on Phetchaburi Road, is an older, rather scruffy mall that's dedicated to all things electronic. Among the shoddy bootleg software there are stacks of innovative gadgets, as well as shops selling secondhand or new and affordable computers, cell phones, or components for either. Vendors aren't fluent in English, but it may not matter if you are into IT and can speak fluent Nerdish. Open daily 10am to 8pm. It's a 10-minute walk from Ratchathewi BTS.

o **Siam Discovery** ★★★ (www.siamdiscovery.co.th) at the corner of Rama I Road and Phayathai Road is the most design-conscious mall. The market-style setting makes it easy to browse for skincare, paper products, home décor, and fashion—most of which comes from Thai or Asian designers. Each floor is conveniently themed (Her Floor; His Floor; Retail Innovation Lab) but the third floor, dubbed 'creative lab' is where to beeline if you don't have much time or hate shopping but need souvenirs. Look for **Loft** (2nd floor) that embraces Japanese cool; **Objects of Desire** (3rd floor) for homewares crafted by Thai designers; while **ROOM Concept Store** sells modern homegoods from established Asian brands. Open daily 10am to 10pm and connected via the Siam BTS.

o **Siam Paragon** ★★ (www.siamparagon.co.th; © **02690-1000**), on Rama I Road, is one of those glitzy malls that just goes on and on. Downstairs is **Sea Life Ocean World** (www.sealifebangkok.com), where kids can watch the sharks swim; above are floors of brand-name stores such as Hermès, MNG, Zara, and Shanghai Tang. The mall also has an entire floor of fun eateries, as well as a top-class food hall, a department store, and even a gymnasium. Open daily 10am to 10pm. There's direct access via Siam BTS.

TAILOR-MADE CLOTHES

Especially along Sukhumvit Road, tailors are as common as tuk-tuks, and it can be confusing to know where to go. The tailors listed here are reliable and have great reputations but if you choose to go somewhere else there are few things to keep in mind. First, remember that you get what you pay for and bundled packages of a suit, two pairs of pants, and four shirts for $200 won't last more than a few wears and are often ill-fitting. Next, schedule fittings. Any reputable tailor worth their weight will insist on two to five sittings; though men's shirts can often fit perfectly after one. Set aside a week for the whole process. And finally, this is a man's world and few places in town can expertly cut women's clothing beyond a boxy '90s-era business suit. Prices are entirely dependent on which fabrics are chosen but there is something for every budget and style at the following shops.

Tailor on Ten ★★ (93 Sukhumvit Soi 8; www.tailoronten.com; © 084877-1543) runs the most tech-savvy shop in town, and their custom iPad app helps discerning gents visualize the final product. They stock several fine Italian wools, have large fitting rooms, and specialize in modern, slim cuts.

Empire Tailors (124-126 Sukhumvit Rd.; www.empiretailors.com; © 02251-6762) rises above the fray of cheap suits and fast sewing. Popular with Thai businessmen since 1978, they go the extra mile to make sure cut is just right, taking time for multiple fittings. Beyond the pants, shirts, and suits on offer, Empire Tailor expertly crafts tuxedos and overcoats as well.

Pinky Tailor (888/40 Phloen Chit in the Mahatun Plaza; www.pinkytailor.com; © 02252-9680) started in Bangkok in 1980 and has a loyal following of well-dressed ambassadors and businessmen. Pinky's bookkeeping is old-school, but his hand-cut suits are modern. From the buttonhole colors to linings and monogrammed accents, nothing is forgotten.

GIFTS, CRAFTS & SOUVENIRS

Street vendors throughout the city are a good source of affordable and fun souvenirs (though they are currently banned on Monday, for street cleaning). The best stalls are along **Sukhumvit Road,** beginning at Soi 4, and on **Khao San Road.** Little of the stuff sold there is unique, but the prices are reasonable, and many people stock up on gifts such as mango wood bowls, chopsticks, candles, incense, or small decorative lamps made of mulberry paper or coconut shells. Impressive brass, bronze, and pewter items, as well as fine celadon (green ceramic ware), are all available in many outlets on **Sukhumvit** and **Charoen Krung roads.**

Around town, you'll see several **OTOP** stores offering locally made Thai goods, handicrafts, food, and more in one convenient setting. OTOP (One Tambon One Product) promotes sustainability for local villagers and makes for feel-good souvenir shopping. There is an outlet in the airport for last-minute purchases. A well-curated and high-end shop is **OTOP Heritage** (www.otopheritage.com) on the fourth floor of **Central Embassy** (1031 Phloenchit Road).

JEWELRY

Sapphires, rubies, garnets, turquoise, and zircons are mined in Thailand, and nearly every other stone you can think of is imported and cut here. Thai artisans are among the most skillful in the world; work in gold and silver is generally of high quality at very good value. If you're interested in a custom piece, bring a photo or drawing of what you'd like and prepare to discuss your ideas at length or contact one of the vendors below before arriving for price estimates.

You'll find gemstone, silver, and gold stores in every part of town but it can be hard to cut through the noise of what's real and worth the money. Head to the **Jewelry Trade Center** (JTC; www.jewelrytradecenter.com; ✆ 02630-1000), on 919/1 Silom Rd., for more than 300 retails outlets specializing in jewelry, gems, and diamonds. At the JTC, **Tabtim Dreams** (www. facebook.com/TabtimDreams) has a good reputation. The **Asian Institute of Gemological Sciences** (48th floor of the JTC; www.aigsthailand.com) is useful for verifying the quality of cut stones (although it's not an appraiser) and also runs courses in gem identification and jewelry design.

There are several independent stores worth visiting. **Gems Pavilion** (1st floor, Siam Paragon; www.gemspavilion.com; ✆ 02129-4400) sells eye-catching jewelry with imaginative designs. **Lambert Industries** (807-809 Silom Soi 17 in the Shanghai Building; www.lambertgems.com; ✆ 02236-4343) is a well-respected gemstone cutter that has been in business for nearly half a century. Personal service and attention are guaranteed since the store is by appointment only. **S.J. International** (125/8 Sawankalong Rd.; www.sjjewelry.com; ✆ 02243-2446) has a large showroom, certified gemologist, goldsmiths, and diamond graders on staff (along with an on-site workshop to observe the craft) to help source quality materials for custom pieces and ready-made baubles.

MARKETS

Visiting Bangkok's many markets is as much a cultural experience as it is a consumer experience; goods come in from all corners of the kingdom, and bargaining is a fast and furious experience. Smaller markets with fewer tourists are great for wandering. **Bangrak Wet Market,** behind the Shangri-La Hotel, is an early-morning gourmet's delight. **Sampeng Lane** in the heart of Chinatown has narrow lanes and lots of atmosphere. Most tourist markets are generally open daily from 6 to 11pm; exceptions are noted below.

A word of warning: Cheap goods flood many markets in Thailand, and Bangkok is no exception. Most market stalls, such as those in Patpong, are filled with stalls of brand-name purses, sneakers, and watches, all of which are fake.

Amulet Market ★★   Small talismans are the commodity of choice at this bizarre and entirely local market. Devoted amulet shoppers flip through magazines that carefully describe the sacred properties of the amulet and pricing and then carefully inspect the tiny figures with a magnifying glass. Monks and taxi drivers are common patrons, and you'll mostly see Thai men hunched over the stalls hoping to find a little luck. The market is just south of the Phra Chan Pier; open daily 7am to 5pm.

Pak Klong Talad ★★★   Near Saphan Phut (Memorial Bridge), on the fringes of Chinatown, is Bangkok's 24-hour flower market, with huge bouquets of cut flowers passing through here all day and all night. Roses arrive from the north, ice-packed lotus flowers are used for temple offerings, and strands of bright marigolds are hand-woven to adorn spirit houses around town. Add cheer to your hotel room with a pre-arranged bouquet.

Khao San Market ★ The nighttime stalls on Khao San Road cater to young travelers and, as such, this is where you'll find T-shirts with Thai phrases ("same same but different!"), backpacker essentials, and selfie sticks. It's worth the trip for the atmosphere alone—bass-thumping clubs, busy bars, and Internet cafes attract crowds of travelers, going or coming from all corners of Asia. The area just north of Khao San Road is a maze of small department stores, shops, and very affordable retail goods. Open daily from 10am to midnight. In Banglampoo, just north of the Grand Palace area and Ratchadamnoen Rd.

Ratchada Train Market ★★ This is the sister market to Rod Fai, and it has a smaller selection but the same retro vibe with the added bonus of being much closer to downtown Bangkok. Local brands, vintage clothing, fashion accessories, and even a barbershop fill the lanes of this large market. Enjoy boat noodles and cold beers or *som tum* papaya salad and a hydrating coconut; the market has three sections of food stalls, making it near impossible to leave hungry. The evening hours (5pm to 1am Thursday to Sunday) bring a welcome break from the hot sun. The market is pretty famous on Instagram and the colorful roofs of each vendor make great photos. Ratchadpisek Road behind Esplanade Cineplex. 5pm–1am Thurs–Sun. Take the MRT to Thailand Cultural Centre and use exit 3.

Rod Fai Market ★ The market covers a lot of ground and you won't have time to see everything, which is okay, because the goods at the entrance aren't very special and, unless you need a glittery phone case or tuk-tuk ornament, you can keep moving. What you don't want to miss, however, is the large antique section in the Warehouse Zone and a section called Rod's Antiques. There you'll find brick-and-mortar shops selling everything under the sun. Need a vintage Vespa? Check. On the hunt for rare Japanese action figures? Done. The vendors are relaxed and up for a little bit of haggling, but the prices on leather goods, Coca-Cola collectibles, electronics and more are already pretty low. Open-air bars and Thai wannabe rock stars crooning classic American hits make this an enjoyable market worth the schlep in a taxi. Srinakarin Soi 51, behind Seacon Square Shopping Mall. Open Thurs–Sun 5pm–midnight.

Patpong Night Market ★ The Patpong area is famous for its bars, neon lights, girls, sex shows, and massage parlors, but it also hosts a bustling Night Market along the central streets that sell mostly faux brands: pirated CDs and DVDs, designer knock-offs, copy watches, and leather goods stamped with desirable logos (sure to hold up better than cardboard). It's lively and a good place to hone your bargaining skills. Patpong Soi 1, btw. Silom and Surawong rds. Open daily after sundown.

Chatuchak Weekend Market ★★★ This mother of all markets, which is open on Saturdays and Sundays from 9am to 6pm, is filled with a head-spinning numbers of stalls selling everything: souvenirs, art, antiques, fresh and dried seafood, vegetables and condiments, pottery, pets of every sort,

FOOD markets

Markets play an incredibly important role in Thai culture; they're a source of commerce and social connection. The numerous wet markets (fish and meat) across town range from photogenic to downright primal but offer a closer look into the food culture of the city. (Note: for markets where meals are sold, see Chapter 5, p. 94.)

o **Or Tor Kor Market** (Kamphaengphet Soi 1; MRT Kamphaeng Phet; daily 8am–6pm), near Chatuchak Weekend Market (p. 127) is the city's best fruit and agricultural market. Unlike most markets, Or Tor Kor has wide, well-lit lanes without a wriggling catfish in sight. Prices reflect the high cleanliness standards and only wealthy Bangkokians and restaurants can afford to shop here. There's a small food court that makes use of the top produce.

o **Talat Mai** (Charoen Krung Soi 16; MRT Hua Lamphong; daily 6am–6pm) means "new market" in Thai but this Chinese-Thai lane off Yaowarat Road is more than 200-years-old. On the narrow street are vendors babbling in Chinese near hidden Daoist temples, selling traditional Chinese market goods like funeral supplies; it feels more like China than Thailand. Shop the stalls selling dried shrimp and squid, fresh fish, pork rinds, seasonings, loose-leaf

teas, goji berries, and more. Midway down the lane is an unmarked side street with a quiet temple and at the end, you'll find stacks of paper effigies (the latest iPhones, Rolex watches, and Gucci slippers are common sights) along with ceremonial incense, candles, and more used for Chinese funerals. One warning: Motorcycles wiz down the alley without much care or caution for pedestrians' toes, so look out.

o **Klong Toey Market** (The intersection of Ratchadaphisek and Rama IV; MRT Khlong Toei; 6am–2am) is the city's largest wet market. The outer fringes of the market are pretty tame with humongous mangoes, buckets of chili dips, and spiky durian, but move inwards toward the meat section and things get bloody. For meat-eaters, it's all part of the circle of life, but some may not enjoy the sights and smells of goats, ducks, frogs, and more on their way to the city's restaurants. Almost every eatery buys something from this market, so it's teaming with action—especially at odd hours when temperatures are cooler. If you're squeamish or hungover, it might be best to give this one a pass. If you'd like guidance in touring the market, try Cooking with Poo (p. 118).

orchids, and other exotic plants, clothing, and a host of strange exotic foods. A visit here is a great way to introduce yourself to the exotic sights, flavors, and colors of Thai life, and it is the best one-stop shop for all those souvenirs you haven't bought yet. Arrive early in the morning, before the heat and the crowds.

Be realistic and remember that you'll never be able to see it all (this is one of the world's largest markets!), so pick a few sections of interest and explore those. Clothing sections almost exclusively carry Thai sizes so it might not be worth your time. If you see something you like, buy it right away for fear of not being able to work your way back later in the day. Shipping centers are available if you want to ship artwork, housewares, or décor.

When you get hungry, the food section is between sections 6 and 8. Coconuts, ice-cold water, plates of noodles, grilled prawns, fresh fruit juices, beer, and more are available. *Tip:* Despite the overwhelming number of stalls, there actually is some order and organization. Before you enter the bowels of the market, stop and take a photo of the color-coded map. Adjacent to the Mo Chit BTS, at the northern terminus of the BTS. Open Sat–Sun 9am–6pm.

SILK
There are numerous silk outlets throughout the city, from shopping malls to the lobbies of international hotels. Synthetics are frequently sold as silk; if you're in doubt about a particular piece, select a thread and burn it—silk should smell like singed hair. Sometimes only the warp (lengthwise threads) is synthetic because it is more uniform and easier to work with. For some of the city's priciest silk, try such outlets as **Jim Thompson** (9 Surawong Rd.; www.jimthompson.com; ✆ **02632-8100**), or the Thai silk specialists **Almeta** (20/3, Sukhumvit Soi 23; www.almeta.com; ✆ **02204-1413**). They can even offer "silk a la carte," whereby silk is woven to the customer's desired weight and dyed to a particular shade. Products include silk wall coverings, silk robes, bed linens, and casual wear.

BANGKOK ENTERTAINMENT & NIGHTLIFE

Bangkok's reputation for rowdy nightlife tends to precede it; however, it's not all raunchy sex shows and public debauchery. There are plenty of nighttime cultural events, such as music, theater, puppetry performances, and orchestral maneuvers. For the hippest nightlife updates, check out *BK Magazine* (bk. asia-city.com; free and available at bookstores and restaurants). Featuring weekly listings of events as well as up-to-date info about the club scene, it is the best entertainment source in Bangkok.

The Performing Arts

Most travelers experience the Thai performing arts at a commercially staged dance show in a hotel, sometimes accompanied by a Thai banquet. Bangkok, however, does provide a few more appealing ways to enjoy the theater, whether it is the avant-garde choreography seen at the **Patravadi Theatre,** traditional puppet shows at the new **Aksra Theater,** or international music recitals as part of annual festivals.

The **National Theater,** 1 Na Phra That Rd. (✆ **02224-1342**), presents demonstrations of Thai classical dancing and music, by performers from the School of Music and Dance in Bangkok, which are generally superior to those at the tourist restaurants and hotels. There are also performances by visiting ballet and theatrical companies. There is no website so check with your hotel for the current schedule.

The **Thailand Cultural Centre,** Thiem Ruammit Road, off Ratchadaphisek Road, Huai Khwang (✆ **02247-0028**), is the largest performance center in town, offering a wide variety of programs. The Bangkok Symphony performs here during its short summer season. Other local and visiting companies present theater and dance at the center. Again, there is no website so check with your hotel for the current schedule.

Bangkok's unique contemporary dance theater, **Patravadi Theatre,** at Soi Wat Rakheng, off Anamarin Road (www.patravaditheatre.com; ✆ **02412-7287**), occupies a laid-back arty corner of the Thonburi district, and challenges cultural conformity by putting on inspiring performances that combine all manner of Thai and international dance forms, including dazzling *likay* (similar to Broadway musicals). Overseen since its founding by Patravadi Mejudhon, a former Thai classical dancer now in her 60s, the theater is well worth the trip. The website doesn't sell tickets or provide much information on the schedule, so ask your hotel to help.

Families in town should consider a puppet show; they reenact Thai folktales. The **Aksra Theatre** on the third floor of the King Power Shopping Complex at 8/1 Rangnam Rd. (www.aksratheatre.com; ✆ **02677-8888;** Victory Monument BTS) is a good bet. Up to three masters manipulate complex puppets, and their movements are incredibly lifelike. Evening and afternoon shows are available and tickets cost 800B. Another more local options the **Baan Silapin Artist's House ★★** (www.facebook.com/baansilapin; ✆ **02868-5279**) on the Thonburi side of the river. It's a lovely old wooden house that is a hybrid gallery-café-cultural center. Traditional Thai puppet shows are daily (except Wednesday) at 2pm and free for all guests. (Occasionally the puppet masters are booked for private gigs and the show is canceled, so you might want to call and check.) The house is a regular stop on canal boat tours and the café has great Thai food.

Cinema

Bangkok cinemas are almost always located in malls and show Hollywood films with Thai subtitles. Art-house movies are shown at the **Bangkok Screening Room** (https://bkksr.com/movies; at Sala Daeng and Rama IV) or at **Scala** (✆ **02251-2861;** Siam Square Soi 1), the city's oldest and most charming cinema. For general information on what's on, check out www.moveedoo.com. At most theaters in Bangkok, seats are assigned when you purchase tickets. VIP tickets include reclining chairs, blankets, and snacks. Don't forget to stand and put down your popcorn when the king's anthem plays before the film.

The Club & Bar Scene

From cool jazz lounges in top-end hotels to street-side dives in the backpacker district, Bangkok's got somewhere for everyone to feel good after dark. Many bars feature live music, and decor ranges from Wild West Saloon to English pub to futuristic dance club. The city is famed for its go-go bars, but they're clustered in Patpong, Nana Plaza, and Soi Cowboy, so this aspect of the city is easy to avoid if it offends you.

ROOFTOP BARS

Taking an ear-popping elevator ride to a rooftop bar is an iconic Bangkok

experience, and visitors will have their choice of locations across town. Many bars have strict dress codes that forbid flip-flops, shorts, tank tops (for men and women), or athletic clothing.

Moon Bar ★★★ on the 61st floor of the Banyan Tree (21/100 South Sathorn Rd.; www.banyantree.com; © **02679-1200**) is one of the top picks for libation seekers with views of Lumpini Park, Sathorn Road, and across town to the river. **Sky Bar** atop the gilded lebua at State Tower (1055 Silom Rd.; www.lebua.com/sky-bar; © **02624-9555**) was famously depicted in *The Hangover: Part II* and is jam-packed with humanity nightly. The drink prices match the sky-high views (soda water is a whopping 400B!), but it has great views of the snaking Chao Phraya River. CentralWorld shopping mall has two sky-high bars: **CRU Champagne Bar** (999/99 Rama I; www.champagnecru.com; © **02659-9000**) sells creative bubbly-based cocktails while **Red Sky** ★ (999/99 Rama I; www.centarahotelsresorts.com/redsky; © **02100-6255**) has martinis, beers, and well-mixed drinks.

If you're not dressed to impress the bouncers, **Brewski** ★★ (Radisson Blu Hotel, 489 Sukhumvit Rd.; www.radissonblu.com; © **02302-3333**) is a super chilled-out beer bar 30 floors above it all with a variety of IPAs and craft bottles. **AIRE Bar** (22/5 Sukhumvit Soi 24; www.bangkoksukhumvit.place.hyatt.com; © **02055-1234**) at the newly opened Hyatt Place has no dress code and refreshingly caps drink prices at 280B.

JAZZ & BLUES BARS

The **Bamboo Bar** ★★★ at the Mandarin Oriental Hotel (48 Oriental Ave.; www.mandarinoriental.com; © **02659-9000**) was named Thailand's best bar at the Asia's 50 Best awards in 2018, and it's a legendary home to jazz. The intimate setting, outstanding cocktails, and rich history (it first opened in 1953) make this one of the best bars in town. **Brown Sugar** ★ (469 Phra Sumen Rd.; www.brownsugarbangkok.com; © **02282-0396**) is another decades-old jazz hole with a rowdy atmosphere and casual cocktails. A mix of jazz and moody blues are on regular rotation at **Saxophone Pub** (3/8 Phaya Thai Rd.; www.saxophonepub.com; © **02246-5472**). While not much bigger than a walk-in closet, **Adhere the 13th** (13 Samsen Rd.; www.facebook.com/adhere13thbluesbar; © **089769-4613**) is a blues bar where local musicians play soulful tunes to a fun-loving crowd.

CHINATOWN

Once a dead zone for nightlife and cocktails (a beer at 7-Eleven was the best you could do), Chinatown has undergone a major rebirth to become one of the trendiest drinking 'hoods in town. What the bars lack in square footage, they make up for in personality and well-mixed craft cocktails. Soi Nana is ground zero for the neighborhood's nightlife and the resurgence started at **Teens of Thailand** ★★★ (76 Soi Nana; www.facebook.com/teensofthailand; © **081443-3784**), an award-winning gin bar with creative gin & tonics that's not nearly as shady as it sounds. Around the corner, the same team owns **Asia Today** ★★ (35 Soi Maitri Chit; www.facebook.com/asiatodaybar; © **097134-4704**) where the bar is stocked with rum, including a few locally produced options, and a giant shark hangs from the ceiling. **Ba Hao** (8 Soi Nana; www.ba-hao.com; © **064635-1989**) is an art gallery-cum-bar with a cool Hong Kong vibe. The hippest spot on the block is **Tep Bar** ★★★ (69-71 Soi Nana; www.facebook.com/tepbar; ✆ **098467-2944**) where *ya-dong* (herb-infused local alcohol) cocktails are served while Thai twentysomethings play local instruments. The bar at **Rabbit Hill** (1 Santiphap Rd.; www.rabbithillbkk.com; ✆ **091780-8896**) stocks a host of Japanese liquors and beers from a microbrewery in Hong Kong while **23 Bar and Gallery** (92 Soi Nana; search 23 Bar & Gallery on Facebook; ✆ **080264-4471**) is a total dive with lots of charm and American rock playlists.

Elsewhere in the neighborhood is **Tropic City** ★★ (672/65 Charoen Krung Soi 28; www.facebook.com/tropiccitybkk; ✆ **091870-9825**), an indoor/outdoor space fully committed to making tiki bars great again; one sip and you'll see they succeed.

SATHORN, SILOM & SURAWONG

There's always a party at **Revolucion Cocktail** (50 Sathorn Soi 10; www.revolucion-cocktail.com; ✆ **084709-9630**) and the colorful drinks are ripe for Instagram. **Smalls** ★★★ (186/3 Suan Phlu Soi 1; www.facebook.com/smalls bkk; ✆ **095585-1398**) is a shophouse with strong cocktails and it's where Bangkok's bartenders go to drink (with abandon) on their nights off. **Vesper** ★★ (10/15 Convent Rd.; www.vesperbar.co; ✆ **02235-2777**) employs some of the best bartenders in the city and everything from classics to bespoke cocktails are expertly mixed here, and it's the kind of place you could stay all night. **Whiteline** (Silom Soi 8; http://whitelinebangkok.com; ✆ **087061-1117**) turned a four-story warehouse into a hotbed for creative music acts. **Maggie Choo's** ★★ (320 Silom Rd.; www.maggiechoos.com; ✆ **091772-2144**) has a raucous gay night on Sunday that is regularly hosted by Pangina Heals (www.facebook.com/panginaheals), the Ru Paul of Thailand and the country's best-known drag queen. Burgers, Thai beers, and gin drinks go down easy at **Junker & Bar** (454 Suna Phlu Soi 1; search Junker and Bar on Facebook; ✆ **085100-3608**); and **The House on Sathorn** (106 N. Sathorn Rd.; www.thehouseonsathorn.com; ✆ **02344-4000**) is arguably the most beautiful bar in the area. If a night ends at **Wong's Place** (27/3 Soi Sribumphen; Sathorn Soi 1; www.facebook.com/wongs-place-89143925751; ✆ **081901-0235**), Bangkok's legendary after-hours dive bar, you know you've done something right, which will likely feel terribly wrong in the morning.

KHAO SAN ROAD & AROUND

Over on Rattanakosin Island, in Old Bangkok, the backpackers on Khao San Road still party on at **The Club** (123 Khao San Rd.; www.clubkhaosan.com; ✆ **02629-1100**) smack dab in the middle of Khao San Road. It is a mainstay among the small dance clubs that come and go around here. **Brick Bar** (265 Khao San Road (at Buddy Lodge); www.brickbarkhaosan.com; ✆ **02629-4556**) is a basement pub at 265 Khao San Rd. that hosts Thai bands and local patrons, emboldened by whiskey sodas, have been known to dance on the tables by the end of the night. At 469 Phra Sumen Rd., climb three flights of decrepit stairs to reach **Ku Bar** ★★ (www.facebook.com/ku.bangkok; ✆ **02067-6731**), where the décor is plain to better keep the focus on the drinks. The spirit-forward drink menu changes monthly but keeps a fruit and vegetable theme (like lychee or tomato), and the head bartender has stacks of awards to his name. Or head west of Khao San to **Phra Athit Road,** where there are any number of small cafes with live performances of folk, blues, and rock tunes. These small venues are full of Thai college students imitating a kind of beat poetry vibe, but some are well worth checking out like **Jazz Happens** (62 Phra Athit Rd.; www. facebook.com/jazzhappens; ✆ **084450-0505**) where students from Silpakorn University play smooth versions of jazz classics and more. Other standout options for tunes are **Brown Sugar** (p. 131) at 469 Phra Sumen Rd. and **Adhere the 13th** (p. 131) at 13 Samsen Rd. Down the small lane (*sois*) surrounding the Chana Songkhram temple compound (on the river end of Khao San), look for lots of little open-air bars—they're a good place to meet fellow travelers.

SUKHUMVIT ROAD

Foreign Correspondents' Club of Thailand ★ (518/5 Phloenchit Rd.; www. fccthai.com; ✆ **02652-0580**) is a watering hole for the city's creatives, photographers, writers, and more. They host a regularly rotating exhibit of photojournalism, contemporary art, and TED-style talks; check the website for the schedule. In addition to the odd-but-successful Japanese and Peruvian menu, **Above Eleven** (38/8 Sukhumvit Soi 11 at the Fraser Suites; www.aboveeleven.com; ✆ **02038-5111**) offers rooftop drinks with DJ sets. Come down to sea level and look for a broken phone booth and a graffiti wall. Through the phone booth is hidden door leading to **Havana Social ★★** (1/1 Sukhumvit Soi 11; www.face book.com/havanasocialbkk; ✆ **02061-5344**) which feel just like Cuba, complete with cigars, rum, music, and lots of dancing. Another secret spot is **Q&A ★★** (235/13 Sukhumvit Soi 21; www.qnabar.com; ✆ **02664-1445**). It's designed to look like a vintage train car; their negroni is outstanding. With dozens of taps and a super-chill vibe, **Craft** (16 Sukhumvit Soi 23; www.craftbangkok.com; ✆ **02258-0541;** a second location at 981 Silom Road) has lots of space and a sociable atmosphere, making it a great spot to come with friends. **Dim Dim** (27/1 Sukhumvit Soi 33; www.facebook.com/dimdimbarbkk; ✆ **02085-2788**) has six chairs and creative Chinese-themed cocktails. One of the best spots in town to dance and drink the night away is **Sing Sing Theater ★★★** (Sukhumvit Soi 45; www.singsingbangkok.com; ✆ **063225-1331**). Designed by Ashley Sutton, Sing Sing captivates patrons with a Shanghai vibe, hidden rooms, beautiful girls swinging from the ceiling, and all sorts of crazy staff costumes.

Outside of cocktails, **Bottles of Beer** (2/7 Sukhumvit Soi 34; www.bottlesofbeer.co; ✆ **02040-0473**) is tiny but stocked with an impressive selection of crafts from around the world; the staff is incredibly knowledgeable and friendly. **Hair of the Dog** (888/26 Phloen Chit Rd.; www.hairofthedogbkk. com; ✆ **02650-7589**) is another topnotch beer hauns and epitomizes the hold the craft brew movement has held over the capital in the last few years.

THONGLOR & EKKAMAI

Throbbing with nightlife on nearly every corner, this is one of Bangkok's most hopping neighborhood when the sun goes down. Before dipping into all the cocktail bars, start with wine and tapas at **Chez Jay** (49 Terrace, Sukhumvit

Soi 49; www.facebook.com/49terrace; ℭ **092639-2895**); owner Jay is a true wine connoisseur. Hop between **WTF** ★ (7 Sukhumvit Soi 51; www.wtf bangkok.com; ℭ **02662-6246**) an art gallery slash bar beloved by the expat community and the neighboring **Studio Lam** ★ (3/1 Sukhumvit Soi 51; www.facebook.com/studiolambkk; ℭ **02261-6661**) where *molam* (Thai folk music) gets the hipster treatment. Gin aficionados head to **Just a Drink (Maybe)** (44/3 Thonglor Soi 1; www.facebook.com/justadrinkmaybe; ℭ **02023-7285**).

The **Commons** ★★ (p. 98) has a host of restaurants and bars under one roof and it's a popular spot for twentysomething Thais and expat families to gather for wine, beer, and bites. Echoing the vibe of The Commons is **Courtyard 72** (72 Sukhumvit Soi 55; www.72courtyard.com; ℭ **02392-7999**), while the roof-level club, **Beam** (www.beamclub.com), is a fun dance spot. **The Iron Fairies** (394 Sukhumvit Soi 55; www.facebook.com/ironfairiesbkk; ℭ **02659-9000**) has hidden corners, intimate spaces, a fun open-mic night on Mondays—and tons of tiny jars containing colorful glitter the staff calls "fairy dust." Near Thonglor Soi 5 are two unmarked bars: **Rabbit Hole** (125 Sukhumvit Soi 55; www.rabbit holebkk.com; ℭ **081-822-3392**), has a great truffle martini, and **J.Boroski** (behind an unmarked door down an alley between Thonglor Soi 5 and 7; ℭ **02712-6025**), is a hidden, menuless bar where drinks are made only after consulting the bartender. Board games, video games, pool, and burgers make **Game Over** ★ (1000/39 Sukhumvit Soi 55 (in Liberty Plaza); www.facebook.com/gameoverbkk; ℭ **02170-7684**) the rare nightlife venue that's appropriate for all ages (many parents bring their kids here). Near Ekkamai Road (Sukhumvit Soi 63) is **Tuba** (34 Ekkamai Soi 21; www.facebook.com/tubabkk; ℭ **02711-5500**), a neighborhood hangout and if you can find the hidden **Sugar Ray You've Just Been Poisoned** ★★★ (88/2 Sukhumvit Soi 24 Alley; www.facebook.com/sugarraybkk; ℭ **094417-9898**), you'll have found my favorite bar in the city. The owners make everyone feel like friends, the tipples are creative drinks, and the setting is dark but cozy, making the bar feel like a living room speakeasy. **Mikkeller** (26 Ekkamai Soi 10, Yeak 2; www.mikkellerbangkok.com; ℭ **02381-9891**) brings the best Danish brews to the Big Mango in a cool, backyard setting.

The Sex Scene

Since the 1960s—and particularly since the Vietnam War—Bangkok has had a reputation as the sin capital of Asia. First-time tourists are sometimes staggered by the numbers of septuagenarian gentlemen trawling red-light areas looking for sex.

While prostitution is technically illegal in Thailand, this law is rarely enforced, making foreigners feel it is "safe" to pay for sex. But beware—it is not. Too often, the people working in this industry are doing this because they have no choice; and some are underage, though they may purport to be older than they are. Reports about poor families selling their children into prostitution are true—many children are held in brothels against their will. Those adults seen making even the slightest sexual advances toward them, if caught, risk a heavy prison sentence. The worst areas are concentrated around **Patpong** (off Silom Rd.), **Nana Plaza** (Sukhumvit Soi 4), and **Soi Cowboy** (between Sukhumvit Soi 21 and 23) districts.

SIDE TRIPS FROM BANGKOK

There are plenty of easy day trips from Bangkok. Favorites include visits to a floating market and to the ancient capital of Ayutthaya, north of Bangkok, with a stop at the Bang Pa-In Summer Palace. Kids will enjoy most of these listed below.

The Ancient City (Muang Boran) ★★ ENTERTAINMENT COMPLEX A remarkable giant scale model of Thailand, this attraction is spread over hundreds of acres, with more than a hundred models of the country's major landmarks either displayed as life-size or in reduced scale. For visitors short on time, it is an excellent way to get an overview of the country's most impressive buildings, such as the temples at Ayutthaya and Sukhothai and stilted houses from the north, in just 1 day. As you move from one section to another, keep your eyes open for the deer who roam freely through the grounds. The project has been evolving over the past 30 years, financed by a local millionaire who has played out his obsession with Thai history on a grand scale. You'll need to arrange a method of getting around, as it's too far to walk everywhere; choices are your own car and driver (additional 200B fee per person), bicycle (free), golf cart (150B/hour), or the hop-on, hop-off tram tour with guide (free).
Kilometer 33 on the old Sukhumvit Highway, in Samut Prakan Province. ⓒ **02709-1644.** www.ancientcitygroup.net. 600B adult, 350B children. Daily from 9am–7pm.

Bang Krachao ★★ PARK Known as Bangkok's 'green lung' (for its organlike shape), this large park makes for an excellent and hassle-free escape from city traffic and skyscrapers. Once you arrive, rent a bike (100B per day) and pedal on trails that zigzag through mangroves and coconut and banana plantations as well as elevated pathways. If you plan your visit for the weekend, you'll be able to visit the Bang Nam Pheung Floating market, which is photogenic and snack-rich (plan to stay for lunch). To get to Bang Krachao take the BTS to Bang Wa, then hire a 20B motorcycle driver (or cab) to the nearby pier at Wat Bang Na Nork. From there, a 4B ferry will get you across the river.
Ferry service runs daily from 5:30am–9pm.

Floating Market at Damnoen Saduak ★ MARKET This, the best known of Thailand's floating markets, is very photogenic. The sampans on the canals are laden with colorful fruits and flowers, and the vendors dress in traditional costume. But it soon becomes clear that it's all staged for tourists. As it's over 100km (62 miles) from Bangkok, you'll need a very early start to catch the market at its best; if this is not convenient, consider a visit to nearby **Amphawa Floating Market** (a 90-minute drive from Bangkok), which takes place in the afternoon, and is less staged. Some tours combine the Floating Market with a visit to the Rose Garden (see above for info). If you choose to go via organized tour, expect to pay about 1,800B.
Damnoen Saduak, Ratchaburi, around 40 minutes south of Nakhon Pathom/100km (62 miles) from Bangkok.

Phra Pathom Chedi ★ HISTORIC SITE One of Thailand's oldest towns, Nakhon Pathom is thought to be where Buddhism first established a following in this region, over 2,000 years ago. Thus, it is fitting that it should be home to the tallest (120m/394 ft.) and most revered stupa in the kingdom. The site has been abandoned and rebuilt many times through the centuries, and the current structure was the work of Rama IV in 1853. Apart from its sheer enormity, the *chedi* impresses with its range of Buddha images in niches, all displaying different *mudras* (hand gestures). The *chedi* can be visited in combination with a trip to the **Floating Market** (see above) or en route to **Kanchanaburi** (see below).

56km/35 miles west of Bangkok, Nakhon Pathom. Admission 40B. Daily 6am–6pm.

Sites Farther Afield
KANCHANABURI
139km (86 miles) NW of Bangkok

Kanchanaburi lies on the **River Kwae** (*Mae Nam Kwae*, in Thai), better known to the West as the **River Kwai.** The city became famous for a single-track rail bridge, built under the Japanese occupation in World War II by Allied prisoners of war (POWs), linking Myanmar and Thailand. Due to the thousands of servicemen and women who lost their lives in this project, and in the notoriously inhumane Japanese internment camps, it became known popularly as the Death Railway. The town, and the dark times associated with it, came to fame following the hugely successful British film *The Bridge on the River Kwai* (filming took place in Sri Lanka). The original wooden bridge no longer exists, so today's visitors, pilgrims, and former POWs head to a similar, but now heavily commercialized, iron bridge that was built around the same time. Every year, in the last days of November, the city hosts several evenings of light-and-sound shows to commemorate the bombing of the bridge in 1944. Many families of former Allied prisoners, as well as local Thai tourists, fill the city and hotels generally book up fast.

In addition to the bridge, lots of other worthwhile attractions are in the area, including golf courses, bike trails, caves, and waterfalls in the surrounding hills. The area's handful of nice hotels and riverside guesthouses also make this a popular escape from the heat of Bangkok.

Getting to Kanchanaburi
You can connect by railway from the **Thonburi Station** (*©* **02411-3102**) to **Kanchanaburi Station** (*©* **03451-1285**) via rail. Trips here are quite scenic and cost about 100B. The train departs at 7:45am and 1:35pm and takes 2 hours. There are also frequent regular buses from the **Southern Bus Terminal** (*©* **02793-8111**). Buses and minivans cost the same as the train and take 2½ hours.

Where to Stay
There are a couple of new places, both located by the river some distance from town, that offer excellent amenities and efficient service. **The FloatHouse River Kwai** (55 Moo 5 Tambol Wangkrajae; www.thefloathouseriverkwai. com; *©* **02642-5497**) has teak wood and bamboo floating villas on the River Kwai that make for an incredibly chic eco-stay. Rooms have private balconies, modern bathrooms, and the hotel employs people from the ethnic Mon tribe. Rooms start at 4,800B. A cheaper and smaller alternative is the **Oriental**

Kwai (194/5, Moo 1, Tambon Ladya. www.orientalkwai.com; ② **03458-8168**), which has cottages and a pool in a lush tropical garden, and rates beginning at 2,800B including breakfast.

If you'd rather be nearer the town, the pretty **Sabai@Kan** (www.sabai atkan.com; ② **03452-1559;**), at 317/4 Mae Nam Khwae, is a hospitable boutique with a swimming pool that's close to all the tourist spots. Rates include breakfast and start at 1,400B. See **www.kanchanburi-info.com** for more tips on accommodations.

Attractions

The town's sites focus on the World War II history of the area. Start any tour of Kanchanaburi at the so-called **Bridge over the River Kwai,** emulating its more famous predecessor, built by World War II prisoners, and the main backdrop to the suspenseful 1957 film *The Bridge on the River Kwai*, directed by David Lean, which won seven Oscars. The bridge is about 5km (3 miles) north of the Kanchanaburi city center.

The **Kanchanaburi War Cemetery** is where many of the 16,000 POWs who died building the railway are laid to rest; graves are organized by country. It is a sobering thought to realize that over 100,000 people died in the construction of this project, mostly conscripted laborers and prisoners. It's a 10-minute walk from the train station on Saengchto Road. It's open daily 8:30am to 6pm, and charges no entry fee.

Adjacent to the cemetery is the **Thailand–Burma Railway Center** (www. tbrconline.com; ② **03451-2721;** daily 9am–5pm; adults 140B, children 60B), which displays a well-organized collection of photos and memorabilia, with ample English descriptions, maps with detailed historical background, and good audiovisual presentations recounting the terrifying fate of the Allied POWs during World War II. Nearby (just south of the cemetery along the river), find the mustier but no less moving **JEATH War Museum** (Wat Chaichumpol, Bantai, Kanchanaburi; ② **03451-5203;** daily 8:30am–4:30m; admission 50B). JEATH is an acronym for Japan, England, Australia/America, Thailand, and Holland. Here, you'll see haunting photos and artifacts in a rustic bamboo museum adjacent to Wat Chaichumpol. Most poignant are the letters and faded photos of the many GIs who've returned since the end of the war.

Other sites farther afield from Kanchanaburi include the **Hellfire Pass Memorial,** on the route of the Death Railway. Pick up a free audio guide at the museum to hear first-person accounts from survivors. Another option is to visit the **Erawan National Park,** north of town, where you can see one of Thailand's most attractive waterfalls. Walking shoes and a level of physical fitness are required to reach the second and third tiers of the falls (it's a 2km hike). You'll need to catch one of the hourly busses from Kanchanaburi (50B; 90-minutes).

KHAO YAI NATIONAL PARK ★★

120km (75 miles) NE of Bangkok

Located 3 hours from Bangkok, near Nakhon Ratchasima (known as Khorat), on the edge of Thailand's rural northeast, the park is home to some high peaks and therefore boasts cooler temperatures year-round. The best time to visit the park is December to June, but trips can be arranged year-round. Visitors usually spot such wildlife as wild elephants, lar gibbons, barking deer, hornbills, and any number of other bird species. Outside of park attractions, you might be interested to join a wine tour or tasting at either **PB Valley** (www.khaoyai winery.com; © **081733-8783**) or **GranMonte** (www.granmonte.com; © **04400-9543**). Both wineries are on the northwest edge of the park and a 15-minute drive apart. Each facility offers tours, tastings, food, and scenic views. If you're trying to pick between the two, PB Valley edges out GranMonte.

Getting to Khao Yai

Minivans depart Bangkok's **Northern Bus Terminal (Mo Chit)** for Pak Chong every 30 minutes; the trip takes 3 hours and costs 160B. Ten trains leave **Hua Lamphong Station** (© **1690** or **02220-4334**) for Pak Chong; the trip takes 2 to 3 hours and costs 25B to 363B. See p. 408 for information on renting a car (with or without a driver) that will give you more freedom to explore.

Hotels & Resorts

There are a couple of comfortable places to stay near the park, including **Hotel des Artists** (4 Moo 17 Thanarat Rd.; www.hotelartists.com/kaoyai; © **089**) with a large outdoor swimming pool, mountain views, and a French-colonial vibe. Rooms start at 4,600B and villas go for 7,500B. The nicest option is **Sala Khaoyai Resort** (99 Moo 11; www.salahospitality.com; © **089846-0500**) with a hilltop restaurant, 360-degree views, modern furnishings, and deep-soak tubs; rooms start at 7,500B. It's possible to stay in the park, which makes early-morning hiking or animal-watching a simple affair. Contact the Khao Yai National Park (http://nps.dnp.go.th © **086092-6529**) for information on booking a park-run bungalow (expect to pay about 2,000B a night).

AYUTTHAYA ★★
76km (47 miles) NW of Bangkok

The temple town of Ayutthaya and the nearby Summer Palace compound of Bang Pa-In are both popular day trips from Bangkok. Ayutthaya was the capital of Thailand from 1350 until it was sacked in 1767 by the Burmese; thereafter, the capital moved briefly to Thonburi, and then to Bangkok. Ayutthaya's temples are magnificent—both Khmer and Thai-style ruins lie along the rivers here, in what was once Thailand's greatest city. It's also an excellent place to rent a bicycle (the terrain is flat) and worth an overnight, in conjunction with an enjoyable 1-day boat trip. Nearby Bang Pa-In is home to some wonderfully whimsical mid-19th-century royal palaces, set amid splendid gardens with topiary elephants.

For more specific information on Ayutthaya, see chapter 10 "Central Thailand."

THE EASTERN SEABOARD

Tracing the coastline east of Bangkok along the Gulf of Thailand is a trio of major tourist locations: **Pattaya, Ko Samet,** and **Ko Chang,** each with their own distinct character. The biggest advantage of heading to places along the east coast is their proximity to the capital (a 5-hour drive max) and Suvarnabhumi International Airport.

Pattaya is a bit of a Jekyll and Hyde. On the one hand it's a rollercoaster of neon lights, blaring discos, ladyboy bars, beer gardens, and sex—even in the smaller *sois* (lanes). But it also has pleasant strips of sand and a more wholesome vibe outside the central strip. The main draw for most visitors to Pattaya, one of the oldest resort developments in the country, is its proximity to Bangkok. Taxis, minivans, and buses all make the journey from the Thai capital to this hedonistic beach town in 2 hours. Bottom line? Pattaya isn't for everyone and if you have the time in your schedule, hop a flight to Phuket (p. 225), Ko Samui (p. 186), or Krabi (p. 266), where the beaches, food, nightlife and hotels are all better, or keep driving further down the coast. If time is of the essence, then Pattaya is the place to be.

Continuing east away from Bangkok is **Ko Samet,** the closest major island to Bangkok (in Rayong Province); it's equally popular with families and the flashpacker crowd thanks to its handsome beaches. Ko Samet is a low-luxe retreat reachable by a short ferry ride from the mainland town of Ban Phe. Keep going down the coast to find **Ko Chang,** Thailand's second largest island (behind Phuket) and the last holiday stop before Cambodia. Rapidly growing Ko Chang has mass appeal, luring sun-worshipers, partiers, and scuba divers by the score. Postcard-worthy **Ko Mak** and **Ko Kut** are further afield from Ko Chang, but worth the extra travel time for their incredible beaches.

PATTAYA

147km (91 miles) SE of Bangkok

The slow evolution of Pattaya from a sleepy fishing town to a sprawling development of high-rise coastal resorts began in 1959 when U.S. Army GIs, stationed in the northeast, started coming here in their free time. Word spread, and with more U.S. troops arriving to fight in the Vietnam War, the town became a hot

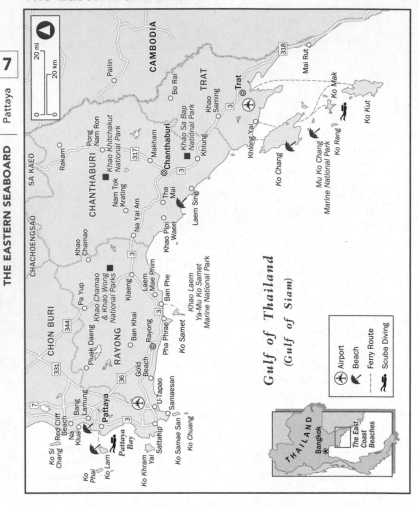

destination for partying and sex. Pattaya today still has an astonishing number of go-go clubs, beer bars, and seedy massage parlors along the beachside.

Tourism boomed in the 1980s, and unchecked resort development was exacerbated by a lack of infrastructure upgrades. Recent years have seen a few civil projects to clean up the bay area with some success, but environmental work is still needed to improve water quality, making swimming an unpleasant experience at times.

The town is trying to create an image as a family destination, expat retirement magnet, and convention hub. However, while these efforts are worthwhile, and though it now has some of the facilities to back this up, the commercial sex trade remains the lifeblood of the city.

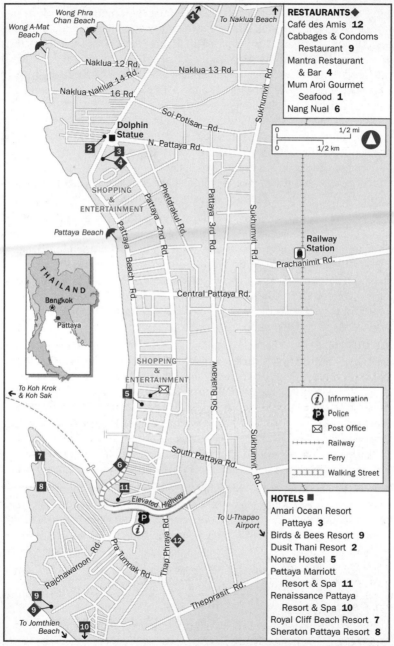

Pattaya

RESTAURANTS◆
Café des Amis **12**
Cabbages & Condoms
 Restaurant **9**
Mantra Restaurant
 & Bar **4**
Mum Aroi Gourmet
 Seafood **1**
Nang Nual **6**

Wong Phra
Chan Beach

Wong A-Mat
Beach

To Naklua Beach

Naklua 12 Rd.

Naklua 14 Rd.

Naklua 13 Rd.

Naklua 16 Rd.

Sukhumvit Rd.

Soi Potisan Rd.

Dolphin
Statue

N. Pattaya Rd.

0   1/2 mi
0   1/2 km

SHOPPING
&
ENTERTAINMENT

Pattaya Beach

Phetdrakul Rd.

Pattaya 2nd Rd.

Pattaya 3rd Rd.

Pattaya Beach Rd.

Sukhumvit Rd.

Railway
Station

Prachanimit Rd.

Central Pattaya Rd.

THAILAND

Bangkok

Pattaya

To Koh Krok
& Koh Sak

SHOPPING
&
ENTERTAINMENT

Soi Buakaow

South Pattaya Rd.

Sukhumvit Rd.

Elevated Highway

To U-Thapao
Airport

Rajchawaroon Rd.

Pra Tumnak Rd.

Thap Phraya Rd.

Thepprasit Rd.

To Jomthien
Beach

(i) Information
P Police
⊠ Post Office
┼┼┼┼┼ Railway
- - - - - Ferry
▭▭▭▭ Walking Street

HOTELS ■
Amari Ocean Resort
 Pattaya **3**
Birds & Bees Resort **9**
Dusit Thani Resort **2**
Nonze Hostel **5**
Pattaya Marriott
 Resort & Spa **11**
Renaissance Pattaya
 Resort & Spa **10**
Royal Cliff Beach Resort **7**
Sheraton Pattaya Resort **8**

Essentials

ARRIVING

BY PLANE The nearest airport is in U-Tapao, 45 minutes east of the city (*©* **03824-5595**). **Bangkok Airways,** which has one flight per day to Phuket (3,900B one-way) and Ko Samui (3,200B one-way). Trip time for both is approximately 1 hour. **AirAsia** has two daily flights to Chiang Mai (850B one-way; flying time 85 minutes) and Phuket (850B to 1,600B; flying time 70 minutes), along with lesser-visited spots in Thailand, like Hat Yai, and international cities like Kuala Lumpur and Macao.

To get to and from the U-Tapao airport to Pattaya, you can arrange a private transfer through your resort. A limo can be as steep as 1,500B, though. If you are arriving at **Suvarnabhumi International Airport** and heading to Pattaya, your only option is by bus or taxi (see below).

The airport is on the cusp of a major expansion and plans are in the works to offer direct flights to most Thai provinces and major cities in China.

BY TRAIN An inconvenient and slow local train chugs away from Bangkok's **Hua Lampong station** at 6:55am; the homebound train departs Pattaya at 2:20pm. The 4-hour trip costs only 31B. Call **Hua Lampong** in Bangkok (*©* **02220-4334** or 1690), or the train station in Pattaya (*©* **03842-9285**). The Pattaya train station is east of the resort strip, off Sukhumvit Road, and *songtaews* (communal pickup trucks) connect with all destinations on the main beach for around 40B. The long-term goal is to connect Pattaya to Bangkok's airports via an express train.

BY PUBLIC BUS The most common and practical form of transportation is the bus. It's also quite safe. Buses depart from **Bangkok's Eastern Bus Terminal,** on Sukhumvit Road (opposite Soi 63, at the Ekkamai BTS; *©* **02391-2504**), every 30 minutes beginning at 4:30am until 11pm every day. For an air-conditioned bus, the fare is 119B. There are also regular buses from **Bangkok's Northern Bus Terminal,** on Kampaengphet 2 Road (near Mo Chit; *©* **02936-2841**) leaving every 40 minutes between 4:30am and 9pm, costing 128B.

The bus station in town is on North Pattaya Road. From there, you can catch a shared ride on a *songtaew* to your hotel for about 40B, or a bit more for a taxi.

BY PRIVATE MINIVAN Most hotels can book a private minivan transfer to the area, so be sure to inquire about rates with the concierge, but expect to pay slightly less than a private taxi. **Bell Travel Service** (www.belltravelservice.com; *©* **03837-0055**) is a reputable vendor.

BY TAXI Taxis from the Suvarnabhumi taxi counter go for 1,050B, and any hotel concierge in Bangkok can negotiate with a metered taxi driver to take you to or from your Pattaya resort, door to door, for about the same fare.

BY CAR Take Highway 3 east from Bangkok stopping to pay a few small tolls along the way. See "Getting Around," below, for info on car rentals.

VISITOR INFORMATION

The **Tourism Authority of Thailand (TAT)** office (609 Moo 10, Pratamnak Rd.; *©* **03842-7667**) is south of Pattaya City, up the hill on the road between

Pattaya and neighboring Jomtien. *Pattaya Mail* is the local English-language paper.

ORIENTATION

Pattaya Beach Road is the heart of the town; a long strip of hotels, bars, restaurants, and shops overlook Pattaya Bay. Pattaya 2nd and Pattaya 3rd roads run parallel to Beach Road and form a busy central grid of small, crowded *sois* bound by North Pattaya and South Pattaya roads, bisected by Central Pattaya Road. At both the far northern and the far southern ends of the beach are two bluffs protecting the bay. North Pattaya is a more upmarket place to relax than Pattaya South, which is the nightlife center of the city. Due south is condo-lined Jomtien Beach—a 15-minute ride from Pattaya. While slightly overdeveloped, it is a pleasant spot and there is a gay-friendly beach at Hat Dongtan. Jomtien Beach is best for active sports like windsurfing and swimming. The northern side of the bay, known as Naklua, is the quietest part of Pattaya.

GETTING AROUND

BY MINIBUS OR SONGTAEW *Songtaews* are red pickup trucks with wooden benches that follow regular routes up and down the main streets. Fares within Pattaya start at 10B while getting to such far-flung beaches as Jomtien costs about 40B. It's important to agree on the fare before getting in, as drivers might charge you a taxi rate if the truck is empty. If you are on a shoestring budget, don't give in; bargain hard or wait for a full truck. Some hotels operate their own minibuses for free; check on this when you book.

BY CAR Car-rental agencies offering discounts in the off-season abound. Well-known car-rental companies, such as **Avis,** have counters at the **Dusit Resort** (© 03836-1627); rates start at about 1,200B per day for a Toyota Vios. **Budget Car Rental,** at Thip Plaza, 219/1–3 Moo 10, Beach Road (© 03871-0717), offers comparable rates. There are plenty of local agencies, but beware of the poor condition of the older-model jeeps; read the contract and check the vehicles before renting

BY MOTORCYCLE You can rent 100cc motorcycles for around 200B a day, or less for a longer period. You just need your passport as collateral—nobody asks to see a license—but insurance is not included, so a significant risk is involved as accidents are common. Big choppers and Japanese speed bikes (500cc) start at around 1,000B per day. Helmets are mandatory by law—so wear one, even if the locals don't.

FAST FACTS

There are many independent **money-changing booths,** 24-hour bank exchanges (with better rates), and **ATMs** at every turn in town. The **post office** is on Soi Post Office. **Bangkok Pattaya Hospital** (www.bangkokpattaya hospital.com; © 03825-9999) has full services and English-speaking staff. The number for the **Tourist Police** is 1155. Internet services are easy to find.

Exploring the Area

Wat Khao Phra Yai is a small temple complex high above town to the south (go by *songtaew* toward Jomtien, and then hop off and climb the steep hill). The temple has excellent vistas and a 10m (33ft.) gold Buddha serenely surveying the western sea.

The **Sanctuary of Truth** was started in 1981 by a Thai millionaire and remains a work in progress to this day. The structure, made entirely without nails, was originally constructed as a statement-making piece of art about the balance of different cultures. It has four wings in total, and they're dedicated to Thai, Khmer, Chinese, and Indian iconography.

Ko Lan is a popular beach escape only 7km offshore. The island is accessible by speedboat in just 15 minutes (approximately 2,000B chartered near Beach Road) or via a ferry leaving from the South Pattaya Pier (30B; 45-minute ride). Ferries are often very crowded and fill up fast, but they leave 11 times a day; the last boat returns around 6pm. On Ko Lan are five white-sand beaches with plenty of places to grab snacks or lunch (they're all indistinguishable from each other, so don't be too picky), and water that is much cleaner than nearby Pattaya. *Tip:* It's best to go early in the morning to claim a quiet spot before the mid-day rush.

Especially for Kids

Art in Paradise, 78/34 Moo 9 Pattaya Sai 2 (www.artinparadise.co.th; Ⓒ **03842-4500)**, uses cleverly drawn 3-D paintings to create wild optical illusions. If ever there was a place for embracing Asia's selfie-taking habit, this is it. Tickets are 400B for adults and 200B for children. Hokier still, **Ripley's Believe It or Not,** 218 Beach Rd. (www.ripleysthailand.com; Ⓒ **03871-0294)** is open daily 11am to 11pm (admission 500B). It's crammed with exhibits highlighting odd facts from around the globe, alongside an infinity maze, and lots of optical illusions. Great for kids and families looking to escape the heat or an occasional rainy day. **Underwater World,** 22/22 Moo 11, Sukhumvit Road (www.underwaterworldpattaya.com; Ⓒ **03875-6879)** is a large aquarium with touch pools, feeding stations for hungry koi fish, and glass tunnels that pass through tanks filled with sharks and colorful fish. Admission is 500B for adults and 300B for children.

Where to Stay

Busy central Pattaya features a range of accommodation, from downright seedy hotels to upmarket international resorts. On the cheaper end you have to be careful: Budget lodgings in Pattaya attract a rough clientele and can be pretty unpleasant. Many have hourly rentals and counters for the mandatory registration of "new friends," meaning prostitutes. It is always worth the extra money stay somewhere on this list. During the high season of December and January, reservations are recommended at least a month in advance.

EXPENSIVE

Royal Cliff Beach Resort ★★ Comprising four hotels (the Royal Cliff Grand & Spa, the Royal Wing & Spa, the Royal Cliff Beach Hotel, and the Royal Cliff Terrace), this luxurious compound is the best-known in town and provides a variety of accommodation and the best range of facilities in Pattaya. High-end **Royal Cliff Grand** and all-suite **Royal Wing** cater to well-heeled business travelers, which means everything is luxe, from the columned public spaces, chandeliers, and fountains to the large and opulent guest rooms. The Grand's spacious rooms are set in a contemporary, scallop-shaped tower and have marble bathrooms with separate shower stalls. The **Royal Cliff Beach Hotel,** the most affordable choice, is Pattaya's top family resort (their two bedroom suites have a central living room and easy beach access, making it perfect for active families to come and go). Rooms here are also spacious, with pastel decor and large terraces, most with bay views. The beachfront **Royal Cliff Terrace** was the resort's first property and is the most secluded. Rooms boast contemporary decor as well as ocean views. The downside, however, is that it is set on the bluff outside of town, so beach trips require more planning.

353 Phra Tamnak Rd. Pattaya 20150 (on the cliff, south end of Pattaya Bay). www.royal cliff.com. ℰ **03825-0421.** 1,072 units. 6,400B–8,200B deluxe double; from 14,400B suite. **Amenities:** All Royal Cliff Beach Resort properties share all facilities, including 10 restaurants; 5 bars (many w/live music); 5 outdoor landscaped pools; golf course; 7 outdoor tennis courts; 2 squash courts; health club; 2 spas; children's playground; concierge; room service; babysitting; Wi-Fi (free).

MODERATE

Birds & Bees Resort ★★ This inviting resort was built by a Thai activist who promotes sex education (hence the name) and rural development projects throughout Thailand. Rooms have a rustic feel, but have all the required amenities. Its primarily attractions are its two pools, a semiprivate beach, and its tucked-away location in a quiet part of Pattaya. The property is family friendly and contains wishing wells and an herb garden (with special exercise bikes designed to irrigate the plant beds). It is also home to the acclaimed Cabbages & Condoms Restaurant (see below), which has a branch in Chiang Rai (p. 382).

366/11 Moo 12, Phra Tamnak 4 Rd. www.cabbagesandcondoms.com. ℰ **03825-0556.** 55 units. 4,500B double; 6,900B suite. **Amenities:** Restaurant; 2 outdoor pools; room service; Wi-Fi (free).

Dusit Thani Resort ★★ This sprawling, manicured resort straddles the cliff on the north end of the main beach and is chock-full of top-notch amenities. Foremost among these: direct access to two beachfronts, a good spa and health club. Tasteful, modern rooms are trimmed with stained wood, and each has fine furnishings and marble bathrooms. Larger rooms and suites have outdoor showers on breezy balconies overlooking Pattaya Bay. Overall, the accommodation is comfortable, with an old-world feel.

240/2 Pattaya Beach Rd. www.dusit.com. ℰ **03842-5611.** 457 units. From 4,000B double; from 13,500B suite. **Amenities:** 3 restaurants; bar; 2 pools; tennis courts; health club; spa; room service; babysitting; Wi-Fi (free).

Pattaya Marriott Resort & Spa ★★ For those wanting to be right in the thick of it, the Marriott is the place to be. In the center of Pattaya and a block from the beach, this resort is abuzz with activities such as biking for adults and yoga for kids. Rooms have wooden floors and spacious balconies with views of gardens or the sea. Bonuses are the resort's beautiful pool area in the well-kept, spacious garden, large health club, and highly regarded spa. The resort contains several restaurants and bars, including the Elephant Bar, a popular meeting place overlooking the pool.

218 Beach Rd. www.marriotthotels.com. ⓒ **03841-2120.** 298 units. 5,500B–6,900B double; from 8,900B suite. **Amenities:** 3 restaurants; 2 bars; outdoor pool; tennis courts; health club; spa; room service; babysitting; executive floor; Wi-Fi (free).

Renaissance Pattaya Resort & Spa ★★★ This swish outpost is among the newer spots in town and all 257 rooms sparkle. The grand open-air entrance is striking, with an abstract installation fixed to the ceiling that represents the soft waves of the nearby sea (the interior design pays homage to Pattaya's former life as a local fisherman's village). Earth tones, light wood, metals, and Thai silks create a chic, beachy vibe, one that's minimalist enough to keep attention on the spectacular sea views. For honeymooners, we recommend the private pool villas. The on-site dining is topnotch, as is the locale: a slice of prime beachfront in Jomtien.

9/9 Moo 3, Na Jomtien. www.marriott.com. ⓒ **03825-9099.** 257 units. 4,500B double; from 8,900B suite. **Amenities:** 3 restaurants; 2 bars; 2 outdoor pools; health club; spa; room service; Wi-Fi (free).

Sheraton Pattaya Resort ★★ Perched in the hills south of Pattaya's main beach, the Sheraton is an excellent choice for a quiet and pampering getaway. The guest rooms and pavilions descend the hillside, flanking a maze of gardens, waterfalls, and freeform swimming pools. Decorated in pleasing pastel peaches and sea greens, the generously sized guest quarters contain king or queen beds. There's an attractive man-made white-sand beach by the water. While the rocky waterfront isn't the most inviting place for a dip, the adventurous will find the water much cleaner than that of Pattaya's main beach.

437 Phra Tamnak Rd. www.sheraton.com/pattaya. ⓒ **03825-9888.** 156 units. 4,500B–9,000B double; **Amenities:** 3 restaurants; bar; 3 outdoor pools; health club; spa; room service; babysitting; Wi-Fi (free with some packages or 450B per day).

INEXPENSIVE

Amari Ocean Resort Pattaya ★★ On the northern end of busy Pattaya, just out of the fray but close enough to walk there, the Amari offers good amenities and helpful staff. The eight room categories all have open-plan bathrooms, ultramodern fixtures and fittings, and superb views of the bay, with suites offering a bit more luxury and club-level access. There's also a playground and lots of space in the grassy central area, including both a kids' pool and an enormous adults' pool. Amari also has good in-house dining (p. 147).

240 Pattaya Beach Rd. www.amari.com/orchid. ⓒ **03841-8418.** 297 units. 2,513B double; from 2,982B suite. **Amenities:** 4 restaurants; 5 bars; 2 outdoor pools; health club; spa; kids' club; room service; babysitting; Wi-Fi (free).

Nonze Hostel ★★ This is one of the most stylish hostels in Thailand and budget travelers will be impressed by the sea views. (Yes, a hostel with sea views!) Private rooms are capsules, which means they're stacked pods. But unlike most hostels, the privacy curtain is an actual door (bonus style points for being canary yellow) that locks. Behind the sliding door is a twin bed with crisp linens, plenty of charging outlets, a safety box, a small closet to hang clothes, a reading light, and a personal air-conditioning unit. Add in free breakfast and coffee, a tour desk, personal lockers, spic-and-span bathrooms with toiletries and hairdryers, and an ironing board and laundry service and well, it keeps getting better. Some capsules are outfitted with two twin beds. However, anyone with even a touch of claustrophobia should find another place to stay.

183/6 Moo 10, Beach Rd. www.nonzehostel.com. ℭ **03871-1112.** 104 units. 550B–3,600B twin. **Amenities:** 1 restaurants; Wi-Fi (free).

Where to Eat

Fresh seafood is abundant in Pattaya, and the highlight of most dining options in town. Outside of those seafood shops, the options for dining can be bleak, and Pattaya is not a foodie's dream space by any stretch of the imagination (it has a lot of multinational chains). The top place for cheap eats is the **Thepprasit Market** (the intersection of Thepprasit and Sukhumvit roads; Fri–Sun 4–10pm).

EXPENSIVE

Café des Amis ★★★ STEAKHOUSE/INTERNATIONAL High-quality cuts of beef are imported fresh (never frozen) from America, Japan, Australia, and New Zealand where they are prepared with much success here. Sous vide, flame grilled, and pan-searing cooking techniques highlight the quality of the meat, like the A5 Japanese wagyu fillet with a marble score of 10—it almost melts in your mouth. Sides like scalloped and mashed potatoes and roasted vegetables accompany the steaks, and fresh crab legs and a catch of the day round out the menu. The gin list is among the best in town.

391/6 Moo 10 (at the end of Soi 11). www.cafe-des-amis.com. ℭ **084026-4989.** Main courses 950B–4,500B; 5-course set menu 2,400B. Mon–Sat 5:30–11pm.

MODERATE

Mantra Restaurant & Bar ★★ INTERNATIONAL Offering a better-than-most hotel dining experience, in the pleasant surrounds of the Amari (p. 146), the Mantra has an eclectic menu of Asian and European cuisines. Despite its age, this restaurant still holds its own, and everything is prepared in seven open kitchens with two stories of dining space overlooking the fashionable dining room. The walk-in wine cellar carries 160 different varieties and offers something for every taste and budget—a rare treat in a country that imposes hefty taxes on wine. The Sunday brunch is a particularly fun event with Alaskan crab, roasts, cheese, and more for 1,990B. The dress code is "chic, smart, and stylish," so that means no shorts, tank tops, or sandals.

Amari Orchid Resort & Tower, Beach Road. www.mantra-pattaya.com. ℭ **0384-29591.** Reservations recommended. Main courses 380B–1,100B. Daily 5pm–1am; Sunday brunch noon–4pm.

INEXPENSIVE

Cabbages & Condoms Restaurant ★ THAI   South of town on Hu Gwang Bay, in the Birds & Bees Resort (p. 145), this is Pattaya's branch of the charitable chain. Both are known not only for their food but also their efforts to educate Thais about HIV/AIDS. The mainly Thai cuisine is good, though, with a wide choice encompassing seafood and other regional specialties. Tastes are only slightly adjusted for the foreign palate, resulting in more authentic than not dishes. The open-concept restaurant is set in the resort's tropical gardens, affording coastal views.

Birds & Bees Resort, 366/11 Moo 12, Phra Tamnak 4 Rd. ℃ **03825-0056.** www.cabbages andcondoms.com. Main courses 80B–250B. Daily 11am–10pm.

Mum Aroi Gourmet Seafood ★ SEAFOOD   This is one the Pattaya's nicest restaurants and it is popular with both residents and Thai visitors. Order Thai lobsters, tiger prawns, oysters, and crabs from nearby tanks and have them cooked to your liking. Go for a steamed fish with lemon and garlic, or the classic hot and sour shrimp soup *tom yam goong*. In addition to premium-quality seafood, it is known for its waterfront views.

83/4 Moo 2 Naklua Banglamung (Near Anaya Beachfront Condominium). ℃ **03822-3252.** Main courses 220B–480B. No credit cards. Daily 11am–11pm.

Nang Nual ★★ SEAFOOD   Head to the southern end of Pattaya Beach Road for excellent seafood at this famed waterfront restaurant. Ice-packed crates of freshwater fish mark the entrance, and you'll point to what you want and indicate a preparation method—we like grilled tiger prawns and steamed sea bass. The Thai menu has large color photos to help make ordering easier. Bring bug spray and request a seat on the terrace overlooking the ocean. There is a second branch near Jomtien Beach.

214 Main Walking St. ℃ **03842-8478.** Main courses 180B–500B. Daily 11am–midnight.

Outdoor Activities
GOLF

The hills around Pattaya are known for their courses, with many international-class greens in a short 40-km (25-mile) radius of the city. Caddy fees are reasonable, around 250B, and golf carts are usually compulsory but rationally priced. Among the recommended are:

o **Burapha Golf Club,** 281 Moo 4, Tambon Bung, Sri Racha (www.burapha golfthailand.com; ℃ **03837-2700**), is the home of numerous tournaments. Greens fees are 2,000B on weekdays and 2,500B on weekends; it's 500B for a golf cart.

o **Laem Chabang International Country Club,** 106/8 Moo 4, Tambon Bung, Sri Racha (www.laemchabanggolf.com; ℃ **03837-2273**), has three 18-hole courses (A, B, and C) designed by Jack Nicklaus and very dramatic scenery. Greens fees are 3,000B on weekdays, 3,500B on weekends.

o **Siam Country Club,** 50/6 Moo 9, Tambol Pong, Banglamung (www.siam countryclub.com; ℃ **03890-9600**), is a short hop from Pattaya and is one of the country's most challenging courses. Greens fees are 3,200B on weekdays and 3,600B on weekends.

WATERSPORTS

For those who come to Pattaya to do more than party, there is plenty on offer, particularly when it comes to watersports. Pattaya's less than pristine beaches are a good excuse to head to outlying areas, where the conditions are more inviting. Day trips to such nearby islands as **Ko Khrok, Ko Lan,** and **Ko Sok** start at around 1,000B per head on a full boat (more for a private charter). To go to far-out Bamboo Island, it will cost you a bit more—about 2,000B. **Paragliding** around the bay behind a motorboat is a popular beachfront activity, and a 5-minute flight starts around 800B.

Jomtien Beach hosts **windsurfing** and **sea kayaking;** boards and boats are rented along the beach for 800B per hour. **Jet ski** rentals are given out to almost anyone without much consideration for age or sobriety. One of the most **common scams** is beach vendors claiming false damage on jet skis upon return. Just like you would a rental car, review any dents or damage with the rental team before getting into the water. If you're uncomfortable with the rental guy, just move along—no jet-ski ride is worth the argument. Always wear a life vest and be aware of snorkelers and swimmers near the shore.

Pattaya is a good place to learn to **scuba dive.** It has a number of reputable dive companies with PADI-certified instructors. The underwater visibility is consistently good, so the sport can be done year-round. There are a few dive sites near the islands, just offshore in **Pattaya Bay,** as well as **Ko Si Chang** to the north—once famous as the summer playground of foreign ambassadors to Siam during the 19th century—and **Sattahip** to the south, with diving to a depth of 40m (131 ft.). **Adventure Divers,** 391/77–78 Moo 10, Tappraya Rd. (www.pattayadivers.com; ✆ **03836-4453**), is one of many PADI-certified companies offering daily trips and courses for all levels.

Nightlife

Nightlife is the biggest draw to Pattaya and the **Walking Street** becomes a pedestrian zone in the evening in South Pattaya, on Beach Roach. Here you will see debauchery at its fullest, with an array of go-go bars, open-air drinking establishments, Thai boxing venues (before you place a bet, know that the fights are all fixed), and, of course, overpriced tourist restaurants. The energy on the street is riotous by evening. In daylight, the passageway is bleak, with bleary-eyed revelers stumbling past seedy storefronts.

Sex for money in Pattaya is an unashamedly direct business. Dubious massage parlors are numerous, especially in northern Pattaya. Despite its prevalence, prostitution in Thailand is illegal, so be prepared to risk a police raid, or hefty bribe to the local police or mafia, not to mention a call to your embassy.

Happily, Pattaya is not entirely sleazy these days. There are still some good bars where you can go to enjoy a drink and listen to live music without being propositioned. Topping the list is the **Hops Brewhouse Pattaya ★★** (219 Beach Rd.; hopsbrewhouse.co.th; ✆ **03871-0650**). Designed like a German brewery, this no-strings-attached spacious watering hole brews its own beer and has an in-house band that plays easy-listening tunes. **Horizon Bar** (at the Hilton Hotel; ✆ **03825-3000**) is a glitzy rooftop 34 floors high that has a buy-one-get-one promotion around sunset and regular DJs.

The town's camped-up cabaret shows are always good, lighthearted fun. Pattaya's sensational *katoeys* (transsexuals) love to don sequined gowns and feather boas and strut their stuff to packed houses nightly. **Tiffany's** (464 Moo 9, 2nd Rd.; www.tiffany-show.co.th; ✆ **03842-1700**) has hilarious shows, much like those in other tourist towns in Thailand.

KO SAMET ★

Ko Samet: 220km (137 miles) SE of Bangkok. Ban Phe: 25km (16 miles) southeast of Rayong City

Tiny Ko Samet, better known simply as Samet (or Samed), is the closest major island to Bangkok but feels world's away from the hectic capital. The island was once a leading backpacker destination, but resorts have popped up to cater to a more affluent group of travelers looking for that easygoing island lifestyle—just with higher thread count sheets. But fire dances, beach barbecues, and young Thais serenading the stars with karaoke songs are still part of the charm of Samet. Just 1km (⅔ mile) wide, the island is a long, triangular pennant shape split by a rocky ridge, with some dazzling beaches on the east coast. Peak season is similar to Pattaya's, with July through October bringing fewer travelers and lower rates, though it's also rainy season.

Local Legend

Samet is well known to Thais through an epic poem by Sunthorn Phu, a venerated 18th-century author who set his famous work, *Phra Aphimani*, in Samet. In the nearly 50,000-line poem, a prince is exiled to an underwater kingdom ruled by a lovesick female giant. The giant holds the prince captive until a mermaid helps him escape to Ko Samet after he defeats the giant with a magical flute. At the Na Dan pier, a commanding statue of a topless female giant is a depiction of the island's most famous literary gift.

Essentials

Ko Samet is a designated national park, and there is a 200B landing fee per adult (children pay half that price). You can pay this fee at the Ban Phe pier.

ARRIVING

BY BUS Buses leave Bangkok every 30 minutes between 4am and 10pm for the 2½-hour journey, departing from **Ekkamai,** Bangkok's Eastern Bus Terminal, on Sukhumvit Road, opposite Soi 63 (✆ **02391-2504**). The one-way trip to Ban Phe costs 157B by air-conditioned bus and takes approximately 3 hours. From Ban Phe, take a ferry to the island (see below).

BY CAR Take the Suvarnabhumi Airport tollway from Bangkok east to Pattaya, then Highway 36 to Rayong, and then the coastal Highway 3145 to Seree Ban Phe (for about 3 hrs.). There are no cars on Ko Samet, so you'll have to pay for overnight parking near Ban Phe. Unless you have plans for a continuing road trip, a rental car is not recommended.

BY FERRY   From the Saphan Nuan Tip ferry pier, there are many ferry companies to choose from, but they all offer the same service and price, so don't hem and haw too long. One-way rides are 70B (return tickets for 100B) and take 40 minutes to reach Na Dan, Samet's main pier. Ferries leave from 8am to 5pm daily; the last boat from Samet to Ban Phe departs at 6pm.

If you've booked a resort on the southern part of the island, catch a ferry to Ao Wong Deuan—sometimes spelled Ao Vongdeuan—beach (90B; 1-hour; three times daily). Speedboats drive direct to your beach of choice charge 200B to 500B one-way, and the driver might wait until the boat is full to leave. Typical travel time is 10 minutes.

FAST FACTS

Ko Samet has a several ATMs. The easiest to find is at the 7-Eleven at the Na Dan pier. The **post office** is at the Naga Bungalows (*©* **03864-4035**), south of Had Sai Kaew. A **health center** is just south of the Na Dan pier before Had Sai Kaew. The **police station** is on the main road near the health center.

GETTING AROUND

Island transport is limited to shared pickups or rented motorbikes, but many people simply choose to walk—it takes about 3 hours to walk the length of the entire east coast, which has most of the island's beaches. Green pickups cost between 20B and 70B, depending on distance and number of passengers. Motorbike rental prices average 300B a day; staff at your resort can arrange this.

ORIENTATION

Had Sai Kaew (Diamond Beach) is on the island's northeastern corner. It's the island's biggest and busiest strip of white sand lined with sun worshipers, jet-skis, open-air restaurants, and sarong hawkers. When the sun goes down, a serious party vibe takes over. **Ao Wong Deuan,** another busy beach, means crescent moon bay in Thai. Resorts, beachside massage huts, and watersports are popular here. The more isolated **Ao Tubtim** is great for families. **Ao Thian** is popular with divers and offers shady spots and a castaway vibe. Right down south are the chilled-out bays of **Ao Kiu Na Nok** (on the east coast) and **Ao Kiu Na Nai** (on the west coast), which are both the exclusive domain of the island's most expensive resort—Paradee. There are also a few upmarket resorts on the northwest side of the island at **Ao Prao** where speedboats take guests over to Ban Phe. In Thai, *had* means "beach," and *ao* means "bay." Most of Samet's beaches are a series of little bays with smooth, clear water.

Where to Stay

While the tides are changing Ko Samet from a backpack hub to a more upmarket island, the bulk of the island's accommodation choices are still simple bungalows and cottages. The few posh resorts fill up fast in high season, but there's typically a bungalow or two with availability for last-minute arrivals.

EXPENSIVE

Le Vimarn Cottages & Spa ★★★   Ao Praov is one of the best beaches on the island and set on it is this small, hillside hideaway for wannabe jet-setters. Accommodations come in three types: deluxe cottages, spa villas, and one spa villa suite. All of the huge thatched villas have four-poster beds and private balconies overlooking the beach and ocean, while the resort's pool villas have Jacuzzis sharing the same wondrous sea views. If flitting between the beaches and seafood joints becomes monotonous, indulge in a spa treatment at the Dhivarin Spa, or take a diving course and explore the vivid underwater world around the island.

40/11 Moo 4, Tambon Phe. www.sametresorts.com. ℂ 03864-4104. 31 units. 10,500B deluxe cottage; 13,000B spa villa; 21,000B spa villa suite inclusive of breakfast. **Amenities:** Restaurant; bar; outdoor pool; spa; Jacuzzi; room service; Wi-Fi (free).

Paradee ★★★   Samet's most exclusive address is this fabulous villa-only resort, right on the island's southernmost tip and straddling two beaches (east and west coast). Expect elegant Thai decor and perks such as tranquil private pools, personal butlers with each villa, and a great bar for sunset. It's ideal for couples (in fact, families are actively discouraged from staying here).

76 Moo 4, Tambon Phe. www.samedresorts.com. ℂ 03864-4283. 40 units. From 17,300B villa. **Amenities:** Restaurant; bar; spa; room service; Wi-Fi (free).

MODERATE

Ao Prao Resort ★★   One of the oldest upscale properties in the area, Ao Prao, located on the west-coast beach of the same name, is still one of the best. The pretty bungalows here make for quaint little vacation retreats. Rooms have delightful teak furnishings and decor, as well as four-poster beds, and some come with enormous double tubs overlooking the blissful scenery. There are plenty of watersports available and direct beach access; the resort is set within a sprawling tropical garden.

60 Moo 4, Tambon Phe. www.samedresorts.com. ℂ 03864-4100. 52 units. 7,100B deluxe. **Amenities:** Restaurant/bar; outdoor pool; room service; babysitting; Wi-Fi (free).

Samed Club ★★   It's fun, it's young, and it's affordable. The Samed Club offers most of the frills of expensive resorts, but for far less. The decor is modern, walls are painted with bright colors, there are walk-in tiled showers, and rooms overlook the central pool, around which sun lovers can chill out under a parasol. The more active have a wide choice of beach sports, sailing, and windsurfing activities on hand. One of the highlights is the great location at Noi Na Beach, a quiet spot on the northern coast but close enough to enjoy a good night out on Had Sai Kaew.

25 Moo 4, Tambon Phe. www.samedresorts.com/samedclub. ℂ 03864-4341. 38 units. 4,000B–5,700B double. **Amenities:** Restaurant; bar; outdoor pool; Wi-Fi (free).

INEXPENSIVE

For cozy huts at good prices (and some great food in Jep's diner next door), head past Had Sai Khaew to Ao Hin Khok, where cool dudes hang at **Jep's Bungalows** (ℂ **03864-4112**); rooms with a fan start at 600B. Farther south still on Ao Tubtim, one of the island's longest-running resorts is **Tub Tim Resort** (no website; ✆ **03864-4025**). It has a variety of Thai-style bungalows with air-conditioning, balconies, and cable TV ranging from 1,000B to 3,300B on a protected bay that is good for swimming.

Where to Eat & Nightlife

The standard fish and rice dishes available at the island's resorts will keep you sated, but it'd be a shame to miss the island's local seafood restaurants. Most bungalows on Samet have their own dining areas for inexpensive, fresh seafood including the area's specialty: locally caught squid and cuttlefish barbecued on skewers. Every day around sunset on **Ao Hin Khok** and **Ao Phai beaches,** tables are set up under twinkling lights for big seafood barbecues brimming with the day's catch.

Jep's Restaurant ★ (✆ **03864-4112**) on Ao Hin Khok, serves-up delicious Thai dishes and so-so Western fare under canopied trees. Hat Sai Kaew isn't known for its culinary options, but the best option in that area (and the island) is **Kitt & Food** ★★ (✆ **03864-4087**), where the fish with salty crust is a top pick. On Ao Phai, **Sea Breeze** ★ (✆ **03864-4124**) does a booming trade in barbecued meats.

Nightlife? Beers and booze are best consumed at these places: **Baywatch Bar** (✆ **081654-1096**) on Ao Wong Deuan, has strong cocktails and a raucous crowd that's a mix of locals and visitors. **Naga Bar** (Ao Whong Deuan beach) is run by some fun-loving locals who can even arrange for fire-twirling lessons. If you'd rather watch the show than fling flames yourself, head to **Ploy Talay Restaurant** (✆ **03864-4212**) for an ice-cold Singha and some music. Take your patience, though, as service can be slow.

CHANTHABURI PROVINCE

250km (155 miles) E of Bangkok

Travelers heading east to rugged Ko Chang (see "Trat & Ko Chang," below) will pass through Chanthaburi province and its capital of the same name. This region is known for its lucrative gem mines that yield sapphires, rubies, and emeralds. Durian, pineapple, *lamyai* (longan), and rambutan thrive here as well. These sweet and sparkling commodities are sold at markets and roadside shops in town. As you drive through Chanthaburi, it's hard to miss the piles of durian that are artfully stacked—with some reaching a whopping 7.9-m (26-ft.) tall. At the end of May or early June, the city holds a fruit festival to celebrate the region's abundance of produce; check with the Tourism Authority of Thailand for exact dates. The city itself is a lot like the fruit festival: not worth making a special trip to see, but an enjoyable local experience if you're passing by.

Essentials

Chanthaburi hugs the Chanthaburi River. The city's main avenue is Tha Chalab Road, and joggers and locals populate the road. The taxi stand is just west of the river, as is the bus station; the latter has departures to Trat and Bangkok.

Buses take 4 hours to reach Bangkok's Eastern Bus Terminal and depart 25 times a day, costing 198B to 290B.

Exploring Chanthaburi

In **Taksin Park** (the center of Chanthaburi), there's a statue of King Taksin on horseback, commemorating the victory over the Burmese in 1767, and a few temples built over Khmer ruins, highlighting the city's Cambodian connections. A Catholic **Cathedral of the Immaculate Conception** ★★ (110 Soi 1, Moo 10; 8:30am–6:30pm; free) is the largest in the country and was formally inaugurated in 1909, but the structure itself dates back to 1711. Beautiful stained glass windows and a Virgin Mary statue outfitted with 200,000 local gems (some estimates put that number closer to 500,000) are highlights.

Gem Markets line the predictably named Gem Street, near the main market. Buying these stones is best left to the gemologists (you don't want to get taken), but it is fun to visit the modest setting in which the vendors sell these high-value stones.

A national park and a beach location lie further afield and make for nice day trips. The 17,000-hectare (42,000-acre) **Namtok Phlio National Park** (admission 200B adults, 100B children; *songtaews* take 30 minutes and cost 50B) is a popular day trip from Chanthaburi offering waterfalls and an easy hiking trail. **Laem Sadet,** a stunning beach and rocky cape located some 35km (22 miles) southwest of the city. Both sites can be visited by private car or taxi; arrange transport through your hotel.

Where to Stay

City lodgings are spartan. **River Guest House** (3/5–8 Si Chan Rd.; ✆ 03932-8211) is not quite downtown but offers homey, air-conditioned rooms (starting at 350B), with quieter (fan only) rooms out back for 190B. **Baan Luang Raja-maitri** (www.tamajunhotel.com; 248 Sukhaphiban Road; ✆ 03931-1977) is the nicest in town with rooms from 1,100B, and the hotel is a good spot for a Thai massage. If you're looking for a real country retreat, consider **Faasai Resort & Spa** ★★ (www.faasai.com; ✆ 03941-7404), a small, award-winning eco-resort on the coast at Khung Wiman, about 30km (18.6 miles) southwest of Chanthaburi. It's run by a Thai–New Zealand couple, and rates are between 900B and 4,100B a night.

Where to Eat

Chanthaburi is famous for its noodles, which are called *sen chan,* which are thin rice noodles many believe are the best noodles to use in *pad thai.* You can taste them at any of the food stalls down by the river, along with Vietnamese spring rolls and *muu liang,* a spicy pork broth. For a wide-ranging menu of Thai and Chinese dishes, such as spicy salads and thick curries with crab, head for **Chanthorn Pochana** (102/5–8 Benchama-Ratchutit Rd.; ✆ 03931-2339). They also serve wines made from local fruits, such as mangosteen, at very cheap prices. Chia tea and biryani are popular dishes at the recommended **Muslim Restaurant** (Soi 4 and Si Chan; ✆ 081353-5174).

KO CHANG

310km (193 miles) E of Bangkok

The capital of Trat Province is Trat, hitherto regarded as the gateway to the Ko Chang National Marine Park. Because of the region's direct transport links, though, visitors can now head straight to any of three piers to access the park's many islands, and Trat is becoming less of a gateway. It offers very little to travelers.

Originally settled by cashew farmers, Ko Chang is the largest of the 52 islands in the archipelago of **Mu Koh Chang National Park.** The interior of the island is forested and mountainous—which makes for some challenging but scenic hiking and trekking experiences. The 30-km (18 miles) long island has a few beaches, and spots for kayaking, snorkeling, and diving. When you look at the number of new hotels, with more opening at a breakneck pace, it is wild to think the island only got 24-hour electricity in the past decade.

Essentials

ARRIVING

BY PLANE **Bangkok Airways** (www.bangkokair.com; ℂ **02270-6699**) has two to three flights daily, depending on the season, between Bangkok and Trat, each taking 1 hour and costing around 2,800B. Airport minivans meet each flight, pick up passengers, drive to and board the car ferry at Ao Thammarat pier, then drop passengers at their resort or guesthouse on the island for a return fee of 800B; get your ticket at the desk at the airport. Most resorts on Ko Chang can arrange airport transfers but at higher rates.

There are also weekly flights to Trat from Phuket via Ko Samui (also on Bangkok Airways), making it possible to hop between the three top island destinations.

BY BUS From Bangkok's two **Eastern Bus Terminals,** at **Ekkamai** (ℂ **02391-2504**) and **Khao San Road** (no phone), there are now dozens of buses direct to the three ferry piers; the trip time is around 5 to 6 hours. Fares range from 250B to 500B; the pricier tickets include the ferry.

Daily minivans operate from Pattaya, via Ban Phe (Ko Samet's ferry port). From Pattaya, allow 4 hours, and from Ban Phe, you'll need 2½ hours; costs are 400B and 300B, respectively.

BY CAR The fastest way from Bangkok is via the Bagna-Trat tollway, past Suvarnabhumi International Airport, and a route via Highway 3 to Chonburi. This route takes about 6½ hours.

GETTING TO KO CHANG & BEYOND

From Trat (the region's capital), *songtaews* (shared pickups) journey between all three piers (Laem Ngop, Center Point, and Ao Thammachat) for around 50B. On the island, *songtaews* charge from 40B to 100B to take visitors to their hotels.

The Ao Thammachat ferry is the shortest, fastest, and safest crossing, with an hourly service year-round (more frequent in high season and on public

Ko Chang

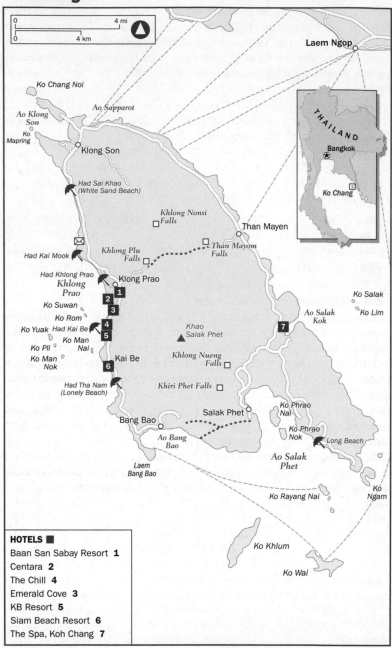

HOTELS ■

Baan San Sabay Resort **1**

Centara **2**

The Chill **4**

Emerald Cove **3**

KB Resort **5**

Siam Beach Resort **6**

The Spa, Koh Chang **7**

holidays), departing daily from 6:30am to 7pm (trip time is 30 min.) and landing at Ko Chang's Ao Sapparos on the north coast. One-way fares cost 60B, and a return trip is 120B. From the **Center Point Pier,** it's 50 minutes and 80B one-way, 160B round-trip. Your slowest option is the cheap but infrequent fishing boat from **Laem Ngob,** costing 100B one-way, which takes an hour to reach Dan Mai Pier, on the east of Ko Chang, but it's often overcrowded. If you are prone to seasickness, be warned that during the monsoon season (July–Sept), the crossing can be rough.

VISITOR INFORMATION

The **TAT** has an office in Trat (Moo 1, Trat-Laem Ngop Rd.; ℂ **03959-7259**) providing information on the nearby islands. The free *Koh Chang Guide* is available in many restaurants and resorts on the island, and it's packed with local information and great beach maps. Another useful website is **www. iamkohchang.com,** run by an expat resident on the island and loaded with restaurant and bar reviews.

The island's narrow, mountainous cliff roads are steep and perilous, so think very carefully before renting a motorbike from your hotel; rates start at 200B per day. For emergencies, call ℂ **1719.** For serious injuries, head for the **Ko Chang International Clinic** (ℂ **03955-1555**), located near the southern end of White Sand Beach (Had Sai Khao).

ORIENTATION

Ko Chang, Thailand's second-largest island after Phuket, is locally known as Elephant Island (*chang* means elephant in Thai) because of the elephant-shaped headland. Thickly forested hills rise from its many bays, which, due to the tides, are narrow and rocky in wet season (June–Oct) and sandier in dry season (Nov–May). Coconut palms (and now billboards) dominate the west coast, which is the most developed part of the island. Ferry piers are all in the north; fishing villages, mangroves, and orchid farms exist on the flatter and more tranquil east coast. In high season, some dive and boat trips leave from **Bang Bao Bay,** on the southernmost tip.

The island's west coast is chock-full with resorts of all types and prices. At the northern end is **Had Sai Khao (White Sand Beach),** the busiest place to hang out. Its kilometer-long (⅔-mile) sands are divided into "north" and "south." More upmarket and family options abound at **Had Klong Phrao,** which has golden sand beaches and smooth waters. Farther south, **Had Kai Be** is a quiet slice of beach that has a mix of rocks and pebbles, but it's a nice place to swim. Last of all, at **Bang Bao,** a stilted fishing village fishmongers have rented parts of their homes to souvenir shacks, dive shops, and budget accommodations. However, the fisherman sell quality fresh fish cooked to order, so stick around long enough for a meal.

Where to Stay

Accommodation-wise, Ko Chang has everything for everyone, from cheap jungle huts to full-on luxury resorts; keep in mind that smaller places will be very much DIY. The buzzing northern strip of Had Sai Khao and Had Kai

Mook tends to pull in budget travelers, while Had Klong Phrao is more upscale. In between, Laem Chai Chet offers a relatively quieter option.

Note: If you arrive after the last ferry and get stranded, head into Trat. The **Muang Trat Hotel,** at 40 Wijitjanya Rd. (℃ **03951-1091**), has 76 very basic rooms: A double with a fan costs 300B, or it's 650B for a double with air-conditioning.

MODERATE

Centara Koh Chang Tropicana Resort & Spa ★   Palm-fringed bungalows scattered across gardens with ponds and tropical flora give this sprawling resort a Robinson Crusoe-like feel. A wide range of rustic bamboo and rattan rooms are on offer; the pricier ones are freestanding. For a small extra charge, opt for one with sea views. All come with tiled bathrooms, indoor and outdoor showers, and petite sun decks. The huge beach restaurant sits on a vast wooden deck next to the crashing surf. The nearby Sunset bar is a pleasant place for sundowners. A professional yoga tutor teaches classes near the beach, and there are sea kayaks for rent.

26/3 Moo 4, Had Klong Phrao. www.centarahotelsresorts.com. ℃ **03955-7122.** 157 units. 5,500B–9,000B superior, deluxe, and suites. **Amenities:** Restaurant; 2 bars; outdoor pool; spa; Wi-Fi (free).

The Chill ★★★   Upmarket resorts are opening all the time on Ko Chang, but most lack the flair of this hotel. Bringing a touch of class to Kai Be Beach, it has a striking modernist design with clean white lines and furnishings in black and white with pops of color from the accent pillows. Rooms range from large deluxe digs to splash rooms with big balconies and pool views, through to Jacuzzi suites and pool villas. Beds are set on platforms in the center of spacious bedrooms, whilst bright windows and sliding doors let plenty of light in, providing a fresh feeling about the place. The Chill has a spa, a library, and chill-out cafe, as well as three pools, including one just for kids.

19/21 Moo 4, Kai Be Beach. www.thechillresort.com. ℃ **03955-2555.** 8 units. From 6,250B double; 10,000B Jacuzzi suite; 15,000B pool villa. **Amenities:** Restaurant; bar; 3 outdoor pools; spa; café; Wi-Fi (free).

The Emerald Cove Koh Chang ★★   Affordable luxury is the watchword at this glamorous resort. The Amari Emerald Cove is truly a study in contemporary comfort. Three-story guestroom wings skirt a delightful courtyard with wooden walkways over lily ponds. A 50m (164ft.) jade-green pool overlooks the ocean with ample lounge chairs and a pool bar, while there's a smaller pool for kids. Rooms are oversized, with slate tile and wood floors, marble bathrooms and thick, soft mattresses on the beds. The resort's restaurants offer an eclectic mix of Thai, modern Italian dishes, and international cuisine.

88/8 Moo 4, Had Klong Phrao. www.emeraldcovekohchang.com. ℃ **03955-2000.** 165 units. From 5,800B double. **Amenities:** 3 restaurants; 2 bars; 2 outdoor pools; health club; spa; room service; babysitting; Wi-Fi (free).

Santhiya Tree Koh Chang Resort ★★   This is another luxurious option on Klong Phrao Beach; its spacious grounds are meticulously manicured, and

the main pool is flanked on one side by a casual bar, on the other by the resort's fine dining restaurant—both with views of the sea. Rooms are set in high-peaked, Thai-style buildings with arching roofs, each with a canopy bed, large sitting area, balcony, and huge stylish bathroom. It's not on a private beach, but the resort is far south of central White Sand Beach, so even in high season you might have a vast stretch of sand to yourself. The excellent spa offers memorable beachside treatments.

8/15 Moo 4, Had Klong Phrao. www.santhiya.com. © **03961-9040.** 50 units. From 7,700B double. **Amenities:** Restaurant; bar; outdoor pool; health club; spa; Jacuzzi; watersports equipment; room service; Wi-Fi (free).

INEXPENSIVE

Baan San Sabay Resort ★   This pocket-sized bungalow resort is on the lower end of Had Sai Khao, opposite the Ko Chang Clinic, on the beach side (though it's a bit of a trek to get there). Rooms are clean, with rattan and wood decor, balconies, and small but adequate en-suite shower rooms. All the basics are available, including air-conditioning, making it a good-value stopover in the busiest part of the island. It's a few minutes to the roadside restaurants. Because it's so small, you should book well ahead.

16/8 Had Sai Khao. © **03955-1061.** 6 units 1,400B–1,800B detached bungalows. No credit cards. **Amenities:** Wi-Fi (free).

Garden Resort ★★   Like many resorts on Ko Chang, this place isn't right on the beach (though it's only about 200m/656 ft. away). However, it is a cozy and welcoming compound with good-sized thatched bungalows at reasonable rates. All the bungalows, which are well-spaced, have big balconies and chunky bamboo furnishings, and they're a decent size, too, especially the family rooms, which are basically two adjoining bungalows. It's under Western management, and there are lots of nice touches like a pool table and computers for guests' use; there's also a small pool.

98/22 Moo 4, Kai Be. www.gardenresortkohchang.com. © **03955-7260.** 20 units. 1,800B-2,500B double. **Amenities:** Restaurant; bar; small outdoor pool; Wi-Fi (free).

KB Resort ★★   Off the busy main drag but still only a short walk to shops, this sprawling bungalow property perches amid well-kept gardens, a few steps from the beach. Freestanding bungalows (of varying size and quality) sleep up to four—making this a good value for families. Resort accommodation runs from basic to top-end beachfront villas. All rooms are decorated with simple wood furnishings and bright yellow walls and regular updates keep the place fresh. The beach here is not as crowded as farther north, and there's a decent pool and Thai massage services.

10/16 Moo 4, Had Kai Bae. www.kbresort.com.© **03955-7125.** 49 units. 1,250B–3,500B. **Amenities:** Restaurant; outdoor pool; Wi-Fi (free).

The Spa, Koh Chang ★★   Far away from the busy west-coast strip, this delightful health retreat offers very reasonably priced 3½- to 9-day detox retreats and colonic cleansing. However, you don't have to detox to stay here as a guest (slightly different rates apply for non-fasters). Rooms are set in stilted one- and two-story houses built of rustic recycled wood, which stand almost hidden from view by a lush hillside garden. The resort's rooms have colorful accent pillows from hill tribes, comfy beds and deep-soaking stone bathtubs, with sleek bathrooms of polished terrazzo, and good-sized balconies. The restaurant serves superb vegetarian food, smoothies, and powerfully cleansing shots of homegrown wheatgrass or the green herb *gotakula*. It has plenty of choices for carnivores, too, and all dishes are made with organic produce when available. A pool sits among sculpted rocks and tropical flora next to a vast pond, yoga and massage pavilion, and delightful sauna.

15/4 Moo 4, Salak Kok. www.thespakohchang.com. ℂ **03955-2733.** www.thespakohchang.com. 26 units. 1,500B–2,900B. **Amenities:** Restaurant; outdoor pool; sauna; Wi-Fi (free).

Siam Beach Resort ★   This popular resort is a good-value hideaway with direct beach access (though take care if swimming here as the current can be treacherous). Older rooms come in two-story (upper or lower) units, built amid gardens, while newer, more expensive beachfront accommodation come with balconies. The best rooms are those called "Deluxe Seaview," located right on the beach where the soothing hiss of the surf creates a calming background. All rooms are airy with glass doors and colorful marine tiles in the bathrooms, and there's in-house dining near the sea, plus a helpful reception staff that can advise on tours.

100/1 Moo 4, Had Tha Nam (Lonely Beach). www.siambeachkohchang.com. ℂ **03955-8082.** 92 units. From 700B deluxe; 4,20000B pool villa. **Amenities:** Restaurant; beach bar; outdoor pool; Wi-Fi (free).

Where to Eat & Drink

For some of the best Thai food on the island, head for **Saffron on the Sea ★★** (13/10 Moo 4; daily 8am–midnight; ℂ **03955-1253**), on Hat Kai Mook, where dishes like steamed lime and chili fish and crispy spring rolls are packed with fresh veggies and have a delightfully crisp wrap. Another simple Thai restaurant worth tracking down is **KaTi Culinary ★★** (48/7 Moo 4; Mon–Sat noon–10pm and Sun 6–10pm; ℂ **081093-0408**) on Klong Phrao Beach. They're famous for their coconut-based curries and spicy Isan salads. They have a kids' menu and offer cooking classes. For a picnic lunch, head to **Crust Bakery ★** (www.facebook.com/CrustBakery.KohChang.Thailand; daily 7am–5pm; ℂ **03955-7157**) for fresh bread, sandwiches, and cakes in Klong Phrao (opposite the temple). Vegetarians should visit **The Spa ★** (ℂ **03955-2733;** p. 159), at Salak Kok on the west coast of the island. On Had Klong Phrao you'll find **Cinnamon ★,** at Aana resort (www.aanaresort.com; ℂ **03955-1359**), which serves up Thai seafood favorites.

Nightlife and cheap eats are available all down the west coast from **Had Sai Khao** (White Sand Beach), through **Had Kai Mook** (Pearl Beach), **Laem Chaichet, Had Klong Phrao, Kai Bae, Had Tha Nam** (Lonely Beach), and **Bai Lan** down to **Bang Bao.** Fresh-caught seafood, like grouper and jumbo Tiger prawns, can also be found at no-name beach shacks on the east coast. Grouper stuffed with chili and lime is an outstanding local specialty.

Outdoor Activities
DIVING & SNORKELING
Dive and snorkeling trips operate here mostly in the dry season, from mid-October until May, but there are a few places that stay open year-round. However, the visibility is so-so outside of the dry season. Most trips head to the islands of Ko Khlum and Ko Wai (a particularly beautiful island), or to Ko Phrao (for wreck dives). **BB Divers** (www.bbdivers-koh-chang.com; ✆ 08615-56212) is the best of the island's many diving outfits, and they have locations around the island. Second place (a near one) goes to **Dolphin Divers** (www.scubadivingkohchang.com; ✆ 086101-4783). PADI-certifications average 3,500B for an introductory lesson and more than 20,000B for a master-dive certification. Most of the diving outfits in town offer snorkeling trips as well or will let surface swimmers tag along on dive trips. If you're lucky, you might share your dive with a whale shark; these non-threatening (they're filter feeders, not predators) underwater giants come around in high season.

KO CHANG ADVENTURE: HIKING, KAYAKING & TREKKING
Several well-marked hiking trails crisscross the island's peaks, but our favorite leads up from Had Klong Phrao to **Klong Plu Waterfall,** which is most spectacular July through August.

Ko Chang also has well-established trekking routes that venture into the lush forest so hikers can view local flora, fauna, and wildlife. While you could strike out on your own, you'll likely spot more fauna, and better identify flora, with a guide. **Evolution Tour** (www.evolutiontour.com; 03955-7078) employs expert local guides who grew up exploring the jungles for both casual family-friendly trips and full-day treks that challenge endurance levels. **Jungle Fever** (www.junglefever.in.th; ✆ 081588-3324) is tops for bird-watching, but also offers scenic hikes to waterfalls and various peaks. Trips start at 700B.

Most hotels rent simple sea kayaks for about 300B per day. However, if you're an experienced kayaker, **KayakChang** (www.kayakchang.com; ✆ 087673-1753) stocks seriously high-end models. Their single and multiday trips are worth joining if you'd like to hop from uninhabited island to uninhabited island with a knowledgeable guide and skilled kayaker. Single day trips start at 3,700B; multiday trips start at 14,000B.

More outdoor fun can be had at the **Treetop Adventure Park** (www.treetopadventurepark.com; ✆ 08431-07600), in Bai Lan, where you can teeter along walkways and whiz along zip lines suspended over the jungle. A half-day swinging through the canopy, including hotel pickup, costs 1,250B.

KOH MAK & KOH KUT
Even more remote than Ko Chang, both of these small islands are a slice of tropical heaven offering castaway vibes, cerulean waters, white sandy beaches, and enough fresh-caught fish to satisfy any craving. In terms of nightlife and restaurants, Koh Mak has more going for it than Koh Kut (often spelled Ko Kood), but both options are super low-key. If you can be moved

from your sandy spot on the shore or the hammock swinging in the breeze, don a snorkel mask and connect with the fishes—it's a major draw here. December to March is the best time to visit these islands and things slow to a halt in May/June to September, with some hotels and restaurants closing during that time.

Ko Mak

Laem Ngop pier: 40km (29 miles) southeast of Trat.

Essentials

ARRIVING

BY PLANE **Bangkok Airways** (✆ **02270-6699;** www.bangkokair.com) has two to three flights daily, depending on the season, between Bangkok and Trat, each taking 1 hour and costing around 2,800B. From there, take a taxi to Laem Ngop pier (260B; 30-minute ride). Catch a speedboat from there.

BY FERRY The Bang Bao Boat (www.kohchangbangbaoboat.com) is the inter-island ferry that runs a loop from Ko Chang to Ko Mak (600B; 1 hour) and on to Koh Kut (900B; 2 hours). Boats leave Ko Chang at 9:30am and noon; frequency has been known to change during high season, so check the website.

BY SPEEDBOAD Speedboats leave from Laem Ngop Pier on the mainland in Trat province and arrive at the piers on Ao Suan Yai and Ao Nid beaches 50 minutes later; cost is 450B.

ON THE ISLAND On Ko Mak you can rent bikes (40B an hour) or motorbikes (200B per day) to zip from beach to beach.

VISITOR INFORMATION AND ORIENTATION

Only 16-square-kilometres (6-square-miles), Ko Mak is tiny. Ao Pra on the west is the best beach on the island, accessible by nearby hotels, like **Cococape Resort**. **Ao Suan Yai** is another lovely beach on the northwestern bay. You'll see Ko Kham in the horizon (a private island, soon to be a resort).

There are **no ATMs,** so stock up on cash before arriving; hotels will sometimes change foreign currencies. There is a small **health center** near Ao Nid pier that can handle sunburns, scrapes, allergic reactions, and basic first-aid. A pinhead-size **police station** is near the health center.

Where to Stay & Eat

Budget accommodations tend to be clustered around Ao Khao on the southwestern side of the island while pricier options call Ao Suan Yai home. **Seavana Beach Resort** (1/23 Moo 2 Tumbon; www.seavanakohmak.com; ✆ **090864-5646**) offers villas with uninterrupted ocean views and direct beach access for 5,200B; rooms in the back of the property go for half that rate. The 26 eco-friendly bungalows at **Ao Kao Resort ★★** (www.aokaoresort.com; ✆ **083152-6564**) all have balconies, rain showerheads, and beach access. On-site are four eateries, and lots of activities (including tennis, badminton, and yoga). Rates start at 2,500B. The best budget pick is **Bamboo Hideaway**

Resort (www.bamboohideaway.com; ✆ 03950-1085) where you'll get a plush mattress in an air-conditioned stilted bungalow made from recycled rubber trees. The American owner makes strong cocktails and proper guacamole; rooms start at 1,000B.

Outstanding massaman curry and drunken noodles with fish or chicken are recommended dishes at **Table Tales** (www.facebook.com/tabletaleskohmak; ✆ **091010-6455**), near the Monkey Island Resort. Practically next door is **Ball Café** (✆ **081925-6591**). Come here for freshly baked bread, sweets, coffee, and bike rentals (100B per day). Khun Bell, the friendly owner and unofficial island ambassador (he runs www.kohmak.com) is a wellspring of local island knowledge and happily passes on his suggestions to curious travelers.

Ko Kut

Laem Sok Pier: 22km (14 miles) southeast of Trat.

Koh Kut's remote location made package holiday deals that bundled private flights with five-figure hotels the norm for a long time. But a more egalitarian vibe is washing over the island, and solo travelers and families are finding their niche on what many call the perfect Thai island. Perfect is a pretty strong descriptor, but for visitors looking for white sandy beaches, few crowds, and a friendly local vibe—Ko Kut is perfect. The island is half the size of Koh Chang.

Essentials

ARRIVING & GETTING AROUND

BY SPEEDBOAD   Speedboats leave from Laem Sok Pier on the mainland in Trat province and arrive 60 minutes later; cost is 500B one-way. Check with your resort to ask which pier is closest to the hotel, noting that the main pier is Ao Salad on the northeast side of the island. **Boonsiri** (www.boonsiriferry.com; ✆ **085921-0111**) runs a catamaran twice a day from Laem Sok to Ao Salad (500B; 90 minutes). **Koh Kood Princess** (www.kohkoodprincess.com; ✆ **086126-7860**) operates a 350B boat from Koh Kut to Trat once a day. The current schedule leaves Koh Kut at 10am and leaves Trat at 12:30pm. The 90-minute ride is free for children 4 years or younger and half price for kids aged 5 to 9.

BY FERRY   The Bang Bao Boat (www.kohchangbangbaoboat.com) is the inter-island ferry that runs a loop from Ko Chang to Ko Mak (600B; 1 hour) and on to Koh Kut (900B; 2 hours). Boats leave Ko Chang at 9:30am and noon; frequency does change during high season, so check the website.

AROUND KOH KUT   A hilly topography makes cycling an arduous task so use the lack of traffic to master your motorbike skills. Bikes are available for 300B a day. Taxis should be booked via your hotel.

VISITOR INFORMATION AND ORIENTATION

During the low season, **boats stop running** and bungalow-type hotels board up for a few months. To give you an idea of how quaint Koh Kut is, imagine this: When the first **ATM** opened on the island in 2015, it was the talk of the town and locals lined up to see the machine in person. The ATM is near the hospital and is often out of cash, so be prepared with baht before arriving. A tiny **hospital** at Ban Khlong Mad takes care of basic first-aid. A **police station** is nearby.

Two waterfalls are easily reached with a short hike. **Nam Tok Khlong Chao** is the bigger and more popular and has a pool for swimming at the base. **Nam Tok Khlong Yai Ki** is other, smaller option and has a small pool.

Where to Stay & Eat

Cozy House (www.kohhkoodcozy.com; ✆ **089094-3650**) is the defacto backpacker hub on the island with fan rooms (600B) and wooden bungalows with air-conditioning (1,200B). There are four hotels on the island named after the "Peter Pan" story, and they offer a great range of accommodations suitable for Lost Boys of all budgets. The nicest of the four is **Peter Pan Resort ★★** (www.peterpanresort.com; ✆ **02966-1800**) where villas have beachfront access, private pools, gardens, and open concept floor plans; rates from 4,000B with midweek discounts. **Bann Makok ★** (www.bannmakok.com; ✆ **081643-9488**) is a boutique hotel in a lush mangrove forest made of recycled timbers that resemble a fishing village; rooms from 3,200B.

Relax House Restaurant ★ (✆ **08651-2779**) at the hotel by the same name has Thai noodles, curries, fish, and classic dishes, along with a few Western snacks and nice cocktails.

One of the most exclusive and luxurious beach resorts in Thailand is **Soneva Kiri Koh Kood ★★★** (www.soneva.com; ✆ **08208-8888**) and it has long been popular with paparazzi-shy celebrities looking for privacy. Here butlers zip-line high tea to treetop canopies, palatial villas are standard issue, and eco-friendly measures are inspiring. Late-night snorkeling, movies under the stars, a kids' club that would make adults envious, and world-class food are all de rigueur. While most guests take planes, ferries, and boats with transfers to the island, the hotel's guests fly on a private plane from Bangkok to Soneva Kiri's private landing strip. Room rates start at 31,000B.

SOUTHERN PENINSULA: THE EAST COAST & ISLANDS

With its postcard-worthy islands and beaches, the Gulf of Siam is truly Thai paradise. Whether you come armed with little money and lots of time, or lots of money and little time, there's an adventure and a little bit of heaven for everyone among its palm-draped beaches, lacy coral reefs, and small mainland towns and fishing villages.

Thailand's slim peninsula extends 1,250km (777 miles) south from Bangkok to the Malaysian border at Sungai Kolok. The towns of Cha-Am and the royal retreat of **Hua Hin** are just a short hop south of Bangkok, and the ancient temples of **Phetchaburi**—the last outpost of the Khmer Empire—are a good day trip from there. Passing through such coastal towns as Prachuap Kiri Khan and Chumphon and heading farther south, you come to Surat Thani, the jumping-off point for islands in the east: **Ko Samui, Ko Pha Ngan, and Ko Tao.** If the beach resorts of Phuket dominate the tourist landscape on the west coast, Ko Samui, a densely developed resort island in the Gulf of Siam, dominates the east. Nearby Ko Pha Ngan, famed for its wild full-moon parties, continues to gain prominence as a rustic resort destination, as does Ko Tao for its access to some of Thailand's best dive sites.

HUA HIN/CHA-AM ★

Hua Hin: 265km (165 miles) S of Bangkok; 223km (139 miles) N of Chumphon. Cha-Am: 240km (149 miles) S of Bangkok; 248km (154 miles) N of Chumphon

Hua Hin and Cha-Am, neighboring towns on the Gulf of Thailand, form the country's oldest resort area. Developed in the 1920s as getaways for Bangkok's elite, the beautiful "Thai Riviera" was a mere 3- or 4-hour journey from the capital by train, thanks to the southern railway's completion in 1916. The Thai royal family was the first to embrace these two small fishing villages as the perfect location for summer vacations and health retreats. In 1924, King Vajiravudh (Rama VI) built the royal Maruekatayawan Palace amid the tall evergreens that lined these stretches of golden sand. Around the same time, the Royal Hua Hin golf course opened, the first of its kind in Thailand. As Bangkok's upper classes began building summer bungalows along the shore, the State Railway opened the Hua Hin Railway Hotel for tourists. King Bhumibol (Rama IX), like generations of royals before him, spent much of his time at his regal residence called *Klai Klangwon* (meaning "Far from Worries") just north of town (note the constant presence of Royal Thai Naval frigates offshore). We can't say the same about the current king, but the spot is still widely associated with royalty. Yet despite the town's venerable connections, the beaches here cannot compare with those on the offshore islands, and the sea is often murky (not appropriate for scuba or snorkeling). However, the proximity to Bangkok (see "Getting There," below) and a booming kiteboarding scene makes this is a solid choice for vacationers short on time or one focused on that sport.

And what about after dark fun? When Pattaya (p. 139), on Thailand's eastern coast, hit the scene in the 1960s, it lured vacationers away from Hua Hin and Cha-Am with promises of a spicier nightlife. Since then, Pattaya's tourism has grown to a riotous, red-light din, and Hua Hin and Cha-Am are a discerning alternative.

While this area is blessed with pleasant weather year-long (November to March is the coolest), visiting between February and June yields the most sunshine and least rain. Kiteboarding is best January through March when the waters are smooth. Note that from about mid-December to mid-January, Hua Hin and Cha-Am reach peak levels, and bookings should be made well in advance. October brings the most rain, but rarely all day long.

Essentials

ARRIVING

BY PLANE   The Hua Hin Airport (code HHQ) is almost exclusively used for private jets. In May 2018, **AirAsia** (www.airasia.com; ✆ **02515-9999**) launched four times weekly flights from Kuala Lumpur; flight time 2 hours.

BY TRAIN   Both Hua Hin and Cha-Am are reached via the train station in Hua Hin, which has been well-preserved and is an attraction in itself. A dozen trains make the daily trek from Bangkok's **Hua Lampong Railway Station** (✆ **02220-4334** or 1690). A second-class seat in an air-conditioned compartment from Bangkok to Hua Hin generally costs 402B, and the trip takes nearly 4 hours.

The **Hua Hin Railway Station** (✆ **03251-1073**) is at the tip of Damnoenkasem Road, which slices through the center of town straight to the beach. Pickup trucks acting as taxis (*songtaews*) and tuk-tuks wait outside to take you to your hotel; fares start at 50B.

Travel Tip: Even if you don't arrive by train, stop and admire the Victorian architecture of the train station built in 1926. Carved wooden pillars and trim decorate the interior. The red-and-white façade is famously replicated around town.

The Southern Peninsula: East Coast

MYANMAR (BURMA)

Thung Wua Laem

Chumphon

Hua Hin/Cha Am

41

Ranong

Lang Suan

Ko Tao

Ko Pha Ngan

Ang Thong National Park

RANONG PROVINCE

Ko Ta Luang

Chaiya

Ko Samui

Don Sak Pier

Suan Mokkh

Surat Thani

Ko Taen

401

Gulf of Thailand

Sichon

(Gulf of Siam)

Phanom

401

Phrasaeng

Tha Sala

4009

41

Thung Yai

Wat Phra Mahathat

Nakhon Si Thammarat

Krabi Town

4

403

41

401

Klong Thom

Hua Sai

Huai Yot

4

Ko Lanta Yai

Trang

Phatthalung

Ko Li Bong

TRANG PROVINCE

Sathing Pra

Andaman Sea

Thung Wa

Songkhla

Hat Yai

Pattani

Ko Tarutao

4

Satun

Narathiwat

Yala

Tak Bai

YALA PROVINCE

MALAYSIA

Sungai Kolok

THAILAND

Bangkok

The Southeast Coast

Airport
Beach
Ferry Route
Scuba Diving

0   30 mi
0   30 km

167

BY BUS/MINIBUS Going by road is the best choice from Bangkok to Hua Hin (expect a journey of 2 to 4 hours) and the best means of transport are a private car or the minibuses that connect with central Cha-Am and Hua Hin. You can arrange **minivan connections** from your hotel in the city. Otherwise, go to any of the bus terminals in the city (such as the eastern at Ekkamai BTS or northern at Mo Chit BTS) and look for the minivans that depart when full throughout the day, costing 180B to Hua Hin.

Buses depart from **Bangkok's Southern Bus Terminal** and **Northern Bus Terminal** around five times per day (155B). There are also hourly buses to Cha-Am between 5am and 8pm (140B). They pull up in Hua Hin on the Phetkasem Road to the south of the town center. From here it is easy to find a *songtaew* or tuk-tuk to take you to your destination. Buses to **Cha-Am** pull up in the middle of town, at the junction of Phetkasem and Narathip Roads.

BY CAR From Bangkok, take Route 35, the Thonburi-Paktho Highway, southwest, then follow Route 4 via Petchburi; allow 2 to 4 hours, depending on traffic. If you'd like a private car, ask your hotel in the city to arrange a trip for you. Expect to pay 1,600B.

SPECIAL EVENTS

The free Hua Hin **jazz festival** attracts thousands of visitors to a unique beach setting, with a stage usually set up in front of the Sofitel hotel. This annual event lasts for 2 or 3 days and features local and international bands and musicians. Spectators sit on the sand or can hire chairs. Extra jazz events take place around town at the same time. Unfortunately, dates are rarely fixed very far in advance, making it hard for tourists to plan to attend. Past years have seen the event take place in May, June, and August. For this year's dates, see tatnews. org, or contact the Hua Hin Tourist Information Center at ☎ **03261-1491.**

CITY LAYOUT

Despite an occasional traffic jam, Hua Hin is easy to navigate. The main artery, Phetkasem Road, runs parallel to the waterfront about 4 blocks inland. The wide Damnoenkasem Road cuts through Phetkasem and runs straight to the beach. On the north side of Damnoenkasem, toward the waterfront, you'll find a cluster of guesthouses, restaurants, shopping, and nightspots lining the narrow lanes. Across Phetkasem to the west are the railway station and Night Market.

Smaller Cha-Am is a 25-minute drive north of Hua Hin along Phetkasem Road. Ruamchit Road, also known as Beach Road, hugs the shore and is lined with shops, restaurants, and hotels. Cha-Am's resorts line the 8-km (5-mile) stretch of beach that runs south from the village toward Hua Hin.

GETTING AROUND

BY SONGTAEW Pickup trucks (*songtaews*) follow regular routes in Hua Hin, passing the railway station and bus terminals at regular intervals. Flag one down that's going in your direction. Fares are 20B within town, while stops at outlying resorts cost up to 50B. If the truck is empty, the driver will likely demand an extortionate fee to hire the whole vehicle; just wait until a shared truck comes along.

BY TUK-TUK   Tuk-tuk rides are negotiable; always agree on a price before you start, but expect to pay at least 50B for a ride within town.

BY MOTORCYCLE TAXI   Within each town, motorcycle taxi fares begin at 30B. These taxis, whose drivers are identifiable by colorful numbered vests, are a good way to get to your resort or hotel.

BY SAMLOR   Trishaws, or *samlors* (bicycle taxis), can be hired for short distances in town, from 40B. You can also negotiate an hourly rate.

BY CAR OR MOTORCYCLE   Avis has an office at 15/112 Phetkasem Soi 29, in Hua Hin ((🕾 03254-7523). **Budget** has an office at the Grand Hotel ((🕾 03251-4220). Self-drive rates start at around 1,200B. Call ahead to reserve at least a day in advance. A cheaper alternative is to rent from one of the small-time agents near the beach on Damnoenkasem Road. Motorbikes (100cc) are available for about 200B per day.

ON FOOT   Hua Hin is a labyrinth of busy streets and narrow alleys, with little guesthouses, colorful local bars, and a wide assortment of casual eating venues. Almost everything in town is accessible on foot.

VISITOR INFORMATION
The **Hua Hin Tourist Information Center** (🕾 03261-1491) is at the junction of Phetkasem and Damnoenkasem Roads near the Starbucks. Opening hours are from 8:30am to 4:30pm daily. The website www.tourismhuahin.com is also quite useful. There's a branch of **TAT** in Cha-Am at 500/51 Phetkasem Rd. (🕾 03247-1005).

FAST FACTS
IN HUA HIN   All major banks are along Phetkasem Road, to the north of Damnoenkasem. The main **post office** (🕾 03251-1567) is on Damnoenkasem Road, near the Phetkasem intersection. The **Bangkok Hospital Hua Hin Hospital** (www.bangkokhospital.com/huahin; 🕾 03261-6800) is in the north of town, along Phetkasem Road. Call the **Tourist Police** for either town at 🕾 03251-5995.

IN CHA-AM   Banks are dotted along Phetkasem Road, and the post office is on Beach Road. The **Cha-Am Hospital** (www.chaamhospital.go.th; 🕾 03247-1007) is at 8/1 Khlong Thian Road to the north of the town center. If time permits, all serious medical needs should be addressed at the Bangkok Hospital Hua Hin.

Exploring Hua Hin
The stunning Khmer-style temples of **Phetchaburi** (see "Side Trips from Hua Hin & Cha-Am," at the end of this section) are the most significant cultural sites near Hua Hin and Cha-Am, but really what attracts so many to this area is what first attracted the Thai royal family: Proximity to the capital; sandy beaches; watersports; and activities such as golf and horseback riding. Hua Hin also boasts some fine resorts, which come with stunning pools, a host of dining options, and top-notch spas.

One of the oldest resorts here is the **Centara Grand Resort and Villas,** originally built as the Railway Hotel for Thai royalty and their guests in the 1920s. Visitors are welcome to wander around its pretty colonial buildings and gardens (don't miss the giant topiary elephant). High Tea at the Centara (daily 10am–6pm) costs 450B per person; it not only offers a chance to sip tea and nibble on sandwiches, cakes, and scones in a lovely original wing of the hotel, but transports guests back in time to the era when Hua Hin was a getaway purely for the Thai upper crust.

If you're in town over the weekend, don't miss the **Cicada Market** (Soi Hua Thanon 23; www.cicadamarket.com) which runs from 4 to 11pm Friday and Saturday and 4 to 10pm on Sunday. The market showcases the best of the region: local snacks; artists selling handmade clothing, jewelry, décor, and art; and buskers and performers taking over the central stage around 8:30pm. The market has four zones (Art of Eating for food; Art of Act for entertainment, Art a la Mode for clothing, and Art Indoors for décor) and is easily manageable and pleasant.

The **Night Market** (on Decha Nuchit Rd., at the northern end of the town center) is much more touristy than the Cicada Market. The market covers a 2-block radius and it's busy from dusk to late with small food stalls and vendors hawking knockoff Nikes, selfie sticks, and cheap souvenirs. Directly southeast of the market are a few shops that sell artwork produced by talented locals.

Bridging the gap between the touristy Night Market and the weekend's only Cicada Market is **Baan Silapin,** which is often called the Hua Hin Artist's Village (4km west of town on Moo 14; © 087047-7125; open 10am–5pm Tues–Sun). A local painter established this artist collective, and today it exhibits the works of 15 local artists in a gallery-style setting. There are classes in painting and sculpture (great for kids!) and the collective promotes the small but passionate group of creatives that call Hua Hin home. The **Plearnwan Vintage Village** (www.plearnwan.com; © 03252-0311; Phetkasem Road between Soi 38 and Soi 40) is a grouping of period-style Chinese-Thai shophouses that harken back to the 1950s. Shops are so-so, but vendors hawk Thai dishes (there's an emphasis on long-forgotten recipes) and traditional teas. The real boon to visitors is the screenings of classic movies at the open-air cinema on the weekend evenings; call for schedule and exact times (info not on website).

The **Maruekhathaiyawan Palace ★★**, often romantically referred to as "the palace of peace and hope" (www.mrigadayavan.or.th; © 086162-0162; Thurs–Tues 8:30am–5pm; 30B), consists of 16 interlinked teakwood buildings and is located on the coast halfway between Hua Hin and Cha-Am; it is one of Thailand's most attractive colonial buildings and a must-see for anyone interested in architecture. Built and designed in 1924 by King Rama VI, it served for many years as the royal summer residence and is now open to the public. A stroll through the preserved rooms with their polished teak floors, period furnishings, and shuttered windows is enough to be transported back to another era. Wander along the raised, covered walkway to the pavilions over the beach (formerly the royal changing rooms) and feel the fresh sea breeze on your face. Shoulders and knees must be covered to visit, and sarongs can be rented for 20B if needed.

The big standing Buddha and viewpoint from spiky **Khao Takiap (Chopstick Hill)**—a small cape 7km (4⅓ miles) south of Hua Hin (hop on a green *songtaew* for 50B to 100B)—is a scenic area worth a visit; if you climb the hill (272m/892 ft.) to enjoy the panoramic view, hang on to your bags and camera, as the local macaques will snatch anything unattended.

Pony riding is popular along the busy beaches at Hua Hin and Cha-Am. Frisky young fillies go for 600B an hour, but you'll need to bargain hard. At 100B for 10-minute kids' rides, you can ride with a Thai escort leading the pony (which is the safest way), or on your own if you're confident. If you're interested, take a walk down to the beach, and you'll be besieged by young men eager to rent out their ponies.

In recent years, Hua Hin has become popular for kiteboarding (see **Activities,** below).

See "Side Trips from Hua Hin & Cha-Am," at the end of this section, for trips to nature sites.

Where to Stay in Hua Hin

Developers have been busy in Hua Hin in recent years, and beside the recommendations below, you can also find hotels run by big-name brands like **Hyatt, Avani,** and **Intercontinental** (good news for award point users). A **Holiday Inn** opened in 2018 and has an on-property waterpark that boasts Thailand's largest waterslide. Because of the proximity of the towns, many hotels in Cha-Am list the better-known town of Hua Hin in their name; be sure to check the exact location if considering a hotel not listed here.

EXPENSIVE

Hotel Bocage ★   Sitting atop hipper-than-hip Seenspace (p. 177), a mixed-use mall where cool Thais come for eating and drinking, the 2017-opened Hotel Bocage is a welcome contrast to the town's frangipani-laden beach resorts. Designed by one of Thailand's most lauded architects, Duangrit Bunnag, the space is starkly contemporary with open floor plans and a crisp industrial color scheme of whites, blacks, and grays. Guestrooms are a sprawling 42- to 75-square-meters (452- to 807-square-feet), but seem even larger as floor-to-ceiling windows open to private terraces overlooking the sea. Luxurious Italian brands outfit the room, from the bed frames to lounge sofas and free-standing tubs. The only bummer: The hotel's swimming pool is shared with mall goers and can get very crowded.

13/14 Seenspace Building, 4th floor, Hua Hin Soi 35. www.hotelbocage.com. ✆ **091712-8822.** 6 units. 6,000B–8,000B double. **Amenities:** Room service; pool; parking (free); Wi-Fi (free).

Centara Grand Beach Resort & Villas ★★   The Centara first opened in 1922 under the name Railway Hotel and was Hua Hin's first hotel. Today it offers some of the classiest accommodations in the area (and is by far the best choice for families, more on that below). Renovations over the years have expanded it into a large and luxurious hotel without sacrificing a bit of its former '20s charm and genteel vibe. The whitewashed buildings, shaded verandas and walkways, fine wooden details, red-tile roofs, and immaculate gardens with topiaries create a cool, calm, colonial effect. There is a small museum of photography and memorabilia, and the original 14 bedrooms are preserved for posterity. These rooms have a unique appeal, but the newer rooms are larger, brighter, and more comfortable, with swank niceties as rain showers and soaking tubs. Though they boast furnishings that reflect the hotel's old beach resort feel, they are still modern and cozy. Many of the room categories are large enough for families, a big perk, as is the superb kid's club which offers a wide variety of activities daily, including some creative ones for parents and kids to do together.

1 Damnoenkasem Rd. (in the center of town, by the beach). www.centarahotelsresorts. com. ⓒ **03251-2021.** 249 units. 2,700–8,845B double; 9,000B–19,700B suite; from 10,000B villa. **Amenities:** 5 restaurants; lounge; bar; 4 pools; lazy river; mini golf; golf course (within 2 miles); health club; spa; children's club; playground; room service; babysitting; Wi-Fi (free).

Chiva-Som International Health Resort ★★★ In the spring of 2018, Conde Naste Traveler named Chiva-Som one of the 25 best spas on the planet. Why? It offers more than 120 treatments and fitness programs, including such unusual ones as Tecar Massage Therapy, Botox treatments, biofeedback, acupuncture, and balneotherapy. (Upon check-in, guests have a brief medical check and meet with an advisor to tailor a program based on needs, goals, and budget). The resort garners accolades for its design and service, too. Guestrooms are set in a collection of handsome pavilions and bungalows dressed in teak and sea-colored tiles, nestled in 2.8 hectares (7 acres) of exotic tropical gardens beside the beach. Décor is super chic and brand new: The resort closed for 3 months in 2018 for a full renovation.

No children under 16 or cell phones are allowed in common spaces (which means no Instagramming the perfectly plated, delicious and healthy meals), and a 3-day minimum booking is required. Day-spa visitors are welcome. It all comes with a high price tag, but it is worth it.

73/4 Phetkasem Rd.; 5-min. drive south of Hua Hin. www.chivasom.com. ⓒ **03253-6536.** 57 units. Contact the resort directly about spa and health packages. Three nights from 75,000B in low-season; from 81,000B in high-season. Rate includes 3 spa cuisine meals/day, health and beauty consultations, daily massage, and participation in fitness and leisure activities. **Amenities:** Restaurant; indoor and outdoor pools; health club w/personal trainer and exercise classes; his-and-hers spas w/steam and hydrotherapy treatments; watersports equipment; bike rental; room service; Wi-Fi (free).

MODERATE

Anantara Resort & Spa ★★★ A series of elegantly designed Thai-style pavilions surround 5.6 hectares (14 acres) of possibly the most exotic gardens you'll see in Thailand, just north of Hua Hin. The open-air *sala*-style lobby tastefully showcases ornately carved teak wooden lanterns, warm wood floors, and oversized furniture with Thai cushions. The Lagoon is an area of teak pavilions surrounded by lily ponds; and from the hotel's most luxurious rooms, you can hear chirping frogs and watch buzzing dragonflies from wide balconies. Other rooms cluster around a manicured courtyard. Superior rooms have a garden view, and deluxe rooms overlook the sand and sea. Lagoon rooms have large patios perfect for private barbecues. All rooms feature vibrant silks, hardwood floors, and high-thread-count sheets. Suites have enormous aggregate bathtubs that open to guest rooms by a sliding door. Fine dining includes an Italian restaurant, and the resort's spa is large and luxurious.

43/1 Phetkasem Beach Rd. www.anantara.com/hua-hin. ✆ **03252-0250.** 190 units. 2,715B–4,275B double; 4,650B–9,150B suite. **Amenities:** 6 restaurants; outdoor pool w/children's pool; health club; spa; room service; babysitting; Wi-Fi (free).

Hilton Hua Hin Resort & Spa ★★
Location is the top reason to pick the Hilton: It's set in the heart of downtown Hua Hin, overlooking the main beach. Its environs are ideal for beach strolls, in-town shopping, and nightlife. Other perks at this 17-story tower include a courteous and professional staff; lots of activities for families (tennis, squash, table tennis, pool and a well-run kids club); and good on-site restaurants, especially the lively Hua Hin Brewing Company, which sells imported beers like Guinness, has a well-rounded selection of spirits, and features live music in the evening.

33 Naresdamri Rd. www.huahin.hilton.com. ✆ **03253-8999.** 296 units. From 3,100 double; from 6,500B suite. **Amenities:** 4 restaurants; 2 bars; tennis and squash courts; game room; outdoor pool; health club; spa; children's center; room service; babysitting; Wi-Fi (free).

Hua Hin Marriott Resort & Spa ★★
From the giant swinging couches in the main lobby to the large central pavilions, this hotel is decked-out in a grand, if exaggerated, Thai-style. The Marriott often attracts large groups but is a good choice for families too, though it's situated quite a way from the town center. Ponds, pools, boats, golf, tennis, and other sports venues dot the junglelike grounds leading to their open beach area, and there is even a "zoo" of pool floats for lounging (selfie opportunities abound). Deluxe rooms are the top choice—large, amenity-filled, and facing out to sea. Terrace rooms at beachside are worth the bump up.

107/1 Phetkasem Beach Rd. www.marriot.com. ✆ **03251-1881.** 322 units. 4,200B–7,200B double. **Amenities:** 3 restaurants; 2 bars; outdoor pool; health club; spa; children's center; room service; babysitting; Wi-Fi (free).

INEXPENSIVE

Because the backpacker crowd rarely makes a stop in Hua Hin or Cha-Am, the budget accommodation in town is quite sparse. Hotels at this price point offer little in terms of style, service or comfort; however we can recommend one guesthouse and one hostel here. The guesthouse, **Big Apple Bed and Pool** (www.bigapplehuahin.com; ✆ **089686-1271**), is a 2-minute walk to the beach and offers spotless rooms (1,200B a night) and apartment-style accommodations (1,800B a night). The property surrounds a large, Technicolor swimming pool. **Chanchala Café and Hostel** ★ (www.facebook.com/chanchalacafe; ✆ **086331-6763**) is close to the train station and a 5-minute walk to the beach. Bunkbed-style rooms (including one women's only room; beds are 350B per night) are super clean, have personal lockers and reading lights, and guests socialize at the on-site café or rooftop lounge. Kudos, too, to the friendly staff.

Where to Stay in Cha-Am

Along the quiet stretch between Hua Hin and Cha-Am, there are several fine resorts. Cha-Am village itself is a bit raucous (the Ocean City, New Jersey, to Hua Hin's The Hamptons) especially along the seedy Soi Bus Station, and most stay outside of town.

MODERATE

Dusit Thani ★   The Dusit has all the amenities of a fine resort, including a marble lobby adorned with massive glass works—chandeliers rippling with crystals, and sculptures that seem to owe a debt to glass artist Dale Chihuly. Guest rooms carry the same elegance and are spacious, with big marble bathrooms, plush headboards on the beds, and plump, overstuffed arm chairs. Room rates vary with the view, and those on the ground floor have private verandas. Suites here are enormous, with real living rooms, plus a full pantry and dressing area. For all its air of formality, however, the resort is ideal for those who want to lounge in swimsuits and T-shirts and a relaxed holiday air pervades. It is a bit far from both Hua Hin and Cha-Am, but the resort is completely self-contained, and has what's needed for a nice holiday.

1349 Phetkasem Rd. www.dusit.com. ℰ **03252-0009.** 296 units. 2,500B–5,800B double. **Amenities:** 4 restaurants; lounge; outdoor pool; beach; health club; room service; babysitting; executive floor; Wi-Fi (free).

SO Sofitel Hua Hin ★★   Did you catch the note above that said oftentimes hotels put Hua Hin in their name even when they're in Cha-Am? This is one of those examples. However, the Sofitel exudes such an uber-cool, pool party vibe that their questionable marketing tactics are forgiven. Rooms achieve a perfect balance of function and artistry, with lots of exuberantly-patterned fabrics, natural woods (in some rooms the bed frames look like tree branches), brushed concrete walls with unique art on them, and gold touches. Despite the swanky vibe, children are never an afterthought, and some rooms include bunk beds and children's forts (we give a big thumbs up to the kids club here, too). The hotel's long pool bellies up to the beach and is a bit of a "see-and-be-seen" spot in town–lots of high-fashion swimwear and contemporary, artistic grounds. There's a second, adults-only pool, too. There is a great happy hour at HI-SO bar (a play on the hotel's name and Thai slang for high-society), a rowdy beach party with DJs the first Saturday of the month, and the hotel breakfast spread is a delicious. The only downside: It's a long drive from town and other restaurants.

115 Moo 7. www.so-sofitel-huahin.com. ℰ **03245-1240.** 78 units. 3,300B–5,300B double; from 5,500B suite. **Amenities:** 2 restaurants; 2 pools; health club; spa; room service; babysitting; Wi-Fi (free).

INEXPENSIVE

The Cha-Am Methavalai Hotel ★   The Methavalai is the best of the ragtag collection in busy Cha-Am town, providing clean accommodations on the main Beach Road, closeby restaurants, shopping, and nightlife. Guest rooms are painted from a pastel palette and are peaceful, all with balconies and sun decks and tidy, but not luxurious, bathrooms. Spacious rooms look out over the good-sized central pool with a large sundeck (front-facing rooms can be a bit noisy, though). If you want to stay in downtown Cha-Am, this is the best choice.

220 Ruamchit Rd. www.methavalai.com. (*) **03243-3250.** 215 units. From 1,450B double; from 5,670B pavilion and suite. **Amenities:** 2 restaurants; lounge; outdoor pool; room service; babysitting; Wi-Fi (free)

Where to Eat in Hua Hin

If you wake up at about 7am and walk to the piers in either Hua Hin or Cha-Am, you can watch the fishing boats return with their loads. Workers sort fish, crabs, and squid, packing them on ice for distribution around the country. In both Hua Hin and Cha-Am, look for the docks at the very north end of the beach; to sample the catch, head for the string of open-air restaurants on stilts, along Naresdamri Road in Hua Hin, where prices are very competitive. Seafood is a big draw here and it would be a shame to leave without pigging out on fresh-caught grouper, prawns, or tilapia.

The resorts have more restaurants than there is room to list, and no matter where you stay, you'll have dining options in-house. In town, there are lots of small storefront eateries and tourist cafes as well.

Baan Itsara ★ THAI   Charm is on the menu, along with top-notch seafood, at this two-story seaside home built in the 1920s. From the noisy, open kitchen to the terrace seating with views of the beach, it's quite atmospheric—a swell place to get together with friends and celebrate the good life. A variety of fresh seafood and meats are prepared steamed or deep-fried and served with salt, chili, or red curry paste. We'd recommend the grilled squid with spicy dipping sauce, though the sizzling hot plate of glass noodles with shrimp, squid, pork, and vegetables is also a specialty here.

7 Napkehard St. (seaside, a 150B tuk-tuk ride north from the town center). (*) **03253-0574.** Reservations recommended for Sat dinner. Main courses 100B–470B. Daily 10:30am–10pm.

Jek Pai ★★ THAI   This family-run market-style eatery debuted more than 50 years ago as a coffee shop. Today it is one of the most popular spots in the area for locals to dine. Arrive in the morning for a quintessential Thai breakfast. Start with Thai coffee, which makes generous use of the cans on condensed milk stacked by the register, and an order of porridge made with rice and a protein. Lunch is more of a free-for-all since there are multiple vendors to choose from (hence the mountains of menus on the table at the front). The seafood salad is world-class and most tables order either the hotpot sukiyaki or glass noodles with prawns.

51/6 Dechanuchit Rd. (no sign; a large wooden complex on the corner). Main courses 40B–200B. Daily 6:30am–12:30pm and 5:30–8pm.

Lung Ja Seafood ★★★ SEAFOOD   In Hua Hin's night market, there are nearly a dozen stalls with ice-packed fish, ready to the hit the grill, and they're all nearly identical at first blush. Lung Ja is the only one that *always* has a crowd; savvy cooking techniques have earned them a loyal following. Fresh seafood arrives daily—grouper ready for the fryer and jumbo prawns that stay plump when grilled—but it's the large lobsters that are the star of the show. Priced by the kilo (about 1,500B per kilo), the lobsters are steamed first and then quickly grilled, which leaves the lobster tender, juicy and full of flavor. Complete the meal with steamed garlicky vegetables or fried rice.

Hua Hin Night Market, at 103/4-5 Dachanuchit Rd. ℭ **082975-9905.** Main courses 80B–1,500B. Daily 6–11pm.

Activities & Tours

GOLF

Probably the most popular activity in Hua Hin and Cha-Am is **golf,** and the town boasts some fine courses. Reservations are suggested and necessary most weekends. Many of the hotels run FOC (free of charge) shuttles, and most clubs can arrange pickup and drop-off to any hotel. The **Hua Hin Golf Center** (www.huahingolf.com; ℭ 03253-0476) rents clubs (around 700B per day), offers information on which courses are top-rated, and can assist with reservations. Expect to pay around 350B for a caddy and 650B for a golf cart.

- **Palm Hills Golf Resort and Country Club,** 1444 Phetkasem Rd., Cha-Am (www.palmhills-golf.com; ℭ 03252-0800), just north of Hua Hin, is a picturesque course set among rolling hills and jagged escarpments (greens fees: 2,500B).

- **Springfield Royal Country Club,** 208 Moo 2, Tambon Sam Paya, Cha-Am (www.springfieldresort.com/golf; ℭ 03270-9222), designed by Jack Nicklaus in 1993, is in a beautiful valley setting—the best by far (greens fees: 3,500B).

WATERSPORTS

While most of the larger resorts will plan watersports activities for you upon request, you can make arrangements with small operators on the beach (for significant savings). Most resorts forbid noisy **jet skis,** but you'll find some young entrepreneurs renting them out on the beach for around 2,000B per hour. **Kiteboarding** is a very popular beach sport; the season runs from November to April (best January to March) and a 3-day beginner's course costs 11,000B. Two first-rate schools have opened to handle the demand: **Kiteboarding Asia** (www.kiteboardingasia.com; ℭ 08159-14593) and **North Kiteboarding Club** (www.northkiteboardingclub.com; ℭ 083438-3833).

ACTIVE TOURS

Pedal pushers with a penchant for history will enjoy the curated tours offered by **Huan Hin Bike Tours** (www.huahinbiketours.com; ℭ 081173-4469). Half-day tours cover a lot of ground, stopping at Hua Hin's main sights with an English-speaking guide. Other tours are longer and visit national parks, beaches, wineries, and more. There are multi-day options (including a ride to Bangkok!) and tours range from easy to challenging. This is also the place to come for high-quality bike rentals (around 500B per day) and suggestions for routes.

Active kayaking tours through the Khao Sam Roi Yot National Park (see Side Trips below) should be booked with the professional and friendly team at **Hua Hin Adventure Tour** (www.huahinadventuretour.com; ✆ **03253-0314**). They also lead guided hikes to waterfalls in the region and wildlife watching trips, but avoid their excursions that include elephant rides, which includes harmful rides atop a carriage on the elephant's back. Tours start at 1,700B.

FOODIE ACTIVITIES

While hotels around town offer cooking classes, a more authentic experience is available at **Thai Cooking Course Hua Hin** (http://thai-cookingcourse.com; ✆ **081572-3805**). Hands-on lessons start with a morning market visit to select produce and other ingredients needed to create the day's menu. This is followed by an in-kitchen session with guests learning to make five Thai dishes. Hotel transfers and a recipe book are included in the 1,500B per person fee.

If you'd prefer to nosh without doing the work, contact the pros at **Feast Thailand** (www.feastthailand.com; ✆ **03251-0207**); they offer five very different tours each week. On the "Foodies' Food Tour," for example, participants sample a whopping 20 snacks from street stands around town, while the "Jing Jing" tour focuses on introducing travelers to Thai specialties they likely haven't tried yet. They even offer a family-friendly tour with adjusted spice levels for little ones. Tours average 1,500B per person (900B for kids 12 and younger) and take between 2½ and 3½ hours.

SPAS

Hua Hin is famous for its spas, and each of the top resorts features excellent services and facilities (see above). Beyond hotel-based spas we highly recommend the ultra-luxe **Chiva-Som ★★★** (73/4 Phetkasem Rd.; 5-min. drive south of town; ✆ **03253-6536**)—there's nothing like it, in terms of pampering and range of options. And far south of town, swank **Six Senses Hua Hin ★★** (9/22 Moo 5; 30km/19 miles south of Hua Hin; ✆ **03263-2111**) is a destination spa worth visiting. Alternative treatments here include chakra balancing and Reiki healing. It's comparable in quality with Chiva-Som.

For those looking for a less pricey experience, there is the **Thai Massage by the Blind** (✆ **081944-2174;** Petchkasem Soi 37). For more than 2 decades it has been offering employment to Hua Hin's visually impaired. Traditional Thai body massages average 200B, the service is highly skilled, and the settings surprisingly nice.

Hua Hin Entertainment & Nightlife

A 15-minute stroll through the labyrinth of *sois* between Damnoenkasem and Dechanuchit roads near the beach reveals all sorts of small places to stop for a beer. If you're after a cocktail or a glass of wine, or prefer a more sophisticated setting, opt for a hotel bar. **HOBS** (House of Beers) and **Oasis**, both at Seenspace (Hua Hin Soi 35; www.seenspace.com/huahin) offer a perfect combo of music, views, well-made drinks and smartly-curated beer menus.

White Lotus Sky Bar (atop the Hilton Hotel) is the place to be when the sun sets. Most of Soi Bintaban is lined with Pattaya-style girlie bars, while Naresdamri Road, which runs north–south parallel to the beach, is home to open-air restaurant-bars for good people watching.

For inspiration and listings of what's happening tonight, the expat-run **Hua Hin Today** (www.huahintoday.com) is a good resource.

Side Trips from Hua Hin & Cha-Am
PHETCHABURI ★★

Phetchaburi, one of Thailand's oldest towns, possibly dates from the same period as Ayutthaya and Kanchanaburi, though it is believed to have been first settled during the Dvaravati period. After the rise of the Thai nation, it served as an important royal military city and was home to several princes who were groomed for ascendance to the throne. In the 17th century, Phetburi, as it's locally known, was a hotbed of trading between Myanmar and Ayuthaya. Phetchaburi's palace and historically significant temples make it an excellent day trip from Hua Hin/Cha-Am or an escape from Bangkok. It is just 1 hour north of Hua Hin.

Western Tours (www.westerntourshuahin.com; © 03253-3303), has day excursions for 1,800B per person that includes most of the sights below, or you can see them on a self-guided day trip by rented car.

The main attraction is **Phra Nakhon Khiri Historical Park ★★★**. The park sits atop Khao Wang (also called Palace Hill), and there is a regal summer palace in the hills that overlooks the city. Built in 1859 by King Mongkut (Rama IV), it was intended not only as a summer retreat for the royal family but for foreign dignitaries as well. Allegedly, the king chose this hilly location as it best suited his favorite hobby: astronomy. Combining Thai, European, and Chinese architectural styles, the palace buildings include guesthouses and a royal Khmer-style *chedi*, or temple. The Phra Thinang Phetphum Phairot Hall is open for viewing and contains period art and antiques from the household. Though it was once accessible only via a 4-km (2½-mile) hike uphill, you'll be happy to hear there's a funicular railway (it's called a "cable car," but that's not an accurate description) to bring you to the top for 40B. Admission is 150B which includes entrance to a museum that displays royal furnishings and belongings. It's open daily 8:30am to 4pm. From the palace, a trio of peaks (accessible via a cobblestone footpath) are each marked with a stupa. Phra That Chom Phet, at the central peak, has a 40-meter-tall white spire and is the most notable of the three peak structures.

Another fascinating sight at Phetchaburi, the **Khao Luang Cave ★★**, houses more than 170 Buddha images underground. The stalactites in the cavern make this one of the most impressive cave-shrines in the country. If you can time it right, arrive in the morning when sunbeams cast a dramatic and photogenic light through the cave's natural 'skylight' of sorts. The cave is accessible via steep but nicely paved stairs. Outside the cave, hundreds of noisy monkeys descend upon the parking lot and food stalls looking for handouts. Sometimes you'll find a guide outside who'll escort you through the caves for a small fee, but it is not necessary to have a guide.

Wat Yai Suwannaram ★ is a stunning royal temple built during the Ayutthaya period. The teak ordination hall was moved from Ayutthaya after the second Burmese invasion of the city (keep an eye peeled for the ax-chop battle scar on the building's carved doors). Inside there are large religious murals featuring Brahmans, hermits, giants, and deities. Scholars believe they date back to 1700, making them among the oldest murals in The Kingdom.

Wat Ko Keo Suttharam ★, also built in the 17th century, should not be skipped. Its stunning, representational murals, painted in the 1730s, even depict some Westerners: There are several panels portraying the arrival in the Ayutthaya court of European courtesans and diplomats (including a Jesuit dressed in Buddhist garb).

Another fabulous temple is **Wat Kamphaeng Laeng** ★, originally constructed during the reign of Khmer ruler King Jayavarman VII (r. 1157–1207) as a Hindu shrine. Made of laterite, it was once covered in decorative stucco, some of which still remains. Each of the five *prangs* (towers) was devoted to a deity—the center *prang* to Shiva is classical Khmer style. During the Ayutthaya period, the Thai people made it a Buddhist temple.

Lastly, the **Phra Ratchawang Ban Peun,** or Ban Peun Palace (© **03242-8506;** daily 8am–4pm; until 4:30pm Sat & Sun; admission 50B), is a nice stop. This royal residence was commissioned by Rama V in 1910. He died the year construction began, and the work finished in 1916. The German-designed grand summer home comes alive with colorful tile work, neoclassical marble columns, and floor motifs. Today it sits on military grounds and is a popular venue for ceremonies and large occasions. The entire space is a beautiful art nouveau structure.

KHAO SAM ROI YOT NATIONAL PARK★

Just a 40-minute drive south of Hua Hin, Khao Sam Roi Yot, or the "Mountain of Three Hundred Peaks," is comparatively small in relation to the nation's other parks, but offers short (but steep) hikes to panoramic views of the sea. Bird populations are abundant here, and more than 300 migratory and resident species call the park home. If you're a budding ornithologist in need of more detailed information, www.thaibirding.com is a wellspring of knowledge. Admission tickets, maps, and information are sold at attractions within the park since there is no official park gate.

Of the park's several caves, **Phraya Nakhon Cave** ★★★ is one of Thailand's most famous caves, housing a *sala* pavilion that was built in 1890 for Rama V. Over the years, jaw-dropping photos of the caved atmospherically bathed in morning light have made the rounds on tourist brochures, traveler's Instagram accounts, and glossy magazines. Plan to arrive around 10:30am to see the famous light in real life. Part of the cave's roof collapsed many years ago (it's a secure structure today, no worries) and there's enough sunlight for photosynthesis to occur, and now trees grow on the cave's floor, adding to the stunning ambiance. Weekends get busy but mornings and evenings are generally people-free. The path to the cave starts at Laem Sala Beach, and it is a 430-meter climb to reach the cave from there. Parts of the climb are steep and rocky, but it's manageable.

A half-day trip to the Pala-U waterfall close to the Burmese border (63km/39 miles west of Hua Hin) is another nature trekking option. Nature trails take you through hills and valleys until you end up at the falls.

PRACHUAP KHIRI KHAN

If you've had enough of Thailand's many overdeveloped beach areas, the small town and coastline near Prachuap Khiri Khan (just a 1-hr. drive south of Hua Hin) might just be the answer. Some of the kindest people in Thailand live here, the beaches are lovely and little-used, and the town begs a wander. There is little in the way of fine dining and accommodations, but it is a good stop on the way south to Chumphon. If you decide to crash for a night, there are a host of guesthouses in town, most of them with shared bathrooms. The nicest is **Prachuap Beach Hotel** (123 Suseuk Rd.; www.prachuapbeach.com; © **03260-1288;** doubles from 900B) with brightly painted walls, firm beds, and (most importantly) a diligent staff keeping it clean. More likely, you'll at least need a place to eat, if so, try the Isan delights at the famed street food shop called **Som Tam Baa Nook** (Suseuk Road just off the beach; approximately 7am to 4pm) or the simply named **Intown Seafood** (no English sign; at the end of Chai Talay Road; © **081705-6507**), where fresh-caught fish is the reason for going.

CHUMPHON

463km (288 miles) S of Bangkok; 193km (120 miles) N of Surat Thani

Chumphon was once known for simply being a stop on the way south, but it's now become a popular jumping off point for trips to offshore islands. Boats leave from here to **Ko Tao** to the southeast and **Ang Thong Marine National Park** due south, both of which are popular diving areas, and ferries continue to **Ko Pha Ngan** and **Ko Samui,** though for these islands the ferry trip is shorter from Donsak Pier near Surat Thani. Surrounded by fruit orchards inland, and a couple of lovely beaches, such as **Sairi Beach,** 22km (14 miles) east of town, and **Thung Wua Laem Beach,** 12km (7½ miles) northeast, it's a good place to unwind before catching the ferry. There's not much to merit an overnight stay.

Essentials

GETTING THERE

BY TRAIN Eleven daily trains stop in Chumphon from Bangkok's Hua Lampong Railway Station. The second-class air-conditioned sleeper fare to Bangkok ranges from 620B and 1,200B. **Chumphon Railway Station** (© **07751-1103**) is on Krom Luang Chumphon Road, where there are oodles of restaurants and guesthouses. Book well in advance.

BY BUS The main Chumphon bus terminal is an inconvenient 16km (10 miles) north of the town center (a tuk-tuk will cost around 150B–200B) and isn't always staffed. While standard air-conditioned buses depart from Bangkok's **Southern Bus Terminal** (℃ **02422-4444**), the arduous trip lasts 8 to 9 hours and costs around 400B.

BY FERRY **Lomprayah** (www.lomprayah.com; ℃ **07755-8212**) and **Songserm** (www.songserm-expressboat.com; ℃ **07750-6205**) run daily express boat services connecting Chumphon with Ko Tao, Ko Pha Ngan, and Ko Samui (approximately a 2-hour trip). Of the two companies, Lomprayah has the better reputation. Expect to pay around 600B/adult and 300B/child.

BY CAR From Bangkok, use Highway 4 or Highway 35 (Thonburi-Pak Tho) and join Highway 4; continue past Phetchaburi, Prachuap Khiri Khan to Chumphon junction, and then turn left along Highway 4001 to reach town.

VISITOR INFORMATION

A **Tourism Authority of Thailand** office (www.tourismthailand.com; ℃ **07750-1831**) is at 111/11-12 Taweesinka Rd. and has free maps. The top English-speaking local tour operator, **New Infinity Travel** (infinity. chumphon@gmail.com; ℃ **07757-0176**), has an office at 68/2 Tha Taphao Rd., a 10-minute walk southeast of the train station.

GETTING AROUND

BY SONGTAEW *Songtaews*, or covered pickups, cruise the main roads and charge about 20B to 40B per trip.

BY MOTORCYCLE TAXI Look for the colored vests designating motorcycle taxi drivers, and bargain hard. Trips start from 20B.

BY TAXI Taxis stop behind the old market, opposite Chumphon Bus Terminal. Vehicles can be hired to Lang Suan, Ranong, and Surat Thani; inquire at your hotel for details. Trips average 50-100B depending on distance.

ORIENTATION

Chumphon's center is small enough to negotiate on foot: Krom Luang Chumphon Road, near the railway station, is the place for dining and accommodation options, and Tha Taphao Road houses a variety of tour operators.

FAST FACTS

Numerous **banks** sit on Sala Daeng Road, which runs parallel to Tha Taphao Road. The main **post office,** on Poramin Mankha Road, is out of the town center but hotels can usually mail a letter. For **police** call ℃ **07751-1300.**

Exploring Chumphon

Most guesthouses and tourist offices can arrange rafting trips and tours to local waterfalls in the nearby rainforest. The best beaches are **Sairi Beach,** for island excursions, and **Thung Wua Laen** beach, to the northeast of town, where kiteboarding is popular. These are nice places to spend the day if you're in town before heading to more tropical parts of Thailand. Diving over Chumphon's offshore pinnacles reveals pristine reefs and abundant marine life—including whale sharks (sightings most likely April, May, and June), turtles, and tropical fish.

The **Chumphon National Museum** (Office of Archeology, Sam Kaew Hill, Na Cha Ang subdistrict; © **07750-4105**; admission 100B) is open 9am to 4pm from Wednesday to Sunday, and covers historic events such as the Japanese invasion in 1941 and the devastation caused by Typhoon Gay in 1989.

Where to Stay
MODERATE

Tusita Wellness Resort ★★ This collection of red-tiled villas sits right on the unspoiled Arunothai beach, one attached to the other with wooden walkways. Thai exteriors shield interiors in a range of styles: Some are blandly contemporary, others are a bit wacky with splotches of primary colors "decoratively" placed on the walls, while still others have a Thai feel with lots of polished dark wood, art on the walls, and hand-woven colorful silk pillows and throws. Whatever style you get, know that the beds will be comfortable, the room will get an abundance of natural light, and these beach villas couldn't get closer to the sea if they tried. Service is excellent and the staff are expert at decoding ferry schedules for onward journeys. A big perk: the elegant onsite restaurant Murraya, serving Thai and international cuisine. The only downside to a stay here: It's a bit far from the heart of town.

259/9 Moo 1, Arunothai Beach. www.tusitawellness.com. © **07763-0920.** 22 units. From 2,000B double. **Amenities:** Restaurant; bar; outdoor pool; health club; spa; Wi-Fi (free).

INEXPENSIVE

Chumphon Cabana Resort & Diving Center ★ Located 30 minutes from town on the fabulously tranquil Thung Wua Laen Beach, this low-rise, family-friendly resort of staggered concrete rooms and bungalows (they're old and are showing wear and tear, but kept clean) has great views, a 30-m (98-ft.) pool, and, most important, an outstanding reputation for its ecological work. Part of the pull is the long list of activities and the organic rice and vegetable gardens. Produce from the latter gets served up in the superb seafood restaurant that's on-site. A regular shuttle bus runs guests to and from Chumphon.

69 Moo 8, Thung Wua Laen Beach. http://cabana.co.th. © **07756-0245.** 118 units. From 1,000B–1,500B double; **Amenities:** Restaurant; lounge; outdoor pool and children's pool; Wi-Fi (free).

Where to Eat & Drink

The best bites are at diners scattered around Tha Tapao and Krom Luang Chumphon roads, or the seafood eateries at the beach hotels. Try **Prikhorn** (32 Tha Taphoa Road), a popular and affordable Thai and seafood restaurant, or **Aeki's Bar,** on Soi Rot fai, which has an authentic island vibe and is very popular with visitors.

SURAT THANI

644km (400 miles) S of Bangkok

Surat Thani, or "Surat," was an important center of the Sumatra-based Srivi-jaya Empire during the 9th and 10th centuries. Today, it is a rich agricultural province yielding rubber and coconuts. Before the opening of the airport on Ko Samui, Surat was constantly busy with travelers heading for the island, but now there's little reason to go there unless you plan to take a ferry to the islands. It is mostly a busy transport hub and apart from the town's night market, its seedy massage parlors and pushy touts give it little appeal. From Surat, you can access ferries to **Ko Samui, Ko Pha Ngan,** and **Ko Tao.** It's not impossibly far to the jungles of **Khao Sok National Park,** or to go west from here to **Phuket, Krabi,** and the **Andaman coast.** Popular local produce includes the Surat oyster and the rambutan (*ngor* in Thai). *Note:* Visitors making their way to Ko Tao or Ko Pha Ngan should depart from Chumphon to save time. Come to Surat Thani if Ko Samui is the final destination.

Essentials

GETTING THERE

BY PLANE   Flights are always cheaper to Surat Thani than to Ko Samui but the trip to the island isn't easy, and it is time-consuming. However, if you do want to fly to Surat Thani from Bangkok, **Air Asia** (www.airasia.com; ℂ **02515-9999**) and **Nok Air** (www.nokair.com; ℂ **1318**) have daily flights (trip time: 70 min.). Expect to pay around 900B one-way. Air Asia offers flight and boat shuttle packages. The airport is 18km west from town, but buses connect passengers to town for around 100B.

BY TRAIN   Eleven trains leave daily from **Bangkok's Hua Lampong station** (www.railway.co.th; ℂ **1690**) to Surat Thani (trip time: 8½ hrs.). Second-class sleepers cost 848B, and second-class seats 578B. Surat Thani station is some 12km (7½ miles) away from the 'city' center in a nondescript town called Phun Phin.

   If you are connecting with the ferry, avoid the aggressive touts and look for representatives from the boat companies **Songserm** (ℂ **07728-9894**) or **Panthip** (ℂ **07727-2230**), who provide buses to meet trains. Otherwise, you can grab a shared minivan to town for around 80B, or a taxi for around 200B.

BY BUS   VIP 24-seater buses leave daily from **Bangkok's Southern Bus Terminal** (ℂ **02422-4444;** trip time: 12 hrs.; 843B). Air-conditioned buses leave daily from **Phuket's bus terminal** off Phang Nga Road, opposite the Royal Phuket City Hotel (ℂ **07621-1977;** trip time: 4 hrs.; 170B). The Surat Thani Bus Terminal is on Kaset II Road, a block east of the main road.

BY MINIVAN   Privately operated air-conditioned minivans offer affordable and regular services from Surat Thani to/from Chumphon, Ranong, Nakhon Si Thammarat, Had Yai, Phuket, and beyond. The best way to arrange these trips is via your hotel's front desk. Expect to pay between 200B and 500B.

BY CAR Take Highway 4 south from Bangkok to Chumphon, and then Highway 41 directly south to Surat Thani (trip time: 12 hrs.).

VISITOR INFORMATION

For information about Surat Thani, Ko Samui, and Ko Pha Ngan, contact the **TAT** office, 5 Talad Mai Rd., Surat Thani (www.tourismthailand.org; ✆ **07728-8818**), near the Wang Tai Hotel.

ORIENTATION

Surat Thani is built up along the south shore of the Tapi River. Talad Mai (meaning new market) Road, 2 blocks south of the river, is the city's main street. The TAT office is on this same road but to the far west of town, en route to the bus and train stations. Ferry piers are on Ban Don, Na Meuang; out of town to the east is the Tha Thong pier. (Depending on your arrival hour, you can get transfers directly to the piers from the bus and train stations without going through town.)

FAST FACTS

Major **banks, exchange kiosks,** and a branch of the **post office** lie along Na Meuang Road, close to Witeetad Road, in the center of town. The **Taksin Hospital** (no website; ✆ **07727-3239**) is at the north end of Talad Mai Road. The **tourist police** (✆ **07728-8818**) are on Talad Mai Road.

Exploring Surat Thani

Surat is a typical small Thai city, with few sites worth mentioning, though the Day and Night Markets are worth a look if you have time to kill. Those with some extra time may want to head to **Khao Sok** and the **Ratchaprapha Dam** surrounded by limestone mountains, or visit the small town of **Chaiya** and its Suan Mokkh monastery, a renowned Buddhist retreat with meditation study programs in English (see "Day Trips from Surat Thani," below). If you are in town at the end of Buddhist Lent (around mid-Oct), it's worth seeing the **Chak Phra festival,** where Buddhist images are towed up the river and boat races take place.

Where to Stay

For most, Surat Thani is just a stopping-off point for trips to the islands. If you have a layover, the best choice in town is the **Wang Tai Hotel** (1 Talad Mai Rd.; www.wangtaisurat.com; ✆ **07728-3020**). It is close to the TAT office with doubles from 800B and a swimming pool too.

Where to Eat

When in season, Surat Thani's famous oysters are on the menu at any streetside cafe; there is a small cluster of open-air eateries along Talad Mai (New Market). **Milano** on Bandon Road (www.facebook.com/surattaneecity; ✆ **084011-2709**) does a booming trade in pizza and pasta.

Day Trips from Surat Thani
KHAO SOK NATIONAL PARK ★★

One of the largest unspoiled areas of rainforest in the south, Khao Sok is known for its stunning scenery, caves, and exotic wildlife. The park is a convenient stop between Surat Thani and Phuket, and the main east–west road (Rte. 401) passes the park headquarters.

The park is some 646 sq. km (249 sq. miles) in area and is traced by jungle waterways; steep trails climb through underbrush, and thick vines hang from craggy limestone cliffs—imagine the jutting formations of Krabi, only inland. Rising some 1,000m (3,280 ft.), the dense jungle habitat is literally crawling with wildlife including the occasional wild elephant, but you may be hard-pressed to actually spot any. More commonly seen are gaur, Malaysian sun bears, gibbons, macaques, civets, and squirrels, along with more than 200 species of such birds as hornbills, woodpeckers, and kingfishers. The flora is equally varied. This is one of the rare places where you may come across the stinking "rotting flesh" odor that typifies the Rafflesia, the largest flower in the world. (The largest blooms are up to 1m/3¼ ft. wide.)

One of the best ways to see the varied fauna of the park is by kayak, along the nether reaches of a large reservoir, about an hour from Surat Thani on Route 415. At **Ratchaprapha Dam,** you can go boating, rafting, and fishing among the limestone cliffs that appear as islands, or stay in beautiful floating bungalows and explore this pristine jungle on foot. Local fisherman will take you out for the day for around 2,000B. **Tham Nam Thalu** and **Tham Si Ru** are the park's two most popular caves and both can be accessed from the southwest shore; the latter was a hideout for communists in the late 1970s.

Farther west, the **park area** (off Highway 401, at kilometer 109) has several resorts in the jungle off the 1½km-long (1-mile) entrance road, some with tree houses. From here, well-marked trails lead you through the park. The park office can provide camping equipment, and guides will offer their services and help plan your itinerary.

Caution: It's important to know that waterfalls and caves pose real risks during rainy season. Both Thai and foreign tourists have lost their lives when flash floods inundated caves in this very park. Chiang Rai made headlines in 2018 when a group of young soccer players and their coach were trapped for more than 2 weeks after flooding trapped them in a cave. Whether visiting the caverns and waterfalls, or considering a jungle hike or tubing down the River Sok, always book through a reputable travel agent so that help is at hand if you run into trouble.

Guesthouses abound near the park and owners can arrange guided tours for a fraction of the price of tour agencies in nearby cities like Phuket. **Art's Riverview Jungle Lodge** (www.artsriverviewlodge.com; ✆ **090167-6818**) has a jungle riverside setting and a swimming hole with pretty great views. Stilted wood-and-brick bungalows start at 1,200B a night.

For a real Thai jungle experience that's high-end "glamping," book a luxury tent at **Elephant Hills** (www.elephanthills.com; ✆ **07638-1703**). The resort offers several soft adventure tours; most popular is an all-inclusive jungle safari, which includes 1 night at the ethical elephant camp where you'll bathe, feed, and bond with rescued pachyderms (no riding). Guided hikes, canoe tours, and meals are included for 18,500B per person for 3 nights or 12,580B for 2 nights.

Contact the **Department of National Parks, Wildlife and Plant Conservation Office** (www.dnp.go.th; *⊘* **02561-0777**), or the TAT offices in Phuket Town (p. 184) or Surat Thani (p. 184), for maps and info. Alternatively, contact **Paddle Asia** in Phuket (www.paddleasia.com; *⊘* **07624-1519**), for details on their kayak adventure trips.

KO SAMUI ★★★

644km (400 miles) S of Bangkok to Surat Thani; 84km (52 miles) NE from Surat Thani to Ko Samui

The island of Ko Samui lies 84km (52 miles) off the east coast in the Gulf of Thailand, near the mainland town of Surat Thani. The island's history dates back to the 1850s when Chinese merchants from Hainan Island in the South China Sea put Ko Samui on the map. The island is said to have more coconut species than any other place in the world, and most of the young coconuts served in restaurants, or sold by roadside vendors around the country, have origins here. The harvesting of coconuts still takes place in the hills of the island's hinterland, but alas, many plantations have given way to wide-scale tourist development, which is now the island's main income. Still, coconut is the second-largest industry, and experts estimate there are 3 million coconut trees on the island with each one producing about 70 coconuts a year.

Once a hippie haven of pristine beaches, idyllic thatched bungalows, and eateries along dusty red-dirt roads, Samui is now packed with upscale resorts, beach bars with fire shows, and posh spa retreats. Despite a voracious tourist onslaught that sees up to 25 flights a day land at Samui International Airport, there are still quiet pockets. If you leave the main tourist hubs (Chaweng and Bophut), Samui still has a few idyllic sand beaches and simple villages, but it is certainly not the sleepy island it was 30—or even 5—years ago, and prices reflect this.

High season is from mid-December to mid-January, but January to April has the best weather—before it gets very hot—with the occasional tropical storm bringing relief; this is the peak of the season for most resorts. October through mid-December are the wettest months, with November bringing heavy rain and winds that make the east side of the island rough for swimming and render nearby islands and marine parks off-limits to boats. July and August see a brief increase in visitors, but during those months, the island's west side is often buffeted by summer monsoons from the mainland. When the sun is shining and the sky is clear, few places in Thailand are as beautiful as Ko Samui.

Ko Samui

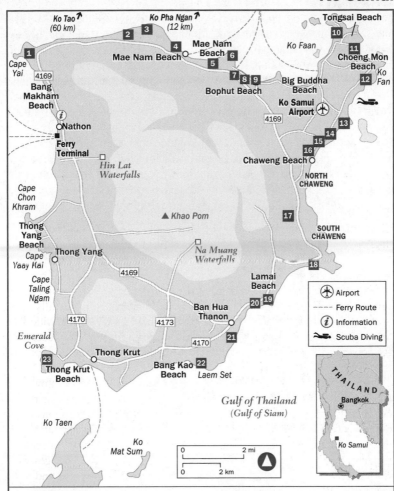

HOTELS

Amari Palm Reef Koh Samui **14**	The Library **16**
Anantara Bophut **9**	Mercure Samui Fenix **19**
Ark Bar Beach Resort **15**	Outrigger Koh Samui Beach Resort **12**
Belmond Napasai **2**	Peace Resort **7**
Bo Phut Resort & Spa **8**	Rocky's Boutique Resort **20**
Casa de Mar **13**	Santiburi Resort **4**
Coco Palm Resort **3**	Sensimar Resort and Spa **5**
Conrad Samui **23**	Six Senses Samui **10**
Four Seasons Resort **1**	Spa Resort **18**
Jungle Club **17**	Tongsai Bay **11**
Kamalaya Koh Samui **22**	W Retreat **6**
	X2 Koh Samui Resort **21**

Essentials

ARRIVING

BY PLANE   While **Thai Airways** (www.thaiairways.com; ☏ **02356-1111**) has a couple of flights each day from Bangkok to Samui, **Bangkok Airways** (www.bangkokair.com; ☏ **02270-6699**) has the lion's share of flights, with up to 25 flights a day in season. Bangkok Airways also has daily flights that connect domestically with Phuket, Pattaya, and Chiang Mai, and international flights to Hong Kong, Singapore, Kuala Lumpur, Chengdu, and Guangzhou. Flights from Bangkok take roughly an hour but cost an average of 4,000B one-way. During high season, book seats at least 2 months in advance.

Ko Samui Airport (www.samuiairportonline.com; ☏ **07724-5600**) is in the northeast corner of the island and boasts open-air pavilions with thatched roofs surrounded by gardens and palms. Most resorts can arrange an airport transfer when you book your room, but some add a hefty fee for this convenience; if it's over 1,000B, you'd be better off taking a cab (those average 500B).

BY FERRY   **Lomprayah** (www.lomprayah.com; ☏ **07742-7765**) links the islands by high-speed catamaran and runs some specialized trips, rates ranging from 400B (Na Thong) to 600B (Surat Thani). **Raja Ferry Port** (www.rajaferryport.com; ☏ **07747-1206**) offers a car and passenger service from Donsak to either Ko Samui (cost 130B per person, or 450B with a car) or Ko Pha Ngan (cost 210B per person, or 550B with a car).

You can buy ferry tickets at the port, although many operators sell a combo bus or train ticket with the ferry ride included from Bangkok or other points in Thailand. Not only does this work out a bit cheaper, but it also means you don't have to be troubled by touts along the way.

If you book ahead at a resort, most will arrange transport from the Samui ferry pier at Nathon to your hotel. Otherwise, *songtaews* (shared transportation run by locals) make the trip to most beaches on the east coast for as little as 70B, if they can get a packed truckload from the boat landing. Songtaews make stops along the way as required, so you can jump on or off. There are also private taxis at the pier; expect to pay around 500B from Nathon pier to Chaweng.

ORIENTATION

Though Ko Samui is Thailand's third-largest island, with a total area of 247 sq. km (95 sq. miles), its entire coastline can be toured by car or motorcycle in about 3½ hours, though if you stop to look at the sights, it can take a full day. The island's main road (Hwy 4169), also called the "ring road," circles hilly, densely forested terrain. The ferries and express boats arrive on the west coast, in or near Nathon.

Samui's best beaches are on the north and east coasts. The long, sandy east coast is home to Chaweng and Lamai beaches, both frenetic in high season. It's here you'll find the heaviest concentration of hotels and bungalows. The south coast has a few little hideaways, and the west coast boasts a handful of sandy strips, but few amenities.

Nathon is where the ferries dock on the west coast, and being the island's main town and community, this is where you'll find banks, the TAT office, and the post office.

The Beaches

Clockwise from Nathon, **Mae Nam Beach,** on Samui's north shore, is 12km (7½ miles) from the ferry pier, facing nearby Ko Pha Ngan. Coarse, golden sand covers the long beach, and palm trees provide shade, making this one of the best beaches on the island. Its peaceful calm bay has water deep enough for swimming; it is often spared the fierce winds that whip up during the stormy months. Although bigger, upmarket resorts have moved in here, there are still some affordable resorts and a number of simple, charming bungalows. Ban Mae Nam, a small commercial hub, is just east of the Santiburi Resort and has a variety of restaurants and shops.

Bophut Beach, the next village along the north coast, is one of the island's fastest-developing areas. Bophut's long coarse-sand beach narrows considerably in the monsoon season, but the water is calm year-round and it's a good spot for swimming. Turning off at "Big Buddha," there's a sign marking the entrance to **Fisherman's Village,** a pleasant street where you'll find restaurants, bars, and guesthouses among a beachside clutch of houses and shops. It's definitely worth a wander, especially when it comes alive on Friday evening (5–11pm) as a car-free walking street.

Big Buddha Beach (Bangrak) is just east of Bophut and has a fairly clean, coarse-sand beach and a calm bay for swimmers (shallow in the low season, May–Oct). Many small restaurants, businesses, shops, and an increasing number of new resorts create a busier pace than is evident at other, more removed beaches. Much of the beach looks out over Ko Faan, the island home of Ko Samui's huge seated Buddha. Haad Rin Queen Ferry leaves from Big Buddha pier, taking Full Moon partygoers to Had Rin on Ko Pha Ngan four times a day. Speedboats also leave from a nearby pier, departing hourly during **Full Moon Party** time (see "Ko Pha Ngan," later in this chapter).

Ko Samui's northeastern tip features the beautiful headland of **Choeng Mon,** with stunning views all around from west to east; this is home to some of the island's most exclusive resorts. Bold rock formations jut from crystal clear waters. Private coves and protected swimming areas abound—though from mid-October to mid-December monsoons can stir up the wind and waves, creating a steep drop-off from the coarse-sand beach, and a strong undertow. **Tongsai Bay** is a beautiful cove dominated by the **Tongsai Bay resort** (p. 196); its privacy is a plus or a minus, depending on what you are looking for.

Southeast of Tongsai, as the road descends from the headland down toward Chaweng, is the fine sandy stretch called **Choeng Mon Beach,** a gracefully shaped crescent about 1km (⅔ mile) long, and lined with shady palm trees (and an increasing number of shops). Swimming here is excellent, with few rocks near the central shore, although the water level can become very low from May to October (low season). Across the way is **Ko Fan Noi,** a deserted island with an excellent beach. You can swim or, if the tides are right, walk there—but be careful of the rocks at low tide. *Note:* Ko Fan and Ko Fan Noi are not the same. Ko Fan is off the northeastern tip of the island and has a famous Buddha image covered in moss.

Although Chaweng is the busiest destination on Ko Samui, if you don't mind the hustle and bustle, it can be great fun. The two Chaweng beaches (**Chaweng Yai** to the north and south is **Chaweng Noi**) are the longest on the island, but, in the north, an offshore reef limits the water to wading depth only—an advantage if you have young children. The swimming is better to the south (though a bit shallow near the shore in low season).

The long sandy beach of **Lamai Bay,** in the southeast, is comparable to Chaweng with clear water that is perfect for swimming. Although many top-range resorts have moved in, there are a few budget options offering bungalows at the north end of the beach. The town area is less developed but does have a wide range of services, cafes, and restaurants, although nightlife tends to center on the small bars on the main street. Samui's waterfalls lie inland of Lamai, toward Ban Thurian at Na Muang.

Laem Set Bay is a small rocky cape on Samui's southeast coast, with dramatic scenery and a few isolated resorts.

On the west coast, you'll find one of Samui's better beaches at Ao Phang Kha (Emerald Cove), south of **Ban Taling Ngam,** on Route 4170. Generally, the west coast beaches are the most isolated on the island, offering few facilities and rocky waters, making the beaches barely swimmable. Many Thai families stop for picnics at **Hin Lat Falls,** a rather uninteresting inland site 2km (1¼ miles) southeast of Nathon.

VISITOR INFORMATION

The **TAT Information Center** is at 370 Thawi Ratchaphakti Rd. just north of the main ferry terminal in Nathon (www.tourismthailand.org; ✆ **07742-0504**). Siam Map Company (www.siammap.com) prints free booklets on the island's hotels, spas, restaurants, and more. They're widely distributed at hotels and the airport, and the *Samui Guide Map* is a terrific resource for tourists.

GETTING AROUND

BY SONGTAEW OR TAXI Pickup trucks (*songtaews,* p. 166) are the cheapest way to get around the island and advertise their destinations with colorful signs. They follow Route 4169, the "ring road," around the island. Hail one anywhere along the highway and beach roads. Most stop after sundown, after which they make a loop of Chaweng. Daytime fares are fixed at around 40B to 60B, but after dark they charge like taxis; night owls face steep fares (500B and up). Taxis are not metered and tend to ask extortionate rates; get hotel staff to help you negotiate a reasonable fare. If you plan to do much exploring on Ko Samui, consider renting a car, with or without a driver.

BY RENTAL CAR Renting a car is far safer than a motorcycle, though be prepared to employ defensive driving skills; you may be required to deal with obstacles such as motorcycles coming at you in your lane or stray dogs meandering across the road. Still, Samui is one of the few destinations in Thailand where having a rental car is a real plus (take just a few taxi rides and you'll have spent far more than you would have on a rental). **Budget Car Rental** (www.budget.com; ☏ **07796-1502**), **Avis** (www.avis.com; ☏ **084700-8161**) and **Hertz** (www.hertz.com; ☏ **07742-5011**) have offices at the airport. All offer a range of vehicles, starting as low as 1,200B, and do pick up and delivery.

Local rental companies and travel agents have good deals for car rentals, starting as low as 900B per day. But don't expect comprehensive insurance coverage; and read all the fine print, particularly how much you must pay in case of an accident.

BY MOTORCYCLE   The roads on Samui are narrow, and filled with novice riders (usually gung-ho foreigners). Road accidents injure or kill an inordinate number of tourists and locals each year, mostly motorcycle riders, but two wheels and a motor is still the most popular way to get around the island. If you must rent a motorcycle, despite this warning, know that a 500B fine is imposed on anyone not wearing a helmet, so keep it on despite the temptation to feel the wind in your hair. Technically, you should have an international license, but small operators rarely ask to see it; they prefer to keep your passport in case of problems. Travel agencies and small operators rent motorcycles, and most resorts can make arrangements. A 100cc Honda scooter goes for around 150B per day, while a 250cc chopper or trail bike starts at around 500B. *Travel tip:* A drive along the coastal road is beautiful, but the interior of the island has steep roads and isn't nearly as scenic.

FAST FACTS

All the major **banks** now have branches in every town, with their main branches in Nathon along the waterfront Thawi Ratchaphakdi Road. You'll find numerous ATMs across every part of the island. There are post offices in Chaweng, Mae Nam, and Lamai—all on the main Samui ring road. The **main post office** is on Chonwithi Road in Nathon, but you probably won't hike all the way back to the main pier just for posting. Most resorts will mail letters for guests; it's possible to purchase stamps in small shops in beach areas.

There are private hospitals and 24-hour rescue and evacuation services if required. **Bangkok Hospital Samui** (www.bangkokhospitalsamui.com; ☏ **07742-9500**) and **Samui International Hospital** (www.sih.co.th; ☏ **07723-0781-2**) provide top-class medical care. **Bandon International Hospital** (www.bandonhospitalsamui.com; ☏ **07724-5236**) is another international facility, with English-speaking physicians who make house calls. All are around Chaweng. The public hospital is **Ko Samui Hospital** (www.samuihospital.com; ☏ **07791-3200**) is near Nathon Beach on the northwest side of the island.

For emergencies, dial ☏ **1155** for the **Tourist Police.**

Exploring Ko Samui

Busy Samui has a host of entertainments apart from the usual beach outings. Have a look at the end of this section, for more outdoor activities.

Samui has several significant temples and Buddhist sites to visit. **Wat Phra Yai** is home to Samui's primary landmark, the **Big Buddha ★★,** more than 12m (39 ft.) tall and the most important temple for the local islanders. Your first glimpse of the temple will be from the airplane window, but further inspection is required. Temples in Thailand are shoe-free so arrive early before the sun heats the concrete to avoid burning the bottoms of your feet climbing the stairs to the top. Bring socks if you go in the mid-day sun. The temple is on **Ko Faan,** a small islet connected to the shore on the northeast coast by a causeway, with tourist shops, ice cream vendors (we like Leonardo's; www.facebook.com/leonardoicecreambigbuddha) and restaurants at the base. Admission is free, but donations are accepted, and the temple is open from dawn to dusk.

Wat Plai Laem is the most picturesque (and newest) temple on the island and features a striking statue of the 18 arm Guanyin, a Chinese goddess of mercy and compassion. A 5-minute drive from the Big Buddha, it's free and open from dawn to dusk.

Two temples in Samui hold bodies of **mummified monks,** which some may find ghoulishly interesting. The most popular is **Wat Khunaram,** along the main road (Rte. 4169) as it shoots inland far south of Lamai. Here the **mummified body** of monk Loung Pordaeng is in the same meditation position, or *mudra*, as when he died while meditating in 1973.

Four engraved imprints of the **Lord Buddha's Footprint** are held in a shrine near the turnoff to the **Butterfly Farm** off the 4170 Road near Laem Din. At the southernmost end of Lamai Beach lie Ko Samui's two famous rocks, **Hin Ta** and **Hin Yai ★,** Grandfather and Grandmother Rock, respectively. They have always caused a bunch of giggles because of their likeness to male and female genitalia (you can guess which is which), and are strong fertility symbols.

Just across Route 4169 from Wat Khunaram is the dirt track leading up to the **Na Muang Falls ★,** to which there is a lower and higher level. The lower reveals a large bathing pool (be careful of sharp rocks), though the upper is more photogenic. You can walk the steamy 5-km (3-mile) trek from the coast road to the upper falls (sometimes called Na Muang Falls 2), but you'll pass through the abysmal Na Muang Safari Park where uneducated tourists pay for elephant rides and to cuddle drugged tigers and leopard cubs.

Where to Stay on Ko Samui

Thirty years ago there were but a few makeshift beachside bungalows along the nearly deserted coast of Samui. Today, luxury resorts stand shoulder to shoulder with upscale beach bungalows, all vying for bookings. The five-star resorts really go all out to impress, with many offering complimentary snorkel trips, branded speedboats, private infinity pools, and personal butlers. So if there was ever a place to splurge in Thailand for a posh resort, Ko Samui is it. But be warned: Ko Samui is one of the more expensive destinations in Thailand, from pricey flights out of Bangkok to unmetered cabs, bills can add up quickly before you even factor in accommodations.

Those traveling with a group of four or more will find the best value in renting one of the island's many villas. **Airbnb** (www.airbnb.com) and **HomeAway** (www.homeaway.com) villas tend to be in the center of Ko Samui with sweeping views of the island and the beach. A search for properties during high season showed four-bedroom villas for around 5,000B per night, and a bit more to rent a home with a pool. That's a big savings, considering double rooms in a hotel will cost between 5,000B to 10,000B, on average.

For more detailed information on each resort locale, check out "The Beaches," on p. 189. The listings below follow a clockwise order around the island, beginning in the northwest corner.

LAEM YAI
Expensive

Four Seasons Resort ★★★ Located on a rocky hillside on the northwest of the island, this is the place to go if you want a luxurious, pampering, and relaxing break. American Bill Bensley designed most of the hotel's newest features, including a sea-facing *Muay Thai* ring and a rum vault with a private tasting room hidden behind an old prison door. All villas and suites enjoy expansive views out to sea, and guests have a choice of swimming at the hotel's private beach, in the communal pool, or in the private infinity pool attached to each villa. Rooms are furnished in sumptuous style with deep soaking tubs, heavenly beds, and cool blues and grays. Golf carts are on hand to run guests up and down the steep hill, and service is both personal and extremely efficient. Guests who want to do a bit of good can participate in the hotel's coral rehabilitation project.

219 Moo 5, Angthong. www.fourseasons.com/kohsamui. © **07724-3000**. 74 units. From 34,000B 1-bedroom pool villa. **Amenities:** 3 restaurants; 2 bars; outdoor pool; tennis court; health club; kids' club; babysitting; spa; room service; Wi-Fi (free).

MAE NAM BAY
Expensive

Belmond Napasai ★★★ This prize resort nestles on a rocky headland leading to the white-sand Baan Tai beach at the western end of Mae Nam. Rooms are in rustic-themed teak cottages with high ceilings, and come with private pools, sumptuous decor, and large bathtubs. The largest is a four-bedroom, oceanfront pool residence that offers total privacy, yet easy access to the resort's services. These include superb spa facilities and excellent in-house dining choices. The only downside to a stay here is the hotel's isolation, though many guests feel little need to leave the premises.

65/10 Baan Tai, Maenam. www.belmond.com. © **07742-9200**. 69 units. 8,900B–12,700B sea-view villa; 10,000B–35,000B 2- to 4-bed villas. **Amenities:** 2 restaurants; bar; outdoor pool; kids' pool; supervised kids' activities; tennis courts; health club; spa; babysitting; room service; Wi-Fi (free).

Santiburi Resort ★★ Just a few steps east of the Napasai, the Santiburi was the first high-end property in the area but has remained fresh and current thanks to several makeovers. The latest renovation added 19 sprawling pool villas surrounded by private gardens. State-of-the-art amenities, like the well-appointed spa, are discreetly infused into the contemporary Thai architecture. The resort's top villas front the beach, while the others are set among lush greenery around a central pool and spa. Each bungalow comes with a large sunken tub. Guests can take advantage of windsurfing and sailing (free), and there is a sailing junk to tour surrounding islands (it's also used for supper cruises). Santiburi also hosts the island's top golf course, **Santiburi Golf,** near the resort.

Santiburi has a slightly more affordable companion in nearby Bophut, called the **Bophut Resort and Spa** (www.bophutresort.com; ✆ **07724-5777)**, at a similar high standard, with 61 luxury seaside villas. The hotel is a member of Small Luxury Hotels, and rates start at 5,500B.

12/12 Moo 1, Tambol Mae Nam. www.santiburi.com. ✆ **07742-5031.** 96 units. 8,800B–12,800B suites and villas; from 13,000B plunge-pool villas. **Amenities:** 2 restaurants; 2 bars; lounge; outdoor pool; golf course (nearby, connected by free shuttle); tennis courts; health club; spa; room service; babysitting; Wi-Fi (free).

W Retreat ★★★ Perched on the peninsula that separates Mae Nam and Bophut beaches on Samui's north coast, this resort sets a benchmark for sleek, design and a contemporary philosophy that is summed up in their "Whatever, whenever" policy to fulfill their guests' every wish. The W factor is in all the facilities–the fitness room is SWEAT, the pool is WET, the bar is the WOOBAR, and the spa is AWAY. The design of the pool villas is hip and modern, with light-wood paneled walls, cool, clean lines and bright red throw rugs and lampshades. Even the minibar menu contains innovative snacks, and the two dining options, The Kitchen Table and Namu, the signature Japanese restaurant, promise exciting culinary adventures.

4/1 Moo 1, Tambon Mae Nam. www.whotels.com/kohsamui. ✆ **07791-5999.** 75 units. 27,000B–157,000B pool villas. **Amenities:** 2 restaurants; 3 bars; outdoor pool; health club; spa; Wi-Fi (free).

Moderate
Coco Palm Resort ★ Well-appointed bungalows bring together bamboo and rattan decorative elements to create a laid-back, casual beach vibe that extends throughout the property. The décor is minimalist and perhaps a little plain, which allows the lush gardens and ocean views from the palm tree-lined pool to shine. The staff are friendly and helpful and are clued-in on good operators for snorkeling trips and boat excursions, and the hotel's shuttle makes getting around the island a breeze. It's a great place for those who want to spend the day island-hopping, exploring the beaches around the island, and enjoying the perks of a pristine beach steps from the room.

26/4 Mae Nam Beach. www.cocopalmbeachresort.com. ✆ **07744-7211.** 91 units. From 2,900B double; from 6,700B pool villas. **Amenities:** Restaurant; bar; outdoor pool; kids' pool; room service; Wi-Fi (free).

Sensimar Resort and Spa ★★ This minimalist-chic resort is adults-only and adheres to an uncluttered design scheme and muted color palette of neutrals, whites, and grays. It feels a little bit like Copenhagen at the beach. In addition to a prime location on a strand that's perfect for swimming, the resort offers heaps of free activities, like kayaking, cooking lessons, cocktail making classes with the resort's mixologist, yoga by the beach, fruit tastings, and guided island tours. When you consider that neighboring properties go for 30,000B a night, Sensimar's service, perks, price-point, and location add up to a great deal.

44/134 Moo 1 Mae Nam Beach. www.sensimarsamui.com. ⓒ **07795-3035.** 125 units. 4,000B—5,200B double. Guests must be 16-years or older. **Amenities:** Restaurant; 2 bars; room service; outdoor pool; fitness center; Wi-Fi (free).

BOPHUT BEACH
Expensive
Outrigger Koh Samui Beach Resort ★★ The biggest benefit of staying at this swish resort is that the beach is nestled between two outcroppings of rocks, essentially making it private. Just offshore is a coral reef teeming with 32 species of tropical fish and 13 types of colorful coral. Tucked away near the Big Buddha temple, the resort features 52 guest rooms all with private pools. Furnishings are very stylish, all made of light wood and with breezy and spacious "open concept" layouts. The excellent spa offers competitively priced treatments. There are cooking courses available at 2,000B per person, and daily activities such as temple tours, Muay Thai lessons and beach yoga; some of these are free, others carry a small charge. There are fab sunset views from the pool, restaurant, and beach, and a shuttle runs guests to Chaweng or Fisherman's Village for shopping or dining.

63/182 Moo 5, Bophut. www.outrigger.com. ⓒ **07791-4700.** 52 units. 6,500B–9,500B villa. **Amenities:** 2 restaurants; bar; outdoor pool; health club; spa; Wi-Fi (free).

Moderate
Anantara Bophut ★★★ This has to be one of Samui's most atmospheric resorts, starting from its grand entrance and high-ceilinged lobby. Generous-sized rooms emphasize classy Thai style décor that make use of exquisite local textiles; each has a private balcony with loungers overlooking the garden or beach. Some of the most attractive features of the resort are the free-form infinity pool with views of nearby Ko Phang Ngan, and the Italian restaurant that enjoys lovely views across to the bay. Anantara provides yoga sessions, Thai cooking classes, wine appreciation instruction, fruit carving lessons, kids' activities, and superb spa therapies. Service is on a par with what you'd find at costlier resorts, though it's not as formal. Anantra is also just a short walk from Fisherman's Village where there are plenty of shops, bars, and restaurants.

99/9 Moo 1, Bophut. www.samui.anantara.com. ⓒ **07742-8300.** 106 units. 4,300B double; 8,000B suite. **Amenities:** 2 restaurants; bar; outdoor pool; tennis court; health club; spa; watersports rental; room service; Wi-Fi (free).

Bo Phut Resort & Spa ★★ Romantic and secluded on one of the island's more upscale beaches, this hotel is popular with honeymooners and others looking for an intimate experience. Rooms are elegantly decorated in classic Thai style with dark wood accents, four-poster bed frames, and silk pillows. Bathrooms have deep-soaking tubs big enough for two and rain showerheads, and some rooms have outdoor Jacuzzis and private pools. The spa has treatment rooms designed to share; free water sports, like kayaking and windsurfing, complete the stay. The hotel is a member of Small Luxury Hotels of the World and service is up to those standards.

12/12 Tambol, Bophut. www.bophutresort.com. ℂ **07724-5777.** 61 units. 5,300B double; 10,000B suite. **Amenities:** Restaurant; bar; outdoor pool; health club; spa; room service; Wi-Fi (free).

Peace Resort ★ Living up to its name, this family-run resort offers eight types of free-standing bungalows set in lush, serene gardens, the largest being a whopping 230 sq. m (2,475 sq. ft.). All villas come with terraces (many with pools) and feature sunny interiors with blue-and-white indigo prints and modern furnishings that have a beachy, rustic quality. Great for families, the large central pool has a separate kids' pool and a playground, with daybeds on the beach and loungers around the pool for relaxation.

178 Moo 1, Bophut. www.peaceresort.com. ℂ **07742-5357.** 122 units. 3,000B–11,000B doubles and villas. **Amenities:** Restaurant; bar; outdoor pool w/kids' pool; spa; children's club; room service; babysitting; Wi-Fi (free)

LAEM SAMRONG
Expensive
Six Senses Samui ★★★ Set on a gently sloping headland among 9 hectares (20 acres) of lush vegetation, this award-winning resort is an ideal honeymoon spot. The hotel effortlessly combines sophisticated ambiance, top-of-the-line amenities, and an environmentally conscious attitude. Facilities include private pools beside most villas and suites, a spa with a comprehensive range of treatments in both indoor and outdoor treatment rooms, and activities such as yoga, island tours, diving trips, and cooking classes. All the villas are equipped with every imaginable comfort and are attended by personal butlers, while the views of nearby islands are simply fabulous. The resort is in Laem Samrong, on the northeastern tip of Samui (just around the promontory that shelters Tongsai Bay). It's home to the fab Dining on the Rocks (p. 202), which has one of the best wine lists outside of Bangkok.

9/10 Moo 5, Baan Plai Laem (northeast tip of island). www.sixsenses.com. ℂ **07724-5678.** 66 units. 11,200B–27,000B villas. **Amenities:** 2 restaurants; 2 bars; room service; babysitting; outdoor pools; health club; spa; Wi-Fi (free).

TONGSAI BAY
Expensive
Tongsai Bay ★★ Built into a lush, tropical hillside that leads to its own beach, this all-suite complex has sweeping views of Tongsai Bay. Each room is designed to maximize a connection to nature, and rooms include large terraces and open-air bathtubs. Even the smallest of the villas is sprawling and at the upper tier multi-room villas host up to 10 people (which appeals to families). There is a beautiful half-moon-shaped pool set in the gardens halfway down, and a large, free-form pool at the beach with a separate children's pool. With only 15 rooms and a large plot of sand, even a full resort will feel like a slice of heaven and never too crowded. The end result is casual outdoors ambiance.

84 Moo 5, Ban Plailaem (northeast tip of island). www.tongsaibay.co.th. ℂ **07724-5480.** 83 units. From 7,300B beachfront or cottage suite; from 10,000B beachfront

suite. **Amenities:** 2 restaurants; 2 bars; 2 outdoor pools; tennis court; health club; spa; room service; Wi-Fi (free).

CHAWENG & CHAWENG NOI BAYS
Expensive
The Library ★★   Black, white, and red all over. This upscale beach resort is famous for its red swimming pool contrasting with the chic white hotel surrounding it. Rooms here are divided into studios and suites (known as pages and chapters), and in keeping with the hotel's name, the resort's main feature is a library with an array of books and films. State-of-the-art digs (with Jacuzzis and rain showers) provide an extraordinary range of luxuries, from huge plasma TVs and iMac computers to light boxes and self-controlled colored lighting. Beds sit atop huge platform structures with carefully curated Buddhist touches. It's cool, it's original, and it appeals to those with a leaning toward techno-Zen.

14/1 Moo 2, Bophut. www.thelibrarysamui.com. ✆ **07742-2767.** 46 units. From 9,000B double; 12,000B suites. **Amenities:** Restaurant; bar; pool; health club; Wi-Fi (free).

Moderate
Amari Palm Reef Koh Samui ★★   This fine-looking hotel has a split personality that combines to create a relaxed beach resort. Near the beach, there are sea-facing suite rooms that merge slick-contemporary with traditional decor. The other half of the hotel is a block of midrange units in a "Thai village" location across the road from the beach and with a separate pool. The central beachside pool area is appealing, as is the dining terrace overlooking it. The resort is far enough from Chaweng strip to be quiet and comfortable (but close enough to party), and their tour desk can fix you up with a motorbike and point you to the best lookout spots on the island. The place is often busy, yet the staff handle everything effortlessly and efficiently, making it a pleasure to stay.

14/3 Chaweng Beach, Ko Samui 84320 (north end of the main strip). www.amari.com/koh-samui. ✆ **07730-0306.** 197 units. 4,000B superior; 8,000 deluxe; 15,000B suite. **Amenities:** 2 restaurants; 2 outdoor pools; health club; spa; Jacuzzi; children's club; babysitting; Wi-Fi (free).

Ark Bar Beach Resort ★★   While certainly not for everyone, Ark Bar is the best choice for party people. Its two-story hotel rooms are squeezed into a narrow strip of gardens leading to the beach right in the heart of Chaweng, but they're all equipped with air-con, minibar, and balconies within walking distance of the famous beach club party. In fact, it's so popular that two further branches have now opened nearby. The restaurant, serving Western and Thai cuisine as well as fresh seafood, is popular, with both indoor and beachside seating. As the sun goes down, Ark Bar becomes one of the main focal areas on Chaweng beach to gather at nighttime. From 2pm until 2am, bikini-clad tourists, frat boy types, and locals join in the fun, when some of the island's best funk and house music DJs perform.

159/75 Moo 2, Chaweng Beach. www.ark-bar.com. ✆ **07796-1333.** 186 units. 2,800B–3,400B double; 4,000B junior suite. **Amenities:** Restaurant; bar; outdoor pool; Wi-Fi (free).

Casa de Mar ★ You won't feel like you're in Thailand at this swish resort: The décor has more of a New York City or Stockholm vibe, with large blond wood planks on the walls, bare hanging Edison bulbs for lighting (in the restaurant), and a color scheme that doesn't stray far from white, gray, and black. It's all highly chic if a bit too "international" for our tastes. That being said the beachfront villas, some with private pools, have fantastic ocean views from the four-poster beds (and are well priced compared with other area hotels). Serving Thai and Western choices, the restaurant overlooks the pool and ocean; in the bar area there are plush beanbag chairs, ideal for taking in the sunset with a cocktail. North of giddy Chaweng, Casa de Mar is close enough to walk to its bars and restaurants.

154/16-17 Moo 2, Chaweng Beach. www.casademarsamui.com. ℂ **07796-9480.** 61 units. From 2,800B double; 3,500B–10,300B villas. **Amenities:** Restaurant; bar; outdoor pool; fitness center; Wi-Fi (free).

Inexpensive

Jungle Club ★ Set high on a hill behind Chaweng Noi Beach, this attractive resort offers something for all budgets, from very basic jungle huts with just a fan, mattress, and mosquito net, to a sturdier jungle bungalow, a spacious jungle house, and luxurious lodges and villas. The setting is truly idyllic, but it is so isolated (only 4WD vehicles and motorbikes can get up the hill), that you'll need to take a shuttle down to the beach or town (free at scheduled times; a taxi is 400B). The views from the bungalows and rooms are sweeping, taking in the lush island interior, white-sand beaches, and nearby islands. Even if you're not going to bed down, Jungle Club runs a popular restaurant by the same name that attracts many visitors to enjoy the view, the romantic, candle-lit setting and the range of Thai and French dishes.

Chaweng Noi Beach, Soi Panyadee (call for pickup). www.jungleclubsamui.com. ℂ **08189–42327.** 18 units. 800B–1,500B jungle hut; 3,000B–3,800B lodge/villa. **Amenities:** Restaurant; outdoor pool; Wi-Fi (free).

LAMAI BAY

Expensive

Kamalaya Koh Samui ★★ Located on the island's quiet southern coast, Kamalaya feels like a (much-needed) escape from reality. Technically, this is a wellness sanctuary, and it's a title they take seriously—there's even is an ancient cave on property that was once used by Thai monks for meditation. Each guest starts their stay with a consultation that addresses their physical, mental, and spiritual well-being and the hotel's team of massage therapists, acupuncturists, life coaches, yoga teachers, and holistic doctors take it from there. Treatments can be booked *a la carte,* but there are outstanding set programs designed to treat exhaustion and health concerns like improving fitness and getting better sleep. There are also detox and yoga retreats with top international teachers. A dozen room categories cater to most budgets and range from suites with balconies to villas with splendid outdoor bathrooms and private pools. While the hotel doesn't specifically limit the guest list to those 18 years and older, this isn't a place for families.

102/9 Moo 3, Laem Set Rd. www.kamalaya.com. © **07742-9800.** 75 units. From 5,900B double; from 12,000B villa; 29,600B penthouse pool suite. A 3-night detox program from 56,500B **Amenities:** Restaurant; 2 outdoor pools; health club; spa; Jacuzzi; room service; Wi-Fi (free).

Rocky's Boutique Resort ★★
Rocky's pushes the boundaries of luxury with two beautiful pools and individually designed one- to four-bedroom villas, which cascade down a rocky hillside to a private sandy beach. Wade out from the beach and find a coral reef that is home to colorful fish and the occasional sea turtle. Just 5 minutes south of Lamai, it's easily accessible—but a hard slog up steep hills for villa residents, though the reward for that cardio is enviable views. Rooms are bright and cheerful and have a sweet Thai touches, like bamboo plants and northern-style décor reminiscent of the Lanna period. The hotel's longtail boat can whisk you to the Marine Park or secluded beaches (for a price). The Dining Room serves delicious French-Mediterranean dishes that make use of the abundance of local seafood.

438/1 Moo 1, Lamai. www.rockyresort.com. © **0773-3288.** 34 units. 4,800B double; 6,200B suite. **Amenities:** Restaurant; bar; 2 pools; room service; babysitting; Wi-Fi (free).

X2 Koh Samui Resort ★★
Pronounced "cross to" this contemporary hotel is known for minimalist décor, polished concrete, and pops of the color. The villas are shrouded in privacy with high walls surrounding each unit—many of which have private pools. For a small fee (often just 1,000B), guests can choose to upgrade to an unlimited spa package and enjoy as many treatments as time allows, including Thai massages, facials, manicures, and more. Emerge from a spa stupor and enjoy the deepest swimming pool on the island, or enjoy Thai fusion dishes at 4K (pronounced "fork").

442 Moo 1, Hua Thanon Beach. www.x2resorts.com. © **07733-2789.** 26 units. 4,250B garden villa (5,700B with unlimited spa treatments); 6,900B pool villa (8,180B with unlimited spa treatments); 12,400B pool villa suite (13,500B with unlimited spa treatments). **Amenities:** Restaurant; bar; outdoor pool; health club; spa; Jacuzzi; room service; Wi-Fi (free).

Inexpensive
Mercure Samui Fenix ★
If you don't need direct beach access and you'd like to save a bit of baht, the Mercure Fenix offers a good alternative to the pricey options that dominate the island. The resort is a 5-minute ride from the restaurants and bars of Lamai, accessible by shuttle. Rooms are not huge, but they're chicly designed and all have the essentials—modern furnishings, satellite TV, work desk, and safety boxes. There's an average-sized pool, exercise room, and smart restaurant, and it's located right next to one of Samui's best-known sights—the "Grandfather and Grandmother Rocks." (p. 192). The beach is a short walk from the hotel, and there you'll find over-sized lounge sofas.

26/1 Moo 3, Lamai. www.mercure.com. © **07742-4008.** 85 units. From 1,700B double; 2,940B suite. **Amenities:** Restaurant; bar; outdoor pool; exercise room; Wi-Fi (free).

Spa Resort ★★ This family-operated wellness retreat has been around for years and is known for its cleansing programs, hypnotherapy, Reiki, Chinese cupping, vegetarian/raw food, and yoga and meditation courses. This hotel is an example of a spa-centric holiday that doesn't have to break the bank. There are two resorts on Samui: The original **Samui Beach Resort,** comprising a laid-back cluster of rustic A-frame bungalows and a pool just north of Lamai, and **Samui Village,** a hillside retreat studded with rock formations (it was undergoing renovation when we visited). Rooms at both locations range from simple bungalows to large private suites with large balconies. Spa Village has a pool, herbal steam bath in a large stone grotto, massage, body wraps, and facial treatments—and is open to day visitors. Due to the price and great word-of-mouth reviews, rooms tend to fill up quickly.

Samui Beach: 171/2 Moo 4, Lamai Beach. www.thesparesorts.com. ⓒ **07723-0855.** 34 units. 700B–1,200B double; **Amenities:** Restaurant; outdoor pool; spa; sauna; Wi-Fi (free).

WEST COAST

Expensive

Conrad Samui ★★★ As soon as you reach the arrivals desk of the resort in the extreme southwest corner of the island, you know you're somewhere special. The sweeping views out to sea and the relaxed and assured manner of the staff are just the beginning of a truly unforgettable experience. The supermodern one- and two-bedroom pool villas have huge TVs, stylish marble bathrooms with over-sized free-standing bathtubs, and the sunset views across the infinity pool, looking over a cluster of islands toward the mainland, are to die for. Jahn (p. 204), their signature fine dining restaurant, is out-of-this-world-good. The beach in front of the resort is not great for swimming as there are some rocks in the bay, but few will worry about this as all villas have their own pool. Enjoy gratis snorkeling trips to nearby islands or stake a claim to your own "island" on a floating hammock in the sea—a butler will even bring drinks. As with most ultra-luxe resorts on the island, the Conrad is built into a cliff, and golf carts whisk guests from the room to restaurants and back again.

49/8-9 Moo 4, Hillcrest Rd., Tambon Taling Ngam. http://conradhotels1.hilton.com. ⓒ **07791-5888.** 66 units. From 15,000B pool villas. **Amenities:** 3 restaurants; 2 bars; outdoor pool; health club; kids' club; spa; children's club; Wi-Fi (free).

Where to Eat on Ko Samui

Since most people wile away their days on Samui lounging by the pool, on a boat, or enjoying a pampering day at the spa, there's plenty of time to make the day's most important decision—where to dine. There are so many options out there that you could spend months eating somewhere different every day and still not exhaust Samui's culinary possibilities. Here is a robust list to whet your palate, but to ponder a wider range of dining venues, pick up a free copy of *Eating on Samui* or log on to www.samuirestaurantguide.com. Restaurants on the island come and go at a breakneck pace, so there is always something new to discover.

It comes as no surprise that **seafood** is the number one choice for visitors to Samui, and you'll find simple shacks on every beach serving up fresh fish, shrimp, and squid in a huge variety of preparations. We also recommend such casual local seafood restaurants as **Jun Hom** (✆ **07760-2008**) on Bangpor beach, just west of Mae Nam beach, and **Sabeingle** (✆ **07723-3082**), which is perched above the south end of Lamai beach.

In the same way that Thai food in the northern provinces, like Chiang Mai (p. 311), tastes different than in Bangkok (and absolutely different than it does at home), you'll find a unique flavor to Southern Thai food. Indian influences are found in the use of cardamom and cloves, while a Malaysian population turns out cracking biryanis (*khao mok*) and a famous Muslim curry, known as *massaman.* Outside of the island's hotels, where everything is cooked with mild spices, Thai dishes in the south tend to be the hottest in the entire country. If you're particularly spice-adverse, stick to curries that use the island's coconuts, and remember the essential phrase: *mai phet (not spicy)!*

MAE NAM BEACH

The Farmer ★ THAI/INTERNATIONAL   It may not be on the beach, but there's a wonderful ambiance at this classy joint located in the middle of rice paddies, where you can sit on the terrace soaking up the view or more comfortably in the air-conditioned interior. Take your pick from classic Thai dishes such as *yam hua plee* (a spicy banana-flower salad), the famous duck, or international favorites like grilled sirloin steak and marinated rack of lamb. The menu is rounded out with a wide choice of cocktails and a healthy selection of wines. A definite plus is that service, which can often be sloppy (read inattentive) on Samui, is spot-on here. The restaurant also has well-regarded cooking school and hosts rice-planting lessons.

1/26 Moo 4, Ban Tai, Mae Nam. ✆ **07744-7222.** www.thefarmerrestaurantsamui.com. Main courses 300B–1,500B. Daily 11:30am–10:30pm.

BOPHUT & FISHERMAN'S VILLAGE

Take the time to wander through the Fisherman's Village area, located more or less in the middle of Bophut beach. The houses that once belong to the island's fisherman have been transformed into foodie havens, and there are several atmospheric pubs and small upmarket restaurants along the water's edge.

You can savor good seafood at the perennially popular and antique-laden **Krua Bophut** (www.kruabophut.com; ✆ **07743-0030**), toward the western end of the village. It serves delicious fried snapper and squid, and features traditional musicians some evenings. **Café 69** ★ (www.facebook.com/cafe69kohsamui; ✆ **081978-1945**) serves Thai fusion in a relaxed café; their green curry pie is legendary. **Café de Pier x Samui** ★ (www.facebook.com/cafedepier; ✆ **07743-0680**) does a booming trade in artisan cocktails and French-Thai dishes in a hip, industrial space. And if you missed the hotel breakfast or want something different, **Bar Baguette** ★★ (www.barbaguette-samui.com; ✆ **094804-1221**) has healthy smoothies, eggs with smoked salmon, pancakes, and delicious lunch options. The food is Instagram-worthy, and there is a second location on Chaweng Road, but this is the original.

Along the main drag with tables on the beach, it is impossible to miss the ice-packed crates of fresh-caught fish and employees begging for your attention. Price don't fluctuate shop-to-shop, so pick one that has an appealing atmosphere and get ready to feast. Grilled prawns with spicy dipping sauce or garlic-fried sea bass never disappoint.

Chez Francois ★★ FRENCH   Chef Francois Porte makes the most out of whatever is fresh that day from the island's produce markets and fisherman. No *a la carte* menus are offered. Instead diners choose between a four- or five-course set menu which often includes Norwegian salmon, sea bass, quality cuts of lamb, duck breast, and more, all complemented by local vegetables. Chez Francois only has a few tables, and they always book up in advance, so make reservations ahead of time. From each table, guests can peek into the open kitchen and watch Francois work his culinary magic.

33/2 Moo 1, Fisherman's Village. www.facebook.com/chezporte. ℭ **07743-0681.** Reservations required. Set menus 1,700B–1,950B. Tues–Sun 6pm–11pm.

Dining on the Rocks ★★★ FUSION   This is Ko Samui's most memorable dining experience. The ten-tiered verandas at the Six Senses Resort give each table privacy, with 270-degree ocean views that are incredible at sunset. The menu focuses on sustainability, creativity, and organic products. While *a la carte* menus are available, the set menus allow the culinary team to really shine. These change seasonally, but the prawn and sea bass ceviche, tooth fish with white bean puree, and pork belly with homemade pear-juniper jam are breathtakingly good and usually available. There is an entire set menu devoted to vegan delights. The sommelier offers wine pairings built from the walk-in cellar's collection of rare old and new world bottles.

9/10 Moo 5, Baan Plai Laem (northeast tip of island). www.sixsenses.com. ℭ **07724-5678.** Reservations required. Set menus from 2,800B (vegan); 3,400B per person to 13,000B for two. Daily 5–10pm.

H Bistro ★★ MEDITERRANEAN/THAI   The signature restaurant at Hansar Samui, H Bistro is located right next to the beach with a breezy terrace and cozy interior. The menu is a mix of elevated Thai classics, like stir-fried soft shell crab with yellow curry sauce, and European dishes (white truffle risotto, perhaps). The menu has a heavy focus on seafood, and the most tempting options include a tower of imported oysters, a duo of lobsters from Phuket and Maine, and a lovely pomelo (it's like Thai grapefruit) salad with grilled prawns. There are enough choices to please a group, but diners won't be overwhelmed with a tome-like menu.

Hansar Samui, 101/28 Moo 1, Bophut. www.hansarsamui.com/hbistro. ℭ **07724-5511.** Main courses 250B–1,650B. Daily 11:30am–5:30pm and 6:30–11pm.

Peppina ★★ ITALIAN   After much praise from picky Bangkokians, Peppina has expanded into a mini empire around Thailand, and it's all thanks to their Neapolitan pizzas. Their Ko Samui location is in partnership with the island's best-known bar, CoCo Tam's (p. 207), making this a one-two punch for those looking for quality dining and nightlife. The open-air restaurant is casual but cool with Edison light bulbs and bamboo ceilings. Neapolitan pizzas come with a host of classic toppings, from Parma ham to artichokes, and there are fresh salads with nuts and cheese, and a variety of grilled cuts of meat. Craft beer and wines from Thai vineyards make this an easy place to linger.

62/1 Moo 1 Bophut Beach. ℂ **07724-5511.** www.peppinabkk.com. Main courses 260B–1,250B. Daily 1pm–1am.

CHAWENG

Chaweng has tons of eateries, with everything from fast food to the finest dining. Increasingly, larger resorts in the area are setting up freestanding restaurants for both in-house and outside guests.

Poppies (www.poppiessamui.com; ℂ **07742-2419**), on South Chaweng, is famous for its beachside dining, Balinese fare, and romantic atmosphere, and brings in guest chefs from around the world; reservations are necessary. Look out also for **Red Snapper** (www.redsnappersamui.com; ℂ **07730-0200**), which serves up not only great Mediterranean fusion food but also live jazz nightly. If you've enjoyed the pastries at your hotel's breakfast, they most likely came from **Clyde Café** (www.clydecafe.com; ℂ **07760-1402**). In their shop, they have outstanding coffee and sandwiches on fresh-baked bread.

The **Laem Din Market** (Soi Reggae) is where many restaurants stock up on produce and meat, and it's a fun place to wander and grab some fruit or pre-made packets of spices to make curries at home. When the sun goes down, hawkers sell fried-chicken and noodles at the night market.

In addition to the places reviewed below, it's worth dropping by for lunch or a sundowner at **Dr Frog's** (www.drfrogssamui.com; ℂ **07741-3797**), which sits on the hill between Chaweng and Lamai. It's a popular spot with a big marketing budget (you'll see signs everywhere around the island) known for basic Thai grub and well-made Western food, like pasta, grilled meats, and seafood, but the real attraction is spectacular views over the bay.

The Larder ★★★ INTERNATIONAL   Run by Martin Selby, a Brit with an impressive culinary resume, The Larder is one of Ko Samui's top restaurants for those looking for a break from Thai dishes. Ingredient sourcing is paramount, and the menu focuses on boat- and farm-to-table specialties. Truthfully, everything is good but the gastro-pub fare is the best. Enjoy sea bass fish and chips, Scotch eggs, and crab cakes with poached quail eggs. There is a robust wine list and the cocktails here are outstanding and innovative. The Old Fashioned Swine uses house-infused bacon bourbon, maple syrup and orange bitters; the Winter Garden blends gin, elderflower, sake and fresh cut herbs.

9/114 Moo 2, Bophut. www.facebook.com/thelardersamui. ℂ **07760-1259.** Reservations recommended. Main courses from 400B–1,100B. Daily 2–10pm.

LAMAI

Radiance ★★ INTERNATIONAL   Inside the Spa Resort (p. 200), this restaurant is ideal for those trying to eat more healthfully: Dishes are made almost entirely from organic fare and tend to be veggie-forward (this is a terrific place for vegans, with many options for them, along with fish and meat dishes). Open from breakfast time, it serves up super smoothies, fresh guacamole, an amazing variety of tofu dishes (the tofu burgers are huge), and delicious curries—along with excellent Thai food.

Rte. 4169, at the north end of Lamai beach. www.thesparesorts.net. ℂ **07723-0855.** Main courses 70B–280B. Daily 7am–10pm.

WEST COAST

Big John's Seafood ★ SEAFOOD   The clientele here are a mix of raucous revelers and Thai families out to graze, and most come in the early evening for the spectacular sunset views. Order the day's catch as you like, and accompany it with a delicate Thai curry or stir-fry. Big John's overlooks a pretty stretch of palm-lined beach and has live entertainment nightly.

The Lipa Lovely Resort, 95/4 Moo 2, Lipa Noi Beach. www.thelipa.com. ℂ **07748-5775.** Seafood priced by kilo and other mains from 150B—400B. Daily 8am–10pm.

Jahn ★★★ THAI/INTERNATIONAL   Unless you're lucky enough to be staying at the Conrad Samui, getting to this restaurant is quite an adventure as it's in a remote southwest corner of the island. We'd say the flair and imagination of the chef make the trek worth it. As do the items on the set menus, like wagyu beef with massaman curry sauce (a culinary masterpiece), and the *tom yum goon,* the famous Thai soup, which arrives deconstructed with the hot broth in a glass teapot. Just as famous as the food and outstanding wine pairing are the superb sunset views—get an early evening reservation.

Conrad Samui, 49/8–9 Moo 4, Hillcrest Rd. ℂ **07791-5888.** http://conradhotels1.hilton.com. Reservations required. Set menus from 3,300B; main courses 950B–1,800B. Daily 3–11pm.

Exploring Ko Samui
SCUBA & SNORKELING

Serious dive fans will want to head to Ko Tao (p. 217). Not only is the marine wildlife more robust, but prices are more affordable (boats need less gas to reach top dive sites). However, if Samui is home base, there are certainly great dives and snorkeling excursions here, as well as PADI schools for beginners. Many shops trips offer trips ranging far afield to some of the 80 or so islands scattered across this archipelago. The **Ang Thong Marine National Park** ★★ has 40-something islands and makes a great destination from Samui, for either diving or a day's sightseeing. *Note:* There is a **hyperbaric chamber** near the Big Buddha; call ℂ 07742-7427 for info.

As for which scuba/snorkeling shop on island to use: The team at **100 Degrees East** (www.100degreeseast.com; ℂ 07742-3936) are total pros, with snorkeling or diving trips around Samui and beyond. **The Life Aquatic** (www.thelifeaquatic.asia; ℂ 086030-0286) is another top choice, offering guided dive trips (from 4,600B; two dives, hotel transfer, lunch, gear) and snorkel trips (from 2,700B; hotel transfer, lunch, gear). Safety records for both are impeccable, and both offer all sorts of PADI courses and daily dive tours. We almost must praise their nice boats, good equipment, and complete insurance packages. A 3-day open water certification costs around 15,000B.

Some of the better **snorkeling** off Ko Samui is along the rocky coast between Chaweng Noi and Lamai bays. Several shops along Chaweng Beach rent snorkeling gear for about 200B per day.

GOLF

Samui boasts the picturesque hilltop Santiburi Golf Course, part of the **Santiburi Samui Country Club** (12/15 Moo 4, Baan Dansai; www.santiburigolf samui.com; ✆ **07742-1700**). It sits high in the hills on the north end of the island and regularly hosts the PGA Asian Tour. Greens fees start from 5,600B for 18 holes (2,825B for 9 holes).

KAYAKING

Blue Stars Sea Kayaking at 83/23 Moo 2, Chaweng Lake Road (www.blue stars.info; ✆ **07741-3231**) takes people kayaking and snorkeling to the Ang Thong Marine National Park at 2,500B for adults, 1,600B for children. The rubber kayaks are perfect for exploring the caverns tucked underneath limestone cliffs.

CRUISING, SAILING & KITEBOARDING

Red Baron (www.redbaron-samui.com), which operates from Bangrak, offers sunset dinner cruises on a **Chinese junk boat** with billowing red sails. The sunsets are outstanding, but the food is only satisfactory. It also offers brunch cruises, and trips to Ang Thong Marine Park. Tours start at 2,500B.

For **speedboat, catamaran** or **yacht sailing,** check out **Oceana Samui Charters** (www.oceanasamui.com; ✆ **083503-5088**). Private charters start at 12,000B, and there are half-day package tours that are also private. To rent from other shops and private owners, look at **GetMyBoat.com**.

There's now a growing number of **kiteboarders** descending on Samui in the peak season (Nov–Mar and April–Oct). Book group lessons (1-day 4,000B; 3-day 11,000B) or private sessions (8,000B) with the pros at **Kiteboarding Asia** (www.kiteboardingasia.com; ✆ **083643-1627**).

Cultural Activities

COOKING COURSES

Almost every hotel from luxury to mid-range will offer on-site cooking classes, but we recommend escaping the resort grounds for one of the daily Thai cooking and fruit-carving lessons at **Samui Institute of Thai Culinary Arts** (**SITCA;** www.sitca.com; ✆ **07741-3172**). It's a highly professional operation with friendly, knowledgeable teachers. And a class here is a great way to meet other visitors—especially if your beach plans get rained out. Classes meet daily at 11am and 4pm and cost 1,850B.

Island Organics Thai Cooking Class (www.islandorganicssamui.com; ✆ **089731-6814**) sources almost all the ingredients needed for class from their organic garden where more than 70 types of herbs, fruits, and vegetables grow. Students not only cook, they pick Thai eggplants for green curry, chilies for spice, and fruits like rose apple for dessert. The open-air kitchen has individual cooking stations for hands-on learning and the affable husband and wife duo that run the class keep things personal and informative. Learn to make four dishes for 2,200B. Classes available Monday, Tuesday, Thursday, and Friday.

SPA, SPORTS & WELLNESS

Like many places in Thailand, the spa scene has really taken off on Samui. All the big, international five-star resorts, such as **Four Seasons** (p. 193), offer top-range (and top-priced) treatments by well-trained staff. But there are also some reasonably priced spas too, including a number of good day spas for those wanting a serious and dedicated wellness retreat that won't leave them financially destitute. Whether as an escape from the kids on a rainy day or as part of a larger health-focused mission, Samui has all the services you'll need.

Ban Sabai, on Big Buddha Beach (www.ban-sabai.com; ℭ **07724-5175**), has a wide range of therapies that take place in one of two Thai teak houses or in a beachside *sala*. Personal attention is the hallmark of this little Garden of Eden. Two houses are available for booking as part of a package or simply as a relaxing accommodation. A blissful 2 hours of treatments start around 2,600B.

The highly respected day spa **Tamarind Springs** ★★ (www.tamarind springs.com; ℭ **07723-0571**) is set on a palm-clad hillside just above the beach at Lamai and is a rare place that truly takes you back to nature. Lounge in the natural herbal steam room sandwiched between huge, smooth boulders before slipping into the outdoor plunge pool or enjoying a Thai massage. Make sure you book in advance.

Absolute Sanctuary (www.absolutesanctuary.com; ℭ **07760-1190**) couples detox programs and nutrition consultations with spa treatments, yoga, and Pilates. The programs take place at the retreat's Moroccan-inspired compound on the beach. A 3-day signature detox package starts at 44,900B.

Traditional massage is available at any number of storefronts in Chaweng and along the beach. Expect to pay between 200B and 400B per hour; it's much the same as the average spa, but without the pomp, ceremony, or incense.

The best place to learn the "art of eight limbs" is **Lamai Muay Thai Camp** (www.lamaimuaythaicamp.com; ℭ **087082-6970**). Training sessions start at 300B, but longer lessons and accommodation are available, too. The World Muaythai Council manages the camp and trains everyone from newbies to pros.

Shopping

There is very little in terms of local craft production on the island—almost everything is imported from the mainland—so save the big purchases for Bangkok or Chiang Mai. The Fisherman's Market is the place to go for souvenirs, like T-shirts, bowls made from coconut shells, and inflatable unicorns for lounging in the pool.

Ko Samui Entertainment & Nightlife

Several times a day the Chaweng strip is disrupted by roaming pickup trucks with crackling PA systems blaring out advertisements in Thai and English for local **Thai boxing bouts.** The fights are a fun local activity. If you're interested in seeing a match, grab a flyer for times and locations—they vary day-to-day. Hotels will have information on the fight schedule, too.

Paris Follies Cabaret (search Paris Follies Cabaret on Facebook; ✆ 087030-8280) is a rollicking cabaret with 1-hour *kathoey* shows featuring cross-dressers and transgender performers. Nightly shows are 8pm, 9pm, 10pm, and 11pm. Admission is technically free, but you're required to buy a drink, which is around 300B.

When it comes to cocktails, Ko Samui's five-star resorts (listed earlier in this chapter) all have outstanding bars—especially the Four Seasons (p. 193) and the W Hotel (p. 207). Hotel bars offer stunning views and have bartenders who really know their stuff. However, the prices typically match the million dollar views. For an affordable tipple, try the following watering holes.

In party-centric Chaweng, there is something for everyone. **Bees Knees Brewpub** (www.samuibrew.pub; ✆ 085537-2498) is best for suds enthusiasts with five homemade beers on tap, like the easy-drinking wheaty bee and a stoutlike black bee (they're more flavorful than local lagers, like Chang). The brewery is behind a glass wall in the bar. **Ark Bar** (www.ark-bar.com; ✆ 07796-1333) is home to a loud but fun all-day, all-night (well, 1am) beach club where DJs play house music, and fire shows and glow sticks light up the night. **Magic Alambic Distillery ★★** (www.facebook.com/rumdistillery; ✆ 091816-7416) produces agricole-style rums distilled from fermented sugarcane. Part of the experience here is the 5-minute distillery tour, which includes a video on the distilling process before guests do a tasting at the open-air bar. Their coconut rum is a best seller and uses fresh coconuts from the island. The French owners serve up a nice selection of French and Thai dishes, making this a fun mid-day stop for lunch and a cheeky drink. **Legends** (www.fb.com/Legends-187991928019590; ✆ 081747-0937) proudly proclaims "no techno, no Spice Girls, no boy bands" and plays mostly classic rock and blues. It's a bit of a hole-in-the-wall, but it's a good place for cheap beer and people watching.

Lava Lounge in Lamai (✆ 080886-5053) has 79B drinks at happy hour from 4 to 9pm, and it's a nice cocktail bar with a laidback island vibe. In Bo Phut, **Woobar ★★★** (www.wkohsamui.com; ✆ 07791-5999) at the swish W Hotel is a must-go place for sunset: The drinks are strong, and the music is upbeat house music, a welcome reprieve from the island's bad cover bands doing Maroon 5 and John Denver. The island's best-known bar is **CoCo Tam's ★★★** (www.facebook.com/CoCoTams; ✆ 091915-5664) in Fisherman's Village. It is the epitome of beach bar with swings replacing barstools, beanbags on the sands, shisha pipes with fruit-flavored tobacco, strong rum cocktails, and fun music. Fire dancers perform on the beach nightly, and the show is one of the best on the island.

On the secluded west coast of the island, **Nikki Beach ★** (www.nikkibeach.com/kohsamui; ✆ 07791-4500) hosts fabulous parties and brings in a string of top-rated international DJs to keep the jet-setting crowd dancing all night. Nearby, **Air Bar** (www.samui.intercontinental.com; ✆ 07742-9100) drips with romance. Enjoy breathtaking views and crafted cocktails made with local fruits, like a lychee martini. There is a two-for-one happy hour from 7 to 8pm and sushi and Thai tapas for light bites.

Side Trips from Ko Samui
ANG THONG NATIONAL MARINE PARK ★★

Ang Thong National Marine Park comprises over 40 islands northwest of Samui and is well known for its scenic beauty and coral reefs. Many of these islands are limestone rock towers of up to 40m (131 ft.), fringed by beaches and tropical rainforest. February, March, and April are the best months for visiting the park; heavy monsoon rains in November and December often close the park.

Ko Wua Talab (Sleeping Cow Island) is the largest of the 40 and is home to the **National Park Headquarters,** where there is some very basic four- to eight-person accommodation (book through the park headquarters www.dnp. go.th; ✆ **07728-6025**), but most just visit for the day. The island has freshwater springs and a park-run restaurant. *Note:* Pack a pair of sturdy walking shoes for the steep hills; flip-flops won't be able to take the gradient.

Ko Mae Ko (Mother Island) is known for both its beach and Talay Noi, an **inland saltwater lake** with a hidden outlet to the sea. Boats crowd the area because this spot was the inspiration behind the famous Leonardo DiCaprio film *The Beach.* Known to the Thais as **Ang Thong,** or "Golden Bowl," this turquoise-green lagoon gave its name to the entire archipelago. Endless companies offer day trips by speedboat. Some include snorkeling and kayaking trips with a range of prices; **Blue Stars** (www.bluestars.info; ✆ **07741-3231**), in Chaweng, is a good operator to try.

KO TAN ★★ & KO MAT SUM★

Just a 15-minute boat ride from the shores of Ko Samui, Ko Tan, and Ko Mat Sum feel worlds away. The islands have pristine white-sand beaches, and the human traffic is minimal, so you'll feel like the mayor of your own private island. Fishmongers slowly buzz by on rickety boats, and a few speedboats pop in and out during the day—but the rest of the time is blissful solitude. Schools of colorful fish live just off shores of Ko Tan so plan to bring a mask (or rent one in Samui from a number of dive and snorkel shops) or just enjoy the island views and swimming in the crystal-clear water. On Ko Tan, guests can enjoy a leisurely walk along an elevated wooden platform through the island's mangrove forest. Ko Mat Sum is much smaller than Ko Tan but has a swell castaway vibe. A few enterprising locals rent beach chairs and sell bags of chips and ice-cold beers. If you think you'll want to stay a full day, you might want to ask your hotel to prepare a picnic lunch, otherwise, there are a few beach huts that sell basic Thai dishes, like fried rice, coconut curries, and—if the fisherman have stopped by that day—grilled prawns or steamed sea bass.

To get to Ko Tan or Ko Mat Sum, hire a longtail boat from the Thong Krut Pier on the south coast of Ko Samui. Most drivers charge between 1,500B and 2,000B for a half-day trip (around 4 or 5 hours). Make sure you've agreed upon terms before getting on the boat. The driver will drop you near the shore and come back at the assigned time (but its smart to get his phone number). Ko Mat Sum is about a kilometer east of Ko Tan, so ask the boat to take you there. One more thing: Like many islands and places in Thailand, Ko Tan has

> ## Watch out for the Jellies!
>
> Nothing will spoil a fun day at the beach faster than a jellyfish sting, and swimmers need to be extra cautious in the waters around Ko Tao, Ko Pha Ngan, and Ko Samui. The venomous box jellyfish that float in the waters, especially after heavy rains and during monsoon season, have a potentially lethal sting that can immobilize humans. Most beaches post warnings when box jellyfish are likely to be in the water, and many keep vinegar jugs nearby; if you're stung, liberally apply the vinegar to the affected area. Rash guards can help protect the skin from stings. Seek medical attention if symptoms are ongoing. If you don't see a sign, check with a nearby dive shop or follow the crowds; carefree locals swimming in the water is a good sign that you have the all clear.

several names. Ko Tan is the most common name, but some call it Ko Tean, and the island is listed as Tean Island on Google Maps.

KO PHA NGAN ★

644km (400 miles) S of Bangkok to Surat Thani; 75km (47 miles) NE from Surat Thani to Ko Pha Ngan

While Ko Pha Ngan lost its innocence years ago to the Full Moon partygoers (see below), the island still remains a more pastoral alternative to busy Ko Samui. When the moon is waning and waxing, the island, just like a chameleon, changes back to a laid-back, tropical paradise where almost 90% of the island is covered in tropical forest. Just off the shores are top-rated diving and snorkeling sites.

Easily visible from Ko Samui but about two-thirds its size, with similar terrain and flora, Ko Pha Ngan boasts beautiful beaches and some secluded upscale resorts on the farther reaches of the island—the rugged north and west coast areas are accessible only by bumpy road, or chartered boat. The southeastern peninsula of **Had Rin** (also written Haad Rin) is home to the now-infamous monthly **Full Moon Party,** a night-long beach rave that attracts thousands of revelers who pack the island to groove to every kind of dance music—and guzzle buckets of alcohol. If that's your idea of a vacation, but you can't make it for Full Moon, there are also smaller Half Moon parties—check out http://fullmoonparty-thailand.com for dates. These events are not like the hippy, trippy, love fests of the '70s, but blatantly commercial gigs geared to squeeze as much cash out of revved-up partygoers as possible. At Full Moon, even the basic bungalows go for double (or more) the normal rates. As a result, **Leela Beach,** on the northern spur, now pulls more backpackers than the noisier beach at Had Rin Nok (known as Sunrise Beach).

A word of warning: Party time is also a petty thief's paradise. Do yourself a favor and lock all your valuables in the hotel safe before you party—as experienced thieves take the opportunity to rob hotel rooms while you're having fun.

Boats from Ko Samui leave at regular intervals all day and night on full moon nights from either Big Buddha Beach or Bophut (running from 5pm; returning

SOUTHERN PENINSULA: THE EAST COAST & ISLANDS | Ko Pha Ngan

Just Say "Mai!"

When it comes to doing drugs in Thailand, remember that "mai" means "no." Thai authorities issue harsh penalties to anyone dealing, in possession of, or using drugs. Numerous undercover drug busts are staged, not just at Full Moon parties, but at bungalow hotels, and at pre- and post-party roadblocks. Many of these stings are setups that you'll never be able to disprove. Dealers and police often work in cahoots, and the lackadaisical Thai legal system offers you no protection or parole. Even scarier, recent reports have highlighted not just the selling of dodgy pharmaceuticals but the lethal herbal hallucinogen *ton lamphong*, a poisonous weed. Every month, local hospitals repeatedly find themselves treating tourists suffering severe psychological damage after taking recreational drugs or hallucinogens—they are the lucky ones; for some partygoers, the drug is fatal.

between 3 and 8am). Many revelers just make a night of it, crash on the beach, and come back to Samui in the morning. At other times, the small area of Had Rin is busy with young travelers. You'll find New Age crystal, trinket, and T-shirt shops, vegetarian restaurants, masseurs, cheap beer, and bungalows just a frisbee's throw away from perfect white-sand beaches. Be careful of the riptides here in monsoon months, and pay attention to the attendant lifeguards.

Don't be too put off by Ko Pha Ngan's party reputation. Had Rin can be avoided altogether and, even during the full moon, you can find peace and quiet in any of a number of tranquil hideaways on the island, such as **Thong Nai Pan,** to the north, and **Had Salad** or **Had Yao,** to the west. **Ko Ma** is a small island connected to Ko Pha Ngan by a sandbar on **Had Mae Had** beach. It's a paradise surrounded by an amazingly colorful, living reef—making it an ideal location for snorkeling or learning to dive.

The weather is the same as Ko Samui, but April, May, and June are typically the quietest party months.

Essentials
ARRIVING

Frequent boats link the mainland towns of Chumphon or Surat Thani with the islands of Ko Samui, Ko Pha Ngan, or Ko Tao. From Samui's Nathon Pier, the trip to Thong Sala, in Ko Pha Ngan, takes 45 minutes with the **Songserm Express Boat** and costs 200B (www.songserm.com; ℓ **07742-0157**). The **Seatran** ferry service (ℓ **07723-8129**) is three times daily, takes 30 minutes, and is 300B.

The fastest way to Ko Pha Ngan from Samui is by the twice-daily **Lomprayah** (www.lomprayah.com; on Samui, ℓ **07742-7765;** on Ko Pha Ngan, ℓ **07723-8412**), which leaves from **Wat Na Phra Larn** on Maenam Beach. The crossing takes about 20 minutes and costs 300B. Lomprayah also makes daily connections on to Ko Tao (500B–600B; 1 hour) and back to the mainland at Chumphon. The **Haad Rin Queen** also runs a service four times daily (double that number the day after a Full Moon party) from Big Buddha beach directly to Had Rin Pier that takes 50 minutes for 200B. Boats can also be chartered from **Petcharat Marina** at Samui's Big Buddha Beach (© **07742-5262**) or Bophut Beach (expect inflated during Full Moon parties). Beware of bad weather and rough waves between November and December, as freak storms have canceled boat trips and put lives at risk.

At press time, the construction of a small airstrip on Ko Pha Ngan had stopped over legal disputes that the project was causing irreparable damage to the island's protected national parks. So there is no way, currently, to get to the island by air.

FAST FACTS

The **tourist police** operate a small information kiosk on the north end of the ferry offices at Thong Sala pier; contact **1155** in an emergency. There are bank branches with **ATMs** both along the main street of Thong Sala and in Had Rin. For more information about the island, visit www.phangan.info; the website is a bit simple, but the information is current. On www.phanganist.com you'll find listings of current events and Full Moon party schedules.

GETTING AROUND

Motorbike rental on Ko Pha Ngan is available at most tour companies and resorts across the island (basic jeeps run from 1,000B; regular motorbikes run from 200B per day). However, the island roads aren't as easy to navigate as they are in other parts of Thailand. Many interior roads, including the one to secluded Thong Nai Pan in the north, are hilly, muddy tracks, requiring off-road skills. (It's not just the state of the roads, but also the inexperienced riders on the road, that are problematic.) Exercise caution, wear a helmet because it will keep you safe, and because it's the law (officials are starting to enforce that law). Souped-up **scooters** are rented out for about 300B per day, but if you're inexperienced in off-road biking, it's much safer to stick to *songtaews* (communal pickups), which follow the main routes and cost from 50B to 100B, more at night or during party season. Avoid renting bikes during Full Moon party days.

Exploring Ko Pha Ngan

The rugged roads of Ko Pha Ngan beg to be explored, and interior routes connect bays and small towns across unspoiled countryside—a window into a laid-back island lifestyle that's now slowly disappearing.

For a nice, active excursion, considering visiting the multi-tier **Phaeng Waterfall,** the grandest of the island's waterfalls in the center of the island. There is a steep 250-meter pathway to reach the waterfall. To avoid disappointment, remember the falls are mostly dry out of season, but they're fantastic after rainy season. Spend another 15-minutes on the Phaeng-Domsila Nature Trail to reach the **Domsila Viewpoint ★,** with postcard-worthy views. Turn around or continue another 2½ hours on the trail's jungle loop that passes by two other waterfalls. Sneakers and plenty of water are required.

The island has nearly two dozen small *wats* (temples), but none of them are must-sees. However, if you do choose to check out a few, remember to dress modestly and keep shoulders and knees covered. Temples are open during daylight hours.

Wat Khao Tham is a well-known international meditation center and temple compound just north of Ban Tai; see www.kowthamcenter.org for info. Theravada Buddhism-based meditation retreats run in 10 to 20-day courses, and prices start at 5,000B. As with any retreat, rules governing behavior apply, such as "No talking, reading, writing, or body sign language with others"; if this sounds a bit tough, best give it a miss. The temple is also open for day visitors and overlooks one of the most impressive views on the island.

The diving capital of Thailand is Ko Tao (p. 217), so serious divers should head there—it is nearby. However, Ko Pha Ngan offers plenty of outfitters, and the marine life population is healthy—especially near Sail Rock, where lucky visitors will see whale sharks. Ko Ma is a small island just off the northwestern tip that is connected to Ko Pha Ngan via a sandbar. This tiny island is the top spot for snorkelers to dip their mask.

In recent years, free diving (diving without an oxygen tank) has boomed on the island. If you'd like to try, **Apnea Koh Pha Ngan** (www.apneakohpha ngan.com; ☏ 092380-1494) are the pros you want to as your teachers. One-day courses are 4,000B, and 2-day sessions run 7,000B; stick around long enough and become a master for 30,000B.

The team at **Chaloklum Diving** ★★ (www.chaloklum-diving.com; ☏ 07737-4025) are a jack of all trades operator, and this is where to go for PADI dives, ranging from beginning to advanced (from 2,700B for two dives), free-diving, night diving, and snorkeling trips (from 1,000B).

Where to Stay

Visitors to Pha Ngan basically fall into two groups—those coming for the Full Moon Party and those trying to avoid it. Those in the former group inevitably look for somewhere around Had Rin, where the party takes place, and those in the latter group look for somewhere as far from Had Rin as possible. Note that at the time of the Full Moon Party, prices quoted below tend to increase by 20% to a whopping 200%, and many places have a minimum 3- to 5-night stay during this period.

BAN KHAI AND BAN TAI BEACHES

Many visitors head east from Thong Sala to nearby Ban Tai Beach—here they find a quiet stretch of sand away from the hubbub of Had Rin but close enough to visit the party zone and readily accessible by communal taxi (*songtaew*). The water, unfortunately, is often too shallow for proper swimming, but the fine-sand beach is wide, and most resorts now have pools set on the beachfront. The beaches here aren't the prettiest, but accommodations tend to be affordable compared to more desired spots on the island.

Coco Garden ★★   If falling asleep to the sound of waves is appealing, pick this beachfront collection of wooden bungalows. It is one of the best budget accommodations on the island, and it offers a choice of fan and air-conditioned individual bungalows with balconies, hammocks, and lots of character. You won't find cheaper prices, which begin at 450B. Kudos, too, to the kindly staff, and the excellent cooks at the restaurant (the food is so appealing, and so varied, that some guests never dine elsewhere). The hotel's beach bar is a super-popular spot for idling away an afternoon or evening and mingling with fellow sun seekers.

100/7, Moo 1, Ban Tai Beach. www.cocogardens.com ☎ **07737-7721.** 25 units. 450B double with fan; 1,200B double with A/C. **Amenities:** Restaurant; bar; Wi-Fi (free).

Milky Bay Resort ★★ Friendly service and midrange luxury are on tap at this beautifully presented resort set in lush gardens with meandering paths to individual villas. Choose from five room types, each of which is different in style and creature comforts. Most rooms are bright and spacious, apart from the standard bungalows, which are little more than shoeboxes. But all rooms have air conditioning and balconies with sea- or garden views. Next to the oceanfront pool (half in the shade, half in the sun), the restaurant serves delicious BBQ seafood, Thai, and Italian (it has a proper wood-burning pizza oven) and overlooks a white-sand beach lapped by the sea. A couple of pool tables will keep some guests happy, while others can indulge in a wonderful Thai massage.

103/4 Moo 1, Ban Tai Beach. www.milkybaythailand.com. ☎ **07723-8566.** 34 units. 1,800B standard; 9,000B beachfront studio. **Amenities:** Restaurant; bar; outdoor pool; exercise room; steam room; Wi-Fi (free).

HAD RIN

Had Rin (aka Haad Rin), is a narrow peninsula on the island's southeastern tip filled with bungalows, busy shopping streets, funky clothing shops, and an array of restaurants between east-facing Had Rin Nok (Sunrise Beach, where the Full Moon Party happens) and Had Rin Nai (Sunset Beach) on the west side. If you're looking for swimming and white sand, Had Rin Nok is the nicer of the two. Full Moon parties are the biggest money-making days for the cheaper hotels/hostels here and they'll often cram extra cots and mattresses into dorm-style rooms to make the most of the busy days.

This part of the island has fully embraced its Full Moon tomfoolery identity, and techno raves, DJs, and fluorescent paint dance parties break out regularly, making it hard to predict when there might be a lull in the action. If peace and quiet trump rowdy and raucous, find accommodation elsewhere.

If you wish to transcend it all, tucked away on the soft white-sand is **Leela Beach** (aka Had Seekantang), just 5 minutes over the hilltop. There you'll find **Cocohut Beach Resort & Spa** ★★ (www.cocohut.com; ☎ **07737-5368**). Spacious bungalows of all sizes start at 2,600B. Next door, the stylish **Sarikantang** (www.sarikantang.com; ☎ **07737-5055-7**) has beautifully designed and well-equipped rooms that range from 1,700B to 5,400B. Both places have beachside restaurants and pools, and are just far enough from town for a bit of quiet, but are close enough to walk down and join the festivities. **Lighthouse Bungalows** (search Lighthouse Bungalows on Facebook since their website was down at press time; ☎ **07737-5075**) has secluded fan and air conditioning bungalows set around the rocky cape hillside with sea views. Despite a secluded setting, regular DJ parties keep the party going outside of key lunar

dates, which might not be your thing. Rates run between 450B and 1,000B.
Tommy Resort (www.tommyresort.com; © 07737-5215) is a cute little boutique that offers everything from standard rooms and bungalows to pool villas and has a nice pool that leads to a quiet beach with shade from palm trees. It's in the heart of the Had Rin action (for better or worse), and prices start around 2,000B, though pool villas run around 8,000B.

THE EAST COAST

Had Yuan and Had Thian are the main beaches on the southeastern part of the island, which is the most secluded part of the Ko Pha Ngan. You'll need a boat to reach the resorts over here since the roads require four wheels and are often impassable after heavy rains. But if you're after quiet beaches and a bit of isolation, don't let that deter you since the 10-minute long journey on a long-tail boat from Had Rin costs around 300B, and hotels are adept at booking transfers. Had Yuan is a small but beautiful beach that feels worlds away from the Had Rin party scene, and the water is a sparkling shade of blue. A rocky outcrop flanks one end of the beach and the swimming is good.

Pariya Resort & Villas ★ This place claims to be the island's first boutique resort, and there's no denying it's an exclusive little hideaway, with a clutch of smart rooms and villas that cater to the better-heeled traveler. The resort lies on the increasingly popular and totally gorgeous Had Yuan (Yuan Beach) in the east. Being accessible only by boat has guarded it against the crowds, but there's enough going on that you won't feel like a castaway. The style is modern-rustic and some of the spacious rooms can feel a little empty and under decorated. However, outdoor rain showers, terraces, and prime beach location balance out the décor missteps. There's a kiddie pool, lovely spa, hammocks on the beach, and a breezy outdoor bar.

152/2 Moo 6, Ban Tai, Had Yuan. www.pariyahaadyuan.com. © **087623-6678.** 45 units. 3,000B–8,000B double. **Amenities:** Restaurant; bar; outdoor pool and kids' pool; spa; Wi-Fi (free).

The Sanctuary Thailand Spa Resort ★★ Hidden behind trees on Had Thien, just a short boat ride to the north of Had Rin, the Sanctuary bills itself as alternative—and it certainly is, with a dazzling range of wellness, dance, and meditative activities and courses, as well as colonic treatments at its adjacent **Wellness & Detox Center.** As much as its yoga, massage, and cleansing programs, the main draw is its tranquility. Choose from simple, low-cost dorms and yogi rooms to houses tucked away in the jungle. The restaurant is the best vegetarian restaurant on the island, and there is a wide selection of raw, organic, and detoxing meals. Overall, the resort is a stark (and perhaps much needed) contrast to the endless nights of overindulgence at Had Rin. *Note:* Not all rooms allow for advanced booking; dorms and bungalows are on a first come, first served basis. The entire resort is cash only.

Had Thien, Ko Pha Ngan. www.thesanctuarythailand.com. © **081271-3614.** 48 units. From 350B dorm and bungalows; 2,800B–7,300 suites. No credit cards. **Amenities:** Restaurant; bar; spa; Wi-Fi (free).

WEST & NORTH COAST

Both the west and north coast have white-sand beaches and are far from the monthly hippy hoedown at Had Rin, which might be a relief. Resorts are quiet and affordable, and growing in number and quality of attractions. The tranquil Laem Son freshwater lake lies close to Ao Chao Phao, but it's on the site of a former tin mine and is thought to be toxic, so don't try swimming there. The resorts below follow a clockwise route starting at Had Chaophao on the west.

Had Son

Haad Son Resort ★   *Haad Son* means secret beach in Thai, and while not much on the island is a secret any more, this place feels like a find. It's on its own secluded sandy beach over from Had Yao, with good hilltop views of the sea. Room-wise, there is a lot of choose from, including two-story villas and the thatched, lakeside villas; all rooms are comfortably equipped and well-spaced. It's a family friendly place with a big pool as well as a children's pool; kayaks and mountain bikes can be rented. The hotel boasts a chic beach restaurant.

Had Son Beach, Ko Pha Ngan. www.haadsonresort.net. © **07734-9103-4.** 57 units. From 1,050B–2,800B villa; 5,000B penthouse. **Amenities:** Restaurant; bar; 2 outdoor pools; Wi-Fi (free).

Had Yao

Had Yao, or Long Beach, is considered by many to be a perfect beach, a quiet but huge stretch of white sand, good for swimming, with the same sunset views and laid-back vibe that drew the first travelers here. Supermarkets and Internet cafes up on the main road provide the bulk of services you'll need; good eats can also be found along the beach—it's big enough to play soccer on.

There are several bungalow resorts and budget spots. Snap great photos for Instagram from the infinity pool at **Haad Yao Sandy Bay Bungalows** (www. sandybaybungalows.com; © **07734-9119**) or from a private bungalow with an ocean view; rooms from 1,500B. The winning combination of great service, good-value rooms and excellent restaurant makes **Shiralea** (www.shiralea. com; © **080719-9256**) a popular pick. Choose from fan-cooled rooms at 650B or air-con rooms at 1,400B; all have thatched roofs, are raised on stilts, and have balconies with hammocks.

Had Salad

This handsome and secluded sandy beach used to be a pirates' hideout and is good for swimming (Nov–Apr), with a reef about 150m (492 ft.) offshore that is a well-known dive site. The beach has a rustic vibe and Thai fisherman catch fish and naps from the long-tail boats docked off shore.

Salad Hut (www.saladhut.com; © **07734-9246**) has Thai-style bungalows with verandas and a small infinity pool (that doesn't fill up too quickly because the hotel only has a dozen rooms). The staff are good-natured and helpful, and rooms start at 2,200B. The nicest option on this stretch of sand is **Cookies Salad** (www.cookies-phangan.com; © **07734-9125**), a popular resort with an odd name. There's a tiered Jacuzzi and pool and the bungalows are stacked on a hill affording great views from nearly every room; rates from 1,700B.

NORTHEAST/AO THONG NAI PAN

Two adjoining crescent-shaped beaches, 17km (11 miles) north of Had Rin, are differentiated by the suffix *yai* (big) and *noi* (small). This secluded paradise is home to the island's most swank resorts and is easily reached by rented boat, or less easily, by bumpy dirt track. Thanks to a bit of construction work, the road between the two beach is well-kept, and a taxi between the two beaches runs around 100B. **Thong Nai Pan Yai** is quieter, while **Thong Nai Pan Noi** is the island's most beautiful beach and has a more bohemian vibe and a small village with some cool bars and restaurants.

This part of the island is best suited for honeymooners and those looking for luxury—and the prices and accommodations types reflect that. However, there are a few inexpensive places to bed down near these fabulous beaches. **Longtail Beach Resort** (www.longtailbeachresort.com; ℂ 07744-5018), at the southern end of Thong Nai Pan, has a lovely pool with ocean views. Its bamboo bungalows are simple but clean and well kept in a lush garden setting. Fan-cooled rooms start at 720B and air-con rooms range from 850B to 2,500B.

Anantara Rasananda ★★★   The Anantara is the island's most luxurious resort; here the booze-filled buckets popular with the Full Moon crowd are replaced with beach-front champagne service. The hotel offers enormous pool suites, which successfully fuse traditional Thai design with modern architecture. Fancy touches like private sundecks with sunset views, Apple TVs, and espresso machines assure guests will not lack for anything, and the in-room bar with complimentary spirits in local decanters is a spark of genius. Spa facilities are top-notch and include indoor and outdoor treatment rooms. On-site restaurants—including a fine Japanese spot—are superb.

5/5 Moo 5, Ao Thong Nai Pan Noi. www.phangan-rasananda.anantara.com. ℂ **07723-9555.** 65 units. From 7,200B pool suites; from 8,550B pool villas. **Amenities:** 2 restaurants; bar; outdoor pool; room service; spa; Wi-Fi (free).

Panviman ★★★   Designed for sophisticated travelers craving tranquility and natural beauty, this sprawling resort's luxury cottages are scattered over the hillside above Thong Nai Pan Beach. Rooms are handsomely decorated in fine woods, with decorative Thai textiles. Service is of a high standard and the staff do their best to predict every need and remember coffee orders at breakfast each morning. The pool is one of the best on the island, a multi-tiered affair, with views of the bay below. It's a bit of a haul from the hilltop to the beach, but there are convenient shuttles. Dining here is top-notch, too.

22/1 Moo 5, Ao Thong Nai Pan Noi. www.panviman.com. ℂ **07744-5101.** 72 units. From 4,700B superior and deluxe hotel rooms; 7,100B–18,000B pool suites and villas. Room rates include breakfast and complimentary spa treatments if you book 3 nights. **Amenities:** 3 restaurants; 2 bars; outdoor pool; Jacuzzi; room service; Wi-Fi (free).

Santhiya Resort & Spa ★★   The teakwood villas that sprawl across 7.2 hectares (18 acres) of prime beachside property offer every luxury to its pampered guests, and along with near-neighbors Panviman and Anantara Rasananda, this resort provides the top accommodation option on Ko Pha Ngan. All rooms are huge and enjoy fabulous views of the bay, while the top-end villas feature secluded private pools. The Ayurvana Spa is the perfect place to wile away an afternoon after a swim in the 1,200-sq.-m. (12,917-sq.-ft.) pool; and the terrace of the Chantara Restaurant is ideal for a delicious Thai dinner.

22/7 Banthai, Ko Pha Ngan. www.santhiya.com. *(* 07742-8999. 99 units. 10,000B deluxe room; 14,000B sea-view villa suite. **Amenities:** Restaurant; 2 bars; outdoor pool; health club; spa; room service; Wi-Fi (free).

Where to Eat

Cheap eats of every type abound in busy Had Rin and, increasingly, even in the smaller villages here. Luxury resorts in the northeast offer special occasion fine dining options.

Serving up all kinds of tasty seafood treats, **Fisherman's** (www.fishermans phangan.com; *(* 08445-47240) is by the pier on Ban Thai Beach and some tables are converted fishing boats—it's very charming. They're famous for the yellow crab curry, but the fish cakes are fab as are the grilled prawns. Book early; especially during Full Moon days. Near the pier on Had Rin Nai, **Om Ganesh** (*(* 07737-5123) serves up authentic Indian curries and biryanis. It's very popular, so do book ahead. Go to **Ando Loco** (www.andoloco.com; *(* 085791-7600) for margaritas and fajitas when another bowl of curry seems like one too many. If you wake up starving and sick of your hotel's breakfast options, **Nira's** (*(* 086595-0636) is *the* place to go on the island for baked goods and outstanding coffee. Take one bite of the pizzas at **Monna Lisa** (*(* 084441-5871) and you'll smile or try **Fabio's** (*(* 07737-7180) famous seafood risotto (there's a nice selection of wine here, too).

KO TAO ★★

55km (34 miles) N of Ko Samui; 80km (50 miles) SE of Chumphon

In the Goldilocks comparison of Ko Tao, Ko Samui, and Ko Pha Nang, Ko Tao would be "just right". It's an ideal mix Ko Samui's niceties with a touch of the party scene that makes Ko Pha Nang famous.

Some 75 years ago, tiny **Ko Tao,** or **Turtle Island**—so-named for its outline and resident marine life—was a penitentiary for insurgents, though few visitors these days would find any punishment in being marooned on its idyllic shores. Until lately, it has been known almost exclusively as a destination for divers. The island is blessed with ravishing offshore isles, clear turquoise waters, and pristine coral reefs. With the arrival of chic resorts, however, the island's appeal has broadened. Though dive resorts (and a social scene based around the local diving expats) do dominate, there are also lots of rustic budget choices, as well as new high-end hideaways.

Just off the northwest corner lies a trio of islets known as **Ko Nang Yuan** or **Ko Hang Tao** (Turtle's Tail). **Had Sai Ree** and **Ban Mae Had,** both on the west coast, form the main centers, where you'll find most of the budget accommodation and dive resorts. There are excellent restaurants and some fun bars along this long shore. *Note:* As its popularity grows, power outages occasionally plague the island but the laid-back locals take it in stride, and things are sorted pretty quickly.

Essentials

ARRIVING

Songserm Express (www.songserm.com; ✆ **07745-6274**) boats leave from Surat Thani and connect nearby islands; fares from Ko Samui are 500B, fares from Ko Pha Ngan are 350B, plus there's a daily morning boat from Chumphon leaving at 6am for 500B that take 3½ hours. Boats run subject to weather conditions in monsoon season.

Lomprayah High Speed Catamarans (www.lomprayah.com; ✆ **07745-6176**) also makes the connection from Samui, via Ko Pha Ngan, and onto Chumphon twice daily: From the Chumphon pier the fare is 600B (1 hr. 45 min.); from Ko Samui, 600B or 700B (3 hrs.); and from Ko Pha Ngan, 500B or 600B (1 hr.). There are also night boats from Surat Thani and Chumphon with basic sleeping accommodation.

Caution: The south and western beaches can get blasted by the monsoon winds June through October when the normally transparent seas get churned up; but even during November to January (high season), there can be squalls. If you have an onward flight to catch, reserve an extra day or two, in case of delays.

ORIENTATION & GETTING AROUND

All boats arrive in **Ban Mae Had** on the west of the island. Touts from resorts and scuba operators alike line the quay. (*Tip:* You're better off booking scuba packages from the actual shop where you can meet the instructors and see the gear.) A single concrete road connects the northwestern tip of the island to **Ban Had Sai Ree** and heads south (with the island's longest beach running parallel) through **Ban Mae Had** to **Ao Chalok Ban Kao,** but elsewhere the roads are steep, loose dirt tracks, most of which are very challenging. It's possible to walk over the headlands (just be mindful of the occasional dropping coconut). Pickups and motorbike taxis (prices vary from 20B–300B) are easy to find in Mae Had or by the pier, but difficult to find elsewhere. Taxi don't use meters, and fares tend to double after dark. Make sure you negotiate an acceptable fare before setting out.

One can a scooter for upward of 200B per day; it's a good idea to rent from a shop or resort, and not to hire bikes from the cowboys around the pier to avoid paying too much. Road conditions aren't great around the island so wear a helmet and be a defensive driver.

More remote bays, such as the eastern bays of **Ao Leuk, Ao Ta Note,** and **Ao Hin Wong,** are reachable by four-wheel-drive or boat, but most high-end resorts there can simply arrange pickup.

The Tourism Authority of Thailand doesn't have an office on the island, but guesthouses, dive shops, and hotels are happy to help with booking transport, making recommendations, and more. We've found in the Thai islands, they're often more plugged-in to the local scene than government-run tourism stands.

ATMs are easy to find at 7-Elevens and along main roads; expect most places to add a 3% fee to credit card transactions. The tiny **Ko Tao Hospital**

(© **07745-6490**) has just 10 beds but can handle basic needs, like dings from a bike accent, sunburns, cuts, or jellyfish stings. Major problems should be addresses in Ko Samui or Bangkok. Plans are in the works to expand the facility by 2020 to include a hyperbaric chamber and speedboat transfers.

Many people find www.kohtaoonline.com to be a helpful resource for up-to-date info on island life, boat timetables, dive packages, and environmental concerns. **Koh Tao Complete Guide** (www.kohtaocompletcguide.com) is a local guide that is updated quarterly and is free for visitors.

Where to Stay

The diving community dominates the accommodation on the island and many bungalows and guesthouses work closely with dive shops to promote each other. Because the competition is so fierce for tourist dollars, many dive shops offer free or discounted hotel deals as part of multi-day packages; a great arrangement if you're just here to find Nemo and his pals and don't mind basic rooms. The resorts on the island lack the ultra-luxurious properties of nearby Ko Samui. In fact, a few of the nicer spots are starting to show their age. However, the rates for prime beachfront hotels are very reasonable, especially when compared to Ko Samui's not-so-wallet-friendly prices.

MODERATE

Charm Churee Villa ★   The lodgings at this perennially popular resort sit on a forested hill atop a secluded cove, just a 10-minute walk from Ban Mae Had. The resort covers an enormous 120 acres (48 hectares) of hillside and beachside jungle, with stairways carved into massive, smooth boulders giving the place a distinctive character. The designs of the rooms vary slightly, but they all have flamboyant pops of color and a beachy, island vibe with teak hut balconies. The resort sits on a private cove and beach with smooth sand and water that is perfect for swimming and snorkeling. Entry-level rooms (marked as eco and superior) leave a bit to be desired—they're quite worn. Those in the deluxe and above categories are better maintained.

30/1 Moo 2, Jansom Bay (just south of the ferry landings at Ban Mae Had). www.charm chureevilla.com. © **07745-6393**. 40 units. 3,000B double; from 7,000B cottage or suite. **Amenities:** 2 restaurants; bar; spa; outdoor pool; Wi-Fi (free)

Jamahkiri Spa & Resort ★★★   Perhaps the island's most upscale resort, Jamahkiri is accessible only by precipitous mountain track and has lots of steep steps to negotiate on property (it's not a good choice for anyone with mobility issues or for families with small children). That being said, it's a charmer, with a top-notch spa, a very good restaurant, a large pool, and a slice of white sandy beach that's pure bliss. Digs overlook the bay in a clutch of gray-tile and glass pavilions and suites; some are duplexes, and all have oceanview balconies. Room décor is colorful, featuring fine works of Thai art, and such luxe touches as deep soaking tubs.

Ao Thian Ok, on the southern end of the island. www.jamahkiri.com. © **07745-6400**. 20 units. 3,000B deluxe room; 5,000B–12,000B deluxe and suites. **Amenities:** Restaurant; bar; outdoor pool; exercise room; spa; babysitting; Wi-Fi (free).

Sensi Paradise Resort ★★ Smack-dab in the middle of Mae Hat along a pretty stretch of sand this lovely resort draws inspiration from the island's natural elements. The bungalows are surrounded by palm trees and forests and have large, breezy balconies, and billowy netting above the beds. Thai-style platform beds support firm mattress and outdoor sofas are perfect for lazy afternoon naps. The hotel staff is incredibly helpful pre-arrival at arranging transfers, and the service continues during the stay. Enjoy a dip in the pool or a walk along the bustling beach. The noise level from the pier can rise to a bothersome level at times. There is a 2-night minimum during high season.

27 Moo 2, Mae Hat. www.sensiparadiseresort.com. ☏ **07745-6244**. 50 units. From 2,900B double; 5,000B–9,000B suite. **Amenities:** Restaurant; bar; 2 outdoor pools; Wi-Fi (free).

INEXPENSIVE

Had Sai Ree and **Mae Had Beach** both have a huge range of budget options available to walk-in guests, but many are booked through budget scuba packages—popular with long-stay guests who want to get more extensive scuba certification. On Mae Had Beach, one popular all-inclusive scuba resort is **Crystal Dive Resort** (www.crystaldive.com; ☏ **07745-6106**); rooms with or without air-conditioning range from 600B to 1,500B. Crystal Dive is one of the more popular dive schools on the island and accommodation is free for 2 nights of scuba and 4 nights of PADI certification.

New Heaven Resort (www.newheavendiveschool.com; ☏ **07745-6422**) is a popular dive resort, with dorms from 300B. Deep discounts are given if you book dives with the resort (this is true for most dive-centric resorts across the island) and a beachfront bungalow with air-con is 1,800B for non-divers and 1,200B for divers. **Simple Life** ★ (www.kohtaosimpleliferesort.com; ☏ **07745-6142**) is probably the most stylish of these cheap dive resorts. Comfy dorms and bungalows with fans or air-conditioning run from 300B and there are hotel-style rooms for 1,900B; the hotel has a popular bar.

Where to Eat

After a day in the sun, trade your flippers for flip-flops and chow down at one of the island's restaurants, most of which are casual divers' haunts. Sai Ree Beach is home to some of the nicest spots on the island and the chef at **Barracuda Restaurant & Bar** ★★ (www.barracudakohtao.com; ☏ **07745-7049**) made a name for himself cooking for the Thai royal family. The pan-fried barracuda is a dish, yes, fit for a prince, and the fusion menu makes use of local ingredients. **The Gallery Restaurant** ★ (www.thegallerykohtao.com; ☏ **07745-6547**) dishes out an outstanding snapper in red curry, which is served in a coconut, giving it a delightfully sweet taste; the Gallery is a particularly good spot for vegetarians, with lots of veggie options. **995 Roasted Duck** ★★ (near The Gallery Restaurant; no phone) is the most famous street stall on the island, so expect lines. A bowl of roasted duck with noodles soothing to the soul for 70B, while a whole bird with perfectly crisp and sweet skin costs 700B.

In Mae Had, there's **Zest Café** (no website; ☏ **07745-6178**) which serves some of the best java on the island—a blessing after a few days of bad hotel powered mixes. Come for Eggs Benedict in the morning and sandwiches on homemade bread for lunch. **Pranee's Kitchen** ★ (search Pranee's Kitchen Koh Tao on Facebook; ✆ **07745-6478**) is an institution in Ko Tao known for Thai curries. Vegetarians and meat eaters alike will adore **Coconut Monkey** ★★ (www.facebook.com/CoconutMonkeyKohTao; ✆ **093640-4522**), where homemade falafel, cold-pressed juices, and outstanding breakfast wraps are all enjoyed along the beach.

Ko Tao Entertainment & Nightlife

Most of the action is right on Mae Had beach, where you'll find stacks of stylish retro bars, dance spots with international DJs, and fire jugglers performing amid stunning sand sculptures. **Lotus Bar** ★★ (✆ **087069-6078**) has everything you'd want at a beach bar: spectacular sunsets, generously sized boozy drinks, and fire shows when the sun goes down.

Beer drinkers will enjoy the selection at **The Earth House** ★ (www.the earthhouse-kohtao.com; ✆ **098039-8637**), a bungalow-style guest house with a charming beer garden and an international selection of more than 40 beers and ciders.

Fizz (www.facebook.com/fizz.beachlounge; ✆ **080697-8289**) is a quintessential beach club and the neon green beanbags on the beach compliment the electric sunsets. The bartenders here are some of the best on the island and chill house music will keep you there all night. Nearby, **Maya Beach Club** (www.mayabeachclubkohtao.com; ✆ **080578-2225**) is more clublike than Fizz, and DJs keep the action going until 2am.

Outdoor Activities

Known as one of the best diving areas in Thailand, Ko Tao is also an unusually affordable place to dive or learn to dive. Divers of every level will find instructors, dives, or lessons to suit their interests. In fact, Ko Tao issues the most scuba certifications in the world.

There are lots of dive schools vying for your baht, so shop around before committing to a package. Unless you're coming for master accreditation or something beyond a basic open-water certification, you'll be fine booking upon arrival. In Ko Tao, remember that other scuba fans are a great resource for recommending dive operators. Be sure to find an instructor that you jive with and ask about group size and the skill sets of the other divers in your group. If you'd like to do some research in advance, here are professional operators that get our stamp of approval. They offer snorkeling trips as well.

o **Master Divers,** in Ban Mae Had (www.master-divers.com; ✆ **07745-6459**)

o **Big Blue Diving,** near Sai Ree Beach (www.bigbluediving.com; ✆ **07745-6050**).

o **Scuba Junction,** on Sai Ree Beach (www.scuba-junction.com; ✆ **07745-6164**).

o **Crystal Dive,** in Ban Mae Had (www.crystaldive.com; ✆ **07745-6106**)

Side Trips from Ko Tao

Local aquanauts agree that the best **scuba diving** in the region is off nearby **Ko Nang Yuan** (just off the northwest tip of Ko Tao), which benefits from deep-water just offshore and high visibility. Ko Nang Yuan consists of three small islands joined by a spectacular sandbar. Because it's famed for its wonderful snorkeling, numerous companies offer day trips here. Look into unique dive-and-stay packages at **Nang Yuan Resort** (www.nangyuan.com; © **07745-6088-93**), set over the three islands, with rooms starting as low as 2,500B to plush family suites at around 5,2000B.

SOUTHERN PENINSULA: WEST COAST & ISLANDS

Phuket is Thailand's best-known and largest island. It is linked by a causeway to peninsular Thailand and was one of Thailand's first tourist developments. Today it's a perennially popular mass-tourism magnet with daily flights arriving from international destinations. In the dry season (Nov–Mar), Phuket is a swell place to kick back on a soft-sand beach or to island-hop by ferry or longtail boat.

With its increasing wealth and popularity come less savory influences, however: X-rated nightlife and unscrupulous developers keen to earn a fast buck from the once-pristine environment are common, and there's now hardly a stretch of beach that isn't backed by a glut of resorts. Should you avoid Phuket then? No. Read on and we'll show you ways to avoid the seamier side of the island.

The province of **Krabi** has been a bit more eco-savvy and classy than bolder, brassier Phuket, making it popular with those looking for nature, not nightlife. The province encompasses all the land east of **Phang Nga Bay,** including **Ko Phi Phi** and **Ko Lanta.** Close to Krabi town, **Ao Nang Beach** and **Railay** offer backdrops of dramatic limestone cliffs, powder-soft beaches, and high-end resorts. **Ko Phi Phi** is booming with snorkelers and tour boats thanks to its famous cameo in "The Beach"; however, the island's National Park designation (theoretically, meant to preserve its outstanding beauty) was shamefully ignored until recently (more on that below). **Ko Lanta Yai,** better known as **Ko Lanta,** lies southeast of Krabi Town. Once home solely to Muslim fishing villages, it now boasts the whole gamut of resorts from budget to super luxe.

At the southernmost tip of Phuket is the idyllic isle of **Ko Racha** (sometimes called Ko Raja or Raya), with its jade-green seas. Northward is **Phang Nga Bay** with its glorious vistas of karst outcrops, and, on the west coast, **Khao Lak,** the gateway to the **Similan** and **Surin Islands,** rated by many among the top 10 dive sites in the world. To the south, **Trang Province's** white-sand beaches, caves, and waterfalls make it one of Thailand's best-kept secrets.

The Southern Peninsula: West Coast

Mu Koh Surin Archipelago Marine National Park
Ranong
Hat Supin
Chumphon
Ko Tao
Ko Pha Ngan
Ko Chang
Ko Phayam
Kapoe
Ang Thong Marine National Park
Ko Samui
Andaman Sea
Chai Ya
Ban Hin Lad
Ko Phra Thong
Khuraburi
Don Sak
Gulf of Thailand (Gulf of Siam)
Surat Thani
401
4014
Takua Pa
Phanom
Khao Sok National Park
4
Khao Lak
41
4009
Phang Nga
Nakhon Si Thammarat
Than Bokkhorani
Phangnga Bay
Ko Yao Noi
Khao Phanom Bencha National Park
Thung Song
Ao Nang
Krabi
408
Had Nai Yang
Ko Yao Yai
Railway Beach
Krabi Resort
Ko Phuket
Ton Sai
Khlong Thom
403
41
Phuket
Ko Pu
4
Phi Phi Don
Ko Phi Phi
Sikao
Trang
Phattalung
To Similan Marine National Park (50 mi/80 km)
Ko Lanta Yai
Ko Lanta
Hat Yao
Hat Chao Mai National Park
Ko Hai
Ko Li Bong
Rattaphum
Andaman Sea
Thung Wa
406
Pak Bara
4078
Ko Tarutao
Ao Pante
Thale Ban National Park
Ko Rawi
Ko Adang
Tarutao National Marine Park
Satun

THAILAND
Bangkok
The Southwest Coast

Legend
- ✈ Airport
- ☂ Beach
- --- Ferry Route
- ≈ Scuba Diving
- 🐢 Turtle area

0   25 mi
0   25 km

During high season (Nov–Apr), bookings for all west coast resorts should be made well in advance; expect hefty surcharges and mandatory payments (regardless of attendance) for Christmas dinners and New Year's Eve celebrations. This season is tops for all watersports. Many hotels offer discounts in the off-season when heavy rains bring mighty winds and rough seas. Swimming becomes dangerous then, with heavy surf and strong undertow, so pay attention to flags flown on beaches that indicate current safety levels. However, islands in the eastern Gulf of Thailand (**Ko Samui, Ko Pha Ngan,** and **Ko Tao**) are more sheltered during those months.

GETTING TO KNOW PHUKET

867km (539 miles) SW of Bangkok

The name "Phuket" comes from the Malay word "Bukit" (meaning hill, and pronounced *poo-ket*); true to the name, lush, green hills dominate much of the island's interior. The ideal way to explore the island is by hiring a car (with or without driver) and taking a hair-raising drive along the cliff roads and through the island's interior.

Most visitors come to Phuket for two reasons: blissful days at the beach or the island's hedonistic nightlife scene. But one doesn't have to come for *both*. It's easy to avoid the bar areas with their sex shows, sex workers, and sex-hungry patrons. Travelers seeking more wholesome activities can head to the Phuket Elephant Sanctuary (p. 237), the island's first and only ethical elephant camp; spend an unforgettable day sea kayaking (p. 235), and seeing awe-inspiring offshore caves and limestone *hong* (literally "rooms"—hidden lagoons with sheer walls that become accessible at low tide); or island hopping on a motorized vehicle.

What's less easy to avoid is Phuket's hideous overdevelopment. Much of Phuket is covered with unsightly concrete bunkers patronized by budget tour groups from Asia, Russia, and Europe. Areas such as Patong, with its seedy commercial strip and sleazy nightlife, can be a bit much for families or single women travelers, but Patong does have some very good restaurants—Acqua (p. 254) and Suay (p. 259)—so it shouldn't be avoided altogether. And though there is a mafia presence (the sky-high taxi prices are a result of the local taxi mafia) it doesn't endanger tourists; crime issues for visitors tend to begin and end with pickpockets.

In dry season, Phuket is at its optimum: You'll find long sandy beaches, warm water, snorkeling and scuba diving, and an up-and-coming surf scene. It also boasts some of the most delectable seafood in Thailand, not to mention some of the best international gourmet food available anywhere in Thailand. Sure, its prices are more than a tad overblown, but for well-heeled fun-seekers who want to be at the heart of the action, Phuket is a fabulous choice. While there are days without a cloud in the sky and very little rain, the monsoon season of mid-May to October is often disappointing to visitors.

If escape at any cost is what you need, Phuket has heaps of elegant resorts designed for tropical solitude; an increasing number offer private villas and

Phuket

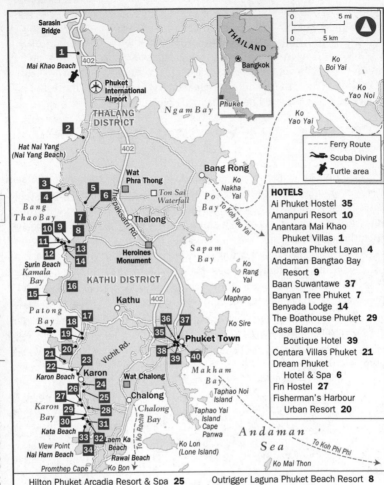

HOTELS

Ai Phuket Hostel **35**
Amanpuri Resort **10**
Anantara Mai Khao
   Phuket Villas **1**
Anantara Phuket Layan **4**
Andaman Bangtao Bay
   Resort **9**
Baan Suwantawe **37**
Banyan Tree Phuket **7**
Benyada Lodge **14**
The Boathouse Phuket **29**
Casa Blanca
   Boutique Hotel **39**
Centara Villas Phuket **21**
Dream Phuket
   Hotel & Spa **6**
Fin Hostel **27**
Fisherman's Harbour
   Urban Resort **20**

Hilton Phuket Arcadia Resort & Spa **25**
In On the Beach **23**
Kata Rocks **30**
Katanoi Resort **32**
Katathani Phuket Beach Resort **31**
Keemala **16**
Le Meridien Phuket **22**
Manathai Surin **12**
Marina Phuket **26**
The Memory at On On Hotel **38**
Mövenpick Resort & Spa **24**
The Nai Harn **34**
Novotel Phuket **17**

Outrigger Laguna Phuket Beach Resort **8**
Paresa **15**
Patong Backpacker Hostel **18**
Phuket Pavilions **5**
Rommanee Boutique Guesthouse **36**
Royal Phuket City Hotel **40**
Sawasdee Village **28**
The Shore **33**
The Slate **2**
The Surin Phuket **11**
Trisara **3**
Twinpalms Phuket **13**
Wire Hostel **19**

pools. Evason Phuket even provides a honeymoon villa on its own island, Ko Bon. Expect superlative facilities with levels of service beyond that in Europe. But with prices here way above those even in Bangkok, it's not suited to travelers on a tight budget. If you need to keep costs down, consider staying in Phuket Town, the cultural hub of the island, from where you could visit a different beach each day.

Arriving

BY PLANE There are more than 50 daily flights from Bangkok's two airports to Phuket, making last-minute bookings easy and giving travelers a choice of flight times. **Thai Airways** (www.thaiair.com; ℂ 02545-3691) flies ten times daily from **Suvarnabhumi International Airport** (trip time: 1 hr. 20 min.) for around 1,200B. **Bangkok Airways** (www.bangkokair.com; ℂ 02270-6699) connects Phuket with Ko Samui four to five times daily for around 2,000. **Air Asia** (www.airasia.com; ℂ 02515-9999) and Bangkok Airways make the 2-hour journey from Chaing Mai to the island for 1,100B.

Almost all Southeast Aisa's budget airlines fly to Phuket from Bangkok and beyond, including **Air Asia** and **Nok Air** (www.nokair.com; ℂ 1318). From Bangkok, most budget carriers operate from Don Mueang International Airport for around 800B. Connecting with Singapore is **Silk Air** (www.silkair.com; ℂ 07630-4020). Budget carriers **Tiger Airways** (www.tigerairways.com; ℂ 80060-15637) and Qantas subsidiary **Jetstar** (ℂ 02267-5125; www.jetstar.com) also have regular connections from Phuket to Singapore; Jetstar flies directly to Australia. As a testament to the island's popularity, it's now possible to fly direct to Phuket from Dubai, Seoul, Beijing, Moscow, Kuala Lumpur, and more. If Phuket is your last stop before flying home, these routes can save you a few hours catching a connecting flight back to Bangkok.

GETTING FROM THE AIRPORT TO TOWN The modern **Phuket International Airport** (www.phuketairportonline.com; ℂ 07632-7230-7) is in the north of the island, about a 45-minute drive from Patong Beach in off-peak hours, or an hour in rush hour (8–9am and 4–7pm). There are ATMs, money-changing facilities, car-rental agents (see "Getting Around," below), fast-food joints, and a post office at the airport. For a fee, most resorts will pick you up at the airport; check if this is included in your booking.

Just outside the terminal to the right is a **meter taxi** stand. With the 100B airport tax imposed your ride will likely cost 600B to 800B. There is a ready supply of taxis upon exiting the terminal. Limos (aka well-kept sedans) and minivans are available at the airport for fixed rates depending on destination.

Travel Tip: Because metered taxis are so rare, consider getting the phone number of the meter taxi driver from the airport—especially if they didn't pump the breaks so much you got nauseous. Another reliable option is downloading the **Grab** app (www.grab.com/th; available in the Google Play and iTunes App Store). Grab drivers are required to use a meter, and they're much cheaper than Phuket's unregulated taxis.

BY BUS Bus travel isn't that much more economical than flying (see above and below). Still if you're long on time and short on cash, there are three air-conditioned VIP buses leave daily from **Bangkok's Southern Bus Terminal** (② **02422-4444**), costing 998B, and taking 12 hours. Numerous regular air-conditioned buses go each day and cost around 600B. Standard buses make frequent connections to Surat Thani and nearby towns on the mainland (to Surat is 5 hrs. and about 160B).

BY MINIVAN Minivans to and from Surat Thani, Krabi, Nakhon Si Thammarat, Ranong, and other southern cities leave on regular schedules throughout the day. In each city, minivan operators work with the hotels and arrange free pickup, so it is best to book through your hotel front desk or a travel agent. Tickets to destinations in the south, to such places as Surat Thani, go for between 200B and 500B.

Visitor Information

The **Tourism Authority of Thailand (TAT)** has an office in Phuket Town at 191 Thalang Rd. (www.tat.org; ② **07621-2213**), but, in general, hotel concierge or independent tour desks offer more up-to-date information. There are lots of free maps on offer (financed by advertisements). Restaurants and hotel lobbies are good places to pick up any of a number of free local publications: *What's On* has some useful information on Phuket, Ko Phi Phi, and Krabi. Also look online at www.thephuketnews.com for current events.

Island Layout

If you arrive by car or coach, you'll cross into Phuket from the mainland at the northern tip of the island via the **Sarasin Bridge,** along Route 402. Phuket Town, the island's historic and commercial center, is in the southeast of the island at the terminus of Route 402. Phuket's picturesque stretches of sand dot the western coast from Nai Harn, on the southern tip, to Mai Khao, about 48km (30 miles) north, via Kata Noi, Kata, Karon, Patong, Kamala, Surin, Bang Tao, and a number of smaller beaches north along this corridor. A busy coastal road links the popular tour towns in the south, but stops north of Patong, requiring a short detour from the main highway. The four corners of Phuket are linked with just a few busy main arterial roads. Renting a vehicle is the best way to tour the island's smaller byways or make the trip to jungle parks, such as **Khao Phra Thaew National Park,** in the northeast, famed for diverse flora and fauna. The western beaches have all the services visitors might need, but everything comes with resort prices—and don't expect to find any real Thai feel here. For a taste of Thai life, affordable services, and authentic restaurants, explore Phuket Town (especially if this is your only urban destination down south).

THE BEACHES There's a beach for everyone in Phuket, from private stretches artfully cordoned off by exclusive resorts to public bays lined with beach chairs and buzzing with jet skis. Each is distinct, and selecting the appropriate area makes all the difference.

Nai Harn, the southernmost bay on the west coast, is home to several swank beachfront resorts, but also has a host of smaller family-friendly resorts set back from the coast. With fine sand and deep water, Nai Harn attracts surfers and other watersports enthusiasts. As a public beach, with a few local eateries, it makes for a nice day trip if you're staying in Phuket Town or at a more populated beach and want to run away for the day (a long motorbike/car ride south of Kata/Karon).

Rawai Beach and Chalong Beach are two well-known, eastern-facing beaches, both hosting a few resorts, and some outdoor seafood or barbecue restaurants. Cape Panwa, between Chalong and Phuket Town, also has hidden scenic beaches with a range of hotels and restaurants.

North of Nai Harn on the west coast are the more popular developed beaches: Kata, Kata Noi, and Karon beaches. Though they are quite developed, they've not reached the levels of over-the-top Patong. Along this section of sandy, picturesque coastline, you'll find resorts large and small. In general, this area is quite ritzy, though there are a few budget places that haven't been bulldozed and made high-end yet. This area (Kata is the quieter of the two) has more restaurants than the remote bays and some shopping, nightlife, and travel agents as well. But you won't find rowdy crowds here and, even with all the development, the area manages to maintain a laid-back character.

Heading north of the Kata and Karon bays, you'll pass Relax Bay, a small cove with a few resorts, before rolling down the mountain to Patong Beach, the most famous (perhaps infamous) strip on the island. Patong's draw is its seamy Patpong-style nightlife, bustling shops and restaurants, and brash, in-your-face beat. Not surprisingly, commercial sex workers flock here. Accommodation runs the gamut from five-star resorts to budget motels. Love it or hate it, the town has the most diverse selection of dining and highest concentration of tour and dive operators, watersports, and entertainment. The drawbacks, however, are all too visible—endless parades of pushy touts and hawkers. While some adults may find the nightlife titillating, families will want to avoid some of the lurid, and often obscene, displays on Bang La Road. If you love to be in the center of it all, stay in Patong; if you want some peace, stay away.

North of Patong, Kamala Bay, Surin Beach, and Bang Tao Beach have more secluded resorts on lovely beaches for those who want the convenience of nearby Patong but cherish serenity. Be prepared to dig deep for the privilege, though; this stretch is sometimes referred to as "the millionaire's mile."

About two-thirds of the way to the northern tip of the island, Bang Tao Beach is home to the Laguna Phuket, a partnership of world-class resorts sharing excellent facilities and a fabulous beach. The beach area was once home to a tin mine, but no traces of its industrial past remain. While this area is rather far from both Patong Beach and Phuket Town, the many dining and activity options make it quite self-sufficient for those with money. The vibe is relaxed.

Far north of the main resort areas, Nai Thon and Nai Yang Beaches have limited facilities and may not appeal to most, but for real beach lovers, they are a dream come true. Nai Thon is one of the most beautiful beaches on the entire island, while at Nai Yang there is a coral reef 1,000m (3,280 ft.) offshore, just a short ride in a longtail boat. If you are looking to get back to nature, these two beaches or Mai Khao, a little farther north, are your best bet.

Mai Khao, about 17km (10½ miles) long, is the northernmost beach in Phuket and is famed as being prime habitat for leatherback and hawksbill sea turtles. To protect the turtles, and the tropical coral reefs below the water, part of the beach is designated to the Sirinath Marine National Park. But with all the development in the area, few sea turtles are returning here to lay eggs. This steep and wide beach is well-shaded by casuarinas trees and sections of it are still deserted, though it now hosts several luxury resorts, all of which claim to respect the local ecology.

Getting Around

If you've spent any time in other parts of the country, you'll know that the covered pickup trucks that cruise the streets picking up and dropping off passengers are called *songtaews,* while the noisy motorized three-wheel vehicular demons are known as tuk-tuks. Not on Phuket: Here, locals call communal pickup trucks tuk-tuks, while *songtaews* are the giant colorful buses that ply the main roads (also called baht buses).

Public transportation on Phuket is a massive problem with little plans for improvement. Here's the problem: *Songtaews* are only permitted to travel from a beach to Phuket Town (not from beach to beach), which means lengthy, unnecessary journeys. Tuk-tuk drivers have exclusive rights to transport people between beaches, so the "service" is run as a racket—pay the fare they demand, or walk. At night, tuk-tuk drivers are known to charge solo passengers up to 1,000B to go from Karon to Patong Beach, but they are the only game in town. Budget travelers on limited funds must bear this in mind to avoid getting stranded late at night. If you plan to stay several days and want to explore the island, renting a car or scooter is the obvious answer.

BY SONGTAEW   The local bus terminal is in front of the Central Market, on Ranong Road, in Phuket Town. Fares to the most popular beaches range from 20B to 30B. *Songtaews* leave when full, usually every 30 minutes, and they run from 7am to 6pm between Phuket Town and the main beaches on the west coast.

BY TUK-TUK   Within Phuket Town, tuk-tuks charge 100B to 200B even for the shortest trips, but they can get away with it because there's no alternative for short hops. They provide the most convenient way to get to the bus station or Phuket Town's restaurants.

In the busy west-coast beaches, tuk-tuks and small Daihatsu mini trucks roll around town honking at any tourist on foot, especially in Patong. It is the only way to travel between beaches. Bargain hard and be aware that these guys will try to eke every baht out of you. Expect to pay about 600B from town to the airport, 500B from town to Patong Beach, and 200B from Patong Beach to Karon Beach. At night, you'll usually pay double the normal day rates.

BY MOTORCYCLE TAXI Motorcycle taxi drivers, identifiable by colored vests, make short trips within Phuket Town or along Patong Beach for fees as steep as 100B. Don't let them talk you into anything but short in-town rides unless you're looking for a death-defying F1-style race along the switchback highways between beaches.

BY CAR Roads between the main beaches in the west and connecting with Phuket Town across the center of the island are dangerously steep and winding, with more than a few hairpin turns and lots of unpredictable traffic. Having said that, renting a vehicle here offers maximum freedom to explore the island, and road surfaces are generally in good condition. You could always get a car and driver for around 2,000B a day. As in other parts of the kingdom, drivers pass aggressively, even on blind curves, and self-driving visitors should be defensive and alert at all times.

Avis (www.avis.com; ℂ **07635-1244**) and **Hertz** (www.hertz.com; ℂ **07632-8545**) have counters at the Phuket airport. You'll spend around 1,200B per day for the cheapest four-door sedan. **Budget** (www.budget.com; ℂ **07632-7744**) charges similar rates. All international renters have sound insurance coverage available, which is highly recommended. Check the vehicle carefully for minor scratches before signing any agreement to avoid issues later.

If you plan to spend most of your time at the beach or island hopping but want to get out and explore one day, you might consider asking your hotel their rates for a car and driver. In researching this book, we found 1,200B an hour for a sedan and 1,700B an hour for a luxury Mercedes to be the going rates, which likely includes cold water, cold towels, and fresh-cut fruit. Many hotels were willing to offer discounts for guests looking to book a full day.

BY MOTORCYCLE Around the island, car-rental offices will offer cheap bike rental as well at roadside shops, and most hotels can arrange for bike drop-off. A 100cc Honda scooter goes for 150B to 200B per day, while a 400cc Honda Shadow chopper will set you back at least 600B per day. Significant discounts can be negotiated if you plan to rent for a longer time. As with other spots in Thailand, many shops will request your passport as a deposit. Always wear your helmet, as police enforce fines of 500B for going without, and practice extreme caution while driving.

[FastFACTS] PHUKET

Banks Banks are located in Phuket Town, with many larger branches on Ranong and Rasada roads. There are bank branches of major Thai banks at Chalong, Nai Harn, Kata, Karon, and Patong beaches. **Money-changers** are located at the airport, in major shopping areas on each beach, and at most resorts. Banks offer the best rates. **ATMs** are in abundance across Phuket.

Hospitals There are three major private hospitals, all with English-speaking staff: The best facility is **Phuket International Hospital** (www.phuketinternational hospital.com; ℂ **07624-9400**) at 44 Chalermprakiat Ror 9 Rd., next to Big C Shopping Mall, outside Phuket Town. **Bangkok Phuket Hospital,** at 2/1 Hongyok-Uthit Rd. (off Yaowarat Rd., in Phuket Town; www.phukethospital.

com; (☎ **07625-4425**), has high-quality facilities. **Mission Hospital** also offers decent medical services and is at 4/1 Thepkasattri Rd., Phuket Town (www.mission hospitalphuket.com; (☎ **07623-7220**). Both

Phuket International Hospital and Bangkok Phuket Hospital both have diving decompression chambers.

Police The emergency number for the **Tourist Police** is (☎ **1155** or 1699;

for **Emergency Police,** dial (☎ **191;** for **Marine Police,** dial (☎ **07621-1883.**

Post Office The **General Post Office,** in Phuket Town ((☎ **07644-3081**), is at 158 Montri Rd.

Special Events

If you are on Phuket around October/November and have a strong stomach, don't miss the **Vegetarian Festival.** The name is misleading—it is not about animal rights or being health conscious, but a Thai-Chinese tradition on Phuket (and now celebrated widely throughout southern Thailand) that corresponds with the Buddhist Lent. Celebrated during the first 9 days of the ninth lunar month, not only do devotees refrain from eating meat and dairy or drinking alcohol, but many also submit to violent public acts of self-mutilation through piercing their bodies with long skewers, swords, knives or odd items like tree branches, lamps, and shovels. The human skewers are often mediums temporarily possessed by spirits of the nine deities invoked during the festivals. Lay people inflict pain by walking over hot coals. The festival began as an act of penance to the spirits to help early inhabitants ward off malaria, but these days, the rituals are more for young men to prove themselves and for gaining merit and good luck. Early-morning processions flow through the streets of Phuket Town with floats, music, and children in costume parading to the major temples around the island, with onlookers clad in white for the occasion. Shop owners construct makeshift alters outside their stores with offerings of nine cups of tea, candles, incense, fruit, and firecrackers. If you still have an appetite after all that stomach-churning gore (it can get a little bloody), you can also on terrific vegetarian buffets at many restaurants on the island. See **www.phuketvegetarian.com** for exact dates and more info.

EXPLORING PHUKET

You can spend a lot of time on Phuket and still not do everything. Below are some of the island's cultural highlights, and below that is information on Phuket's adrenaline pumping adventures. The beachfront areas are full of tour operators, each vying for your business and offering similar trips (or copycat tours). Listed below are the most reputable firms, but ask lots of questions before signing up for anything, so there are no surprises.

Phuket's Cultural Side

You'll find the most authentic aspects of Phuket's culture at Muslim fishing villages, small rural temples, and in the backstreets of Phuket Town.

More or less in the center of the island, the **Heroines' Monument** is a good place to get a taste of local history. It was erected in honor of two women who rallied the troops and saved the town from an attack by the Burmese in 1785.

Locals frequently arrive to make offerings and prostrate themselves before the monument, making it more than a simple statue.

Thalang National Museum, just off Highway 402 beside the Heroines' Monument (© **07631-1426;** 100B), exhibits Phuket's indigenous cultures, the history of Thai settlements on Phuket, and crafts from the southern Thai regions as well as a 9th-century statue of the Hindu deity Vishnu—evidence of early Indian merchants visiting the burgeoning kingdom. At the time of this update, the museum was closed for renovations but will reopen midyear in 2019 with new hours of operation.

There are a few Buddhist temples on the island that are notable: The most interesting is **Wat Phra Thong** (daily 6am–6pm), along Highway 402, in Thalang, just south of the airport. Years ago, a boy fell ill and dropped dead after tying his buffalo to a post sticking out of the ground. It was later discovered that the post was actually the top of a huge Buddha image that was buried under the earth. Numerous attempts to dig out the post failed—during one attempt in 1785, workers were chased off by hornets. Everyone took all this failure to mean that the Buddha image wanted to just stay put, so they covered the "post" with a plaster image of The Buddha's head and shoulders and built a temple around it.

The most famous temple among Thai visitors here is **Wat Chalong** ★ (daily 6am–6pm). Chalong was the first resort on Phuket, back when the Thais first started coming to the island for vacations. Nowadays, the discovery of better beaches on the west side of the island has driven most tourists away from this area, but the temple still remains the center of Buddhist worship. The temple is on the Chaofa West Road, about 8km (5 miles) south of Phuket Town. On a hilltop to the west of Wat Chalong, sits an enormous (45-m/148-ft. high) **Big Buddha** ★ (daily 6am–6pm), which has quickly become one of the island's main attractions both to pay homage and to admire the peerless views, which include Kata and Karon beaches to the west.

Sea Gypsies, or *Chao Leh,* are considered the indigenous people of Phuket. This minority group used to shift around the region, living off subsistence fishing, but commercial fishing interests and shoreline encroachment have virtually eliminated their lifestyle and livelihood. Related to the Malaysian Orang Laut people and the southern Thai Sakai tribes, Phuket and Phang Nga's Sea Gypsies have a few tiny settlements on Phuket island: One on Ko Siray (aka Ko Sire), east of Phuket Town, and another at Rawai Beach, just south of Chalong Bay. The villages are simple seashore shacks, with vendors selling souvenir shells. Though it should be educational to visit these people and their disappearing culture, sadly the experience on tours is tantamount to visiting a human zoo, with tourists taking photos of unkempt, unwashed kids who ask for handouts.

Beachfront Watersports

Jet skis are technically illegal, but alas, you'll hear them all along the length of Patong. (Most of the noisier watersports activities are concentrated along Patong Beach.) Accidents are so common (some resulting in amputations or death when a swimmer or diver comes into contact with a jet skier) that areas are now being cordoned off from these aquatic toys.

You'll find small **sailboats and kayaks** for rent along many of the island's beaches. Kata is a good place to rent a kayak and play in the waves for 200B per hour but ask about the strong riptides before paddling away from shore. The trendiest beach activity is **kiteboarding** or **kitesurfing,** and a few companies, such as **Kiteboarding Asia** (www.kiteboardingasia.com; ✆ **08159-14594**), offer 3-day introductory courses for around 11,000B. The best beaches for kiteboarding on Phuket are Rawai and Chalong in the south and Nai Yang in the north, though which beach is best depends on the time of year—check with a local school for current conditions. While you can kitesurf any month, peak season is May to October.

While it can't compare to other Asian surfing destinations, like Bali and Sydney, Phuket has a growing **surf scene.** Go with the pros at **Phuket Surfing** (www.phuketsurfing.com; ✆ **089874-9147**) where an hour-long private lesson on Kata Beach is 1,200B, while 2 days of rental and 4 hours of lessons runs 3,800B. There are longer lessons and rentals of surfboards and stand up paddleboards.

Day Cruising & Yachting

The turquoise waters of the Andaman Sea near Phuket are every city dweller's dream. Every December, Phuket hosts the increasingly popular **King's Cup Regatta,** in which almost 100 international racing yachts compete. For more information, check out www.kingscup.com.

All the tour stands around town can assist with booking multi-island group speedboat trips. They're all pretty cookie cutter the only difference usually being the size of the boat; smaller boats with fewer people make for a more enjoyable experience. Many diver operators and speedboat tour companies have offices at luxury hotels and give discounted rates for guests. If you'd like something private, Phuket is chockfull of yachts and boats available for private rental. Check out **Sweet Dreamers** (www.sailingtourphuket.com; ✆ **087277-7395**) for a well-maintained fleet of yachts and catamarans from 28,000B a day, include things like meals, drinks, and a Thai crew. They also offer small group (3,500B a day) and private (37,000B a day) speedboat tours. **Andaman Cruises** (www.andaman-cruises.com; ✆ **07631-6562**) has some of the best yachts in Thailand. If spending several days at sea sounds like an ideal vacation, the pros at **Sunsail** (www.sunsail.com; ✆ **07633-6212**) rent yachts for several days at a time for very completive rates. Finally, the website **GetMy Boat.com** is a bustling marketplace for both private and public boat tours and charters (both bare-boat and crewed). Because there are so many entities on it, the competition often causes prices to drop below what we have above.

Fishing

Phuket Fishing Charters (www.phuketfishingcharters.com; ✆ **062060-0220**) are deep-sea fishing experts with well-equipped boats. They'll take you out for marlin, sailfish, swordfish, and tuna with top of the line equipment. Read tour descriptions carefully because some trips are for casual visitors looking for a day on a boat with stops for snorkeling and casting reel (around 2,100B) while others are for serious fisherman (3,900B–69,000B for private yacht).

Golfing

There are some superb golf courses on Phuket attracting enthusiasts from around the globe. Golf package tour companies offer some great discounts on greens fees; try **Phuket Golf Holidays** (www.phuketgolfholidays.com). Below is a selection of some of the best courses on the island.

o **The Blue Canyon Country Club,** 165 Moo 1, Thepkasattri Rd., near the airport (www.bluecanyonphuket.com; ℰ **07632-8088**), has two courses: the Canyon Course, a par-72 championship course with natural hazards, trees, and guarded greens, and the Lakes Course, which features water hazards on 17 holes. Greens fees: 4,900B in low season and 5,100B in high season at Canyon Course; 4,100B in low season and 4,300B high season at Lakes Course.

o **Laguna Phuket Golf Club,** 34 Moo 4, Srisoonthorn Rd., at the Laguna Resort Complex on Bang Tao Bay (www.lagunaphuket.com/golf; ℰ **07627-0991**), is a par-71 championship course with many water features. Greens fees: 3,950B to 5,700B; guests of Laguna resorts receive a discount.

o **Mission Hills Golf Resort & Spa,** 195 Moo 4, Phla Khlok (www.mission hillsphuket.com; ℰ **07631-0888**), was designed by Jack Nicklaus and offers ocean views over 18 holes and a 9-hole bay view, and night course. Greens fees: 4,500B.

Sea Kayaking

Phang Nga Bay National Park, a half-hour drive north of Phuket is an outstanding spot for sea kayaking. The scenery is stunning, with limestone karst towers rising from the bay of more than 120 islands. These craggy rock formations were the backdrop for the James Bond classic *The Man with the Golden Gun* and most visitors call this **James Bond Island.** Sadly, due to unfettered commercialism, the most frequently visited islands are overrun with tour groups dropping litter as they reach for a selfie stick. To avoid the crowds, **Sea kayaks** are the way to go. They'll allow you to explore the many breathtaking caves and chambers that hide beneath the jagged cliffs in peace. Check with the operators below, but all should include the hour-plus ride to and from Phang Nga, the cruise to the island area, paddle-guide, kayak, and lunch.

John Gray Sea Canoe (www.johngray-seacanoe.com; 124 Soi 1, Yaowarat Rd.; ℰ **07625-4505**) is the most respected, low-impact, eco-tour operator on Phuket and a pioneer of sea kayaking in the region. Their main trip is a *"hong by starlight"* tour (3,950B adults, 1,975B children; age 6 and under free), which includes kayaking in the *hongs* (sea caves) and a seafood buffet in Phang Nga Bay. Their day trip is now only available for private charter (29,00B for a group of four). A guide will paddle you dexterously in and out of the caves—which is frustrating if you actually like paddling—but the caves are stunning, and there's free time for paddling on your own later. Multiday and more adventurous "self-guided" tours are also offered.

The folks at **Paddle Asia** (www.paddleasia.com; 18/58 Rasdanusorn Rd.; ℂ **08189-36558**) make Phuket their home and do trips throughout the region, with a focus on custom adventure travel, rather than day junkets. They have options for beginners to experts, and on any trip, you'll paddle real decked kayaks, not inflatables. A highlight is their trip to **Khao Sok National Park** (p. 185), a 3-day adventure in which you may even spot jungle wildlife. Due to tragedies in this park in rainy season, Thai authorities often close it during storms, so stay abreast of the weather, especially in monsoon season. In Phuket, Paddle Asia can arrange offshore trips to outlying islands, kayak surfing on Kata Beach, or custom-made adventures ranging as far as Laos.

Scuba Diving

Because it's world-renowned for its access to nearby Surin Islands Marine National Park, which is home to the **Surin** and **Similan Islands** (rated by many among the world's best dive sites), scuba diving is a huge draw to the island of Phuket. Manta rays are common, and whale sharks come to feed on the plankton near the Similan Islands between January and May. For real diving junkies, a liveaboard scuba trip is the most appealing option and ups the chances of seeing oh-my-Buddha-worthy sea creatures.

For newbies, Thailand is one of the most affordable places to get into this hugely rewarding sport, yet it is not without its risks—safety is paramount when choosing your operator. When you are selecting a company, always check that it is PADI certified. Many of the storefront operations are just consolidators for other companies (meaning you get less quality care and pay a fee to a middleman), so ask if they have their own boats and make sure you'll be diving with the folks you meet behind the counter. Also check about the ratio of divers to instructor or dive master; anything more than five-to-one is less than ideal, and it should be more like two-to-one for beginner courses.

Below are a few of the best choices in Phuket. All these companies can arrange day trips to the nearby coral wall and wrecks, as well as overnight or long-term excursions to the Similan Islands (also PADI courses, Dive Master courses, or 1-day introductory lessons and Open Water certification). Multiday "Open Water" courses begin at around 15,000B.

- **Dive Asia** is a highly reputable firm on Phuket that appeals to serious divers. Their main office is at 24 Karon Rd. near Kata Beach (www.diveasia.com; ℂ **07633-0598**). Dive packages include 4-day PADI certification courses, while full-day trips around Phuket run between 3,400B and 3,900B (for experienced divers only), including two or three dives.
- **Sea Fun Divers** (www.seafundivers.com; ℂ **07634-0480**) are staffed with total pros who making learning to dive, and discovering the underwater life in Phuket, a blast. They offer trips Tuesday to Sunday that cover a variety of must-see spots sights like wrecks, walls, and reefs. 3,900B will get you 2 days of dives and equipment rentals are 650B. Those interested in an Open Water Diver certification should plan to pay 18,400B. This outfit has an office at the Le Meridien in Patong and another in Kata Noi.

- **Thailand Divers** (www.thailand-divers.com; © **07662-6067**) provides competitive services and they have their own boats. This outfitter is a good choice for those looking to add to their list of specializations, like wreck divers, rescue divers, and more. Private lessons for PADI certifications start at 15,000B; live aboard trip in the crystal clear waters around Similan are also available.

Snorkeling

In the smaller bays around the island, such as Nai Harn Beach or Relax Bay, you'll come across some lovely **snorkeling** right along the shore. For the best coral just off the shoreline, trek up to **Nai Yang Beach** for its long reef in clear, shallow waters. Nearby Raya Island is also popular, and many venture farther to the **Similan Islands** or **Ko Phi Phi**. The best times to snorkel are from November to April before the monsoon comes and makes the sea too choppy. Almost every tour operator and hotel can book day trips by boat that include hotel transfers, lunch, and gear for about 1,000B per person. The biggest thing to ask each provider is the route of the boat and how many people will join. Avoid boats with 40 or more people, if possible. The trip is more enjoyable with fewer people. If you're traveling with a bubble blower and you'd prefer to stay at the surface, most of the diving outfits listed above offer add-on snorkel packages.

Back to Nature & Other Activities

To experience the wild side of Phuket's interior, try a **rainforest trek** through the **Khao Phra Thaew National Park** in northeast Phuket; it's still relatively rich with tropical trees and wildlife. The park trails are well-maintained and the reserve also houses the **Gibbon Rehabilitation Project** (see below).

Even though elephants are not indigenous to Phuket, there are dozens of places around the island looking to capitalize on tourist dollars. Of those we can only recommend one: **Phuket Elephant Sanctuary** ★★★ (www.phuketelephantsanctuary.org; © **07652-9099**) is a safe haven for rescued pachyderms to happily live out their days without ever hauling a log or tourist again. Guests can feed the elephants and closely observe their natural interactions with other elephants as they happily roll around in the river. Famed animal rights activist Leonardo DiCaprio (yup, the Hollywood actor) visited the camp and is a major supporter of the ethical work it does and the strides it is making to improve elephant tourism in Thailand. Full day programs are 6,000B per adult, 3,000B per child; half-day programs are 50% cheaper. The Phuket Elephant Sanctuary accepts weeklong volunteers and the 16,000B fee goes directly to the large costs incurred for caring for the animals as well as three vegetarian Thai meals a day and a place to stay. Book well in advance.

River Rovers (www.riverrovers.com; © **07628-0420**) is one way to see Phuket's nature; this cruise takes in mangrove swamps (with monkeys clambering in the branches), and fish and mussel farms. Guests have the chance to do a bit of exploring by kayak, and eat a fabulous fresh seafood lunch at a floating restaurant.

ANIMAL ABUSE—AND volunteer OPPORTUNITIES

A word on those adorable monkeys you'll see in tourist areas across Thailand. The fragile primates known as **Lar Gibbons** are poached as pets when young, and caged until they are mature—and become aggressive. At this point they are usually sold to a bar, where they are dressed in children's clothes, and fed amphetamines to stay awake at night. If you watch *The Hangover: Part II*, the monkey in the movie is a riff on real-life monkeys who are taught to smoke cigarettes for shows in Thailand. Posing for photos with these monkeys unwittingly exacerbates the problem; some simple advice is: don't do it, though you'll see them in numerous places in Phuket.

Many gibbons develop psychological problems and become extremely menacing, which is when the owners want to get rid of them. **The Gibbon Rehabilitation Project** ★★ in the northeastern corner of the island (www.gibbonproject.org; 𝄞 **07626-0492;** it is operated by the Wild Animal Rescue Foundation) cares for mistreated gibbons, and volunteers are always welcome. Guides offer tours of the facility, open daily from 9am to 4:30pm. Admission is free, but donations are expected.

Another reputable animal foundation that is always looking for volunteers is the wonderful **Soi Dog Foundation** ★★ (www.soidog.org; 𝄞 **07668-1029).** Donate your time socializing with dogs (and cats), teaching them to trust humans, and learning how to walk on a leash—all essentials for finding them forever homes, the foundation says.

For land-based touring, the **Amazing Bike Tour** ★ (www.amazingbiketoursthailand.asia; 𝄞 **087263-2031**) lives up to its name. This half-day tour covers villages in the northern part of the island. The company also offers off-island trips to Ko Yao Noi, Khao Sok National Park, and Krabi. Trips start at 1,900B.

Sirinat National Marine Park ★★, 90 sq. km (35 sq. miles) of protected land and sea (mostly the latter) in the northwest corner of the island, is a peaceful retreat from the rest of the island's tourism madness. There are two fab reasons to make the journey out to the park. The first is for Phuket's largest coral reef in shallow water, only 1,000m (3,280 ft.) from the shore. The second is for the chance of spotting the endangered Olive Ridley turtles that come to nest every year between November and February. The second reason: Nai Yang beach in the park is home to Phuket's **kitesurfing** scene. The park headquarters (www.dnp.go.th; 𝄞 **07632-8226**) is a very short hop from Phuket Airport off Highway 402.

The **Phuket Aquarium** (www.phuketaquarium.org; 𝄞 **07639-1126**), at the **Phuket Marine Biological Center** (51 Moo 8, Sakdidet Rd.), seeks to educate the public about local marine life and nature preservation. It also hosts a science and nature trail along the adjoining coast. A number of the signs throughout are in Thai, but it is still worth a trip for the kid-friendly exhibits, underwater tunnel, and coral reef displays. It's open daily 8:30am to 4:30pm, and admission is 180B for adults, 100B for children.

You'd never think seashells were fascinating until you visit the **Phuket Shell Museum** (12/2 Moo 2, Viset Rd., Rawai Beach, just south of Chalong

Bay; tel. **07638-1266;** admission 200B adults, 100B for kids). Billed as "the largest shell museum in the world," it's actually not the quantity that amazes, but the quality; don't miss the world's biggest golden pearl. As always, the gift shop sells a range of tempting high-quality shell products; however, these days, any eco-savvy traveler will be well aware that the retail shell industry is depriving a sea creature of a home, and that such countries as Australia actively prohibit their import. The museum is open daily from 8am to 6pm.

Spas

If you've come to Phuket to relax, there's no better way to accomplish your goal than to visit one of the island's many spas. Luxurious hotels like **Keemala, Banyan Tree, Anantara Mai Khao,** and **The Nai Harn** all have top-rated spas but even the smallest resorts offer full spa service. As well, you can find good, affordable massages along any beach and in storefronts in the tourist areas.

Let's Relax (www.letsrelaxspa.com) is a chain with five locations across the island, so you'll never be too far from a super-pampering four-hand massage (that's where two masseuses work out the knots at once) for 1,100B. There are foot massages in La-Z-Boy-like massage chairs for 450B an hour.

WHERE TO STAY IN PHUKET

The hotels and resorts below are divided by beach area to simplify your choices on the island. In Phuket, the peak season runs from December 15 to January 15. In low season (May 1–Oct 31), rates can drop as much as 50%. For apartment-style accommodations and full homes that are ideal for groups, checkout **Airbnb** (www.airbnb.com), **HomeAway** (www.homeaway.com) and **FlipKey** (www.flipkey.com). All three have dozens of options around the island, many of which will be significantly cheaper, on a per person basis, than a hotel will be, the amount of savings going up with the size of your party.

Nai Harn Beach

Blissfully secluded with great sunset views from Promthep Cape, this area is less busy than other parts of Phuket. But this is where you'll find one of the island's most-famous resorts and an outstanding beach. There are limited restaurants on this strip of sand.

EXPENSIVE

The Nai Harn ★★★ Perched above the northern edge of Nai Harn Beach, the hotel of the same name was one of the earliest forms of luxury accommodation in Phuket (established by Mandarin Oriental in 1987 it later served as the Royal Yacht Club). Yet it still rivals anything on the island for setting and comfort. The pagoda-style foyer/lobby overlooks terraced gardens overflowing with pink and white bougainvillea. The whitewashed walls with light woods and punchy accents give the resort swish Côte d'Azur-like vibe with the turquoise waters of Nai Harn Bay glistening below. Most rooms have large balconies with four-posted sun beds. Villas have a button that, when pushed, immediately alerts your private butler to bring a bottle of champagne. Rooms are spacious with freestanding bathtubs, high-end bath products, and extra-fluffy bath robes. The hotel's wines were curated by wine expert James Suckling and the spa is one of the best on the island.

23/3 Viset Rd., Nai Harn Beach. www.thenaiharn.com. © **07638-0200.** 130 units. From 3,500–6,900B double (varies with view and season); from 10,560B suite. **Amenities:** 2 restaurants; 2 bars; outdoor pool; health club; spa; room service; babysitting; Wi-Fi (free).

Kata Beach

One of Phuket's best tourist beaches, Kata is a wide strip of soft, white sand and rolling surf, with Kata Noi located beyond a headland to the south. Rent an umbrella, get a massage, or grab a kayak or surfboard and hit the waves (there's decent surf April–November). Prime beachfront real estate on Kata Beach itself is taken up by the sprawling **Phuket Club Med** (www.clubmed. com; © **07633-0455;** rates from 5,000B), an all-inclusive, club-style resort, but its beach is open to all. In the evening, Kata comes alive in the tasteful bars and music cafes along the beach roads.

EXPENSIVE

The Boathouse Phuket★★ At the quieter south end of Kata Beach, the Boathouse is a small inn that has been a longtime favorite with many returning visitors. In December 2017, under new ownership, it received a top-to-bottom renovation that has provided the inn with a contemporary yacht theme (think: ship's rope and vintage looking oars on the walls). Comfortable, attractive rooms all face the sea, each with a terrace overlooking a pool and beach beyond; they're all equipped with writing desks and luxurious bathrooms. The Boathouse Wine & Grill is a well-regarded dining option, and its chef teaches fantastic 1-day and 2-day cooking classes that include market visits and lunch with wine pairings from local vineyards. This is an ideal spot for those looking for a slice of tranquility near the buzz of Kata.

182 Koktanod Rd., Kata Beach. www.boathouse-phuket.com. © **07633-0015-7.** 38 units. 4,300B–10,700B double; 14,000B–19,000B suite. **Amenities:** Restaurant; lounge; outdoor pool; spa; room service; babysitting; Wi-Fi (free).

Katathani Phuket Beach Resort ★★ The Katathani is on a quiet cul-de-sac and dominates a large slice of the lovely Kata Noi Beach, a haven of luxury. Rooms are contemporary, but cozy—all with large balconies and indoor sitting areas; top-end rooms are beachfront while cheaper rooms are set back from the beach in the Bhuri Wing. Wide, well-groomed lawns surround six sizable pools (having so many makes the resort feels far less crowded during high occupancy days) and lead to the graceful curve of the pristine cove. There is a nightly poolside buffet in high season. Service is excellent, and kids have their own pools and a nifty club supervised by specially trained activity and arts instructors. Since it is very popular with families this is not the resort for a quiet, romantic getaway; if that's what you're after, check out their sister hotel **The Shore** (see below), where kids are not allowed.

14 Kata Noi Rd., Kata Noi Beach. www.katathani.com. © **07633-0124-6.** 479 units. 3,950B–8,550B double; 10,050B–25,500B suite. **Amenities:** 6 restaurants; 6 bars; bar; 6

outdoor pools; 2 outdoor lit tennis courts; health club; spa; room service; babysitting; Wi-Fi (free).

Kata Rocks ★★★ Seclusion, privacy, and service—those elements make Kata Rocks a worthwhile "splash out" choice. This all-villa resort comes with personal 'rock stars' aka private butlers who handle everything from unpacking luggage to arranging for in-villa spa treatments or full-day yachting excursions. Rooms and common spaces feature lots of white-on-white décor with a pop of color coming from the private infinity pool in each room that ranges from 7- to 14-meters long. Villas are more like apartments with full kitchens, Nespresso machines, and indoor-outdoor living spaces. In-room iPads control the sound system, electric blinds, and temperature, and can be used to order room service. There are anti-jetlag pods in the spa for napping and a spa menu that marries traditional Thai and western techniques.

186/22 Koktanode Rd. Kata Noi Beach. www.katarocks.com. ℂ **07637-0777**. 35 units. Villas 16,000B–20,000B. **Amenities:** 2 restaurants; 2 bars; health club; spa; room service; babysitting; Wi-Fi (free).

The Shore ★★ This all villa property is on a steep hill just south of the main resort, and aims directly at the romantic getaway market with its secluded, luxurious pool villas; in fact, no children under 12-years-old are allowed to stay here. With a size of 130 sq. meter (1,399 sq. ft.), the pool and ocean view villas are wonderfully spacious, and along with a private infinity pool with day bed built into the pool, each contains a living/dining area, a bedroom, and an ample bathroom with a deep bathtub designed for two people. The two-bedroom pool villas are twice as big. Facilities include a top-class restaurant, The Harbor, a relaxing bar, and, of course, a spa.

14 Kata Noi Rd., Kata Noi Beach. www.theshore.katathani.com. ℂ **07633-0124**. 48 units. 24,000B pool and sea-view villas; 48,000B 2-bedroom pool villas. **Amenities:** Restaurant; bar; health club; spa; Wi-Fi (free).

MODERATE

Sawasdee Village ★★ A 10-minute walk from Kata Beach (or short ride on the complimentary shuttle), you'll pass a small portico of stone with some Khmer statuary; walk in and you'll discover a little Eden. An attractive garden surrounds a small pool with ornate fountains, waterfalls, and overflowing greenery. For digs, you have two choices: garden rooms that are fairly compact but stylish, with canopy beds and outdoor rain showers. Or the stunning pool access Baray Villas which are enormous, featuring a delightfully ornate blend of Moroccan and Thai design. The spa mixes treatments from those two cultures, too.

38 Katekwan Rd., Kata Beach. www.phuketsawasdee.com. ℂ **07633-0979**. 86 units. 2,900B–3,500B garden room; 7,500B Baray Villas. **Amenities:** 2 restaurants; bar; 3 outdoor pools; spa; Wi-Fi (free).

INEXPENSIVE

Fin Hostel ★★ This cheery hostel is walking distance to Kata Beach, the surfing hub of Thailand. The good-natured staff at Fin make it easy to catch a wave with in-house surfboard rentals (150B/hour; 500B day). Relax after a day at the beach in the impeccably clean dorms or the more luxurious "capsules", which have double and single beds behind private curtains. There are private rooms, too, which have brightly colored accent pillows. A small pool, laundry facilities, and communal area round out the services. Advanced payment can only be made by bank transfer but websites like Booking.com offer online payments.

100/20-21 Kata Rd. www.finhostelphuket.com. ⓒ **088753-1162.** 15 units. Dorms and capsules 300B–1,000B; 1,000B–3,000B private room. **Amenities:** Restaurant; bar; outdoor pool; Wi-Fi (free).

Katanoi Resort ★ This tiny resort is dwarfed by the enormous Katathani, which stands right across the road. But with smart rooms that cost a fraction of the price and its location just 2 minutes' walk from Kata Noi beach, it's an excellent value. Guests have a choice between apartments that are small but well-equipped with cable TV, small balconies and decent-sized bathrooms; and two-bedroom villas with fully fitted kitchens. There is a small swimming pool, a bar with inexpensive local beers, laundry service, and helpful staff.

37 Kata Noi Rd., Kata Noi Beach (Kata Noi is south of Kata Beach). www.katanoiresort. com. ⓒ **07633-3078.** 15 units. 1,200B apartment; 1,900B villa. **Amenities:** Restaurant; bar; outdoor pool; Wi-Fi (free).

Karon Beach

Karon Beach is a long stretch of beach lined lots of big hotels with multiple pools and every amenity imaginable…except direct beach access (for most). The northern end is where you'll find the nicest sand, and there are heaps of tailors, gift shops, bars (some are kind of sleazy), small restaurants and cafes, dive operators, local markets, and minimarts jumbled together behind the length of the beach. Sandwiched between classy Kata and hedonistic Patong, Karon has the niceties of Kata mixed with the girly bars of Patong; however, here the sex tourism is low-key.

MODERATE

Centara Villas Phuket ★★ Set on a hillside perch on the north end of Karon Beach—along the crest of a hill between Karon and Relax Bay—this hideaway consists of freestanding, luxury bungalows in tropical garden surrounds, overlooking the majestic crashing surf. The room decor is tasteful with slick, modern bathrooms with skylights. The restaurant is first-rate, and this self-contained gem has a friendly staff that can handle any issue; they drive the zippy golf carts that transport guests around the expansive property. The outdoor waterfall pool overlooks the sea, and their outdoor spa *salas* add a touch of nature to a relaxing treatment. Thai cooking classes and in-villa dining with a private chef are on offer, as well.

701 Patak Rd., Tambon Karon. ⓒ **07628-6300.** 72 units. 3,000B–14,000B villas. **Amenities:** 2 restaurants; bar; 2 outdoor pools; room service; babysitting; Wi-Fi (free).

Hilton Phuket Arcadia Resort & Spa ★★ This sprawling resort is a great choice for families. It has dedicated family rooms with interconnecting doors, kid-friendly menus, a kids' pool and play area, water slides, game room, family brunch on Sunday, and much more. Staff members happily lead young guests on resort treasure hunts and hold art classes while mom and dad catch a spa treatment. But other guests will also enjoy this modern, full-facility resort, set in 30 hectares (74 acres) of lawns and lush tropical gardens (many of the stylish guest rooms overlook Karon Beach). The hotel has a large "spa village" with 15 purpose-built villas connected by raised wooden platforms in a mellow, wooded glen at the heart of the resort. The in-house dining choices are top-notch (do try the Thai restaurant), and everything about the place is classy, with snappy service.

333 Patak Rd., Karon Beach (middle of Karon Beach Rd.). www.hilton.com. © **07639-6433.** 676 units. 2,810B–4,800B double; from 4,500B suite. **Amenities:** 4 restaurants; lounge bar w/live band; 5 pools; golf course nearby and putting green on-site; outdoor lit tennis courts; health club; spa; watersports equipment; room service; babysitting; Wi-Fi (free).

Le Meridien Phuket ★★★ Tucked away on secluded Relax Bay, the Le Meridien features a 549-m (1,800-ft.) beach—with trained lifeguards—and 16 hectares (40 acres) of tropical greenery, making it one of the largest resorts on the island. The resort caters to families with plenty of activities, a day-care center, and kid-centric meals. The large self-contained complex combines Western and traditional Thai architecture, and one of the advantages to its U-shape layout is that it ensures that nearly all the rooms face the ocean, with the lowest category getting a garden view. The cheerful modern furnishings in the rooms are of rattan and teak; each room has a balcony with comfortable deck chairs. Seven restaurants are on property, meaning lots of dining choices.

29 Soi Karon Noi, Relax Bay. www.lemeridien.com. © **07637-0100.** 470 units. 4,200B–6,500B double; from 8,510B suite. **Amenities:** 7 restaurants; 3 bars w/games and live shows; 2 large outdoor pools; outdoor lit tennis courts; squash courts; health club; spa; kids' club; room service; babysitting; Wi-Fi (free).

Marina Phuket ★ These simple cottages tucked in the jungle above a scenic promontory between Kata and Karon beaches provide an adequate level of comfort in four room types. Rates vary according to the view, but all have a jungle bungalow feel, connected by hilly walkways and boardwalks past the lush hillside greenery (keep your eyes peeled for wildlife). It is a hike down to the rocky shore and the swimming isn't great, but they have a good seaside restaurant, **On the Rock,** and their in-house **Marina Divers** (www. marinadivers.com; © **07633-0272**) is a PADI International Diving School, which conducts classes, rents equipment, and leads good multiday expeditions. *Travel Tip:* Book on the hotel's website for free airport transfers.

47 Karon Rd., Karon Beach (on bluff at south end of Karon Beach Rd.). From 3,900–6,500B double. www.marinaphuket.com. © **07633-0625.** 89 units. **Amenities:** 4 restaurants; spa; outdoor pool; room service; Wi-Fi (free).

Mövenpick Resort & Spa ★★ Big, big, big! Occupying a huge area opposite the center of Karon Beach, this Swiss-run, luxury hotel is ideal for those who want everything on-site. Rooms range from garden view doubles in the main building to plunge pool villas decorated in Balinese-style, with thatched roofs, and massive, two-bedroom family suites. Guests have a choice of four pools, as well as several restaurants and bars scattered around the site. There's a play zone for kids and a spa, fitness room, and PADI diving courses, run by the reliable Euro Divers, for adults.

509 Patak Rd., Karon Beach. www.moevenpick-hotels.com. ✆ **07639-6139.** 364 units. From 2,900B double; from 5,000B plunge pool villa. **Amenities:** 4 restaurants; 3 bars; 4 outdoor pools; 2 tennis courts; health club; fitness room; spa; Wi-Fi (free).

INEXPENSIVE

In On the Beach ★★   One of only a few acceptable budget accommodation offerings, In On The Beach is also one of the only spots with direct beach access on this part of the island. Rooms are a reasonable size and most have sea views. They're sparsely but smartly furnished and underwent an update in 2018. Bathrooms have everything you'll need: hot showers, good water pressure, a vanity large enough to unpack toiletries, and good lighting. There is a pool just steps from the beach and complimentary breakfast with an impressive fresh fruit display to enjoy on a quiet terrace.

695/697 Moo 1, Patak Rd., Karon Beach. www.karon-inonthebeach.com. ✆ **07639-8220.** 30 units. 1,100B–3,500B double. **Amenities:** Restaurant; outdoor pool; Wi-Fi (free).

Patong

Once the popular haunt of the U.S. Navy's 9th Fleet, Patong built its nightlife on cheap sex and even cheaper beer. Today, this is Phuket's most divisive destination, with plenty of affordable shopping, dining, clubbing—and prostitution. The main strip never shies away from what it really is: a place where—for a price—any sexual desire becomes reality, and it's all accompanied by the constant beeping of tuk-tuks attempting to take tourists for a ride (in both senses). The main street is a free-for-all with ping-pong shows (Google if you dare), lady-boy bars, and wide-eyed men trolling the streets as a walking advertisement for a midlife crisis.

That being said, it's not all bad: Patong has some good accommodation and nice places to eat, and its white-sand beach is bustling with wholesome activities (and quite a few hungover sun worshippers) during the day. But many travelers will find the scene here depressing.

MODERATE

Fisherman's Harbour Urban Resort ★   Despite the neighborhood's lowbrow nightlife, the hotel has managed to create a family-friendly space—and a quarter of the 390 rooms have bunk beds for kiddos, extra beds, and a spacious living room. Rooms are crisp and cool with deep bathtubs and fun turquoise murals of the local sea life. There's a kids' club, a swim-up bar for mom and dad, and bike rentals to keep the family active. Book on the hotel's website for added perks like spa discounts and late checkout.

2/21 Siriraj Rd., Patong. www.fishermansharbour.com. ✆ **07638-0400.** 390 units. 2,200B–4,500B double. From 5,000B suites. **Amenities:** Restaurant; bars; outdoor pool; room service; babysitting; kids' club; fitness center; Wi-Fi (free).

Novotel Phuket ★★   Located on a hillside toward the northern end of Patong beach (the quieter end), this resort offers most of the facilities of a top-end hotel at midrange prices. Bright, tiled rooms all have balconies, most with views of the bay, and stylish furnishings are complemented by murals depicting Thai temples and scenery. There are plenty of facilities to keep guests entertained and well-fed, include several restaurants and bars, a three-tiered swimming pool, Muay Thai lessons for kids and adults, and a tour desk where you can plan tailor-made adventures. Service is smooth and efficient.

Kalim Beach, Patong. www.novotelphuket.com. © **07634-2777.** 215 units. 2,200B–4,000B double. From 6,200B suites. **Amenities:** 2 restaurants; 2 bars; 2 outdoor pools; room service; babysitting; kids' club; spa; Wi-Fi (free).

INEXPENSIVE

Budget lodgings are difficult to find on Patong beach, and what there is tends to be in the backstreets where it's a bit of a trek to the beach. If you need to find a room for a few thousand baht, you'll fare better in Phuket Town or on the beaches farther south at Kata and Karon. Of the budget accommodation at Patong, the following offer reasonable value:

Wire Hostel (www.facebook.com/WireHostelPatong; © 07660-4066; 66/10 Bangla Rd.) has dorms from 340B to 500B that fill up quickly with travelers looking to be in the heart of Patong, and the hostel is on bustling Bangla Road. Clean bathrooms, a cool communal area but it does get a bit noisy.

Patong Backpacker Hostel (no website so book on www.hostelworld.com; © **07634-1196;** 140 Thawiwong Rd.) keeps tidy dorms that have three to 10 bunks and private lockers, some have attached bathrooms. Rates: 300B to 550B.

Kamala & Surin Beaches

These two attractive beaches, both flanked by cliffs and steep hillsides, are home to some of Phuket's most exclusive hideaways, so the area is worth considering if your main objective is honeymoon-style romance or tropical escapism. However, all the luxury comes at a price, and this part of the island offers few selections for budget travelers.

In 2016, Phuket's police cracked down hard on unlicensed beach vendors, bars, and restaurants. Few places felt the impact quite like Surin Beach, where the once-bustling beach is now a bit like a ghost town. While the expat community might mourn the loss of their go-to place for a buzzy weekend in the sun, many visitors and sun worshipers will be happy to enjoy lazy days in the sun without the disturbance of rogue hawkers selling everything from local lagers to beach mats and plates of *pad Thai*.

EXPENSIVE

Amanpuri Resort ★★★ The adjectives to describe this Aman-owned property are as endless as the ocean views from the rooms, and luxurious, private, peaceful, exclusive, and blissful all spring to mind. Located on a quiet peninsula on the west coast, the hotel has access to a private beach and uninterrupted views of the Andaman Sea. Traditional in design, the pavilions are oversized with outdoor sitting areas (most with private pools), elegant Thai art pieces, sprawling bathrooms, and verdant surrounding gardens. Try surfing or Thai boxing at the beach (and book a massage in the sumptuous spa to sooth post-sport pains) or paddle offshore in a kayak. The resort is serious about wellness, from yoga classes and healthy food to carefully calibrated programs designed to help with emotional well-being, physical fitness, and improved happiness. But even without an expert-led program, you'll leave this magnificent resort restored and relaxed.

Pansea Beach, Cherngtalay. www.amanresorts.com. © **07632-4333.** 71 units. From 23,000B pavilion; from 78,000B pool pavilions. **Amenities:** 4 restaurants; bar; outdoor pool; spa; watersports equipment; room service; babysitting; Wi-Fi (free).

Keemala ★★★ This design-centric hotel is built into the lush, forested hills just up from Kamala Beach, and it is one of the most magical hotels in Thailand. The hotel has gone viral on social media thanks to its "bird's nest villas" that appear suspended in the air in front of private infinity pools. There are three other room categories: an entry-level clay pool villa with dazzling views, a safari-style tent (with a private pool, naturally), and a double-decker tree pool villa that feels plucked from a modern, very luxurious, very sexy take on "Robinson Crusoe." But there is so much more to the property than photo opportunities: There is a hotel pool with swim-up bar, a wine cellar for private meals, and healthy food options including raw, macrobiotic, vegan, and gluten-free menus both through room service and at the hotel's restaurants. The spa is set in eight podlike treatment rooms, and there are opportunities to join guided jungle hikes, yoga class, or Muay Thai sessions. Commendably, the hotel prides itself on treating animals ethically and does not promote elephant camps or visits to dolphin shows—and there are even rescued water buffalos on site!

10-88 Nakasud Rd. www.keemala.com. © **07635-8777.** 38 units. Villas from 16,000B. **Amenities:** 2 restaurants; bar; outdoor pool; spa; room service; Wi-Fi (free).

Paresa ★★★ "Paresa" is a Sanskrit word meaning "heaven of all heavens," and while this may seem an extravagant claim to make, this award-winning resort nestled into the hills of Phuket does instill a feeling of peace and contentment in its guests. Paresa offers an idyllic location (on a steep hillside with private infinity pools that seem to merge with the Andaman Sea beyond) and stylish luxury (spacious brick villas with wood floors and solid wood furnishings). The resort sprawls over such a wide area that a fleet of golf carts and SUVs are needed to transport guests to and from their villas, which come in five categories of ascending magnificence. Facilities are all top class, including Diavolo restaurant, and the luxurious spa. Bring a notebook to jot down techniques at the state-of-the-art, on-site cooking school.

49 Moo 6, Layi-Nakalay Rd. (to the south of Kamala Beach). www.paresaresorts.com. © **07630-2000.** 49 units. 17,000B–60,000B suites and villas. **Amenities:** 2 restaurants; bar; outdoor pool; health club; room service; spa; Wi-Fi (free).

The Surin Phuket ★★★ The Surin commands an excellent view of Pansea Bay and has its own private stretch of sand, with shady wooden walkways under the cover of lush coconut groves. From the exotic lobby, with columns and a lily pond, to sleek private bungalows, it is one of the most handsome properties on the island. True, the quality comes with a big price tag, but this romantic getaway has all the details down pat. From the beach, grab a snorkel, body board, yoga mat, or try windsurfing. Each room is a thatched mini-suite with a private sun deck and top amenities, and some of them are just steps from the sand. The black-tile swimming pool is large and luxurious. The fine service here caters to the likes of honeymooners and celebrities, but everyone is treated like a VIP.

118, Moo 3, Surin Beach Rd., Cherng Talay (next to the Amanpuri). www.thesurinphuket. com.℃**07662-1580.** 108 units. From 5,300B cottage; from 8,800B beach suite. **Amenities:** 3 restaurants; bar; outdoor pool; 2 outdoor lit tennis courts; spa; watersports equipment & dive center; room service; babysitting; Wi-Fi (free).

Twinpalms Phuket ★★★   The brainchild of a Swedish entrepreneur, this gorgeous Thai contemporary resort has sublime charm and cutting-edge style. A stunning, open-rafter lobby with glassy stone floors makes way to a vast pool lined with towering palm trees and shaded cabanas, the photogenic centerpiece of the property. Guests have use of an excellent spa and highly acclaimed restaurant, **Oriental Spoon,** as well as an extensive wine room. The airy Lagoon rooms and suites feel like true tropical escapes, some of which have terraces that go straight into the water. The rooms flow perfectly from spacious bathrooms with heavenly showers to billowy bedding that ensures sweet dreams. Twin Palms is the place to be after dark too, as its nearby **Catch Beach Club** is one of the hottest spots for Phuket scene-makers to be seen. The Sunday brunch at **Twinpalms** is legendary.

106/46 Moo 3, Surin Beach Rd. http://twinpalms-phuket.com. ℃**07631-6500.** 97 units. From 6,300B deluxe palm room; from 10,000B deluxe lagoon room; from 19,400B 1-bedroom deluxe pool suite; 21,000B 2-bedroom penthouse residence with private pool. **Amenities:** 2 restaurants; bar; outdoor pool; watersports equipment; room service; babysitting; Wi-Fi (free).

INEXPENSIVE

Benyada Lodge ★   With simple rooms and an all-around relaxed, low-key vibe, this hotel is the ideal choice for those who are keen to be on Surin beach but don't want to blow lots of baht on a big-name resort. Large rooms are contemporary Thai with crisp bedding on wooden platform beds or more dramatic four-poster beds, all with Thai silk accent pillows. Everything is well-kept if slightly old-fashioned, but the proximity to the beach is a major boon. The friendly staff fumbles a bit when trying to communicate with their international guests but they always have a good attitude.

106/52 Moo 3. www.benyadalodge-phuket.com. ℃**07627-1777.** 29 units. 1,800B–3,500B double; 1,6250B–3,500B junior suite. **Amenities:** Restaurant; bar; room service; Wi-Fi (free).

Manathai Surin ★★   The birdcage motif that is echoed throughout the entrance is a nod to the local tradition of caging birds and releasing them for good luck—you'll see many Thai houses on the island display beautiful bird cages in front of their home. In the lobby, however, the cages are reimagined as chic, minimalist chairs and as light fixtures. The uber-stylish rooms are bright and cheerful with rattan blinds and Thai handicrafts used for tasteful decorations. For the price and the location (steps from Surin Beach), the hotel is a win-win combo. There is a nice Thai restaurant, an authentic cooking class here, a charming spa, and a small pool for quick dips.

121/1 Moo 3, Srisunthorn Rd. www.manathai.com.© **07636-0250.** 66 units. 1,700B–3,200B double; 3,500B–5,300B suite. **Amenities:** Restaurant; bar; outdoor pool; spa; room service; Wi-Fi (free).

Bang Thao Bay (Laguna)

Twenty minutes south of the airport and just as far north of Patong Beach on the western shore of Phuket, this isolated area is Phuket's high-end, "integrated resort" of several properties that share some of the island's top-rated facilities. It can feel a little too corporate until you get off "campus" and explore local fisherman's villages or stake claim to a pretty patch of sand on the stunning Bang Thao Beach.

EXPENSIVE

Banyan Tree Phuket ★★★ This is one of Phuket's most famous hideaway for honeymooners, sports stars, and high society. Private villas with walled courtyards, many with private pools or Jacuzzis, are spacious and grand, and lavishly styled in teakwood with outdoor bathtubs. The main pool is truly impressive—a free-form lagoon, landscaped with greenery and rock formations—with a flowing water canal. In a small village-like setting, the spa provides a wide range of beauty and health treatments in luxurious rooms. The resort can arrange barbecues at your villa, or you can dine at the Tamarind Restaurant, which serves delicious health food. The Banyan Tree garners many international awards, especially for its eco-friendly stance. The staff are affable and the concierge is well-connected and informed about day trips to secluded islands and local's only restaurants.

33/27 Moo 4, Srisoonthorn Rd. (north end of beach). www.banyantree.com. © **07632-4374.** 150 units. 14,000B–80,000B villas. **Amenities:** 5 restaurants; lounge; outdoor pool; golf course; 3 outdoor lit tennis courts; health club; spa; watersports equipment; room service; babysitting; Wi-Fi (free).

Outrigger Laguna Phuket Beach Resort ★★ Situated on the northern fringe of the Laguna complex, Outrigger consists of two sections: one with detached, spacious villas of two to four bedrooms, some with a private pool, and another section that contains the lobby, an inviting angular pool, health club, and a seven-story block of one- to three-bedroom suites. The latter occupy the top floor and boast rooftop private pools with impressive views across the Laguna complex. All suites have huge open-plan living, dining, and cooking areas with floor-to-ceiling windows and big balconies, plus cozy bedrooms and sparkling-clean bathrooms. There's free bicycle use for all guests and a cheery kids' club right next to the pool and lobby. The resort's main restaurant, Panache, serves a tempting range of Thai and Mediterranean dishes.

323 Moo 2 Srisoonthorn Rd. www.outrigger.com. © **07636-0600.** 255 units. 12,700B–19,400B 1- to 3-bedroom suites; 14,400B–37,900B 2- to 4-bedroom villas. **Amenities:** 2

restaurants; bar; 2 outdoor pools and outdoor kids' pool; health club; bikes; children's club; Wi-Fi (free).

MODERATE

Andaman Bangtao Bay Resort ★ Bungalows at this small, friendly resort are just 20 steps from the beach and the rooms adhere to a classic Thai style. While there aren't flashy modern amenities, the rooms are spick and span, and the bathrooms are spacious. Everything here, from the staff to the service, is pretty laid-back, but it suits easy going Bang Thao just right. A small pool overlooks the ocean and lounge chairs are set up on the beach each morning.

82/9 Moo 3. www.andamanbangtaobayresort.com. ℭ **07631-4214.** 22 units. 1,500B–7,900B doubles. **Amenities:** Restaurant; outdoor pool; Wi-Fi (free).

Dream Phuket Hotel & Spa ★★ While always hospitable, helpful and polite, Thai hospitality standards are traditionally more formal, which is part of the reason we love the energetic team at Dream, who are Phuket's "cool kids" and well-informed on the hippest beach clubs, restaurants, and shops. Modern rooms compliment the contemporary hotel layout, which surrounds a wide pool with a well-stocked swim-up bar (a handful of ground-level rooms have swim-up access). Guest rooms have a cool mid-century meets ikat vibe that's hip and curated looking, but I generally feel the villas aren't worth the extra baht. There's a rooftop infinity pool with great sunset views. At the hotel's Dream Beach Club international DJs entertain travelers as they hang in spacious cabanas or enjoy a pool party with new friends.

11/7 Moo 6. www.dreamhotels.com. ℭ **07660-9888.** 172 units. 2,250B–7,000B doubles; Suites and villas from 17,000B. **Amenities:** 2 restaurants; 2 outdoor pools; 2 bars; spa; beach club; fitness center; Wi-Fi (free).

Layan Beach

EXPENSIVE

Anantara Phuket Layan ★★★ With pride in protecting Phuket's wildlife and a passion for service and style, this resort ticks all right boxes. That includes a secluded beach where kayaks and water sports await, a fab watering hole next to the swimming pool, and complimentary use of a 4G smartphone for all guests. Pool villas each come with their spacious sundeck, outdoor living spaces, and a private plunge pool. Like Thailand's other Anantara resorts, this property effortlessly blends Thai details with contemporary design to create chic, relaxed rooms. The spa has a number of unique treatments, including one in which a mixture of heated seashells and herbs are suppose to release tension in the muscles with the calcium ions helping rejuvenate the skin. Once a year, in partnership with the Mai Khao Marine Turtle Foundation (www.maikhaomarineturtlefoundation.com), the hotel releases 40 endangered turtles off Layan Beach, and guests are invited to participate.

31/1 Moo 6, Cherng Talay. www.thepavilionsresorts.com/phuket. ℭ **07631-7600.** 81 units. From 5,900B double; from 14,000B pool villa. **Amenities:** 2 restaurants; bar; spa; tennis courts; 2 outdoor pools; kids' club; Wi-Fi (free).

Phuket Pavilions ★★ "No tan lines" is the catchphrase at this intimate escape, by which guests should understand that they can enjoy total privacy within the grounds of their spacious pool villa. The resort is situated on a hill just north of the Laguna complex, and while it's a bit of a trek from the beach, most guests will settle for lounging around the luxurious pavilions. Furnishings are super-modern and comfortable, and each pavilion has its private pool, as well as fantastic views out to sea. Two-, three-, and four-bedroom villas are ideal for groups looking for a tranquil retreat. Golf carts are on hand to run guests to the Plantation Club restaurant or 360° Lookout bar, and spa treatments are offered in specially constructed rooms beside each private pool. No children under 16 are admitted.

31/1 Moo 6, Cherng Talay. www.thepavilionsresorts.com/phuket. ⓒ **07631-7600.** 49 units. From 5,500 suites; from 12,000B pool villa; 25,000B 3-bedroom pool villa. **Amenities:** Restaurant; bar; room service; spa; Wi-Fi (free).

9 Nai Thon & Nai Yang Beaches

Nai Thon and **Nai Yang Beaches** form part of the **Sirinath National Marine Park,** which was established to protect offshore coral reefs and turtles that nest in this region. These casuarina-fringed stretches of sand are quite isolated meaning that, generally, apart from a few posh resorts, there are limited facilities in this remote corner of the island.

Nai Yang is known for its annual release of hatchling sea turtles into the Andaman Sea. Mature sea turtles weigh from 45 to 680kg (100 to 1,500 lbs.) and swim the waters around Phuket, and though the law is supposed to protect them from fishermen and poachers, who collect their eggs from beaches, their numbers are dwindling. If not for the efforts of international volunteer groups who have spent years working out of a small conservation center at Ko Phra Thong near Khuraburi, about 100km (62 miles) north of Phuket, these creatures would probably have become extinct already.

Nai Thon is just south of Nai Yang (closer to Laguna) and is home to a handful of resorts. It is one of the quietest beaches, yet is also possibly the most picturesque, on the entire west coast of Phuket.

EXPENSIVE

Trisara ★★ Tisara affords a high level of comfort in a clutch of private, contemporary pool villas right at the seaside. It's definitely not as classy as The Surin, nor as celebrity-friendly as The Banyan Tree, but it would like to think it outdoes both; at times, you'll rub up against a distinct attitude here. Still, its private spaces are picturesquely flamboyant, with pools overlooking the blue water below—it should appeal to those who enjoy the isolation. Book a half- or full-day cruise on the hotel's private boat the explore nearby islands and snorkeling destinations in ultimate luxury.

60/1 Moo 6, Srisoonthorn Rd. www.trisara.com. ⓒ **07631-0100.** 39 units. 26,800B–38,650B room/suite; from 85,600B 2-bedroom villa. **Amenities:** 2 restaurants; bar; private outdoor pool; seaside public pool; tennis courts; health club; spa; children's center; room service; babysitting; Wi-Fi (free).

MODERATE

The Slate ★★ Named in honor of Phuket's mining past, The Slate is a chic design hotel close to quiet Nai Yang Beach. Without an experienced designer, all the industrial elements could feel too sterile, but American-born and Thailand-based Bill Bensley (of Four Season Tented Camp fame) carefully guided the hotel to a place where harsh lines meet tropical fauna to create something magical. There are three pools on the property, including an adults-only infinity pool, and many of the rooms include private butlers and in-room massage facilities. Speaking of the rooms, they're total sanctuaries with lots of space to relax, exotic flowers, and natural elements. The restaurants are trendy and guests enjoy modern takes on Thai classics, happy hour at the bar, and craft beer promotions on Fridays. Surprisingly, the place is tops for families and there is a kids' pool, kiddie cooking classes, scavenger hunts, and a kids' club.

Nai Yang Beach 116 Moo 1. www.theslatephuket.com. © **07632-7006.** 177 units. 3,500B–14,000B suites; 14,000B–25,000B villas. **Amenities:** 6 restaurants; 2 bars; 3 outdoor pools; health club; spa; children's club; room service; babysitting; Wi-Fi (free).

Mai Khao Beach

Mai Khao is a wide sweep of beach on the northeastern shore close to the airport. It is Phuket's longest beach and is the site where sea turtles lay their eggs during December and January.

EXPENSIVE

Anantara Mai Khao Phuket Villas ★★★ Behind the tall laterite wall that separates the Anantara from the outside world lies a wonderland of tropical gardens and lagoons with secluded pool villas and a stretch of beach shaded by casuarina trees. The villas are artfully designed, with lots of traditional Thai ornamentation and the utmost in creature comforts—and they each include a private pool plus sun loungers, a sala, a huge outdoor bath, and a choice of indoor or outdoor showers. The two restaurants are both extremely stylish—La Sala serving Thai and Sicilian cuisine all day and Sea Fire Salt specializing in seafood, with a resident salt sommelier sharing his secrets with diners. The signature treatment at the nature-inspired spa uses warmed bamboo sticks with aromatic oils to ease muscle tension. The beautiful grounds are a delight to stroll around, and there's even a thatched villa on a tiny island for the resident population of ducks.

888 Moo 3, Mai Khao. www.anantara.com. © **07633-6100-9.** 91 units. Villas from 15,500B. **Amenities:** 2 restaurants; bar; outdoor pool; health club; spa; Wi-Fi (free).

Phuket Town

Most just pass through the island's commercial hub, but Old Phuket culture abounds in the many colorful Sino-Portuguese homes and shophouse-style architecture, and it's the best place to base yourself if you want to explore all the island's beaches. This charming area is packed with cute coffeehouses, colorful street art, and affordable places to bed down, from adorable boutiques to hip hostels. Even if you stay on the beach, it's well worth a visit to see the cultural hub of Phuket.

INEXPENSIVE

Ai Phuket Hostel ★   This is one of Phuket's more stylish hostels; its colorful walls have hand-drawn illustrations of the houses in the neighborhood while the ceilings feature ancient maps and Chinese art. There is a lot on offer here: bunk-style rooms with six beds in a women-only room, eight beds in a mixed dorm, and private doubles with and without a private bathroom. We'd say go for the latter: even in high season, a private room with a small but bright and clean bathroom only costs 850B, a great deal.

88 Yaowarat Rd., Phuket Town. www.aiphukethostel.com. ℂ **07621-2881.** 6 units. 220B–299B dorm; 490B–850B double. **Amenities:** Wi-Fi (free).

Baan Suwantawe ★   With 20 well-equipped rooms, this place is a smart base for those who have aged out of the hostel life but don't want to spend 10,000B a night for a place to sleep. It is set in the most charming part of town, and while rooms don't share that charm they're solidly comfortable with good quality beds, cable TV, a desk, central air-conditioning, rain showerheads, and a balcony. There's even a small pool. There's no restaurant, but plenty of eateries nearby and the staff are very helpful.

1/9-10 Dibuk Rd., Phuket Town. www.baansuwantawe.com. ℂ **07621-2879.** 20 units. 1,400B–1,700B studio; 2,200B–3,000B suite. **Amenities:** Outdoor pool; Wi-Fi (free).

Casa Blanca Boutique Hotel ★★★   Few places in Phuket can match Casa Blanca in terms of style for price: the hotel is a whitewashed and elegantly revamped Sino-Portuguese mansion. Rooms have tasteful and graphic wallpaper, modern art, and the charm and intimacy of a bed-and-breakfast. There's a notable café in the hotel along with a small pool and a tour desk to help arrange island excursions and transfers.

26 Phuket Rd., Phuket Town. www.casablancaphuket.com. ℂ **07621-9019.** 17 units. 1,300B–2,800B double. **Amenities:** Outdoor pool; café; Wi-Fi (free).

The Memory at On On Hotel ★★   There's close to a century of history packed into this enchanting Old Town boutique, which first opened in 1929. Today its rooms have modern amenities and curated Old World charm. Shutters open to the bustling neighborhood below and rooms have each have slightly different décor with bright walls, cozy sitting areas, and great natural light. The lobby and check-in retain a lovely sense of period style, with painted tiles on the floor, exposed teak beams, and tropical orchids in beautiful planters. On an island where historic buildings and budget-friendly hotels are frequently razed in favor of another big chain resort, it's nice to have a place to stay that delivers style, friendly service, and a touch of the past.

19 Phangnga Rd., Phuket Town. www.thememoryhotel.com. ℂ **07636-3700.** 35 units. 1,300B–3,300B double. **Amenities:** Wi-Fi (free).

Rommanee Boutique Guesthouse ★★   Right in the heart of the colorful Soi Romanee—think of this street at Phuket's answer to Copenhagen's famous Nyhavn—this is an artsy, modern hotel. Rooms feature cool murals, bright colors, and funky lamps; the whole effect is very stylish. With seven rooms over three floors, attention is personal—just be sure to ask the hotel staff haul any heavy bags up the steep stairs. Bathrooms are small but efficient.

15 Soi Rommanee, Phuket Town. www.facebook.com/therommanee. ⓒ **089728-9871.** 7 units. 1,200B–2,800B double. **Amenities:** Wi-Fi (free).

Royal Phuket City Hotel ★ For a small town like Phuket, this hotel is surprisingly cosmopolitan and ideal for those who are looking for some nice facilities without breaking the bank. There is a large and modern health club, a full-service spa with a non-nonsense Thai massage, a spacious outdoor swimming pool, and an executive business center. Above the outdated marble lobby, guest rooms are smart with simple, contemporary furnishings, and comfortable beds. Views of the busy town below pale in comparison to the beachfront just a short ride away.

154 Phang Nga Rd. www.royalphuketcity.com. ⓒ **07623-3333.** 251 units. 1,800B–2,700B double; from 7,000B suite. **Amenities:** 3 restaurants; bar; outdoor pool; health club; spa; room service; Wi-Fi (free).

WHERE TO EAT IN PHUKET

Bangkok is the culinary capital of Thailand. But Phuket isn't far behind, chock full of five-star dining options, plus street food that is a delicious hybrid of Thai and Chinese flavors. And for fresh seafood, Phuket can't be beat.

Kata & Karon

The busy road between Kata and Karon (as well as the many side streets) is crammed with small cafes and restaurants serving affordable Thai and Western food. There are also lots of outdoor beer bars and cafes on the far southern end of Kata Beach that rock till late and are handy for grabbing a quick bite, local style. Of those low-key joints on Kata Yai, the best seafood stall is **Kata Mama** (ⓒ 07628-4006), a longstanding shop with friendly Thai staff. The simply named **Istanbul Restaurant ★★★** (www.istanbulrestaurantphuket. com; ⓒ 091820-7173) does Turkish breakfasts, kebabs, and regional favorites like minced beef atop eggplant. Its prices are low, and its staff are a delightful bunch. **Red Duck ★★** (www.facebook.com/redduckrestaurant; ⓒ **084850-2929**) has tons of regular clients who come back for the vegan selections, seafood curries, and the vegetable *larb*—all made without MSG.

For a casual meal in Karon, try **The Pad Thai Shop ★★** (look for an orange sign with blue font). As the name suggests, it's all about noodles at this humble roadside shop, but the fried rice with veggies and crabmeat is equally famous; closed on Friday. **Eat Bar & Grill ★★★** (www.eatbargrill.com; ⓒ 085292-5652) is another real standout. It does a bang-up job with beef burgers, steaks and other western fare. Book in advance during high season to avoid waiting.

Boathouse Wine & Grill ★★★ THAI/INTERNATIONAL So legendary is the Thai and Western cuisine at the Boathouse that, after numerous requests over the years, the management now arranges cooking lessons with the chef. A large bar and separate dining area sport nautical touches, and through huge picture windows, or from the terrace, guests can watch the sun set over the watery horizon as they dine. The cuisine combines the best of East and West and utilizes only the finest ingredients—top-quality steaks, fresh fish, colorful veggies, and fruits. The Boathouse also has an excellent wine room with over 800 labels. Private dining rooms elevate a romantic meal, the Friday wine lunches (1,000B) include three courses and free-flow wine, and there is an over-the-top brunch on the last Sunday of the month (from 1,200B).

182 Koktanode Rd. (at The Boathouse Hotel). www.boathousephuket.com. © **07633-0015.** Reservations recommended during peak season. Main courses 3000B–1,600B. Daily 6:30am–11pm.

Mom Tri's Kitchen ★★ INTERNATIONAL/THAI   Located in the Villa Royale Resort, Mom Tri's Kitchen serves fancy fare from a perch above the ocean. It's regularly honored with awards from international publications. The menu includes such favorites as pork belly, crab soufflé, jumbo Thai prawns in curry, and more. Over 700 wine labels, including several organic wines, are stocked to accompany the Thai and international cuisine here. Service is precise but warm.

Villa Royale, 12 Kata Noi Rd. www.momtriphuket.com. © **07633-3569.** Reservations recommended. Main courses 460B–2,000B. Daily 11am–11pm.

Patong

If you have a hankering for seafood (and who doesn't at the seaside?), head to the southern end of the beach drag (Thaweewong Road). What was once just a collection of wooden shacks is now a long strip darn good seafood shacks with reasonable pricing. Most of the restaurants offer identical menus and have a wide selection of fresh seafood, which will be displayed at the front of each shop. So pick based on atmosphere and view; they're all worthy of your baht. For a more formal meal, try one of the restaurants below.

Acqua ★★★ SEAFOOD/ITALIAN   Few have helped to elevate the fine dining scene in Phuket like Sardinian-born chef Alessandro Frau. Guests are able to watch him in action most nights in the open kitchen here, as he carefully orchestrates the service, making sure the pacing of the meal is just right, and that each dish is artfully plated. He does this in a chic black and white space which has both romantic two-top tables and booths for groups. One could cherry pick dishes from the extensive *a la carte* menu (loaded with great fish dishes and homemade pastas), but the curated degustation menus features the best of the best, so go for the gold. Highlights include sous vide octopus, a 55-minute slow cooked egg, saffron risotto with caviar and urchin, scallops with foie gras, and the signature Sardinian roasted suckling pig. Frau personally oversees the selection of some pretty rare wines, and the wine pairings are so generous you'll need a taxi back to the hotel. Acqua is a real treat.

324/15 Prabaramee Rd. www.acquarestaurantphuket.com. © **07661-8127.** Reservations required. Main courses 600B–1,550B; set menus 2,500B and 3,500B. Daily 5pm–11pm.

Baan Rim Pa Patong ★★ ROYAL THAI   In a handsome Thai-style teak house, Baan Rim Pa comes with a high price tag, especially if you order a bottle of wine. Still, the restaurant has much going for it, not the least of which are its stunning ocean views—be sure to reserve early so that you can get a seat on the outdoor terrace. As guests dine on very tasty Thai fare, a pianist tinkles the ivories, adding the ambiance. The owner of Baan Rim Pa has opened up a few other restaurants next door on the cliffside, including **Joe's Downstairs,** for cool cocktails and tapas (✆ **07661-8245**).

223 Kalim Beach Rd. (on the cliffs just north of Patong Beach). www.baanrimpa.com. ✆ **07634-0789.** Reservations required. Main courses 425B–1,350B. Daily noon–11pm.

Kamala Bay

The restaurants in Kamala Bay tend to cater to European taste buds and budgets, so we have no good budget suggestions for this area.

Plum Prime Steakhouse ★★ INTERNATIONAL   If the craving for a good steak hits, make a beeline to Plum for some of the best imported cuts on the island. Japanese grain-fed, Australian angus, and French *Charolais* are among the choices, expertly seared on a bamboo charcoal grill to the "done-ness" preference of each diner. Equal attention is given to the large seafood selection, including towers of fine de claire and belon oysters along with filets plucked from the sea earlier that day. The breezy dining room overlooks a lovely infinity pool and has fab ocean views. Service is polished, and the wine list is a rounded balance of new and old world bottles.

18/40 Moo 6, Nakalay Rd. (at the Cape Sienna Hotel). www.capesienna.com/restaurants/plum-prime-steakhouse. ✆ **07633-7300.** Reservations recommended. Main courses 3,000B–4,000B. Tues–Sun 6pm–11pm.

Bang Tao Bay (Laguna)

The many hotel restaurants of the five-star properties in the Laguna Complex could fill a small guidebook of their own. We'd say the **The Banyan Tree Phuket** (p. 248) tops the lot for sheer style and enormous variety (try the pan-Asian delicacies at **Saffron**) while **Dee Plee** at the **Anantara Layan** is another ace choice. Outside the complex, here are a few great spots to try:

Bampot Kitchen & Bar ★★ INTERNATIONAL   Bampot Kitchen and Bar has a cool New York City bistro vibe but, unlike the Big Apple where tables are smushed together, there's elbow room galore here. From their roomy perches, guests can peer into the bustling open kitchen, the equally buzzy bar area, stocked with international wines and local spirits; or at the art on the walls, much of which comes from talented local artists. The Scottish chefs here balance the menu between small plates and heartier mains. The rib-eye carpaccio, grilled squid in its own ink, and the sea bass ceviche are affordable enough (150–300B) that a table of friends could order a few to share. Of the entrees, the Maine lobster mac and cheese, and the vegan asparagus risotto are top choices. It's a welcome foil to Phuket's traditional Thai restaurants.

19/1 Moo 1, Lagoon Rd. www.bampot.co. ℭ **093586-9829.** Main courses 300B–1,200B. Daily 6pm–midnight; open for Saturday lunch noon–3pm.

Project Artisan ★ INTERNATIONAL   This indoor-outdoor space does a booming breakfast trade with a menu of acai smoothie bowls, organic eggs cooked to order, homemade granola, fresh-baked nut bread, and fresh pressed juice. It's a smooth transition to lunch, where organic salads and sandwiches on crispy French baguettes are top picks. Everything is organic and local where possible, and there is a counter of pre-made sandwiches and snacks that are ideal for taking to a nearby beach for a picnic lunch.

53/17 Moo 6, Choeng Thale. www.projectartisan.com. ℭ **093790-9911.** Main courses 120B–350B. Daily 8:30am–11pm.

Siam Supper Club ★ INTERNATIONAL   Anchored by a sociable bar, and all done up in men's club style burnished woods, this restaurant feels more American than Thai. Which can make for a nice change. Dishes tend to be more western, too, like the delicious French onion soup, a Wagyu beef carpaccio, crab cakes, and their locally famous salt and pepper calamari. Generously portioned mains like lobster ravioli, yellowfin tuna, and a pan-fried barramundi fish showcase the local bounty of seafood. It all pairs beautifully with old and new world wines from the United States, France, South Africa, and Italy wines, or balanced but strong cocktails. Mondays feature popular jazz sessions.

36-40 Lagoon Rd. www.siamsupperclub.com. ℭ **07627-0936.** Reservations recommended. Main courses 120B–350B. Daily 6pm–1am.

Tatonka ★★ INTERNATIONAL   Billed as "globetrotter cuisine," dining at Tatonka is indeed a foray into the realm of global gastronomy. The owner is a well-traveled chef (check out his résumé written on the bathroom wall) and dishes reflect his meanderings. Among our favorites on the menu are a Peking duck pizza and green curry pasta. This is a local hangout of the off-duty hotel managers, and it gets busy in high season.

382/19 Moo 1, Srisoonthorn Rd. www.phuket.com/tatonka. ℭ **07632-4349.** Main courses 275B–560B. Thurs–Tues 6–10:30pm.

Chalong Bay & Rawai

In the far south of the island at Chalong Bay's **Kan Eang Seafood** (www. kaneang-pier.com; 9/3 Chaofa Rd., Chalong Bay; ℭ 07638-1323) is a good bet for fresh seafood. We're talking whole fish or Phuket lobster (a giant clawless langoustine) plucked from the ocean just hours before. If you've rented a car, a ride down this way makes for a fun day out. **Nikita's** (www.nikitas-phuket.com; ℭ 07628-8703) on the Rawai seafront is a breezy seaside hangout with lite bites, wood-fired pizzas. It's popular for sundowners. **Rum Jungle** (search Rum Jungle on Facebook; ℭ 07638-8153) is the pick of the restaurants in this area with homemade pasta, cuts of New Zealand lamb, and a menu that changes weekly to make use of the best produce; book ahead in

Where to Eat in Phuket

SOUTHERN PENINSULA: WEST COAST & ISLANDS

high season. A final option: go for a stroll around Rawai Beach and check out the **local seafood shacks**. Each will have ice-packed crates of the day's catch ready to be cooked to your liking.

Phuket Town

Though quite a long ride from the West coast beach areas, a night out in Phuket Town is worth it for a taste of local culture. The range of dining options is as good a reason as any to base yourself in town. Oh, and here's a tip we learned from a hotel GM: the best pizza on the island is at **Crust ★★★** (www.facebook.com/crustphuket; ℰ **093763-0318**), just north of Phuket Town.

Abdul's Roti Shop ★ THAI/MUSLIM   For more than 75 years, this family-run *roti* shop has used the same recipes. Don't believe us? The frozen-in-time décor and decades-old newspaper clippings on the wall that surrounded the metal tables should convince you. Light and flakey like a perfect French croissant, the *roti* bread is perfect, and it is an ideal vehicle for dipping into a curry of spicy chicken, massaman with fish, or beef. If sweet sounds more appealing than savory, try the grilled banana version with a generous drizzle of condensed milk. Healthy? Nah. But it's finger-lickin' good. This is a popular spot for locals to catch up on gossip over breakfast.

Thalang Road (at the intersection of Thepkassattri Road). No phone. Main courses 40B. 7am–4pm Mon–Sat; 7am–noon Sun.

Blue Elephant ★★ ROYAL THAI   Set in a Sino-Portuguese mansion, known as the Governor's Mansion, this is one of the most romantic spots for Thai food on the island. Blue Elephant specialized in royal Thai cuisine and bringing life to centuries-old recipes while adding new twists to classic dishes. Order one of the colorful herbal salads tossed in a delicious fish sauce, palm sugar, and lime juice dressing to start, before opting for the braised lamb with *roti* and jasmine rice, or a whole sea bass steamed with fresh-cut lemongrass. The chef also offers a hands-on cooking class with lunch scrved in the elegant dining room.

96 Krabi Rd. www.blueelephant.com/phuket. ℰ **076354-3557**. Main courses 250B–500B. Daily 11am–midnight.

Ka Jok See ★★ THAI   A truly special find, Ka Jok See is a smart and intimate European-styled venue set in an old Sino-Portuguese house. But what really sets it apart is the nightly dancing here, led by the friendly and fun-loving staff. The place has been here for years hiding mysteriously behind a façade dripping with ivy, and is patronized by well-heeled local professionals; it's so well known, there is no sign (look for the small Kanasutra Indian restaurant next door). The friendly vibe of the place extends to the menu comprised of Thai dishes designed to share. Though its name means "stained glass," the decor opts for ceilings of huge wooden beams, giant plants, and candlelight instead.

26 Takua Pa Rd. ℰ **07621-7903**. Reservations recommended. Main courses 380B–620B. Tues–Sat 6:30–11:30pm.

Kopitiam by Walai ★ THAI   First things first: there is *a lot* of bad pad Thai in Thailand because (spoiler) Thai people don't eat the rice noodle dish with the fervor that American takeout menus might lead you to believe. But the good folks at Kopitiam by Walai are known for their authentic Phuketian-style pad Thai, which means the noodles are thin, the shrimp is fresh from the sea, and there's a major spice level. The other reason the lines are long here is for *mee sua*, a sautéed noodle dish that perfectly combines egg, squid, sea bass (or other white fish), prawns, fried egg, and Chinese cabbage. Yum!

18 Thalang Rd. www.facebook.com/kopitiambywilai. 🕐 **083606-9776.** Main courses 95B–200B. Mon–Sat 11am–10pm.

Le Gaetana Restaurant ★★ ITALIAN   This intimate, family-run Italian restaurant just south of Old Town is incredibly popular with longtime locals and Phuket's expats. The Italian owner, Gianni Ferra, and his Thai wife are consummate hosts, flitting from table to table to recommend starters, like the mixed carpaccio of salmon, beef, and tuna, or suggest the perfect Italian wine to go with homemade pasta. Many of the dishes on the menu are family recipes that Gianni brought to Thailand, and there are family photos on the menu and a great sense of pride in the cooking and ownership. During low season, the restaurant closes for a few weeks while the owners travel to Italy.

352 Phuket Rd. 🕐 **07625-0523.** Search La Gaetana Restaurant on Facebook. Reservations essential for dinner. Main courses 250B–550B. Lunch: noon–2pm Mon, Tues, Fri; Dinner: 6–10pm Thurs–Tues.

Lock Tien Food Court ★★ THAI   For more than 50 years, locals and tuned-in visitors have come to this open-air food court to feast on Thai-Chinese dishes. There are about ten restaurants under the blue tile roof, and a waitress brings a stack of English language menus to the table, so this is a great place for visitors to experience street food without the language barrier. Among the top restaurants is the eponymous Lock Tien, where locals line up for 50-baht bowls of *mee nam tom yam kong,* a spicy and sour noodle soup with shrimp. Perfect the flavor with a dash of dried chilies or vinegar from the condiments on the table. Pork *(moo)* satay with a cucumber and onion relish and peanut sauce is popular, too, with 15 sticks costing 70 baht. Look for a woman in the corner making paper-thin sheets of spring roll paper from a springy ball of dough. Those freshly made papers are sold to local restaurants and used in the fresh (not fried) spring rolls with a sweet and sticky tamarind sauce. Finish the meal with brightly colored sweet jellies over crushed iced with a sweet syrup, which the Thais call *nam kang sai.*

Dibuk Road (at the intersection of Yaowarat Road). 🕐 **087387-3703.** Main courses 30B–100B. Daily 10am–5pm.

Raya ★★ THAI   A Sino-Portuguese home with original mosaic flooring and a collection of gramophones, Raya stands untouched and unfazed by Phuket's love of new and shiny. There's a lot to choose from, but we'll cut through the noise: get the crab-meat curry with coconut milk. It features jumbo lumps of crab meat that are flavorful and tender and blend in perfect harmony with the sweet coconut milk. The stink bean salad with fish paste and grilled shrimp is also a winner, as is braised pork with pepper and garlic that so tender it falls apart with the prod of a fork. But did we mention the crab curry? That's what why everyone is here, so don't go without. Raya's sister restaurant, **One Chun,** also serves the famous crab curry along with a host of cheaper Thai classics, like roasted duck in red curry. Find One Chun at 48/1 Thepkasattri Rd.; ℂ **07635-5909,** open daily from 10am–10pm.

48 Dibuk Rd. ℂ **07621-8155.** Main courses 20B–600B. Daily 10am–10pm.

Suay ★★★ THAI/FUSION A truly delightful find, this charming place with an attractive garden stands out for its superb preparation of classic Thai and fusion dishes. Chef Tammasak 'Noi' Chootong, a rising star in the Thai culinary scene, helms the restaurant and oversees the artful presentation and sourcing of top ingredients. It all comes together beautifully in the lemongrass lamb chops with papaya, the Isan-style spicy tuna salad, and the beef cheek massaman curry. Vegetarians are well looked after here, too. Popularity demanded a second location in the center of the island at 177/99 Moo 4, Baan Wana Park; ℂ **093339-1890;** Daily 4–11pm.

50/2 Takua Pa Rd. ℂ **087888-6990.** www.suayrestaurant.com. Reservations recommended. Main courses 300B–700B. Daily 5pm–midnight.

Shopping

The shopping in Chiang Mai (p. 343) is the best in the country, so save your baht for up north, or for the markets in Bangkok (p. 121). Phuket pales in comparison to those two cities. Patong Beach is teeming with storefront tailors (give them a pass; the quality is bad), leather shops (again, skip), jewelers, and ready-to-wear clothing boutiques. Vendors line the sidewalks, selling everything from bras to batik clothing, arts and crafts, northern hill-tribe silver, and of course the usual fake Nikes and selfie sticks. Most prices are inflated compared to Bangkok or other tourist markets in Thailand even when you're able to bargain the price down. Many items, such as northern handicrafts, are best if purchased closer to the source.

If the hotel's body wash or the aromatherapy from a massage left you smelling delightful, it probably came from **Lemongrass House** (www.lemongrass housethailand.com; ℂ **0762-5501**). This Phuket-based shop has locations across the island and outfits many of Thailand's hotels and spa with personal care products.

Phuket Town is your best shot for finding something special; don't miss a walk down Thalang Road, both for the shopping and the old architecture. While you're cruising the street, keep an eye out for **Drawing Room** (96 Phang-Nga; ℂ **086899-4888**) for funky local art and **Ranida** (119 Thalang Rd.; ℂ **077621-4801**) for Asian decorations and some Thai-inspired clothing. The **night market** runs from 4 to 10pm on Saturday and Sunday. The car-free streets are a mix of buskers, people selling handmade goods, and street food vendors selling everything from noodles to fruit to fresh coconut ice cream. It's as much of a social event as it is for shopping.

Phuket Entertainment & Nightlife

Patong is the center of infamous nightlife on the island, though it serves up the same old sordid stuff as Patpong, in Bangkok; you'll find plenty of bars, nightclubs, karaoke lounges, billiard parlors, and dance shows with pretty sleazy entertainment. While some wide-eyed teenagers or washed-up barflies may find it titillating to trawl the hundreds of hostess bars, many people find these venues a complete turnoff. Lit up like a seedy Las Vegas in miniature, the Patong bar areas are filled with (often underage) working girls and boys in pursuit of wealthy foreign men. Since the Vietnam War, prostitutes have plied Patong's girlie bars.

Thankfully, there are upscale places to grab a drink, and every hotel in the "expensive" and "moderate" category has an established bar that offers some combination of well-made cocktails, sunset views, craft beers, and a nice selection of wines. Because it can take more than an hour to get from end to end in Phuket, ask your hotel which resorts nearby have nice spots to grab a drink.

One of the best drinking-related activities on the island is to visit the **Chalong Bay Distillery ★★★** (www.chalongbayrum.com; ✆ **093575-1119**). Bar none—no pun intended!—this white rum is Thailand's most famous boutique spirit, and you'll find it at bars across the country. Thibault Spithakis and Marine Lucchini, a French couple who each grew up in wine producing families, started the company, and this small-scale craft distillery uses French copper stills and traditional distillation methods to make natural rum made from organic Thai sugarcane. The result is a full body, smooth white rum that is knockout good in mojitos, and you'll get to sample a mojito after the 30-minute tour (450B; daily on the hour from 2–6pm). Cocktail making classes (2 hours; 1,700B; Monday and Thursday) are fun for groups and great for a rainy day. The popularity of the rum in Thailand and abroad (not to mention a rack of awards) brought expansion to the brand, and now it adds Thai flavors, like lemongrass and kaffir lime, to the line of rums.

BARS

Craft Beer Lounge ★ (www.grandmercurephuketpatong.com; ✆ **07623-1999**) has more than 30 beers, including a nice international selection and a few Thai crafts. On the vino front is **Luca Cini – A Wine Story ★** (www.lucacini.com; ✆ **094804-4461**), which carries more than 100 different types of Italian wines pairing them with a mouthwatering selection of imported meats and cheese. Considering the premium products, the prices are affordable, and a glass of wine starts at 260B. Keeping with the wine trend, **Drinks & Co.** (search Drinks & Co. Phuket on Facebook; ✆ **086309-1392**) has more than 250 bottles with tons of selection for under 1,000B. The helpful staff can offer opinions for bottles to open and enjoy there or select a bottle or two for a beach picnic.

For mixology and cocktails, these are a few spots we love. **Garden's Gastronomy Bar** (www.facebook.com/GardensBarPhuket; ✆ **062242-0210**) carries a premium selection of tonics and gins and the menu is a mix of classics, like a French 75 and a negroni, along with more innovative cocktails that use

Asian spirits like soju and sake. For cocktails with a view, try **Nikita's** (www. nikitas-phuket.com; ✆ **07628-8703**) where the lychee gin smash and the fresh-fruit margaritas are irresistible. Delicious wood-fired pizzas are also sold to help soak up all the booze in the blood stream. Inside a Sino-Portuguese shophouse in Old Town is **Dibuk House** ★★ (www.facebook.com/dibukhouse; ✆ **082733-0442**) where posh bartenders in slick uniform shake and stir pineapple-infused rum drinks and fab martinis.

In Phuket Town, there are a few dives with live music that are worth visiting. Consider starting at **Timber Hut** (search Timber Hut on Facebook; ✆ **07621-1839**) a two-story pub that has nearly 30 years of history to its name, which might be some kind of record in fickle Phuket. The live music is a grab bag night-to-night, so it might be hip-hop, pop or rock but it's almost always good; stop in for a beer. Or head to **Rockin' Angels Blues Café & Band** (www.facebook.com/RockinAngelsCafe; ✆ **089654-9654**) where bike gear and records line the wall and house the blues start around 9 or 9:30pm. We're also fans of **Ka Jok See** (www.facebook.com/kajoksee; ✆ **07621-7903**) where there's music and mayhem most nights when the owner hands out tambourines and encourages guests to dance on the tables (there's even an occasional cabaret). Reservations are essential a month in advance is you decide to dine here.

BEACH CLUBS

One of the most popular places to enjoy Phuket's nightlife—and daytime parties—is at a beach club, where combinations of international DJs, fancy buffets with ice-packed towers of crab claws, and swim-up bars make for a full day of fun. **Dream Beach Club** (www.dreambeachclub.com; ✆ **07668-4964**) caters to trendy Millennials who are ready to swipe right on a dating app while big-name DJs thump in the background, **Café del Mar** (www.cafedelmarphuket.com; ✆ **061359-5500**) is more family-friendly and loved by expats looking to unwind. Landing somewhere in the middle is **Catch Beach Club** ★★ (www.catchbeachclub.com; ✆ **065348-2017**) where white-washed wood decks flow seamlessly into the soft sand. There's great food, coffee, and lots of bubbles and sangria to make for a perfect afternoon.

CABARET

On the south end of Patong, crowds of tourists pack the long-established transgender **Simon Cabaret** (www.phuket-simoncabaret.com; ✆ **07634-2011**). There are three shows each evening (6, 7:30 and 9pm) featuring flamboyantly clad transsexuals lip-syncing their way through popular Asian and Western pop songs. Can't quite picture it? Well, imagine if the Radio City Rockettes got a Thai ladyboy makeover. Its burlesque humor draws busloads—especially Asian grannies who happily dance along in their seats. The sets are impressive and costumes are covered in glitter, rhinestones, and feathers. Tickets are 1,000B and should be booked a few days in advance because, even with 600 seats, the show sells out most nights.

SIDE TRIPS FROM PHUKET: KHAO LAK & OFFSHORE ISLANDS

Khao Lak

Travel Tip: The best time to visit the islands in this section is December to May. In recent years, the Thai government has completely shut down the Ko Smilan National Marine Park and Ko Surin National Park from May to October or November to allow the marine life a much-needed break from the onslaught of boats and humans in high season.

Just over an hour from the northernmost tip of Phuket, in the province of **Phang Nga,** the coastal town of **Khao Lak** was the area hardest hit by the 2004 tsunami. Now entirely rebuilt, it's a burgeoning eco-tourism destination with some magnificent resorts and spots for bird-watching and visiting waterfalls. However, the town's main attraction is as a jumping-off point for visits to some superb dive sites around **Ko Similan National Marine Park ★★★**. Admission to the park is 400B for adults, 200B for children.

Comprising nine islands, the **Similan Islands** are rated in the top ten best dive sites in the world for their array of unspoiled corals, sea fans, and sponges, as well as angelfish, parrotfish, manta rays, and, sometimes, whitetipped sharks. Numerous local dive operators offer short (approx. 3 hrs. by speedboat) or long trips to these regions from Thap Lamu Pier, 8km (5 miles) south of Khao Lak. For information about bungalows or camping on the islands, contact **Similan National Park** (local office ✆ **07645-3272**). An aircon bungalow costs 2,000B a night, while a fan room is 1,000B.

To the north of the Similan Islands lies **Ko Surin National Park ★★★** (✆ **07647-2145**), which comprises five islands with some of the best shallow water corals you could wish to see (great for snorkeling!). Whale sharks are known to frequent these waters, which, in the past, were once the exclusive domain of Phuket's indigenous people, the Sea Gypsies—known in Thai as "*chao ley*," or "sea people" and they live in simple thatched-roof boats bobbing on the limpid waters offshore. At park headquarters, a fan-cooled bungalow costs 2,000B and an air-conditioned bungalow with two bedrooms costs 3,000B.

Boats to Ko Surin leave from Khuraburi Pier, north of Khao Lak, with a journey time of 4 hours to the islands; as we said above, islands are closed to visitors from mid-May to mid-November. From Khuraburi, fans of marine life can take a day trip to isolated **Ko Phra Thong** to visit the island's conservation center. Manned (only in dry season) by an international team of experts and volunteers, it surveys and protects rare turtles and the region's disappearing, yet ecologically vital, mangroves. See www.naucrates.org for info.

Other local attractions include miles of peaceful white-sand beaches, temple tours, white-water rafting, and jungle treks. Visit **Khao Lak Land Discovery** (www.khaolaklanddiscovery.com; ✆ **07648-5411**) for info.

WHERE TO STAY

Many visitors who are tired of Phuket's full-on party vibe head up here for a tranquil break at properties ranging from dreamy resorts to simple shacks. As with most tropical destinations, the more you spend, the closer to the beach you'll be. The budget options tend to be closer to the town's congested center but nothing is too far from the water.

Expensive

La Flora Resort & Spa ★★　This stylish resort is the ideal place for a romantic getaway, with an attractive garden, a good swimming beach, and excellent service. Rooms are fitted out in contemporary Asian style, and most have balconies with daybeds. There are pool access rooms and family suites with two-bedroom villas right on the beach with Jacuzzis and outdoor rain showers. Check their website for a list of nature tours organized by local guides, and for information on available Thai cooking and boxing classes. There's lots to do besides hang by the beach.

59/1 Moo 5, Kukkak. www.lafloraresort.com. ℂ **07642-8000.** 138 units. From 5,900B deluxe room; from 11,745B villa. **Amenities:** Restaurant; bar; 2 outdoor pools; tennis court; health club; spa; Wi-Fi (free).

The Sarojin ★★　This multiple-award-winning property set on 4 hectares (10 acres) of beachside land offers the opportunity for either complete relaxation or adventures in the forest or out at sea with the aid of its "imagineers"—personal concierges intent on satisfying guests' every whim, from private snorkeling safaris to romantic dinners on the beach. The suites and residences are surrounded by lush gardens and feature wooden floors, floor-to-ceiling windows, intimate baths for two, complimentary Wi-Fi, and daily fruit baskets. The hotel's 56 rooms allow for a more intimate stay than booking at one of the mega resorts nearby. The Pathways Spa blends ancient massage techniques with modern comforts, while the two dining options, Ficus and The Edge are truly top class.

60 Moo 2, Kukkak, Takuapa. www.sarojin.com. ℂ **07642-7900-4.** 56 units. 5,600B garden residence; 8,900B pool residence. **Amenities:** 2 restaurants; bar; outdoor pool; health club; spa; Wi-Fi (free).

Moderate

The Haven ★★　It is places like The Haven that make people fall in love with Thailand. The lengthy resort occupies a fine slice of Khuk Khak Beach and there is a massive 5,000-square-meters (53,800-square-feet) of salt water turquoise pools to admire the ocean from. The rooms are contemporary in style and are quite spacious, some with private outdoor Jacuzzi. Spend your days enjoying a Thai cooking class or reading at the beach. The Haven requires that guests be 12-years or older to stay at the resort.

61/4 Moo 3, Khuk Khak. www.thehavenkhaolak.com. ℂ **07642-9900.** 110 units. From 1,800B deluxe room; 5,500B deluxe pool access; 7,500B oceanfront Jacuzzi. **Amenities:** 3 restaurants; many bars; 5 outdoor pools; spa; fitness center; room service; Wi-Fi (free).

Inexpensive

On the budget end, there are bungalows in a coconut grove near the beach at **Phu Khao Lak** (www.phukhaolak.com; ℂ **07648-5141**), with fan rooms starting at 600B, and air-con rooms from 1,500B. **Fasai House** (www.fasai house.com; ℂ **07648-5867**) is another good choice, with super clean air-conditioned rooms and a small pool; here rooms cost between 600B and 950B. Both are good spots to swap diving stories with fellow travelers.

WHERE TO EAT

Khao Lak isn't a foodie destination. But it boasts a diverse range of options from hotel restos to places in town. Among the best is **Takieng** ★★ (26/43 Moo 5; ℂ 86952-7963), just north of town. It serves steamed fish in curry sauce, outstanding grilled squid with a spicy dip, and a slightly overwhelming number of other Thai classics. To get to **Go Pong** ★ (10/1 Moo 7; ℂ 081907-7460) you'll either follow the smell of the aromatic noodle soups or follow the crowds of locals that adore this authentic street-side, casual restaurant. The stir-fried noodles are outstanding here. **Siam Tumeric** ★(17/11 Moo 2; ℂ 07649-0564) is run by the affable Raj who serves some of best Thai on the island. English-speaking staff helpfully offer suggestions but don't miss the tableside BBQ of fresh-caught seafood like prawns and squid. **One warning:** A number of eateries close during the low season (May–Oct), so contact them to check that they're serving before heading out.

Ko Yao Yai & Ko Yao Noi Islands ★

In the middle of Phang Nga Bay, about halfway between Krabi and Phuket (an hour's boat ride from Phuket's Bang Rong Pier), the twin islands of **Ko Yao Yai** and **Ko Yao Noi** ("Big Long Island" and "Little Long Island") are where nature lovers head to enjoy awe-inspiring scenery and relax on islands populated by Muslim fisherman. The islands are part of the Ao Phang-Nga National Park and exotic looking karsts jut from the water in such a spectacular way that it is impossible to take a bad scenic photo here. A world apart from the clamor of Ko Phi Phi, Phang Nga Bay's two largest islands never get very touristy and are tops for cruising by motorbike or mountain bike (available for rent on both islands at around 200B/100B per day).

A couple of reasons these islands never became as popular as Ko Phi Phi is that most beaches are rather stony and the sea is not as clear as around nearby islands, so they are not great for swimming. The nearest things to civilization on Ko Yao Noi are a few beachside seafood spots, a 7-Eleven store and ATM. There's still not a traffic light to be seen. Yet, despite being the smaller of the two islands, this is the more developed of the two, with a road running all the way around it and a rapidly growing choice of resorts (mostly on the east coast). Ko Yao Yai, by contrast, has just a few roads and a handful of places to stay.

Active travelers can go kayaking, bird-watching, or head off to snorkel and explore nearby uninhabited islands by longtail; any resort can make arrangements. In addition, there's fishing, jungle walks, or the exhausting sport of hammock swinging. It all makes for a perfect island escape.

Ferries to both islands leave Bang Rong Pier approximately hourly throughout the day and cost 120B. Call ahead to your accommodation to arrange transport from the pier.

WHERE TO STAY

Some resorts on Ko Yao Noi open all year, while others close during the rainy season (May–Sept). There's such a range of choice that you might pay anywhere between 500B and 50,000B for a night's stay. For an easygoing budget bungalow resort, try **Sabai Corner Bungalows** (www.sabaicornerbungalows. com; ℂ **07659-7497**), which has a handful of bungalows from 500B; each has a different design but all have spacious balconies and hammocks. The restaurant here serves up tasty Thai and Italian dishes. An even better budget choice **Suntisook** ★★ (www.fb.com/suntisook-resort-koh-yao; ℂ **07558-2750**) is situated on a lovely, tranquil beach at the south end of the island, with rooms from 2,000B (often closed May–Sept); it also has a dive shop, a very good restaurant, and tons of hammocks. Right next door (though vegetation is so dense that guests probably never know) is the tiny, upscale **Koyao Bay Pavilions** ★(www.koyaobay.com; ℂ **07659-7441**), where the gorgeous suites, cottages, and private pool villas go for between 5000B and 10,000B, and the Hong Islands in the distance make for stunning scenery. You'll find similar prices and facilities at **Ko Yao Island Resort** ★★★ (www.koyao.com; ℂ **07659-7474**), about halfway down the east coast in a former coconut plantation. This bliss-inducing resort has 15 open-concept (meaning no locks on the doors, but there are safes) thatched and well-spaced villas with indoor and outdoor bathrooms and tip top service.

If you need a break from your chosen resort on Ko Yao Noi, head on over to **Chaba Café** (www.facebook.com/chabacafeandwinelounge; ℂ **087887-0625**) on the east coast, where they serve a grab bag of dishes like avocado smoothies, salads, sandwiches, pasta, and Thai food with much success. **Pizzeria La Luna** (www.lalunakohyao.com; ℂ **0850689-4326**) serves woodfired pizzas and pastas to a regular list of island dwellers. They've added delivery services and breakfast to their menu, too.

On **Ko Yao Yai,** the **Santhiya Koh Yao Yai** (www.santhiya.com/kohyao yai; ℂ **07659-2888**) has rooms with lots of teak wood, several pools, and ravishing sunset views. However, we noticed the staff being short-tempered with several guests on our recent stay. Rates run a wide range: 2,250B for a deluxe double to 23,500B for a four-bedroom villa. **Thiwson Beach Resort** (www.thiwsonbeach.com; ℂ **081956-7582**) offers great value for money with breezy bungalows ranging from 2,000B to 3,500B. There's a nice pool, and it's on a pretty stretch of beach.

Six Senses Yao Noi ★★★   What most people gasp at first here are the stunning views—the surrounding seascape is studded with karst outcrops.

Second gasp might be the transportation options: instead of roughing it on a longtail ferry, guests are whisked to and from the island by swanky speedboat, or helicopter. Third gasp? The prices. But for those who can afford it, rooms are equipped with every conceivable luxury, including chilled wine cabinets, and each villa is assigned a personal butler who can arrange private longtail boats for island hopping or point out the best spots for snorkeling. The simple but stylish teak architecture is a treat for the eyes, and true to its name, Six Senses leaves no sense unfulfilled, with superb cuisine in the Dining Room and Living Room, a host of watersports including sailing classes, and the usual range of heavenly spa treatments. The only downside is that while paying hotel guests are treated like royalty, the hotel staff get a bit surly towards outside visitors who come for dinner or sunset drinks.

56 Moo 5. www.sixsenses.com. © **07641-8500.** 54 units. 18,500B–51,500B pool villa. **Amenities:** 2 restaurants; bar; tennis court; health club; spa; watersports equipment; bikes (free); Wi-Fi (free).

Racha Islands & Phang Nga Bay ★★

From Chalong Bay at the south end of Phuket, there's a daily ferry service to the idyllic islet of **Ko Racha** (aka Ko Raya or Ko Raja), a delightful getaway with a perfect white-sand beach. It's hugely popular with day-trippers in the dry season. Sybarites in search of seclusion can also splash out on a pool villa at **The Racha ★★★** (www.theracha.com; © **07635-5455**), a magnificent contemporary-styled luxury hotel that cascades down the hill to the cerulean sea. (The hotel offers speedboat transfers to its guests.) You'll need deep pockets for their premium Lighthouse suite, which costs 35,000B, but if that seems a bit steep, you can get deluxe villa (rates online 6,300B). The hotel is a member of Small Luxury Hotels of the World and the service is ace.

   Phang Nga Bay, with its towering karst limestone spires, is a very popular day trip by boat. Some might say it's *too* popular, with hordes of tour groups descending on its tiny beaches, but it depends where you go—some of the smaller islands are still not overrun. A more peaceful trip around the bay by sea kayak is possibly a better bet. **Ko Phi Phi** is another oversold day trip for snorkeling, or more commonly an overnight stay from Phuket (p. 225).

KRABI ★★ (AO NANG, RAILAY & KHLONG MUANG BEACHES)

814km (506 miles) S of Bangkok; 165km (103 miles) E of Phuket; 42km (26 miles) E of Ko Phi Phi; 276km (171 miles) N of Satun; 211km (131 miles) SW of Surat Thani

For many tourists, Krabi has become an eco-friendly alternative to the heavily commercialized Phuket and resort boomtown of Ko Phi Phi. For others, it's an easy stop along the way. Flights connecting with Krabi's international airport mean visitors can bypass Bangkok and arrive directly from Singapore, Kuala

Lumpur, Ko Samui. It is also possible to arrange a road transfer from Phuket International airport; the journey is 2½ hours. Ferries and minivans from other destinations connect via *songtaew* (p. 230) and boats to the nearby tourist strip of Ao Nang and farther-flung beaches. Railay, with its famed soft sands, and limestone cliffs with ample rappelling opportunities, is accessed by boat (from either Krabi Town to the northeast, or more commonly from Ao Nang Beach to the west). Khlong Muang Beach, more recently developed, lies just north of Ao Nang by road.

The best time to visit the Krabi area is November through April, with January and February the ideal months. The rainy season runs May through October when the wet weather and choppy seas drive away all but the hardiest.

Essentials

GETTING THERE

BY PLANE   **Tiger Airways** (www.tigerairways.com; ✆ **80060-15637**) has direct flights from Singapore. **Thai Airways** (www.thaiair.com; ✆ **02356-1111**), **Bangkok Airways** (www.bangkokair.com; ✆ **02270-6699**), and **Air-Asia** (www.airasia.com; ✆ **02515-9999**) all fly from Bangkok. Air Asia also connects Krabi with Chiang Mai and Bangkok Air has direct flights from Ko Samui. With advanced purchase, flights from Bangkok should cost around 1,200B; flying time 85 minutes.

From **Krabi airport** (✆ **07563-6541**), you can hire a taxi to go into town for around 350B. To go directly to Ao Nang beach, a taxi is about 600B.

BY BOAT   Boats leave from Ko Phi Phi to Krabi (9am, 10:30am, 1:30pm, 3pm; trip time 90 min.; 350B). There is one boat that goes from Ko Lanta to Krabi in the high season (11:30am; trip time: 2 hrs.; 400B) while rainy season travelers will have to take a minivan (frequent departures; trip time: 2½ hrs.; 250B–300B).

BY BUS OR MINIVAN   Two air-conditioned VIP 24-seater buses leave daily from **Bangkok's Southern Bus Terminal** (✆ **02422-4444;** trip time: 12 hrs.; 970B) to Krabi Town. Frequently scheduled air-conditioned minibuses leave daily from Surat Thani to Krabi (trip time: 2¾ hrs.; 250B). Air-conditioned minivan travel daily from Phuket Town to Krabi (trip time: 3 hrs.; 140B).

VISITOR INFORMATION

Most services in Krabi town are on Utarakit Road, paralleling the waterfront (to the right as you alight the ferry). Here you'll find the **TAT Office** (www.tourismthailand.org; ✆ **07562-2163**) and a number of **banks** with ATM service. The **post office** and **police station** (✆ **07561-1222**) are located south on Utarakit Road, to the left as you leave the pier. **Krabi Nakharin International Hospital** (www.krabinakharin.co.th; ✆ **07562-6555**) is at 1 Pisanpob Rd. on the northwest part of town.

Check the small shops around town for a copy of the local free map of the resort area, town, and surrounding islands.

GETTING AROUND

Krabi Town is the commercial hub in the area, but few bother to stay. There is frequent *songtaew* (p. 230) service between Krabi Town and Ao Nang Beach; just flag down a white pickup (the trip takes 30 min. and costs 50B).

Railay Beach and the resorts on the surrounding beaches are cut off by a ridge of cliffs from the mainland and, therefore, are accessible only by boat. From the pier in Krabi Town, you'll pay 100B during the day and 150B at night; trip time 30 min.). From the beach at **Ao Nang** (at the small pavilion across from the Phra Nang Inn), the trip takes just 20 minutes and costs 80B.

Khlong Muang beach is some 25km (16 miles) northwest of Krabi Town. Expect to pay at least 500B for a taxi.

The limestone formations around the coastline here are not only gorgeous visually, but also are fun spots to explore by small boat. Some, such as the famous **Ko Hong** ★★, to the northwest of Ao Nang, are almost entirely enclosed—with brilliant blue lagoons at their heart. Boats slip inside them at low tide via almost invisible, narrow chasms; ask at your resort for information about boat tours.

If you're checking in at any resort, ask about transportation arrangements (which are often included) and prevailing weather conditions.

Exploring Krabi

Krabi has a number of sites, but most visitors head straight for the beaches to relax. Popular activities are day boat trips, snorkeling, and rock climbing at Railay East.

Just north and east of Krabi Town, though, you will find **Wat Tham Seua** ★★ (The Tiger Temple), a stunning hilltop pilgrimage point. (Thankfully, the name has nothing to do with any animals kept here.) A punishing 30 to 40-minute climb up 1,272 steep steps brings you to the rocky pinnacle where a collection of Buddhist statuary overlooks the surrounding area stretching from Krabi Town to the cliffs near Railay. There is a large monastery and temple compound built into the rock at the bottom of the mountain, where you may chance upon a monk in silent meditation or chat with one of the friendly temple stewards (most are eager to practice English). The abbot speaks English and welcomes international students of Vipassana meditation. If you decide to climb the steep temple mountain, go in either the early morning or the late afternoon to beat the heat. The view from above is worth it. *Note:* Be careful of the many monkeys here. Don't hold anything tempting in your hands or it will be taken. Be sure to bring water.

The beaches and stunning cliffs of **Railay Beach** ★★★ are certainly worth a day trip, even if you don't stay there. Divided into Railay East and West, the former offers challenging rock-climbing cliffs, situated next to mud flats. The West has the sort of soft powdery sands that attract beach bunnies, though longtails dock right here and the resulting noise of the motors can ruin the peacefulness of the gorgeous cerulean sea.

The craggy limestone cliffs of Railay make it one of the best-known **rock-climbing** spots in the world and with more than 1,000 routes, it is a mecca for bolder lovers. (Climbing information is available at www.railay.com.) It is certainly not for the fainthearted; nevertheless, the whole cliff area is well organized (with mapped routes) and safety bolts drilled into the rock. There are heaps of companies offering full- and half-day courses, as well as equipment rental. There are also many routes suitable for beginners. Climbing schools set up "top rope" climbing for safety, whereby climbers are attached by a rope through a fixed pulley at the top, and to a guide on the other end, holding them fast. The schools all offer similar rates and have offices scattered around Railay Beach, with posters and pamphlets everywhere. Two of the most reputable climbing schools are **King Climbers** ★ (www.railay.com; ℂ **07566-2096**) and **Hot Rock** (www.railayadventure.com; ℂ **085641-9842**). Half-day courses start at about 1,000B, full-day courses from 1,800B, and 3-day courses run from 6,000B. Deep-water soloing is on the rise. That's a sport where strong climbers traverse the rocks without ropes until falling safely into the water below. **Basecamp Tonsai** ★ (www.tonsaibasecamp.com; ℂ **081149-9745**) offers half-day lessons in that for 800B and full-day lessons for 1,500B.

Near Railay Beach is **Phra Nang Beach** ★, a secluded section of sand that is either a short 50B boat trip from Railay proper, or a cliffside walk east, past Rayavadee Resort and south along a shaded cliffside path (again, watch out for monkeys). From here, you can swim or kayak around the craggy hunk of rock just a few meters away offshore, or explore the **Tham Phra Nang,** or Princess Cave, a small cavern at the base of a tall cliff, filled with huge phallic sculptures where, legend has it, donors attain fertility. The cliffs are stunning and the sunsets spectacular.

Along the path to **Phra Nang Beach,** you'll find signs pointing up to a small cleft in the rocks. After a short hike up a steep escarpment and then an often treacherously muddy downward climb (use the ropes to avoid slipping), you'll arrive at a shallow saltwater lagoon. How it got up here is anyone's guess.

Full-day boat trips and **snorkeling** to **Ko Poda** ★ can be arranged from any beachfront tour agent or hotel near Krabi, which will take you to a few small coral sites as well as any number of secluded coves and islets (or *hongs*); **Sea Kayak Krabi** (www.seakayak-krabi.net; **07563-0270**) run a number of half- and full-day excursions lead by knowledgeable and fit guides. Most recommended is to Ko Hong (full day 2,200B) to see the famed emerald lagoon but there are other great trips to see karsts and sea caves at Ban Bho Tho (full day 2,200B) or half-day tours for 900B around the island. There are countless operators along Ao Nang or Railay that rent snorkel masks and flippers for about 150B per day.

Cycling is a fun way to explore the area. **Krabi Eco Cycle** (www.krabieco cycle.com; ℂ **081607-4162**) visits villages, hot springs and more on a half-day (1,500B) or full-day (3,000B) tour.

There are some dive operators in Krabi, but you'll have to travel practically back to Phuket to reach the better sites, so most people prefer to book from Ko Phi Phi (p. 274) or Phuket (p. 225). There are local operators in Railay who will take bubble blowers out to Ko Poda; inquire at shops along the beach. Based in Ao Nang, **The Dive** (www.thediveaonang; ✆ **082282-2537**) runs local trips and does Open Water certifications for 14,900B. Another great choice is **Acqua Vision** (www.diving-krabi.com; ✆ **086944-4068**), where you can scuba and snorkel.

Where to Stay

In general, Krabi tends to be a fairly expensive place to bed down, but there are lots of low season deals. Book high season rooms well in advance and remember that even budget hotels have compulsory dinners on Christmas and New Year's Eve. Read the fine print because some of those dinners could add 5,000B to 10,000B per person to the final bill.

KRABI TOWN

Despite a booming number of guesthouses, few travelers will choose to stay in Krabi Town as there's no beach there. But if you're stuck or are too tired to leave, **Maritime Park & Spa** (1 Tungfah Rd.; www.maritimeparkandspa.com; ✆ **07562-0028**) is clean and dependable with rooms from 1,200B. **Pak-Up Hostel** (87 Utaraki Rd.; www.pakuphostel.com; ✆ **07561-1955**) is the most popular hostel in Krabi; its spic-and-span dorms start at 380B and rooms are 850B. There is a fun-loving bar outside the hostel with open-mic nights and beer pong and a generous happy hour that goes until 9:30pm.

RAILAY BEACH
Expensive
Rayavadee ★★★ Rayavadee offers unique two-story rondavels (circular pavilions), most of which are large, and all of which are luxurious. They come with every modern convenience and then some, and are set in enclosed gardens, making them unusually private and quiet. Ground-floor sitting rooms have a central, double-sized hanging lounger with cushions. Upper-story bedrooms are all silk and teak, and private bathrooms have oversized Jacuzzi tubs. The resort grounds lie at the base of towering cliffs on the island's most choice piece of property, with direct access onto the beautiful Phra Nang beach. It all feels very much like a peaceful village, with paths meandering among private lotus ponds and meticulous landscaping. Many couples choose the hotel for weddings because of the excellent food, beverages, service, and setting.

214 Moo 2, Tambol Ao Nang. www.rayavadee.com. ✆ **07562-0740.** 102 units. 14,000B–45,000B pavilions. **Amenities:** 4 restaurants; lounge; outdoor pool w/children's pool; health club; spa; watersports equipment; room service; Wi-Fi (free).

Inexpensive
Anyavee Railay Resort ★ It's hard to improve the value for location ratio at this fun, relaxed resort. Rooms have balconies (some with ocean views) and while perhaps an update to make them more modern might be needed, they're clean, spacious, and have comfortable beds. The resort is surrounded

by the jungle and the long pool in the heart of it all overlooks stunning karst formations just out at sea. The Anyavee Resort collection has another location on quiet Tubkaak Beach but this is the better of the two resorts.

390 Moo 2, Railay Beach (on Railay Beach, longtails from Ao Nang pull up onshore). www.anyaveerailaybeachresort.com.© **07581-9437.** 62 units. 620B–1,050 twin; 1,300B–3,500B superior. **Amenities:** Restaurant; outdoor pool; spa; watersports equipment; Wi-Fi (free).

Sunrise Tropical Resort ★ Classic Thai designs dominate the rooms which, for some, means the rooms can feel a bit outdated with all the wood elements and ornately carved four-poster beds. However, the chalets and villas are spacious and a great deal considering the prime location. A number of rooms connect if needed, making this an appealing pick for groups. The resort is sandwiched between two beaches, Railay West and Phra Nang Beach, and has a small pool.

39 Moo 2, Railay West. www.sunrisetropical.com. © **081979-6299.** 28 units. 1,100B–3,500B. **Amenities:** Restaurant; bar; outdoor pool; Wi-Fi (free).

AO NANG BEACH
Moderate
Phra Nang Inn ★ The Phra Nang Inn is famed for its eccentric décor—think "Thailand meets Mexico" with lots of bright colors. Rooms are light and breezy though a touch small, but the beds are big and comfy, and the beachfront bar oozes island cool. The hotel's two wings are on either side of the busiest intersection in Ao Nang, and the helpful staff can help arrange tours and onward boat travel (from right across the street). The hotel has two pools.

119 Moo 2, Ao Nang Beach. www.phrananginnkrabi.com. © **07563-7130.** 88 units. 1,200B–4,500B double. **Amenities:** 2 restaurants; 2 bars; 2 outdoor pools; spa; sauna; room service; Wi-Fi (free).

The ShellSea Krabi ★★ Sleek low-rises stick to a charming nautical motif with seashell accents and sailboats dominating the décor—the lobby even has a wicker seashell daybed that is big enough for two people. The hotel's enviable location offers the best of both worlds: it is steps away from the beach and just a 10-minute car ride from busy Ao Nang. Rooms are contemporary and classic with natural linen sofas and bedding so luxurious you might be tempted to unmake the bed to see where it's from. The hotel caters to couples (there are rooms with private pools and outdoor Jacuzzis) while families will enjoy the kiddie pool, kids' club, and family-friendly activities. Join a guided bike ride or nature walk, or stretch out after a long flight in a complimentary yoga class. The ShellSea offers an all around lovely experience. The hotel is a short walk from Krabi's **Fossil Shell Beach** which is home to slabs of fossils formed from snail shells—and one of only three known formations in the world.

999 Moo 6, Sai Thai. www.theshellseakrabi.com.© **07581-0519.** 85 units. 4,500B–9,000B double. **Amenities:** Restaurant; bar; outdoor pool; room service; spa; kids' club; room service; Wi-Fi (free).

Inexpensive

The Thai architect who owns **Glur** (www.krabiglurhostel.com; ℂ **07569-5297**) created super-cool dorms and rooms from old shipping containers. A night in a dorm is 600B and private rooms go for 1,500B. It's our favorite, but there are tons of other hostels and budget guesthouses here. Book early as they do fill up in high season.

KLONG MUANG BEACH

Following the coast north of the busy Ao Nang strip, you'll come to quiet Khlong Muang with a long stretch of quiet beach. This area is number of top-flight resorts.

Expensive

Nakamanda ★★★ This slickly designed resort sits on the far northern end of Krabi (just past the Sheraton; see below), and consists of a collection of luxurious private villas sprinkled among indigo pools, pavilions, and meticulously kept gardens. The name means the "sacred sea dragon," and this stylish outcrop does look otherworldly. Public spaces are delightfully spartan; the eclectic decor tends to mix Angkorian antiquities with a cool contemporary style. Villas are aligned for optimal privacy, and inside everything is a harmonious blend of light wood and granite. Rooms range from a basic villa to a couple of over-the-top private-pool villas with huge terraces and sea views. The spa is inviting; the seaside pool, an oasis; and the resort restaurant, excellent.

126 Moo 3, Klong Muang Beach. www.nakamanda.com. ℂ **07562-8200.** 39 units. 4,000–9,500B *sala* villa; 13,000B Jacuzzi villa; from 20,000B pool villa. **Amenities:** Restaurant; 2 bars; outdoor pool; health club; spa; watersports rentals; room service; Wi-Fi (free).

Phulay Bay, A Ritz-Carlton Reserve ★★★ Hands down, this elegant ultra-luxury resort is the best in Krabi and honeymooners will rave about their private suites and villas for years to come. Verdant gardens filled with rooted banyan trees, blankets of pink and purple bougainvillea, and fragrant frangipani cover the property. In the suites and villas, each room category has its own design but all feature elegant Thai furnishings with cool Moroccan elements, like lamps and cutouts in the doorframe. And each has heavenly beds and spacious bathrooms with silk robes hanging on the back of the door. Butlers attend to every need, from unpacking to advising on the merits of a Thai massage, and the hotel's staff are friendly, and quick to remember your name and drink order. Complimentary longtail boats to nearby islands are a nice perk, but it is an amenity built from necessity because the hotel's beach is too rocky for lounging and swimming. The food is outstanding, the spa luxury incarnate.

111 Moo 3, Nongthalay. www.ritzcarlton.com/en/hotels/phulay-bay. ℂ **07562-8111.** 54 units. 12,000B–14,000B suites; 19,000B–41,000B villas. **Amenities:** 4 restaurant; 2 bars; outdoor pool; health club; spa; watersports rentals; room service; Wi-Fi (free).

Moderate

Dusit Thani Krabi Beach Resort ★★★ A large circular drive and luxurious modern lobby pavilion usher you into this expansive resort. Rooms are set across a sprawling low-rise complex and they offer great privacy. Moderate-sized rooms are a fusion of simple lines and Art Deco details, with a few Thai decorative features thrown in as well. Services range from fine-dining choices in the main building to more laid-back fare taken by the large, luxurious beachside pool. Also on hand are plenty of fitness facilities, which offer a great variety of programs (from kickboxing to meditation), after which a treatment at the spa will dispel all aches or stress. The service is of a high standard; they have a fleet of concierge staff with their finger on the pulse of the city.

155 Moo 2, Klong Muang Beach. www.dusit.com/dusitthani/krabibeachresort. (℃)**07562-8000**. 246 units. From 3,300B double; 15,500B suite. **Amenities:** 4 restaurants; 3 bars; outdoor pool; tennis court; health club; spa; watersports equipment; bikes; children's club; room service; babysitting; Wi-Fi (free).

Sofitel Phokeethra Krabi ★★★ This is among the nicest of the luxury resorts to grace this pretty coastline and it has extensive manicured lawns, and a gigantic sculpted pool, surrounded by coconut groves. Boasting an opulent mix of Thai and colonial architecture, this awesome property features a palatial lobby and magnificent views. The vast rooms are classically furnished, with polished teak floors, broad balconies, and a warm butterscotch-and-cream decor. Because it caters not only for upscale tourists but also to large conference groups and wedding parties, expect high standards of service and dining—including a spa with a long menu of options, a wide range of business facilities, and a children's playground. If you like to stay active on vacation, you'll love the breadth of classes on offer, from yoga and tai chi to Pilates and golf.

Klong Muang Beach, Tambon Nongtalay. www.sofitel.com. (℃) **07562-7800**. 276 units. 3,900B–5,900B superior ocean view; 6,200B–17,000B club level and suites. **Amenities:** 3 restaurants; 5 bars; outdoor pool; health club; tennis court; spa; watersports rentals; room service; Wi-Fi (free).

Where to Eat

Apart from the better-than-most dining choices at the many resorts listed above, here are a few more recommendations around the region: In the north end of Krabi Town, the **Night Market**, just off Utarakit riverside road, on Maharaj Soi 10, is the place to try such local specialties as deep-fried oysters, papaya salads, and noodles—most places have English menus, too. For good Western food with an Asian twist, try **Gecko Cabane ★★** (www.facebook.com/GeckoCabaneRestaurant; (℃) **081958-5945**) where the massaman curry with lamb is outstanding.

In Ao Nang, the beachside tourist street is already turning into a mini-Patong, with heaps of neon-lit shops and storefront eateries: Try **Last Fisherman** ((℃) **081267-5338**) for a sunset drink in this longtail-shaped bar before feasting on fish at **Krua Ao Nang Cuisine** ((℃) **07569-5260**), a reliable seafood restaurant with great views. Ice-packed crates of fish let you know what was freshly caught, and fish is priced by the kilo. Let the fisherman do the catching while you catch a great sunset at **Lae Lay Grill** ★ (www.laelaygrill.com; ✆ **07566-1588**) where everything from lobster to scallops with XO sauce comes fresh from the sea. On Railay, the beachside bars and bungalows serve good Thai and continental nosh at affordable prices, and **Last Bar** ★ (✆ 93683-7229) has fire shows on the beach and tiki drinks behind the bar.

KO PHI PHI

814km (506 miles) S of Bangkok, then 42km (26 miles) W of Krabi; 160km (99 miles) SW of Phuket

Phi Phi is, in fact, two islands: **Phi Phi Leh** and **Phi Phi Don.** The latter is the main barbell-shaped island whose central isthmus (the barbell handle) was hit badly by the 2004 tsunami. Ko Phi Phi is a popular choice for day trips, snorkeling, and scuba junkets from Krabi and Phuket. Crowds of noisy tourists used to descend upon **Maya Bay,** on Phi Phi Leh, where filmmakers shot the Hollywood film *The Beach*, with Leonardo DiCaprio. But in October 2018, Thailand's Department of National Parks, Wildlife and Plant Conservation announced that Maya Bay will close indefinitely, due to overuse and degradation of the environment. No timeline was given for reopening, so check before making plans to go there.

All visitors arrive at the busy ferry port in south-facing **Tonsai Bay.** The beach is quite attractive but the constant coming and going of boats makes it inadvisable for swimming. Most people just walk the 300m (984 ft.) across the barbell handle to north-facing **Loh Dalam Bay,** a spectacular, horseshoe-shaped crescent of blinding-white sand. Small beachfront outfits rent snorkel gear and conduct longtail boat tours to quiet coves with great views of coral reefs and sea life for as little as 1,000B for an all-day trip. You can rent kayaks and do a little exploring on your own, or hike to one of the island viewpoints and soak up the memorable view of back-to-back bays and rugged limestone cliffs.

Phi Phi Ley is famed for its coveted **swallow nests** and the courageous pole-climbing daredevils who collect them (the saliva-coated nests fetch a hefty price as the main ingredient in a much-favored but ethically questionable bird's-nest soup). Though nobody lives on Phi Phi Ley, it is frequently visited on day trips as there are some good snorkeling areas nearby, like Bamboo Island.

Before the 2004 tsunami, many of the settlements and hotels on Phi Phi Don had been built illegally by squatters on land belonging to the once-pristine National Marine Park. These facilities were—almost literally—wiped off the map by the tragic disaster. Now crowds have returned to the island en mass, but unfortunately so has the unplanned chaos of pre-tsunami days. Beaches are once again crammed with hotels, low-end guesthouses, sleazy bars, and backpackers. In terms of wholesale environmental degradation, we are, sadly, right back to square one.

Getting There

Boats from Krabi Town run at least four times daily (9am, 10:30am, 1:30pm, and 3:30pm; more in high season) and cost from 350B. From Phuket, ferry services leave at around the same time and charge the same fee, but some include hotel pickup as well. The journey from either place takes 1½ hours to 2 hours.

Where to Stay

We're not really sure why someone would want to spend the night on Ko Phi Phi—especially when amazing accommodation and beaches are found nearby and daytrips are popular. There are no hotels on Ko Phi Phi Leh and camping is now outlawed which sends the masses to Ko Phi Phi Don. You must book early and expect to pay out the wazoo for even mediocre spots. Small island bars have a 2am cutoff but most of the time the partying lasts until sunup.

Those who do want to give it a go should manage expectations and book one of these recommended spots. Remember, *The Beach* is not the reality of visiting Ko Phi Phi. However, if you'd like to try and recreate the movie, consider booking a night on the **Maya Bay Sleepaboard** (www.mayabaytours.com). Camping is not allowed on Maya Bay anymore but this boat docks overnight just offshore. You'll be in a sleeping bag under the stars where dreams come easy as the gentle waves rock you to sleep. The rate of 3,500B per person includes the sleeping bag, food, and national park fee. If you don't want to hang out overnight, they have information about a sunset cruise on their website.

Holiday Inn Resort Phi Phi ★ The Holiday Inn has a lot of things going for it—a nice location on Laem Tong beach, manicured lawns, hammocks gently swaying under beachfront palm trees. The bungalows are comfortable enough, with spacious balconies, though the rooms lack local touches to give them character. A step-up are the studios in the Coral Wing, featuring big balconies and TVs. There are plenty of activities to keep guests busy, such as a dive center, game fishing, and cookery classes, and the restaurants offer grub that satisfies but doesn't thrill.

Laem Thong Beach, Ko Phi Phi. www.phiphi.holidayinn.com. ✆ **07562-7300.** 97 units. 3,500B-5,700B double. **Amenities:** 2 restaurants; bar; 2 outdoor pools; health club; spa; Jacuzzi; watersports rentals & dive center; room service; babysitting; Wi-Fi (free).

Phi Phi Island Village ★★ Accessible only by a 30-minute boat ride (regular shuttles are available from the ferry pier), this is a top choice among the islands' more far-flung resorts. Deluxe bungalows offer private balconies and open-plan bathrooms; with such unrivaled ocean views, it's not surprising this place proves a popular choice for honeymooners. A luxury spa, two large pools, good-dining options, and an in-house tour program service and scuba school complete the picture. Apart from a few nearby jungle walks, it's all about relaxing here. This is one of the nicest spots in Ko Phi Phi.

Loh Ba Kao Bay at the northeast end of the island. www.phiphiislandvillage.com. ⓒ **07562-8900.** 201 units. 4,800B–9,800B double; from 26,000B villa. **Amenities:** 3 restaurants; 3 bars; 2 outdoor pools; spa; watersports equipment; babysitting; Wi-Fi (free).

Zeavola ★★ Many Thais long for a return to their rural village roots, a time when life was simple. That is what Zeavola, tucked away in the northeast corner of the island, is all about—a return to traditional Thai living (just ignore all the house music thumping in the distance). Sand walkways cut through palm trees, leading to freestanding thatch-roofed teak suites. Each is luxuriously appointed with polished teakwood floors, oversized daybeds, and both indoor and outdoor rain showers. The living areas extend past glass doors to covered teakwood patios, where electronically controlled bamboo blinds offer privacy. What makes the suites truly unique, however, are the rustic flourishes: old-fashioned copper piping, wooden taps, pottery sink basins, and *mon khwan* cushions (the traditional triangular Thai pillows) for the patios. The resort also has a PADI dive center and private dive boat.

11 Moo 8, Laem Tong Beach. www.zeavola.com. ⓒ**07562-7000.** 52 units. 5,500B–11,000B village suite; 22,000B beachfront suite. **Amenities:** 2 restaurants; saltwater pool; spa; watersports equipment; Wi-Fi (free).

Where to Eat & Drink

Phi Phi Don is packed with eateries. In downtown central Tonsai, look out for **Unni's** (www.facebook.com/unnis.phiphi; ⓒ **091837-5931**) a specialist in breakfast and "hangover food" while **Efe** (www.facebook.com/eferestaurant; ⓒ **095150-4434**) does authentic Mediterranean. **Ton Sai Seafood** (in front of the Phi Phi Banyayn Villa)**, Jasmine** (Laem Thong Beach), and **Papaya Restaurant** (ⓒ **087280-1719;** in Ton Sai Village) are good for Thai food. You'll also find a few little halal food stands and vendors with wheeled carts making Southern-style sweet *roti* (pancake) with banana.

Once a Muslim village, Phi Phi now parties into the night at such places as **Banana Bar** (Ton Sai Village)**, Slinky** (ⓒ **086067-7339**) for a great fire show around 10pm, **Relax Bar** (Ton Sai Village; no website or phone number)**,** and **Carlito's** (Ton Sai Beach; no website or phone number); there's even an Irish pub and a sports bar. Don't miss the laid-back, beachfront **Sunflower Beach Bar and Restaurant** (no website or phone number) on Loh Dalam Bay or the live music at **Kong Siam** (no website or phone number).

Ko Phi Phi Activities

Kayaks can be rented on the beach for leisurely paddling for around 200B per hour. **Snorkeling** trips around the island are popular and you can sign up for a group tour with any hotel or with any of the many beachfront travel agencies for around 800B–1,200B per day. To hire a longtail boat with pilot for a half-day private trip, expect to pay around 1,200B.

Scuba diving ★★ is quite popular here, too, and **Princess Divers** (www. princessdivers.com; 🕽 **088768-0945**) and **Blue View Divers** (www.blueview divers.com; 🕽 **0945920-0184)** are the ones to pick for full-service and expert staff; they offers everything from day trips to multiday adventures, as well as all the requisite PADI course instruction.

Phi Phi Climbers ★ (www.phiphiislandclimbers.com) operates rock-climbing trips around the gnarled cliffs of the two Phi Phi islands; prices run from 800B for a 2-hour intro class to 2,000B for a full day.

KO LANTA ★

70km (43 miles) SE of Krabi

The two islands of Ko Lanta Yai (Big Lanta Island) and Ko Lanta Noi (Small Lanta Island) are a few hours' car and boat trip from Krabi airport. Ko Lanta Yai is a bohemian alternative to heady Samui or pricey Phuket. But the crowds that love Ko Phi Phi have started to head here, too. However, the island is big enough that, during the high season (Nov–Mar), small pockets of seclusion can be found—especially in the far south and over on the east coast, where Muslim fishing villagers carry on with their traditional economy, ignoring the rolling cement trucks and noise of construction on the upper west coast, where most resorts are located. Despite the island's growing popularity, the endless white-sand beaches are far from crowded. When the sun goes down, there's fun nightlife with an island vibe. During March, when the crowds have left, locals head to historic Lanta Old Town for the annual Laanta Lanta Festival— a celebration of street art, performance, cultural shows, music, dance, fun, and games; check www.tourismthailand.org for exact dates. During low season, many hotels and restaurants shut down.

Getting There & Information

Ban Sala Dan has two boat piers, one for passengers and one for vehicles. **Tigerline Ferry** (www.tigerlinetravel.com) runs in high season between Phuket and Ko Lanta (1,500B; 2 hrs.). Ferries from Koh Phi Phi run all year and take 90 minutes for a price of 300B; speedboats make the trip in an hour for 700B. Two additional passenger boats leave Krabi in the morning during high season for 400B at a travel time of 2 hours. The popular **12go.asia** is a top resource for managing and booking travel to Ko Lanta. The website presents all travel options (boat, car, flight, train) and gives pricing, so it's easy to make a decision based on your time and budget. Another perk: Paying online with a credit card!

There are two **police stations** (one on Phra Ae beach and the other at Ban Sala Dan). **Ko Lanta Hospital** (🕽 **07569-7017**) can help with basic injuries like sunburns, cuts, jellyfish stings, and more. **ATMs** are all along the island and everywhere along the west coast.

To book a diving lesson or excursion, contact the good folks at **Scubafish** (www.scubafish.com; 🕽 **07566-5095**). A 1-day intro course is 5,200B and they have a class on underwater photography.

For all things Ko Lanta, check out: www.lantapocketguide.com. It's a helpful resource for up-to-date travel info and what's happening around the island.

Where to Stay

EXPENSIVE

Layana ★★ An award-winning, small boutique resort located near the northern end of the west coast, Layana has an excellent spa and offers stylish, contemporary thatched bungalows close to the ocean, many of them snuggled around a grand pool. Each room has an open, airy feel with a decor of hard woods, silks, and local art. It carries a high price tag, but the resort's high-quality facilities and service make it worth considering. This resort is for over-18s only.

272 Moo 3, Saladan, Phra-Ae Beach. www.layanaresort.com. ℂ **07560-7100.** 50 units. Between 4,500B and 7,900B double; from 14,700B suite. **Amenities:** Restaurant; bar; outdoor pool; health club; spa; watersports rentals; bikes; room service; Wi-Fi (free).

Pimalai Resort & Spa ★★ Located in the far southwest of the island, close to the National Park headquarters, Pimalai was the first luxury resort on the island. Designed by a young, eco-sensitive Thai architect, it continues to win awards in hospitality and environmental awareness. A fine marriage of comfort and proximity to nature, these stylish villas sprawl down rolling hills and gardens right onto the pristine beach. Shady walkways have been built around the trees and the infinity pool is beautiful; there's first-rate dining in a large open-air *sala*, or down on the beach in a funky thatched bar hewn from logs. The design throughout—from the simple thatched treatment *salas* and trickling waterfall in the spa, to the many small Thai art pieces—flows in harmony.

99 Moo 5, Ba Kan Tiang Beach. www.pimalai.com. ℂ **07560-7999.** 118 units. From 6,000B double; 36,000B three bedroom pool villa. **Amenities:** 5 restaurants; 3 bars; outdoor pool; tennis courts; health club; spa; watersports equipment; bikes; room service; Wi-Fi (free).

MODERATE

Costa Lanta ★★ Lauded for its unique architectural design, the Costa Lanta boasts sleek rooms that balance Western minimalism and Thai rustic décor with a pool deck that overlooks a long, rectangular pool. The resort has also garnered positive reviews for its innovative back-to-nature approach, and for its restaurant, which offers some of the island's best cuisine and cocktails. In the interest of environmental preservation, the resort is built back from the beach under the natural tree line. It caters to well-to-do Thai visitors as much as to foreign tourists.

212 Moo 1, Saladan. www.costalanta.com. ℂ **07566-8186.** 22 units. 2,000B–9,700B double. **Amenities:** Restaurant; bar; outdoor pool; watersports rentals; Wi-Fi (free).

INEXPENSIVE

Mango Guesthouse ★ This unique guesthouse is on the east coast, in an area that was once a hub of Chinese mercantile trade. The studio rooms and two- and three-bedroom villas here are historic Thai fishermen's homes built on stilts over the sea, though not all rooms have air-con. The solid post and beam structures feature modern touches of Chinese décor (it is rumored to have once been an opium den), with spectacular views from private seafront patios. Downstairs, there's the Mango Bistro for eats, and occasional parties with international DJs.

45 Sriraya Rd., Moo 2, Lanta Old Town. www.mangohouses.com. © **095014-0658.** 4 units. 1,500B–6,400B double. **Amenities:** Restaurant; bar; Wi-Fi (free).

La Laanta Hideaway Resort ★★ Located right near the national park and on a quiet section of beach, this collection of thatched bungalows has a cool castaway vibe. An artist friend of the Thai-Vietnamese owners painted hip murals in the rooms and the beds sit on traditional Thai platforms and are adorned with silk pillows. The bathrooms bring the wow factor, especially the deep soaking tub—something rarely seen at this price level. Play volleyball with fellow travelers on the beach or nosh on some really delicious Thai food.

188 Moo 5, Bamboo Beach. www.lalaanta.com. © **087883-9966.** 20 units. 1,200B–6,500B double. **Amenities:** Restaurant; bar; Wi-Fi (free).

Where to Eat & Drink

Cool places to chill on Ko Lanta include **Red Snapper** ★★ (www.facebook.com/RedSnapperLantaThailand; © **07885-6965**), which specializes in fusion food and **Drunken Sailors** ★ (www.facebook.com/drunkensailors; © **07566-5076**), which has stir-fries, curries, and some pretty tasty Western food. **El Greco** (© **083521-6613**) sells gyros the size of your head and **Kwan's Cookery** (© **088446-2167**) has fresh Thai food and offers a fun cooking class. Another great spot for a cooking class is the beloved **Time for Lime** (www.timeforlime.net; © **07568-4590**). **Patty's Secret Garden** (© **098978-8909**) does great breakfast in a pleasant setting.

Ko Lanta can't compare with Ko Phi Phi for nightlife, but there are a few beachfront bars on Ao Phra-Ae (aka Long Beach) that advertise weekly parties. Of those nightly specials, **Irie** (© **084170-6673**) is among the best for Monday night reggae jam sessions.

TRANG ★

129km (80 miles) SE of Krabi

Trang Province, south of Krabi, is where it's at if you're looking for a real Thai-style beach holiday in the south. Popular with Thai tourists, the large province is spectacularly placed, with unspoiled national parks and 46 islands. The jumping-off point for the islands is at **Pak Meng Beach,** about 40km (25 miles) west of the small town of Trang. Day tours for snorkelers are affordable and the scenery is much like nearby Krabi, but cheaper and without as many tourists. Bear in mind that during the monsoon season (May–Oct), there are no day tours and many resorts close down.

For mainland nature, visit wildlife sanctuaries such as **Namtok Khao Chong** and **Khlong Lamchan Park,** which boast waterfalls, trails, and caves. The **Southern Thailand Botanical Garden** (Thung Khai), on the Trang-Palian Road (Hwy. 404), offers stunning nature trails through lowland jungle and tropical gardens. For keen adventurers, there are some remote islands— one such island is **Tarutao Marine National Park,** which lies close to the Malaysian border, in Satun province. This region is great for kayaking and pristine diving. For more adventure tour info, see **www.paddleasia.com.**

Just like in Phuket, Trang celebrates the 9-day vegetarian festival in the first 2 weeks of October. It's a foodie fest without the gore and mutilation that goes on in Phuket. To read about the origins of the festival, see p. 232.

Trang Province is also top for light adventure activities such as sea kayaking and diving. **Had Chao Mai National Park ★★**, which consists of several islands, including the ones listed below, has some secluded islands with upscale bungalows, fresh seafood shacks, fantastic snorkeling, and very little nightlife.

Ko Kradan ★★, is one of the Andaman's real gems, with healthy coral reefs, azure seas, and powder-soft sands. The pinhead size island is mostly visited on snorkeling day trips, but it does have a few places to sleep, the nicest of the handful of options is **Seven Seas Resort ★★** (www.sevenseas resorts.com; ℂ **0752033-8990**) with rates around 6,000B a night. While Ko Kardan's beaches are divine, the island is famous for hosting underwater weddings on Valentine's Day where brides and grooms get hitched in scuba gear underwater.

Ko Mook (Muk) **★★**, famous for the Emerald Cave, a hidden lagoon (it is accessible only at low tide), is growing in popularity every year and has some good budget beach accommodation. Check out **Koh Mook Hostel** (kohmook-hostel@gmail.com; ℂ **089724-4456**) for simple but clean dooms from 400B. **Sivalai ★★★** (www.komooksivalai.com; ℂ **089723-3355**) has wooden bungalows that—quite literally—just four steps from the water.

The most convenient island for a base is **Ko Ngai,** a short boat ride from Pak Meng Beach, and it has a few dive shops that offer lessons and snorkel gear, hotels, and a spot to book snorkeling boat tours. There are two nice spots to stay on the island: **Thanya Resort ★★** (www.kohngaithanyaresort.com; ℂ **094583-2888**) has teak bungalows, a pool overlooking the ocean, and a dive center with rooms from 3,800B. Another recommendation is **Coco Cottage ★★** (www.coco-cottage.com; ℂ **07522-4387**), which is the most romantic choice on the island. Rooms have floor-to-ceiling ocean views with walls made of coconut shells and there's an outdoor spa; rates from 3,300B.

Getting There

BY PLANE   There are six daily flights from Don Muang airport in Bangkok to Trang. **Nok Air** (www.nokair.com; ℂ **1318**) and **Air Asia** (www.airasia. com; ℂ **02515-9999**) make the journey in 90 minutes for around 1,500B. It is then around 100B to reach hotels in Trang by taxi. If you're going onward to one of Trang's islands, book a combo taxi-boat ticket from an airport agent for around 1,000B. Hotels can assist, too.

BY TRAIN   Trang city is connected by train with Bangkok on the main north–south line. Two daily departures make the 16-hour trek. Ask for details at **Bangkok's Hua Lampong Station** (℡ **1690**) but expect to pay 1,600B, which is more than the short flight.

BY BUS   There are frequent buses from Bangkok's **Southern Bus Terminal** (℡ **02422-4444**) but it's a long 12-hour ride (about 650B). Minibus connections from Krabi (2 hours; 125B) and Surat Thani (4 hours; 150B). When you arrive in Trang, connect by minibus with Pak Meng Beach for around 50B per person, or 500B to hire the entire vehicle; it's about a 1-hour ride.

Ferryboats to the outlying islands regularly leave all day from Trang's Pak Meng Pier on the north end of the beach. It costs around 1,000B to 1,500B for an all-day tour by boat (including lunch), and they can drop you off at any number of islands (Ko Ngai, Ko Mook, or Ko Kradan); though, if you are staying at one of the island resorts, your hosts will usually arrange transfers.

Where to Stay & Eat

Yamawa Guesthouse (www.yamawagesthouse.com; ℡ **099402-0349**) is rustic but cozy with owners who are passionate about making sure their guests discover all that Trang has to offer. Rooms range from 350B fill up early for high season. **Mitree House** (℡ **07521-2292**) is a charming guesthouse with lots of space to spread out. Some of the rooms don't have windows but the bathrooms are big and bright. A helpful staff, fast Wi-Fi, and cozy communal areas round out a stay; rooms from 750B.

Sin Ocha (on Kantang Road; no ℡) has nearly 70 decades of business to its name and locals come here for dim sum, great breakfast, and roasted pork. It's old-school Thai-Chinese and a real institution. The **night market** near Praram VI Road has some really amazing Thai dishes including fried chicken, tons of curries, deep-fried hunks of tofu, noodles, fruit, and more. Come hungry, it's open daily from 4-9pm.

WHERE TO STAY ON THE ISLANDS

If you prebook a stay on the nearby islands, the resorts will help with transfers; otherwise, head for the ferries that leave frequently from Pak Meng Pier. **Ko Ngai** (aka Ko Hai) is the most developed island, with half a dozen smart places, including the quaint **CoCo Cottages** (www.coco-cottage.com; ℡ **07522-4387**), an environmentally friendly cluster run by a cheerful Thai family; beach cottages range from 3,300B to 6,800B. Another good bet is right next door, where the **Thapwarin Resort** (www.thapwarin.com; ℡ **081894-3585**) has big, comfy bamboo and rattan cottages for similar rates. **Thanya Resort** (www.kohngaithanyaresort.com; ℡ **07520-6967**) has a gorgeous pool, dive center, great Thai restaurant, and rooms from 3,700B.

On **Ko Mook,** go for **Sivalai Resort** (www.komooksivalai.com; ℂ **08972-33355**), which stands on a dramatic spur of land that is the best on the island with a beach on both sides; rooms start at 5,000B. Finally, on gorgeous **Ko Kradan,** the best place to stay is the **Seven Seas Resort** (www.sevenseas resorts.com; ℂ **07520-3389;**), where rooms and villas go for 6,000B to 12,000B. If that's too much, try **Kalume** (www.kalumekradan.com; ℂ **080932-0029**) where beachfront bungalows are no frills but go for 1,200B a night.

CENTRAL THAILAND

Going north from Bangkok, travelers who trace the route of the Chao Phraya River will feel as if they are traveling back in time. Starting with the ruins of Ayutthaya, as you go north, you will discover a series of former capitals: After **Ayutthaya** comes **Lopburi.** Farther north, the nation's most famous architectural wonder, **Sukhothai,** is traditionally considered the seat of the first Thai kingdom, from 1238. Beyond Sukhothai, to the north of the Central Plains, is the mountainous land once called Lanna, or the "Land of a Million Rice Fields." This distinct ancient kingdom meandered between Chiang Mai and Chiang Rai (see chapters 11 and 12), and brought totally different customs and architecture.

Central Thailand is also the country's "Great Rice Bowl," known for its agricultural abundance. Winding rivers cut through a mosaic of rice fields, and smaller villages and towns provide a window into the heart of Thailand's rural culture.

10

AYUTTHAYA ★★

76km (47 miles) N of Bangkok

Ayutthaya is a highlight of any trip to Thailand. Many travelers take the day tour from Bangkok, which allows about 3 hours at the sites (the majority of these lie inside the Historical Park), but for anyone with a strong interest in archaeological ruins, Ayutthaya justifies an overnight or more.

From its establishment in 1350 by King U Thong (Ramathibodi I) until its fall to the Burmese in 1767, Ayutthaya was the capital of Siam, home to 33 kings and numerous dynasties. At its zenith and until the mid-18th century, Ayutthaya was a majestic city with three palaces and 400 temples on an island threaded by canals. The former capital rivaled European cities in splendor and was a source of marvel to foreigners.

Then, in 1767, after a 15-month siege, the town was destroyed by the Burmese. Today there is little left but ruins and rows of headless Buddhas where once an empire thrived. But the temple compounds are still awe-inspiring even in disrepair, and a visit here is memorable and a good starting point for those drawn to the relics of history.

The Central Plains

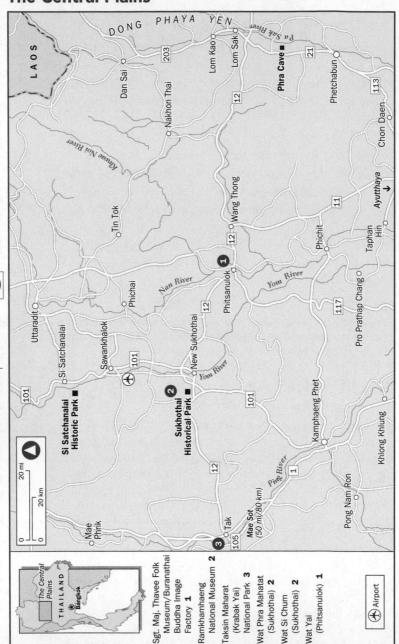

LAOS

DONG PHAYA YEN

Dan Sai

Nakhon Thai

Lom Kao

Lom Sak

Pa Sak River

Phra Cave ■

203

12

21

113

Phetchabun

Chon Daen

Khwae Noi River

Tin Tok

Wang Thong

Ayutthaya →

11

Phichit

Taphan Hin

Phichai

Nan River

Phitsanulok

1

12

Yom River

Uttaradit

Si Satchanalai

Sawankhalok

New Sukhothai

12

117

Pro Prathap Chang

Si Satchanalai Historic Park ■

101

101

✈

Yom River

Sukhothai Historical Park ■

2

101

Kamphaeng Phet

Khlong Khlung

Mae Phrik

12

Ping River

1

Tak

105

3

Mae Sot
(50 mi/80 km)

Pong Nam Ron

20 mi

20 km

0

0

The Central Plains

THAILAND

● Bangkok

✈ Airport

284

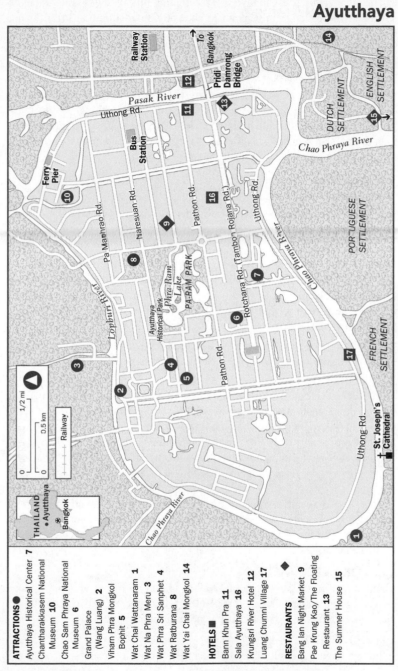

Ayutthaya

ATTRACTIONS●

Ayutthaya Historical Center **7**
Chantharakkasem National
  Museum **10**
Chao Sam Phraya National
  Museum **6**
Grand Palace
  (Wang Luang) **2**
Viharn Phra Mongkol
  Bophit **5**
Wat Chai Wattanaram **1**
Wat Na Phra Meru **3**
Wat Phra Sri Sanphet **4**
Wat Ratburana **8**
Wat Yai Chai Mongkol **14**

HOTELS■

Bann Khun Pra **11**
Sala Ayutthaya **16**
Krungsri River Hotel **12**
Luang Chumni Village **17**

RESTAURANTS◆

Bang Ian Night Market **9**
Pae Krung Kao/The Floating
  Restaurant **13**
The Summer House **15**

Railway Station

Pridi Damrong Bridge

To Bangkok

Pasak River

Uthong Rd.

Bus Station

Ferry Pier

Pa Maphrao Rd.

Naresuan Rd.

Pathon Rd.

Lopburi River

Ayutthaya Historical Park

Phra Ram Lake

PA-RAM PARK

Rotchana Rd. (Tambon Rojana Rd.)

Uthong Rd.

Chao Phraya River

Pathon Rd.

Uthong Rd.

St. Joseph's Cathedral

Chao Phraya River

DUTCH SETTLEMENT

ENGLISH SETTLEMENT

PORTUGUESE SETTLEMENT

FRENCH SETTLEMENT

1/2 mi
0   0.5 km
Railway

THAILAND
• Ayutthaya
✴ Bangkok

10

CENTRAL THAILAND | Ayutthaya

285

The architecture of Ayutthaya is a fascinating mix of styles. Tall, corncob-shaped spires, called *prangs*, point to ancient Khmer (Cambodian) influence (best seen in Bangkok at Wat Arun, p. 113). These bear a resemblance to the architecture of Angkor Wat, in Cambodia. The pointed stupas are ascribed to the Sukhothai style.

In 2018 a breakout Thai TV show "Buppaesannivas" portrayed a present-day archeologist who wakes up in Ayutthaya in the mid-1600s after a car crash. As a result, groups of young Thais have been flocking here in traditional dress to recreate shots from the series. Sure, there are a few more people than normal, but seeing locals in period-specific garb is great fun, and heightens the lost-in-time feeling of the temples.

Essentials

ARRIVING

BY TRAIN   Starting at 4:20am, trains depart nearly every 40 minutes from Bangkok's **Hua Lampong Railway Station** (℃ **1690;** trip time 80 minutes; 65B first class, 45B second class; 15B third class).

BY BUS OR MINIBUS   With regular departure times from sun up to sun down (5am to 8pm) from Bangkok's **Mo Chit Northern Bus Terminal** (℃ **02936-2841**), the 1½ hr. ride averages 50B. Minibuses leave every 20–30 minutes from Victory Monument (on the BTS). They cost around 70B and take just an hour to arrive.

BY CAR   Outside of the congestion of the big city, the 90-minute drive is a cinch, but the ease and affordability of public transportation should sway you from renting a car for this occasion. If you do drive plan to pay 130B in tolls.

BY BOAT   All-day river cruises are a popular option, but we would advise against them since most of the travel is done by bus with only short stints along rivers near Bangkok. There is, however, one notable exception for getting to Ayutthaya by boat. That exception requires 3 days but you'll be traveling upriver aboard a sumptuously chic renovated teak rice barge. Three-day, two-night trips sail from Bangkok, stopping at local temples. Aboard the ship, the crew serves cocktails, snacks, high tea, and Thai meals in a covered lounge. Guests spend an afternoon in Ayutthaya in the company of a knowledgeable guide. Inclusive of meals, tours, and transfers (but not alcohol) the cost is 64,767B. To learn more, contact **Anantara Cruises** (www.bangkok-cruises.anantara.com).

VISITOR INFORMATION

There is a **Tourism Authority of Thailand (TAT)** office at Si Sanphet Road (www.tourismthailand.org; ℃ **03524-6076**), opposite the Chao Sam Phraya National Museum. Stop by for maps and other information.

CITY LAYOUT

Ayutthaya's old city is surrounded by a canal fed by three rivers—Chao Phraya, Lopburi, and Pasak—and thus is often referred to as the "island." The main ferry pier is located on the east side of the island, just opposite the train station.

GETTING AROUND

A tuk-tuk from the train station into town will cost about 50B. Then the absolute best way to visit the ruins is by renting a bicycle (about 50B per day) from any guesthouse or hotel. If you're feeling lazy, speak with a rider of a *samlor* (bicycle taxi); enlist the help of hotel staff to negotiate, or this will cost an arm and a leg. You can also hire a tuk-tuk for 200B an hour. **Fun to know:** Ayutthaya's tuk-tuks have a dome-like hood that is unique to this province, and they come in a variety of colors with larger bench seats. The most likely reason for this difference is they were imported from Japan.

FAST FACTS

Bank of Ayudhya (which uses a different spelling of the city's name and is often known as Krungsri) has a branch on U Thong Road next to the ferry pier, across the river from the train station, and there are plenty of ATMs in the city. The main **post office** is also on U Thong Road in the northeast corner of town (but any hotel or guesthouse can help with posting mail). **Phra Nakhon Si Ayutthaya Hospital** on U Thong Road is where to head for emergency care.

Exploring Ayutthaya

In its heyday, Ayutthaya was home to more than 400 temples. Today, most of the main historical sites here are concentrated on the "island," with ancient ruins interspersed with the modern buildings that have risen around them. The Ayutthaya Historical Park lies in the center of the island, but the sites below are just a few of many, and a guide who can offer historical context is helpful (you'll find well-reviewed guides at GetYourGuide.com and Viator.com).

Most temples sell tickets from 8am (opening time) until 4:30pm and close at 5pm. If you plan to visit several temples, there is a six-in-one **package pass** that costs 220B available at all temples; it grants access to the six main temples, saving 80B per person. Though you can't go inside the temples after dark, several of the exteriors are dramatically lit at night, and worth seeing on their own. Hotels can arrange night tours to look at these illuminations. Brightly caparisoned elephants are on hand for short rides around the center of the ancient city, but consider the ethics (p. 44) before hopping on for a ride. Be sure to give the **Inter Market** (near the Floating Market) a miss; it's a heartbreaking display of mistreated animals.

MUSEUMS

Ayutthaya Historical Study Center ★ MUSEUM   Financed by the Japanese, the center's detailed dioramas bring to life how the ancient city, rural villages, and the port area looked in its heyday. If you're interested in seeing historical artifacts from the Ayutthaya era, however, you'd be better off visiting the nearby Chao Sam Phraya National Museum (p. 288).

Rotchana Road between Si San Phet and Chikun roads. © **03524-5124.** Admission adults 100B; children 50B. Daily 9am–5pm.

Chantharakasem National Museum ★ MUSEUM The Chan Kasem Palace was built in 1577 by King Maha Thamaraja (the 17th Ayutthaya monarch) for his son, who became King Naresuan. It was destroyed when the Burmese sacked Ayutthaya in 1767 but was later restored by King Mongkut (Rama IV) in the 1850s. Today, this is where you'll find a small collection of gold artifacts, jewelry, carvings, Buddha images, and domestic and religious objects from the 13th to the 17th century. More than anything, it's a nice air-conditioned spot to cool down.

Northeast part of the island. ℂ **03525-1586.** Admission 100B. Wed–Sun 9am–4pm.

Chao Sam Phraya National Museum ★★ MUSEUM This museum, one of Thailand's largest, boasts a comprehensive collection of antique bronze Buddha images, carved panels, religious objects, and other local artifacts found during excavation of the city. Though most of the city's treasures were plundered by the Burmese in the 18th century or moved to the National Museum in Bangkok, it's still worth taking a look at the collection of gold objects that includes a relic casket from Wat Mahathat, a jewel-encrusted sword, and a kneeling elephant studded with gems that was found in the crypt at Wat Ratburana.

Rotchana Rd. (1½ blocks west of the center near the junction of Si Sanphet Rd.) ℂ **03524-1587.** Admission 150B. Daily 9am–4pm.

THE TEMPLES & RUINS

Viharn Phra Mongkon Bophit ★ RELIGIOUS SITE Home to one of Thailand's largest seated bronze Buddhas (55.5-feet/17-meters with the base), this sanctuary was rebuilt in the 1950s with funding from the Burmese who destroyed the original a couple of centuries ago (can you say karmic atonement?). The area was originally designated for royal cremation ceremonies, and the *viharn* (assembly hall) was later constructed to house the Buddha image. It is the only newish building in the ancient city and is generally the first port of call for Thai visitors, who come to pay their respects to the huge Buddha image.

West of Wat Phra Mahathat and near Wat Si Sanphet. Free admission. Daily 8am–5pm.

Wat Chai Wattanaram ★★ HISTORIC SITE This impressive off-island temple on the southwest side of the city is too far to walk from the other main sights, but accessible by bike (bring water!). It is a well-preserved example of Khmer architecture in the Ayutthaya period, and it looks a lot like Cambodia's Angkor Wat. You can climb to the steep steps of the central *prang* for superb views of the surrounding countryside. Its intact structure offers visitors a good sense of what a working temple might have looked like some 300 years ago.

Opposite bank of the Chao Phraya River, southwest of town. Admission 50B. Daily 8am–5pm.

Wat Na Phra Meru ★★ HISTORIC SITE Because it was used as a base for the invading Burmese army, Wat Na Phra Meru is one of the few temples that escaped unharmed during the siege of 1787. A Burmese king died here when his cannon backfired during an attack, an event Thais feel adds to the spiritual power of the temple. Most visitors flock to it, however, because it is a rare intact example of 16th century architecture, and quite beautiful, its central sanctuary featuring stunning vaulted ceilings supported by ornate columns. The temple houses a 1.8m-tall (6-ft.) Buddha dressed in "royal attire" (a common practice in the 18th century). It's located on the Lopburi side of the river.

Across the Lopburi River, north of the Grand Palace area. Admission 20B. Daily 8am–5pm.

Wat Phra Mahathat ★★★ HISTORIC SITE

The most striking of all the temples in Ayutthaya, Wat Phra Mahathat was built in the heart of the city in 1374 during the reign of King Borom Rachathirat I, and it was one of the most important temples in the area. Today, it is a shell of its former self and, typical of Ayutthaya ruins, has large crumbling stupas surrounded by low laterite walls and rows of headless Buddhas. One Buddha head remains a draw for merit-makers and photographers alike: Looking like a work of contemporary art, it's famously embedded in the gnarled roots of a bodhi tree.

Along Chee Kun Rd., near the intersection with Naresuan. Admission for 50B. Daily 8am–5pm.

Wat Ratburana ★★ HISTORIC SITE

Opposite Wat Phra Mahathat and built in 1424, this wat is splendidly restored. The towering monuments (both rounded Khmer-style *prangs* and Sukhothai-style pointed *chedis*) have even retained some of their original stucco. King Borom Rachathirat II built the temple to honor his two brothers, who killed each other in a duel for the throne, leaving him king. In the two crypts (visitable, but not recommended for those with fear of heights, confined spaces or bats), excavators found bronze Buddha images and votive tablets, as well as golden objects and jewelry, many of which are displayed in the Chao Sam Phraya National Museum (p. 288).

Along Chee Kun Rd., near the intersection with Naresuan. Admission for 50B. Daily 8am–5pm.

Wat Phra Si Sanphet ★★ HISTORIC SITE

Built in the 14th century for private royal use, this was the city's largest temple. Now little remains apart from brick foundations and three well-preserved 15th-century *chedis*, enshrining the ashes of several Ayutthayan kings. This is one of the only temples in the park that you're allowed to climb, which makes it the most photographed sight in the historical park. Nothing remains of the **Grand Palace,** just to the north, which is included in the same ticket, apart from the foundations of three buildings and a wall around the compound. If the temple looks familiar, it is because it was the model for Bangkok's Wat Phra Keo at the Grand Palace.

Next to Viharn Phra Mongkul Bophit in the northwest end of the island. Admission 50B. Daily 8am–5pm.

Wat Yai Chai Mongkhon ★ HISTORIC SITE   Visible for miles around, the huge, brick *chedi* of Wat Yai is a long walk (or a short bicycle ride) southeast of ancient Ayutthaya (across the river and out of town). King U Thong founded the temple in 1357, and the white reclining Buddha near the entrance was built by King Naresuan. The massive pagoda celebrates the defeat of the Burmese at Suphanburi in 1592, and King Naresuan's triumph over the crown prince of Burma in an elephant joust. The rows of Buddha images draped in saffron robes make for Instagram-worthy photos. Stick around for sunset if you can—it's a real experience to see the sun dip below the ancient ruins here. However sunset viewing is not exactly a well-kept secret, so arrive 30 minutes early to claim a spot.

East of the city, across the Pridi Damrong Bridge and south on Dusit Rd. Admission 20B. Daily 8am–5pm.

Where to Stay

So-so facilities in town and proximity to the capital means that most people visit Ayutthaya on a day trip and depart by 4pm so they can make it back to Bangkok for dinner. That's great news for those who plan to stay the night and explore a few well-lit ruins around sunset—you can make reservations at the last minute no problem. In town, Naresuan Road, which is like a smaller version of Khao San Road in Bangkok, has a slew of backpacker-style accommodations. A few waterfront boutiques are charming, like Sala Ayutthaya and Luang Chumni Village (p. 291). However, most of what Ayutthaya offers is pretty bland, lacking in both style and service. Here are the options we can heartily recommend.

MODERATE

Sala Ayutthaya ★★★   Sala is both Ayutthaya's newest and swankiest hotel and its nighttime views of the illuminated Wah Phutthai Sawan are ace—similar to the views of Wat Arun from the Bangkok branch (p. 71). The décor is quite chic—white walls and polished concrete, timber four-poster beds, crisp white bedding, free-standing deep soak tubs, and floor-to-ceiling windows. Five room categories range from spacious doubles to rooms with private pools and a river view duplex. Don't miss the topnotch on-site restaurant.

9/2 Moo 4, U-Thong Rd. www.salahospitality.com/ayutthaya. ✆ **03524-2588.** 26 units. 4,948B room; from 7,990B suite including breakfast. **Amenities:** Restaurant; bar; outdoor pool; spa; Wi-Fi (free).

INEXPENSIVE

Baan Bussara ★★   This spic-and-span small hotel feels like staying at the home of your Thai auntie; the kindly owners offer very personalized service, which ranges from recommending expert but inexpensive massages, to steering guests towards the best street food. Well-maintained bikes are available for rent, and the hotel's prime location makes reaching the top ancient sights on two wheels a breeze. Rooms are simple but spacious and have Western-style bathrooms and small refrigerators.

64/14 Soi Bua Wan. www.facebook.com/baanbussara. © **081655-6379.** 10 units. From 600B double. Amenities: Restaurants; Wi-Fi (free).

Luang Chumni Village ★★   Half a dozen multi-story teak houses make for a charming, Thai-style overnight stay. Absolutely sprawling balconies are the highlight of each room and the welcoming staff are very helpful. Superior rooms and standard rooms are the same size, but guests in the superior category have a bit more privacy and better views.

2/4 Rojana Rd. www.luangchumnivillage.com. © **03532-2990.** 6 units. 920B standard; 1,500B superior all rooms inclusive of breakfast. No online booking so email yourhost@ luangchumnivillage.com. **Amenities:** Restaurant; Wi-Fi (free)

Where to Eat

Particularly if this is your first stop outside of Bangkok, don't miss the **Bang Ian Night Market,** on its namesake street, with fresh produce and a wide selection of Thai-Muslim dishes. The market exudes a great local vibe and the dishes are authentic. The **Floating Market** is a giant tourist trap but is a surprisingly nice place to grab a snack, like homemade coconut ice cream that hits the spot on a hot day. The guesthouses along **Naresuan Road** serve decent Thai fare geared to foreigners, and this area also hosts a few **open-air bars** right on the street, a great place to meet, greet, eat, and party.

Pae Krung Kao ★★ THAI   On low floating pallets at the riverside, this restaurant (known locally as the floating restaurant) has swell views of the overworked tugboats pulling heavy barges filled with rice. Inside, it's charmingly cluttered with knick-knacks, all displayed without regards for spacing or style. The satisfying Thai-Chinese stir-fry and curries are good, but the reason everyone is here is the giant river prawns. Go with the flow and order the signature dish grilled with a spicy dipping sauce. Lick your lips and say "*aroy mak*"—very delicious!

4 Moo 2, U Thong Rd. (west bank of Pasak River, north of Pridi Damrong Bridge). © **03525-1807.** Main courses 60B–500B. Daily 5–10pm.

The Summer House ★★★ THAI   Popular with Thailand's social-media twenty- and thirtysomethings, this riverside restaurant is a beguiling place to spend an evening relaxing with friends, meeting locals eager to practice their English, and enjoying a good meal. Everything here looks Instagram-worthy, from the artfully plated trays of river prawns, colorful Thai curries, generously portioned salmon fillets, and fruit juices—all complimented by Scandinavian-style décor. Listen to live music while lounging on a beanbag in the backyard.

71/1 Koh Raen. www.facebook.com/thesummerhouse.ayutthaya. © **094224-2223.** Main courses 110B–500B. Daily 10am–9:30pm.

10

CENTRAL THAILAND — Ayutthaya

Day Trip from Ayutthaya
BANG PA-IN★★

Only 61km (38 miles) north of Bangkok and 20km (12 miles) south of Ayutthaya, this delightful **royal palace** (admission 100B; 8am–4pm, last admission 3:15pm) is usually combined with Ayutthaya in 1-day tours. The palace's eclectic mashup of architectural styles stands in fascinating contrast to Ayutthaya's crumbling temples.

The 17th-century temple and palace at **Bang Pa-In** were originally built by Ayutthaya's King Prasat who later abandoned the space when the capital moved in the late 1700s. The palace sat dormant for nearly a century before King Rama IV rebuilt it in the 1800s, and it became a favorite summer home for King Rama V until tragedy struck. In 1880, the pregnant queen and her daughter died when a boat capsized en route to the palace. Her horrified subjects and on-lookers stood by and watched, and could have easily saved her, had it not been for a Thai law that forbade commoners from touching the royal family. The grief-stricken King Rama V changed the law and built a marble obelisk in her honor.

On the banks opposite the palace is **Wat Niwet Thamprawat,** the only temple in Thailand with European architecture. It is small but stunning; featuring stained-glass windows, a belfry, and neo-Gothic style resembling a cathedral. In the center of the small lake, **Phra Thinang Aisawan Thippa-At** is a pavilion that is an excellent example of classic Thai style architecture. Behind it, in Versailles style, are the former **king's apartments,** which today serve as a hall for state ceremonies. The **Phra Thinang Wehat Chamrun,** also noteworthy, is a Chinese-style building (open to the public), where court members generally lived during the rainy and cool seasons. It was custombuilt with materials from China and showcases jade and porcelain from the Ming era.

It closes early, and you're best moving on to Ayutthaya or Bangkok for any major meal or for a place to sleep. If you're not on a pre-arranged tour, a taxi from Ayutthaya will cost several hundred baht, so you're better off asking your hotel (in Bangkok or Ayutthaya) to pre-book a round-trip minivan or taxi. On your way in or out of Bang Pa-In, make a detour to visit the **Bang Sai Arts & Crafts Centre ★★**, a space dedicated to preserving traditional Thai arts. Workers demonstrate the skills needed to make more than 30 local crafts, like ceramics, glass blowing, khon mask making, hyacinth weaving, and more. There is a small souvenir shop to buy local crafts after the tour.

LOPBURI

77km (48 miles) N of Ayutthaya; 153km (95 miles) N of Bangkok; 224km (139 miles) S of Phitsanulok

Lopburi is best known for being one of Thailand's oldest cities, and scholars say it was developed during the Dvaravati period (6th to 10th centuries). Famous attractions are 14th- to 17th-century temple ruins and, possibly even more so, the troops of monkeys that call them home. The town hosted kings and emissaries from around the world some 400 years ago, and archaeological evidence suggests a highly developed Buddhist society was here as early as the 11th century. These days, Lopburi is a popular day trip from Ayutthaya or a good stopover on the way to northern cities like Chiang Mai.

Essentials

ARRIVING
Lopburi is along Highway 1 just past Saraburi (connect with Lopburi via Hwy. 3196 to Rte. 311). The fastest way to go straight there from Bangkok is by minivan from Victory Monument (accessible by BTS) for 100B. Regular buses connect to Lopburi via Ayutthaya from Bangkok's **Northern Bus Terminal** (© **02936-2841**) for the same price. Numerous trains make a daily connection with Lopburi via Ayutthaya from Bangkok's **Hua Lampong Railway Station** (© **1690**), from 28B upward.

VISITOR INFORMATION & CITY LAYOUT
The **TAT Office** is located in a teak house built in the 1930s just a short walk from the train station (follow the signs) on Ropwat Phrathat Road (© **03642-2768**). They have a useful map and can point you to sights within walking distance.

Exploring Lopburi

You should visit Lopburi by approaching its attractions in a clockwise circle pattern—touring the town is a half-day activity. From the train station, stop at **Wat Phra Si Ratana Mahathat** just out front. Built in 1257, Mahathat is a stunning ruin that has undergone heavy reconstruction over the years, much like the temples of Ayutthaya (admission 50B; daily 7am–5pm). The central *prang* is the tallest in Lopburi.

Directly west of the TAT, the large complex of **Phra Narai Ratchaniwet (King Narai's Palace)** was built in 1666. Palace buildings are now a large museum of Lopburi antiquities with the *wats* and palace of the king. When nearby Ayutthaya was little more than a marsh, King Narai hosted emissaries from around the world (note the many Islamic-style doorways). The museum also houses displays of Thai rural life and traditions, from weaving and agriculture to shadow puppetry (admission 150B; daily 8:30am–4:30pm). After leaving the museum, take some time to saunter around the atmospheric palace grounds.

From Narai's palace, head north through the town's small streets and market areas to **Wat Sao Thong Thong,** which houses a large golden Buddha and fine Khmer and Ayutthaya period statues. Heading farther north brings you to **Ban Vichayen,** the manicured ruins of the housing built for visiting dignitaries (admission 50B; 9am–4pm).

Going east along Vichayen Road, toward the town center, the three connected towers at **Phra Prang Sam Yot** are handsome examples of the Khmer influence on what is known as "Lopburi style." This is the site where you'll find the town's famous monkeys most hours of the day (admission 50B; daily 7am–6pm). Be careful around these mischievous apes: They have been known to get aggressive. You can take pictures, but keep a tight grip on your camera, don't carry any food, and watch your glasses.

Reaching Prang Sam Yot brings you full circle back to the town's roundabout. Ask about the occasional *macaque* **banquets,** where a formal table is set for the little beasts, who tear it to bits—they've no manners at all—as thanks to the gods for answering prayers. Most days they are fed at a temple just east of Sam Yot, called **San Phra Khan** (across the train tracks). Groups of the mischievous animals trapeze along the high wires and swoop down on shop owners armed with sticks, who keep a close eye on outdoor merchandise. It's a different kind of rush hour altogether.

Where to Stay & Eat

Few stay in little Lopburi, instead visiting the town on a day trip from Ayutthaya or as a brief stopover on the way to points north. If you do choose to stay here, try the **Noom Guesthouse** (15-17 Phayakamjad Rd.; www.noomguesthouse.com; (**036642-7693**), with shared bathrooms for 250B and bungalows for 590B. They can arrange half-day rock-climbing trips to **Khao Chin Lae,** where dozens of roped routes leading to the top of **Wat Pa Suwannahong.** Climbing is nowhere near the quality of Krabi (p. 266) but it's a nice touch of adventure in this quiet temple-dotted region.

There are lots of small open-air restaurants in and around town. One of the best options is the Thai-Chinese **Khao Tom Hor** (Na Phra Kan Road near the train station; 5pm to late). They're famous for deep-fried salted fish, which is authentically delicious and cheap. An ice-cold Singha pairs perfectly with it.

PHITSANULOK

377km (234 miles) N of Bangkok; 93km (58 miles) SE of Sukhothai

Phitsanulok is a bustling agricultural, transportation, and military center nestled on the banks of the Nan River. It is the crossroads of Thailand, located in the center of the country and roughly equidistant from Chiang Mai and Bangkok. Like most transportation hubs, it's hectic, noisy, and just a stopover for most people on their way to the more charming Sukhothai.

There was a 25-year period in between the fall of Sukhothai and the rise of Ayutthaya, where Phitsanulok served as the kingdom's capital, and it is the birthplace of King Naresuan the Great, the Ayutthayan king who, on elephantback, defended Thailand from the Burmese army during the 16th century.

When a tragic fire burned most of the city in 1959, one of the only building to survive was **Wat Phra Si Ratana Mahathat,** famed for its unique statue of Buddha; the temple is now a holy pilgrimage site. For travelers, Wat Yai is worth a visit on the way west to Sukhothai or farther to the Burmese border. Phitsanulok is also famous for the Bangkaew dog, a notoriously fierce and faithful breed that's prized globally, and is thought to have originated from the Bang Rakham District.

Outside of town, the terrain is flat and the rice paddies are endless—they turn a vivid green from July to August. In winter, white-flowering tobacco and pink-flowering soybeans are planted in rotation. Rice barges, houseboats, and longtail boats ply the Nan and Song Kwai rivers, which eventually connect to the Chao Phraya River and feed into the Gulf of Thailand.

Essentials

ARRIVING

BY PLANE   Nok Air (www.nokair.com; ✆ 1318) and AirAsia (www.air asia.com; ✆ 02515-9999) each have three flights daily to Phitsanulok from Bangkok (flying time: about 1 hr.; 500B–1,000B one-way). Taxis from the airport to town run approximately 150B.

BY TRAIN   About 10 trains per day travel between Phitsanulok and Bangkok. The trip time is about 7 hours and costs range from 69B to nearly 1,700B, and the price is determined by class of train and speed— "rapid" trains add an extra 2 hours to the journey. There are six daily connections between Phitsanulok and Chiang Mai (7 hr.; fare 440B). For information and reservations, call Bangkok's **Hua Lampong Railway Station** (✆ 1690), **Chiang Mai Railway Station** (✆ 05324-5363), or the **Phitsanulok Railway Station** (✆ 05525-8005).

In front of the station in Phitsanulok, throngs of *samlors* (pedicabs) and motorcycle taxis wait to take you to your hotel. The station is right in town, so expect to pay 60B to get where you need to go. The bidding will start at around 120B; smile and get ready to haggle.

BY BUS   Standard air-conditioned buses leave daily every hour for the trip to Phitsanulok from Bangkok from 7am to midnight (trip time 6 hr.; about 475B). The VIP bus leaves at midnight and is about the same price; the wide seats recline enough to get a decent sleep, and the overnight trip is a timesaver. Buses depart from Chiang Mai in similar numbers. Frequent non-air-conditioned buses connect with Sukhothai. The intercity bus terminal in Phitsanulok is 2km (1¼ miles) east of town on Highway 12 (about 50B by tuk-tuk or taxi). Contact **Bangkok's Northern Bus Terminal** (✆ 02936-2841), the **Arcade Bus Station** in **Chiang Mai** (✆ 05324-2664), or the **Phitsanulok Bus Terminal** (✆ 05521-2090).

VISITOR INFORMATION

The **TAT office** (✆ 05525-2742) on Boromtrailokanat Road has handy maps.

CITY LAYOUT

The town is fairly compact, with the majority of services and sights for tourists concentrated along or near the east bank of the Nan River. Naresuan Road extends from the railway station and crosses the river from the east over the town's main bridge. Wat Yai is north of the bridge and just a hitch north of busy Highway 12. The main **market,** featuring souvenirs during the day and **food stalls** at night, is just south of the bridge on riverside Phutta Bucha Road. One landmark is the clock tower at the southern end of the commercial district, Boromtrailokanart Road.

GETTING AROUND

BY TUK-TUK & SONGTAEW Tuk-tuks (called taxis here) stop near the bus and train stations. Negotiate hard for in-town trips, usually 30B to 60B. *Songtaews* (covered pickup trucks) follow regular routes outside of town.

BY BUS There's a city bus system with the main terminal south of the train station on A-Kathotsarot Road. Trips are about 10B, but you're just as well off to hire tuk-tuks. There are frequent (every half-hour 6am–6pm) buses from the intercity bus terminal east of town to **New Sukhothai** (trip time 1 hr.; fare 42B).

BY HIRED MINIVAN Any hotel in Phitsanulok can arrange minivan tours in the area and to Sukhothai. Expect to pay around 2,000B with a driver, plus fuel. We highly recommend this option for a full day of exploration.

BY RENTAL CAR Budget (© 05530-1020) and **Avis** (© 08996-8672) have offices at the airport.

SPECIAL EVENTS

The **Buddha Chinarat Festival** is held annually on the 6th day of the waxing moon in the 3rd lunar month (usually late Jan or early Feb). Then, Phitsanulok's Wat Yai is packed with well-wishers, dancers, monks and abbots, children, and tourists, all converging on the temple grounds for a 6-day celebration.

FAST FACTS

There are plenty of exchange services and ATMs, most of which are on Naresuan Road. The **General Post Office** is on Phuttha Bucha Road, along the river 2 blocks north of Naresuan Road.

Exploring Phitsanulok

Most use Phitsanulok as a jumping-off point for Sukhothai, but there are a few sights in the town proper—with Wat Yai being the foremost among them (see below).

The Sgt. Maj. Thawee Folk Museum ★ MUSEUM This small campus of low-slung pavilions houses a private collection of antiques and oddities from the country's rural life. Farming and trapping equipment (ever seen a rat guillotine?), household items, and old photographs of the city are lovingly displayed by the sergeant major, with descriptions in English. This museum is far more worthy of your time than the more official sounding **Museum of Phitsanulok,** which has virtually no English descriptions. Just across the road is the **Buranathai Buddha Casting Foundry** (admission free), where you can see the carving and casting of large Buddhas, most of which are copies of the Chinarat Buddha image from Wat Yai. The foundry is also operated by Maj. Thawee, as is the adjacent **Thai Bird Garden** (daily 8:30am–5pm; admission 50B), which contains examples of some of the country's most colorful species, including a hornbill and a silver pheasant.

26/43 Wisut Kasat Rd. © **05521-2749.** Admission 50B adults; 20B children. Daily 8:30am–4:30pm.

Wat Chulamanee ★★ TEMPLE   The oldest temple in the area and the site of the original city, about 7km (4 miles) south of the modern city, Wat Chulamanee is still an active monastery. The temple was restored in the 1950s and is admired for the fine, laterite, Khmer-style *prang* that dates back to the Sukhothai era and its elaborate stucco work; also look out for the finely carved lintels above the doorways. It's best to have your own transport if you want to visit, or you may find yourself stranded due to limited public transportation.

7km (4⅓ miles) south of the Nakon Sawan Hwy., on Boromtrailokanart Rd. Suggested donation 20B. Daily 6am–7pm.

Wat Phra Si Ratana Mahathat ★★★ TEMPLE   Known as **Wat Yai,** meaning the Great Temple, it's one of the most important temples in Thailand. The reason is its Phra Buddha Chinarat statue, a bronze image cast in 1357 under the Sukhothai King Mahatmmaracha. Its most distinctive feature is its flame-like halo (*mandorla*), which symbolizes spiritual radiance. Only the Emerald Buddha in Bangkok (p. 106) is more highly revered by the Thai people.

The *viharn* housing the Buddha is a prized example of traditional Thai architecture, with three eaves, overlapping one another to emphasize the nave, and graceful black and gold columns. The mother-of-pearl inlaid doors leading into the chapel were added in 1756 as a gift from King Borommakot of Ayutthaya. Inside, you'll discover an Italian marble floor, two painted *thammas* (pulpits), and murals illustrating the life of Buddha. Other than the *viharn* and *bot* (ordination hall), the *wat*'s most distinctive architectural feature is the Khmer-style *prang*, rebuilt by King Boromtrailokanart. It houses the Buddha relic from which the *wat* takes its name; *mahathat* means "great relic." The small museum holds a collection of Sukhothai- and Ayutthaya-era Buddhas.

The *wat* is always packed with worshipers paying their respects and making offerings. Conservative dress is obligatory—this means clothing that covers the shoulders, elbows, and knees; you'll also need to remove your shoes before entering the *wat*. Early morning (say, 7am) is a calm, tranquil time to visit.

1 block north of the Hwy. 12 bridge and just a short walk east of the river. Admission 50B. Wat daily 6:30am–6:30pm; museum Wed–Sun 9am–4pm.

Where to Stay

The bright, clean rooms at the characterless **Lithai Guest House** (73/1-5 Phayalithai Rd.; © **05521-9626**) are a welcome addition to the city's budget accommodation options; the price (300B single; 580B double) includes breakfast. Most of the budget options are bunk beds in dorms, so if those aren't your thing, here are three more private options. Sleep tight!

MODERATE

Pattara Resort & Spa ★★★   A charming retreat to return to after a day of exploring, the Pattara offers Sukhothai-style chalets surrounding a lovely pool with wood decking, fountains, and palm trees. Rooms are breezy, with patios near lotus ponds, and floods of natural light. The décor follows a similar aesthetic, and citron green pillows add a pop of color to the timber-and-white décor. There are two villas available, and while the pool villa feels more appropriate for Ko Samui, it offers total privacy and lots of space.

349/40 Chiyanupap Rd. www.pattararesort.com. ℂ **05528-2966.** 64 units. 3,000B superior; from 7,500B suite. **Amenities:** Restaurant; outdoor pool; small fitness center; spa; room service; Wi-Fi (free).

Yodia Heritage Hotel ★ This is among the most attractive options in the city that thanks to its tranquil location on the Nan River. Rooms have Thai-centric names like *saranjai* (happy mind) and *saranrom* (happy mood) that reflect the tranquility of the property. Rooms are spacious, attractive, and quiet, with local art adding a touch of color, and deep-soaking tubs adding relaxation. Stay in a suite for swim-out pool access and let the helpful front desk book tours or arrange for rental cars with drivers.

89/1 Phuttabucha Rd. www.yodiaheritage.com.com. ℂ **055214-677.** 22 units. 2,150B–3,500B double; from 9,000B suite. **Amenities:** Restaurant; pool; room service; Wi-Fi (free); parking (free); tour desk.

INEXPENSIVE

Karma Home Hostel ★★ The word "home" is key here. Owner Mark has a talent for hospitality, and a way of making all guests feel like family. That translates to spontaneous communal meals, cooking classes, guided tours of the temples (for a small donation), and evening nightlife excursions with other guests. As for the rooms: They're basic but immaculate, and do have air-conditioning. Many guests, however, decide to forgo indoor sleeping, and spend the night on the roof, which is slung with hammocks just for that purpose (it's a wonderful place to relax during the day, too). Well-located and with a spirit that is quite rare, Karma Home is one of the most welcoming hostels in Thailand.

26-64 Lang Wat Mai Apaiyaram. www.facebook.com/karmahomehostel. 20 units. From 360B per person, per night. **Amenities:** Roof deck, included breakfast, social activities for guests, Wi-Fi (free).

Where to Eat

No fine-dining options exist in Phitsanulok, which is okay because it fits the low-key vibe of the town. There are, however, lots of small eateries in and around the train station. Be sure to try the local specialty, *khaew tak*, sun-dried banana baked with honey; packages are sold everywhere and cost just 30B. Don't miss Muslim delights like roti and curry on Pra Ong Dam Road. At the **Night Bazaar,** there is a fun local tradition of serving "flying vegetables"—morning-glory greens sautéed, tossed high in the air, and adeptly caught in the chef's wok or even tossed to a nearby waiter who plates the veggies in the air!

Pae Fa Thai Floating Restaurant ★ THAI The best of many similar places along the riverbank, just in front of the main tourist attraction, Wat Yai, Pae Pha Thai is a friendly, casual eatery with no pretense. Indulge in the kind of spread you might find in a Thai home—*tod man plaa* (deep-fried fish cakes), *kai phad kaprow* (chicken with basil and chili), *tom yum* soup, and a whole fish encrusted with garlic and lemon.

Phutta Bucha Rd. (on Nan River in front of Wat Yai). © **05524-2743.** Main courses 100B–200B. Daily 11am–11pm.

SUKHOTHAI ★★★ & SI SATCHANALAI HISTORICAL PARKS ★★★

Sukhothai: 58km (36 miles) E of Phitsanulok; Si Satchanalai: 56km (35 miles) N of Sukhothai

The emergence of Sukhothai ("Dawn of Happiness") in 1238 is considered the birth of the first Thai kingdom. For a brief but wondrous time (1238-1376) it was the capital of Thailand. Under King Ramkhamhaeng the Great, Sukhothai's influence covered a larger area than that of present-day Thailand. The ruins here are more intact and less encroached upon than those in Ayutthaya, making this the country's most gratifying historical site.

Within the Old City is **Sukhothai Historical Park,** the main attraction, which is a World Heritage Site situated 12km (7½ miles) west of the town of Sukhothai, also known as **New Sukhothai.** Not surprisingly, the new town lacks any of Old Sukhothai's historic grandeur but it's where to head for hotels, a touch of nightlife, market culture, and bowls of the region's famous noodles.

Si Satchanalai, north of New Sukhothai, is another legacy of the Sukhothai kingdom. Visitors often enjoy these ruins the most as they are less frequented and therefore quieter, so they are certainly worth the 1-day detour.

Essentials
ARRIVING
BY PLANE From Bangkok, **Bangkok Airways** (www.bangkokair.com; © **02270-6699**) operates at least one daily flight connecting Bangkok with Sukhothai through their private airport 27km (17 miles) from Sukhothai. Contact them at the Sukhothai airport (© **05564-7224**). **You're not seeing things.** Yes, that's a heard of zebra and three giraffes roaming in pens near the landing strip. No, you're not in Tanzania; there's a small zoo next to the airport.

BY TRAIN The nearest rail station is in Phitsanulok (p. 294). From there, you can connect by local air-conditioned bus, leaving hourly for New Sukhothai (trip time 1 hr.; fare 42B) from the intercity terminal on Highway 12.

BY BUS Daily first-class, nonstop, air-conditioned buses leave from Bangkok at all hours of the day (trip time 7 hr.; fare 400B for VIP bus), departing from the **Northern Bus Terminal** (© **02936-2841**). There are also more arduous second-class buses, but avoid them unless you're desperate. Several air-conditioned buses leave daily from Chiang Mai's **Arcade Bus Terminal** (© **05324-2664**) for the 5½-hour trip (fare 249B for second class with A/C).

VISITOR INFORMATION

The **TAT** office in Sukhothai is at 130 Charot Withi Thong Rd. (© **05561-6228**). **ATMs** abound in both New and Old Sukhothai. There's a **tourist police point** (© **1155**) opposite the Ramkhamhaeng National Museum. The main police station is at the junction of Singhawat and Si Intharathit roads. The **Sukhothai Hospital** (© **05561-1720**) is at 2/1 Jarot Withithong Rd. The **post office** is down near the river on Nikhon Kasem Road.

CITY LAYOUT

Sukhothai Historical Park (or *muang kao*, "old city") lies 12km (7½ miles) west of **New Sukhothai.** Built along the banks of the Yom River, New Sukhothai has lots of accommodation options, though there are now several fancy places near the Historical Park and in the surrounding countryside. The selection is growing—whether you're looking for laid-back cool or decked-out comfort, you're likely to find your desired niche. **Si Satchanalai Historic Park,** also along the Yom River, is 56km (35 miles) north of New Sukhothai.

SPECIAL EVENTS

The **Loy Krathong** ★★ festival here is an exceptional spectacle. Sukhothai is the birthplace of this multi-day festival, which is held on the full moon of the 12th lunar month (usually Nov). Crowds gather at rivers, *klongs* (canals), lakes, and temple fountains to drop small banana-leaf floats or *krathong,* bearing candles, incense, and a flower. As the *krathong* glides downstream, it symbolizes a letting go of the previous year's sins and unhappiness. Sukhothai celebrates with fireworks, traditional dancing, and a music and light show in the Historical Park; book accommodation early.

Exploring Sukhothai ★★★

In 1978, UNESCO named Sukhothai a World Heritage Site, and the Thai government, with international assistance, completed the preservation of these magnificent monuments and consolidated them with an excellent museum into one large park. Every Saturday night from 8pm, a **Walking Street** outside the historical park comes alive with food, handicrafts, and cultural shows.

TOURING THE SITE   The tuk-tuks that cruise around New Sukhothai can be hired to whiz you out to the monuments on a 4-hour tour around the park for about 500B, but if you have the energy it's much more rewarding to rent a bike from shops outside the park entrance; prices start at 30B. At peak times, there is a tram service that runs visitors around the central zone for 60B, starting near the national museum, but it's not that enjoyable since you'll have little time to explore each temple on your own before being corralled back into the tram. Maps are available at the museum or at the nearby bicycle-rental shops. The park is open daily 7:30am to 6:50pm; Saturday nights, temples are illuminated and open until 9pm. Admission is 100B to the central area within the park walls plus an extra 10B per bike and 20B per motorcycle, with additional charges of 100B for each of the four zones outside the walls of the park.

Be sure to bring water and go early in the morning to beat the heat and tour buses. Or consider coming back in the evening with picnic provisions, when it's cooler and the sun is going down. **Important Tip:** Download a QR scanner before arriving; all the temples have codes in English, Thai, Japanese, and Chinese, so you can listen to short historical sound bites as you tour around.

If you'd like a pro to show you the historical sites and surrounding rural areas, **Cycling Sukhothai** (www.cycling-sukhothai.com; ✆ **05561-2519**) run one of the best operations in town with good commentary and well-maintained bikes. Prices start at 800B and include historical and countryside rides for a half-day or full-day, or join a great sunset tour.

THE HIGHLIGHTS
RAMKHAMHAENG NATIONAL MUSEUM ★   Located in the center
of the old city near the park entrance, this museum houses a detailed model of the area, and an admirable display of Sukhothai and Si Satchanalai archaeological finds, including what scholars believe to be the earliest example of Thai writing. Before exploring the temple sites, breeze through here for an overview of the history, and to collect maps and information. It's open every day from 9am to 4pm; admission is 150B (unfortunately that's for the museum alone, not for the museum and park). Call ✆ **05561-2617** for info.

WAT PHRA MAHATHAT ★★★   The most extraordinary monument in
the park, this temple is dominated by a 14th-century lotus-bud tower and encircled by a lotus-filled moat. Surrounding its unique Sukhothai-style *chedi* are several smaller towers of Sri Lankan and Khmer influence, and some of the stone remains of Buddha figures (originally thought to number more than 100) sit in among the ruined columns. An imposing cast-bronze seated Buddha used to be in front of the reliquary but this image, Phra Si Sakaya Muni, was removed in the 18th century to Bangkok's Wat Suthat. Be sure to examine the lowest platform (south side of Wat Phra Mahathat) and its excellent stucco sculpture, the crypt murals, and two elegant Sri Lankan-style stupas at the southeast corner of the site. Some of the finest architectural ornamentation in Sukhothai is found on the upper, eastern-facing levels of the pediments in the main reliquary tower. Dancing figures, Queen Maya giving birth to Prince Siddhartha, and scenes from Buddha's life are among the best-preserved details.

WAT SI CHUM ★★★   Outside the temple walls, this complex holds one
of the more astonishing and beautiful monuments in Sukhothai: a majestic seated Buddha 15-m (49-ft.) tall, in the Subduing Mara pose (cross-legged with the left hand resting palm-up in the lap). The fingers of this Buddha, draped over the right knee and frequently smothered with gold leaf, provide one of the country's most iconic images. (Thais purchase paper-thin gold leaf bits the size of a coin to place on the Buddha as an act of merit making.) Hidden mostly by a tall wall with only a sliver of the face shown at first, the Buddha reveals more of itself the closer you get, adding to the beauty.

OTHER MONUMENTS IN THE PARK Southwest of Wat Phra Mahathat, you'll come to the 12th-century Hindu shrine **Wat Si Sawai,** later converted to a Buddhist temple. It's surrounded by a crumbling laterite wall. The architecture is distinctly Khmer, with three Lopburi-style *prangs* commanding center stage, and is commonly thought to be the oldest structure in the complex. Just west of the palace is **Wat Traphang Tong,** set on its own pond. Though little remains other than an attractive *chedi*, the vistas of the surrounding monuments are among the most superb in the park. North of Wat Phra Mahathat is **Wat Chana Songkhram,** where there's a Sri Lankan-style stupa of note. Nearby is **Wat Sa Si,** located on the island in the middle of Traphang Trakuan Pond. Here, a large Buddha overlooks columns of the ruined temple and overlooks the lake, which was used by temple monks for religious ceremonies. The annual Loy Krathong festival is centered here.

Outside the Old City walls, **Wat Phra Phai Luang** lies 150m (492 ft.) beyond the northern gate and is somewhat isolated. Originally a Hindu shrine, it housed a *lingam*, a phallic sculpture representing Shiva, and features impressively large 12th-century Khmer-style towers.

A few kilometers west of the old city walls, the ruins of **Wat Saphan Hin** sit atop a hill that's visible for miles. Its name translates to 'stone bridge' and you'll understand why as you make the steep ascent to visit the Phra Attaros Buddha, his right hand raised in the Dispelling Fear pose and towering above the *wat*'s laterite remains. This is a good spot to come for perspective as to how large and impressive the Sukhothai grounds once were.

LUNCH AT THE HISTORICAL PARK There are a number of small storefront eateries in and among the bike-rental shops and souvenir stands at the gate of the park (just across from Ramkhamhaeng Museum).

Where to Stay
MODERATE
Sukhothai Heritage Resort ★★ Set on an organic farm right next to Sukhothai Airport, this place offers a quiet, rural retreat (aircraft land here rarely) and the chance to learn more about rice culture at the neighboring research center. Superior rooms in this two-story hotel are not huge but are comfortably furnished, and they all look out over a pool. When the heat becomes too much, come enjoy a mid-afternoon cocktail at the bar surrounded by lotus blooms or take a dip in the outdoor pools. Bicycles are on hand for exploring the area (free for guests), and staff can arrange transport to the Historical Park.

999 Moo 2, Tambon Klongkrajong. www.sukhothaiheritage.com. ✆ **05564-7567.** 68 units. 1,215B–3,500B double; 6,500B suite. **Amenities:** Restaurant; bar; 2 pools; Wi-Fi (free).

Sriwilai Sukhothai Resort & Spa ★★ Interestingly, this swank hotel has become a go-to alternative to a beach vacation for many Bangkok residents. It has that same kind of resorty-vibe, with an infinity pool overlooking the rice paddies (as well as a separate kids pool), and a swellegent spa, but has the plus of being just a 5-minute drive from the historic park (or a 10-minute bike ride). Rooms have a Lanna-Sukhothai look, with high-pitched ceilings, finely carved wooden furnishings, and hand-embroidered throw pillows (all linens and pottery here was created locally). Ethical tourism is also a hallmark, which means that solar panels are responsible for much of the electricity, water is recycled ("brown" water is filtered to water the plants in the garden), and plastic use is kept to a minimum.

214/4 Moo 2, T. Mueangkao A. Mueang. http://sriwilaisukhothai.com. (C) **66 55 697 445.** 50 units. Doubles from 3,4000B. **Amenities:** Restaurant, bar, room service, spa, fitness room, 2 pools, Wi-Fi (free).

INEXPENSIVE

The Legendha Sukhothai Resort ★★★   The hotel is designed to feel like a traditional Thai village, which is something it does with much success; never worn-out, never cheesy. Spacious rooms have working desks, Thai-style daybeds, and are decorated with punchy colors and crisp white bedding, all of which feel authentically Thai. The service-minded staff are among the most helpful in the region, so trust their recommendations for guides or food. The hotel's restaurant features traditional dance at dinner, along with classic Thai fare.

241 Moo 3, Old City. www.legendhasukhothai.com. (C) **02642-5497.** 64 units. 1,600B double; from 4,400B suite includes breakfast. **Amenities:** Restaurant; outdoor pool; room service; Wi-Fi (free).

Tharaburi Resort ★   After being remodeled from a simple backpacker pad to a high-style haven, this is now one of Sukhothai's most happening boutiques, with rooms, suites, and dorms covering a huge range of prices. The design scheme borrows from Moroccan, Japanese, and Chinese decor, making use of silks and replicated antiques. Luxurious double rooms and suites are fitted with Jacuzzis, flatscreen TVs, and spacious balconies. Dorms are simpler but still quite spiffy. The original guesthouse, Baan Thai, can accommodate a large family with its seven rooms and four bathrooms. Individual rooms in the house are also available.

11/3 Srisomboon Rd. www.tharaburiresort.com. (C) **05569-7132.** 20 units. 600B dorm with shared bathroom; 1,500B–4,200B double; 5,000B–7,800B multi-room suites and the house inclusive of breakfast. **Amenities:** Restaurant; outdoor pool; room service; Wi-Fi (free).

Wake Up at Muang Khao ★★   Flashpacker is a cheeky term for backpackers who prefer nice accommodations, and that's exactly who this hotel serves. The open-air lobby won't win awards for style but the rooms are spacious, very clean, comfortable, and adorned with lotus and koi fish stenciling on the walls. Bathrooms are small and are a typical Asian shower-toilet combo, but the location and price are hard to beat. The locals who run the place are very friendly.

1/1 Route 12. www.facebook.com/WakeUpAtMuangKaoBoutiqueHotel. (C) **05561-2444.** 5 units. 900B–1,500B double including breakfast. **Amenities:** Restaurant; Wi-Fi (free).

10

CENTRAL THAILAND

Sukhothai & Si Satchanalai Historical Parks

Where to Eat

Eating in Sukhothai is all about sampling the city's famous dish, *kwaytiaw sukhothai,* or **Sukhothai noodles**—a mouth-watering bowl of rice noodles with crispy pork, garlic, green beans, cilantro, chili, and peanuts in a broth seasoned with soy sauce. For one of the best versions, try **Baan Kru Iew** on Vichien Chamnong Road or Jayhea (see below). New Sukhothai's **night food stalls** (close to the bus stop for the Historical Park) are also good for casual grazing. For a touch of nightlife with your meal, **Chopper Bar** (Prawet Nakhon Road opposite a 7-Eleven) has live music, a rooftop terrace, and drinks while **Poo Restaurant** (24/3 Jarodvithithong) has a terrible name but a good selection of Belgian beers.

Dream Café ★★ THAI/INTERNATIONAL   This is a cozy place bathed in warm, soft light. With its oddball collection of ceramics, memorabilia, and old jewelry, it looks more like an antique store than a restaurant. In addition to Thai dishes, including many family recipes, you can try excellent European and Chinese cuisine. If you don't mind doing a bit of work, opt for the Sukhothai Fondue, a hot pot of meat, veggies, and noodles. *Tip:* Remember that Dream Café has been in the biz for more than 2 decades, and their default when confronted with a foreign diner is to opt for very mild levels of spice— so ask them to kick it up a notch and request dishes to be *phet* (spicy) if you want heat.

86/1 Singhawat Rd. (center of new city). ℂ **05561-2081.** Main courses 100B–250B. Daily 5pm–11pm.

Jayhea ★★★ THAI   Funnily enough, I discovered this haunt by asking a cab driver to take me to his favorite place for Sukhotai Noodles (a travel strategy I highly endorse). When the place was filled with Thai families and was near spotless, I guessed I'd hit a goldmine, and I knew for sure once I tried the food. There isn't an English menu available but know that the "Sukhothai noodles" come in either 40B, 60B, or 80B portions. Add a side of satay if you're extra hungry.

Jarodvithithong Road (look for the words "welcome" and "Jaehea" among the Thai signs). ℂ **05561-1901.** Main courses 40B–80B. Daily 8am–4pm.

Ruean Thai Restaurant & Bar ★ THAI/INTERNATIONAL   Many of the local restaurants in and around town are tin-roof, open-air food stalls. If you want a meal where you can linger at the table, the Ruean Thai Hotel's restaurant is a comfortable place and does local food well (try the green curry made with coconut milk, garlic prawns, or cashew chicken). Stay away, however, from international fare like spaghetti and cheese pizza—those dishes are given weird Asian interpretations and dosed with too much sugar. *Note*: There is additional seating by the pool and garden if the weather isn't too hot.

181/20 Soi Pracharuammit. www.rueanthaihotel.com. ℂ **05561-2444.** Main courses 120B–250B. Sun–Thurs 11:30am–2pm (lunch), 5–10pm (dinner); Fri–Sat 11:30am–2pm (lunch), 5–11pm (dinner).

Exploring Si Satchanalai Historical Park ★★

This is the most important satellite city of the Sukhothai era, and visitors often enjoy the secluded ruins and lush temple grounds at Si Satchanalai even more than those at Sukhothai. Si Satchanalai's riverside site was crucial to the development of its famous ceramics industry. More than 1,000 kilns operated along the river, producing highly prized pots that carried a greenish-gray glaze known as celadon. These were eventually exported throughout Asia. Academics believe that ceramic manufacture began more than 1,000 years ago at Ban Ko Noi (there's a small site museum 6km/3¾ miles north of Satchanalai), and ceramic shards today are sold as souvenirs. Just like Sukhothai, the ruins have QR codes that scan to brief overviews, although one or two have melted off in the heat.

GETTING TO THE SITE Si Satchanalai is north of New Sukhothai on Route 101. Buses from Sukhothai bound for Si Satchanalai depart every hour from the bus stop on Jarot Withithong Road for 49B; it's a 90-minute journey. If you're one of the handful of Chiang Rai-bound buses, ask the driver to let you off at "*muang kao*" (Old City). There are two stops; the second is closer to the park entrance, across the river. A taxi, private car, or guided tour can also be arranged through your hotel or guesthouse.

An adventurous alternative, if you are starting in Bangkok, is to go by train. A "Sprinter" express runs daily at 10:50am (fare 482B) from Bangkok to Sawankhalok, 20km (12 miles) south of Si Satchanalai park, stopping at Phitsanulok on the way, and arriving 7 hours later. The line to Sawankhalok is a spur that King Rama VI had built so that he could visit the ruins at Si Satchanalai, and the well-preserved station seems trapped in a time bubble. The train returns to Bangkok at 7:40pm. It is second-class, with air-conditioning but no sleepers, and fare includes dinner and breakfast. From the station, charter a *songtaew* for the remaining 20km (12 miles).

TOURING THE SITE There is an **information center** at the park, which is open daily from 8am to 5pm. Admission to the historical park is 100B, or 220B including entrance to Chaliang (for Wat Phra Si Ratana Mahathat) and the ancient pottery kilns of Sawankhalok. Bike rentals are available at the entrance (40B for singles; 80B for doubles) and many have child seats attached to the back, making this a fun, active trip for families. The roads are flat, devoid of everything except for the occasional motorbike, and it's a really enjoyable way to see this beautiful slice of history. Next to the bike rental store are stalls to buy water, soda, bags of chips, and a few Thai snacks. Best to grab a few things here before biking into the park.

THE HIGHLIGHTS

WAT CHANG LOM & WAT CHEDI JET THAEW The discovery of presumed relics of Lord Buddha at this site during the reign of King Ramkhamhaeng prompted the construction of the temple, an event described in stone inscriptions found at Sukhothai. Thirty-nine elephant buttresses surround a central stupa—it's unusual to find so many elephant forms intact. If you climb the steps to the stupa's terrace, you can admire the 19 Buddhas installed in niches there. Opposite Wat Chang Lom to the south, within sandstone walls, Wat Chedi Jet Thaew is distinguished by a series of lotus-bud towers and rows of *chedis* resembling those at Sukhothai's Wat Phra Mahathat and thought to contain the remains of the royal family.

OTHER MONUMENTS IN THE PARK   You can see most of the monuments within the ancient city walls in an hour's drive. Nothing compares to **Wat Phra Si Ratana Mahathat ★★★**, located 1km (⅔ mile) southeast of the big bridge and directly adjacent to the footbridge connecting to the main road. The exterior carving and sculpture are superb, particularly the walking Buddha done in relief.

   Wat Khao Phnom Phloeng ★★   You'll feel like Indian Jones (and, probably, a bit winded) after climbing the 114 steps made of laterite to reach this former monastery atop a hill. The bell-shaped principal stupa has a lotus flower base, though erosion makes it hard to see. Look for offerings of joss sticks (a type of incense) and water inside the stupa and peek through the overgrown bushes for a great hilltop view. You'll likely have this ancient space all to yourself.

SAWANKHALOK KILNS ★   During the 14th and 15th centuries, there were hundreds of kilns operating in this area, producing some of the best ceramics in all of Asia from local clay. You can take a look at some of these excavated kilns at the **Sawankhalok Kiln Preservation Centre** (daily 9am– 4:30pm; admission 100B or included in 220B ticket for the historical park), which is located a few kilometers along the Yom River from the historical park.

TAK PROVINCE: MAE SOT & THE MYANMAR BORDER

Tak: 138km (86 miles) W of Phitsanulok. Mae Sot: 80km (50 miles) W of Tak

Tak Province doesn't get a lot of tourists, possibly because there are no major attractions in the provincial capital. In fact many come here simply to use Mae Sot for an easy "visa run"—entering Myanmar for the day to get an exit stamp and renew their Thai visa. But the region is certainly not lacking in natural beauty thanks to a prime location at the beginning of the mountainous north. It is home to the **Bhumibol Dam,** the country's largest, and the area is covered in lush forests that offer a quiet retreat at **Taksin Maharat** and **Lan Sang** national parks, both about 25km (16 miles) west of Tak. Just a few kilometers from the border with Myanmar, **Mae Sot** displays all the hallmarks of a small border town. For decades it has played host to camps that take in an endless stream of refugees fleeing from Myanmar, many of whom are from the persecuted Karen tribe, and there is a palpable Burmese influence in the way people dress and what they eat. The area is known for trading teak wood and gemstones (buyer beware) along with a black-market border crossing of drugs and sex workers. Because of these border tensions, the province is likely to stay relatively undeveloped in terms of tourism for the foreseeable future, though there are no real safety concerns for tourists visiting today. Most visitors in Mae Sot are on their way to **Umphang,** some 150km (93 miles) south along one of the country's truly hair-raising roads. Umphang boasts **Ti Lor Su ★★,** Thailand's most spectacular waterfall, and some of the best trekking and white-water rafting in the kingdom, making the arduous journey there worthwhile.

Essentials

ARRIVING

BY PLANE   Nok Air (www.nokair.com; ℂ 1318) has six daily flights from Bangkok to Mae Sot (airport code MAQ). The airport is about 2km (1.2 miles) west of the town center. Flying time 70-minutes and tickets are 1,900B.

BY BUS   From Bangkok to **Mae Sot's bus terminal** (ℂ 05556-3435), there are seven to eight connections a day. A VIP bus (660B), a first-class bus (335B). The bus terminal is 1½km west of town and the trip is 8 hours.

Privately operated minivans connect Tak and Mae Sot, leaving from the bus station when they're full (about every half-hour), for about 60B per person. The trip time is 1½ hours. There are good buses operated by the **Green Bus Line** (ℂ 05553-6433) from Mae Sot to Tak and on to Lampang and Chiang Mai (first-class buses depart daily at 8am from Mae Sot; 6 hr. to Chiang Mai; 304B).

From the bus terminals in Tak and Mae Sot, motorcycle taxis, *samlors*, and *songtaews* wait to take you to any hotel for about 50B. *Songtaews* also make the dizzying 5-hour drive between Mae Sot and Umphang several times daily and charge about 120B.

VISITOR INFORMATION

Tak has a **TAT** office near the bus terminal, at 193 Taksin Rd. (ℂ 05551-4341); Mae Sot does not have a TAT office, so ask a guest house for information. In Mae Sot, **tourist police** (ℂ 1155) are on Intharakhiri Road east of the town center. Near the Friendship Bridge is an **immigration office** (ℂ 05556-3000) who have very basic visa services available.

SPECIAL EVENTS

Every year from December 28 to January 3, the **Taksin Maharachanuson Fair** is held in Tak to honor King Taksin the Great, who liberated the Thais from Burmese control in 1767. The streets around his shrine (on Taksin Road at the north side of town) fill with food vendors, dancers, musicians, and monks. The shrine is decorated with floral wreaths and gold fabric to welcome pilgrims. The fair coincides with a New Year's Eve festival in town.

FAST FACTS

In Tak, there are a handful of **ATMs** along Mahat Thai Bamrung Road, and, where it meets Thetsaban 1 Road, there's a **police station.** In Mae Sot, banks with ATMs are located on the main thoroughfare, on Prasat Withee Road. The

post office in Mae Sot is on Intharakiri Road opposite the main police station.

Exploring the Area

Along Highway 105, 20km (12 miles) west of Tak, a left turn leads to **Lan Sang National Park** (✆ **05557-7207**), where there are hiking trails and waterfalls, and on weekdays usually no visitors, so you might have the place to yourself. About 5km (3 miles) farther along H105, a right turn leads to **Taksin Maharat National Park** (✆ **05551-1429**), known as the home of *Krabak Yai*, Thailand's largest tree. A hike brings you to this colossal tree beside a stream—it takes 16 people's stretched arms to wrap around the conifer. Accommodation is available at both parks and admission to each is 200B for adults and 100B for children. For more information, check out the Thai national parks website, www.dnp.go.th.

Mae Sot is perched on the Myanmar border, and the area is always buzzing with trade. The town has a surplus of Burmese woven cotton blankets, lacquerware, jewelry, bronze statues, cotton sarongs, and wicker ware. Business is conducted in Thai baht, U.S. dollars, or Myanmar kyat.

There is a dark side to the border, though: Trade means the movement of not just produce and crafts, but also drugs, precious stones, and women (and even children) for prostitution. There's something disquieting about the many European luxury cars parked in front of two-story brick homes lining this village's main street—they hint at the substantial illegal profiteering. Be careful about buying gems unless you know what you're doing; you can find yourself walking away with a handful of fakes and a dent in your wallet. The border also sees a heavy flow of refugees, and there are a number of camps in the surrounding hills. Speak with your hotel or guesthouse about how to donate financially to these camps, some of which accept volunteers for the day.

The border between Mae Sot (at the town of Rim Moei) and Myawaddy, Myanmar, is open daily from 8am to 4:30pm, and—when relations are good—you can cross the bridge on foot or by car for a day for 500B. You'll need to leave your passport at the Myanmar immigration booth, and pick it up by 4:30pm. Many visitors cross just for a walk around Myawaddy, a glimpse of Burmese culture, or to say they've 'been' to Myanmar. But in reality, there isn't much here to make it worth the journey. Remember that any official fees you pay to the Myanmar government only add to the coffers of a regime that recently committed genocide (in its treatment of the Rohingya people in 2018).

Trekking and rafting in the area around Umphang is very popular, especially to visit the fabulous **Ti Lor Su waterfall,** which cascades down a cliff in several plumes, and is at its best around October and November. **Umphang Hill Resort** (www.umphanghill.com; ✆ **05556-1063**) provides basic lodging (rooms 500B–2,000B) in the tiny town of Umphang, and organizes a variety of trekking and rafting tours in the region, lasting between a day and a week. Prices work out to around 1,500B per person per day, depending on the size of the group.

Tak Province: Mae Sot & the Myanmar Border

CENTRAL THAILAND

Where to Stay

Mae Sot has many small, affordable guesthouses lining the main street, most of which were purpose-built to cheaply house the ever-growing number of itinerant NGO workers that pass through town. **Ban Thai** (740 Intharakiri Rd.; ℂ **05553-1590**) is a local hotel popular with NGO workers which offers air-conditioning rooms from 300B.

MODERATE

Centara Mae Sot Hill Resort ★   This contemporary hotel is built in two long wings fanning out from a classy open atrium lobby and is the highest standard hotel in town. While the purple, white and green motif won't win any awards for style, the rooms have modern facilities and views of the mist-shrouded, wooded hills. The staff are fluent in English and a helpful resource for arranging tours and onward travel.

100 Asia Rd. www.centarahotelsresorts.com. ℂ **05553-2601.** 120 units. From 2,800B double; from 4,000B suite. **Amenities:** 2 restaurants; lounge; 2 outdoor pools; 2 outdoor tennis courts; room service; Wi-Fi (free).

Irawadee Resort ★   Embrace the gaudy red-and-gold Burmese décor, like the royal-looking four-poster beds on a platform decorated with inlay designs, and enjoy the attention given by the kindhearted staff. Why not? Rooms are comfortable, clean, and have open-air showers. Temple bells, rhinoceros-shaped fountains, Thai garden gnomes, and gold Buddhas add to the kitsch. The hotel offers yoga classes and free loaner bokes.

758/1 Intrarakeeree Rd. www.irawadee.com ℂ **05553-5430.** 15 units. 1,200B double; 2,200B suite including breakfast. **Amenities:** Café; spa; Wi-Fi (free); yoga classes.

Where to Eat in Mae Sot

Mae Sot is a hotbed for non-Thai cuisine, which is as good a reason as any to make the journey through. Just a stone's throw away from Myanmar, this is an outstanding place to sample traditional Burmese dishes, like tea-leaf salads and curries. A fish and rice noodle soup called *mohinga* is Myanmar's best-known dish, and a great place to grab a bowl is at the **municipal market** (Prasatwithi Road; approximately 6am to sunset). Most locals and guesthouses refer to it as the day market to distinguish it from the nearby **night market**, which is a nice place for Thai-Chinese dishes (lots of noodles) from 6pm until late. **Muslim restaurants** are gathered in a cluster just south of the main mosque, which is **Nurul Islam.** Top-rated dishes at the Muslim restaurants are flaky roti, rich curries, and turmeric chicken. Wash it all down with the traditional tea, which tends to be very sweet.

All the options below are not only incredibly affordable but offer a deep-dive into the culinary and culturally complex part of Thailand. Here are a few great places to go for a more traditional dining experience.

INEXPENSIVE

Borderline Shop ★★★ BURMESE   If you've made it to Mae Sot, that likely means you've been in Thailand awhile and have enjoyed many meals sampling the local cuisine. Come to this café to see if your taste buds can pick up the difference between Thai and Burmese dishes, like authentic tea-leaf salads, noodles, samosas, and sweets. The owners do their best to source only organic produce, fish, and meat and engage in eco-friendly efforts like reducing single-use plastics. To learn more about the intricacies of the Burmese cuisine, enroll in the shop's **cooking course**, which includes a visit to a local market and lunch in the café; lessons 500B-1,000B per person. The **fair-trade shop** is great for hill-tribe goods and locally made souvenirs. With so much going on, it's a can't-miss spot in town.

674/14 Intharakeeree Rd. www.borderlinecollective.org. ℂ **05554-6584.** Main courses 50B–120B. Tues-Sun 7:30am–9pm.

Khaomao-Khaofang Restaurant ★ THAI

This little oasis along the Burmese border verges on the surreal in looks, but the food is much better than the décor. Be sure to go to the bathroom, because the washrooms are large grottos with flushable fixtures at odd heights and stalactites hanging from the ceiling. The menu surveys the whole country, with an emphasis on curries and authentic spice. Portions are small and Thai-style and designed to share with a group. To find it look for the ponds overgrown with lush vegetation and orchids surrounding an enormous thatched pavilion.

382 Moo 9. www.khaomaokhaofang.com. ℂ **05553-2483.** Main courses 100B–260B. Daily 11am–3pm and 5pm–9:30pm.

Krua Canadian ★ INTERNATIONAL

This restaurant's name is Thai for "Canadian kitchen," and that's just how it feels—as if you've been invited into the home of Canadian Dave and his wife, Chulee, the owners and chefs. From this simple, central storefront, they serve hearty Western-style breakfasts, local coffee, and a unique tofu burger that is both messy and delectable. You can also just drop in for a drink and for some advice on local happenings.

3 Sri Phanit Rd. www.facebook.com/com/KruaCanadianRestaurant. ℂ **05553-4659.** Main courses 50B–280B. Daily 7am–10pm.

CHIANG MAI

I t would be difficult to find a city that reflects more of the country's diverse cultural heritage and modern aspirations than Chiang Mai. The largest city in Northern Thailand, its heart is its Old City, which has regal roots—this was the capital of the Lanna kingdom from 1296 to 1768 (after which it was the capital of the Chiang Mai Kingdom until 1899). Today, the Old City is surrounded by the vestiges of ancient walls, bastions, and a moat originally constructed for defense. But it lies in the shadow of an increasingly expanding metropolis, encircled by gargantuan concrete highways, giant billboards and superstores. Modern tour buses crowd Burmese-style wats (temples) ablaze with monks in saffron robes chanting ancient mantras. Vendors dressed in hill-tribe costume sell souvenirs in tourist areas. Narrow streets lined with ornately carved teak houses lie in the shadow of contemporary skyscrapers. It's a hodgepodge, but a splendid one.

Before we go any further, its important to give a bit of context. From 1296, under King Mengrai, Chiang Mai (meaning the "New City") was the cultural and religious center of the northern Tai. The city was overtaken and occupied by the Burmese in 1558 until Chao (Lord) Kavila retook the city in 1775, driving the Burmese forces back to near the present border. Burmese influence on religion, architecture, language, cuisine, and culture, however, remained strong (as it does today). Local feudal lords (sometimes referred to as princes) carrying the title chao, remained in nominal control of the city in the late 18th and early 19th centuries, but under continued pressure from King Chulalongkorn (Rama V), the Lanna kingdom was brought under the control of the central government in Bangkok. In 1932, the city was formally and fully integrated into the kingdom of Thailand, becoming the administrative center of the north.

Today's Chaing Mai is a bastion of local art. Streets are teeming with galleries, motivated designers are filling boutiques with their wares, and a vibrant coffee scene fuels all that creativity. It is important to note that art galleries in town are generally quite small, often showcasing just a few works at a time. The best way to explore the current offerings is to pick up a free copy of the excellent **Chiang Mai Art Map** (www.cac-art.info/map for locations; free). It's an annually updated listing of all the best major galleries, artist's studios, and more. The detailed map makes an afternoon of self-guided gallery hopping—an easy, enriching experience.

From March to October, the North's climate follows the pattern of the rest of the country—hot and dry followed by hot and wet. March and April are known locally as the "smoky season," named for the haze that fills the sky when local farmers burn their crops. This can be a rough time of year to visit Chiang Mai, with low visibility and poor air quality. Yet from November to February, it's almost like another country, with cool breezes blowing down from China, bright sunny days, and rarely a cloud in the sky. During these cooler months, Chiang Mai is an excellent base for exploring the north.

ESSENTIALS

Arriving

Before the 1920s, when the railway's Northern Line to Chiang Mai was completed, one traveled throughout this area by either boat or, more exotically, by elephant. So, when your train ride gets boring or the flight is crowded, remember that not so long ago the trip here from Bangkok took 4 to 6 weeks.

BY PLANE Chiang Mai International Airport (airport code CNX; ℂ **05327-0222**) is about 3km/1¼ miles and a 10-min. ride from the Old City. When planning your trip, keep in mind that Chiang Mai has a growing number of international links with major cities throughout the region. You can directly connect with Yangon, Singapore, Kuala Lumpur, Hong Kong, Shanghai, Guangzhou, and more.

Domestically, **Thai Airways** (www.thaiair.com; ℂ **05392-0999**) flies from Bangkok to Chiang Mai several times a day (trip time 70 min.); schedules adjust with the tourist season. There are direct flights from Chiang Mai to Phuket, Krabi, and Koh Samui. **Bangkok Airways** (www.bangkokair.com; ℂ **05328-1519**) flies at least six times daily from Bangkok; it also operates a direct daily flight to Ko Samui. Flying is, by far, the easiest and most economical way to get to Chiang Mai. Flights are an incredibly reasonable 1,200B from the capital and average 2,4000B from islands like Phuket. During high season, expect to see an uptick in pricing, but thanks to budget airlines like AirAsia, Thai Smile, Nok Air, Vietjet, there are flights every hour (or more) giving visitors a plethora of choices.

The airport has several banks for changing money, a post, an information booth, luggage storage for 200B a day. Taxis from the airport start at 120B to town, a bit more for places outside of Chiang Mai proper.

BY TRAIN Train travel is an arduous way to get back to Bangkok. The station in Chiang Mai is not well kept and derailments on the line happen with shocking frequency. Frankly, the rise of budget airlines has made train travel back to the capital a locals-only affair, although the Thai government has been discussing the creation of a high-speed train. Of the five daily trains from Bangkok to Chiang Mai, the 8:30am *sprinter* (trip time 12 hrs.; fare 611B for a second-class air-conditioned seat) is the quickest, but you sacrifice a whole day to travel. The other trains take between 13 and 15 hours; for overnight trips, second-class sleeper berths are a good choice (881B lower berth, air-conditioned; 791B upper berth, air-conditioned). Private sleeper cabins are also available, which cost 1,353B.

Purchase tickets at Bangkok's **Hua Lampong Railway Station** (𝄞 **02220-4334**) up to 60 days in advance. For local train information in Chiang Mai, call 𝄞 **05324-5363**; for advance booking, call 𝄞 **05324-4795**. The State Railway's website (www.thairailwayticket.com) is wonky and frequently shut down, so using the phone is the most reliable way to reserve, along with using a third-party booking site like http://12go.asia/en.

BY BUS Buses from Bangkok to Chiang Mai are many and varied: From rattletrap, non-air-conditioned numbers to reclining-seat, VIP buses. The trip takes about 8 to 10 hours. From **Bangkok's Northern Bus Terminal,** close to the Mo Chit BTS (𝄞 **02936-2841**), six daily 24-seater VIP buses provide the most comfort, with larger seats that recline (fare 806B). There is also a frequent service between Chiang Mai and Mae Hong Son, and Chiang Rai.

Most buses arrive at the **Arcade Bus Station** (𝄞 **05324-2664**) on Kaeo Nawarat Road, 3km (1¼ miles) northeast of the Thapae Gate; a few arrive at the Chang Puak station (𝄞 **05321-1586**), north of the Chang Puak Gate on Chotana Road. Expect to pay 80B to 150B for a tuk-tuk (motorized three-wheeler) into town, and around 30B for a red pickup, *songtaew,* to the town center and your hotel.

Visitor Information

The **TAT** office is at 105/1 Chiang Mai–Lamphun Rd., 400m (1,312 ft.) south of the Nawarat Bridge, on the east side of the Ping River (www.tourism thailand.org; 𝄞 **05324-8604**). You can also find any of a number of detailed maps distributed free.

City Layout

The heart of Chiang Mai is the **Old City,** a squared section of land surrounded by a massive restored wall and moat. Today, the remains of the wall's five gates, serve as a handy reference points, particularly **Thapae Gate** to the east. The most important temples are within the walls of the Old City.

All major streets radiate from the Old City. The main business and shopping area is the 1-km (⅔-mile) stretch between the east side of the Old City and the **Ping River.** Here you will find the **Night Bazaar,** many shops, art galleries, trekking agents, hotels, guesthouses, and restaurants—plus some of the most picturesque backstreets.

To the west of town and visible from anywhere in the city is the imposing wall of Doi Suthep Mountain (1,685m/5,528 ft.), where, near its crest, you'll find the most regal of all Chiang Mai Buddhist compounds, **Wat Phra That Doi Suthep,** standing stalwart as if to give its blessing to the city below. The road leading to the temple takes you past a big mall, a strip of modern hotels, the zoo, and the university.

The Superhighway circles the outskirts of the city and is connected by traffic-choked arteries emanating from the city center. If you're driving or riding a motorbike in Chiang Mai, the many one-way streets in and around town are confounding. The moat that surrounds the city has concentric circles of traffic: The outer ring runs clockwise, and the inner ring counterclockwise, with U-turn bridges between. The streets in and around the Night Bazaar are all one-way as well. This means that even if you know where you're going, you'll have to pull your share of U-turns.

Getting Around

BY BUS   Chiang Mai has a few irregular bus routes that are more useful for locals than visitors. Your best bet is to look out for the ubiquitous *songtaews* and flag one down.

BY SONGTAEW   *Songtaews* (red pickup trucks known locally as *rot daang*) cover all routes and these beloved trucks even have a craft beer named in their honor. Fitted with two long bench seats, they are also known locally as *seelor* (four-wheels). They follow no specific route and have no fixed stopping points. Hail one going in your general direction and tell the driver your destination. If it fits in with the destinations of other passengers, you'll get a ride to your door for around 20B to 40B. Some drivers will ask for exorbitant fees to hire the complete vehicle when they're empty; let these guys just drive on. If you can deal with a bit of uncertainty along the confusing twist of roads, a *songtaew* is an ideal way to explore the city.

Songtaews will also head up to the temple on Doi Suthep Mountain for 50B, and only 40B for the easier downhill return trip. A cluster can usually be found outside the zoo at the western end of Huay Kaeo Road. The road up the mountain is very steep so hold on tight or call a taxi for more comfort.

BY TUK TUK   The ubiquitous tuk-tuk is the next best option to the *songtaew* for getting around Chiang Mai. Fares are negotiable—and you will have to bargain hard to get a good rate—but expect to pay at least 60B for any ride.

BY TAXI   Chiang Mai has metered taxis but taxi drivers are generally unwilling to use the meter, so rates are commonly fixed. Trips in town are generally less than 160B. While Uber left Southeast Asia in 2018, the popular ride-hailing app **GrabTaxi** performs the same function (www.grab.com; available in the iTunes store and Google Play).

BY CAR   There really is no need to rent a car in Chiang Mai, especially if you don't have onward plans for sites farther afield, like Chiang Rai or Pai. However, if you need wheels, **Avis** has an office conveniently located at the airport (www.avisthailand.com; ✆ **05320-1798**). Avis self-drive rental rates for Chiang Mai are the same as they are elsewhere in Thailand, from 1,400B and up for a compact sedan. **Budget** (www.budget.co.th; ✆ **05320-2871-2**) has an office at the airport and offers comparable rates and services. Both companies offer comprehensive insurance and provide good maps.

BY MOTORCYCLE Motorcycle touring in northern Thailand is another option and best done in the cool season (Nov–Feb). For up-to-date info on the best routes to follow, check out the **Golden Triangle Rider** website (www. gt-rider.com); you can pick up their map of the Samoeng Loop or Mae Hong Son Loop at many outlets in Chiang Mai (listed on the website).

In the city, a simple scooter is a much better option for getting around than a bulky motorcycle. Many guesthouses along the Ping River and shops around Chaiyaphum Road (north of Thapae Gate, in the Old City) rent 100cc to 150cc scooters for about 150B to 200B per day (discounts for longer durations). Larger 250cc Hondas and other international brands with good suspension are commonly available and are the best choice for any trips upcountry because of their added power and large fuel tanks; they rent for about 700B. **Tony's Big Bikes** (17 Ratchamankha Rd.; www.chiangmai-motorcycle-rental. com; ☎ **083865-0935**), is an outstanding resource for motorcycle tours, bike rentals, and road knowledge. Helmets are mandatory—and while locals may be able to wriggle out of arrest, as a foreigner, you won't be let off lightly. Expect to leave your passport as security (don't leave any credit cards).

BY BICYCLE Cycling in the city is fun and practical, especially for getting around to the temples within the Old City. Avoid rush hour and take great care on the busy roads outside of the ancient walls. Bikes are available at any of the many guesthouses in or around the Old City and go for about 50B per day.

[FastFACTS] CHIANG MAI

ATMs ATMs are located across Chiang Mai and you'll find them outside most convenience stores, such as 7-Elevens. For the most convenient major bank branches look around the Night Bazaar.

Embassies & Consulates There are many representative offices in Chiang Mai. Contacts are as follows: **American Consulate General,** 387 Wichayanon Rd. (☎ **05310-7700**); **Canadian Honorary Consul,** 151 Super Highway Rd. (☎ **05385-0147**); **Australian Honorary Consul,** 165 Sirimungklajarn Rd. (☎ **05349-2480**); and **British Consul,** 198 Bumrungraj Rd. (☎ **05326-3015**).

Doctors & Dentists The Consulates detailed below will supply you with a list of English-speaking dentists and doctors. There are also several medical clinics, and standards are very high; but for serious illness, you should seek professional and advanced care in Bangkok.

Emergencies Dial ☎ **1155** to reach the Tourist Police in case of emergency.

Hospitals Try the private **McCormick** hospital, on Kaeo Nawarat Road (☎ **05392-1777**), out toward the Arcade Bus Terminal. The **Ram** (www.chiangmairam.com) and **Lanna** (www.lanna-hospital.com) hospitals are also popular choices for expats.

Internet Access Most hotels and guesthouses provide Internet access, often free of charge. All around the city, there are numerous small, inexpensive cafes with service sometimes costing only 30B per hour. **Starbucks** offers free Wi-Fi access at half a dozen locations, including Chaiyaphum Road opposite Tha Pae Gate and at the Suriwong Hotel on Chang Klan, in the Night Bazaar area.

Mail & Postage The most convenient post office branch is at 186/1 Chang Klan Rd. (☎ **05327-3657**). The General Post Office is on Charoen Muang (☎ **05324-1070**), near the train station. **UPS** has an office at 77 Sri Phum Rd. (☎ **05341-8767-9;**

Mon–Sat 9am–5:30pm), making it easy to send your finds back home.
Pharmacies There are dozens of pharmacies throughout the city; most are open daily 7am to midnight. Bring any prescriptions that you need filled from home.

Police For police assistance, call the **Tourist Police** at © **1155,** or see them at the TAT office (see p. 313).

FESTIVALS

Northern Thailand celebrates many festivals—even the nationwide ones—in different ways than the rest of the country. Many Thais travel to participate in these festivals, and advance booking in hotels is a must.

Northern Thailand Calendar of Events

Many of these annual events are based on the lunar calendar. Contact the **Tourism Authority of Thailand** (**TAT;** www.tourismthailand.org) for exact dates and for other events.

JANUARY

Umbrella Festival, Bo Sang. Held in a village of umbrella craftspeople and painters, about 9km (5⅔ miles) east of Chiang Mai, the Umbrella Festival features handicraft competitions and a local parade. Third weekend of January.

FEBRUARY

Flower Festival, Chiang Mai. Celebrates the city's undisputed accolade as the "Rose of the North," with a parade, concerts, flower displays, and competitions. A food fair and a beauty contest take place at Buak Hat Park, on the first weekend in February.

King Mengrai Festival, Chiang Rai. Known for its special hill-tribe cultural displays and a fine handicrafts market. Early February.

Sakura Blooms Flower Fair, Doi Mae Salong. Sakura (Japanese cherry trees) were imported to this hilly village 50 years ago by fleeing members of China's Nationalist, or Kuomintang, party (KMT). Their abundant blossoms bring numerous sightseers. Early to mid-February.

MARCH

Poy Sang Long. A traditional Shan ceremony ordaining Buddhist novices—particularly celebrated in the northwestern town of Mae Hong Son, but can also be seen in Chiang Mai. Late March or early April.

APRIL

Songkran (Water) Festival. Thai New Year is celebrated at home and in more formal ceremonies at *wats* (temples). Presents and merit-making acts are offered, and water is "splashed" over Buddha figures, monks, elders, and tourists to encourage the beginning of the rains and to wish good fortune. Those who don't want a good soaking should avoid the streets. The festival is celebrated in all Northern provinces and throughout the country, but Chiang Mai's celebration is notorious for being the longest (up to 10 days) and the rowdiest. The climax comes April 12 to April 14, days that are official holidays.

MAY

Visakha Bucha. Honors the birth, enlightenment, and death of the Lord Buddha. Celebrated nationwide, it is a particularly dramatic event in Chiang Mai, where residents walk up Mount (Doi) Suthep in homage. On the first full moon day in May.

Lychee Festival, Kho Loi Park, Chiang Rai. This festival honors the harvest of lychees, a small, fragrant fruit encased in bumpy red skin. There is a parade, a lychee competition and display, a beauty contest to find Miss Lychee, and lots of great food. Mid-May.

Mango Fair, Chiang Mai. This fair honors the mango, a favorite local crop. Second weekend in May.

AUGUST

Longan (lamyai) Fair, Lamphun. Celebrates North Thailand's most dearly loved fruit and one of the country's largest foreign-exchange earners. There is even a Miss Longan competition. First or second weekend of August.

OCTOBER

Lanna Boat Races. Each October, Nan Province holds 2 days of boat racing, with wildly decorated, long, low-slung crafts zipping down the Nan River. The Lanna Boat Races are run 7 days after the end of the Buddhist Rains' Retreat, which generally marks the beginning of the dry season. In mid- to late October.

NOVEMBER

Loy Krathong. Occurs nationwide on the full moon in the 12th lunar month. Small *krathongs* (banana-leaf floats bearing candles, incense, and garlands) are sent downriver to carry away the previous year's sins. In Chiang Mai, the waterborne offerings are floated on the Ping River. In the city, enormous 1-m (3¼-ft.) tall paper lanterns *(khom loy)* are released in the night sky, and there's a parade of women in traditional costumes. Late October to mid-November.

DECEMBER

Day of Roses, Chiang Mai. Exhibitions and cultural performances are held in Buak Hat Park. First weekend in December.

EXPLORING CHIANG MAI
The Wats (Temples)

Chiang Mai has more than 700 temples, the largest concentration outside of Bangkok, and unique little sites are around every corner. You can hit the highlights in Old Chiang Mai by tuk-tuk, but even more fun is to arm yourself with a map and wend your way from one side of the Old City to the other, weaving in and out of temple compounds. Most temples open from 6am until 6 or 8pm but sporadic closings do happen. If you find yourself locked out during regular visiting hours, find a local monk to open the temple. Donation boxes are in lieu of formal ticket fees.

Wat Chedi Luang ★★★ TEMPLE   Because this temple is in the heart of the Old City, most visitors begin their sightseeing here, where there are two *wats* of interest. This complex, which briefly housed the Emerald Buddha (now at Bangkok's Wat Phra Kaew; p. 104), dates from 1411 when King Saen Muang Ma built the original *chedi* (stupa). The already-massive edifice was expanded to 84m (276 ft.) in height in the mid-1400s, only to be ruined by a severe earthquake in 1545, just 13 years before Chiang Mai fell to the Burmese. Some of the elephants around its base were restored in the 1990s, but the spire was never rebuilt. Buddhas sit in niches facing the cardinal points, and it is not unusual to spot a saffron-robed monk bowing to them as he circles the *chedi*. The huge *chedi* is especially atmospheric during the *puja* festivals, when monks and laymen circumambulate it carrying candles, flowers, and incense.

Wat Phan Tao, in the northeast corner of the same compound, has an impressively large teak wood *viharn* (assembly hall) that once served as a royal residence and is adorned with a striking mosaic of a peacock and dog above the main door (a nod to the astrological sign of the former royal resident). After leaving the temple, walk around to the monks' quarters on the side, taking in the traditional teak northern architecture and delightful landscaping. This is a very atmospheric wat to explore.

Prapokklao Road, south of Ratchadamnoen Road. Suggested donation 20B. Daily 6am–6pm.

Wat Chiang Man ★ TEMPLE   Thought to be Chiang Mai's oldest *wat*, it was built around 1296 by King Mengrai, the founder of Chiang Mai, on the spot where he first camped. Like many of the *wats* in Chiang Mai, this complex reflects many architectural styles. Some of the structures and artworks are pure Lanna. Others show influences from as far away as Sri Lanka, like the typical row of elephant supports around the small stupa behind the *viharn*. Wat Chiang Man is most famous for its two Buddhas: Phra Sae Tang Khamani (a miniature crystal image also known as the **White Emerald Buddha**) and the marble **Phra Sila Buddha,** believed to have been carved in Sri Lanka over 1000 years ago. Unfortunately, the small *viharn* that safeguards these religious sculptures (to the right as you enter) is almost always closed.

Ratchapakinai Road, south of the Sri Phum Road moat. Suggested donation 20B. Daily 6am–6pm.

Wat Jed Yod ★★ TEMPLE   Also called Wat Maha Photharam, Wat Jed Yod ("Temple of the Seven Spires") is one of the city's most elegant sites, though it is located northwest of the center, beside the Superhighway. The *chedi* was built during the reign of King Tilokkarat in the late 15th century (his remains are in one of the other *chedis*), and, in 1477, the World Sangkayana convened here to revise the doctrines of the Buddha.

The unusual design of the main rectangular *chedi* with seven peaks was copied from the Maha Bodhi Temple in Bodhgaya, India, where the Buddha first achieved enlightenment. The temple also has architectural elements reflecting Burmese and early Chinese influences supposed to date back to the Yuan and Ming dynasties. The extraordinary proportions; the angelic, levitating *devata* (Buddhist spirits) bas reliefs around the base of the *chedi;* and the juxtaposition of the other buildings make Wat Jed Yod a masterpiece.

Superhighway, near the Chiang Mai National Museum (north of the intersection of Nimmanhaemin and Huai Kaeo rds., about 1km/⅔ mile on the left). Suggested donation 20B. Daily 6am–6pm.

Wat Phra Singh ★★★ TEMPLE   This compound was built during the zenith of Chiang Mai's power and is one of the more venerated temples in the city. It is still the focus of many important religious ceremonies, particularly the Songkran Festival. More than 700 monks study here and you will find them especially friendly with tourists.

King Phayu, of Mengrai lineage, built the *chedi* in 1345, principally to house the cremated remains of King Kamfu, his father. As you enter the grounds, head to the right toward the 14th-century library. Notice the graceful carving and the characteristic roofline with four separate elevations. The sculptural *devata* figures, in both dancing and meditative poses, are thought to have been made during King Muang Kaeo's reign in the early 16th century. They decorate a stone base designed to keep the fragile *saa* (mulberry bark) manuscripts elevated from flooding and vermin.

On the other side of the temple complex is the 200-year-old **Lai Kham (Gilded Hall) Viharn,** housing the venerated image of the Phra Singh or **Lion Buddha,** brought to the site by King Muang Ma in 1400. The original

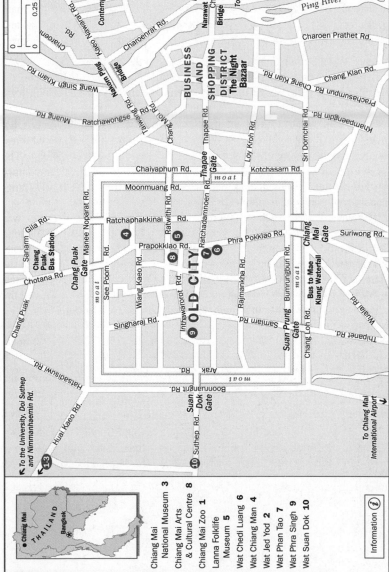

1/4 mi

0.25 km

To Arcade Bus Station & Chiang Rai

To the MAIIAM Contemporary Museum

Bumroongrasd Rd.

To the Railway Station

To Sankampaeng craft villages

Bus to Lamphun, Pa Sang

Charoen Muang Rd.

Chiang Mai-Lamphun Rd.

Ping River

Charoenrat Rd.

Kaeo Nawarat Rd.

Charoen Rd.

Narawat Bridge

Nakorn Ping Bridge

Wang Singh Kham Rd.

Muang Rd.

Ratchawongse Rd.

Taiwang Rd.

Moon Muang Rd.

Chang Moi Rd.

BUSINESS AND SHOPPING DISTRICT The Night Bazaar

Charoen Prathet Rd.

Chang Klan Rd.

Prachasumpun Rd., Chang Klan Rd.

Khampaengdin Rd.

Sri Dornchai Rd.

Chaiyaphum Rd.

Thapae Rd.

Thapae Gate

Kotchasarn Rd.

moat

Moonmuang Rd.

Loy Kroh Rd.

Sanarm Gila Rd.

Manee Noparat Rd.

Ratchaphakkinai Rd.

Ratwithi Rd.

Ratchadamnoen Rd.

Phra Pokklao Rd.

Chiang Mai Gate

Suriwong Rd.

Chang Puak Bus Station

Chang Puak Gate

See Poom Rd.

④ ⑤ ⑦ ⑥

Prapokklao Rd.

⑧

Chotana Rd.

Wiang Kaeo Rd.

Inthawarorot Rd.

Rajmankha Rd.

Bumrungburi Rd.

Bus to Mae Klang Waterfall

Chang Puak

Hatsdiswipi Rd.

Singharaj Rd.

⑨ OLD CITY

Samlarn Rd.

Suan Prung Gate

Chang Loh Rd.

Wualai Rd.

Thipanet Rd.

moat

To the University, Doi Suthep and Nimmanhaemin Rd.

Hual Kaeo Rd.

Suthep Rd.

⑩

Suan Dok Gate

Arak Rd.

Boonnangrit Rd.

moat

To Chiang Mai International Airport

13

THAILAND

Chiang Mai

Bangkok

Chiang Mai National Museum **3**

Chiang Mai Arts & Cultural Centre **8**

Chiang Mai Zoo **1**

Lanna Folklife Museum **5**

Wat Chedi Luang **6**

Wat Chiang Man **4**

Wat Jed Yod **2**

Wat Phan Tao **7**

Wat Phra Singh **9**

Wat Suan Dok **10**

Information *i*

319

Buddha's head was stolen in 1922, but the reproduction in its place doesn't diminish the homage paid to this figure during Songkran. Inside are frescoes illustrating the stories of Sang Thong (the Golden Prince of the Conchshell) and Suwannahong. These images convey a great deal about the religious, civil, and military life of 19th-century Chiang Mai during King Mahotraprathet's reign.

Samlarn and Ratchadamnoen rds. Suggested donation 20B. Daily 6am–8:30pm.

Wat Phra That Doi Suthep ★★★ TEMPLE   The jewel of Chiang Mai, Wat Phra That Doi Suthep, glistens in the sun near the summit of the mountain known as Doi Suthep. One of four royal wats in the north, at 1,300m (4,265 ft.), it occupies an extraordinary site with a cool refreshing climate, expansive views over the city and the mountain's densely forested slopes, which form part of the Doi Suthep–Doi Pui National Park.

In the 14th century, during the installation of a relic of the Buddha in Wat Suan Dok (in the Old City), the holy object split in two, with one part equaling the original size. A new wat was needed to honor the miracle. King Ku Na placed the new relic on a sacred white elephant and let it wander freely through the hills. The elephant climbed to the top of Doi Suthep, trumpeted three times, made three counterclockwise circles, and knelt down, choosing the site for Wat Phra That Doi Suthep.

The original chedi was built to a height of 8m (26 ft.). Subsequent kings contributed to it, first by doubling the size and then by adding layers of gold and other ornamentation to the exterior; it now measures 16m (52 ft.) tall. The slender, gleaming chedi and the gilded-copper decorative umbrellas around it provide one of the most iconic images of North Thailand.

Other structures were raised to bring greater honor to the Buddha and various patrons. The most remarkable is the steep *naga* (sacred river snake) staircase, added in 1557, leading up to the wat—one of the most dramatic approaches to a temple in all of Thailand. To shorten the 5-hour climb from the base of the mountain, the winding road was constructed in 1935 by thousands of volunteers under the direction of a local monk.

Visitors with exposed legs are offered a sarong at the entrance. Most Thai visitors come to make an offering—usually flowers, candles, incense, and small squares of gold leaf that are applied to a favored Buddha or to the exterior of a chedi—and to be blessed. Believers kneel down and touch their foreheads to the ground three times in worship. Some shake prayer sticks to learn their fortune.

Wat Phra That Doi Suthep is open daily 6am to 6pm; come early or late to avoid the crowds. To get here, take a *songtaew* from in front of the zoo (40B per person) or in front of Wat Phra Singh (50B per person); chartered rides are 300B one-way and 500B return. The ride can get cool, so bring a sweater or jacket in the cool season. If you'd rather not climb the 306 steps, a special part of the experience, there's a funicular railway to the top for 20B. You can simplify matters by booking a half-day trip through any tour agency for around 600B, including a stop at Phuping Palace (when it's open).

What do you say to these tonsured men in orange robes one sees piously padding barefoot around Thailand? The answer is: "Hello. How are you?" Monks, especially seniors, deserve a special level of respect, of course, but are quite human, and the best way to find out is to stop by a temple for a monk chat. It is a mostly informal discussion about one's own country or sports—young novices are nuts about English Premier League soccer (football), and the more senior monks can give you some insights into Buddhist practice and monastic life. The most popular location for these chats is under a shady tent at Wat Chedi Luang (p. 317) during temple hours. Wat Srisuphan has chats between 5:30 and 7pm before a free evening meditation course. Please not that you can engage in these chats at temples around Thailand, but we've found the monks in Chiang Mai to be particularly open and informative. Be sure to cover your knees and shoulders and women should avoid touching the monks.

After visiting the Doi Suthep, many make their way to **Phuping Palace** which is 4km (2½ miles) beyond the temple, 22km (14 miles) west of the Old City off Route 1004. It is the summer residence of Thailand's royal family, but when the royal family isn't present (usually January to March; ask hotel staff to check for you), visitors are allowed to enter and stroll through its beautiful gardens. The hours are Friday to Sunday 8:30–11:30am and 1–3:30pm, and admission is 50B. You really have to dress conservatively for this one; military guards at the gate act like the fashion police.

Huay Kaew Doi Suthep. Admission 30B. Daily 6am–6pm.

Wat Suan Dok ★★ TEMPLE   This complex is special, less for its architecture (the buildings, though monumental, are undistinguished) than for its contemplative spirit and pleasant surroundings. The temple was built amid the pleasure gardens of the 14th-century Lanna Thai monarch, King Ku Na. Like several of Chiang Mai's other *wats*, Wat Suan Dok functions as a study center for monks who have isolated themselves from the distractions of the outside world.

Among the main attractions in the complex are the *bot*, with a very impressive **Chiang Saen Buddha** (one of the largest bronzes in the north) dating from 1504 and some garish murals. Also of interest is the *chedi*, built to hold a relic of the Buddha, and a royal cemetery with some splendid shrines. An informal "monk chat" is held here each week (see the box, above).

Suthep Rd. (from the Old City, take the Suan Dok Gate and continue 1.6km/1 mile west). Suggested donation 20B. Daily 6am–6pm.

Museums & Sights

Tip: Tickets to the three historical museums below (Chiang Mai City Arts & Cultural Centre, Chiang Mai Historical Centre, and the Lanna Folklife Museum) are all covered by a single ticket costing 180B adults and 80B for children. The ticket is valid for a week and amounts to a small 90B savings for adults.

Chiang Mai City Arts & Cultural Centre ★ MUSEUM   Using dioramas, photos, artifacts, and audio displays, this museum presents an informative overview of Chiang Mai's past, from pre-historic times through today. There's also a rotating cast of temporary exhibits. You'll find the museum in a well-preserved, colonial building dating back to 1927, set behind the Three Kings Monument (they were the founders of Chiang Mai) in the heart of the Old City. *Tips:* School groups can crowd the museum in the mornings but afternoons are normally peaceful; the café is a nice spot to relax and plan your next move.

Phra Pokklao Road. www.cmocity.com. ℂ **05321-7793.** Admission 90B for adults, 40B for children. Tues–Sun 8:30am–5pm.

Chiang Mai Historical Centre ★ MUSEUM   More history here, but this time the story of the province is covered, including the founding and creation of the capital, the occupation of the Burmese, and the modern cultural awakening. The main focus of the museum's exhibits and dioramas is the Lanna period. Visitors can also view the active archaeological dig of an ancient temple wall taking place in a downstairs gallery. While not Chiang Mai's top museum, history buffs will enjoy the visit, which can be accomplished in an hour or less. The museum is set right behind the Chiang Mai City Arts & Cultural Center.

Ratwithi Road. ℂ **05321-7793.** Admission 90B for adults, 40B for children. Tues–Sun 8:30am–5pm.

The Chiang Mai Zoo ★ ZOO   While better than most in Thailand in terms of animal welfare, the Chiang Mai zoo can feel a bit worn and sad. Locals love the pandas and they're the stars of the extensive zoo. There's an extra admission fee to see the pandas (100B adults, 50B children), as there is for other new attractions—the **snow dome** (adults 150B, children 100B) with real snow, and a murky **aquarium** (adults 450B, children 330B) that isn't worth the extra fee. The site is too large to see everything by walking so take the shuttles (the monorail no longer runs). It makes for a good day out with kids who may be wilting from temple overdose (not to be underestimated).

100 Huai Kaeo Rd. (west of town, on the road to Doi Suthep). www.chiangmai.zoo thailand.org. ℂ **05335-8116.** Admission 150B adults, 570B children. Daily 8am–4:30pm.

Lanna Folklife Museum ★★ MUSEUM   The Thai-colonial building that houses this museum is a former Provincial Court dating back to 1935. As you make your way through the rooms, life-size dioramas show what life might have been like for Lanna villagers. Scenes depict monastic life, the importance of dance rituals, pottery making, and more. The explanations of the symbolism on Lanna-style monasteries are an excellent primer for visitors who will soon be seeing those buildings (usually with no-one around to discuss why they were built the way they were).

Phra Pokklao. ℂ **05208-1737.** Admission 90B adults; 40B students; Tues–Sun 8:30am–5pm.

MAIIAM Contemporary Art Museum ★★ MUSEUM   When this museum opened in 2015, it cemented Chiang Mai's status as the art capital of Thailand. Today, it is a creative home for the new wave of artists who call Chiang Mai home and are working diligently to make the city an artists' haven. The museum is housed in an old warehouse and a mirrored façade gives way to bright gallery rooms housing 50 pieces in a permanent collection, including photography installations, artistic takes on politics and culture, splashy paintings, and more. TED-style talks and lectures are regularly on rotation here. The café and gift shop are worth visiting.

122 Moo 7 Tanpao. www.maiiam.com. ✆ **05208-1737.** Admission 150B adults; 100B students; 12 and under free. Wed–Mon 10am–6pm.

Cultural Activities
THAI COOKING SCHOOL

If you love Thai food, consider taking a cooking class in Chiang Mai. The priciest cooking classes are offered at top resorts like the **Dhara Dhevi** and **Four Seasons** (covered later) and they're informative and hands-on. But very reasonable courses abound in town as well, such as those offered at **Chiang Mai Thai Cookery School,** the oldest establishment of its kind in Chiang Mai. It has 1- to 5-day courses, each teaching basic Thai cooking skills; daily menus feature up to seven dishes per day. You'll have hands-on training and a lot of fun. Classes start at 10am, last until 4pm, and cost 1,450B for the day. Contact them at their main office at 47/2 Moon Muang Rd., opposite the Thapae Gate (www.thaicookeryschool.com; ✆ **05320-6388**).

Foodies who want to focus on eating more than cooking should consider a street food tour. The aptly named **Chiang Mai Street Food Tours** (www. chiangmaistreetfoodtours.com; ✆ **085033-8161**) offers morning and evening tours through the markets with a focus on Northern Thai dishes. Tours are 750B.

MASSAGE SCHOOL

The **Thai massage schools** in Bangkok and Phuket teach the southern style of Thai massage, which places pressure on muscles to make them tender and relaxed. Northern-style Thai massage is something closer to yoga, with the masseuse physically stretching and elongating the client's muscles to enhance flexibility and relaxation. There are a number of schools teaching this style of massage in Chiang Mai, ranging from vocational schools, to one-day classes that teach the basics. We recommend the long-established **Lanna Thai Massage School** (www.lannathaimassageschool.net; ✆ 05323-2547), near Wat Chomphu. This government-recognized school employs expert teachers for 1-day classes on back and neck massages or on how to make herbal compresses (multi-day courses focus on the full body). Prices range from 1,500B to 9,500B for a 10-day session. Other options offering similar programs and pricing are **Sabai De Ka** (www.masssage-chiangmai.com; ✆ **081881-3697**) and **Art of Massage** (www.artofmassage.webs.com; ✆ **083866-2901**).

MEDITATION COURSES

Volumes have been written about the practice of Vipassana, but the main idea is to develop mindfulness and observe one's body, mind, and emotions—to eventually gain "insight" and to see things as they are, without delusion. The **Northern Insight Meditation Center,** at Wat Rampoeng (Kan Klongchonprathan Road; www.watrampoeng.net; ✆ **05327-8620**) is a serious and well-respected center for learning Vipassana meditation during a 26-day course (day courses are sometimes available). Most temples offer courses as well, and the **Doi Suthep Vipassana Meditation Center** (www.fivethousandyears. org; ✆ **05329-5012**) is a first-rate choice for all levels with courses lasting between 3 and 21 days. Participants are commonly asked to wear white, loose-fitting clothes, which are available in temple stores. Courses are frequently free, but you will be asked to make a donation to the temple of whatever amount you see fit. If you only have a few hours, drop-in at **Namo** (www. namochiangmai.org; ✆ **05332-6648**) for workshops specializing in chanting, meditation, Ayurveda, and yoga.

CHIANG MAI ACTIVITIES

Tours, Treks & Outdoor Adventure

TREKKING TOURS

There are so many tour groups in Chiang Mai that specialize in trekking that it can seem impossible to choose one. Below are some of most reputable operators for each type of trip. Most of the smaller companies have offices along Thapae Road, in guesthouses, and all along the major tourist routes in the city, and they are always happy to talk about what's on offer. Many adventure tours mix mountain biking or motorcycling with tribal village tours. See chapter 12 for more information on the hill-tribes themselves, descriptions of what to expect on tours and how to select a good operator.

For **jungle trekking,** one of the most efficient and reliable organizations is **Active Travel** (www.activethailand.com; ✆ **05385-0160**). Combining treks and village stays with multisport adventures by jeep, bicycle, and kayak, the folks at Active can cater a tour to any need and price range. They also offer more traditional itineraries with visits to caves, and relaxing bamboo-raft river trips, and their English-speaking guides are the best in the area. Treks from Chiang Mai stop at Lisu, Lahu, and Karen villages. A 2-day/1-night trip is 4,600B per person if you join their regular tour, or 5,600B per person for a private group trip. A 3-day/2-night trip, which takes you to a greater variety of villages, is 5,500B per person if you join their regular tour or 6,850B per person for a private group. Their office in Chiang Mai is at 54/5 Moo 2, Soi 14, Tambol Tasala.

Another company with lots of experience specializing in customized trekking tours (with a focus on bird-watching or rare orchids, for example) is the **Trekking Collective** (www.trekkingcollective.com; ✆ **05320-8340;** 3/5 Loy Kroh Soi 1). Expect to pay around 3,000B to 5,500B per person per day, depending on the group size and itinerary.

BOAT TRIPS

Within the city, a **boat trip** along the Mae Ping River is a happy diversion. Two-hour rice barge tours depart hourly from 9am to 5pm (minimum 2 people, 250B per person including hotel pickup), operated by **Mae Ping River Cruise Co.** (133 Charoen Prathet Rd.; www.maepingrivercruise.com; ✆ **05327-4822**). From the deck you'll get great views of old teak riverside mansions, behind which rise the tall skyline of this developing burg. While on the outskirts of the city, you'll see villages that offer scenes of rural living.

History buffs, however, might prefer to cruise the river in a **scorpion-tailed boat** of the kind that used to be poled up and down the river in the late 19th century when first missionaries and later teak traders turned up to try their luck in this remote outpost. The modern version is propelled by an engine, but visitors can look forward to a running commentary on the historical significance of places passed along the route. Contact **Scorpion-Tailed Cruises** (www.scorpiontailedrivercruise.com; ✆ **05324-5888**). Rates vary by number of passengers.

ELEPHANT ENCOUNTERS ★

One of Thailand's greatest treasures, the domesticated Asian elephant, has worked alongside men since the early history of Siam, and these gentle giants are an important symbol of the kingdom. Elephant training culture is strongest in parts of Isan (the northeast) and the far north. In and around Chiang Mai there are a growing number of elephant camps that try to cash in on the popularity of these gentle giants. Remember, not all elephant camps are ethical: At shoddier camps, creatures are drugged to keep them placid, and conditions are grim, so choose your elephant camp wisely. Fortunately, camp owners are finally starting to realize that visitors would much rather get up close and personal with the elephants than watch them performing in a show, and this has softened their treatment at many camps. (See p. 46 for information on elephant camps in Thailand.) Resort-run elephant camps, such as that shared by the **Anantara** (p. 388) and **Four Seasons Tented Camp** (p. 388), north of Chiang Rai in the Golden Triangle, are among the most humane. Another popular and ethical place nearer Chiang Mai is the **Patara Elephant Camp** ★★ (www. pataraelephantfarm.com; ✆ **08199-22551**), located on the Samoeng Road to the southwest of town. It runs an enjoyable program called "Elephant owner for a day," in which visitors spend a day feeding, bathing, caring for, and riding their own elephant bareback. Rates start at 3,200B and include professional photos and videos. **Elephant Nature Park** ★★ (www.elephantnaturepark. org; ✆ **05381-8754**) was one of the first camps in Thailand to give a home to rescued elephants and now leads the charge for ride-free interactions. Tourists work alongside a mahout (elephant trainer), helping feed and wash their assigned elephant. Elephants wander semi-wild and form herds, with older females caring for young that were orphaned or abandoned. The park is 60km outside of Chaing Mai and a day costs 2,500B. Longer volunteer vacation options are available, too.

MOUNTAIN BIKING

In the fresh air in the hills outside of town, you can get a slower, closer look at nature, sights, and people. Many small trekking companies and travel agents offer day trips, but I recommend the folks at **Mountain Biking Chiang Mai** (www.mountainbikingchiangmai.com; ✆ **081024-7046**) for their 1-day excursion cycling down Doi Suthep mountain, and for multiday adventures in the region for everyone from beginners to experts. Bikes and gear are well maintained and included in the trip costs. Day trips start at 1,600B.

Cultural and temple tours in Chiang Mai itself are offered by **Click and Travel** ★★ (www.chiangmaicycling.com; ✆ **05328-1553**). The tours' information is engaging for children as well as adults and adult-child tandem bikes make this a great choice for families. Rates start at 950B.

Golf

For Thais and Western retirees, golf is a favored hobby in Chiang Mai, especially in the cooler months. All courses below are open to the public and offer equipment rental. Call ahead to reserve a tee time.

o **Summit Green Valley Chiang Mai Country Club,** located in Mae Rim, 20 minutes north of town on Route 107, 186 Moo 1, Chotana Rd. (www. summitgreenvalley.com; ✆ **05329-8220**), is in excellent condition with flat greens and fairways that slope toward the Ping River (greens fees: Apr–Oct. 1,800B, rest of year 2,400B).

o **Lanna Golf Club,** on Chotana Road, 2km (1¼ miles) north of the Old City (✆ **05322-1911**), is a challenging, wooded 27 holes, and a local favorite with great views of Doi Suthep Mountain (greens fees: weekdays 1,200B, weekends 1,400B).

o **Royal Chiang Mai Golf Club,** a 30-minute drive north of town toward Phrao (www.royalchiangmail.com; ✆ **05384-9301**), is a pleasant 18-hole course designed by Peter Thompson (greens fees: 2,800B for 18 holes plus a mandatory caddie fee of 300B).

Spas & Massage

The spa industry is big business all over Thailand, and Chiang Mai is no exception. There are a few fine, full-service spas in and around town. As well, many hotels offer massage and beauty treatments in typical private rooms with soothing music. You can pay a fraction of the cost for the same treatment (without the frills of fancy treatment rooms) at one of the many small storefront massage parlors in and around any tourist area of the city.

Some of the best spa experiences, both high-end and affordable:

The Dhevi Spa ★★★ (51/4 Chiang Mai–Sankampaeng Rd., 5km/3 miles east of town; www.dharadhevi.com; ✆ **05388-8888**) is an enormous complex built of teak to mimic a Burmese palace. The treatments and spa environment are extensive, with the unusual addition of a starlit sauna, or *rasoul,* and therapies that reflect local Lanna culture.

Oasis Spa ★ offers a high standard of service at its two locations in town: At 102 Sirimangkalajarn Rd. and 4 Samlan Rd. For reservations, call ✆ **05392-0111**

or visit www.chiangmaioasis.com. A luxury campus of private spa villas, Oasis Spa offers a long roster of treatments and provides free pickup and drop-off from hotels in Chiang Mai.

Ban Sabai (219 Moo 9, San Pee Sua; http://bansabaivillage.com; ☎ **05385-4778**) is the bridge between the expensive services of a five-star spa and the affordable street-side places. You get the best of both worlds here: A stylish facility at affordable rates. The spa is located in a rural setting 5km (3 miles) northeast of town.

Let's Relax (www.letsrelaxspa.com) has three bright, clean, and affordable locations around town. The one in the Chiang Mai Pavilion (on the second floor, 145/27 Chang Klan Rd.; ☎ **05381-8498**) is perfect for a quick recharge after wading through the Night Bazaar area.

Vocational Training Center of the Chiang Mai Women's Correctional Institution ★ (100 Ratwithi Rd.; ☎ **05312-2340**) employs well-trained and non-violent female inmates as part of the prison's job training rehabilitation. The women complete 180 hours of training so the massages are outstanding, well-priced, and the spa environment echoes that of any other casual spot in town. Foot massages and Thai massages go for 180B an hour.

Other Activities

One of the most popular activities around Chiang Mai is to spend a day on the zip lines at **Flight of the Gibbon** (www.treetopasia.com; ☎ **05301-0660-3**). A day tour includes hotel pickup, a few hours on a zip line canopy adventure, and a 1-hour trek in the rainforest, and costs around 3,000B.

Rock climbers can get their kicks at the North's main climbing area near Sankampaeng, about 35km (22 miles) east of Chiang Mai. Hundreds of routes have been pegged on the Crazy Horse buttress. If you're a beginner and you'd like to learn the ropes, so to speak, contact **Chiang Mai Rock Climbing Adventures** (www.thailandclimbing.com; ☎ **05320-7102**), which organizes 1- to 3-day introductory courses for 2,795B and 8,995B, respectively.

Learn the "art of eight limbs" at a **Muay Thai camp**; many in Chiang Mai have trained top Thai fighters along with game foreigners. Most hotels offer 1-hour lessons if you're looking to get your heart rate up, but more technical skills can be acquired at camps like **Chai Yai Muay Thai** (www.chayyaimuay thaigym.com; ☎ **082938-1364**), which has been around for nearly 30 years and offers half-day classes for 400B, private lessons for 850B. East of town is **Santai Muay Thai** (www.muay-thai-santai.com; ☎ **082528-6059**), a gym that specializes in getting hard-bodied boxers ready for competition. Join the sweaty fun for a week of training, lodging, meals, and more for 4,000B.

WHERE TO STAY

City accommodation listed below is separated as follows: Outside of town; east of town near the Ping River/Night Bazaar area; within the Old City walls; or west of town, on the road to Doi Suthep (near the university). Airbnb and other vacation rentals haven't caught on here as they have in other parts of the country, so stick with a traditional hotel. The hotels along the Ping River are within close striking distance for sightseeing and shopping and, in general, offer more tranquility than those within the Old City walls. Splashy resorts, like the Four Seasons, are outside of town but are the most glamorous.

Outside Chiang Mai
EXPENSIVE

The Dhara Dhevi ★★★ About 20 minutes east of central Chiang Mai, this super-luxe resort is designed like an enclosed Lanna city, complete with a small moat, grand city gate, delightfully lush gardens, and flowering trees—all over 60 acres. The resort comprises immaculate suites and rustic, free-standing villas, all sumptuously decorated. Standard perks in the villas include a sauna, piano, sun deck, and Jacuzzi. Around a working rice paddy lie well-placed pool villas with outdoor pavilions, and even hill-tribe-style stilt cottages next to a working vegetable patch. All units have large balconies, but the rice barns offer two stories of teak-lined luxury. Colonial suites have Persian rugs, pretty fretwork, high ceilings, and pleasant pastel hues. At times the more over-the-top suites may teeter on kitsch, but it somehow seems to work well with the contrasting rustic ambiance. There are few spas in town as pampering as here.

51/4 Chiang Mai–Sankampaeng Rd. www.dharadhevi.com. ℂ **05388-8999.** 123 units. 8,000B–17,000B villa (varies by season); 10,000B–19,500B colonial suite; 50,500B grand deluxe 2-bedroom villa; 280,000B royal residence inclusive of breakfast. **Amenities:** 3 restaurants; 3 bars; babysitting; 2 pools; health club; spa; bikes; kids' club; room service; Wi-Fi (free).

Four Seasons Chiang Mai ★★★ About 30 minutes north of Chiang Mai in the Mae Sa Valley, the Four Seasons was Chiang Mai's first five-star hotel and still sets the standard for luxuriously equipped rooms, the range of facilities and activities on offer and, perhaps most important, efficient and personalized service. The spacious pavilions, each with its own covered outdoor veranda (gorgeous mountain views!), are set among rice paddies looked after by local farmers. Top reasons to choose this property: its entertaining cooking school and five-star spa. The traditional Lanna design of the complex and its rural setting creates a memorable experience, as does a visit (and photo session) with the resident albino water buffalos. A shuttle into and out of the city leaves at regular intervals.

502 Moo 1, Mae-Rim. www.fourseasons.com/chiangmai. ℂ **05329-8181.** 99 units. From 14,000B pavilion. **Amenities:** 3 Restaurants; bars; outdoor pool; large health club; spa; tennis courts; yoga instruction; shuttle; kids' club; babysitting; room service; Wi-Fi (free).

Near the Ping River
EXPENSIVE

137 Pillars House ★★★ This well-dressed resort offers colonial luxury with tasteful elegance where no design detail has gone unnoticed. The collection of suites are centered around a Baan Borneo—a teak home that once

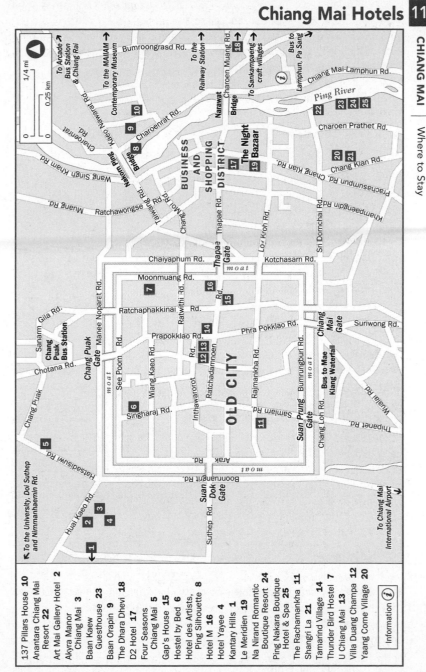

137 Pillars House **10**
Anantara Chiang Mai Resort **22**
Art Mai Gallery Hotel **2**
Akyra Manor Chiang Mai **3**
Baan Kaew Guesthouse **23**
Baan Orapin **9**
The Dhara Dhevi **18**
D2 Hotel **17**
Four Seasons Chiang Mai **5**
Gap's House **15**
Hostel by Bed **6**
Hotel des Artists, Ping Silhouette **8**
Hotel M **16**
Hotel Yayee **4**
Kantary Hills **1**
Le Meridien **19**
Na Nirand Romantic Boutique Resort **24**
Ping Nakara Boutique Hotel & Spa **25**
The Rachamankha **11**
Shangri La **21**
Tamarind Village **14**
Thunder Bird Hostel **7**
U Chiang Mai **13**
Villa Duang Champa **12**
Yaang Come Village **20**

Information *i*

belonged to the son of Anna Leonowens (of *Anna and the King* fame)—and rooms overlook a lush garden and large swimming pool. Each has indoor/outdoor showers, Victorian bathtubs, four-poster beds, and Thai silks in warm tones. The hotel's food is superb, and Jack Bain's is a sumptuously decorated cocktail bar that stocks local spirits.

2 Soi 1 Nawatgate Rd. www.137pillarschiangmai.com. ℰ **02079-7137**. 30 units. From 9,700B suite. **Amenities:** 2 restaurant; bar; outdoor pool; health club; spa; room service; Wi-Fi (free).

Anantara Chiang Mai Resort ★★★　On what was once the site of the venerable British Consulate, The Anantara (formerly The Chedi) is a luxurious oasis facing the scenic Ping River. Because of that location, and the hotel's pretty lawns, it brings a resort feeling to downtown Chiang Mai. The Anantara's rather daunting exterior of minimalist wooden slats gives way to a crisp interior of large reflecting pools and polished concrete paths leading to a gem of a colonial mansion, a pleasing mix of modern and colonial. Rooms are not all that Thai looking, but rather contemporary (lots of polished woods, and neutrals interrupted by pops of color), and all offer a private courtyard entrance. The glassy pool is lovely, and the spa boasts an expert staff (I had one of the best massages of my life there).

123 Charoen Prathet Rd. www.anantara.com/en/chiang-mai. ℰ **02365-9110**. 84 units. 8,500B deluxe double; 14,600B suite. **Amenities:** Restaurant; 3 bars; outdoor pool; health club; spa; room service; babysitting; Wi-Fi (free).

MODERATE

Dusit D2 Hotel ★★　Every corner of this hotel is bathed in a postmodern minimalist cool. In a country so often decorated in Thai silks and teak woods, here the design aesthetic is of the moment, the furniture and decor seamlessly blending sharp lines with rounded edges, and pops of orange. Everything flows. Rooms are very livable and have all the finer creature comforts: Daybeds, roomy living areas, and well-stocked bathrooms. An upgrade to the deluxe club level allows access to the chic club lounge, with free cocktails and snacks. The hotel's staff are fun hipsters (they dance the conga at shift changes) but all are very attentive and helpful. Its location in the heart of the shopping district couldn't be better. Overall, this is an enjoyable and unique choice.

100 Chang Klan Rd. www.dusit.com ℰ **05399-9999**. 131 units. 2,600B–4,000B deluxe; 8,000B club deluxe; from 12,500B suite. **Amenities:** Restaurant; bar; outdoor pool; health club; spa; room service; babysitting; Wi-Fi (free).

Hotel des Artists, Ping Silhouette ★★　Located on the east side of the Ping River in Wat Ket, a vibrant area that used to be a multicultural trading neighborhood with Chinese influence, all of Chiang Mai's highlights are nearby when you stay here. And the neighborhood's past is tastefully reflected in the design of the rooms and common spaces, which are very modern (bright white walls and fluffy duvets), with Chinese-style elements, like the prints hanging on the walls, blue-and-white pots adorning the courtyards, and brushed brass and marble accents in the bathrooms. The hotel is set in a former Shan mansion; all rooms have balconies.

181 Chareonraj Rd. www.hotelartists.com.com. © **05326-0666.** 14 units. 4,000B–4,800B. **Amenities:** Restaurant; outdoor pool; Wi-Fi (free).

Le Meridien ★★ With an ideal location on Changklan Road, right next to the Night Bazaar, this large hotel is an imposing presence in central Chiang Mai. The spacious and well-lit rooms are packed with state-of-the-art furnishings that combine European and Asian touches. Yes, some vacationers might find rooms, with their neutral-toned décor, too corporate-looking, but we find them restful. Try and snag one of the upper-floor rooms that have views of the nearby mountain, Doi Suthep. The hotel's restaurants and bars offer an appetizing array of culinary delights, exotic cocktails, and fruit infusions. *Important:* This is a rare example of an area hotel with wheelchair access.

108 Changklan Rd. www.lemeridienchiangmai.com. © **05325-3666.** 384 units. From 4,275B double; from 12,600B suite. **Amenities:** 2 restaurants; 2 bars; pool; fitness facility; spa; sauna; babysitting; Wi-Fi (free).

Na Nirand Romantic Boutique Resort ★★★ The hotel makes a striking impression on guests who are immediately greeted by a palm tree-lined pool and an indigenous, century-old rain tree; as the name states, it's all very romantic. Rooms are spread among six residences that harken back, in their design, to the Lanna-Colonial period of 19th century. The result is rooms with a harmonious blend of Thai teak wood, rattan made by local artisans, Lanna art, and crisp colonial touches. Upper level rooms have private balconies, and a lovely breakfast (don't miss the homemade jams) is served in a tranquil setting overlooking the Ping River.

1/1 Soi 9, Charoenprathet Rd. www.nanirand.com. © **062875-2401.** 39 units. From 5,000B–7,000B double. **Amenities:** Restaurants; bar; outdoor pool; spa; sauna; Wi-Fi (free).

Ping Nakara Boutique Hotel & Spa ★★★ Taking its inspiration from the teak boom in Chiang Mai in the late 19th century, this award-winning boutique property has an elegant colonial design, with delicately carved woodwork around the eaves and balconies. The theme continues in the rooms, where antique telephones, wrought iron beds, fans, and fine carpets hark back to another era. The essential fixtures and fittings, however, are thoroughly modern. All 19 rooms are named after different Thai flowers and are individually decorated, giving each a separate identity. Hotel facilities include an infinity pool, an Ayurvedic spa, a small but smart restaurant, and a cozy library. The high staff to guest ratio guarantees prompt and attentive service.

135/9 Charoen Prathet Rd. www.pingnakara.com. © **05325-2999.** 19 units. 4,300B–9,500B double. **Amenities:** Restaurant; bar; infinity pool; spa; library; Wi-Fi (free).

Shangri La ★★ Located in a lush garden setting in the heart of the city's business district, the Shangri La caters equally well to families and biz travelers. It is just a few steps away from the Night Bazaar, a 10-minute ride from the city's airport, and within easy reach of all major sights, and offers a broad range of facilities, including the CHI Spa with Shangri La's inimitable service. The hotel has excellent dining and drinking options, including an impressive breakfast spread. But most impressive is the doting treatment little ones receive including cartoon-themed comforters on their beds, loaner teddy bears, tiny robes, and more. A very nice, Thai-style hotel.

89/8 Changklan Rd., Chiang Mai 50100. www.shangri-la.com. ⓒ **05325-3888.** 281 units. From 4,500B double; from 9,350B suite. **Amenities:** Restaurant; 3 bars; pool; spa; kids' corner; babysitting; Wi-Fi (free).

Yaang Come Village ★★   Named after the massive 50-year-old yaang tree that provides shade for the reception area, the Yaang Come is an unusually quiet hotel for bustling Chiang Mai. The resort aims to re-create the feel of a traditional Thai Lue village (the Thai Lue migrated from Yunnan Province to northern Thailand a couple of centuries ago), so the lavishly decorated open-air reception leads to an inner courtyard (dominated by a swimming pool). Flanking the pool area are the guest rooms, housed in brick buildings with Lanna-style roofs, red-tile floors, balconies, glossy tile bathrooms, four-poster beds, and unique wall murals painted by local artisans. The hotel is tucked away from the bustle of the Night Bazaar, yet still within striking distance.

90/3 Sri Dornchai Rd. (btw. Chang Klan and Charoen Prathet roads, just off Sri Dornchai Road). www.yaangcome.com. ⓒ **05323-7222.** 42 units. From 2,400B double; 8,500B family room; 9,000B suite. **Amenities:** Restaurant; bar; outdoor pool; Wi-Fi (free).

INEXPENSIVE

Baan Kaew Guesthouse ★   This motel-style guesthouse—an enclosed compound in a quiet neighborhood—just a short walk south of the Night Bazaar, has a well-tended garden, a manicured lawn and one of the friendliest staffs in town. Rooms are very simple but spotless, with new floor coverings (guests are asked to remove shoes before entering), fridges, A/C, balconies, and tiled bathrooms with hot-water showers. Breakfast is served in a shaded pavilion. You're close to the market, but the place is quiet.

142 Charoen Prathet Rd. (south of Sri Dornchai Rd., opposite Wat Chaimongkol; enter gate, turn left, and find guesthouse well back from street). www.baankaew-guesthouse. com. ⓒ **05327-1606.** 20 units. 700B double. **Amenities:** Restaurant (breakfast only), Wi-Fi (free).

Baan Orapin ★★★   For those looking for a more intimate and personal stay in Chiang Mai, Baan Orapin is the choice. Owned and operated by Khun Opas Chao, who spent over a decade studying and working in the U.S. and U.K., the hotel is set on land that has been in his family since 1914. Two-story Lanna-style buildings surround the 90-year-old mansion and attached gardens. While the rooms and suites are rustic in comparison with the larger resorts and hotels, they are stylish and extremely clean, with sturdy teak-wood furniture, mosquito netting for the beds, and handicrafts to add some local flavor. Large bathrooms are outfitted in beautifully polished, locally-made green-and-blue tiling. Khun Opas knows a wealth of information about the town and its history; he and his staff will bend over backward to attend to your every need.

150 Charoenraj Rd., Chiang Mai 50100 (east side of river, north of Narawat Bridge). www.baanorapin.com. © **05324-3677.** 15 units. From 1,800B superior including breakfast. **Amenities:** Restaurant; outdoor pool; Wi-Fi (free).

In the Old City

EXPENSIVE

The Rachamankha ★★★ This graceful hotel feels miles away from the city but is set right in the heart of the Old City. Just south of Wat Phra Singh, the unique boutique property is designed in a courtyard style, much like a Thai temple—though the rooms are far more luxe than monks ever get. We're talking cool terra-cotta tile floors, high ceilings, traditional Chinese furnishings, and plenty of stunning Lanna antiques. The architecture is inspired by 11th-century Chinese dwellings, from which Northern Thai décor has its roots. Deluxe rooms are just larger versions of superior ones (so only upgrade if you really like a lot of space) and all the bathrooms are bright and big. An indigo pool lies in the peaceful courtyard. Hotel dining is in either a gravel courtyard or the long, peaceful antiques-laden hall. Upstairs is a spectacular boutique.

6 Rachamankha 9 (on the western edge of the Old City). www.rachamankha.com. © **05390-4111.** 24 units. From 7,000B–10,000B superior double; 12,268B deluxe double. **Amenities:** Restaurant; bar; outdoor pool; room service; Wi-Fi (free).

MODERATE

Tamarind Village ★★ After passing down a long, shaded lane lined with new-growth bamboo, and following meandering walkways among the gobo buildings of this stylish little hideaway in the heart of the Old City, it'll be hard to believe that you're in Chiang Mai (though you can still hear the traffic). Rooms at the Tamarind are marvels of polished concrete burnished to a shining glow, complemented by straw mats and chic contemporary Thai furnishings, all making for a pleasing minimalist feel. Bathrooms are spacious, with large double doors connecting with the guest rooms, topped off with vaulted ceilings. There's an almost Mediterranean air to the whole complex—with all of the arched, covered terra-cotta walks joining buildings in a village-style layout. There's a satisfactory pool and an excellent restaurant, Ruen Tamarind, serving delicious Thai fare, plus the staff members are helpful and an atmosphere that's quite unique.

50/1 Ratchadamnoen Rd. (a short walk to the center of the Old City from Thapae Gate). www.tamarindvillage.com. © **05341-8896.** 45 units. 4,200B double; 5,600B deluxe; from 9,800B suite. **Amenities:** Restaurant; bar; outdoor pool; Wi-Fi (free).

U Chiang Mai ★ With an ideal location right in the center of the Old City—the Sunday Walking Street (p. 345) sets up right in front!—U Chiang Mai is an easy to walk to the city's main temples. Rooms are on the small side, but they're tastefully equipped in Lanna style, and guests have use of the gym, infinity pool, bike rentals, and spa facilities. Added touches, such as the ability to check in at any time (most hotels insist you check in after 2pm on the day reserved), breakfast whenever and wherever you like it, plus the on-site restaurant and free Wi-Fi, make this an attractive option.

70 Ratchadamnoen Rd. www.uhotelsresorts.com. ✆ **05332-7000.** 41 units. From 3,500B double. **Amenities:** Restaurant; bar; outdoor pool; health club; spa; babysitting; Wi-Fi (free).

INEXPENSIVE

Gap's House ★ Gap's House is tucked down a quiet lane just inside the city wall near Thapae Gate. Long popular among budget travelers, the hotel boasts a calm atmosphere, with an almost jungle-like central garden area (it's very leafy) surrounding a large, teak Lanna pavilion. Rooms are in freestanding teak houses and feature woven rattan beds and small tiled bathrooms. Time is taking a toll on the room facilities: The rustic charm borders on just plain tatty in some rooms, though they are large with working A/C. Management is rather indifferent. It's still a cheap, atmospheric choice in the town center, though, and its cooking classes are particularly popular. No advance bookings are accepted, so call on arrival.

3 Ratchadamnoen Rd. Soi 4. (1 block west of Thapae Gate on left). www.gaps-house. com. ✆ **05327-8140.** 20 units. 470B–1,00B double inclusive of breakfast. Amenities: Vegetarian restaurant; Wi-Fi (free).

Hostel by BED ★★★ The elevated, minimalist-chic style of this hostel, combined with high standards of cleanliness and an ace location, make this a no-brainer choice for budget travelers. Bunks are available in twin or queen size, or opt for a private room with an en-suite bathroom—all options have lovely linens. Lockers, reading lights, privacy curtains, free toiletries, and hairdryers complete the appeal. Make food in the modern communal kitchen or run a load of laundry before heading out to explore the city.

54/2, 54/4 Singharat Rd. www.hostelbybed.com. ✆ **05321-7215.** 450B–700B dorm; 1,250B double. **Amenities:** Kitchen; Wi-Fi (free).

Hotel M ★ Formerly the Montri Hotel, this was the earliest address of note for foreigners in Chiang Mai, and it is still a convenient, inexpensive choice just inside the Old City—and across from Thapae Gate. Modern, clean rooms are comfortable, with a soft sofa, wide-screen TV, and free Wi-Fi. Bathrooms are small but functional, with a walk-in shower. The hotel's main advantage is its location. *Note:* Ask for a room at the rear; you'll get more peace and quiet; from the higher floors you can see the outline of Doi Suthep.

2–6 Ratchadamnoen Rd. (just northwest across from Thapae Gate). www.hotelmchiang mai.com. ✆ **05321-1069.** 75 units. From 1,300B double. **Amenities:** Restaurant; Wi-Fi (free).

Thunder Bird Hostel ★★★ Honing in on a trendy industrial vibe, this hostel has cool street art, bathrooms with clean lines, and simply decorated rooms that are damn near spotless. Dorms are booked in four-, six-, or eight-bed configurations, so things never get too busy or noisy at night. Private rooms are available, too, but they use the communal bathrooms. The hostel operates a coffee shop and bakery (which are worth a stop even if you're not staying there) so there's always a crowd of people to mingle with and swap travel tips.

181 Moonmuang Rd. www.thunderbirdhostel.com. ✆ **05328-9654.** 6 bunk rooms; 2 private rooms. 400B–550B bunk; from 1,500B private room. **Amenities:** Café; Wi-Fi (free).

Villa Duang Champa ★ This cute, refurbished colonial house is full of character and superbly located for sightseeing in the heart of the Old City. There are just 10 rooms in the main building, each individually furnished using eclectic furniture, and a restful spa in the wooden villa out back. Some rooms have small balconies and others have views of the nearby mountain. It lacks such amenities as a restaurant and bar, but there are plenty of places just a few steps away, and the friendly staff members are happy to give advice.

82 Ratchadamnoen Rd. www.villaduangchampa.com. ✆ **05332-7198-9.** 10 units. 1,800B–3,000B double inclusive of breakfast. **Amenities:** Breakfast room; spa; Wi-Fi (free).

West Side/University Area
MODERATE

Akyra Manor Chiang Mai ★★★ This contemporary boutique hits all the right notes: a photogenic rooftop pool (the only one in town) with a full bar, a prime location, and one of the best concierge teams in Chiang Mai. The all-suite rooms boast hardwood floors, Egyptian cotton bedding, freestanding tubs, sculptural lighting, and designer sofas all amounting to a sexy-cool vibe. There is even a courtyard-within-a-room concept that gives the feeling of an outdoor shower. Enjoy on-site facilities like free bike rentals, art exhibits, and a top-notch spa.

22/2 Nimmana Haeminda Rd. Soi 9. www.theakyra.com. ✆ **02514-8112.** 30 units. 5,540B–8,700B suite. **Amenities:** Restaurants; bar; outdoor pool; health club; room service; Wi-Fi (free).

Art Mai Gallery Hotel ★★ In the trendy Nimmanhaemin neighborhood, this hotel is perfectly suited for travelers drawn to Chiang Mai's creative and artistic side. The lobby plays hosts to rotating art exhibits while the eight floors of rooms, themed around art genres like pop, abstract, and impressionism, offer their own creative touches. Each floor has one suite that doubles as a private gallery, exhibiting works from well-known Thai artists, while the other rooms follow the floor's art theme. Modern bathrooms with rain showerheads, ample closet space to unpack, firm beds, and working desks are standard amenities. If a creative spark ignites, easels with paper and drawing pencils are in every room.

21 Soi 3. Nimmanheimin Rd. www.artmaigalleryhotel.com. ✆ **05389-4888.** 79 units. From 2,600B double. **Amenities:** Restaurant; outdoor pool; health club; Wi-Fi (free).

Kantary Hills ★ This complex of serviced apartments serve as a swell base near the fashionable Nimmanheimin Road, which is lined with boutiques, restaurants and cafes, to the west of the city center. Studios and one- and two-bedroom apartments are all bright and spacious, some with private balconies, and views of Doi Suthep mountain. While this is not the most up-to-date hotel in town, guest quarters are unusually roomy with a living room, bedroom, and dining area, modern furnishings, and wood floors. On-site there's a reading room, pool, and health club, and the staff take great pleasure in assisting guests.

44, 44/1-2 Nimmanheimin Rd. www.kantarycollection.com. (C) **05340-0877.** 174 units. From 2,400B studio; 4,300B 1-bedroom apartment; 6,300B 2-bedroom apartment. **Amenities:** Restaurant; pool; health club; sauna & steam room; Wi-Fi (free).

INEXPENSIVE

Hotel Yayee ★★ Perhaps it was a conscious design decision, but almost every corner of this hotel seems to have been meant for Instagram; it's photogenic through and through. There is an arresting black-and-white portrait of the beloved King Rama IX behind the check-in desk, and a hand-drawn map of Chiang Mai hangs in sections over the two-story lobby. A mashup of vibrant accessories adorn the rooms, like colorful rugs and hand-dyed fabrics. The highlight of the property is the stunning rooftop bar (a rare find in Chiang Mai!) that has the best views of Doi Suthep.

17/4-6 Soi Sai Nam Phueng. www.facebook.com/hotelyayee (use www.booking.com or www.agoda.com for reservations). (C) **099269-5885.** 14 units. From 1,865B double. **Amenities:** Restaurant; bar; Wi-Fi (free).

WHERE TO EAT

Northern-style Thai cooking is influenced by the nearby Burmese, Yunnanese, and Lao cuisines. Many northern Thai dishes are not served with steamed rice, but *khao niaow* (glutinous or sticky rice), which can be cooked as an accompaniment to a savory dish or used in a dessert. Sticky rice is sometimes served simply in a knotted banana leaf or in a small cylindrical basket with a lid, and it is eaten with the hands, by squeezing it into a small ball then pressing it into dips or sauces. Chiang Mai specialties include *sai ua* (Chiang Mai sausage), *khao soi* (a spicy, yellow Burmese-style curry and both fried and boiled noodles), and many other slightly sweet meat and fish curries. You may be relieved to know that chili peppers are used less than in other Thai regional cuisines. The formal northern meal is called *khan toke* and refers to the practice of sharing a variety of main courses, with guests seated around *khan toke* (low, lacquered teak tables); eating is done using the hands.

Near the Ping River

EXPENSIVE

David's Kitchen ★★ FRENCH/INTERNATIONAL Surprisingly, Chiang Mai has several very good French restaurants. So when noodles and rice become ho-hum or dining with white tablecloths is preferred, make a reservation here, for both classic French grub and fusion dishes. In the latter category, we're particularly fond of the foie gras with sweet mango, and the pot au feu with Thai lobster. Other reasons to come: an excellent wine list, intimate

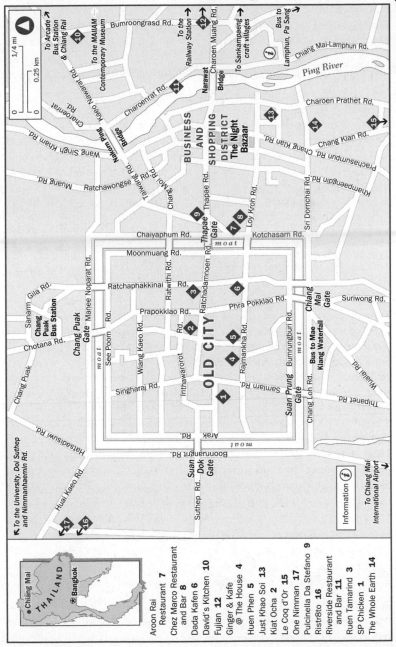

Aroon Rai Restaurant **7**
Chez Marco Restaurant and Bar **8**
Dada Kafen **6**
David's Kitchen **10**
Fujian **12**
Ginger & Kafe @ The House **4**
Huen Phen **5**
Just Khao Soi **13**
Kiat Ocha **2**
Le Coq d'Or **15**
One Nimman **17**
Pulcinella Da Stefano **9**
Ristr8to **16**
Riverside Restaurant and Bar **11**
Ruen Tamarind **3**
SP Chicken **1**
The Whole Earth **14**

nooks for couples wanting privacy, and space for group events. The restaurant has been jam packed since it opened in 2013, so reservations are highly recommended.

113 Bamrungrad Rd. www.davidskitchen.co.th. ℃ **091068-1744.** Main courses 300B–1,000B. 5–10pm Mon–Sat.

Fujian ★★★ CHINESE   Set in an elegant 1930s Sino-Portuguese mansion, at the entrance to the traditional Lanna village that contains the Dhara Dhevi hotel (p. 328), this restaurant turns out some of the tastiest Chinese cuisine to be found in Thailand. Dim sum lunches, with bite-sized dumplings arriving in bamboo steamer baskets (around 800B for all you can eat), are lots of fun and a very good value. Dinner is more formal, and includes Peking duck along with Cantonese and Sichuan specialties. While eating, diners are invited to taste the black tea from Fujian Province after which the restaurant is named.

51/4 Chiang Mai–Sankampaeng Rd. (4km/2½ miles east on Charoen Muang). www. dharadhevi. ℃ **05388-8888.** Main courses 520B–950B; set dinners 800B–1,500B. Daily 11:30am–2:30pm and 6–10:30pm.

Le Coq d'Or ★★ FRENCH   In a colonial house setting, Le Coq d'Or has been around for decades and is known for its intimate atmosphere and good service. The menu offers imported beef, lamb, and local fish prepared in French and Continental styles. We'd particularly recommend the chateaubriand, or the poached Norwegian salmon as a lighter choice. For starters, the foie gras is deservedly popular, as is a unique salmon tartare served with toast and a sour-cream-and-horseradish sauce. Live jazz is performed from Monday to Saturday evenings; kick back and enjoy it while tippling on something nice from the unusually extensive wine list here.

11 Soi 2, Koh Klang Rd. (5-min. drive south of the Mengrai Bridge, following the river). www.lecoqdorchiangmai.com. ℃ **05314-1555.** Reservations recommended for dinner Sat–Sun. Main courses 580B–1,850B; set dinner around 2,000B. Daily noon–2pm and 6–10pm.

MODERATE

Chez Marco Restaurant and Bar ★★ FRENCH   The western end of Loy Kroh Road is shoulder-to-shoulder girlie bars—an odd place to find one of the city's best gourmet restaurants, but that doesn't prevent its patrons from packing the place most evenings. Following the simple principles of using fresh ingredients that are sensibly combined and subtly flavored, Marco manages to impress diners with his French-influenced fare. Choose between indoor and outdoor tables, and from a mouth-watering range of dishes, including daily specials on a chalkboard. The coq a vin and pates are topnotch. There's a long drinks list and tempting desserts as well.

15/7 Loy Kroh Rd. ℃ **05320-7032.** Main Courses 200B–800B. Daily 5–11pm.

The Whole Earth ★ VEGETARIAN/INDIAN   Featuring Asian foods, mostly Indian and Thai, prepared with light, fresh ingredients in healthy and creative ways, this 30-year-old restaurant still feels like a find. Set in a traditional Lanna Thai pavilion, it has an indoor air-conditioned section, and a long open-air veranda with views of the gardens. The menu is extensive, and the Indian dishes are especially toothsome. Try the spicy house vegetarian curry with tofu, wrapped in seaweed, and finish with a fresh mango lassi. Service is often slow and reservations are recommended for parties of four or more.

88 Sri Donchai Rd. ℰ **05328-2463.** Main courses 250B–420B. Daily 11am–10pm.

INEXPENSIVE

Just Khao Soi ★ NORTHERN THAI   If you'd like to try Chiang Mai's signature dish, *khao soi* (a curry noodle dish), but are wary of those hole-in-the-wall places where they sell it, then head for Just Khao Soi; it elevates the dish to fine-dining status. So what if you're paying several times the going rate? It is still reasonably cheap, and you get to choose from different strengths of broth and a wide range of accompanying side dishes here, all served on a giant artist's palette with the topping taking the place of the paint. Add the spotless, smart surroundings and attentive staff, and you have the perfect setting in which to enjoy this memorable dish.

108/2 Charoen Prathet Rd. (1 block east of the Night Bazaar). ℰ **05381-8641.** Main courses 99B–249B. Daily 11am–11pm.

Riverside Restaurant and Bar ★ THAI/INTERNATIONAL   Casual and cool is what Riverside is all about. It is split into two parts: an old wooden building overlooking the river, and a smart new place across the road. Hugely popular among both Thais and foreigners, make sure you get there before the dinner rush to get your pick of tables (some are right on the river). There's live music, from blues to soft rock, tasty Thai and Western food (including burgers), and a full bar. Even if you just stop by for a beer, it is a jovial place that always has a crowd of revelers.

9–11 Charoenrat Rd. (east side of river, north of Nawarat Bridge). www.theriverside chiangmai.com. ℰ **05324-3239.** Main courses 90B–330B. Daily 10am–1am.

The Old City
MODERATE

Ginger & Kafe @ The House ★★ THAI/INTERNATIONAL   Centrally located and sharing space with the trio of charming boutiques known collectively as "The House", Ginger & Kafe is a favorite for visitors and locals alike. It is set in an old 1960s edifice that's been lovingly restored; the eclectic mix of décor, and the eatery's bright colors, give the place a fun "Alice in Wonderland" vibe. On the menu traditional Thai dishes are presented artfully, the standouts being the soft-shell crab with black pepper, *sam tam* with organic coconut rice, and the coriander marinated pork neck salad. A selection of Western dishes come with Thai twists, like the pasta with spicy Chiang Mai sausage.

199 Moon Muang Rd. (north of Thapae gate on the inside edge of the city moat). www. facebook.com/thehousebyginger. ℰ **05341-9014.** Main courses 20B–850B. Daily 10am–11pm.

Ruen Tamarind ★ THAI/INTERNATIONAL   Part of Tamarind Village, Ruen Tamarind offers a nice selection of northern Thai dishes with a couple of international favorites thrown in for the less adventurous. A must-try is the *tort mun pla,* or fried fish cakes, a common dish with a unique twist: The cakes are marinated with small chunks of banana and peanut sauce. Delicious. In the evenings, the restaurant's candlelit tables spread onto the lovely pool deck.

At the Tamarind Village, 50/1 Ratchadamnoen Rd., Sriphum (a short walk toward the center of the Old City from Tha Pae Gate). www.tamarindvillage.com/en/dining.php. ⓒ **05341-8896.** Main courses 180B–480B. Daily 7am–11pm.

INEXPENSIVE

Aroon Rai Restaurant ★★ NORTHERN THAI   How good is the food here? The restaurant does a brisk trade selling prepackaged spices and recipes for make-it-yourself dishes (so that local home cooks can pass off the grub as their own). Since you likely won't have a kitchen while you're in town, get a table in this nondescript-looking garden restaurant, one of the city's longest-running eateries. Their *khao soi,* filled with egg noodles and crisp-fried chicken bits and sprinkled with dried fried noodles, is spicy and coconut-sweet at the same time. Chiang Mai sausages are served sliced over steamed rice; puffed-up fried pork rinds are the traditional cholesterol lover's accompaniment. Dishes are all made to order in an open kitchen, so you can point to things that interest you, including the myriad fried insects and frogs' legs cooked with ginger, for which this place is famous.

45 Kotchasarn Rd. (2 blocks south of Thapae Gate, outside Old City). ⓒ **05327-6947.** Main courses 50B–110B. No credit cards. No reservations. Daily 9am–10pm.

Dada Kafe ★★ VEGETARIAN   For the most part, it is pretty easy to make Thai dishes vegetarian, so those going meat-free should find plenty of options around town. But finding something veggie-friendly that is more Western is challenging. Enter Dada Kafe. This simple shop in the Old City makes tasty smoothies with local fruits and adds wheatgrass, chia, goji berries, or bee pollen for an extra health kick. Its veggie burger is topnotch as are the veggie-laden curries, sandwiches, and salads on the menu.

Ratchamankha Road (a block west of Mueang Road). ⓒ **05344-9718.** Main courses 80B–200B. 10am–9:30pm Mon–Sat; 10am–2:45pm Sun.

Huen Phen ★★ NORTHERN THAI   Just south of Wat Chedi Luang, Huen Phen is not only a convenient spot for lunch when temple touring but also among the best places in town to sample authentic Northern Thai food. Lunch is served from a simple, open kitchen by the street, though there is an air-conditioned room, too. There's fabulous *khao soi* here, Chiang Mai's famed Burmese curry with noodle, and another tasty (but fiery) dish, *khanom jeen nam ngua,* a beef stew in a hearty broth over rice noodles. In the evening, the quaint, antique-strewn house out back provides a classier setting for a feast, including *kaeng haeng lay,* a thick pork and ginger curry, and *nam phrik ong,* a delicious ground pork and chili dip served with raw vegetables and pork crackling. Arrive early to beat the crowds.

112 Rachamankha Rd. ⓒ **05327-7103.** Main courses 40B–160B. Daily 9am–4pm and 5–10pm.

Kiat Ocha ★★ THAI/CHINESE   If it weren't for the mobs of people surrounding this canteen, it would be very easy to miss. And that would be a shame because this is one of the most famous places for chicken and rice (*khao man gai*). Orders come as platters mixed with white meat and some organs, but if you'd prefer just the white meat, ask for it *nuea luan*. The rice strikes the perfect balance of not being too oily and maintaining a fragrant aroma while the chicken is flavorful and insanely tender and moist. Pork satay skewers (20 skewers for 100B) are equally famous here, so don't fill up on chicken and rice too fast.

42/43 Intawarorot Rd. (no English sign but it's just south of the Three Kings Monument). ℂ **05332-7262.** Main courses 100B. No credit cards. Daily 6am–3pm.

Pulcinella Da Stefano ★ ITALIAN   Da Stefano's is in a narrow lane off Tha Pae Road; it's a lively and popular place with an extensive catalog of northern Italian cuisine, from steaks to excellent pizzas and pastas. Portions are big, the wine list has a few good choices (wine isn't very popular in Thailand), and there are daily set menus and specials. The boss is often on hand to advise, if you can't make up your mind, and reservations are a good idea. You'll meet lots of young backpackers splashing out after long treks around the northern hills here.

2/1–2 Chang Moi Kao Rd. (just to the east of Tha Pae Gate). ℂ **05387-4189.** Reservations recommended. Main courses 150B–320B. Daily 11:30am–10:30pm.

SP Chicken ★★ THAI   The city's best grilled chicken (*gai yang*) is at this tiny open-air shop near Wat Phra Singh. Most order a whole chicken since they're pretty small. The rotisserie-style birds are best when dipped in the spicy sauces that accompany each order. Thai-style salads are another nice option on the menu but every table has at least one order of chicken.

9/1 Soi 1 Samlan Rd. ℂ **080500-5035.** Main courses 90B–170B. No credit cards. Daily 11am–9pm.

Westside Specialty Shops

One Nimman ★★ INTERNATIONAL   The group of cafes and restaurants in this community center are a one-stop-shop for hungry travelers who might want to do a little shopping. The open-air space, called One Nimman, opened in 2018 to great fanfare; it is akin to New York City's famous Chelsea Market or San Francisco's Ferry Building. Inside is a mix of fashion retail, souvenir shopping, and places to eat. **Ginger Farm Kitchen,** is one of them, a spinoff of the popular Ginger & Kafe (p. 339). Like the original it offers refined takes on Thai classics. **Cha Tra Mue** is recognized as one of the original purveyors of Thai tea and has been in business for more than 70 years. In addition to tea, it sells desserts made from Thai tea, and its vintage tins of loose-leaf tea make great gifts. If you need a coffee fix, **Nine One Coffee** uses single-origin beans in great hot and cold drinks. Satisfy a chocolate craving at **Melt Me,** where Japanese precision is applied to a host of delicious treats.

1 Nimmanhaemin Rd. ℂ **05208-0900.** www.onenimman.com. Daily 11am–10pm.

Ristr8to ★★★ CAFE   The locals take their coffee very seriously, and the best place to grab a latte or flat white in town is at Ristr8to. The Thai owner spent time in Sydney studying English and working in coffee shops before setting up shop in Chiang Mai. The baristas are famous for their latte art and even took sixth place in the 2011 World Latte Art Championships. (We looked it up and, yep, that's a real competition.) Ristr8to's success has allowed them to pop up around town like mushrooms after a rainstorm and there are currently three branches in town with more to come. The main shop is listed below, but there is a **Ristr8to Lab** at 14 Soi 3, Nimmanhaemin Road and a **Doppio Ristr8to** on Thapae Road.

15/3 Nimmanhaemin Rd. www.facebook.com/ristr8to. 🕐 **05321-5278.** Daily 7am–6pm.

Food Markets

Eating at street stalls in Chiang Mai is not only an incredibly affordable way to dine it often yields more delicious fare than at formal restaurants. Here is a quick primer on where to go and what to eat.

Somphet Market, on the northeast corner of the city, is visited by most cooking schools during the day when it's a food market packed with produce. At night, it bustles with locals and young backpackers looking for cheap meals. The number of stalls fluctuate depending on the time of day (there's mid-day lull) but 20 to 30 hawkers sell a wide variety of noodles, fresh fruit shakes, satay, and more here.

Phatu Chang Pheuak (North Gate Market) gets its name for its location just west of the northern gate. This is a delicious place to be when the sun goes down (it's open 5–11pm). The most famous vendor at the market can be

---

khao soi: THE ONE DISH YOU MUST TRY IN CHIANG MAI

Chiang Mai folks take their khao soi pretty seriously. It is considered the "national dish"...of the city (so to speak). Khao soi (sometimes spelled kow soy) is an egg-noodle dish served in a coconut milk curry topped with pickled vegetables, shallots, and deep-fried noodles for a crispy texture. While generally on the mild side of Thai spicy, some dishes can pack heat; it all depends on the broth. The origins of the dish are murky, but it is believed to have traveled from China to Myanmar and Thailand with the Yunnan traders in the 18th and 19th centuries. Served mostly at lunchtime because it's cheap, filling and fast, all the venues listed here sell bowls for 40B to 60B. One of the best in town is at **Khao Soi Lam Duan Fah Ham** (352/22 Charoenrat Rd.; 9am–4pm) located along the east bank of the Ping River. If you want to compare and contrast, order just one bowl here and then walk north to the nearby **Khao Soi Samerjai** (391 Charoenrat; 8am–5pm) to taste the difference in the recipes of these family-run shops. **Kao Soi Fueng Fah** (Charoen Phrathet Soi 1; 7am–9pm), another highly recommended vendor, is on Halal Street and the nearby **Khao Soi Islam** (Chang Moi Soi 1; 8am–5pm) makes a delicious halal version.

identified by her cowboy hat. Her culinary contribution, a slow-cooked pork leg, was famously enjoyed by Anthony Bourdain when he filmed an episode of *Parts Unknown* in Chiang Mai.

Chiang Mai Gate, on the south side of the Old City, is a reliable spot for takeaway dishes, fruit smoothies, Muslim rotee, and red curry stir-fry. The morning shuffle (5am–noon) is busy with working locals grabbing snacks and lunches to bring to work. The 6pm to midnight shift offers more filling options like soups and curries for the throngs of hungry people.

In addition to the markets above, we heartily recommend the walking streets that are only open on Saturday and Sunday for food as well as souvenirs.

SHOPPING

If you plan to shop in Thailand, save your money for Chiang Mai. Quality craft pieces and handmade, traditional items still sell for very little, and large outlets for quality antiques and high-end goods abound in and around the city. Many shoppers pick up an affordable new piece of luggage to tote their finds home and, if you find that huge standing Buddha or oversized Thai divan you've been searching for, almost all shops or hotels can arrange shipping—or head to the **UPS** office at 77 Sri Phum Rd. (✆ **05341-767-9;** Mon–Sat 9am–5:30pm).

What to Buy

Thailand has a rich tradition of handicrafts, developed over centuries of combining local materials, indigenous technology, and skills from Chinese and Indian merchants. Drawing on such ancient technologies and the abundance of hardwoods, precious metals and stones, raw materials (for fabrics and dyes), and bamboo and clay, modern craftsmen have refined traditional techniques and now cater their wares to the modern market. Below is a breakdown of what you might find; and in the coming pages are shops and streets where you'll find all of these crafts.

Tribal weaving and craft work is for sale everywhere in the Lanna capital and you can come away with some unique finds. Check out the highly innovative **Sop Moei Arts,** at 150/10 Charoenrat Rd. (www.sopmoeiarts.com), whose homegrown crafts and ceramics help sustain Pwo Karen hill-tribes, or the well-known **Mae Fah Luang** shops (a branch is at Chiang Mai airport), which is part of a different charity assisting hill-tribe communities and abused women.

These days, **hill-tribe embroidery crafts** are employed to produce more modern items; you'll find everything from chic shoulder bags and backpacks to vibrant pillow covers, and wall hangings. The hill-tribes' **hand-woven textiles** are rich in texture and natural tones, and dyed with natural plant dyes. Cool, ready-made cotton clothing can also be found anywhere for a song.

Some of the city's best **art galleries** and **craft stores** are all clustered along Charoenrat Road and wandering the street is a pleasure. A few minutes' walk toward the Nawarat Bridge, at numbers 30 and 36, are **Vila Cini** (✆ **05324-6246)** and **Oriental Style** (✆ **05324-5724**); both have racks of stunning **silk** collections and tasteful **souvenirs,** with some truly outstanding **hand-loomed silk furnishings.** Hand-painted elephants in sizes ranging from paperweights to life-like are found further up the road at **Elephant Parade House** (www. elephantparadestore.com; ✆ **05311-1849**). Figurines have been painted by international and local celebrities and 20% of the proceeds go to elephant welfare and conservation efforts.

For books, **Backstreet Books** (✆ **05387-4143**) and **Gekko Books** (formerly Gecko Books; ✆ **05387-4066**) are neighbors on Chang Moi Kao, a side street north of eastern Thapae Road just before it meets the city wall. Both have a good selection of new and used books and do exchanges at the usual rate (two for one, depending on the condition). Perhaps those books inspired you to pen your own tome or start a travel journal. If so, **HQ Paper Maker** at 3/31 Samlan Rd. (www.hqpapermaker.com; ✆ **05381-4717**) is the finest paper purveyor in town. It exhibits a small collection of local art upstairs, and classes are available for further learning and crafting.

Silver works are synonymous with Chiang Mai, and the silversmiths working around Wua Lai Road occupy Chiang Mai's last remaining artisan's quarter. Early smiths are believed to have emigrated from Myanmar (Burma) with the coming of Kublai Khan, and skills have been passed from generation to generation. While silver is not a local resource, early raw materials were acquired from coins brought by traders. Traditional bowls feature intricate raised *(repoussé)* floral designs—the deeper the imprint, the higher quality the silver (some up to 92½ percent). Some hill-tribe groups are known for their quality **silver jewelry**—necklaces, bangles, and earrings—in unusual traditional ethnic designs or more ordinary Western styles. For all hill-tribe handicrafts, the best places to shop is at the Night Bazaar or Sop Moei Arts.

Modern **jewelry** is available in strikingly original designs at **Nova Collection,** 179 Tha Pae Rd. (www.nova-collection.com; ✆ **05327-3058**), while farther up the road, **Shiraz Jewelry** (170 Tha Pae Rd.; ✆ **05325-2382**) offers more traditional designs and a passion for local gemstones. On Nimanhemin Road, local artist Sirilak Samanasak owns **Medal Studio Jewelry** (www. metal-studio-thailand.com; ✆ **05321-4806**). Her contemporary and sculptural pieces have won favor with fashion plates like Kate Middleton.

The lords of Lanna commissioned carvers to produce wood furnishings for use in palaces, thrones, temple doors and adornments, carriages, pavilions, *howdahs* (seats for riding elephants), and royal barges. The excellent quality of hardwoods in Thailand's forests allowed these items to be adorned with grand and intricate woodcarvings. The skills survived, and talented craftspeople still produce furniture, boxes, and all varieties of gift items imaginable. When you can find the real stuff, that is. Of all the crafts made in Chiang Mai, **woodcarving** is perhaps the most influenced by foreign preferences, and pieces are often mass-produced. The best way to ID the real thing is ask for a certificate of authenticity (fairly common). In Chiang Mai (and Thailand, really) assume that anything sold in a market setting is machine made.

Lacquer skills came from China with early migrants. Sap is applied in layers to bamboo items and can be carved, colored, and sometimes inlaid with mother-of-pearl for a very elegant finished product. Today it is acknowledged as a traditional Chiang Mai craft, having been perfected over centuries by the Tai Khoen people who live in communities outside the city. **Lacquerware** vases, boxes, bangles, and traditional items are lightweight gifts, practical for carrying home. Larger tiered boxes and furnishings can be shipped.

Celadon pottery is elegantly simple in tones of the palest gray-greens. The distinctive color of the glaze comes from a mixture of local clay and wood ash. Chiang Mai has some of the largest and best celadon factories in the country. The best places to purchase celadon are at the beautiful Lanna-style compound of **Baan Celadon** (www.baanceladon.com), 10km (6¼ miles) out of town, or at the large factory outlets.

Authentic antiques, except for furniture, are virtually extinct in the tourist areas of Chiang Mai. Most furniture is from China. Some shops may offer certificates of authenticity, but as anywhere, the rule is "buyer beware." If you do get your hands on the genuine article, you may have a problem getting it home (see "Customs," in chapter 2).

Markets

The **Night Bazaar** ★ has traditionally been regarded as the city's premier shopping location, and it's still a good place to find a wide range of souvenirs, but with the success of the Saturday and Sunday **Walking Streets** in recent years, the Night Bazaar has waned in popularity and many vendors are moving out. Located on Chang Klan Road, between Thapae and Sri Dornchai roads, the market starts around 6pm each night and winds up at about 11pm. The actual Night Bazaar is a modern three-story building, but the street-side stalls extend south for several blocks. Inside the Night Bazaar building, there are mass-manufactured Chinese goods such as low-cost fashions and souvenirs. More interesting are the tribal bric-a-brac stalls or items sold by wandering vendors dressed in hill-tribe get-up.

The **Anusarn Night Market,** which runs between Chang Klan and Charoen Prathet roads south of Suriwongse Road, features more hill-tribe goods in authentic traditional styles as well as several dining options. It's easy to combine a walk round here with a visit to the Night Bazaar.

The **Warorot Market,** on Chang Moi and Wichayanon roads, opens every morning at 6am and stays open until 6pm. This central indoor market is geared to locals rather than tourists and is the city's oldest public market. Produce, colorful fruits, spices, and food products jam the ground floor. On the second floor, things are calmer, with dozens of vendors selling cheap cotton sportswear, Thai-made shoes, and some hill-tribe handicrafts and garments. It's fun and inexpensive. You'll likely want to save souvenir shopping for other markets and stores, but this is an authentic look into Thai market culture. Adjacent to the market is **Talat Ton Lam Yai,** the city's 24/7 flower market bursting with colorful and fragrant blooms—it is most active after dark.

The **Walking Streets** take place on Saturday along Wualai Road (directly south of the Old City) and on Sunday along Ratchadamnoen Road (between Tha Pae Gate and Wat Phra Singh, in the Old City); both streets are closed to traffic from midday to midnight on the appointed day, rain or shine. The **Sunday market** ★★ is bigger and is a great place to mingle with locals and other tourists (as long as you don't mind crowds—it can get packed sometimes) as well as pick up a few cheap but unique gifts. Many of the vendors have booths at both markets, so it isn't that necessary to visit both if you're in town over a weekend.

City Center, Riverside & Old Town

Small shops and boutiques line tourist streets such as Tha Pae and Loy Kroh and there are many local designer boutiques on Nimmanhaemin Road (see "West Side of the Old City," below). **Ginger** ★★ (199 Moon Muang Rd. Soi 7, ℂ 05341-9014 and 6/21 Nimmanheimin Rd., ℂ 05321-5635) is a Thai-Danish affair selling contemporary day wear, fun accessories, and fabulous twinkly costume jewelry. **Nova Collection** (see p. 344) carries a unique line of decorative jewelry in contemporary styles with Asian influences. They make custom pieces and even offer courses in metalwork and jewelry making. **Chiang Mai Cotton** ★★ (141/6 Ratchadamnoen; www.chiangmaicotton. com; ℂ 05381-4413) specializes in quality natural cotton clothing with Western cuts and sizes. **Mengrai Kilns** ★ (79/2 Arak Rd., Soi Samlarn 6; www. mengraikilns.com; ℂ 05327-2063) is in the southwest corner of the old city and specializes in celadon and decorative items. There are lots of silk dealers and tailors in and around town of varying quality. Try **City Silk** (336 Thapae Rd., 1 block east of the gate; ℂ 05323-4388) among the many for its good selection and affordable tailoring. Just past Sop Moei Arts on Charoenrat Road is **Vila.**

West Side of the Old City

On the lanes off affluent **Nimmanhaemin Road** ★★ and along the street itself are boutiques selling crafts and designer wear. These make for good one-stop shopping if your time is short. Soi 1 is especially good for textiles, homewares, and candles. Look for **Gong Dee Gallery** (www.gongdeegallery. com; ℂ 05322-5032). It's an art gallery with an extensive collection of gifts and original artwork. **Wit's Collection** ★ (ℂ 05321-7544), also on Soi 1, is a truly sublime, all-white boutique featuring a treasure-trove of fantastic contemporary furniture, ceramics, and homewares. Opposite Soi 1, at 6/23–24 Nimmanhaemin Rd., **Gerard Collection** ★ (www.gerardcollection.com; ℂ 05322-0604) features beautifully made bamboo furniture. Swish home and fashion accessories are sold at **Hilltribe Products Promotion Center** (21/17 Suthep; ℂ 05327-7743) and the money goes directly to hill-tribe assistance programs. **Studio Naenna** (22 Nimmanhaemin Soi 1; www.studio-naenna. com; ℂ 05322-6042) offers vibrant ikat and brocade fabrics that are crafted into fashion accessories.

Wulai Road

Chiang Mai's silver industry is just south of Chiang Mai Gate. **Siam Silverware** (5 Wua Lai Rd., Soi 3; ℂ **05327-4736**) tops the list of many offering crafted jewelry and silver work.

Sankampaeng Road

Shopaholics will be thrilled by the many handicraft outlets along the Chiang Mai–Sankampaeng Road (Rte. 1006, aka the Handicraft Hwy.), particularly since you can wander around the workshops, watch the craftsmen at work, and take photos of the processes, too. There are several shops, showrooms, and factories extending along a 9km (5⅔-mile) strip here. Talk to any concierge or travel agent about a full- or half-day shopping tour. *Important:* Do not arrange a day of shopping with a tuk-tuk or taxi driver, as they will collect a commission and drive up the price of your purchases.

The many shops along Sankampaeng feature anything from lacquerware to ready-made clothes, and from silver to celadon pottery. Among the many, try **Laitong Lacquerware** (140/1 Moo 3, Chiang Mai–Sankampaeng Rd.; www.thailacquerware.com; ℂ **05333-8237**), which carries a host of special lacquer gifts (among other items). Some of the smaller items, such as jewelry boxes, can be quite lightweight, good news for travelers, as you'll be able to easily carry them home. *Saa* (mulberry bark) paper cards with pressed flowers, stationery, notebooks, and gifts are not only top quality, but perfect for traveling light. There are plenty of outlets along the Handicraft Highway, with a particular concentration in Bor Sang village, also known as the **Umbrella village** since most people who live here are involved in the production of umbrellas made with *sao* paper. There is a large **Umbrella Making Center** (11/2 Moo 3; ℂ **053-338324**) where local artist demonstrate painting techniques, sell umbrellas of all sizes, and will paint anything from clothing to luggage.

To view a large selection of olive-green celadon, for which North Thailand is renowned, in traditional Thai as well as modern designs, head for **Baan Celadon,** which has an attractive rustic compound at 7 Moo 3, Chiang Mai–Sankampaeng Rd. (www.baanceladon.com; ℂ **05333-8288**). Smooth and lustrous vases, jars, bowls, and decorative objects spring to life, and even the salt and pepper shakers catch the eye.

Shinawatra Thai Silk, 145/1-2 Sankampaeng Rd. (www.shinawatrathaisilk.co.th; ℂ **05322-1076**), has been weaving traditional silks in rich colors since 1911; there is a showroom at 18 Huay Kaew Rd. Another option is **Vila Cini's** ★★ branch The Dhara Dhevi (on Sankampaeng Rd.); a bigger selection is available at the Charoenraj Road shop (see above). Though focusing less on fashions and more on silk furnishings, this homegrown silk merchant outdoes even Jim Thompson's (p. 109) for creativity and sumptuously stylish designs, all following traditional Lanna hues and inspiration.

Nearby Villages

Many of the handicrafts you'll find in town—and out at Sankampaeng Road—are the fine work of local villagers around Chiang Mai. They welcome visitors to their villages to see their traditional craft techniques that have been handed down through generations. Purchase these items directly from the source, and you might save, though you'll need a guide to find some of them as they're off the beaten track.

East of Chiang Mai, **Sri-pun-krua** (near the railway station) specializes in bamboo products and lacquerware. On the Sankampaeng Road, **Bor Sang** (10km/6 miles outside the city) is a nationally renowned center for painted paper umbrellas and fans made of *saa* paper. Just west of Bor Sang, the village of **Ton Pao** (about 8km/5 miles outside the city) also produces *saa* paper products. Just to the south, **Pa Bong** (about 6km/3¾ miles down Superhighway 11) manufactures furnishings and household items from bamboo.

South of the city, **Muang Kung** (along Hwy. 108) is a center for clay pottery, while **Ban Tawai** (14km/8⅔ miles south near Hang Dong) is the north's capital for woodcarvings and wooden furniture.

ENTERTAINMENT & NIGHTLIFE

Pick up a copy of any free magazine (or head to their online site)—such as *Welcome to Chiang Mai & Chiang Rai*, *Guidelines* (http://guidelineschiang mai.com) or *Citylife* (www.chiangmaicitylife.com)— for listings of special events and concerts in town during your stay. Most folks will spend at least one evening at the Night Bazaar (see above). For an impromptu bar scene, you can duck into one of the back alleys behind the Night Bazaar mall for streets lined with tiny bars.

If you get tired and hungry during shopping or barhopping at the Night Bazaar, you could stop at **Kalare Food & Shopping Center,** 89/2 Chang Klan Rd., opposite the main Night Bazaar building (℃ 05327-2067). Free nightly traditional Thai folk dance and musical performances, beginning around 8:30pm, grace an informal beer garden, where shoppers can stop for a drink or pick up inexpensive Chinese, Thai, and Indian food from the stalls there.

For a more studied **cultural performance,** the **Old Chiang Mai Cultural Center ★**, 185/3 Wua Lai Rd. (www.oldchiangmai.com; ℃ 05320-2993), stages a solid show starting at 8pm every night for 420B, which includes dinner. Live music accompanies male and female dancers who perform traditional dances, such as a rice-winnowing dance and a sword dance, while dressed in lavish costumes. A dinner is served on a *khan toke* (low table on the floor) and, despite the crowds, the wait staff is attentive. Yes, it is touristy—busloads find their way here—but the quality of the food and entertainment are surprisingly high. Call ahead and they'll plan transportation from your hotel.

For **live music,** one of the best hunting grounds is along the east bank of the River Ping, north of the Nawarat Bridge. Here you'll find three of the city's most popular bar/restaurants that popular with a mix of locals and tourists. **Good View** (13 Charoenrat Rd.; www.goodview.co.th; ℃ 05324-1866) and **The Riverside** (9/11 Charoenrat Rd.; www.theriversidechiangmai.com; ℃ 05324-3239) both feature live music after 7pm with the beat getting progressively faster as the evening wears on. (The food is kind of crummy so plan to come for drinks and music only.) For something all around wholesome with knee-slapping good music, **Piccolo Wine & Tapas** (www.facebook.com/piccolowineandtapas; an extension of David's Kitchen, p. 336) is the place to be. A great wine list and Spanish tapas accompany jam sessions played on fiddles and acoustic guitars.

Jazz fans should head to the **North Gate Jazz Co-op ★★★** (Sri Phum Rd.; www.facebook.com/northgate.jazzcoop; 🕿 **081765-5246**), just a few steps east of Chang Puak Gate inside the north moat of the Old City, to listen to top local talent or to join in the Tuesday jam sessions.

The bars at the western end of Loy Kroh Road constitute the town's red-light district, with many hostess bars doubling up as brothels or pickup joints. If you're curious to see how the students from Chiang Mai University spend their evenings, head along to **Warm Up Cafe** (40 Nimmanheimin Rd; www.facebook.com/warmupcafe1999; 🕿 **05340-0676**), where various DJs compete for the attentions of the crowds. Beer geeks will love the selection of micro-brews at the tiny **Mixology** (61/6 Arak; www.facebook.com/Mixology Chiangmai; 🕿 **093192-4951**); they also have easy-drinking cocktails. **Beer Lab** (Nimmanhaemin Soi 12; www.facebook.com/beerlabchiangmai; 🕿 **097997-4566**) offers more atmosphere and 80 beers to choose from. You don't have to be a journalist to drink at **Writers Club & Wine Bar** (141/1 Ratchadamnoen; 🕿 **05381-4187**) but come with a story because it's a great place to meet fellow travelers over a glass of wine.

DAY TRIPS FROM CHIANG MAI

The most popular out-of-town trip is to Wat Phra That Doi Suthep (p. 320), Chiang Mai's famed mountain and temple; however, don't miss nearby Lampang or Lamphun, both sleepy rural towns with old teak homes and exquisite Lanna temples.

Lamphun ★★

The oldest continuously inhabited city in Thailand, just 26km (16 miles) south of Chiang Mai, Lamphun was founded in A.D. 663 by the Mon Queen Chama-devi as the capital of Nakhon Hariphunchai. Throughout its long history, the Hariphunchai Kingdom, an offspring of the Mon Empire, was fought over and often conquered; yet it remained one of the powers of the north until King Mengrai established his capital in neighboring Chiang Mai. Like Chiang Mai, it is surrounded by crumbling walls and a moat.

The best way to get there is by car, taking the old highway, Route 106, south to town. Superhighway 11 runs parallel and east of it, but you'll miss the tall *yang* (rubber) trees, which shade the old highway until Sarapi, and the bushy yellow-flowered *khilik* (cassia) trees. Buses to Lamphun and Pasang leave from the **Chang Puak Bus Station** (🕿 **05321-1586**), while *songtaews* regularly leave from just south of the TAT office on the Chiang Mai–Lamphun Road.

The town holds historical *wats*, including excellent Dvaravati-style *chedis*, and a fine museum. Longan (*lamyai*), a native fruit that resembles clusters of fuzzy brown grapes—which peel easily to yield luscious, crisp white flesh—are popular here. The trees are identified by their narrow, crooked trunks and long, droopy oval leaves. On the second weekend in August, Lamphun goes wild with its **Longan Festival,** with a parade of floats decorated only in longans, a fruit in the same family as the lychee, and a beauty contest to select that year's Miss Longan. Lamphun and Pasang (to the south) are also popular with shoppers for their excellent cotton and silk weaving.

The highlight of Lamphun is **Wat Phra That Hariphunchai ★★**, one of the most striking temples in all of Thailand. (Wat Phra That Doi Suthep was modeled after it.) The central *chedi*, in Chiang Saen style and said to house a hair of the Buddha, is more than 45m (148 ft.) high and dates from the 9th century, when it was built over a royal structure. The nine-tiered umbrella at the top contains 6,498.75g (229 oz.) of gold, and the *chedi's* exterior is of bronze. Also of interest in the temple complex are an immense bronze gong (reputedly the largest in the world), and several *viharn* (rebuilt in the 19th and 20th c.) containing Buddha images. According to legend, the Buddha visited a hill about 16km (10 miles) southeast of town, where he left his footprint; Wat Phra Phuttabat Tak Pha marks the site. During the full-moon day in May, there's a ritual bathing ceremony for the Phra That.

The **Hariphunchai National Museum ★**, Amphur Muang (www.thailand museum.com/thaimuseum_eng/haribhunchai/main.htm; ✆ **05351-1186**), is across the street from Wat Phra That Hariphunchai's back entrance. It is worth a visit to see the bronze and stucco religious works from the *wat.* The museum also contains a collection of Dvaravati- and Lanna-style votive and architectural objects. It's open Wednesday to Sunday from 9am to 4pm; admission is 100B.

Wat Chamadevi (Wat Kukut) ★ is probably one of the most distinctive temple complexes in the country, located less than 1km (⅔ mile) northwest of the city center. The highlights here are the superb examples of late Dvaravati-style (pyramid) *chedis*, known as Suwan Chang Kot and Ratana, built in the 8th and 10th centuries, respectively, and thought to be modeled on those in Sri Lanka's ancient capital Polonnaruwa. The larger one is remarkable for the 60 standing Buddhas that adorn its niches. Khmer artisans built the original temple for King Mahantayot around A.D. 755. The relics of his mother, Queen Chamadevi, are housed inside, but the gold-covered pagoda was stolen, earning this site its nickname Kukut (topless).

Lampang ★

The sprawling town of Lampang (initially called Khelang Nakhon) was once famous for its exclusive reliance on the horse and carriage for transportation, even after the "horseless carriage" came into fashion. These often florally adorned buggies can still be rented near the center of town next to the City Hall or arranged through any hotel for about 300B per hour; it's an enchanting mode of transport and a pleasant (and more eco-friendly) way to see some of the city's sights.

Lampang showcases some of the best Burmese temples in Thailand. Because of the region's fine kilns, there are dozens of ceramics factories producing new and reproduction "antique" pottery. For visitor information, contact the **Lampang Tourist Office,** Thakhrao Noi Road, near the central clock tower (**℃ 05423-7229;** Mon–Fri 8am–4:30pm, Sat–Sun 10am–4pm). The easiest way to reach Lampang from Chiang Mai is by car, taking Route no. 11 southeast for about 100km (62 miles). Buses to Lampang leave throughout the day from **Chiang Mai's Arcade Bus Terminal** (**℃ 05324-2664**). The 1½-hour trip costs about 67B.

For an overnight sojourn, the atmospheric **Riverside Guest House** (286 Talat Kao Rd.; www.theriverside-lampang.com; **℃ 05422-7005**) is the best place to lay your head; it's a lovingly maintained old wooden house and some rooms have delightful river views. Rates range from 300B for a small fan room to 1,800B for a luxurious suite. The best hotel as such in town is **Wienglakor Hotel** (138/38 Phaholyothin Rd.; www.wienglakor.com; **℃ 05422-4470**), with a few stylish Thai touches in the rooms (they start at 1,400B).

Lampang's *wats* are best toured by car or horse and carriage (the only town in Thailand to still use horse carts), as they are scattered around. **Wat Phra Kaew Don Tao ★** is 1km (⅔ miles) to the northeast of the town center on the other side of the Wang River. For 32 years, this highly revered 18th-century Burmese temple housed the Emerald Buddha that's now in Bangkok's Wat Phra Kaew. Legend has it that one day the prince of Chiang Mai decided to move the Emerald Buddha from Chiang Rai to Chiang Mai. His attendants traveled there with a royal elephant to transport the sacred icon. But when the elephant got to this spot, it refused to go on to Chiang Mai with its burden, and so a *wat* was built here to house the image. There's an impressive carved wooden chapel and Buddha: A 49-m (161-ft) high pagoda houses a strand of the Buddha's hair. Poke around in the dusty **Laan Thai Museum** toward the back of the compound; it contains some lovely woodwork and an old *sarn phra phum* (Spirit House).

Wat Phra That Lampang Luang ★★★ is in Koh Kha, 18km (11 miles) southwest of the center of Lampang. This impressive temple complex is considered one of the finest examples of northern Thai architecture. If you mount the main steps, you'll see a site map, a distinguished *viharn* (inspired by Wat Phra That Hariphunchai in Lamphun), and, behind it to the west, a *chedi* with a seated Buddha. Go back to the parking area and pass the huge Bodhi tree—whose stems are supported by dozens of bamboo poles and ribbons—and you'll see signs for the Emerald Buddha House. The small Phra Kaew Don Tao image wears a gold necklace and stands on a gold base; it's locked behind two separate sets of gates and is difficult to see.

Doi Inthanon National Park ★★★

The turnoff for Thailand's tallest mountain, **Doi Inthanon**—2,565m (8,415 ft.)—is 55km (34 miles) southwest of Chiang Mai along H108. It crowns a

482-sq.-km (186-sq.-mile) national park filled with impressive waterfalls and wild orchids. A good, sealed road climbs 48km (30 miles) to the summit. At the base of the climb is the 30-m (98-ft.) high **Mae Klang Falls,** a popular picnic spot with food stands. The road to the top of the mountain features pretty views and three more falls, **Wachirathan, Sirithan,** and **Siriphum,** all worth exploring. At the end of the park road, you are at the highest point in Thailand. There is a small visitor's center and a short trail into a thick wooded area of mossy overhanging trees called the **Ang Khang Nature Trail,** which makes for a short but picturesque walk.

Admission to **Doi Inthanon National Park** is 200B (children 100B). It's open daily from sunrise to sunset. Tents and bungalows are available to rent— contact the **Department of National Parks** at ✆ **02561-0777** or visit www. dnp.go.th.

The area is a popular day-trip destination for residents of Chiang Mai, particularly in the cool season when occasionally frost (an alien concept in the tropics) can be seen near the summit. Day trips organized by Chiang Mai tour companies will cost around 1,000B, including lunch and a few other stops for sightseeing. You can always use your own rented car, too—as long as you are confident driving on switchbacks and steep slopes; take Route 108 south through San Pa Tong, then turn right after 55km (34 miles), and follow the signs to the top of the mountain. You can take a 13-km (8-mile) side trip to Lamphun on Route 1015.

Mae Sa Valley ★

The pleasant Mae Sa Valley area is about 20km (12 miles) northwest of Chiang Mai. A rash of condo construction and the sprouting of roadside billboards all indicate that Mae Sa Valley is being developed as a rural tourist resort, but it still has an unhurried feel. The top attraction here is the **Queen Sirikit Botanic Gardens** (www.qsbg.org; ✆ **05384-1000;** daily 8:30am–4:30pm; admission 40B adult, 10B child, 100B car), and orchid nurseries. Chiang Mai tour operators package some of these attractions as a half-day trip costing about 700B. The Four Seasons is found in the Mae Sa Valley.

Chiang Dao ★★

The town of Chiang Dao, 72km (45 miles) north of Chiang Mai, and its environs offer several small resort hotels and a few fun activities, but if you don't have a car, the easiest way to sightsee is by joining a day trip organized by Chiang Mai operators, which costs about 1,500B per person (half-day trips are also available). *Note:* You'll likely be encouraged by locals to visit the Elephant Training Center Chiang Dao, which offers *howdah* rides and performances. But we're including mention in the book **not** as a recommendation, but as a plea *not* to visit, as we don't feel the elephants are ethically treated here.

Sixteen kilometers (10 miles) north of the elephant camp is the **Chiang Dao Cave (Wat Tham Chiang Dao) ★★,** one of the area's more fascinating sites. Electric lights illuminate two caverns, and you can see a number of Buddha statues, including a 4-m (13-ft.) long reclining one. The row of five seated Buddhas in the first cavern is particularly impressive. Legend says the cave was the home to a hermit with magical powers. The cave and two connected caverns extend over 10km (6¼ miles) into the mountain, but you'll have to hire a local guide with a lantern to explore the unlit areas. It is open daily from 8:30am to 4:30pm. Admission is 40B and a guide fee is 100B.

The peak of Chiang Dao, called **Doi Luang** (2,240m/7349 ft.), is Thailand's second-highest mountain, and also its most dramatic, with sheer sides rearing up from the rice paddies. The summit can be reached by an arduous but scenic day-long trek that is one of North Thailand's top experiences, best done between November and February. Local guesthouses, such as lovely **Chiang Dao Nest** (www.chiangdao.com; ✆ **05345-6242**), can arrange for expert guides and put you up before and after the trek. Rooms start at 900B and the award-winning restaurant is an outstanding choice for dinner (their saffron risotto is famous) after a day of exploration.

EXPLORING THE NORTHERN HILLS

12

Northern Thailand feels, and *is*, set apart the rest of the country. Its food, customs and geography are very different, and there's even a tonal shifts in the language. Journey beyond Chiang Mai and its satellite cities and you'll find blissfully unplugged, remote towns that offer an escape to the countryside—but which country is the question? Burmese-style architecture is seen in most of the temples, while Laotian flavors and ingredients permeate the cuisine. Once here there are prehistoric caves to explore, elephants to hand-feed bananas, rivers to raft, mountains to climb, and lost-in-time ethnic hill-tribe groups to meet.

Connected by highways that undulate through forested mountains, descend into picturesque valleys, and pass through quaint farming villages, the country's northern points are best explored overland, with a rented vehicle. There are lookout viewpoints along the way, and plenty of places to refuel, relax, and stay. Travelers can choose from a number of routes: Over several days, the classic route covers a scenic slice of country that includes the rugged area northwest of Chiang Mai, which is encircled by the Mae Hong Son Loop (p. 359). From there, continue on to Chiang Rai and further north to the Myanmar-Laos-Thai border at the Golden Triangle.

THE LAND & ITS PEOPLE
The Region in Brief

Northern Thailand is composed of 17 provinces and borders Myanmar to the northwest and Laos to the northeast. This verdant, mountainous terrain, which includes Thailand's largest mountain, 2,565-m (8,415-ft.) Doi Inthanon, supports nomadic farming, teak plantations on the hillsides, and systematic agriculture in the valleys. The hill-tribes' traditional poppy crops have long been replaced with rice, coffee, tea, soybeans, corn, and sugar cane. In the fertile Chiang Mai valley, lowland farmers also cultivate seasonal fruits such as strawberries, longan (*lamyai*), mandarin oranges, mango, and melon. The lush fields and winding rivers make sightseeing—particularly in the cooler

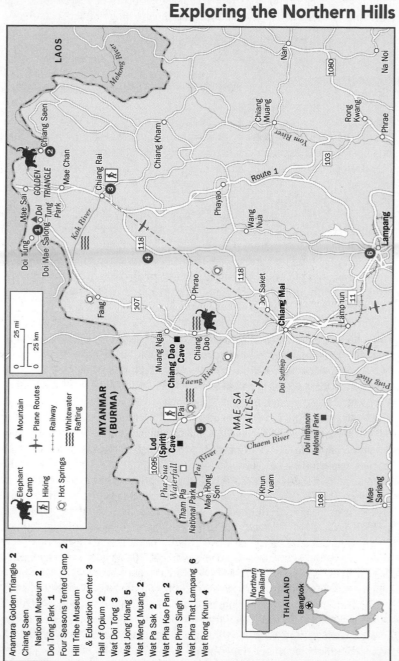

LAOS

Mekong River

Chiang Saen 2

GOLDEN TRIANGLE

Mae Sai

Doi Mae Salong 1 Doi Tung Park

Mae Chan

Chiang Rai 3

Doi Tung

Doi Mae Salong

Kok River

Faang

307

118 4

Phrao

118

Muang Ngai

Chiang Dao Cave

Chiang Dao

Taeng River

Pai

5

Lod (Spirit) Cave

1095

Pha Sua Waterfall

Tham Pla National Park

Mae Hong Son

MYANMAR (BURMA)

MAE SA VALLEY

Chaem River

Khun Yuam

Mae Sariang

108

Pai River

Doi Suthep

Chiang Mai

Doi Saket

Lamphun

11

Lampang 6

Lampang

Nan

Na Noi

1080

Chiang Muang

Rong Kwang

Phrae

103

Route 1

Chiang Kham

Phayao

Wang Nua

Yom River

Ping River

Doi Inthanon National Park

0 ____ 25 mi
0 ____ 25 km

Elephant Camp

Mountain ▲
Plane Routes ✈
Railway +++
Whitewater Rafting ≋

Hiking 🔥
Hot Springs ⊙

Northern Thailand

THAILAND

Bangkok ✴

months of November to January—a visual treat. Textiles, handicrafts, and tourism-related industries also contribute to the growing northern economy.

A Portrait of the Hill-Tribe People

The north is a tapestry of the divergent customs and cultures of the many tribes that migrated from China or Tibet to Myanmar, Laos, and Vietnam and ultimately settled in Thailand's Northern provinces such as Chiang Rai, Chiang Mai, Mae Hong Son, Phayao, and Nan. The six main tribes are the Karen, Akha (also known as the E-Kaw), Lahu (Mussur), Lisu (Lisaw), Hmong (Meo), and Mien (Yao), each with subgroups that are linked by history, lineage, language, costume, social organization, and religion.

Hill-tribes in northern Thailand are subdivided into Sino-Tibetan speakers (Hmong, Mien) and Tibeto-Burman speakers (Lahu, Akha, Lisu, and Karen), though most now speak some Thai.

In addition, tribes are divided geographically into lowland, or valley, dwellers, that grow cyclical crops such as rice or corn, and high-altitude dwellers, that traditionally grew opium poppies. The so-called indigenous tribes, who have occupied the same areas for hundreds of years, are those that tend to inhabit the lower valleys in organized villages of split-log huts. The nomadic groups generally live above 1,000m (3,280 ft.) in easy-to-assemble bamboo and thatch housing, ready to resettle when required.

Unlike the rest of Thailand, where more than 95% of the people are Buddhist, highland minorities believe in spirits, and it is the role of the village shaman, or spiritual leader, to understand harbingers and prescribe appeasing rites. Before choosing to visit a hill tribe, read our guide to being an ethical trekker on page 50 in chapter four, and use one of our recommended outfitters.

KAREN An estimated 400,000 Karen make up the largest tribal group in Thailand, accounting for more than half of all tribal people in the country. In nearby Myanmar, it is estimated that there are more than 6 million people of Karen descent who are practicing Buddhists and Christians. For years, the Burmese government has been suppressing Karen independence fighters who want an autonomous homeland. Many Burmese Karen have sought refuge in Thailand. Practicing either Buddhism or an amalgamation of Christianity absorbed from missionaries and ancient animism, the Karen are among the most assimilated of Thailand's hill-tribes, making it difficult to identify them by any outward appearance. However, the most traditional tribespeople wear silver armbands and don a beaded sash and headband, while unmarried women wear white shift dresses. The Karen tribe is known for their high-quality weaving and beadwork, which you'll find in shops in the north.

The Paduang tribe, more commonly known as "long neck" villagers, are a subsect of the Karen tribe. This tribe is the most commonly known among foreign visitors, who have seen images of smiling women with gold coils wrapped around their neck. For young Paduang girls, the long neck process can start as young as 5-years-old and a new ring is added each year. The heavy bands, which can be more than 10 pounds each, push down on the collarbone to create the illusion of an elongated neck.

HMONG (MEO) The Hmong are a nomadic tribe scattered throughout Southeast Asia and China. An estimated 150,000 Hmong live in Thailand, with the greatest number residing in Chiang Mai, with others in Chiang Rai, Nan, Phetchabun, and Phrae provinces; there are approximately 4 million Hmong living in China. Within Thailand, there are two main subgroups; the Hmong Daw (White Hmong) and the Hmong Njua (Blue Hmong) are the main divisions. The Hmong Gua Mba (Armband Hmong) is a subdivision of the Hmong Daw.

Hmong live in the highlands, cultivating corn, rice, and soybeans, which are grown as subsistence crops. Their wealth is displayed in a vast array of silver jewelry. Women are easily recognized by the way they pile their hair into an enormous bun on top of their heads and by their elaborately embroidered, pleated skirts.

Hmong are pantheistic and rely on shamans to perform spiritual rites. Hmong place particular emphasis on the use of doors: Doors for entering and exiting the human world, doors to houses, doors to let in good fortune and to block bad spirits, and doors to the afterlife. The Hmong also worship their ancestors—a reverberation of their Chinese past. Because they're skilled entrepreneurs, Hmong are increasingly moving down from the highlands to ply trades in the lowlands.

LAHU (MUSSUR) The Lahu people (pop. around 100,000) are composed of two main bands: The Lahu Na (Black Lahu) and the Lahu Shi (Yellow Lahu), with a much smaller number of Lahu Hpu (White Lahu), La Ba, and Abele. Most Lahu villages are situated above 1,000m (3,280 ft.), in the mountains around Chiang Mai, Chiang Rai, Mae Hong Son, Tak, and Kamphaeng Phet, where "dry soil" rice, corn, and other cash crops are grown.

The lingua franca in the hills is Thai, but many of the other groups can speak a little Lahu. The Lahu are skilled musicians, and their bamboo and gourd flutes feature prominently in their compositions—flutes are often used by young men to woo the woman of their choice.

Originally animists, the Lahu adopted the worship of a deity called G'ui sha (possibly Tibetan in origin), borrowed the practice of merit-making from Buddhism (Indian or Chinese), and ultimately incorporated Christian (British/Burmese) theology into their belief system. G'ui sha is the Supreme Being who created the universe and rules over all spirits. Spirits inhabit animate and inanimate objects, making them capable of benevolence or evil, with the soul functioning as the spiritual force within people. In addition, they practice a kind of Lahu voodoo, as well as following a messianic tradition. The Lahu warmly welcome foreign visitors.

YAO (MIEN) There are now estimated to be 40,000 Yao living in Thailand, concentrated in Chiang Rai, Phayao, Lampang, and Nan provinces. The Yao are still numerous in China, as well as in Vietnam, Myanmar, and Laos. Like the Hmong, tens of thousands of Yao fled to northern Thailand from Vietnam and Laos after the end of the Vietnam War.

Even more than the Hmong, the Yao (the name "mien," also used to refer to the Yao, is thought to come from the Chinese word for "barbarian") are closely connected to their origins in southern China. They incorporated an ancient version of southern Chinese into their own writing and oral language, and many Yao legends, history books, and religious tracts are recorded in this rarely understood script. The Yao people also assimilated ancestor worship and a form of Taoism into their theology, in addition to celebrating their New Year on the same date as the Chinese, using the same lunar calculations.

Yao farmers practice slash-and-burn agriculture with their main crops of soil-grown rice (not paddy fields) and maize. The women produce rather elaborate and elegant embroidery, which adorns their baggy pants, while their black jackets have scarlet, fur-like lapels. Their silver work is intricate and highly prized, even by other tribes, particularly the Hmong. Much of Yao religious art appears to be strongly influenced by Chinese design, particularly Taoist (Daoist) motifs, clearly distinguishing it from other tribes' work.

LISU (LISAW)   The Lisu represent less than 5% of all hill-tribe people. They arrived in Chiang Rai province in the 1920s, migrating from nearby Myanmar, and, in time, some intermarried with the Lahu and ethnic Chinese. The Lisu occupy high ground and, traditionally, grew opium poppies as well as other subsistence crops. Their traditional clothing is vibrant, with brightly colored tunics punctuated by hundreds of silver beads and trinkets. In a region of flamboyant dressers, the Lisu still steal the show.

The Lisu live well-structured lives; everything from birth to courtship to marriage to death is ruled by an orthodox tradition, with much borrowed from the Chinese.

AKHA (E-KAW)   Of all the tradition-bound tribes, the Akha, accounting for only 10% of all hill-tribe people living in Thailand, have probably maintained the most profound connection with their past. At great events in one's life, the full name (often more than 50 generations of titles) of an Akha is proclaimed, with each name symbolic of a lineage dating back more than 1,000 years. All aspects of life are governed by the Akha Way: An all-encompassing system of myth, ritual, plant cultivation, courtship and marriage, birth, death, dress, and healing.

The first Akha migrated from Myanmar to Thailand at the beginning of the 20th century, originally settling in the highlands above the Kok River in Chiang Rai province. Today, they are increasingly migrating to the lower altitudes within China and Indochina in search of more arable land. They are "shifting" cultivators, depending on subsistence crops planted in rotation and raising domestic animals for their livelihood.

The clothing of the Akha is regarded as one of the most attractive of all the hill-tribes. Simple black jackets with skillful embroidery are the everyday attire for men and women alike. Women often also wear stunning silver headdresses, with different subgroups sporting different designs. Akha shoulder bags—woven with exceptional skill—are adorned with silver coins, cowrie shells, and all sorts of baubles and beads.

ALONG THE MAE HONG SON LOOP

The heart and soul of Northern Thailand is The Mae Hong Son Loop. For most visitors, the loop is the *raison d'être* for venturing beyond Chiang Mai, and the route spans a truly beautiful slice of Thailand. Covering more than 600km (373 miles), the path sweeps around almost 2,000 bends as it heads through the rugged hills northwest of Chiang Mai to the well-loved tourist destinations of **Pai** and **Mae Hong Son,** then continues south to out-of-the-way **Mae Sariang** and returns to **Chiang Mai** on H108. We suggest a week or more on the route, but if that's not doable, it can be accomplished in 4 days accounting for 1 night in each of the aforementioned spots. Organized tours or a hired car with driver is an option, but a self-guided tour means freedom to take side trips and explore at one's own pace. The road, especially on the northernmost points, is serpentine and precipitous but is easily manageable for visitors who drive on the other side of the road (as in the United Kingdom). Traffic usually is not an issue, but drivers should be on the alert for everything from water buffalo to slow-moving, smoke-belching trucks.

An outstanding resource for a self-guided tour by car or motorbike is the map titled *Mae Hong Son, The Loop* (published by Golden Triangle Rider; www.gt-rider.com). The GT-Rider map gives exact details of even the smallest dirt track as well as useful sitemaps of each town. You can pick it up in many bookstores, guesthouses, and restaurants in Chiang Mai (see the website for outlets). The TAT offices in Chiang Mai (p. 313) or Mae Hong Son (p. 368) are also good resources for maps and advice on side trips.

ESSENTIALS
Arriving & Getting Around
BY PLANE   Nok Air (www.nokair.com; ✆ 1318 or 02627-2000) flies from Bangkok to Mae Hong Son (airport code HGN) on Sunday, Wednesday, and Friday. Flying time is almost 2 hours, and tickets are 1,900B. Flights on **Bangkok Airways** (www.bangkokair.com; ✆ 1771) have a layover in Chiang Mai before making the 45-minute connecting flight. Tickets are 3,500B.

BY CAR   This is undoubtedly the best option for making the loop or even just touring the hills around Pai and Mae Hong Son. See "Getting Around," in chapter 14. Travel agents can arrange a car with driver for 2,000B per day.

BY MOTORCYCLE   Though an increasingly popular option, this mode of transport is recommended only for experienced riders. Motorcycle travel around the Mae Hong Son Loop means less traffic than your average Thai highway, but the same warnings apply as anywhere: Wear a helmet, be defensive, and remember that there's not much between you and the road. In Chiang Mai, **Tony's Big Bikes** (www.chiangmai-motorcycle-rental.com; ✆ 083865-0935) is the place to go for well-maintained motorcycle rentals, lessons, repairs, questions about where to ride or to join a guided tour.

BY SCOOTER   Scooter rental places are common in the region with hires averaging an affordable 250B per day. If this entry-level two-wheeled option is appealing, get at least a 150cc motorbike, so it has the pep to get up the hills.

BY BUS   Regular public buses ply the winding tracks between all towns on the loop (Chiang Mai, Pai, Mae Hong Son, and Mae Sariang), but offer limited ability to explore the countryside. Bus tickets from Chiang Mai average 400B and can be booked from any of the countless tour agencies in town.

Pai ★

831km (516 miles) NW of Bangkok; 135km (84 miles) NW of Chiang Mai

Halfway between Chiang Mai and Mae Hong Son, the mountain road makes a winding descent into a broad green valley carpeted with rice paddies and fruit orchards. Mountains rise on all sides, and on warm afternoons, butterflies flit along the streets. Here you'll find a village called Pai—pronounced more like *bye* than *pie*—named after the river that runs through the valley. Pai is a speck of a place with main roads littered with homegrown guesthouses, laid-back restaurants and bars, local trekking companies, and small souvenir shops. Its metamorphosis from being unknown in the 1980s into one of the most popular destinations in North Thailand is impressive. The 2009 release of "Pai in Love"—a cheesy Thai rom-com—boosted tourist numbers and to this day, buses of Thai and Chinese tourists come to town to pose for photos in front of the film's iconic spots. Famously, there are 762 turns on the road from Chiang Mai to Pai, and T-shirts and coffee mugs are for sale in town to commemorate the windy journey—it's a souvenir vibe akin to Route 66 swag in America.

While Pai is an incredibly popular stop on the Mae Hong Song Loop, it's a worthy destination in its own right, and many come to the region just for hippie-dippy Pai. We've heard off-putting comparisons made between Pai in high season and Bangkok's infamous Khao San Road, but we don't get it. Yes, Pai is crowded in the winter, but it's also devoid of the sex shows, vendors selling grilled cockroaches and whippits that make Khao San Road famous. The most "wild" thing you'll likely encounter here is a twentysomething backpacker drunk from too many Chang beers.

Today, Pai attracts mostly New-Agers, musicians, and the backpacker crowd on the Southeast Asian circuit (Thailand, Laos, Vietnam, and Cambodia), and it's known more as a place to kick back and relax than run around looking at temples and museums. This chilled out vibe is very appealing, and Pai can get very crowded in the cool season when Thais from Bangkok flock here for the beautiful weather.

ESSENTIALS
Arriving
BY AIR   Tiny Pai has an airstrip, but it's not serviced. The rumor mill swirls that regional airlines will return to Pai. Before coming, it's worth checking to see if regular flights have returned.

The Mae Hong Son Loop

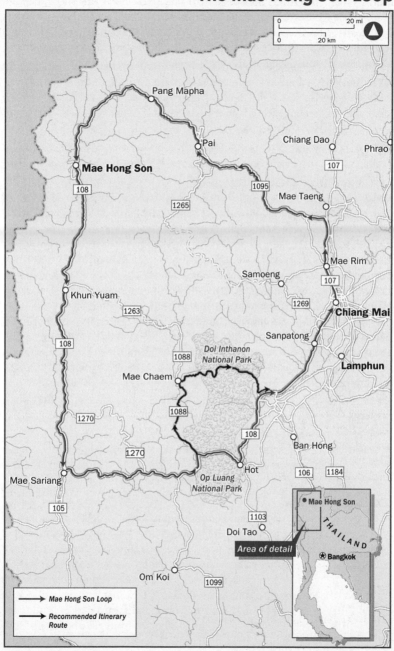

BY BUS   Several public buses leave each day for Pai from Chiang Mai (trip time 3–4 hrs.; fare 100B) and continue to Mae Hong Son (trip time 3 hrs.; fare 100B). The **Chiang Mai Arcade Bus Terminal** is off Kaew Nawarat Road, northeast of the Old City across the Ping River (*Ⓒ* **05324-2664**). The **bus terminal** in **Mae Hong Son** is on Khunlumprapas Road (the main street), about 1km (⅔ mile) south of the town center.

BY MINIVAN   Frequent minivans (called *rot too*) can be hired for connections between Chiang Mai, Pai, and Mae Hong Son for about 150B for each leg and these can be quicker than regular buses. Contact any storefront travel agent or bus station for details.

BY CAR   The scenic route is long, with steep winding roads that make for beautiful rural scenery. From Chiang Mai take Route 1095 northwest to Pai.

City Layout & Getting Around

You won't find a formal tourist information booth in Pai, but restaurateurs, bungalow owners, and fellow travelers are usually happy to share their knowledge and experience. Most guesthouses and restaurants offer photocopied maps of town and the surrounding areas. Tiny Pai consists of four main streets: Route 1095, or the Pai–Mae Hong Son Highway (colloquially known as Khetkelang Rd.), runs parallel to Rangsiyanon Road, which is the main commercial street; Chaisongkhram and Ratchadamnoen roads run perpendicular, and many guesthouses and restaurants are in or around this central grid (with more guesthouses in the surrounding countryside). You can walk the town in 15 minutes; renting a motorcycle is the best way to explore the hills around Pai. Mountain bikes and motorbikes are available at guesthouses or shops along the main streets for about 50B and 200B per day, respectively.

Fast Facts

ATMs are available on the main roads and at some hotels. The **Pai Hospital** (*Ⓒ* **05369-9031**) is open 24 hours a day. The mom-and-pop **pharmacies** in town often don't have Roman script signs, but they're easy enough to recognize and are the best spots to go for small ailments, like sunburn or an upset stomach; anything more serious should be addressed at the hospital. There is a **post office** south of the walking street on route 1095.

EXPLORING PAI

Pai has a few nice temples and some top-notch nature sites to visit, but no "bucket list" items, and that is part of the charm since most people simply come to put their feet up. While in town, make like a local and rent a motorbike because Pai is a great place to explore along country lanes. The **Pai River** itself is one of the main attractions here. Outfitters organize rafting adventures on some pretty raucous rapids from July to January. Trekking is also popular, with 2- and 3-day organized treks to **Karen, Lahu,** and **Lisu villages.** And many simply strike out on their own, grabbing local maps from guesthouses for self-guided hikes to nearby waterfalls and caves. Every day feels like a lazy Sunday in Pai, and local business owners are foreigners, or bohemian Thais, who come here for a slower pace than bustling Bangkok or Chiang Mai.

If you're thinking of leaving your hammock for a trip to the Chinese village of **Ban Santichon** or going to view the **Memorial Bridge,** might we suggest that you stay put? The former is a cheesy photo-op spot, and the latter is a recreation of the original bridge. If all that relaxing has you feeling restless, there are a few small temples and sites worth visiting.

Boon Ko Ku So Bridge ★ PARK   This elevated bamboo walkway is about a half-mile long and zig-zags through rice paddies and among herds of local water buffalo being looked after by local farmers. A few viewing platforms make this a relaxing spot to bring a picnic lunch or a book. Combine this excursion with Pai Canyon for a pleasant half-day experience.

5.6km from town on an unmarked road but easily reachable on a motorbike, in a car, or by taxi. Ask your hotel for a map and specific directions. No phone. Free. Daily 8am–sunset.

Nam Tok Mo Paeng Waterfall ★ PARK   Visitors arriving in Pai from October to mid-December (the post-rainy season months when the waterfall and pool is full and flowing) might be interested in heading out for a swim at this popular waterfall. At the bottom of the cascading water, pristine pools form, and they're ideal for swimming. The waterfall's proximity to town makes for a nice, easy excursion, which could be tackled on foot or bike.

9km from Pai along the road that leads to Wat Nam Hoo. No phone. Daily approximately 8am until dusk.

Pai Canyon ★★ PARK   While it is certainly not Thailand's answer to American's Grand Canyon, Pai Canyon is a pretty spot with lovely views. On the road to Chiang Mai and about 8km from the center of Pai, look for clearly marked signs identifying the turnoff from Highway 1095. From there, climb the concrete staircase to reach the panoramic viewpoint of the Pai Valley. The canyon is a popular lookout spot and a place to catch a good sunset.

8km from town off Highway 1095. No phone. Daily dawn–dusk.

Pai Hot Springs ★ PARK   Set in the Huai Nam Dang National Park, this hot spring has an average temperature of 176°F (80°C) with steam from the water filling the air. It's a pleasant place to go for a dip, and nearby streams offer cooler water. Several of the spas in town use the water from the hot springs in their treatments. We'd recommend the **Pai Hotsprings Spa Resort** (84-84/2 Moo 2; www.paihotsparesort.com), which has rooms starting at 1,000B but you don't need to be a hotel guest to enjoy a thermal water soak or deep-tissue massages, the latter of which brings sweet relief after hiking.

2KM off Route1095 at the 87KM marker. No phone. 300B adult; child 150B. Daily 8am–6pm.

Wat Phra That Mae Yen ★ TEMPLE   This temple on the hill—known locally as the White Buddha on the hill—is more a destination for photos and good views than it is for outstanding or noteworthy architectural achievements. There are 353 steps to climb before reaching the westward facing

Buddha, but you'll be rewarded with valley views and an exceptional spot for sundowners.

Look for signs off Rural Road Mae Hong Son 4024 (the temple is easily spotted from town). No phone. Daily 7am–6pm.

OUTDOOR ACTIVITIES & ORGANIZED TOURS

Locally operated small trekking companies are sprinkled around town and at nearly every guesthouse all along the main streets. Of the many options, we recommend **Duang Trekking** (at Duang Guesthouse, across from the bus terminal; ℭ 05369-9101) and **Back Trax** (17 Chaisongkhram Rd.; ℭ 05369-9739; backtraxtour@gmail.com) for the quality of their guides. Expect to pay in the region of 900B per day per person.

The **Pai River** is really the most exciting attraction going. Overnight **white-water rafting** trips take you through thrilling rapids as well as more scenic spots, like canyons walled with prehistoric fossilized lime and a wildlife sanctuary. A pioneer of the rafting business is longtime resident Guy Gorias who runs **Thai Adventure Rafting ★★** (16 Moo 4, Rangsiyanon Rd., in the town center; www.thairafting.com; ℭ 05369-9111). He offers regular trips from June to January. Two-day adventures begin and end in Pai, at a cost of 2,500B per person. There are many copycats in town (in both name and tour routes), but Thai Adventure Rafting is the best, and they're known for high safety standards and quality equipment. They can also help arrange accommodation in Pai or make the necessary arrangements for pickup and drop-off in Mae Hong Son.

WHERE TO STAY

There are several posh resorts and a larger congregation of guesthouses in the center of town—some of which are pretty rough dives at 200B a night. Many midrange places are on the outskirts in Ban Mae Yen, Ban Mae Hi, and Ban Juang but transportation is easy, cheap, and plentiful, so don't let that sway you.

Moderate

Hotel Des Artists ★★   Once a mansion belonging to noble Thais, this 14-room boutique is a truly charming riverside retreat just steps from "downtown" Pai. With the property's original architecture intact, colorful touches, like bright pillows made by hill tribes, complete the welcoming, open-air lobby. Rooms are smaller than average, but the beds are top quality, and the showers are strong. If budget allows, river view rooms are worth the extra 800B, but all room categories have private balconies. A nice on-property café completes the appeal.

99 Chaisongkhram Rd., www.hotelartists.com. ℭ **05369-9539.** 14 units. 2,060B double room; 3,850B suite. **Amenities:** Restaurant; bar; Wi-Fi (free).

Reverie Siam ★★★   Offering unparalleled value for money, this boutique hotel has a European country-house vibe but doesn't feel cheesy—a common pitfall in Thailand. The family that owns the property took great care in decorating the rooms, and all 18 suites are individually outfitted. Expect deep soaking tubs, four-poster beds (in some), spacious rooms, handsome wood furnishings, and total privacy. The staff here are genuinely hospitable, and they're a wellspring of information on where to go in Pai. Plan to have a Med-inspired meal (with a great charcuterie board) at the hotel's Silhouette Bar.

476 Moo 8, Vieng Tai Pai. www.secret-retreats.com/reveriesiam. © **05369-9870.** 18 units. From 3,300 double. **Amenities:** Restaurant; 2 outdoor pools; Wi-Fi (free).

Inexpensive
Belle Villa Resort ★★   A friendly resort 15-minutes outside of Pai, Belle Villa is ideal for *really* getting off the grid. The resort's stilted bungalows (called "cottages" on the booking site) sit along a quiet, rural stretch of the Pai River. These bungalow digs boast contemporary conveniences such as digital safes and cable TV without sacrificing the rustic charm of thatched roof and bamboo walls. Deluxe rooms have a lower price point and mirror a traditional hotel in décor; some have direct pool access. The peace, quiet, and scenery are all good reasons to pick this resort.

113 Moo 6, Huay Poo-WiangNua Rd. www.bellevillaresort.com. © **05369-8226.** 47 units. From 1400B double room; from 2,600B cottage. **Amenities:** Restaurant; outdoor pool; Wi-Fi (free).

Pairadise Guest House ★★   Located across the river from town (about a 10- to 15-minute walk) and overlooking the Pai Valley this adorable resort is a top pick. Sway in the hammock on your private balcony or swim in the purpose-built lake. Comfortable, Western-style beds and bedding ensure a peaceful and relaxing night of sleep, and Thai-inspired murals are a nice touch. Rooms, as opposed to bungalows, don't have AC but they're half the price and include a private bathroom.

98 Baan Maeyen. www.pairadise.com. © **05369-8065.** 15 units. 130B–1,500B double. **Amenities:** Restaurant; Wi-Fi (free); parking (free)

WHERE TO EAT
Pai plays host to a bevy of restaurants as well as a whole range of street-side dining, and vegetarian options are easy to come by in this hippie hamlet. For a casual, inexpensive meal, head to **Talart Don Bai** market off Raddamrong Road, 2pm until sundown. Hill-tribe women sell fresh produce and local snacks there, like fermented sausage, fresh-cut fruit with a sugar-and-chili dipping sauce, and noodle dishes are available. Pai's popular **Walking Street** also has food stands, with kebab, roti, and noodle vendors interspersed among the souvenir stalls.

Cafecito ★ TEX-MEX   If a hankering for Tex-Mex strikes, head to Cafecito, which is near the Pai police station, for tacos, burritos, and quesadillas—and a hearty dash of the homemade salsa. The shop is also a café with a nice list of hot and cold java drinks meaning you can complete your meal with either an iced black or a cold Corona. Funky local art adorns the walls.

258 Moo 8 (across from the police station). www.facebook.com/cafecitopai. © **088499-2456.** Main courses 150B. 9am–5pm Fri–Wed.

Krazy Kitchen ★★ THAI   To say this place is a hole-in-the-wall would imply that there are walls—which there aren't. But Mama Sue doesn't need walls—just a really old wok—to make her famous 50B *pad Thai* to perfection. Seasonal fruit juices here are utterly refreshing.

88 Moo 3 (on highway 1095 approaching the memorial bridge from Chiang Mai). ℂ **05306-5738.** Main courses 50B–90B. No credit cards. Daily 8am–8pm.

Larp Khom Huay Poo ★★★ THAI   In my reporting, I found the food in Pai to be mostly satisfying but never very memorable. One of the few exceptions: the *larp moo* at this open-air shop about a kilometer outside of town. This is a traditional northern dish of minced pork fried with local herbs, and it's perfect with a basket of sticky rice and an order of sun-dried beef.

270m east of the airport on Highway 1095. ℂ **05369-9126.** Main courses 50B–100B. Daily 9am–9pm.

Om Garden Café ★★ INTERNATIONAL   Single-origin beans, strong espresso, and breakfast burritos paired with fresh-pressed juices are the main draw here, but they do a booming lunch business, too, thanks to salads and Middle Eastern dishes that are fresh and filling and a welcome change from Thai food. Vegetarians will find the meat-free options on the menu to be the best in town. There's a funky, hippie vibe to the place.

60/4 Wiant Tai. www.facebook.com/OmGardenCafePa. ℂ **082451-5930.** Main courses 80B–150B. Daily 8:30am–5pm.

NIGHTLIFE

One hotel general manager told me during my recent reporting trip that nightlife spots in Pai generally "live as long as a fruit fly." But while watering holes may come and go, spots for live music seem to endure. Two standouts are **Mojo Café** (61/2 Moo 2; www.facebook.com/mojocafepai), where crowds pour out into the street as local Thai bands play everything from jazz to Western covers, and **The Jazz House** (24/1 Moo 3; www.facebook.com/pai-jazzhouse), a chilled-out spot known for good food, good vibes, and good cocktails. The latter has a popular open-mic night and happily singing along to "Wonderwall" at full volume with strangers-turned-friends is a rite of passage in this town. **Jikko Beer** (65/1 Moo 3; ℂ **081938-8244**) is a small street side bar that is leading the craft beer movement in Pai. Jikko mostly serves imported bottles with a particular focus on European and American IPAs with standard local lagers are on tap. The affable guys who run the bar are legends in Pai, and they've been here since 1982.

Between Pai & Mae Hong Son

Either as a day trip from Pai or as a stop on the way to Mae Hong Son, the best little detour going is **Tham Lot** ★★ off Route 1095 (about 30km/19 miles northwest of Pai on Route 1095 in the town of Soppong, and then about 8km/5 miles north of the highway). This large, awe-inspiring cave is filled with colorful stalagmites, stalactites, and small caverns. The mile-long cavern here was discovered in the 1960s and was jam-packed with antique pottery dating from the Ban Chiang culture—read more about them on p. 396. There are three caverns within the cave. The first chamber is a magnificent grotto and the second contains a prehistoric cave painting of a deer (which unfortunately has been largely blurred by curious fingers). In the third cavern, visitors view prehistoric coffins made from wood and shaped like canoes; carbon dating puts the creation of these coffins as far back as 2,200 years ago.

A guide for all three caves costs 150B, with a gas lantern rental included. 'Guide' in this case is more a literal guide and not so much a tour guide to who will highlight key features, though some English-speaking guides will offer a few insights. If you want a proper guide, hire the pros from **Cave Lodge** (see below). Be sure to take the canoe ride to the third cave (the ferryman will hit you up for an extra 300B one-way and 400B return), where, especially in the late afternoon and evening, you can see clouds of bats and swallows vying for space in the cave's high craggy ceiling (the boat ride is fun, too). Pay again to get back by boat, or you can follow the clear jungle path a few kilometers back to the parking lot. *Important:* The park no longer allows for self-exploration, and some smaller chambers in the cave can only be reached by a ladder.

There are lots of little guesthouses along the road near the entrance to the Spirit Cave in Soppong; hands down the best is **Cave Lodge** ★★★ (15 Moo 1; www.cavelodge.com; ℂ **05361-7107**) within walking distance of Tham Lot. It offers a variety of room types, all loosely based on hill-tribe architecture, with rates ranging from 180B for a dorm bed to 700B for a bungalow. More than just an agreeable place to rest your head, the lodge is run in part by John Spies, a longtime resident who studied the area's caves for more than 30 years and is a true expert (he enjoys sharing his insights with guests). Everything from cave tours to kayaking and multi-day hill-tribe treks can—and should—be booked through the lodge, and they offer handy maps for self-exploration, and copies of Spies' book on the region's caves, called *Wild Times.*

As the road curves south heading into Mae Hong Son, you'll encounter **Tham Pla Park** (17km/11 miles north of Mae Hong Son on Rte. 1095), a small landscaped park leading up to the entrance of Tham Pla, or Fish Cave. Here you'll find a small grotto crowded with carp (legend says there are 10,000 of them) that Thais believe are protected by local spirits. You can buy fish food in the parking lot, but the fish don't eat it, preferring vegetables. Have a look—it is meant to be good luck and is also a good leg stretch after the long drive.

In the Tham Pla Park interior 10km (6¼ miles) away is the huge **Pha Sua Waterfall,** which tumbles over limestone cliffs in seven cataracts. The water is at its most powerful after the rainy season in August and September. The Hmong hill-tribe village of Mae Sou Yaa is beyond the park on a road suitable for jeeps, just a few kilometers from the Burmese border.

Mae Hong Son ★

924km (574 miles) NW of Bangkok; 355km (221 miles) NW of Chiang Mai via Pai; 274km (170 miles) NW of Chiang Mai via Mae Sariang

Not far from the Burmese border, Mae Hong Son, the provincial capital of Mae Hong Son province, is the urban center of this large patch of scenic woodlands, waterways, and unique hill-tribe villages. The town's surrounding hills, famed for their eerie morning mist, burst into color each October and November when *tung buatong* (wild sunflowers) come into bloom. The hot season (Mar–Apr) has temperatures as high as 104°F (40°C), and the rainy season is long (May–Oct), with several brief showers daily.

The mountains around Mae Hong Son are scarred by slash-and-burn agriculture and evidence of logged teak forests from departed hill-tribe settlements. Roads, airfields, and public works projects have since opened up the scenic province, as poppy fields gave way to terraced rice paddies and garlic crops. At the same time, the surge in tourism brought foreigners trekking into villages where automobiles were still unknown. Although the busy town of Mae Hong Son continues to grow and develop, its picturesque valley setting and lovely Burmese-style *wats* (temples) are still the star attractions here, it has a uniquely Thai-Burmese vibe, and it's a lot less crowded than Pai.

ESSENTIALS
Arriving
BY PLANE **Nok Air** (www.nokair.com; ℂ **05392-2183**) runs flights a few times a week to Bangkok. **Bangkok Airways** (www.bangkokair.com; ℂ **1771**) has a daily 5:05pm flight to Chiang Mai; the 40-minute flight averages 1,090B. The **Mae Hong Son Airport** (airport code HGN) is about 10 minutes from the town center. Tuk-tuks and *songtaews*, or pickups, are always waiting for passengers outside the airport.

BY BUS Buses connect with Pai (trip time 4 hrs.; fare 70B) or beyond to the **Chiang Mai Arcade Bus Terminal** (trip time 7 hrs.; fare 350B). Buses to Mae Sariang to the south (trip time 4 hrs.; fare 100B–200B) run about four times daily. The bus terminal in Mae Hong Son is on Khunlumprapas Road (the main street), about a kilometer south of the main intersection.

BY CAR The 8-hour journey to Mae Hong Son from Chiang Mai is a pleasant mountain drive with spectacular views and some fun attractions (see "Between Pai & Mae Hong Son," above). The road is winding but paved and safe, with places to stop for gas, food, and toilets, as well as scenic pull-offs. Take Route 107 north from Chiang Mai to Route 1095 northwest through Pai. For car-rental info, see chapter 11, "Chiang Mai."

Visitor Information
The **TAT** office (ℂ **05361-2982**), 58000 Khunlumprapas Rd., opposite the post office, has helpful staff and maps. The **Tourist Police** office (ℂ **05361-1812** or 1155), Singhanat Bamrung Road, is open daily from 8:30am to 5pm.

Mae Hong Son ★

0   1/10 mi

0   0.10 km

Thanon Sirimongkol

1095

Thanon Panishwattana

Wat Hua Wiang

Morning Market

Night Market

Thanon Khunimprapas

Thanon

Pradit Jongkham

Singhanat Bamrung

Airport Terminal

Thanon U-Domchaoitesh

Thanon Channahsathi

Sri Sangwarn

Jong Kam Lake

1

(i)

✉

Wat Dol Kung Mu

Thanon Padungmaaytan

2

3

Wat Chong Klang

Wat Chong Kham

Mae Hong Son

THAILAND

Bangkok

Thanon Khuaphuek

4

108

5

6
↓

ACCOMMODATIONS ■

Fern Resort **6**
Imperial Mae Hong Son **5**
Mae Hong Son Mountain Inn **4**
Piya Guest House **2**

DINING ◆

Fern Restaurant **3**
La Tasca **1**

✈ Airport
🚌 Bus Station
✚ Hospital
(i) Information
✉ Post Office

City Layout

Mae Hong Son is small and easy to cover on food. Khunlumprapas Road, part of the Pai–Mae Sariang Highway (Rte. 108), is the town's main street and home to travel agents, hotels, and restaurants. The main sights are **Jong Kham Lake,** just east of the main street, and **Wat Phra That Doi Kong Mu,** which overlooks town from the west.

Getting Around

You can walk to most places in town, but there are tuk-tuks parked outside the market for longer trips. At some guesthouses, you'll find bicycle rental for 50B or 100cc motorbikes for rent at 150B to 200B per day.

FAST FACTS

There are major **banks** with ATMs and currency exchanges along Khunlumprapas and Singhanat Bamrung roads. The **Sri Sangawan Hospital** is east of town on Singhanat Bamrung Road (© **05361-1378**). The **post office** is opposite the King Singhanat Rajah statue.

EXPLORING MAE HONG SON

Wat Jong Klang and **Wat Jong Kham** are reflected in the serene waters of Jong Kham Lake, in the heart of town. Their striking white and gold *chedis* (stupas) and dark teak *viharn* (assembly hall) are symbols of Burmese influence. Wat Jong Klang was constructed from 1867 to 1871 as an offering to Burmese monks who made the long journey here for the funeral of Wat Jong Kham's abbot. Inside is a series of folk-style glass paintings depicting the Buddha's life and a small collection of dusty Burmese wood carvings and dolls. Next door, the older Wat Jong Kham (ca. 1827) was built by King Singhanat Rajah and his queen and is distinguished by gold-leaf columns supporting its *viharn.* Don't miss the colorful Burmese-style donation boxes; they're like musical arcade games with spinning discs and cups to drop your change in, only the end result is not "game over" but "make merit."

Wat Phra That Doi Kong Mu ★★ (also known as Wat Plai Doi) dominates the western hillside above the town, particularly at night when the strings of lights rimming its two Mon pagodas are silhouetted against the dark forest. King Singhanat Rajah constructed the oldest part (ca. 1860) of this compound, and a 15-minute climb up its *naga* (snake) staircase rewards one with grand views of the mist-shrouded valley, blooming pink cassia trees, and Jong Kham Lake below. Below Wat Phra That Doi Kong Mu, there's a 12-m (39-ft.) long **Reclining Buddha** in Wat Phra Non.

For everything from short **single-day treks** to multi-day journeys in the region, **Nature Walks** ★★★ (www.naturewalksthai-myanmar.com; © cell: **089552-6899**) is the best outfitter in town. Mr. Chan, a native of Mae Hong Son, is an encyclopedia on the region's flora and fauna and he has a solid relationship with the region's hill tribes. Some tours include village home stays.

There are three **Padaung villages** close to Mae Hong Son populated by the famed **"long-neck" Karen people,** so called because their women wear layers of brass rings around their necks, continually adding rings to give them elongated necks. However popular they remain, visits to these villages are controversial, and some describe them as human zoos. These villagers are refugees—caught in limbo between being exiled from Myanmar and without citizenship in Thailand. For these once independent farmers, the main source of income is now selling handicrafts and snacks to visitors. The reality is that these villagers see little of the entrance fee and a way to support them is through peer-to-peer spending.

WHERE TO STAY

Mae Hong Son offers something for every budget, and there are a few lovely hotel options in the center of town. Prices are slashed up to 50% in the offseason, making for some very affordable options.

Moderate

Imperial Mae Hong Son ★ Though it's some 2km (1¼ miles) south of town, the hotel's style, service, many amenities, and upkeep set it above the rest. Guest rooms have French windows that open to private terraces overlooking a teak forest, garden, and stream. Blond wood and wicker furnishing dominate the décor scheme of the rooms, and suites are large and comfortable. Lounge on the wooden pool deck or nosh on Thai classics at the open-air restaurant with garden views. The staff can help with any eventuality, from day tours to flat tires.

149 Moo 8. www.imperialmaehongson.com. ℱ **05368-4444.** 104 units. 2,464B double; from 3,653B suite. **Amenities:** Restaurant; 2 bars; lounge; outdoor pool; health club; sauna; room service; Wi-Fi (free).

Inexpensive

Fern Resort ★★★ In a quiet valley 8km (5 miles) south of town and surrounded by rice paddies and running creeks, the Fern Resort is a dreamy eco-resort. Tai Yai (Shan)-style wooden bungalows have simple but comfortable locally inspired furnishings with leaf roofs. Bathrooms have slate-tiled showers with reliable hot water. As you might expect in a bona fide eco-resort, there are no TVs or phones in the rooms, but this only adds to the appreciation of sounds from the jungle around. Grab one of the hotel's trail maps and explore the adjacent Mae Surin National Park; experienced guides are available for more extensive treks. Shuttles whisk passengers into town, and most of the employees are members of the Karen villages.

64 Moo 10. www.fernresort.info. ℱ **05368-6110.** 35 units. 1,130B–3,000B inclusive of breakfast. **Amenities:** 2 restaurants; 1 bar; outdoor pool; Wi-Fi (free); pets (free); shuttle into town (free); parking (free).

Mae Hong Son Mountain Inn ★ Originally built as the headquarters and shooting locations for '90s American films like "The Quest" and "Air American," you can't miss the angular spire of the oversized Thai Yai-style peaked roofs marking the entrance to this compound. After filming, it was reborn as a simple hotel. What décor there is a mixture of Burmese, hill tribe, and Thai elements; the guest rooms are arranged in two stories around lush gardens. For those who decide to upgrade, there are mountain-view superior rooms and a suite with a private balcony.

112/2 Khunlumprapas Rd. www.mhsmountaininn.com. © **05361-1802.** 69 units. From 860B double; from 4,500B suite. **Amenities:** Restaurant; Wi-Fi (free).

Piya Guest House ★★ This is the best budget choice on beautiful Jong Kham Lake, easily the nicest part of town—and a short walk to the two lakeside temples. Piya offers 16 one-story bungalows that circle a garden courtyard and swimming pool. Rooms are basic but clean with private bathrooms, hot-water showers, and air-conditioning.

1/1 Khunlumprapas, Soi 3 (east side of Jong Kham Lake). www.facebook.com/piyaguest houseMHS. © **05361-1260.** 14 units. 665B bungalow. No credit cards accepted. **Amenities:** Restaurant.

WHERE TO EAT

The local **Night Market,** on central Khunlumprapas, is the busiest venue in town for diners. There you can sample noodle soups, crisp-fried beef, dried squid, roast sausage, fish balls, and other snacks sold by vendors for very little. It's open until approximately 9pm daily.

Ban Din Coffee ★ THAI/CHINESE This tin-roofed pavilion has more style than most: Overhead lights are shaded by straw farmer's hats, and Formica tables are interspersed between bamboo columns. The Thai and Chinese menu include a kai-mook salad (a tasty blend of crispy fried squid, cashews, sausage, and onions), and a large selection of light and fresh stir-fried dishes. There's a nice tea selection, a nod to the town's Yunnanese population.

23 Udom Chaonitesh Rd. © **05361-2092.** Main courses 60B–190B. No credit cards. Daily 9:30am–2pm and 5:30–11pm.

Fern Restaurant & Bar ★★ THAI/INTERNATIONAL Not sure what you're in the mood for? Then go to Fern, set in the hotel of the same name, for an especially wide variety of Thai and international dishes for this part of the country—all of it well prepared. The hotel's bar has live music most nights. There is also a nice view of the mountaintop temple, Wat Phra That Doi Kong Mu, in the evening glow.

87 Khunlumprapas Rd. © **05361-1374.** Main courses 80B–250B. Daily 10am–10pm.

La Tasca ★★ ITALIAN In the town center, look for a little Italian storefront pizza joint. It serves real coffee in the morning and surprisingly authentic pasta and pizza. A highlight: their famous calzone.

88/4 Khunlumprapas Rd. © **05361-1344.** Main courses 80B–180B. Daily 10am–10pm.

Mae Sariang: Completing the Mae Hong Son Loop

180km (112 miles) W of Chiang Mai; 130km (81 miles) S of Mae Hong Son

The tiny, little-visited burg of Mae Sariang is a cozy river town dotted with rows of wooden shophouses. Spend time exploring nearby national parks or floating on the Salawin River near to Myanmar. (Both **NG River Guides,** www.ng-river-guides.com, or **Dragon Sabaii Tours**, www.thailandhilltribe holidays.com are reputable outfitters for that.) The utility of Mae Sariang is that it's the best halfway stopover on the long southern link between Mae Hong Son and Chiang Mai. Driving in the area, along Route 108, takes you past pastoral villages, scenic rolling hills, and a few enticing side trips to small local temples and an educational stop at an informative World War II museum.

GETTING THERE

BY CAR   Navigation is a cinch, but watch out for bends (there must be a thousand between Mae Hong Son and Mae Sariang). Just follow Route 108 between Mae Hong Son, Mae Sariang, and Chiang Mai.

BY BUS   Standard and air-conditioned buses connect Mae Hong Son, Mae Sariang, and **Chiang Mai Arcade Bus Terminal** (© 05324-2664) along the southern leg of Route 108. Tickets for the 8- to 9-hour journey and cost between 200B and 300B.

EXPLORING MAE SARIANG

The road is good, and the scenery is lush on the long stretch of Route 108 west of Chiang Mai. There are decent side trips to break up the drive, and roadside facilities are limited but adequate.

In the village of **Khun Yuam,** 63km (39 miles) south of Mae Hong Son, you'll come to a junction with a road that no longer exists: A ghost trail remembered as "The Road of Japanese Skeletons," the path of retreat for Japanese soldiers fleeing what was Burma (now Myanmar) at the end of World War II. The road lives only in the memory of those who met the starved and dying troops, an estimated 20,000 of whom lie in mass graves in the surrounding area. The **World War II Museum** (on the grounds of the Khun Yuam Indigenous Cultural Center along Rte. 108; 100B; daily 8:30am–4:30pm) commemorates this little-known chapter in World War II history. The museum features rusting tanks and weaponry, photos, personal effects, and written accounts (translated to English) of soldiers' struggles and the kindness of the locals.

Mae Sariang has a few outfits offering day treks and rafting (stop in any of the riverside cafes or hotels), but most people just spend a night here before making their way to Chiang Mai. It's worth a stroll around the small town center, particularly for the atmospheric, Burmese-style temples of **Wat Si Boonruang** and **Wat Utthayarom** (also known as Wat John Sung, built in 1838) on Wiang Mai Road. Wat Si Boonruang, built in 1896, has beautifully carved roofs, a Shan-style chedi, and a white jade Buddha from Myanmar that is nearly 7-feet tall, and is the more interesting to explore of the two.

Between Mae Sariang and **Hot,** you'll pass a turning on the left to **Mae Chaem** (H1088), a route that leads into **Doi Inthanon National Park** from the west. It is possible to return to Chiang Mai by this extremely scenic route, going over Thailand's highest peak (well, near the top anyway), though the more straightforward alternative (with fewer curves!) is to keep on H108 to Hot, where the road turns north and passes through Chom Thong en route to Chiang Mai.

WHERE TO STAY & EAT

There are lots of budget accommodation along the Mae Yuam River in the town center. The best choice is the 1,800B a night **Riverhouse Resort** (6/1 Moo 2, Langpanich Rd.; www.riverhousehotelgroup.com; ℂ **05368-3066**), a small grouping of cozy wooden pavilions overlooking the Yuam River. The same owners run the Riverhouse Hotel, which is slightly cheaper at 1,000B a night. Riverhouse's **Coriander in Redwood** is also the best bet for dining in their riverside *sala* (open pavilion) that is a century old. A stroll through town will take you past any number of local greasy spoons, where the adventurous eaters can find everything from Burmese pancakes, to grilled eel, and one-dish noodle or rice meals for next to nothing.

CHIANG RAI ★

780km (485 miles) NE of Bangkok; 180km (112 miles) NE of Chiang Mai

Chiang Rai is Thailand's northernmost province. The Mekong River marks the country's borders with Laos to the east and Myanmar to the west. The smaller yet scenic Mae Kok River, which supports many hill-tribe villages along its banks, flows right through the provincial capital of the same name.

Often characterized as the "poor cousin" of Chiang Mai, Chiang Rai City lies in a broad fertile valley, with tree-lined riverbanks and a refreshingly cool climate (at least by Thai standards). That moniker isn't all bad though, and while popular sites are more subdued than in Chiang Mai, like the Night Market and Walking Street, Chiang Mai lures travelers weary of traffic and pollution in Chiang Mai. Chiang Rai is a lush place to bed down for a night or two before going further afield for trekking and trips to Chiang Saen and the Golden Triangle.

Because the journey from Chiang Mai takes only 3 hours, it is possible to see Chiang Rai and the Golden Triangle in a very aggressive day trip, but you'll need to get an early start and allow a full day of car travel.

Essentials

ARRIVING

BY PLANE　Thai Airways (www.thaiairways.com; ℂ **02356-1111**) and its subsidiary, **Thai Smile** (www.thaismileair.com), have daily flights to Chiang Rai from Bangkok's main airport. Budget carriers like **Nok Air** (www.nokair. com; ℂ **1318**), **Bangkok Airways** (www.bangkokair.com; ℂ **1771**), and **Air-Asia** (www.airasia.com; ℂ **02515-9999**) fly daily from both of Bangkok's airports. Flying time is 80-minutes and prices hover around 600B for a one-way ticket but can be as low as 350B with advanced purchase.

　Chiang Rai International Airport (ℂ **05379-8000**) is about 10km (6¼ miles) north of town. The airport is fairly primitive, but there is a money exchange, a few restaurants, post office, and several car rental companies have offices there. Taxis hover outside and charge 200B to town.

BY HELICOPTER　A scenic but pricey option is chartering a private helicopter to fly from Chiang Mai to Chiang Rai. The hour-long flight offers

Chiang Rai

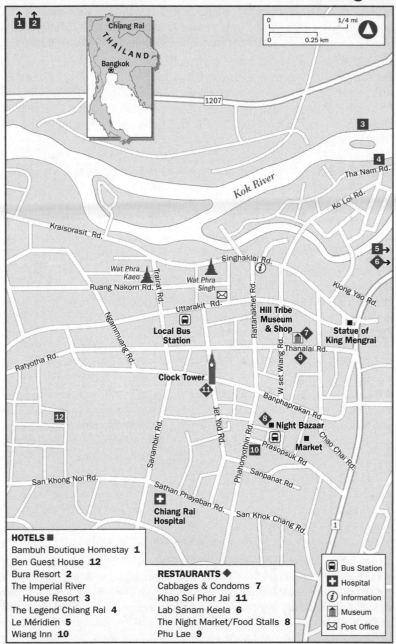

HOTELS ■
Bambuh Boutique Homestay **1**
Ben Guest House **12**
Bura Resort **2**
The Imperial River
  House Resort **3**
The Legend Chiang Rai **4**
Le Méridien **5**
Wiang Inn **10**

RESTAURANTS ◆
Cabbages & Condoms **7**
Khao Soi Phor Jai **11**
Lab Sanam Keela **6**
The Night Market/Food Stalls **8**
Phu Lae **9**

🚌 Bus Station
➕ Hospital
ⓘ Information
🏛 Museum
✉ Post Office

postcard views of the Northern Thai countryside and the Mekong River. **Advance Aviation** (www.advanceaviation.com; © **085055-4444**) can arrange helicopter flights. Uber-luxury resorts, like the Four Seasons, arrange to fly guests between their Chiang Mai hotel and their Golden Triangle property. Charter fees are around 75,000B each way.

BY BOAT   While not advisable for travelers pressed for time or those who can't let go of certain creature comforts, longtail boats with large, loud motors make the 130km/81-mile journey on the Mae Nam Kok from Tha Ton to Chiang Rai. They're normally canopied boats, allowing you enjoy the verdant landscape in the shade as you pass by rice fields, riverside temples, orchid farms, banana trees and thirsty water buffalo. During rainy season when the water is high (July to December), boats depart at 12:30pm from the Tha Ton Pier for a 4-hour journey (400B per person; a minimum number of passengers required for departure).

BY BUS   Buses and minivans depart Bangkok nearly every hour daily from Bangkok's **Northern Bus Terminal** (© **02936-2841**) to Chiang Rai (trip time 11 hrs.; fare 500–1,000B). Buses leave hourly between 6am and 7:30pm from **Chiang Mai's Arcade Bus Terminal** (© **05324-2664**; trip time 3½ hrs.; fare 106B non-A/C; 280B VIP). Chiang Rai has two bus terminals. The original is Khon Song Bus Terminal (© **05371-1224**), but most operators call it the **Old Bus Station** or Terminal 1. It is near the night market in the center of town. Today, most busses, including those from Bangkok, now stop at an unnamed **New Bus Station** or Terminal 2 (© **05377-3989**) 6km (3½ miles) south of town. A 15-minute shuttle service (15B) operates between the two stations, and tuk-tuks and *samlor* (motorized pedicabs) connect to hotels for 30B to 100B, depending on which station you arrive at and the hotel's location.

BY CAR   The fast, not particularly scenic, route from Bangkok is Highway 1 North. It leads direct to Chiang Rai in 11 hours. The direct route from Chiang Mai, along Route 118, takes 3½ hours. A slower, but attractive approach on blacktop mountain roads, is on Route 107 north from Chiang Mai to Fang, and then Route 109 east to Highway 1. That journey is 4½ hours.

VISITOR INFORMATION
The **TAT** (© **05374-4674**) is located at 448/16 Singhaklai Rd., near Wat Phra Singh on the north side of town; and the **Tourist Police** (© **1155**) are located on Phaholyothin Road, by the junction with Wisetwiang Road. Either the TAT office or your hotel can provide you with a map of the town.

CITY LAYOUT & GETTING AROUND
BY SAMLOR OR TUK-TUK   You'll probably find walking to be the best way to get around town as the center is so small. However, there are *samlors* (a Thai rickshaw), and tuk-tuks charge between around town that charge 40B to 100B for in-town trips.

BY BUS   Chiang Rai's frequent local buses are the easiest and cheapest way to get to nearby cities. All leave from the bus station on Prasopsuk Road and advanced booking of more than a day isn't necessary.

BY MOTORCYCLE   Motorcycling is another good way to get out of town. There are bike shops on nearly every corner, and they're indistinguishable from each other in price and types of bikes. Expect to pay 150B per day for a 100cc motorbike.

BY CAR   **Budget** and **Avis** have offices at the airport and can arrange hotel drop-offs for an additional fee if needed. Both rental companies have a standard rate of 1,500B per day for an automatic compact car.

FAST FACTS

Several **bank** exchanges are located on Phaholyothin Road in the center of town and are open daily from 8:30am to 10pm, while **ATMs** are easy to spot around the city. The **post office** is on Utarakit Road, 2 blocks north of the Clock Tower. Several branches of the popular **Boots** pharmacy are around town, and this is your go-to for topical creams, pain medication, antibiotics, and the like. English-speaking pharmacists are generally available.

Exploring Chiang Rai

Chiang Rai is a small city, with most services grouped around the main north–south street, Phaholyothin Road, while Singhaklai Road is the main artery on the north side of town, parallel to the river. Chiang Rai itself has few must-do attractions, so a casual walk around the city will take a few hours.

Direction-givers usually orient restaurants, markets, and other attractions based on their proximity to two local attractions: the Clock Tower and Night Market. The gilded **Clock Tower** in the city center is at the junction of Banphaprakan and Jet Yod Roads. It was designed in 2008 by local artist Chalermchai Kositpipat of White Temple fame (see p. 379) and serves as a landmark and traffic circle. Every night it is briefly illuminated with multicolored lights and accompanying music nightly at 7, 8, and 9pm. If you happen to be by the Clock Tower, stop for the "show", otherwise it's not worth deviating off track.

The other reference point is the **Night Market** is on Phaholyothin Road, next to the bus station, and the **Saturday Walking Street** on Thanalai Road, running east to west from just south of the King Mengrai statue. Both the walking street and the night market will feel familiar to counterparts in Bangkok and Chiang Mai. But as with most things, the further from the urban center you go, the more local the patrons and the commodities tend to be. That's true here, but if you arrive at the Night Market thinking of it more as cultural anthropology rather than a shopping destination, your expectations will be in line with reality.

Baan Dum (Temple) ★   In bizarre, eerie contrast to the white Wat Rong Khun (p. 379) is this all-black multi-home complex that is an interpretation of hell by the Thai artist Thawan Duchanee. The main temple-like building is centered around a wooden dining table with chairs made from antlers; shockingly long snake skins act as a runner. Taxidermy is used in nearly every design decision, although the artist claims the animals were collected after dying of natural causes. However, the bones, skins, and dark colors coalesce into something creepily intriguing. There are no signs in English or Thai to explain the artist's thoughts, which will leave you making "heads or tails" of it yourself.

Off Route 1 13km north of Chiang Rai. Daily 9am–noon; 1–5pm.

Hilltribe Museum & Education Center (Museum) ★★   Especially if you plan to visit one of the region's hill-tribe communities, devote an hour-and-a-half to learning more about these minority groups, their struggles, and their beliefs. Kick things off with a 20-minute slideshow on the hill tribes before wandering through the informative collections which shows native clothing and explains the traditions that each group follows. The museum is run by the **Population & Community Development Association (PDA),** and it's worth asking a staff member to speak about the group's community efforts and offering an opinion on what the future looks like for hill tribe people. Book a trekking tour with PDA while you're there; they have superb programs, ones are beyond the norm in terms of both ethics and service— see p. 51.

620/1 Thanalai Rd., 3rd floor PDA building. www.pdacr.org. © **05374-0088.** 50B. Mon–Fri 8:30am–6pm, Sat–Sun and holidays 10am–6pm.

Oub Kham Museum (Museum) ★★   Small but mighty, this museum on the outskirts of town packs more than a 1,000-years of Tai and Lanna history and artifacts into its displays. The private collection belongs to curator Julasak Suriyachai, a descent of a Lanna royal family, and he regularly leads tours himself—just ask. Set among several historic buildings the museum contains impressive coronation robes from 15th-century Lanna kings and a 400-year-old golden throne of the Tai Yai royals from the Shan State in Myanmar.

81/1 Nakhai. © **05371-7433.** www.oubkhammuseum.com. Only in Thai. 300B adults; 100B children. Daily 8am–5pm.

Wat Doi Tong (Temple) ★   Doi Tong is the tallest mountain in Chiang Rai at 6,560-feet above sea level and near the summit of the mountain sits this Burmese-style temple. Journey up a steep staircase off Kaisornrasit Road for a panoramic overview of the town and the Mae Kok valley, along with vivid sunset vistas. It is said that King Mengrai himself chose the site for his new Lanna capital from this very hill. The circle of columns at the top of the hill surrounds the city's new *lak muang* (city pillar), built to commemorate the 725th anniversary of the city and the late King Bhumibol's 60th birthday. (You can see the old wooden *lak muang* in the *viharn* of the *wat*.)

Off Kaisornrasit Road. © **05371-7433.** Daily 8am–dusk.

Wat Phra Kaew (Temple) ★★   The most sacred temple in Chiang Rai, it once housed the Emerald Buddha (made of jade) that is now at Bangkok's Grand Place (see p. 106) in a temple of the same name. Near its Lanna-style chapel is the *chedi,* which (according to legend) was struck by lightning in

1434 to reveal the precious green jasper Buddha. There is now a green jade replica of the image on display in a pavilion behind the *viharn*. The murals depict the journey of the original Emerald Buddha and tells the story of how the current one arrived in Chiang Rai. View Lanna artifacts in the adjacent wooden museum. Two blocks east is **Wat Phra Sing** (donation suggested; daily 7am–dusk), a restored temple dating back to the 14th-century that is known for its replica of the Phra Sihing Buddha, a highly revered Theravada Buddhist image; the original was moved to Chiang Mai's Wat Phra Singh.

Off Trairat Road on the northwest side of town. ✆ **05371-1385.** Temple daily 7am–7pm; museum daily 9am–5pm.

Wat Rong Khun (Temple) ★★ Make the 13km (8 miles) journey south on Highway 1 to visit Wat Rong Khun, aka The White Temple. Upon approach, the dazzling white structure shimmers in the sun thanks to mirrored mosaics on the white exterior. Cross the footbridge above a pond filled with reaching hands (a symbol of desire) before entering the temple. Buddha's life story typically adorns the walls of most temples, but here, contemporary takes on pop culture are on the walls. See if you can find Harry Potter reaching for the golden snitch, Hello Kitty, Keanu Reeves' Neo from *The Matrix,* and darker elements like an airplane crashing into the Twin Towers on September 11th. The temple is the brainchild of Thai artist Chalermchai Kositpipat (the artist behind the Clock Tower in the center of town), and he and a team of 40-plus artists started the project in 1997. Comparisons are often made between Chalermchai and Antoni Gaudí because the Thai artist doesn't expect the temple to be finished in his lifetime, which, since he was born in 1955, means a lot of construction is left.

Off Route 1. No phone. 50B for foreign tourists. Daily 8am–5pm.

Organized Tours

Most of the **hill-tribe villages** within close range of Chiang Rai have long ago been set up for routine visits by group tours; a clear example is the "Union of Hilltribe Villages," located north of the Chiang Rai airport, where members of various tribes are herded together for the convenience of tourists. The vibe in such villages is more like a human zoo than an insight into a disappearing lifestyle.

That being said, there are ethical ways to experience the diversity of the hill tribe cultures, like joining the **Population and Community Development Association** ★★★ (www.pdacr.com; ✆ **05374-0088**) for authentic hill-tribe encounters. A professional and experienced organization it offers an array of tours with particular attention given to ethical interactions with hill-tribe people. **Longer treks** are a 2- to 3-day sojourns with overnight stays with Akha and Lahu tribes. PDA offers tours where tribal people participate in the tourism by offering guided tours instead of simply watching Westerns walk around their village. Half-day tours, sightseeing trips, and day trips to Myanmar and Laos are also on the menu.

Where to Stay

A large selection of accommodations is available in every price range. Most mid-range hotels are within walking distance of the sights and shopping, while fancier resorts are located further afield, by the river or out of town.

MODERATE

Bambuh Boutique Homestay ★★★ This idyllic guesthouse is encircled by verdant rice paddies and gardens, with mountain views in the distance. So, not right in the heart of the city (it's about 10 km out), but the Thai-Dutch couple who run the hotel (consummate hosts!) work with a few taxis to get their guests into town for a reasonable amount. Four guestrooms are in a stilted traditional Thai home, the other two are in a detached house surrounded by a lotus pond. All are handsomely turned out, with comfortable platform beds, pieces of Thai art, fine wooden furnishings and bathrooms tiled with river stones. For those who do yoga, there's a view-rich deck on which to practice sun salutations. The owners also supply free bikes for exploring the surrounding countryside—take advantage of them, as the area is exquisite.
82 Moo 3, Tambon Naglea. www.bambuhboutique.com. ℗ **086919-3370.** 6 units. 1,250B–1,950B double. Guests must be at least 15-years-old to stay. **Amenities:** Restaurant; in-room massages; Wi-Fi (free).

The Imperial River House Resort ★ The River House is a leafy campus just across the river from town, with loaner bikes and a free shuttle available for guests. Set around a large pool flanked by laughing elephant sculptures, rooms here feature wooden built-ins, furniture, and flooring, meaning that it feels very Thai—though it is all a bit dated, unfortunately. Still, the 39 rooms are all well maintained and roomy, and the views from the second-floor rooms overlook farmers' fields and the riverside. There are also a few more basic cottages on the grounds, surrounded by greenery. The resort has a full-service spa for Thai-style pampering.
482 Moo 4, Mae Kok Rd. www.imperialriverhouse.com. ℗ **05375-0829.** 39 units. From 1,600B double. **Amenities:** Restaurant; bar; outdoor pool; health club; spa; room service; Wi-Fi (free).

The Legend Chiang Rai ★★ A modern Lanna vibe permeates this elegant, understated resort along the river. Rooms feature rustic stone floors and beds evocatively draped in netting. Each is flooded with light though pricier rooms overlook the river, while others line a narrow garden pond. All have pleasant indoor and outdoor sitting areas and include large shower areas, some with a soaking tubs. In the common areas you'll find an infinity pool and the spa's outdoor *salas* on the riverbank, plus indoor treatment rooms. The Legend may not have the reputation, or all the facilities, of the international chain hotels, but offers a good dollop of charm at a slightly lower nightly rate.
124/15 Moo 21 Kohloy Rd. www.thelegend-chiangrai.com. ℗ **05391-0400.** 78 units. 3,900B–5,900B studio; 8,100B pool villa. **Amenities:** Restaurant; bar; outdoor pool; spa; room service; babysitting; Wi-Fi (free)

Le Méridien ★★   In a picturesque setting by the Kok River a few kilometers from the town center, Le Méridien has pampering down to a fine art. The service is all smiles, all the time, and very helpful. Rooms are huge and newly renovated, with pine floors, a trendy gray, black and white color palate (love the geometric wallpapers), and useable desks. There are plenty of activities on-site, such as spa treatments, yoga classes, and a well-equipped gym. The helpful tour desk can arrange excursions, while a free shuttle service is available for trips in to town.

221/2 Moo 20 Kwaewai Rd. www.lemeridienchiangrai.com. ℂ **05360-3333.** 159 units. 2,500B–5,000B double; 10,000B–14,000B suite. **Amenities:** 2 restaurants; 2 bars; outdoor pool; spa; free shuttle; Wi-Fi (450B per day).

INEXPENSIVE

Ben Guesthouse ★★   Ben Guesthouse is an absolute gem for budget-savvy travelers, and it ticks all the boxes: it's spotless, in a good location, and has real personality. Private rooms with hot shower bathrooms (almost always private) are spread across a multi-floor, teak wood house resplendent with carvings and period-piece art. For those looking to save a lot, there are affordable fan-cooled rooms; those who can splash out choose suites with air-con (there are loads of options in between). Enjoy a refreshing dip in the pool or rent a motorbike on-site for exploration around town, which is 1.2km away.

351/10 Soi 4, Sankhongnoi Rd. www.benguesthousechiangrai.com. ℂ **05371-6775.** 28 units. 400B single (shared bathroom); 900B superior; 1,500B suite. **Amenities:** Restaurant; outdoor pool; Wi-Fi (free).

Bura Resort ★★★   Those who have journeyed to Chiang Rai to connect with nature will find a welcoming, tranquil home at Bura Resort. Decks from some of the rooms and the restaurant overlook a rolling waterfall and the flower-covered grounds. Generous-sized rooms draw on the nature theme, too, in a way that's quite unusual: The wooden backboards of the beds sweep up and over the walls in a scalloped and wavy pattern, echoing the look of the curvy built in's across the room. It's a stunning effect. Bathrooms are also quite handsome, featuring deep soaking tubs and rainfall showers. The staff are as kind as can be and go out of their way to make every guest feel important.

224 Moo 13, Ban Hua Fai, Tambol Bandoo. www.bura-resort.gochiangraihotels.com/en. ℂ **082192-4518.** 8 units. 1,800B–2,500B double. **Amenities:** Restaurant; Wi-Fi (free)

Wiang Inn ★   We're recommending this one with some caveats. The exterior feels very 1970s Americana, and is off-putting. The hotel is also designed to cater to the business conference crowd, and large tour groups, which means that service can be a bit impersonal. But on the plus side, tastefully decorated rooms have Lanna-style murals over the beds and everything you'll need for a good night's sleep, like a cozy bed and comfortable layout. Plus the price is a great the value for money, and the location can't be beat, right in the heart of the city.

893 Phaholyothin Rd. www.wianginn.com. ℂ **05371-1533.** 260 units. 2,800B–3,200B double; from 6,000B suite. **Amenities:** Restaurant; bar; outdoor pool; room service; babysitting; Wi-Fi (free)

Where to Eat

Be sure to sample some northern dishes, such as the *kaeng hang lay* or Burmese-style pork curry, the lychees, which ripen in April, and the sweet pineapple wine.

Cabbages & Condoms ★ THAI   The northern branch of this community-focused restaurant was opened by the Population & Community Development Association to promote their humanitarian work in the region. The extensive Thai menu is tasty and features local catfish. They play host to lots of events and live bands, and an exhibit space upstairs (see "Exploring Chiang Rai," above). It gets hectic on Saturdays when the Walking Street is in full swing in front.

620/25 Thanalai Rd. © **05371-9167.** Main courses 80B–200B. Daily 10am–11pm.

Khao Soi Phor Jai ★★ THAI   The Bumese-style curry *khao soi* is an unforgettable dish. If you haven't had a bowl (or need more!) Khao Soi Phor Jai makes one of the best in town. And don't just take my word for it: This place is filled with cab drivers coming for a quick lunch and locals loudly slurping. There isn't a sign in English, but the bright blue and white walls make this open-air shop is easy to spot. Lunchtime is crowded but tables turn over quickly.

1023/2 Jetyod Rd. © **05371-2935.** Main courses 40B–60B. Daily 7am–4pm.

Lab Sanam Keela ★★ THAI   This open-air shop is popular with locals and foreign visitors looking for authentic flavors not found in the area's hotel restaurants. Northern specialties are the menu highlights, so expect minced meat salads with baskets of local herbs and spicy dipping sauces. Yang ruam is a mixed meat salad and one of the restaurant's specialties; it's a mix of mostly pork, with everything from loin to intestines, or beef. The meats on the mixed plates are also delish: Smoky and sweet, they pair well with the accompanying spicy dipping sauce. Steamed fish overloaded with roasted garlic and a side of sticky rice is another must-have dish. Photo menus help to make ordering easier.

123 Moo 22. © **087173-2498.** Dishes 90B–199B. Daily 10am–9pm.

The Night Market/Food Stalls ★ THAI   Every night after 6pm, the cavernous, tin-roofed Municipal Market at the town center comes alive with dozens of chrome-plated food stalls that serve steamed, grilled, and fried Thai treats. This is where locals meet, greet, and eat. It's really the heart of the town (and a busy mercantile market as well), so don't miss a wander here even if you're not into street-eats.

Phu Lae ★ THAI   The teak wood tables at this simple but clean restaurant are often filled with locals coming here for one dish: the Burmese curry with pork. Richly seasoned but tender, it's the best version in town. That being said, the homemade Isan-style sausage, sun-dried pork, and *tom yum* soup are also quite tasty, so order a few different types of dishes to share.

673/1 Thanalai Rd. © **05360-0500.** Dishes 80B–300B. Daily 11:30am–3pm and 5:30–11pm.

Shopping & Nightlife

Local markets and walking streets are the name of the game in this town for both shopping and nightlife options. Luckily, midweek visitors are rewarded as equally as weekenders, so there is always something to shop for and explore. *Our tip*: If you've seen one market in Chiang Rai, you've pretty much seen them all. Most of the vendors double-down on the market scene and make appearances at the pedestrian-only **Saturday Walking Street** (4–10pm on Thanalai Road) as well as the **Sunday Night Market** (6–9pm on Sankhongnoi Road), and the ever-present **Night Market** (6–11pm), a daily bazaar adjacent to the bus terminal. These markets are a fraction of the size of the mother of all markets—Bangkok's Chatuchak Weekend Market (p. 127)— and are more manageable than Chiang Mai's **Night Bazaar** (p. 345), so browsing the stalls can be done at a leisurely pace. Touristy souvenirs are omnipresent but Hill-tribe handicrafts are also available, though you'll get better deals (and your money will help the local people more) when buying directly from the tribe on a trekking tour (see p. 51). If you're not planning on a tour, then go ahead and stock up here.

About 12km north of Chiang Rai on the road to Mae Sai is a gem of a pottery place called **Doy Din Dang Pottery** ★★ (49 Moo 6; www.dddpottery. com; ✆ **05370-5291**). Here, the lush grounds of the multi-building showroom are an inspiration to the Thai artists who craft wheel-thrown pieces finished in traditional celadon or contemporary styles. The English-speaking staff can help arrange shipping, and there is a nice coffee shop on the property.

Jetyod Road is the main drag for beer bars and watering holes that all start to blur together—especially after a beer or two. They essentially offer the same thing, which is an open-air place to grab a cold Singha, super-sweet Long Island Iced Tea, or an unbalanced vodka soda. Do a lap around the block to survey the land, then head to **Cat Bar** (1013/1 Jetyod Rd.; 5pm–1am) for pool and live music or **Peace House Bar** (1013/3 Jetyod Rd.; approximately 5pm–1am) for reggae and impromptu jam sessions.

Chiang Rai to Mae Sai

Mae Sai—the northernmost point in Thailand and 60km (37 miles) north of Chiang Rai—is a popular "visa run" town where foreign residents go to renew their visas by crossing into Myanmar at the edge of town. This cross-border trip is the liveliest part of Mae Sai, and as such, most visitors coming from Chiang Rai give the dusty little border town of Mae Sai a miss, choosing to move onward and head instead for Chiang Saen and the Golden Triangle. Since gambling is illegal in Thailand, locals will cross into the tiny Burmese town of **Thachilek** to spend their baht at a trio of casinos.

Back in Mae Sai, the town's market is a hotbed of Thai-Burmese trade where the region's hill-tribe people, citizens from Myanmar, and local Thai come together. You can't miss this **busy market** right at the border gate to Myanmar. Throngs of stalls sell stock-standard souvenirs, but the primary market draw is silver jewelry brought from Myanmar and exotic gemstones like Burmese rubies, jade, and cornflower blue sapphires. Buyer beware: There are no GIA certificates and, more often than not, the gems are a scam. But looking is fun! In the winter, the real gem is the ripe, sweet strawberries grown in Mae Sai.

If you need a place to crash for the night, the hotel used mostly by Thai tourists and gem traders is the **Wang Thong Hotel** (299 Phaholyothin Rd.; ✆ **05373-3389; 900B**). It offers little in the way of charm but has spacious rooms, a pool, and a restaurant-bar. Accommodations are better further afield in Chiang Saen.

THE GOLDEN TRIANGLE REGION

935km (581 miles) NE of Bangkok; 239km (149 miles) NE of Chiang Mai

The fabled Golden Triangle is the point where Thailand, Myanmar, and Laos meet at the confluence of the broad, slow, and silted Mekong and Ruak rivers. They create Thailand's northern border, separating it from overgrown jungle patches of Myanmar to the west and forested, hilly Laos to the east. Most know the region for its host of illicit activities and trade. The region's involvement in the production of opium dates back to the early 20th century, and for more than 100 years, the area was the leading grower of poppy crops. The geographical proximity facilitated largely unchecked overland drug transportation of opium and heroin in its first steps toward international markets.

To understand the drug culture of the region is to know the most famous trader of opium in Southeast Asia: Khun Sa, a Shan-born drug lord who ran the region's opium monopoly from the mid-1970s. In 1996, with U.S. drug agents closing in, he self-surrendered to Burmese officials who refused to extradite him. He died in Yangon in 2007, but his surrender marked the end of the opium trade in the region. In 2018, Afghanistan's Golden Crescent is the leading producer of opium. Modern-day Thailand's opium trade has essentially vanished—thanks in part to government programs that encourage alternative crops. So, while some illegal activity goes unchecked, the area is hardly dangerous, and any tourist drug encounters in this region are contained to museum displays. Myanmar, however, is facing an epidemic of a more modern enemy: methamphetamines. And a 2016 study by the United Nations Office of Drugs & Crime reported that clandestine makeshift labs in the region were worth an estimated US$40 billion.

Today, Golden Triangle is still the most commonplace, blanket term for the region. Several villages dot the area with noteworthy places to explore.

Chiang Saen

The village of Chiang Saen, the best gateway to the Golden Triangle area, has a sleepy, rural charm as if the waters of the Mekong carry a palpable calm from nearby Myanmar and Laos. The road from Chiang Rai (59km/37 miles) follows the small Mae Nam Chan River past coconut groves and lush rice paddies. Poinsettias and gladioli decorate thatched Lanna Thai houses with peaked rooflines that extend into Xs like buffalo horns. This elaborately carved roof decoration, called a *galae*, is a defining aspect of Lanna architecture.

Little Chiang Saen, the birthplace of expansionary King Mengrai, was abandoned for the new Lanna capitals of Chiang Rai followed by Chiang Mai, in the 13th century. The Burmese sacked the town in 1588, and a fire took out what was left of the ancient ruins in 1786. Today, the rural pace, decaying regal *wats*, crumbling fort walls, and an overgrown moat contributes to its appeal.

Chiang Saen is a quaint and pleasant place to spend time, unlike **Sop Ruak,** the Thai town at the junction of the Kok and Mekong rivers, which is a long and disappointing row of souvenir stalls, with a few "Golden Triangle" signs for photo ops. If you're staying either of the region's most opulent resorts—**Four Seasons Tented Camp** (p. 388) or the **Anantara Golden Triangle** (p. 388)—you'll depart from Sop Ruak. While there, stand at the crook of the river and see Laos to the right and Myanmar on the left. When the river is low, a large sandbar appears that is apparently unclaimed by any authority.

A common route here is to leave from Chiang Rai by car (or motorbike) and travel directly north to the Burmese border town of **Mae Sai,** where locals trade goods at a bustling market. Then follow the Mekong River going east along the border, making a stop at **The Hall of Opium,** and the town of **Sop Ruak,** before catching the museum and many temples of Chiang Saen. If you're overnighting in the area, the fanciest places are in the Golden Triangle proper.

Essentials

ARRIVING

BY BUS   Buses from **Chiang Rai's Bus Terminal** (p. 362) leave from 6am to 7pm (trip time 1½ hrs.; fare 38B). The bus drops you on Chiang Saen's main street, where the museum and main temples are within walking distance.

BY CAR   Take the Superhighway Route 110 north from Chiang Rai to Mae Chan, and then route 1016 northeast to Chiang Saen.

CITY LAYOUT

Route 1016 is the village's main street, also called Phaholyothin Road, which terminates at the Mekong River. Along the river road, there are a few guest-houses, eateries, and souvenir, clothing, and food stalls.

The Golden Triangle and the town of Sob Ruak are just 10km (6¼ miles) north of the town of Chiang Saen, and the choicest accommodations (the Anantara and the Four Seasons) is just a few clicks west from there. Mae Sai is 30km (19 miles) west of the Golden Triangle.

GETTING AROUND

ON FOOT   There's so little traffic it is a pleasure to walk around here; the main temple ruins are within a 15-minute walk of the town center, though you'll need transport for the more far-flung sites.

BY BICYCLE & MOTORCYCLE   It's a swell bike ride (45 min.) from Chiang Saen to the prime nearby attraction, the Golden Triangle. The roads are well paved and pretty flat, though you should keep an eye out for speeding vehicles. Bicycles are also ideal for exploring Chiang Saen's more remote temples. The main road is littered with shops renting bikes for 50B per day, and 100cc motorcycles for 200B per day.

BY SONGTAEW   Public *songtaews* make frequent trips between Chiang Saen and the Golden Triangle for about 50B. They leave from the eastern end of Phaholyothin Road, near the river.

BY LONGTAIL BOAT   Longtail boat captains hang out by the river and offer Golden Triangle tours for as little as 500B per boat (seating five) per hour. Typical routes gaze at the Myanmar plots of land before stopping at the Lao island of Don Sao and plying the river towards the Golden Triangle. Any pier along the river will have boats waiting to be booked; prices are fixed, and a 50B tip is appreciated for a smooth ride.

FAST FACTS

A **Siam Commercial Bank** is in the middle of the town's main street, Phaholyothin Road, Route 1016. It's close to the **bus stop,** the **post and telegram office** (with no overseas service and few local telephones), the **police station,** and such attractions as the Chiang Saen National Museum. There are **currency exchange** booths at the Golden Triangle.

Exploring Chiang Saen & the Golden Triangle

Allow half a day to see all of Chiang Saen's historical sights before exploring the Golden Triangle. To help with orientation, make the museum your first stop. There is a good map of local historical sites on the second floor.

The **Chiang Saen National Museum** ★ (702 Phaholyothin Rd.; ✆ 05377-7102; Wed–Sun 8:30am–4:30pm; admission 100B) houses a small but very fine collection of this region's historical and ethnographic products. Spend an hour viewing the bronze and stone Buddha images (c. 15th to 17th centuries), pottery from Sukhothai-era kiln sites, and handicrafts and cultural items of local hill tribes. Burmese-style lacquerware, Buddha images, and wood carvings reinforce the similarities seen between Chiang Saen and its spiritual counterpart, Pagan (in Myanmar).

Wat Pa Sak ★★, the best-preserved *wat* here, is set in a landscaped historical park that contains a large, square-based stupa and six smaller *chedis* and temples. The park preserves what's left of the compound's 1,000 teak trees. The *wat* is said to have been constructed in 1295 by King Saen Phu to house relics of the Buddha, though some historians believe its ornate combination of Sukhothai and Pagan styles dates it later. The historical park is about 200m (656 ft.) west of the Chiang Saen Gate (at the entrance to the village). It is open daily 8am to 5pm; admission is 50B.

The area's second-oldest *wat* is still an active Buddhist monastery, and it is located right next to the National Museum. **Wat Phra That Chedi Luang** has a huge brick *chedi*, often draped in moss, that dominates the main street—and it should; it's the tallest religious structure in the Chiang Rai region. The *wat* complex was established in 1331 under the reign of King Saen Phu and was rebuilt in 1515 by King Muang Kaeo. The old brick foundations of the *viharn*, now supporting a very large, plaster seated Buddha flanked by smaller ones, are all that remain. Small bronze and stucco Buddhas excavated from the site are now in the museum. It is open daily from 8am to dusk. Admission is free.

There are several other *wats* of note in the town center. **Wat Mung Muang** is the 15th-century square-based stupa seen next to the post office. Above the bell-shaped *chedi* are four small stupas. Across the street, you can see the bell-shaped *chedi* from **Wat Phra Buat.** It's rumored to have been built by the prince of Chiang Saen in 1346, though historians believe it is of the same period as Mung Muang.

If you're exploring by bicycle or motorbike, head for **Wat Phra That Chom Kitti ★**, in the northwest corner of the Old City. Its main feature is a slender, slightly leaning, 25-m (82-ft.) *chedi*, but the site is also worth visiting, as it sits on a small hill and offers great views of the town and across the river to Laos.

Sop Ruak

This is the so-called center of the Golden Triangle and where to get a look at at the home of ethnic hill-tribes and their legendary opium trade. Sop Ruak doesn't offer much in the way of sites to see or things to do, but what it does have is a can't-miss pair of museums that center on the geopolitical curiosity of the opium trade. The pinhead size town is made of thatch roof souvenir stalls, cheap noodle shops with river views, and large, fancy hotels.

The Hall of Opium ★★★ MUSEUM   Founded by the Mae Fah Luang Foundation, a non-profit group that works to improve the lives of rural people in Thailand, the museum is under royal patronage. A sprawling, lush complex overlooks the Mekong; plan for 2-ish hours to tour the facilities. You enter the museum and follow a long corridor through a mountain, which is designed to create an "opium experience." Having never tried opium, it is hard to tell if it's successful or gimmicky. Nevertheless, in the dark, all you can see are murals portraying the pain and anguish of addiction. You then emerge in a grand atrium with a giant glowing golden triangle (the irony is a bit much) and a field of poppies. From there a multimedia romp of films and displays tell of the 5,000-year history of the drug, its vital importance in British and international trade with China and how the plant is cultivated. The many conflicts over opium are covered, as is the drug's influx into Thailand, and recent efforts to suppress smuggling and address rampant addiction throughout the region. There is even a self-aware exhibit on the global epidemic of methamphetamines.

Media-savvy exhibits are in both Thai and English. The "Hall of Excuses" at the end highlights (or lowlights?) many of the world's most well-known addicts and the museum ends in the "Hall of Reflections," where guests are invited to ruminate on their experience. And it *is* an experience, and there's nothing like it anywhere else in Thailand.

11km/6¾ miles north of Chiang Saen. ⓒ **05378-4444.** Admission 200B. Tues–Sun 8:30am–4pm.

House of Opium ★ MUSEUM If the massive Hall of Opium only whets your thirst for more knowledge, then stop here for a deep dive into the world of poppies. If, however, you've overdosed (!) on opium knowledge from the main museum, go ahead and give this one a pass. Its most interesting exhibits showcase the tools and farming equipment used to plant and harvest poppy seeds, and the containers used for trading opium. Drug paraphernalia like pipes, scales, weights, and scrapers are on display as well.

212 House of Opium, Chiang Saen (just opposite the golden Buddha, at the very heart of the Golden Triangle). ℭ **05378-4060.** Admission 50B. Daily 7am–7pm.

Where to Stay

If budget allows, there are two once-in-a-lifetime resorts in the Golden Triangle area that are worth every baht. A nice in-town option and a mountainous eco-lodge are other standouts.

EXPENSIVE

Anantara Resort & Spa Golden Triangle ★★★ The Anantara is a triumph of upscale, but local design. Every detail reminds you that you're in the scenic hill-tribe region; and the resort's elegance and style are heightened by locally produced weavings and carved teak panels. The balconied rooms have splendid views of Thailand, Laos, and Myanmar, and are so spacious and private that you will feel utterly secluded. Tiled foyers lead to large bathrooms with the biggest bathtubs we've ever encountered, and bedrooms are furnished in teak and traditional fabrics. The hotel supports a small elephant camp, which offers natural and informative encounters with these gentle giants under the expert watch of local elephant caretakers and experts. Grab a sundowner at the Elephant Bar and Opium Terrace before enjoying the resort's culinary magic.

229 Moo 1, Chiang Saen (above river, 11km/6¾ miles north of Chiang Saen). http://goldentriangle.anantara.com. ℭ **05378-4084.** 77 units. From 30,000B double. **Amenities:** 2 restaurants; lounge and bar; outdoor pool; outdoor tennis courts; health club; spa; room service; babysitting; Wi-Fi (free).

Four Seasons Tented Camp ★★★ This once-in-a-lifetime stay regularly makes media roundups of best resorts in the world—and for good reason. If you want to imagine that you're a 19th-century explorer in the wilds of Asia, but with all modern comforts, here's the place to indulge yourself. The resort's 15 tents, all enjoying total privacy, are tents only in name. These palatial lodgings on a hillside above the Golden Triangle include freestanding brass bathtubs atop smooth wood floors, outdoor showers, full bars, and explorer-themed touches like telescopes. This resort is all-inclusive, so the rates include everything, from fantastic gourmet meals to spa treatments, and boat trips on the river to mahout training classes at the resort's elephant camp. Have a drink at Burma Bar where Myanmar is close enough to touch, sample local wines in the wine and cheese vault, enjoy pampering treatments at the outdoor spa, or enjoy the idyllic sounds of elephants playing and eating in the forest below. It is overwhelming and memorable.

Next to Anantara on the Ruak River. www.fourseasons.com/goldentriangle. ℂ **05391-0200.** 15 units. From 80,000B tent. **Amenities:** Restaurant (meals included); bar; spa; outdoor pool; Wi-Fi (free); tours (free); elephant camp (included). Children must be 10-years-old to stay at the camp.

MODERATE

The Imperial Golden Triangle Resort ★ If travel plans have led to an overnight in the souvenir village of Sop Ruak, this hotel is the best option by far. Modern, spacious guest rooms with pastel and rattan decor have large balconies, and the more expensive rooms overlook the confluence of the town's three famous rivers. Bathrooms are adequate, roomy, and functional but they're overdue for an upgrade. The bar here is a nice place to head for sundowners, even if you're not a hotel guest.

222 Golden Triangle (in Sob Ruak, 11km/6¾ miles north of Chiang Saen). www.imperialhotels.com. ℂ **05378-4001.** 73 units. 960B–2,719B double; from 4,862B suite. **Amenities:** Restaurant; bar; lounge; outdoor pool; Wi-Fi (free).

Lanjia Lodge ★★ Get lost in nature at the eco-friendly, community-based lodge in the mountains of northern Thailand. The four bamboo houses and guests are attentively looked after by local hill-tribe people, and rates include sustainable and complimentary tours for guests to experience tribal life. Fan-cooled rooms are comfortably simple, with billowing mosquito nets hovering over beds decorated with hill-tribe fabrics. Lanjia means peaceful in the Hmong language, and that's exactly what this retreat offers. A portion of the fees for each stay help support community projects that improve the lives of local villagers.

347 Kiewkan Village, Moo 6. www.asian-oasis.com/chiang-rai-thailand. ℂ **083540-9529.** 16 units. 4,500B double. **Amenities:** Restaurant; tours; Wi-Fi (free).

EXPLORING ISAN: THAILAND'S FRONTIER

13

The 20 provinces of northeastern Thailand are collectively called Isan (*e-sahn*) and account for roughly one-third of the country's landmass, and a third of the population. Bordered by Laos to the north and east (along the Mekong) and by Cambodia to the south, the area resembles Laos and is quite distinct from mainstream Thai culture (many joke about *Prathet Isan*, or "the Nation of Isan," for its unique culture, and stubbornly snail-like pace). Life can hard on the scorched plains of Isan, but the friendly people of this region welcome travelers warmly—you'll experience something along the lines of America's southern hospitality. There are lovely river towns, finely made crafts, and fiery food. The areas in the far north and along the Mekong are particularly worth the trip.

That being said, Isan doesn't get the tourist numbers that other parts of the country get; most of its towns are small with little night-life. However, the tides are beginning to shift as more decide to visit the region's important archaeological sites (from the Khmer period) and try its famous local cuisine. A fresh crop of riverside retreats and boutique hotels, run by media-savvy thirtysomethings, represent a new wave of entrepreneurs looking to entice tourists and backpackers who are on the hunt for "the new Chiang Mai," and a glimpse into laid-back and authentic Thailand. Most importantly, budget airlines just recently began offering daily flights from Bangkok across the region making it easier than ever before to get here.

The region is best explored by car, allowing for the piquant lure of the region's famed and fiery cuisine to merit roadside stops. And if, as we suspect, you fall in love with a spicy plate of *larb*, a regional foodie favorite, or the tranquility of watching local fisherman navigate the placid Mekong, the general availably of accommodations encourages spontaneity in exploring. While some provinces offer more attractions than others (more on that below), Isan is ideally suited for return visitors to The Kingdom who have previously ticked the boxes of Bangkok and Chiang Mai but are looking for a deeper appreciation and understanding of Thailand and its people. The weather is especially hot in Isan but follows a pattern much like the rest of Thailand: It's coolest from November to February; hot and dry from March to May; and rainy from June to October. Windswept, flat, and infertile in parts, but verdant along the Mekong, the region's farmers live a tough life, and many families send relatives to urban parts of Thailand to earn wages to send back to Isan. Strike up a conversation with a cab driver in Bangkok, or resort staff in the south, and odds are good that they'll hail from Isan, and you'll be rewarded with an ear-to-ear smile for knowing just a little bit about the region.

Isan's major cities, which, for the sake of clarity, are defined as the ones with airports, offer little more than a place to bed down and onward transportation. Hard-earned tourist dollars and vacation days are better spent exploring the countryside and getting a real taste of the region. For many, Isan serves as an ideal jumping-off point to nearby Laos.

ESSENTIALS

Airlines covering this region include **Thai Airways** (www.thaiairways.com; ✆ 02356-1111), **Nok Air** (www.nokair.com; ✆ 1318), **Bangkok Airways** (www.bangkokair.com; ✆ 1771), and **AirAsia** (www.airasia.com; ✆ 02515-9999). There are also regular bus and train connections throughout Isan. In more remote parts, however, buses are slow and won't stop near sights, so we recommend arranging a tour, renting your own vehicle, or hiring a driver with car. The latter is a relatively affordable proposition; expect to pay about 2,000B per day, plus fuel. Little traffic and flat roads make driving in Isan on your own a very manageable prospect, too and allows for the most flexibility in your schedule. If you decide to do a tour, contact **Isan Discovery Travel** in Khon Kaen (www.thaitraveldreams.com; ✆ 04332-1268), a small, expat-owned company. Don't be discouraged by their dated website; they're pros at arranging private itineraries around the region.

There are **Tourist Authority of Thailand (TAT)** offices in bigger towns in the region (though they're not conveniently located). Check out www.tourismthailand.org, or call ✆ 1672 for assistance. In our travels, we have found **12Go's** (www.12go.asia/en) English-language website takes the hassle out of booking regional trains or buses, and it accepts credit cards. For tips on using 12Go and additional information for booking transportation around Thailand, see p. 407 in chapter 14.

NAKHON RATCHASIMA (KHORAT)

259km (161 miles) NE of Bangkok; 150km (93 miles) W of Buriram; 305km (190 miles) S of Udon Thani

Nakhon Ratchasima, popularly known by its older name Khorat, isn't a wildly interesting city, but it's close to Bangkok and makes a good base for

Isan

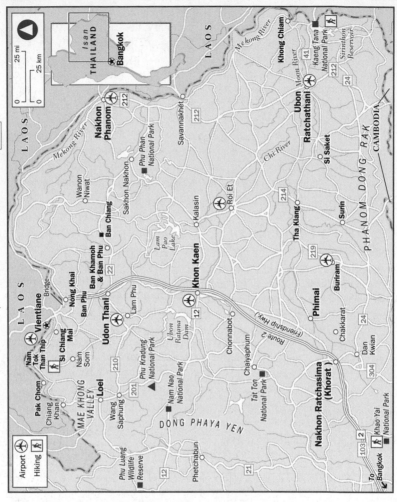

excursions to beautiful **Khao Yai National Park** (see "Side Trips from Bang-kok," in chapter 6; Khao Yai trips most commonly depart from Bangkok) and the Khmer temple at **Phimai.** It is a rapidly developing industrial city and is called the "Gateway to Isan" because it is located in the southwest corner of the region and all train lines, bus routes, roads, and communications from Bangkok pass through it. There is little in the way of local public transporta-tion, and it's a significant distance between key sites, so plan to explore this area by car. There are some comfortable accommodations in Khorat and a few temples and city monuments worth seeing. The city also gives its name to the

Khorat Plateau, which occupies most of Isan. The plateau is made of sandstone, which accounts for the region's lack of fertility, and stands about 200m (656 ft.) above sea level.

Getting There

Between **Nok Air** (www.nokair.com; ℘ **1318**) and **AirAsia** (www.airasia.com; ℘ **02515-9999**), there are five flights per day from Bangkok to Khorat. There are also numerous daily trains from Bangkok's **Hua Lampong Station** (℘ **1690**), and frequent bus connections from Bangkok's Northern Bus Terminal, **Mo Chit** (℘ **02936-2841**). It's about a 5-hour journey by train or bus, with an average cost of 500B, while the 1-hour flight is typically 600B.

Exploring Khorat

A trip to **Pimai**, 60km (37 miles) northeast of town, is highly recommended to appreciate the wonders of Khmer archaeology, particularly if you have not visited Cambodia's Angkor Wat. **Prasat Hin Pimai** temple complex (daily 7am–6pm; 100B) has been artfully restored by the same experts who renovated Angkor Wat. Wander the well-maintained grounds and discover Khmer temples that date back to the 11th century, with a few temples in near-perfect condition. While you're there, stop by the on-site **Phimai National Museum ★★** (daily 9am–4pm; 100B) to view centuries-old artifacts from the Dvaravati (estimated 6th to 11th centuries) and Khmer (10th to 14th centuries) eras. The showpiece of the museum is an impressive stone statue of King Jayavarman VII of Angkor Thom.

In Khorat, the most intriguing temple houses a sandstone image of Phra Narai (Vishnu), a sacred Hindu deity, at **Wat Phra Narai Maharat** (daily 8am–8pm), along Prajak Road, where you'll also find the **City Pillar Shrine**, which serves as the founding stone for the provincial town.

Where to Stay & Eat

Multiple dining options, a pool, fitness center, and a spa make **Sima Thani ★** (2112/2 Mittraphap Rd., west of town; www.simathani.com; ℘ **04421-3100**) a bargain for 1,200B a night. As well, rooms have above-standard amenities. A slightly less dated choice is **The Imperial Hotel & Convention Centre ★★** (1137 Suranarai Rd.; www.imperialkorat.com; ℘ **04425-6629**) with similar rates and amenities and the option to upgrade to a spacious suite. **Kantary Hotel Korat ★★** (899/1, 899/2 Mittraphap Rd., along the main road; ℘ **04435-3011;** www.kantarycollection.com) has stylish, clean and up-to-date rooms from 2,000B with an on-site a workout facility, pool, and an Italian restaurant.

When it comes to dining, you can't do better than to head for the reliable **Cabbages & Condoms ★** (86/1 Seub Siri Rd.; ℘ **04425-3760**), a branch of the Population & Community Development Association-run chain just west of the train station. Profits from the restaurant go to promoting health education and safe sex. With a shady terrace, an extensive menu of such Thai classics as *tom kha kai* (chicken in coconut soup), and a decent wine list, it's an ideal spot to while away a lazy evening. Western dishes with a European influence (the chef hails from Switzerland, which explains the fondue on the menu) are found at **Chez Andy** ★★ (5–7 Manat Rd.; ✆ **04428-9556**) in the southwest corner of the Old City.

KHON KAEN

449km (279 miles) NE of Bangkok; 190km (118 miles) N of Nakhon Ratchasima; 115km (71 miles) S of Udon Thani

Thanks to a prominent university and two major television studios, Khon Kaen is Isan's most heavily populated and busiest city. Its prime location along Route 2, and connections to Bangkok via rail and a large commercial airport, make this city a common stopover en route to places like Udon Thani and Nong Khai. But don't write off Khon Kaen as a flyover town; it boasts an upbeat market culture and good mid-range hotels, both of which have contributed to an uptick in tourist numbers in recent years. Another boon to the tourist biz: Laos and Vietnam have established consulates in town, making Khon Kaen a charming pit-stop to acquire visas, and a branch of the well-established **Thailand Creative Design Center** (TCDC), a bastion for local art and creatives opened in 2018.

Getting There

Collectively, **Thai Airways** (www.thaiairways.com; ✆ **02356-1111**), **Nok Air** (www.nokair.com; ✆ **1318**), **AirAsia** (www.airasia.com; ✆ **02515-9999**), and **Thai Regional Airlines** (www.thairegionalairlines.com; ✆ **02134-7152**) offer more than a dozen flights per day from Bangkok's airports, Suvarnabhumi Airport and Don Mueang International Airport. There are also four trains running daily from Bangkok, and bus services abound. However, with some advanced purchase, the short 45-minute flight can cost as much as the 7-plus-hour train, which is around 700B.

Exploring Khon Kaen

The town's most striking monument is the nine-tiered **Wat Nong Wang,** located at the southern end of Klang Muang Road. Supposedly inspired by the Shwedagon Pagoda in Myanmar, its white, red, and gold coat glows in the early-morning and late-afternoon sun, an ideal Instagram opportunity. Conveniently located to the east of the temple is **Beung Kaen Nakhon,** a large lake that attracts walkers, joggers, and cyclists to its perimeter path (bikes can be rented for a small fee) in the mornings and evenings, and itinerant vendors selling snacks.

Models of dinosaurs dot the city and major intersections of this "Dinosaur City" thanks to a discovery in 1996 of a small (6-m/l20-ft. long) fossil of a 120-million-year-old dinosaur at **Phuwiang,** about 90km (56 miles) northwest of Khon Kaen. Phuwiang has now been protected as a national park, but, in truth, there is little to see there apart from a few dusty old bones.

Where to Stay & Eat

Khon Kaen is a busy regional convention center with many rooms available, from international chains to no-frills budget accommodations. The top choice in town is the **Avani Khon Kaen Hotel & Convention Centre ★★★** (999 Moo 4; www.minorhotels.com; ✆ **02365-9110**), which has creature comforts like crisp bedding and rain showerheads, and palatial suites with living rooms, deep-soaking tubs, and four-poster beds. The hotel has a full-service spa and an international restaurant on-site, with doubles from 1,500B and suites from 3,700B. Another stronghold, the **Pullman Khon Kaen Raja Orchid ★★** (9–9 Prachasamran Rd.; www.pullmanhotels.com; ✆ **04332-2155**) features stylish rooms, fast and free Wi-Fi, an array of F&B options, and doubles from 1,800B.

For a truly memorable stay, book one of the three villas at the amiable **Supanniga Home Boutique Hideaway ★★★** (130/9 Potisarn Rd.; ✆ **089-444880;** www.secret-retreats.com/supanniga). The tranquil property is reason enough to visit Khon Kaen, and it occupies 6 hectares of land richly covered in local flora, including the bright yellow supanniga flower, which is native to the region. Pick a fresh mango ripe from the vine while chatting with the owner before retreating into the cottage-style villas furnished with handmade lace and antique furnishings. The hotel regularly hosts weeklong meditation retreats with local Buddhist monks (email for the schedule), but that Zen-like quality is consistent year-round. Villas from 4,800B.

Khon Kaen's **Walking Street Market** (Na Soon Rachakarn Rd.; Saturdays from approximately 5–10pm) is a top place to mingle with the locals and grab a bite to eat. Local buskers and live bands line the corners and vendors sell street food delights like *hoi tod* (deep-fried mussels) and *som tom* (Thailand's famous papaya salad). Similar snacks are found mid-week at the **Ton Tann Market** (Mittraphap Rd.), which is more like an outdoor shopping center than a traditional market, with local artists and designers selling their goods alongside open-air stalls, restaurants, and beer bars.

Gai Yang Rabeab Khao Suan Kwang on Thepharak Road is a reliable option for well-made Isan delights; nosh on their signature BBQ chicken (*gai yang*) with spicy dipping sauce, minced meat salads (known as *larb),* and sun-dried pork. Dinner at **Supanniga by Khun Yai ★★★**, at the hotel by the same name; see above, is where Trat-style family recipes, like crispy catfish and crab curry, have been preserved for three generations. The Supanniga group has expanded to include four restaurants and a dinner cruise in Bangkok, but it all started here in 2012 with dishes from the owner's grandmother.

UDON THANI & BAN CHIANG

564km (350 miles) NE of Bangkok; 305km (190 miles) N of Nakhon Ratchasima

"No sweat, man," was once a common saying among tuk-tuk drivers here. The use of 1960s slang reminds tourists that Udon Thani (or Udon) was home to a large contingent of U.S. armed forces during the Vietnam War and memories of that time still linger. Today, the town remains a key industrial province and is mostly known for a large-scale sugar-cane and rice production

Udon Thani itself has few attractions, so don't plan to linger for too long, but it is a good jumping-off point to such small towns as Loei, to the west (p. 397), and Ban Chiang, an important archaeological site, to the east.

Getting There & Getting Around

Thai Airways (www.thaiairways.com; ℂ **02356-1111**) offers daily flights to the area, as do budget carriers **Nok Air** (www.nokair.com; ℂ **1318**) and **AirAsia** (www.airasia.com; ℂ **02515-9999**). Numerous trains (best as an overnight in a second-class sleeper) connect from Bangkok's **Hua Lampong Station** (ℂ **1690**) daily via Khon Kaen, and there are bus connections from Udon across the region. All transport options cost less than 1,000B (with some 11-hour bus routes selling for 400B), so pick based on your timetable; a 1-hour flight or 9-hour bus or train ride. Major car rental companies, like **Budget Car Rental** (ℂ **04224-6805**), have offices at the airport and online reservations aren't necessary. This option is best for travelers setting off on a multi-city Isan tour. If you just plan to hangout in Udon Thani, the best way to get around the surprisingly sprawling town is by tuk-tuk, which, oddly, are called "skylabs" here. From Udon Thani it is easy to explore the Mekong Valley to the north (see the following sections).

Exploring Udon Thani & Ban Chiang

The tiny hamlet of Ban Chiang, approximately 50km (31 miles) east of Udon Thani on the Sakon Nakhon highway, boasts a history of more than 5,600 years; the area was declared a UNESCO World Heritage Site in 1992. It was—quite literally—stumbled upon in 1974 and, since then, has been excavated by an international team. The findings at **Ban Chiang National Museum ★★** (open Tues–Sun, 9am–4pm; 150B) prove the existence of a distinct and very sophisticated Bronze Age culture in Southeast Asia, long before any earlier findings. The museum itself has a '70s vibe, and not much has changed since it opened, including some facts that accompany exhibits! Historians have revised the dates to more recent time periods, but those changes aren't reflected in most of the museum's displays. Nevertheless, the museum, which was partially funded by the Smithsonian Institute, houses a fine collection of whorl-designed pottery, intricate bronze jewelry, arrowheads, and ladles.

Next swing by the nearby **Wat Po Si Nai** (daily 9am–6pm; 150B) excavation pit to see the elaborate interments of these ancient people. Along the main road to the sites, look for villagers producing replica Ban Chiang ceramic ware, with its distinctive spiral design.

If you're in town in December, January or February, take a worthwhile and photogenic half-day trip to the **Red Lotus Sea**, or *Talay Bua Dang,* on Nong Han Lake. Join a pontoon boat tour (all boats are created equal here so take the first available option) from Ban Diem Pier (100B for 90-minutes; approximately 500B for a private tour) from 6am to 5pm and float among innumerable

For a holistic understanding of Isan, plan to see at least three or four towns on your journey. The Mekong Valley Loop, in a way, is like a greatest hits track of Isan. It includes an archeological adventure in **Udon Thani** (p. 395), stopping in charming **Loei** (see below) for a dose of nature and national parks. Next it heads along the Mekong River, the natural Thai–Laos border, through **Nong Khai** (p. 398), and on to **Nakhon Phanom** (p. 400). With a side trip to **That Phanom** (p. 401), you return to Udon Thani, from where you can catch the lotus ponds in bloom or sample some local rum before headed back to Bangkok. Another option is to follow the Mekong all the way south from Nakhon Phanom to **Ubon Ratchathani** (p. 403), and then hop on a flight back to Bangkok. This is an off-the-beaten track option, and it's best accomplished by car (see "Information & Tours," at the beginning of this chapter). The road that strings together these towns is easy for outsiders to navigate, but major rental car companies can provide a driver with the car.

vibrant pink lotus flowers. The blooms open early and close in the mid-day sun, so arrive before 10am for the best viewing and to beat the crowds.

Where to Stay & Eat

Udon's best hotel, for those who want a lot of amenities is the **Centara** ★ (277/1 Prachak Silpakorn Rd., west of the railway station and adjacent to the mall; www.centarahotelsresorts.com; ✆ 04234-3555). It is up to the international brand's standards, with a nice fitness center and pool, and doubles from 2,000B. But we prefer the simple and very friendly, **Baan Rare Guesthouse** ★★★ (4/8 Po-Sri Rd., near the large Nongprajak Park; www.facebook. com/baanrare; ✆ 08126-0133) where 300B rooms have homey touches like *pakaoma* (local gingham) pillows and bike rentals. The architect owner runs a bike-tour company that can arrange rides in the region and to nearby Laos.

LOEI

520km (323 miles) NE of Bangkok; 344km (214 miles) N of Nakhon Ratchasima

Chilly in the winter, scorching in the summer, and often rainy because of its higher elevation (the town is reputedly the coldest spot in the kingdom), little Loei is a lazy riverside town worth an overnight stop, but this route is more about the beautiful road journey and nearby national parks than the town of Loei itself. Dan Sai, 80km (50 miles) southwest of Loei, hosts the annual **Pi Tha Khon Festival** (June/July), a raucous, Thai-style Mardi Gras where townspeople elaborately dress as spirits and go crazy in the streets. "The devil made me do it!" is the excuse for all kinds of outlandish behavior; it's lots of fun. South of Loei town is **Phu Kradung National Park** ★ (admission 400B adults, 200B children), one of Thailand's most dramatic sights: a bell-shaped, table-top mountain of 1,300m (4,265ft.) that can be climbed in around 3 to 4 hours (porters can be hired to carry bags) and has rustic log-cabin huts (900B–3,600B double) and camping facilities on the summit. The park is 82km (51 miles) from Loei and well worth the trip, especially in December and January when temperatures drop and scarlet maple leaves fall. The park is closed during the rainy season (June–Sept) and very crowded during school holidays (Mar–May).

Getting There

Nok Air (www.nokair.com; 🕾 **1318**) and **AirAsia** (www.airasia.com; 🕾 **02515-9999**) fly to the small Loei Airport about four times a day from Bangkok's Don Mueang Airport. Loei does not have its own train station, but the region's bus systems make stops in town.

Where to Stay & Eat

Loei Village ★★ (17/62 Nok Kaew Soi 3; www.loeivillages.com; 🕾 **0428-11132**) has charming service and very helpful staff. Enjoy bike rentals, a better-than-most buffet breakfast, free Wi-Fi, and affordable rooms (from 1,200B per double).

For food, **Ban Thai** (🕾 **04283-3472**) at 22/58-60 Chumsai Rd., is the pick. It can satisfy a craving for Western food with steaks, pizzas, good beer, and coffee, but also turns out a good range of tasty Thai dishes—it's ideal for a group of diners with different tastes.

ALONG THE MEKONG FROM LOEI TO NONG KHAI

One of the most scenic areas in Thailand—and delightfully secluded—the northwestern perimeter of Isan runs along the wide Mekong River, which forms the border with Laos. Buses and *songtaews* don't make connections at every village, so you'll need to have your own transport, but the terrain is flat and the roads are well maintained.

The loop begins in Loei and ends in Nong Khai. Directly north of Loei, you'll reach the uber-charming riverside town of **Chiang Khan,** a popular destination for young Thais to vacation with their friends. The small riverside "promenade" is lined with teak guesthouses that have an appealing French-Lao influence. For our money, we'd choose the friendly **Husband & Wife Guesthouse** ★ (241 moo 1, Chai Khong Road; www.withaviewhotel.com; 🕾 **0910-58185**), which combines Isan-style décor with groovy new age touches in rooms that aren't luxe but are clean and comfortable. In the back is a garden with a large "cat jungle gym" for the 11 felines that live here. The guesthouse also has a popular coffee shop on-site; rooms from 750B.

Visitors often offer fruit, rice, or small donations (a process known as making alms) in the early morning with local monks and at night enjoy **Chiang Khan Walking Street** in the center of town. This market runs nightly from 5 to 10pm, and it's a great place to snack on Isan bites, shop for locally-made goods, and take in the charm of this laid-back town. During the day, plan time for a visit to **Wat Si Khun Muang** with its Lao-style stupa, interesting murals, and topiary. If all temples are being to look the same, rent bikes from any guesthouse, or ask them to book a trip to see the rapids at **Kaeng Kut Khu** by longtail boat for around 1,000B for a couple of hours.

From Chiang Khan, Route 212 follows the Mekong east to **Pak Chom, Sangkhom,** and **Si Chiang Mai** before arriving in Nong Khai. The route passes lush banana plantations, terraced fruit farms, and wonderful river views. Cotton and tomato fields fan out along the verdant floodplains of the Mekong basin. Farther inland are attractive waterfalls, such as **Than Thip** (between Pak Chom and Sangkhom), which are fun for hiking and ideal for picnics. Road signs in English will mark the way.

If you're looking for a stopover along this route, a luxurious place to bed down is **Mekong Villas** ★★ (96 Moo 6, Leab Mekong River Rd.; www. secret-retreats.com/mekongvillas; ℰ **02222-1290**) where private houses are secluded along the riverbank and come with such niceties as satellite TV, crisp linens, and breezy balconies. The owners can arrange canoe trips or home-made meals; doubles from 4,000B.

As you head east from Sangkhom beside the river, don't miss **Wat Hin Mak Peng ★,** a meditation temple some 30km (19 miles) west of Si Chiang Mai, which occupies a glorious site overlooking the Mekong, or, just before reaching Si Chaing Mai, look for the unique gold tower of the **Prasutham Chedi** beside the main road.

Si Chiang Mai is opposite Vientiane, the Laos capital, and is but 58km (36 miles) due west of Nong Khai. The town is just a quiet Thai backwater. Walks along the long concrete pier or relaxing and watching Laos and Thai longtail boats load and unload or chug up- and downriver is about all that's going on here. In the evenings, join in a game of badminton or a circle of people juggling a *takraw* (a small rattan ball). There are lots of little open-air eateries at the riverside and a few small guesthouses along the quay at the town center.

NONG KHAI

615km (382 miles) NE of Bangkok; 51km (32 miles) N of Udon Thani

The little border town of Nong Khai is nothing special but its sprawling riverside market **Tha Sadet** is full of interesting goods from Laos and China. Around town, there's a fun rum distillery, and the place has a palpable calm with some good, laid-back riverside guesthouses. Nong Khai is a popular jumping-off point for travel to Laos.

Getting There

The nearest airport is in Udon Thani (p. 395), but Nong Khai is the terminus of the Northeast train line from Bangkok and is an enjoyable, if rocky, over-night journey. Regular buses connect with points throughout the region, too.

Exploring Nong Khai

Tha Sadet, or the **Indochina Market** (daily 8am–6pm), located at the heart of town at the riverside, is the main attraction in Nong Khai and it is certainly worth a wander. Also check out **Sala Kaew Ku Sculpture Park** (about

4km/2½ miles east of town, on Rte. 212), where you'll find concrete Buddhas, Hindu deities, and other fantastic statues of enormous proportions in an attractive garden setting—all the brainchild of the eccentric Mr. Luang Phu Boonlua Surirat. He studied with an Indian guru in Vietnam and later taught in Laos, and his mummified body can be viewed on a tour of the main temple building (he also built a similar sculpture garden just across the river near Vientiane, Laos). Entry is 20B, and the site is open daily from 7am to 6pm.

On the way in or out of town, stop by the open-air, utterly charming (but utterly small) **Issan Rum Distillery** (www.facebook.com/pages/Issan-Rum-Distillery/758004334355373). It's about 20km/12 miles outside of town on an unnamed road, but message the amiable French owner, David Giallorenzo, on the Facebook page and he'll send you a pin location. It's worth the journey to sample the award-winning organic agricore rum made with sugarcane grown, harvested and processed on-site. Only 10,000 bottles are produced a year, most of which ship to Europe and Bangkok, and the brand employs 20 Isan farmers.

Good day trips from Nong Khai include a day (or overnight) across the Thai-Laos Friendship bridge to **Vientiane** (visas are available at the border); and the **Phu Phrabat Historical Park,** some 70km/43 miles southwest of Nong Khai. The latter site is a unique grouping of natural sandstone towers that were fashioned into rudimentary cave dwellings.

Where to Stay & Eat

Budget accommodations line the small streets across town. **Mutmee Guesthouse ★★** (1111/4 Kaeworawut Rd.; www.mutmee.com; ℂ 04246-0717) is foreign-run, tremendously friendly, and a comfy budget choice (from 220B for dorm beds; from 320B per double). It's also a great place to get good local info and a bite to eat, and they can try to help with booking excursions, cars, or tours. A charming riverside hotel is **Na Rim Khong River View ★★** (432 Moo 5 Rd.; www.narimkhong-riverview.com; ℂ 0424-12077) with rooms starting at 2,500B. It's in a prime location to explore town on foot and the rooms are simple but clean and basic amenities are included.

For good local dining, **Daeng Namnuang** (on a small side street just off the central market; ℂ 04241-1961) has become a bit of an institution thanks to its popular do-it-yourself Vietnamese pork spring roll. Alternatively, stop by **Café Thasadej** (just around the corner at 387/3 Soi Thepbunterng; ℂ 04242-3921), where you can choose from Thai favorites, German sausage, or spaghetti Bolognese—the restaurant has the best liquor list in town if you're in the mood for cocktails.

NAKHON PHANOM

740km (460 miles) NE of Bangkok; 252km (157 miles) E of Udon Thani; 481km (299 miles) NE of Nakhon Ratchasima

Travelers rarely make it out to these parts of Thailand; apart from a few good riverside hotels catering to Westerners, the place is pretty sleepy. But that's the allure. Most visitors are happy just walking riverside streets and looking for the old Vietnamese clock tower—a gift from grateful Vietnamese Catholic refugees escaping Ho Chi Minh's Communists in North Vietnam—or visiting the **Phra Pathom Chedi.** This towering chedi stands at 120-m (393-ft.), making it the tallest chedi in Thailand and one of the world's tallest Buddhist monuments. Originally erected in the 4th century and later reduced to ruins during regional conflict, the structure was rebuilt in by Rama IV in 1853. The nearby Wat Phra Pathom Chedi Museum offers little of note, so go ahead and move along when you're done.

South of town is **That Phanom** (see Exploring Nakhon Phanom, below), an important pilgrimage site for Thai Buddhists; from there, pass through Sakon Nakhon to return to Udon Thani (with a possible side trip to Ban Chiang) completing the loop. If you have more time, follow the Mekong south from Nakhon Phanom all the way to Ubon Ratchathani, where you can fly on AirAsia or Nok Air or catch a train back to Bangkok. Each year, Nakhon Phanom hosts the famed "Lai Rua Fai," or **Fire Boat Festival,** where barges float downstream, twinkling with small candles in the night (also dragon boat races by day), all to celebrate the end of the rains in October.

Getting There

Nakhon Pathom's tiny airport is serviced twice daily by **Nok Air** (www.nokair.com; ℭ **1318**); the 1-hour flight sells for 800B. VIP buses from Bangkok take about 12 hours and cost around 1,000B, see p. 411 for details.

Exploring Nakhon Phanom

The city's *wats* are built in a distinctive Thai and Laoation styles, and the exterior bas-reliefs, attributed to the Laotian Lan Xang kingdom, are said to date back some 300 years. An hour to the south, **Wat Phra That Phanom** is a temple built around a tall 9th-century stupa that collapsed in 1975 and was rebuilt in 1978. It's an important pilgrimage site for Thai Buddhists and makes for a pleasant trip. The 53-m (174-ft.) tall stupa itself is built in Laos style, with its tapering, curved sides decorated with gold patterns on a white background and topped off with a gold umbrella. There's always a reverential aura around the place, particularly at the annual **That Phanom Festival,** usually in February, when it is crowded with pilgrims, both Thai and Lao, for 10 days.

Where to Stay

The River Hotel ★★ (35/9 Nakornphanom Rd.; www.therivernakhonphanom.com; ℭ **0836-692999**) has well-furnished rooms and you can book a river view room for postcard views, starting at 790B.

SURIN

457km (284 miles) NE of Bangkok; 227km (141 miles) W of Ubon Ratchathani

Surin is elephant country and is famed (or infamous, see below) for its annual roundup (in Nov), a nearly 200-year tradition; many of Thailand's *mahouts* or elephant trainers, come from Surin and a long family lineage of working with these gentle giants. The city is also a good base for exploring far-flung Khmer ruins. More than one-third of Surin's population is Khmer.

Getting There

Nok Air (www.nokair.com; ✆ **1318**) and **AirAsia** (www.airasia.com; ✆ **02515-9999**) both have a couple of flights a day from Bangkok to nearby Buriram. Frequent trains connect Surin from Bangkok via the spur line from Khorat (about 8½ hrs.), and there are numerous buses; see p. 319 for details.

Exploring Surin

If you haven't come with your own guide, the best way to visit the scattered sites around Surin is to book a tour or car hire with **Saren Travel & Tour** (202/1-4 Soi Thesaban 2; www.facebook.com/sarentravel; ✆ **0445-13599**). Popular tours in and around the province include secluded Khmer temples, handicraft villages, and trips to the weekend market at the Cambodian border. Expect to pay 1,500B per person.

The **elephant roundup** that takes place on the third weekend of November is Surin's biggest claim to fame, and more than 300 elephants are brought to town for the 11-day event. The roundup started as a pilot project to resettle homeless and abandoned street elephants (and transition them to the Elephant Nature Park in Chiang Mai; see page 46). But today it is a sad spectacle of elephants padding around in chains and being made to dance in battle gear, play games of soccer, and test their strength with a tug of war. Directing these creatures to make them docile enough for such events involves an often torturous training, and animal rights activists condemn the event. If you still decide to go, book a room months in advance and reserve tickets through the Tourism Authority of Thailand (www.tourismthailand.org); accommodations prices make a big jump during this time.

Make the short 8 km/5-mile drive from the city center to see the craftspeople at **Ban Tha Sawang ★★** (✆ **0878-714449;** 7am–7pm), a renowned silk village with looms using more than a hundred heddles. The village itself is a worthy visit, and the specialist weavers hone their craft in ancient houses. Brocade fabrics from this village are normally used in the royal court, but big-spending tourists (expect 1-meter pieces to start at 30,000B) can custom order pieces with threads of real gold and silver. If you're looking for well-made but more affordable options, outside the village neighborhood shops sell more reasonably priced pieces that make lovely souvenirs.

Outside of Surin

Buriram is about halfway between Surin and Khorat, and easily reached overland or by **Nok Air** (www.nokair.com; ✆ **1318**) or **AirAsia** (www.airasia.com; ✆ **02515-9999**) from the capital. It's the best base (a little nearer than Khorat) to visit **Phanom Rung** (daily 6am–6pm; admission 100B), a stunning Khmer ruin which was deserted in the late 13th century, rediscovered in 1935, and restored in the 1970s. This Khmer temple was built during the 11th century and stands in a direct line between Angkor in Cambodia and Pimai, a little farther northwest. Like Pimai, it has benefited from a loving restoration by the Fine Arts Department and is in some ways even more impressive than Pimai with its hilltop location and intricate carvings on the main *prang* (central tower). It's worth stopping by the **visitor center** (9am–4:30pm) to get an overview of the temple's most significant aspects.

An additional popular side trip from Surin is **Khao Phra Viharn,** another striking Khmer temple site, on the Cambodian border, with some wonderful lintel carvings, though not restored as meticulously as Pimai or Phanom Rung. The temple has been closed to the public due to a border dispute. At press time, tensions were beginning to thaw, so check locally whether it has re-opened before setting out on the long journey. When it is open, admission for foreigners is 400B.

Where to Stay

There are no standout hotels in Surin but here are two reliable choices with good locations. **Maneerote Hotel** ★ (Soi Poi Tunggor; www.maneerotehotel. com; ☏ 0445-39477) is near the fresh market with good-for-the-value rooms starting at 450B and an attached coffee shop. **Surin Majestic Hotel** ★ (99 Jitbumrung Rd.; www.surinmajestic.com; ☏ 0447-13980) offers clean, well-lit rooms and suites near the bus station. Starting at 1,200B, room rates include breakfast and access to the swimming pool and fitness center.

UBON RATCHATHANI

606km (375 miles) NE of Bangkok; 173km (107 miles) E of Surin

Few tourists find their way to Ubon Ratchathani—often shortened to Ubon—one of Isan's largest urban centers. Highlights of downtown include a surprisingly informative museum and a massive statue of a votive candle in **Thung Si Muang Park.** The statue is a reference to the town's unusual annual **Candle Festival,** which takes place in July and involves huge wax carvings (the size of parade floats) being towed around the town's streets and displayed in the city's temples for several months after.

Known as 'Royal City of the Lotus' Ubon Ratchathani is a smart launch point to nearby national parks, the highlight of which is **Phu Chong Nayoi,** a jungle area tucked away between Thailand's borders with Cambodia and Laos that is often called the Emerald Triangle—a nod to the Golden Triangle of the north.

Getting There

AirAsia (www.airasia.com; ☏ 02515-9999) and **Nok Air** (www.nokair.com; ☏ 1318;) fly from Bangkok's Don Muang Airport, while **Thai Airways** (www.thaiairways.com; ☏ 02356-1111) operates out of Suvarnabhumi Airport. Bus connect Ubon with Bangkok, and VIP vans abound; we recommend **999 VIP.** Overnight express trains service the capital as well, and daytime departures make regional stops before reaching Bangkok. The 11-hour journey on a train or bus hovers around 500B while the hour-long flight typically costs 800B.

Exploring Ubon

While the city itself is ho-hum, a worthwhile stop is a visit to the **Ubon Ratchathani National Museum** ★ (Wed–Sun 9am–4pm; 100B), which showcases a 2,500-year-old bronze drum from Vietnam's Dong Son culture and an assortment of Dvaravati-era antiques. The centerpiece of the collection is a 9th-century Ardhanarishvara statue, a composite male-female figure of the Hindu god Shiva with his consort Parvati. Also of interest, **Wat Si Ubon Rattanaram** (daily 8am–4pm) holds the Topaz Buddha; at 3-inches wide and 5-inches tall, this is the city's holiest image, and it's paraded around town during April's Songkran festival. Nearby national parks include **Pha Taem** ★ (admission 200B adults, 100B children), home to ancient rock paintings dating back 3,000 and 4,000 years that overlook the Mekong River, and **Kaeng Tana** (admission 100B adults, 50B children), which has waterfalls, caves, and rock formations.

The **Night Market** (daily 4–11pm) and weekend **Walking Street Market** are good places for local Isan food. For nightlife, **U-Bar** (www.facebook.com/ubarUB; ℂ 0452-65141) on Thepyothi Road is home to a buzzy crowd and surprisingly fun and funky live bands from Bangkok.

Where to Stay

Tip-top service, private gardens, large rooms, and interiors finished in reclaimed wood are the lures at **Outside Inn** ★ (11 Suriyat Rd.; www.theoutsideinn ubon.com; ℂ 0885-812069), doubles from 650B. The hotel's Thai-American owners run an on-site restaurant that is also a hit.

PLANNING YOUR TRIP TO THAILAND

This may well be the chapter of the book that saves you the most money. Read it to learn about the best ways to get discounts on transportation to the country (always a big expense), average costs on the ground, what you need to know about different types of Thai accommodations, healthcare issues, etiquette, and more.

GETTING THERE

Getting to Thailand
BY PLANE

There is no longer a direct flight from the U.S. to Thailand, although, in mid-2018, news outlets were reporting that Thai Airways was hoping to relaunch their Bangkok to U.S. route, pending FAA approval. Until that happens, flights from major U.S. cities have layovers across the Asian continent, including Hong Kong, Tokyo, Dubai, Abu Dhabi, Doha, and Seoul. Depending on your origin city, expect travel from the U.S. to Thailand to take 22 to 30 hours. But with those layovers come some opportunities, since Thailand has more than one international airport. While most international flights arrive at Bangkok's **Suvarnabhumi International Airport** (airport code BKK; ✆ **02132-1888**) some do land at **Don Muang Airport** (airport code DMK; ✆ **02535-1111**). One can also fly directly to **Phuket** (airport code HKT; ✆ **07632-7230-7**), **Ko Samui** (airport code USM; ✆ **07724-5600**), **Chiang Mai** (airport code CNX; ✆ **05327-0222-33**), and **Chiang Rai** (airport code CEI; ✆ **0537-98000**) from certain regional destinations such as Beijing, Singapore, or Hong Kong, which can mean a savings for those planning a Thai vacation that does not include Bangkok. That being said, international round-trips into Bangkok tend to be about $200 cheaper than those into other gateways. One can also catch flights to Kuala Lumpur and Singapore from **Hat Yai** (airport code HDY; ✆ **07422-7000**) and fly to and from Yangon from **Mae Sot** (airport code MAQ; ✆ **05556-3620**). Direct flights from major European cities, like London, Munich, and Copenhagen to Bangkok take about 11 hours.

Where to Search for Airfare

At Frommers.com we did a major study on which search engines are best for international airfares and found that **Momondo.com** and **Skyscanner.net** had the best track records, by far, for finding the lowest prices. This conclusion was based on several thousand searches, which included a number of gateways, and different timings (last-minute bookings, those well in advance, holiday travel and more).

Timing is also important. Tuesday flights are statistically cheapest for those flying into and out of the country, and prices are lowest in **April, May,** and **September.**

BY TRAIN

Thailand is accessible via train from Singapore and peninsular Malaysia. **Malaysia's Keretapi Tanah Melayu Berhad (KTM)** begins in Singapore (ⓒ **65/6222-5165**), making regional stops in places like Kuala Lumpur before heading for Thailand, where it joins service with the State Railway of Thailand. Arrive at Bangkok's **Hua Lampong Station,** which is in the heart of Chinatown on Krung Kasem Road (ⓒ **02220-4334**). Taxis, tuk-tuks, and public buses wait outside the station and access to the MRT (subway) is a few steps away. These trains are equivalent to the ones that run in country, in terms of comfort and service. For a discussion of those trains, see p. 56.

Saccharine travel posters and refrigerator magnets all agree: It's more about the journey than the destination. That phrase is rarely more applicable than aboard The *Eastern & Oriental Express*' (www.orient-express.com) 2-night/ 3-day journey between Singapore and Bangkok or Kuala Lumpur and Bangkok, with service out of Bangkok as well. The romance of 1930s colonial travel is joined with modern luxury in Pullman, State, or Presidential cars, plus fine-dining in the restaurant car, a bar car, a saloon car, and an observation car. Along the way, stop in Kuala Kangsar and Kanchanaburi (River Kwai) for guided tours and sightseeing. Current fares per person one-way start from $2,290.

BY BUS OR CAR

Neighboring countries of Laos, Cambodia, Myanmar, and Malaysia have sanctioned border-crossing points to exit or enter Thailand. Most buses, private cars, or shared taxis cannot cross the border point, and the onward leg of the journey is another bus, private car, or shared taxi on the other side of the border. Visa on arrival services are available at these points, but remember to bring the necessary paperwork, visa photos, and crisp U.S. dollars in the correct amount. You can change Thai baht at airports across the country or, if you're in Bangkok, **Super Rich** (www.superrichthailand.com) offers the best rates. Look out for locals offering to coordinate health checks or expedite visa services—these are always a scam. At press time, these are the current visa fees: Laos charges $35 (for U.S., Europe, U.K. citizens), $42 for Canadians, and Australians. Most others pay $30. Cambodia charges $30 for most nationalities and requires a passport photo (or else pay a $2 fine and skip the photo).

Myanmar charges $50 for an online e-visa ($56 for 24-hour turnaround). Visitors from most countries can enter Malaysia without a visa.

BY SHIP

Star Clipper Cruises run leisurely cruises that stop at several picturesque Thai islands on the weeklong journey from Singapore to Phuket. For more information visit www.starclippers.com.

To see more of mainland Thailand, consider a river cruise. Active on-land activities are guided by experienced tour professionals, and more-than-comfortable cabins are standard issue. **Mekong Kingdoms** (www.mekong kingdoms.com), in partnership with Minor Hotels, offers small-group and private cruises that include onboard cooking classes, sunrise yoga, and sundowner cocktails as the fleet sails from northern Thailand's Golden Triangle to Luang Prabang, Laos. The Laos to Thailand route sails on a four-person boat for 4-nights/3-day on a full-board package is US$5,450. Day trips are available as well.

For more information on Bangkok-based cruises (including a list of recommended dinner cruises), see page 286.

Getting Around Thailand

Thailand's domestic transport system is accessible, generally efficient, and inexpensive. A robust network of domestic flights (from Don Mueang and Suvarnabhumi International Airports, as well as other Thai cities) and an onslaught of budget airline carriers make air travel a breeze. But if you have the time to take in the countryside, travel by bus, train, private car, or for the really adventurous, by motorcycle (see p. 48 for details).

In our travels, we have found the English-language website **12Go** (www.12go.asia/en) to be an invaluable one-stop resource for booking travel. Their website compares timetables and pricing, allowing you to choose the best option for your schedule and budget. For example, a search from Bangkok to Chiang Mai instantly priced out VIP buses, coach buses, overnight sleeper train cars, flights, and even private cabs. Ferry pricing and schedules are included when applicable. Handy icons indicate amenities, like air-con, food, on-board stewards, and TVs. The peer reviews on the site are also helpful.

To book domestic flights, **Skyscanner** (www.skyscanner) and **Momondo** (www.momondo.com) typically outperform the competition by including a larger number of Asian budget carriers in their search results.

For tips on deciphering Thai addresses, especially in Bangkok, see p. 58 in chapter 5.

BY PLANE

Domestic air travel in Thailand is a safe and convenient way to get around. Flights from Bangkok depart from **Suvarnabhumi Airport** and **Don Muang Airport,** so make sure which one you're headed for, as they are a long way apart. Airports outside of Bangkok, Phuket, and Chiang Mai usually tend to be more basic but will have necessities such as money-changing facilities, information kiosks, and waiting ground transportation.

There are heaps of domestic flights on **Thai Airways** (www.thaiairways. com; ℭ **02356-1111**), with Bangkok as its hub. Flights connect Bangkok with such popular domestic destinations as Chiang Mai, Chiang Rai, Ko Samui, Krabi, and Phuket. There are also connecting flights between these cities. **Bangkok Airways** (www.bangkokair.com; ℭ **1177**) flies to more than two dozen destinations across Asia and domestically is the sole operator of the Phuket to Ko Samui and Bangkok to Trat routes.

The budget subsidiary of Thai Airways, **Nok Air** (www.nokair.com; ℭ **1318**) services more than two dozen spots in Thailand and they offer easy to book 'fly and ferry' combos to beach locations like Koh Lipe and Koh Phi Phi from Bangkok. Another budget option is **AirAsia** (www.airasia.com; ℭ **02515-9999** in Bangkok). They travel across Thailand from Bangkok's Don Mueang and offer good-value fares internationally. **Pro Tip:** While appealing at first glance, especially if you'll be traveling in Asia for several weeks, AirAsia's Asean Pass is a headache-inducing service and not worth your money.

With most budget airlines, you'll need to pre-pay for checked luggage to avoid steep fees (and delays) at the airport. Normally, the fee for checking bags is cheaper when done in advance.

See individual chapters for details of the most convenient connections in different regions of the country.

BY CAR OR MOTORBIKE

Renting a car is easy in Thailand, but driving it is another matter. Driving in Bangkok is particularly hard; the one-way streets, poor and even misleading road signage, and constant traffic jams prove frustrating. Outside the city, once you've managed to avoid local farm animals and the occasional water buffalo herd, driving is doable, but can be hair-raising. Thai drivers are unashamedly reckless—many ignore basic rules, and have a total disregard for road safety. Foreign drivers must reorient themselves fast and Americans need to adjust to driving on the left.

Among the many car-rental agencies, both **Avis** (www.avisthailand.com; ℭ **02251-2011**) and **Budget** (www.budget.co.th; ℭ **02203-9294-5**) have convenient offices around the country. In theory, drivers are required to have an international driver's license, but this is rarely enforced. Gas stations are conveniently located along major roads throughout the country. Esso, Shell, Caltex, and PTT all have competitive rates and are full-service. Say "top up" while raising your palm upwards to request a full tank.

Self-drive rates start around 1,200B per day for a family-sized sedan, more for luxury vehicles or SUVs. When renting a car, check insurance coverage and if you're wary of driving yourself, **ask about rates for a car and driver,** which can be very reasonable. How reasonable? About 3,200B will pay for a car, driver, gas, tolls and parking for 10 hours, and 5 hours is usually 2,200B.

These are the rates for Bangkok, so booking this type of service in areas like Isan and Chiang Rai should be cheaper. And the fees *end* here. If the driver has to stay overnight, his expenses usually come out of the rates listed above.

In towns like Chiang Mai, Pai, Phuket, or Ko Samui, **motorbike rentals** are cheap and found on nearly every street corner. There are plenty of rental shops in Bangkok, **but I strongly advise against renting a motorbike unless you're a very skilled driver** with lots of patience for traffic and chaos. Typically, rentals cost 200 to 450 baht per day and include helmets, which have been used by other sweaty riders many times before. Scooter pricing is based on engine sizes, which typically range from 110 to 150cc. If your goal is casual cruising around town, a smaller bike will do the job and, for more inexperienced riders, a smaller engine will be a smoother ride and easier to handle. When venturing into more mountainous regions (see p. 324 for great rides outside of Chiang Mai), you'll want more pep in your step, so opt for the 150cc models, especially if you'll be carrying a passenger. Be sure to test drive rentals for comfort and confidence. It's not uncommon for rental shops to request to keep your passport in lieu of a deposit.

BY TRAIN

Bangkok's **Hua Lampong Railway Station** (see "By Train," under "Getting There," above) is a convenient, user-friendly facility. Ticket windows open at least 15 minutes before departure and clear signs point the way to public toilets, the food court, ATMs, and the baggage check (sometimes called a cloakroom).

From this hub, the **State Railway of Thailand** (www.railway.co.th; ✆ **1690**), or SRT, provides regular service across the country, including destinations as far north as Chiang Mai, northeast to Nong Khai, east to Pattaya, and south to Thailand's southern border, where it connects with Malaysia's Keretapi Tanah Melayu Berhad (KTM), with service to major cities like Kuala Lumpur and Singapore. Complete routes, schedules, and fare information is on the SRT website.

If you've zig-zagged around Europe or Japan on trains, Thailand's rail system will seem like a stuck-in-time option, with slow service and no state-of-the-art cabins to speak of. However, the Thai countryside is beautiful, and it's a generally relaxing, albeit sometimes slow, way to get around. The SRT runs several different trains, each at a different speed, and priced accordingly. Class of service varies significantly depending on speed of the train, but generally, first-class sleepers are an air-conditioned, two-bunk compartment with wash basin; second-class sleepers bench seats that convert into fold-down bunks with a ceiling fan or air-conditioning, depending on the ticket price. Third-class carriage cars are rows of bench seats that often hold more than the designated two or three people; commuter trains in Bangkok are all third-class. The fastest is the Special Express, which is the best choice for long-haul, overnight travel. These trains cut travel time by as much as 60% and have sleeper cars—which are a must for long trips. Rapid trains (an over-generous use of that adjective) are the next best option. Prices vary for class,

KNOW BEFORE YOU GO: thai etiquette

Thai customs can be confusing. Foreigners are not expected to know and follow local etiquette to the letter, but good manners and appropriate dress will earn you instant respect. A few small gestures and a general awareness will help foster a spirit of goodwill.

GREETINGS

Thais greet each other with a graceful bow called a **wai** (pronounced like the letter Y). Palms and fingers are pressed flat together, fingers pointing up; the higher they are held, the greater the respect, with fingertips touching the top of the forehead forming the most respectful *wai*. Younger people are expected to *wai* an elder first, who will usually return the gesture. Foreigners are more or less exempt from this custom, though many new arrivals, eager to show their familiarity with Thai culture, *wai* everyone they meet, which is unnecessary and a little silly. In hotels, doormen, bellhops, and waitresses will frequently *wai* to you. It's not necessary to return the greeting; a simple smile of acknowledgment or a nod of your head is all that's needed. In situations where a *wai* is appropriate, such as when meeting a person of obvious status, a friend's mother or father, or a monk, don't fret about the position of your hands. To keep them level to your chest is perfectly acceptable. Two exceptions—never *wai* a child, and never expect a monk to *wai* back (they are exempted from the custom).

CONFRONTATIONS

An important aspect of the Thai character is that they expect a certain level of **equanimity, calm, and light-heartedness** in any personal dealings. Displays of anger and confrontational behavior, especially from foreign visitors, get you nowhere. Thais believe such outbursts are an indication of a less-developed human being. Getting angry and upset is in essence "losing face" by acting shamefully in front of others, and Thai people will walk away or giggle, to spare revealing their embarrassment. Travelers who throw fits often find themselves ignored or abandoned by the very people who could help.

So what do you do if you encounter a frustrating situation? The Thai philosophy advocates **jai yen,** meaning, "Take it easy. Chill." If it's a situation you can't control, such as a traffic jam or a delayed flight—*jai yen*. If you find yourself at loggerheads with the front desk, arguing with a taxi driver, or in any other truly frustrating situation, keep calm, try a little humor, and find a non-confrontational compromise that will save face for all involved.

TAXI ETIQUETTE

To hail a taxi or call someone toward you, point your palm to the ground and beckon with your fingers towards your body. Basically, the opposite of how you would motion someone to come your way in the West. Another option for

from air-conditioned sleeper cars in first class to air-conditioned and fan sleepers or seats in second, on down to the straight-backed, hard seats in third class.

Reservations can be made 60 days before departure at any train station or local travel agency. Agencies normally add a service charge to the price of the ticket, but often the convince factor outweighs the additional cost. To book long-distance tickets prior to arrival in Thailand, email your request to SRT (passenger-ser@railway.co.th), and they will email confirmation so you can pick up tickets at the departure station.

calling a taxi is to hold out your hand like you would in New York City. If the light on the left-hand side of the dashboard is illuminated, that means the taxi is open. Many drivers will roll down the window and ask you where you're going before accepting your ride. It's a common annoyance in Bangkok.

RELIGION & POLITICS

The Thais hold two things sacred: Their religion and their royal family. In temples and royal palaces, **strict dress code** is enforced. Wear long pants or skirts, with a neat shirt, and tops with shoulder-covering sleeves. Remove shoes and hats before entering temple buildings and give worshipers their space. Some temples will rent women a sarong to cover their lower half for just a few baht, but it might be easier and more enjoyable to carry your own in a bag. Young Thai society may seem very liberal, but it is in fact curiously conservative and sartorially prudish. Offices have dress codes and workers are often given uniforms to wear.

While **photographing** images is generally allowed, do not climb on anything or pose near it in a way that could be seen as showing disrespect. In the *I-did-it-for-the-Instagram-era*, this advice is particularly prudent. Women should be especially cautious around monks, who are not allowed to touch members of the opposite sex. If a woman needs to hand something to a monk, she should either hand it to a man to give to the monk, or place the item in front of him.

Never, ever, say anything critical or improper about the **royal family,** past or present, not even in jest. Never deface images of royalty (on coins, stamps, or posters); this could result in a hefty prison sentence. This same rule applies for offering your opinion on Thai politics—just don't do it. And when in doubt zip your lip. In movie theaters, everyone is expected to stand for the national anthem, which is played before every screening.

TOUCHING & GESTURES

Thais avoid **public displays of affection.** While straight members of the same gender often hold hands or walk arm in arm (this includes men), you'll rarely see a Thai man and woman acting this way. Thai women who date foreign men flaunt these rules openly but, as a rule of thumb, Thais frown upon lovers who touch, hug, or kiss in public.

Buddhists believe **the feet** are the lowliest part of the body, so using the foot to point or touch an object in Thailand is unbelievably insulting. Do not point your feet at a person or a Buddha image, or use your foot to tap a runaway coin (it bears the king's image).

In contrast, **the head** is considered the most sacred part of the body. Don't touch a Thai on the head or tousle a child's hair, but rather offer a friendly pat on the back.

BY BUS

In the farthest and more remote destinations in the country, buses are the cheapest and fastest public transportation. However, the frequency with which wrecked buses appear in Thai newspapers shows that taking the bus carries an inherent risk. (A 2015 study, the most recent data available at press time, by the World Health Organization said Thailand's roads are the second deadliest in the world.) If you go for it, the major choices are public or private and air-conditioned or non-air-conditioned. Longer bus trips usually depart in the evenings to arrive at their destination early in the morning. Whenever you can, opt for the **VIP buses,** especially for overnight trips. Some have 36 seats; better ones have 24 seats (non-VIP buses double the number of passengers). The extra cost is well worth it for the legroom. Also, stick to government-subsidized buses operated by the **Transport Company** (✆ **1490**), commonly known as Baw Khaw Saw or BKS, from each city's proper bus terminal. Many private companies sell VIP tickets for major routes, but sometimes put you on a standard bus. *Scam Alert:* In tourist centers or backpacker hubs, like Bangkok's Khao San Road, third-party vendors sell bus tickets. While some are reliable, others are scams or include unscheduled commission-making stops (at souvenir stands and the like). Better not to risk it.

BY TAXI, TUK-TUK, SONGTAEW & SAMLOR

By law, **taxis** must charge by the meter and the flag fare is 35B. However, outside Bangkok they rarely use them, so you'll need to negotiate upfront. *Farang* passengers, essentially any non-Thai, are likely to be scammed at least once during a trip to Thailand, so adopt the laidback Thai attitude of *mai pen rai,* or no worries, and don't lose your cool. The most common annoyance is refusing to use the meter or claiming that it's broken. Get out and find a new taxi if that happens. A taxi driver often refuses crosstown trips, especially when it's coming up to a shift change (3–4pm) or if the traffic is bad.

In 2018, Uber sold its Southeast Asian operations to **GrabTaxi** (www. grabtaxi.com), an Uber-like smartphone app that partners with local taxis, cars, and even motorbikes. Prices are known to be nominally higher (between 10B and 60B), but that price bump is outweighed by convenience, since many taxi drivers speak little English, which eliminates any price negotiation. Surge pricing goes into effect when demand is high (often when it rains) making this a pretty pricey transportation option then.

Immortalized on postcards of Thailand, a ride in a three-wheeled **tuk-tuk** is a must-do for most visitors. But these iconic rides can be a bit of pain: Drivers speak little English, never carry change and have over-inflated prices. Plus in bad traffic they're pollution chariots. Be sure to bargain hard, and don't let them take you to their uncle's tailor or brother-in-law's gemstone store in exchange for free fare—that's the oldest scam in Thailand!

WHO ARE farang?

Caucasians are known as *farang* (a word that originally meant French, referring to the nation's earliest Western visitors). *Farang* is not necessarily a racist term, but, yes, foreign tourists are ritually overcharged and some take this personally as a form of discrimination. Look at this from a Thai, not Western, perspective. Thais believe if you have more, you are expected to give more; the rule applies to Thais as well, regardless of your budget. As a *farang* you are *automatically* seen as wealthy in Thailand. Skills in bargaining will come in time if you practice. Just remember that Thais really appreciate the generosity, rather than someone who makes a big deal about haggling over a 20 or 40 baht.

In provincial areas and resort islands, small pickup trucks called *songtaews* cruise the main streets offering a communal taxi service at cheap, set fees. As with tuk-tuks, always agree on your fare before engaging a driver. A *samlor* is like a rickshaw where the driver pedals a three-wheeled bicycle. These are mostly used in remote regions, and you're more like to see cabbages and carrots than people in the open carriage.

Pro Tips: Even cosmopolitan Bangkok, taxi, tuk-tuk or *songtaew* drivers speak basic English at best, so grab your hotel's business card to show to your driver to (hopefully) prevent getting lost. Rounding up on the meter or leaving the coins is enough of a tip for taxis, and negotiated rates don't require tipping.

PUBLIC TRANSPORT (BANGKOK ONLY)

Bangkok is the only city in Thailand that has traditional forms of mass transit, like a subway, and it's an incredibly cheap and efficient way to beat the traffic. See page 56 for tips on using the BTS and MRT, and there is a transportation map on the inside front cover.

TIPS ON PLACES TO STAY

Almost every type of accommodation will add a 10% service charge and a 7% value-added tax (VAT) to the final bill. Often, these two fees combined are listed as ++, or plus plus. Be sure to check if those numbers are included before making any bookings.

Across the country, particularly in Bangkok, Phuket, and Koh Samui, **Airbnb** (www.airbnb.com) and **Wimdu.com** are blooming in popularity. If you're a budget traveler, these option can be an outstanding value and a great way to connect with local expat or Thai hosts. (Airbnb designates top property managers as Superhosts, and they're normally a goldmine for local tips.)

If you're traveling with a group of friends of a large family—especially to a tropical part of the country—check out **VBRO** (www.vbro.com), **FlipKey** (www.flipkey.com), or **HomeAway** (www.homeaway.com) for villa listings that include drool-worthy private pools and multiple rooms. These can be a major money-saver in beach locations, especially for groups. We find these rental sites less fruitful for city locales though (use Wimdu or Airbnb for those).

Price Ranges

HOTELS: Frommer's guides have three designations of price-points, so all lodging in this guide is either **expensive, moderate,** or **inexpensive.**

As a guideline, the expensive distinction is 6,000B or more per night, but do note that there are a number of hotels in this category that go well beyond 10,000B. I love to travel, and I am lucky that my job takes me to some magical places, but I know there are few travel frustrations as great as spending a lot of hard-earned cash on a place that doesn't live up to the hype. So I promise the top-dollar properties in this guide are *really* worth the splurge and are

Best Strategies for Booking Online

While our robust hotel recommendations have been personally vetted, and cover a wide breadth of styles and prices, you'll still need to go on the trusty World Wide Web to book. So, for just a moment, put down this guide (long live print!) and make use of our pro tips for booking accommodation in Southeast Asia. First, remember that traditional websites aren't mandatory for Thai businesses to thrive, and often social media pages like Facebook, Instagram, or LINE, a regional messaging platform, play the role that a formal website would in the west. SEO (that's search engine optimization, in tech terms) isn't great here either, so official hotel booking sites are often buried on the second or third page of a Google search. Second, book smarter! A 2018 study by Frommers.com found that **Agoda.com** offered the best rates for Asia, by far. Other good options include **Booking.com** and **Hotels.com**. On the latter, you'll earn 1 free night for every 10 nights booked on their free rewards program. And, finally: **Ask for a discount!** While it's not a particularly helpful strategy at big chains, you shouldn't hesitate to politely request a small discount in person, especially for last-minute deals or during off-peak tourism times. Be sure you're asking the right person though: Usually you'll need to speak with a manager or owner to get the money off.

perfect for honeymooners, anniversary celebrators, and once-in-a-lifetime trip seekers.

You'll find that more than half of our hotel recommendations are in the moderate category. We hope you'll be spending a lot of time *outside* your hotel, exploring side *sois,* meeting with kind-hearted locals, chowing down on a perfect bowl of 35B noodles, and taking lots of photos. But we also know how crazy Thailand—especially Bangkok—can be, and how having a place to cool your heals and decompress can be lifesaving for a jet-lagged traveler. Moderate hotels have all the creature comforts and then some, and you'll find charming boutiques, chain hotels, and beachside hangouts in this category, which we're defining as 3,000B–6,000B per night. That's a wide price range (about $90–$180 U.S. dollars), so you'll be able to cherry-pick options that fit your exact financial plan.

The inexpensive category is 2,999B or less and covers a wide range of boutiques, guesthouses, and hostels that are always clean and comfortable. Options at the lower end of this range, which is to say 500B or less per day, are going to be barebones. If air-con or hot showers aren't included, we'll be sure to mention that upfront.

DINING: Expensive means that a meal for without drinks will probably cost more than 1,000B; in **moderate** places, expect to pay from 500B to 1000B; **inexpensive** means you'll pay less than 500B per person—often as little as 40B a plate! For tips on eating in Thailand, the foodie culture, and more, see Chapter 3.

SPECIAL-INTEREST TRIPS

Destination chapters will have robust recommendations for adventure-seekers (as will chapter 4), food tours, cooking classes, bike trips, trekking adventures, walking tours, scuba certifications, meditation courses, yoga retreats, spa lessons, and more. The possibilities are endless in Thailand. What follows are some organizations have offerings in all parts of the kingdom.

Volunteer Vacations

Most volunteer vacations require a commitment of 2 weeks or more. However those who experience the country in this way are guaranteed closer contact with Thais than those on the tourist circuit, a usually gain a deeper appreciation for the culture. The most common opportunities in Thailand involve teaching English, but those who can teach computer skills or other subjects are also in demand. Below are some organizations that offer the chance to do voluntary work in Thailand; most require a donation to cover expenses such as accommodation and food.

Volunteer Work Thailand (www.volunteerworkthailand.org) is a good place to start, as it is an umbrella site that provides links to a host of organizations looking for volunteers in the country, ranging from the Thai Society for the Conservation of Wild Animals to United Nation Volunteers. Grassroots-level volunteer jobs of all sorts are also available at **Kaya Responsible Travel** (www.kayavolunteer.com), which lists opportunities ranging from animal care to cleaning up national parks to working with children, and more.

For would-be English teachers, the best resource is **Lemon Grass Volunteering** in Bangkok (www.lemongrass-volunteering.com).

If you're an animal lover, check out the **World Wildlife Fund's** website (www.wwf.or.th) for a summary of the country's many problems. There are organizations trying to protect animals like gibbons from exploitation and extinction, such as the **Gibbon Rehabilitation Project** (see p. 238). The Phuket-based **Soi Dog Foundation** (www.soidog.org) is always in need of volunteers in their Phuket office to help socialize rescued street dogs with human interaction, walks, and supervised play with other dogs. The foundation also uses volunteers to help re-home these animals abroad and ask for travelers to help transport animals on their flights. There is no cost to the traveler and the foundation handles all necessary paperwork and fees.

Those seriously interested in marine conservation can join the volunteer team at Ko Phra Thong north of Phuket, where an Italian-led organization called **Naucrates** (www.naucrates.org) has spent over a decade educating local communities on ecological issues and monitoring the decline of local turtles. It also runs a mangrove revitalization scheme.

HEALTHCARE IN THAILAND

High standards of personal and food hygiene should reassure most visitors to Thailand. That being said, the same precautions for visiting tropical climes apply to the more remote areas of the Thai kingdom, where some types of mosquito can transmit malaria or dengue fever. The **Center for Disease Control (CDC)** recommends that travelers are up-to-date on routine vaccinations, like measles-mumps-rubella (MMR) and an annual flu shot, as well as getting current immunizations for hepatitis A and typhoid. Stay abreast of the most up-to-date CDC information at www.cdc.gov.

General Availability of Healthcare

Dispensaries and hospital facilities in Thailand, especially in urban centers, are generally excellent. In Phuket and Samui, hospitals are familiar with the needs of vacationers, especially victims of car and motorbike crashes. Smaller towns will usually have a basic clinic, but getting back to Bangkok is always the best bet. (See "Fast Facts," in individual destination chapters for info.) Throughout the country, there are drugstores stocked with brand-name medications and toiletries, plus less expensive local brands. Pharmacists often speak some English, and a number of drugs that require a prescription elsewhere can be dispensed over the counter.

Private and public hospitals in Thailand both have English-speaking staff. In Bangkok, world-class hospitals like **Samitivej Hospital** (www.samitivej hospitals.com), **Bumrungrad International Hospital** (www.bumrungrad. com), and **BNH Hospital** (www.bnhhospital.com) do a booming business in medical tourism (see below). If your ailment isn't an emergency, these are outstanding options for visitors.

Medical Tourism

Medical tourism is a tour de force for the Thai economy, surpassing US$4.6 billion in 2016, the last year records were kept, with no signs of slowing down or stopping. World-class hospitals, a high ratio of staff to patients, and affordable post-op care are driving forces for elective cosmetic procedures and scheduled surgeries like knee replacements or root canals. As the industry skyrockets, medical centers have started offering facilities for drug and alcohol dependent people to go to rehab in relaxed temple settings or on tranquil beaches. Tour outfitters have joined the medical tourism movement, and websites like www.topdoctors.co bundle pre-travel doctor consultations and surgeries with recovery time at a beachfront resort, including care from registered nurses if needed.

Common Ailments
STOMACH TROUBLE

Often the change in diet will provoke **diarrhea** in travelers to Thailand. You can best avoid upset stomachs by sticking to bottled water at all times, and drinking lots of it. *Note:* Carry a roll of toilet paper or packet of tissues since Thai toilets do not always provide this. Pharmacies here, such as Boots or Watson's, have a wide range of Western brand drugs, including Imodium. 7-Eleven stores sell single toilet-paper rolls and ready-to-go electrolyte drinks and packets as well as the familiar items and brands such as Bayer, Tylenol, and Eno antacids.

While restaurant hygiene throughout the country is generally excellent, be wary of street-side food stalls where the food is sitting out.

TROPICAL ILLNESSES

Major tourist areas, such as Bangkok, Phuket, Ko Samui, and Chiang Mai, have very few cases and are considered **malaria free.** However, malaria is still a problem in rural parts, particularly territories in the mountains to the north and near the borders with Cambodia, Laos, and Myanmar. The best way to prevent malaria transmission or catching any other diseases listed here is to cover up with light-colored clothing and wear long pants and sleeves after dark. Sleep with **Permethrin**-treated mosquito netting well tucked in, and use repellents. And make sure your repellent contains a high percentage of DEET. If you do get bitten and you develop a fever within 2 weeks of entering a high-risk area, be sure to consult a physician.

Dengue fever has spiked in the last decade. Like malaria, the virus spreads by mosquitos, but this one can bite during the day as well as at night. Symptoms are similar to those of the flu, with high fever, severe aches, fatigue, and possible skin rashes or headaches, lasting about a week.

Japanese encephalitis is a deadly viral infection that attacks the brain and is spread by a mosquito bite. Outbreaks are rare and, typically, vaccinations are only recommended for travelers staying in remote areas for more than a month. As with malaria and dengue, the best protection is to avoid being bitten, but seek medical attention if you develop symptoms such as fever, severe aches, and skin rashes.

Mosquito-born **Zika** can be a concern in Thailand, so if you're pregnant or plan to get pregnant, you should consult with your doctor prior to travel.

BUGS & OTHER WILDLIFE CONCERNS

On jungle hikes in particular, wear long sleeves and trousers instead of shorts, which will protect against not just mosquito bites, but the ubiquitous ticks, leeches, nasty biting giant centipedes, and (rarely seen) snakes. In order to survive the heat and humidity, wear loose cotton pants, socks, and sturdy boots—natural fibers are perfect for this terrain. When venturing into thick jungle terrain, do so with a qualified guide and follow his or her example. Don't pick or touch plants unless the guide says it's safe.

Rabies is not a major risk in Thailand but avoid interacting with stray animals just to be safe. **Coral reefs** pose minor risks from such things as poisonous sea snakes, jellyfish, and sea urchins.

WHAT'S HAPPENING tonight?

If you're looking for a concert and other performance schedules, these English publications are reliable resources for expats and Thais.

The lifestyle section of **Bangkok Post** is called **Guru** (www.bangkokpost.com/guru) and their staff publishes interviews with chefs and a high-brow list of events. **BK Magazine** (www.bk.asia-city.com) is a free weekly paper with its finger on the pulse of the city and a go-to resource to find out where Bangkok's young and trendy are headed any given night of the week. **Bangkok 101** (www.bangkok101.com) is a free monthly magazine with a robust events section and cultural insights.

All three titles are available in coffee shops around Bangkok and online as well. While the primary focus of coverage is the capital, frequent listings for other major cities or islands make it worth a look for other parts of Thailand.

RESPIRATORY ILLNESS

The air in Bangkok at certain times of the year can be smog-laden and Chiang Mai can also be very hazy in March when locals burn their crops. Anyone with respiratory issues such as asthma should carry both regular and emergency inhalers, though common brands are available without prescription.

COPING WITH THE HEAT

The symptoms for **sunstroke** or **heat exhaustion** are unbearable headaches, nausea, vomiting, dizziness, and extreme fatigue. To help avoid these ailments, expose yourself gradually to the heat; wearing a high-SPF sunscreen and a hat which will prevent sunburn but not heatstroke. Low alcohol consumption and light meals will help you to acclimatize much faster.

What to Do if You Get Sick in Thailand

Medical services in Thailand are good, especially in cities (top-notch at Bangkok's private hospitals). Street dispensaries (open-air, shophouse-style pharmacies)—though unregulated—sell most drugs, even those normally available only by prescription overseas. The pharmacist may have an almanac on the counter in English, which you can check for the different brand names of generic pharmaceutical products in your country, but always seek professional advice.

In most cases, your existing health plan likely won't provide the coverage you need. Therefore we recommend buying **travel medical insurance,** a particularly smart move for those with pre-existing medical conditions. Bring your insurance ID card for hospital visits with you when you travel.

If you don't feel well, ask any hotel concierge to recommend a local doctor or clinic. In only very grave cases will you be sent to the emergency room. I list **emergency numbers** under "Fast Facts," p. 420.

If you require an ambulance, the number is **1554** or say *rohng pha yaa baan,* to a taxi driver. In an emergency, some embassies or consulates can offer advice.

Dental clinics are easy to find around the country and prices are normally much cheaper than in the U.S., including pricing for expensive treatments like root canals. In Bangkok, **Thonglor Dental Hospital** (www.thonglordental hospital.com) is a popular choice for expats and upperclass Thais. Outside the capital, hospitals offer dental services and there are plenty of standalone clinics.

MONEY & COSTS

THE VALUE OF THE BAHT VS. OTHER POPULAR CURRENCIES

Thai Baht	US$	Can$	UK£	Euro (€)	Aus$	NZ$
100	US$3.12	C$4.01	£2.33	€2.66	A$4.13	NZ$4.51

The Thai unit of currency is the **baht** (written B, Bt, Bht, or THB) and is divided into 100 **satang**. Small coins of 1B, 2B, and 5B denominations are generally a pain for most tourists, but they'll come in handy for riding the BTS or MRT in Bangkok (see p. 56). The larger, more useful 10B coin is silver with a copper inset and they'll be helpful for cabs or 7-Eleven purchases. Bank bills come in denominations of 20B (green), 50B (blue), 100B (red), 500B (purple), and 1,000B (tan). At some point during your visit, you'll likely encounter a taxi driver, market hawker, or street food vendor who can't—or won't—break a 1,000B bill, so be sure to carry smaller denominations.

14

WHAT THINGS COST IN BANGKOK (THAI BAHT)

A taxi from Suvarnabhumi Airport to the city	250–350
One-day pass on the BTS	130
One-day pass on the MRT	120
Double at the Mandarin Oriental (very expensive)	17,500
Double at the Avani Riverside (moderate)	3,700
Double at Shanghai Mansion (budget)	1,700
Dinner for one, without alcohol, at Le Du (expensive)	1,690
Dinner for one, without alcohol, at 80/20 (moderate)	800
Dinner for one, without alcohol, at a street food vendor (inexpensive)	40
Bottle of beer at a hotel bar	150
Bottle of beer at a local bar	100
Coca-Cola	15
Regular coffee at a mall cafe	100
Admission to the Grand Palace	500
Movie ticket	140

Convenience stores will always make change so pop in for a bottle of water or pack of mints if you're stuck with a 1,000B.

Travel in Thailand is affordable and therefore attracts all types of travelers. In 2018, the average Thai income stood at around US$700 per person, per month, so standards of living and corresponding prices reflect this. Compared to home, many excellent hotels and restaurants cost a fraction of the price in Thailand, and, because of this, Thais consider any foreigner to be extremely well-off (see box on p. 412).

Always bear in mind that throughout Thailand, the baht will be the only acceptable currency, and foreign currency is rarely, if ever, accepted for everyday transactions.

There are no restrictions on the import of foreign currencies, but you must report to customs if you're arriving or leaving with an excess of US$20,000 per person.

In Thailand, like many international destinations, **traveler's checks** are almost entirely phased out, having been largely replaced by ATMs and there is no guarantee that they will be easily accepted.

When using your card in Thai department stores, also be aware that each section must ring up its receipt *separately*—so don't be alarmed if a clerk walks off a little way with your card to process the transaction, but still remain vigilant and take a common-sense approach.

MasterCard and **Visa** are the most widely accepted credit cards in Thailand, followed by **American Express.** Most hotels and restaurants accept all of these, especially in tourist destination areas. **Discover** and **Diners Club** are far less commonly accepted.

[FastFACTS] THAILAND

ATMs ATMs are common around Thailand and generally charge a 150B foreign-transaction fee for non-Thai ATM cards. Remember, your home bank will likely charge an out-of-network fee as well. ATMs issue Thai baht, but there are several machines at Suvarnabhumi Airport that distribute U.S. dollar and euros as well. ATMs dispense 100-, 500-, and 1,000-baht bills

Customs Tourists can enter the country with 1 liter of alcohol and 200 cigarettes (or 250g of cigars or smoking tobacco) per adult, duty-free, and there is no official limit on perfume. Still have questions? Use the handy customs website (www.customs.go.th) as a guide.

However, you should pay more attention to what you can take back with you to your home country. Thai export customs is rather lax, but one exception is cultural treasures: It is forbidden to take antique Buddha images or Bodhisattva images out of the kingdom.

(Amulets are a noted exception.) Special permission is required for removing antique artifacts from the country, and the authorization process takes about 4 days. For further details, contact the **Department of Fine Arts** (① 02628-5033), open weekdays 8:30am to 4pm. **Scam alert:** Remember that antique dealers are out for the sale, and while they might be kind, verify all customs rules and regulations yourself before making a large purchase.

Doctors, Dentists, and Hospitals See "Health," on p. 416.

Drinking Laws The official drinking age in Thailand is 18, though you need to be 20 to enter a nightclub. You can buy alcohol at convenience stores and supermarkets from 11am to 2pm and from 5pm to midnight. On certain religious holidays, and on the eve of election days liquor sales are banned (the government want its voters to be sober and clear of mind). Nightlife venues must close at 1am, and the rule is generally enforced though you'll find exceptions where bars are given "special dispensation" (in exchange for a bribe).

Electricity Thailand uses 220 volts AC electricity. Outlets have two flat-pronged or round-pronged holes, so you may need an adapter.

Embassies & Consulates International embassies are in Bangkok and many countries have consular representation in cities like Chiang Mai and Phuket. Most embassies have 24-hour emergency services. If you are seriously injured or ill, call your embassy for assistance.

Emergencies Throughout the country, the emergency number you should use is ☎ **1155** for the Tourist Police. Don't expect many English speakers at police posts outside the major tourist areas. For an emergency ambulance, call

☎ **1554.** You can also contact your embassy or consulate.

Family Travel A visit to Thailand will certainly broaden the horizons of young visitors, and many families report great experiences in the kingdom, partly because most Thais dote on kids. Larger resorts and hotels, along with many malls, have kid-friendly programs, kids' clubs, sports equipment rentals, and kid-oriented group activities. Many of the larger hotels also offer special deals for families or young children.

In general, 12-years-old is the cut-off for children to share their parents' hotel room for free and not be counted as an extra adult—and often an extra bed can be arranged for an additional fee. There are also a few hotels that require guests to be 12 or older. If there are age restrictions, you'll see them noted in individual listings. If you're looking for a place to stay with a small kitchen or above-average space, consider booking a rental over a hotel (see Tips on Places to Stay, above).

As in other countries, babysitting services are available in top hotels, but few consider this a chore in Thailand, and generally, you can expect hotel and restaurant staff to be falling over each other to amuse the kids while you are eating. You'll never get a dirty look from a Thai for bringing a noisy or active child

around as you might in the West.

Your animal-loving tot might be fascinated with the large numbers of soi dogs and cats roaming the streets of Thailand, but do not let your child touch them. Street animals are more feral than in the West or Europe, and could potentially be rabid.

Uneven sidewalks and crossing major roads via bridges make Thailand less than ideal for those with strollers, so, if you can get away with it, opt for baby carriers instead.

Insurance If your insurance back home doesn't offer international coverage, it's wise to take out travel insurance before heading to Thailand, particularly if you intend to go diving or ride a rented motorbike. Such websites as **SquareMouth. com** and **InsureMyTrip.com** act as clearinghouse sites for policies from the major insurance companies.

Internet Access and Mobile Phones If your phone is unlocked (check with your carrier), pop in a Thai SIM card for a fraction of the price of a data plan. Weeklong packages with unlimited 4G data are around 300B. Buy them at any airport or 7-Eleven. DTAC, and AIS are the major carriers and offer comparable coverage. All hotels in this book have Wi-Fi (and most that aren't in the book will, too.)

Legal Aid As long as you do not break the law in

Thailand, there is no reason that you should require legal aid. Thai police generally avoid having to speak English to foreigners, unless they think you're harboring drugs. Possession and trafficking carry strict punishments, like lengthy jail time or even death. If, however, you feel you have been wrongly accused of, say, causing a road accident, you should consult your nearest embassy or consulate for advice.

LGBT Travelers Thailand is very gay-friendly and the gay nightlife scene is huge. Lesbians are known as tom (more butch, durative of tomboy) or dee (more outwardly femme); are usually less vocal and ostentatious than their male counterparts, or the theatrically inclined lady-boys (katoeys).

There are regular cabaret shows (some light-hearted and fun; other raunchy) and beauty competitions for lady-boys throughout the country. In Bangkok, the most popular and highbrow gay event is Sunday nights at **Maggie Choo's** (www.maggiechoos.com). A go-to resource for the LGBT community in Asia is www.travelgayasia.com, a website with gay-friendly information, event listings, and travel tips. **Out Adventures** (www.outadventures.com) organizes group and tailor-made trips to Thailand for gay travelers.

Regardless of sexual orientation, public displays of affection beyond

hand-holding are generally frowned upon.

Mail Send postcards to the United States for 15B for a standard size postcard and airmail letters cost 19B (17B to Europe). Airmail delivery usually takes 7 to 14 days. Mailing a small package is generally affordable—around 1,000B—and can be done via **Thai Post's** EMS express service. Customs forms are available at the post offices. For a list of locations or more detailed pricing information, visit www.thailandpost.co.th.

Major international delivery services have offices in Bangkok and a network that extends to the provinces. These are **DHL Thailand** (www.dhl.co.th/en), **Federal Express,** (www.fedex.com/th), and **UPS** (www.ups.com). The mother of all markets is Bangkok's Chatuchak Weekend Market (p. 127) and you'll find shipping services on-site. But don't plan to ship goods home unless necessary since these services are quite expensive. Often, paying an airline for an extra bag or an overweight bag is cheaper, and obviously faster, than shipping. If you fall in love with an item that is simply too big (like a table) or fragile (like beautiful pottery in Chiang Rai, p. 383) to fit into a suitcase, ask the seller to arrange shipping and customs for you. Be sure to hold on to a receipt and business card of the vendor in case there are issues.

Pharmacies There are pharmacies everywhere in Bangkok and easy to find on even the smallest of islands. In recent years, officials have been cracking down on distribution of prescription drugs—like Xanax or sleeping pills. In Thailand, many drugs that would require a prescription in the West, like antibiotics and birth control, are available over the counter. Check the expiration dates on drugs and, when you can, buy from a pharmacy with air-conditioning (drugs have longer shelf life when kept cool, generally). **Boots** (www.th.boots.com/en for locations) and **Watsons** (www.watsons.co.th for locations) are Thailand's most popular chains of pharmacies and they have English-speaking pharmacists on-site. There is a Boots after security at Suvarnabhumi Airport.

Safety Violent crime—especially towards foreigners—is rare in Thailand so safety is more about being street-smart. Because **pickpockets** and **scam artists** work the tourist areas and pounce on friendly or naive travelers, keep an eye on valuables in crowded places, and be wary of anyone who approaches you in the street to solicit your friendship or alert you that a major temple is closed. **Snatch thieves** are known for whizzing around on motorbikes and grabbing bags or cell phones from the hands of pedestrians or passengers riding in open-air tuk-tuks, so wear a cross-body bag and be mindful of your possessions. Another tuk-tuk precaution is drivers who end up wasting precious time on "shopping tours," where your "guide" will collect a commission and keep you from getting where you'd like to go—see more in the tuk-tuk section on page 412.

Thai police are some of the lowest-paid civil servants in the country, so it's not surprising that they have a reputation for harassment, intimidation, and bribery. Prostitution is also illegal; see below for info on that.

Since the military coup d'état in September 2014, the political situation in Thailand has moments of instability. Things have calmed down significantly since then but flare-ups do happen. International news outlets, like CNN or the *New York Times*, are the best sources for up-to-date information.

The far southern provinces of Yala, Narathiwat, and Pattani, near the Malaysian border, are subject to ongoing sectarian violence between Thai Muslims and Thai military police. Thai institutions, schools, banks, and Buddhist temples have been targeted with small-scale bombs. Avoid this area, or travel through it with care.

Senior Travelers
Senior citizens are highly revered in Thai society and are treated with deference

and respect, which comes as a pleasant surprise to many first-time Western visitors. Unfortunately, this deference does not stretch to the kind of discounts on transport and admission fees that older travelers are used to back home.

Sex Prostitution in Thailand is technically illegal but is tolerated across the country. Go-go bars and brothels are most common in Bangkok, Phuket, and Pattaya, but they're not hard to find in other parts of the country. Despite its reputation for high numbers of sex tourists (or *sexpats*—a slang term for tourists and expats seeking out sex tourism), go-go bars and sex shows, including the infamous ping-pong shows, are tamer than their illicit reputation. (Although, that is not to say that a seedier, more exploitative sides don't exist because they certainly do.)

Smoking In Thailand, smoking is banned in air-conditioned public places such as restaurants and airports. Most hotel rooms are also non-smoking, so you should specify when booking if you are a smoker. By and large, the law is respected and some open-air bars that don't serve food tolerate smokers, or have created smoker-friendly outdoor spaces, including upmarket private cigar bars. Shops must cover displays of cigarettes, so you'll need to ask for your brand in a shop like 7-Eleven.

Student Travelers
Discounts for students in Thailand and the rest of Southeast Asia are better earned by the tenacity of the individual traveler's bargaining skills and tolerance for substandard accommodation than flashing a student ID. The **International Student Identity Card (ISIC),** however, offers small savings on plane tickets and some entrance fees. It also provides basic health and life insurance and a 24-hour helpline. The card is available for $22 from **STA Travel** (📞 **800/781-4040** in North America; www.sta travel.com), the biggest student travel agency in the world.

If you're no longer a student but are still under 26, you can get an **International Youth Travel Card (IYTC)** for the same price from the same people, entitling you to some discounts (but not on museum admissions). **Travel CUTS** (📞 **800/667-2887;** www. travelcuts.com) offers similar services for both Canadians and U.S. residents.

Taxes The 7% value-added tax (VAT) levied on most goods—just not hotels or food—can be refunded to non-Thai tourists upon leaving Thailand. This is a similar process to claiming a tax refund in other countries, but there are a few rules.

○ You must present your passport during the purchase process and ask the staff to complete the VAT Refund for Application for Tourists form.

- In order to qualify for the refund, you'll need to spend a minimum of 2,000B at each store.
- Goods must be taken out of Thailand within 60 days of purchase and be inspected by a customs officer at the airport—which means you'll need to hand-carry any items you intend to claim for a refund.
- You'll pay a 100B processing fee prior to receiving your refund.
- Be sure to allow ample time for the items to be inspected at the airport and for the refund to be issued. Lines are unpredictable.

For more information and to use The Revenue Department's handy VAT calculator, visit http://vrtweb.rd.go.th/index.php/en/.

Tipping Tipping is not an integral part of Thai culture but, unsurprisingly, Thais are willing to accommodate this generous Western habit, so feel free to reward good service wherever you find it. Hotels and upmarket restaurants add a 10% service charge and no additional tip is needed. Airport or hotel porters expect tips; 20–40B per bag is acceptable.

Tipping taxi drivers is also more or less expected. Carry small bills, as many cab drivers either don't have change or won't admit to having any in the hope of

getting a tip. It's not rude to leave the small change for a cab driver or at a restaurant; so, if your bill is 379B, leave 400B. If you've had a great tour guide, ride, or experience, 10 to 15% is a nice gesture, but your judgment overrides these suggestions, and the local people will be grateful for any tip. Hand a 100-baht bill to a masseuse after an hour-long treatment at a massage shop or spa.

Toilets Western toilets are (to the relief of most of you reading this book) more and more common in Thailand. But the Asian squat toilet, a ceramic platform mounted over a hole in the ground, are common in lesser-visited towns in rural areas. If this is your first experience with such toilets, take note: Near the toilet is a water bucket or sink with a small ladle. The water is for cleaning yourself and flushing the toilet. Many public washrooms normally have one Western toilet. Always carry a pack of tissues with you (they're available at 7-Eleven) since toilet paper is not usually provided.

Water Don't drink the tap water here, even in major hotels. Most hotels provide bottled water for free and you should use it for brushing your teeth. If you're in the shower and absently mindedly forget where you are and swallow a mouthful of water, you'll likely be just fine.

Since Thais do not drink the tap water, bottled water

is easily available across the country, including remote areas. Typically bottles are 10B each and you do not need to buy purification tabs or filtration systems.

Travelers with Disabilities Disabilities shouldn't stop anyone from traveling, but sadly Thailand does not make it easy on the physically challenged. Visitors to Thailand will find that, short of the better hotels in the larger towns, amenities for travelers with disabilities are nonexistent, even in public places. Negotiating sidewalks in cities is hazardous even for the nimble-footed, and crossing roads is a nightmare, so itineraries need to be well-planned. (In May 2018, the Thai government approved a 256-million-baht deal—about $8M U.S. dollar—to install better elevators on the BTS.)

On the positive side, the Thais' warm-hearted and genuinely helpful nature means they go to great pains to make sure visitors are well looked after. One way to guarantee a smooth trip if you have mobility issues is to book a package tour with **Wheelchair Holidays @ Thailand** (www.wheelchairtours.com) or **Accessible Journeys** (www.disabilitytravel.com).

Women Travelers Women travelers face no particular discrimination or dangers in Thailand. Women should, however, be very careful when dealing with monks: Never touch a monk, never hand anything directly to him (it should be set on the floor in front of the monk or given to a man who will hand it to them directly), and don't sit next to monks on public transport or in the monk-only designated areas in waiting rooms. Some parts of temples do not allow women to enter; look for signs indicating this.

At all temples and mosques, be sure to wear a long skirt or pants and have your shoulders covered. Your head should be covered in mosques, but headwear (caps, sun visors) must be removed in Buddhist temples.

USEFUL TERMS & PHRASES

Thai is a tonal language, with low, mid, high, rising, or falling tones. There are five tonal markings:

low tone: `
falling tone: ^
middle tone (no marking)
rising tone: ˇ
high tone: ´

Most important, Thai also differentiates between the language used by a male and that used by a female. Thus, males use **Pŏm** for I, and females use **Deè-chăn**. The suffix **khráp** is an affirmation used by men only, and **khă** is used similarly for women. It can be used as a lazy reply, such as "Uh-huh."

Though it's very difficult for Westerners to pronounce Thai sounds correctly, there are no problems with stress, as all syllables receive equal emphasis. A useful resource for self-study of Thai is **www.thai-language.com.**

BASIC PHRASES & VOCABULARY

English	Thai Transliteration	Pronunciation
Hello (male)	**Sà–wàt–dii–khráp**	sah-wah-dee-kup
Hello (female)	**Sà-wàt-dii-khâ**	sah-wah-dee-kah
How are you?	**Sà bai-dii măi?**	sah-bye-dee-my
I am fine	**Sà bai-dii**	sah-bye-dee
Do you speak English?	**Phûut phaa-săa ang rìt dăi măi?**	poot pa-sah ang-krit dye my?
I do not understand	**Măi khăo jai**	my cow jy
Excuse me/Sorry	**Khăw thôht (-khráp, -khă)**	cor tort (-kup, -kah)
Thank you	**Khòp khun (-khráp, -khă)**	cop koon (-kup, -kah)
No, I do not want . . .	**Măi ao . . .**	my ow . . .
Yes, I want . . .	**Chăi, ao. . .**	chai, ow . . .
Stop here!	**Yùt tĭi nĭi!**	Yut ti nee
Where is the (public) toilet?	**Hâwng nám yùu thĭi năi?**	hong nam yutin nye?
I need to see a doctor	**Pŏm/Deè-chăn tăwng kaan hăa măw**	pom/dee-charn tong-garn haa mor
Call the police!	**Rîak tam-rùat nàwy!**	reeyuk tamru-at noy
Never mind/No problem	**Măi pen rai**	my pen rye
Do you have . . . ?	**Mii . . . măi?**	mee . . . my?

GETTING AROUND

English	Thai Transliteration	Pronunciation
I want to go to . . .	Yàk jà pai . . .	yark jar by . . .
Where is the . . .	Yùu thîi nǎi . . .	yutin nye . . .
taxi	tháek-sîi	tak-see
bus station	sà thǎa nee khǒn sòng	sartarnee kornsong
train station	sà thǎa nee rót fai	sartarnee rot fye
airport	sà nǎam bin	sanam-bin
boat jetty	thǎ reua	taa ru-er
hotel	rohng ra-em	rorngrem
hospital	rohng phá yaa baan	roong-pye-aban
How much . . . ?	Thǎo rai?	tao-rye?
What time (does it depart)?	(Jà àwk) kìi mohng?	(jar ork) kee-mong?

IN A RESTAURANT

English	Thai Transliteration	Pronunciation
coffee	kaa–fae	gar-fay
tea (hot)	chaa–ráwn	char-rawn
bottled water	nám khuàt	nam kwat
water	nám	nam
ice	nám khǎeng	nam keng
beer	bia	bee-ya
noodles	kwǎy tǐaw	kway tee-ow
rice	khâo	cow
fried rice	khâo phàt	cow pat
chicken	kài	guy
beef	neúa	nuhr
pork	mǔu	moo
fish	plaa	blar
shrimp	kûng	goong
mango with sticky rice	khâo nǐaw má mûang	cow neeow mar-mwang
Thai desserts (general)	khà nǒm	knom
I am a vegetarian	Kin a han jae	gin aharn jae
I don't like it spicy	Mâi châwp phèt	my chorp pet
I like it spicy	Châwp phèt	chorp pet
Delicious!	Àh-ròy!	ah-roy
Check/bill please	Khǎw chék –bin	gor chek-bin

SPECIFIC MENU TERMS

Basic Ingredients

bread khà noˇm pan
cake/cookie khà noˇm
egg khài

salt kleua
sugar nám tan

Cooking Methods

grilled pǐng
baked òb
barbecued yâng
boiled dôm
deep-fried tôrt

ground sěe
roasted phǎo
steamed nêung
stir-fried phàt

Fruits

banana klûay
coconut máphráo
custard apple náwy nàa
durian thúrian
guava fà ràng
jackfruit khà nǔn
lime mánao
longan lam yài
mandarin orange sôm

mango mámûang
mangosteen mangkút
papaya málákaw
pineapple sàppàrót
pomelo sôm oh
rambutan ngáw
sapodilla lá mút
tamarind mákhǎm
watermelon taeng moh

Seafood

crab pu
lobster kûng yài
mussel hǒi maeng phû
oyster hǒi naang rom

scallop hǒi shell
shellfish hǒi
shrimp kûng fǒi

Vegetables

beansprouts thùa ngôk
cabbage phàk kà làm
cauliflower kà làm dàwk
corn khâo phôht
cucumber taeng kwa
eggplant mákhěua mûang
garlic kràtiam

lettuce phàk kàat
long bean thùa fàk yao
mushroom hèt
scallions tôn hǎwm
potato man fà ràng
spinach phàk khǒm
tomato mákhěua thêt

GEOGRAPHICAL TERMS

bay	ào	**lane**	soi
beach	hàt	**mountain**	doi
bridge	sà phan	**pier**	thâ
canal	klong	**province**	changwàt
cape	lǎem	**river**	mâe nám
city	ná khon	**street**	thà nǒn
district	amphoe	**town**	muang
hill	khǎo	**village**	bân
island	kò	**waterfall**	nám tòk

DAYS OF THE WEEK & TIME

Days of the Week

Sunday	wan aa thít	**Thursday**	wan phá réu hàt
Monday	wan jan	**Friday**	wan sòok
Tuesday	wan ang kan	**Saturday**	wan sǎo
Wednesday	wan poót		

Time

What is the time? keè mohng láew?
Day wan
Month deuan
Year pcc
Evening yen
Afternoon bai

Morning ton chaó
Now deeo née
This evening yen née
Today wan née
Tonight kern née
Tomorrow prûng née
Yesterday meûa wan née

SHOPPING

English	Thai Transliteration	Pronunciation
It's too expensive	**Phaeng kern pai**	peng kern pye
It's too big	**Yài kern pai**	yai kern pye
It's too small	**Lék kern pai**	lek kern pye
I don't like this one	**Mâi châwp an nîi**	my chorp an nee
Do you have a (smaller/larger) size?	**Mii sai (lék /yài gwà) nîi mǎi?**	mee sai (lek/yai gwa) nee my?
Do you have a black one?	**Mii sǐi dam mǎi?**	mee see dam my?
Can you give me a better price?	**Lót raa kah dâi mǎi?**	lot ra ka dai my?
How much is this?	**Nêe taô rai?**	Nee tao ray
Do you have anything cheaper?	**Toòk gwà nêe mii mǎi?**	Tuk gwa nee me my?

NUMBERS

Numbers	Thai Transliteration	Pronunciation
0	sǔun	soon
1	nèung	nung
2	sǎwng	song
3	sǎam	sam
4	sìi	see
5	hâa	hah
6	hòk	hork
7	jèd	jet
8	pàet	bet
9	kâo	gao
10	sìp	sip
11	sìp-èt	sip-ett
12	sìp-sǎwng	sip-song
100	nèung ráwy	nung-roy
1,000	nèung phan	nung-pan
10,000	nèung mùen	nung mwuen

To conjugate numbers like 30, 40, and so on, you simply say three-ten, four-ten, and so on. For example, 30 is *saam-sip*. Exceptions are:

o Such numbers as 11, 21, 31, and so on use the suffix *et*, not *neung*, so 11 is *sip-et*.

o Number 20 is *yee-sip* or simply *yip*, not *song-sip*.

Therefore, 21 is *yee-sip-et* or *yip-et*, not *song-sip neung*, as one might logically surmise!

Numbers

USEFUL TERMS & PHRASES

Index

See also Accommodations and
Restaurant Indexes

General Index

A

Accommodations

Restaurants

Map List

Photo Credits

p. i, © Phornphan Boonkrachai; p. ii, © 10 FACE; p. iii, © DR Travel Photo and Video; p. iv, © Mikhail Gnatkovskiy; p. v, top, © Omongkol / Shutterstock.com; p. v, middle, © Christian Mueller; p. v, bottom, © neo2620 / Shutterstock.com; p. vi, top, © MOLPIX; p. vi, bottom left, © Tommy love king / Shutterstock.com; p. vi, bottom right, © travelview / Shutterstock.com; p. vii, top, © kan Sangtong / Shutterstock.com; p. vii, middle, © martinho Smart; p. vii, bottom, © benedix / Shutterstock.com; p. viii, top. left, © topten22photo / Shutterstock.com; p. viii, top. right, © leungchopan; p. viii, bottom, © Travel mania; p. ix, top, © CRStudio; p. ix, middle, © martinho Smart / Shutterstock.com; p. ix, bottom, © Sarawut Chamsaeng / Shutterstock.com; p. x, top, © Udompeter; p. x, bottom left, © Maxim Tupikov / Shutterstock.com; p. x, bottom right, © Light Beam / Shutterstock.com; p. xi, top. left, © Kriengsak tarasr; p. xi, top. right, © LEE SNIDER PHOTO IMAGES / Shutterstock.com; p. xi, bottom, © Don Mammoser; p. xii, top, © apiguide; p. xii, middle, © Parkpoom Kotcharat; p. xii, bottom, © Denis Costille / Shutterstock.com; p. xiii, top, © Guitar photographer; p. xiii, bottom left, © Alphonsine Sabine; p. xiii, bottom right, © konmesa; p. xiv, top left, © bumihills / Shutterstock.com; p. xiv, top. right, © Eva Mont / Shutterstock.com; p. xiv, bottom left, © JR AK / Shutterstock.com; p. xiv, bottom right, © Toa55 / Shutterstock.com; p. xv, top, © KAMONRAT / Shutterstock.com; p. xv, middle, © Mongkol_Chuewong; p. xv, bottom, © pang_oasis; p. xvi, top, © Blanscape; p. xvi, bottom, © Akira Kaelyn / Shutterstock.com.

Frommer's Thailand, 13th Edition

Published by
FROMMER MEDIA LLC

Copyright (c) 2019 by FrommerMedia LLC, New York City, New York. All rights reserved. No part of this publication may be reproduced, stored in a retrieval system, or transmitted in any form or by any means, electronic, mechanical, photocopying, recording, scanning or otherwise, except as permitted under Sections 107 or 108 of the 1976 United States Copyright Act, without the prior written permission of the Publisher. Requests to the Publisher for permission should be addressed to the Permissions Department, FrommerMedia LLC, 44 West 62nd Street, New York, NY 10023, or online at http://www.frommers.com/permissions.

Frommer's is a registered trademark of Arthur Frommer. Used under license. All other trademarks are the property of their respective owners. FrommerMedia LLC is not associated with any product or vendor mentioned in this book.

ISBN 978-1-62887-402-0 (paper), 978-1-62887-403-7 (e-book)

Editorial Director: Pauline Frommer
Editor: Pauline Frommer
Production Editor: Lindsay Conner
Photo Editor: Meghan Lamb
Assistant Photo Editor: Phil Vinke
Cartographer: Roberta Stockwell
Cover Design: David Riedy

Front cover photo: Traditional floating market © i viewfinder / Shutterstock.com

Back cover photo: The Marble Temple or Wat Benchamabophit, Bangkok © Noppasin Wongchum / iStockphoto.com

For information on our other products or services, see www.frommers.com.

FrommerMedia LLC also publishes its books in a variety of electronic formats. Some content that appears in print may not be available in electronic formats.

Manufactured in the United States of America

5 4 3 2 1

ABOUT THE AUTHOR

Ashley Niedringhaus is an American lifestyle and travel journalist. Before moving to Bangkok, Ashley called New York City home where she held staff roles at various national women's magazines. She has contributed to several Thailand guides and was the editor of the first-ever Michelin Guide Bangkok, a gastronomic job that taught her to love Thai chilis. Her feature articles on travel, food, and culture have appeared in a wide range of international publications, including *Travel+Leisure*. She hopes the lure of spicy food and ever-evolving, off-the-beaten-path spots in her adopted hometown will enrich your Thailand travels. This is Ashley's first Frommer's guide.

ABOUT THE FROMMER TRAVEL GUIDES

For most of the past 50 years, Frommer's has been the leading series of travel guides in North America, accounting for as many as 24% of all guidebooks sold. I think I know why.

Though we hope our books are entertaining, we nevertheless deal with travel in a serious fashion. Our guidebooks have never looked on such journeys as a mere recreation, but as a far more important human function, a time of learning and introspection, an essential part of a civilized life. We stress the culture, lifestyle, history, and beliefs of the destinations we cover, and urge our readers to seek out people and new ideas as the chief rewards of travel.

We have never shied from controversy. We have, from the beginning, encouraged our authors to be intensely judgmental, critical—both pro and con—in their comments, and wholly independent. Our only clients are our readers, and we have triggered the ire of countless prominent sorts, from a tourist newspaper we called "practically worthless" (it unsuccessfully sued us) to the many rip-offs we've condemned.

And because we believe that travel should be available to everyone regardless of their incomes, we have always been cost-conscious at every level of expenditure. Though we have broadened our recommendations beyond the budget category, we insist that every lodging we include be sensibly priced. We use every form of media to assist our readers, and are particularly proud of our feisty daily website, the award-winning Frommers.com.

I have high hopes for the future of Frommer's. May these guidebooks, in all the years ahead, continue to reflect the joy of travel and the freedom that travel represents. May they always pursue a cost-conscious path, so that people of all incomes can enjoy the rewards of travel. And may they create, for both the traveler and the persons among whom we travel, a community of friends, where all human beings live in harmony and peace.

Arthur Frommer